"One of the best superhero pastiches I've ever read. From his dry take on the old pulp heroes stories to his disturbingly sinister version of Marvel's flagship hero, this is not something I ever expected to find outside of an Alan Moore graphic novel."
Pornokitsch

"Ewing is the kind of writer who loves a challenge like this and is up to the task. It's his willingness to raise the bar that has me along for the ride each and every time. I found myself marvelling at the sword fights, bruised by the super powered encounters and mouth agape at the sci-fi."
Graeme's Fantasy Book Review

"The creative appropriation and relentless inventiveness never flags... From the opening pages to the overall theme (which surprises and delights), this is a book where ingenuity meshes with smart pulp fiction. I finished the book eager for more, and I have no hesitation in recommending it as a real winner."
SF Site

"Ewing is not only a poet of pulp, but a poet of beating-to-a-pulp. For those who want to see some furious ass-kicking rendered with some really good writing, check out Al Ewing. He's got the goods."
Steampunk Scholar

"Ewing's fiction critiques the stasis at the core of reactionary steampunk... his reputation as a visceral 'poet of pulp' is well deserved, but it would be a mistake to underestimate the way he intelligently radicalises steampunk from within."
Foundation Magazine

MBRA

TRILOGY

An Abaddon Books™ Publication
www.abaddonbooks.com
abaddon@rebellion.co.uk

This omnibus first published in 2016 by Abaddon Books™,
Rebellion Publishing Limited, Riverside House,
Osney Mead, Oxford, OX2 0ES, UK.

10 9 8 7 6 5 4 3 2 1

Editors: Jonathan Oliver & David Moore
Cover Art: Mark Harrison
Design: Sam Gretton & Oz Osborne
Marketing and PR: Rob Power
Head of Books and Comics Publishing: Ben Smith
Creative Director and CEO: Jason Kingsley
Chief Technical Officer: Chris Kingsley
Pax Britannia™ created by Jonathan Green

ISBN: 978-1-78108-499-1

Printed in Denmark by Nørhaven

To Ashley,

When! you get to the third book you'll see why you can never give this

away.

Love Matt, Michal Zac + Lani

INTRODUCTION

THE ONE THING I know about steampunk is: it's about *steam*. Electricity does *not exist*.

(Don't put the book down in disgust, casual shopper—I'm going somewhere. Also, here be spoilers.)

El Sombra was the first novel I ever wrote, and as "first novels the author ever wrote" go, it's one I'm happy with. I came to it from my early work in comics, which was how I'd gotten to know Rebellion/Solaris Editor Extraordinaire Jon Oliver, who liked the sound of the pulp action I was proposing. Originally a half-baked idea for a more fantastic world—where some kind of eagle-men would lord it over earthbound humans from a huge eyrie—it really got going when I re-tooled it for *Pax Britannia,* the steampunk line, which Jon Green had started off in the *Ulysses Quicksilver* books.

Jon was in charge of Britain in the *PB* world, and I didn't want to step on his toes, so I set up camp in the Americas, and cheekily reimagined his version of cavorite—borrowed from HG Wells, I believe—as an 'Nth Metal' in the style of Hawkman. (The first of many fairly naked homages to other works.) The one thing I wanted to stick with—the one thing I knew for a *fact* about steampunk—was that there was *no electricity*. Everything was either steam or cavorite or both. So the world of *El Sombra* was full of great clanking steam machines, steam-powered tanks, steam-powered robots, steam-powered everything. I think even the wings on the backs of the Nazi hawk-men were steam-powered, though goodness knows how.

I threw in a few other ideas I thought were good, and we were off to the races. The one thing everyone picked up on at the time was a trick I borrowed from Marv Wolfman's *Tomb of Dracula*—or was it Claremont? He did this, too—which was to give every single character who died at El Sombra's hands, pretty much all Nazis, a relatively rich backstory. Some of them were more human than others, but that meant they were all at least a little humanised— even the very worst of the worst were individuals. And it did a lot to fill up the word count.

The second *El Sombra* novel was going to be called *Odessaland,* and was a murder mystery set in the thriving movie studios of the Eastern Bloc, featuring El Sombra navigating a world of literal vampires and monsters. "*In Odessaland, the mirrors always lie.*" It didn't happen for various reasons—the played-out- ness of vampires at the time might have been a factor. Fine by me; I wrote a zombie novel instead. Zombies are evergreen.

(The fact that I can't remember what the murder mystery in *Odessaland* was or how it resolved itself is telling. I doubt the reader is missing anything better than what they conjure up in their imagination from a brief description and a tagline.)

When I wrote the real second *El Sombra* novel, I kept the central idea of a murder mystery, but moved the action to New York City and brought in the one thing steampunk as a genre needs a lot more of: superheroes.

Gods of Manhattan might be my best genre novel—if we call *Pax Omega* a collection of short stories, it definitely is. It's the one people remember best, for the larger than life characters, the optimistic messages, and most of all for the complete lack of any electricity. (Besides Doc Thunder's 'omega energy,' of course.)

Steampunk is about *steam,* remember.

I was a bit older, a bit more confident, and more than happy to use Mark Harrison's brilliant cover art as motivation—he'd created a perfect movie poster of pulp tropes and I wanted to write a novel that matched it as exactly as possible. The homages came thick and fast—Superman, Doc Savage, Hugo Danner, the Shadow, the Spider, Spider-Man, S.H.I.E.L.D., Bizarro, the Avenger, Lex Luthor, *Death of a Salesman,* the Spirit, and those are just the ones I can remember off the top of my head. Doc Thunder remains one of my favourite creations, which is probably why I eventually made him God.

(Again: here be spoilers.)

Pax Omega is a collection of short stories, but if we're calling it a novel, it's the last steampunk novel I'll ever write. I came to it wanting to close off the trilogy and end the stories of everyone involved, and wanting to experiment and have fun doing it. The particular question I asked myself: if you extend a steampunk world a million years into the past or the future, is it still steampunk? *Pax Britannia* is a steampunk universe in the year 2000 or so—how far can you extend that before it breaks? And also, how did the timeline diverge so that steam became a thing and—as in all steampunk—electricity didn't?

So *Pax Omega* became the long history of the *Pax Britannia* universe as I saw it, from prehistory to the year 1,000,000 AD, and how it might connect with our own. The supporting characters and villains of the earlier books end up being the heroes and saviours of this one, while the heroes end in tragedy because their stories carry on too long. And in the background, along with the usual homages—Jonah Hex, Stan Lee, Andy Warhol, MODOK, the A-Team, Batroc the Leaper, Naori Urasawa's masterful *Pluto* (I made that last one as explicit as humanly possible)—we get the strange deaths of Ben Franklin and Thomas Edison, because steampunk universes don't have electricity in them.

I wrote one more big novel since, *The Fictional Man*, as well as the Dredd novella *Wear Iron*. One day I'll get around to writing *Here Walks Flannery*, the existentialist detective story I've been percolating, and hopefully if you like this, you'll be there for that—until then, you'll find me on the racks of your local comic shop, where I'm very happy.

One of the nice things about comics is that you occasionally get invited to conventions in foreign places by your publishers—I believe, though I could be wrong, that it was on one of these that Ben Smith, of Rebellion, took me out for a drink and we talked about the books. Over the course of the evening, he mentioned how much he'd liked *Pax Omega*, which had either just been published or just gone to print.

"One thing, though," he said. "You know there's electricity in Jon Green's books?"

Those weren't the exact words—I can't remember the exact words—but I do remember that no, I didn't know that. I'd read Jon's books, but somehow the presence of electricity in them had slipped completely out of my memory.

Because I *knew* what steampunk was. It's about *steam!* I was as sure of that fact as anyone is of any fact they don't actually know. And thus, I'd merrily written a steampunk universe where electricity had never been discovered and tamed and—with great care—connected it to a universe where it had been, because why wouldn't it have been?

In other words, I'd written a steampunk trilogy while being completely wrong about what the central defining trait of steampunk actually was.

Oops.

So, in closing—we can add Jon Green's Ulysses Quicksilver to the list of homages and mentions, since the *Pax Omega* trilogy definitively does not take place in the main *Pax Britannia* universe where Ulysses lives. The one with electricity in it.

You can get around that if you're inclined—I won't spoil how, but the means of doing so is in the very last chapter of this omnibus—but otherwise, you hold in your hands every book ever set in *Pax Britannia*'s Universe B, and the entire history of that universe, complete in and of itself. I hope you like it.

This omnibus is dedicated, with apologies, to Jon Green.

Thanks for the opportunity to play in your world, Jon. I'm very sorry I didn't.

Al Ewing
2016

PROLOGUE
THE MAN AND THE DESERT

THE MAN WALKED across the desert.

And the desert destroyed the man.

The sun was a dragon that breathed fire on his neck and his back. Each grain of sand beneath his feet was a branding iron. He wanted to cry, but the desert had stolen his tears. Instead, his eyes wept blood.

In his left hand, he clutched a sash of silk, red stained black with spattered gore. His right hand gripped a sword. The knuckles on both hands were white and straining, almost bulging through the burned skin. He couldn't have opened his hands if he'd wanted to. But he didn't want to.

All the man wanted to do was die.

The wedding had been three days before.

AND OH! WHAT a wedding it had been!

The groom had passed the bride the thirteen coins and the rosary lasso was placed around their shoulders and then Father Santiago had blessed the couple—and when they kissed, you should have heard the noise! The whole town cheered and stamped their feet for joy! Everyone from old Gilberto, who'd crafted a pair of wedding ducks, to little Carina, the madrina de ramo, nine years old and too shy to do anything other than giggle and punch the dashing madrina de laso on the arm. The cheer rang until the mariachis struck up their lively wedding march, and Heraclio led Maria—his Maria!—to his magnificent white horse, Santo. The noble beast stood quietly as his new mistress was lifted onto his back and then bore her with all the grace his old horse body could muster to the Great Square. Heraclio gave the venerable beast a gentle pat on the muzzle and fed him a lump of sugar from his wedding-coat, as the townspeople followed behind, led by the mariachi band, for dancing and laughter and food and good wine.

It was all the little town of Pasito had been talking of for months. The day when Heraclio, the handsome guardsman who rode through the town on his white horse and gave sugar-drops to the children from the pocket of his coat, would marry his Maria, perhaps the most beautiful girl the little Mexican town had yet produced and certainly the very finest dancer. To see her laugh and smile atop the gently pacing Santo was to catch a brief glimpse of what life could offer a man. Miguel the baker, forty-three years old and heavy and fat as his own loaves, drank her in with his eyes, and then turned those green eyes to his wife, with whom he had not shared a bed in more than a decade—and did those laughing green eyes not have a certain unidentifiable sparkle that said: *Come, mi amor! Let us forget the passing of years and find ourselves again under the desert stars!* Little Hector, the madrina de laso, who carried the coins and the lasso, all of twelve years old and looking very handsome in his miniature version of Heraclio's red wedding sash, looked at Maria as though he had never seen her before, never seen anyone before... and this time, when little Carina punched him in his arm, he grinned a cocky grin at her and said, "One day I'm gonna marry you!" Poor Carina, she blushed as red as that wedding sash, and ran to hide behind her father, the chubby jailer Rafael, who chuckled and murmured to his neighbour in the crowd: "That boy, he's muy caballero! Like a little Heraclio, hey? In ten years we'll be going to his wedding!"

"Ah, not if you can catch him first!" chuckled Isidoro the schoolteacher, and Carina blushed even redder but smiled secretly at Hector from the safety of her father's legs.

The only one who could look at Maria and not feel as though life was worth living was the poet Djego. Thin as a rake and soft as dough, with a mane of lank, black hair and a tiny pencil moustache, he might have been considered handsome—even debonair—if not for the air of misery and sorrow that he had carefully crafted to hang around himself like a funeral shroud. He was generally tolerated, occasionally even humoured, but there was not a soul in town who could possibly understand how Djego and Heraclio could be brothers.

The wise old women of the town nodded sagely in their rocking chairs when the question was put to them, and the reply was always the same. "Sometimes, a mother and a father put so much into that first child, that it takes a little out of the womb and the balls, and after that they don't work so good. So the first son is like a god, or maybe they have a princess for a daughter. And after that…" And at this point in the telling Djego would strut past with his nose in the air, frowning as though there was nothing to be enjoyed on a sunny day but his own secret and special pain. And the old wise women would chuckle. "After that… *blehhh*!"

And that was the reaction when Djego walked through the town, composing his awful poems, never turning his hand to anything of value, never allowing his heavy, leaden, rhymeless, metreless verse to breathe or represent something of beauty or worth. *Blehhh*. His brother looked after him, as he always had since their parents had died—because he felt sorry for him. "Djego is an idiot," he would say, "but he is my brother. And one day he will be able to laugh with me."

All of this is not to say that Djego could resist Maria's charms—quite the opposite. But when most men would see the most beautiful girl in Pasito and want to go out and live life, dance, sing, make great plans for themselves— Djego looked upon her and only wished to be transformed into stone.

The reason for this was simple. Djego had been hopelessly in love with Maria since the first moment his brother had brought her home.

THE MAN IN the desert fell to his knees and then fell forward onto his face.

Each breath was agony now. His throat was numb and his lips were swollen with the lack of moisture. His skin was like cracked parchment, burnt red. Blisters covered his feet from the red-hot sand that now seared his body.

In front of him, there was a small cactus, no larger than his head. His eyes could barely focus on it, but some switch in his mind triggered the thought that here was water. If you could question his conscious mind on the matter, he would tell you vehemently that he wanted no water; he wanted nothing but to die, and die soon. But his fingers crept forward, scrabbling at the spines of the cactus, drawing blood, then reaching for the hilt of the sword.

The conscious mind was all but dead. The brave desire to walk himself to death had boiled away in the furnace of the desert sun. All that was left was the instinct to survive. The sword flashed, carving the cactus open, the dry, cracked mouth making a terrible noise of despair and rage as a precious drop of moisture was lost to the sand. Then he was leaning forward to drink in what little liquid there was, eating the pulpy, wet flesh, swallowing and sucking it down, tearing at it with his teeth, breaking away the spines so he could devour the skin of the cactus itself.

When he began to choke on the cactus, he rolled to his side and slumped on the sand, unable to move, the pulpy meat of the plant resting in his arid mouth as the sun beat mercilessly down.

The cactus was of the Trichocereus variety. Originally from Ecuador, it had slowly migrated north through Central America, mutating as it went to survive the greenhouse effect brought down on the planet by Britain's runaway industrialism. Originally, the Trichocereus was used by tribal shamen to provide them with intense, often terrifying visions. Those botanists who had discovered this new variety termed it Trichocereus validus.

This was because its psychotropic qualities were hundreds, perhaps thousands of times more powerful.

The man's eyes bulged. He began to convulse. Foam ran from his lips as from a rabid dog.

He could no longer recall his name, but he remembered very vividly that three days before he had been punched in the face by a woman, for the first and the last time in his life.

THE PROCESSION HAD reached the great square, and there the dancing began. Heraclio danced with his beautiful bride to the strains of the mariachi band, and all around him, the whole town danced in the shape of a heart, as was tradition. Had there ever been a happier moment in the whole time that the town of Pasito had stood? Certainly none anyone could remember, although occasionally a husband would turn to a wife and squeeze their hand a little tighter, the glimmer in their eyes seeming to say: *Yes, I remember it well.*

And then the great circle broke up, and every man in the town took their turn to dance with the lovely Maria, and the women queued to be whirled around by the manly Heraclio, who danced well, but not as well as with Maria, and danced with consideration, slowing his pace where necessary—especially when gently escorting the ninety-five year old Consuela Vasquez, the town's oldest resident, from one end of the square to the other.

Occasionally, Maria would sit herself down in her magnificent white dress, and pass time with the old men and women who, unlike the beloved and venerable Consuela, were unable to dance—either through advanced age, physical disorder or, in the case of Toraidio DeMario, several bottles of good wine. She would also flash her stunning smile at Elbanco the singer and the rest of his band, who would not fail to play whatever song she requested. Even those they did not know, they would do their very best to attempt, plucking the words from the air and making up a tune which fit them. A song called 'The Dark Side of the Moon,' for example, had been the talk of London some ten or twenty years previously. It was a melancholy ballad with subtle undertones of laudanum abuse, and had become so famous that word of it had managed to spread even as far as El Pasito. In the hands of Elbanco's band it became a quick, jolly tune about a cuckold painting his wife's bottom black to discourage the many suitors who came running when she waved it out of the window. Maria laughed and danced to it regardless, and thanked each of the band with another sparkling smile, which they considered ample payment for their labours.

And so, when Djego finally deigned to take the floor and dance, Elbanco and his cohorts were busily attempting to perform an apparently famous European ditty called The Dancing Queen, which allegedly went something like:

She doesn't like to walk and she cannot ride a horse—
But the way she dances? Oh, it's a scandal!

Eyebrows were raised—the venerable Consuela gave a gasp of shock, which was a rare event as she had, it was believed, seen it all. Djego the poet, who was above all petty enjoyments, was moving to dance for the first time! It was scarcely believable. To her credit, Maria acknowledged the rarity of the event, and took him gently in her arms to start a waltz about the floor. Heraclio watched with a proud smile—Djego had never told him his feelings on any matter, and so he assumed he was simply watching his shy younger brother finally coming out of the thick shell he had so painstakingly built for himself. He accepted the hand of the chief bridesmaid, and led her into a stately twirl as Elbanco waved his guitarist into a spirited solo.

Of course, he had no way of knowing what was truly on Djego's mind.

Maria's green eyes sparkled as she looked into his, and the smile on her face held a hint of mischief. "So you've finally decided to enjoy yourself, hah? Is this the start of a trend or a momentary bout of insanity?"

Djego smiled stiffly in response. "I... would like it to be the start of something."

She raised an eyebrow. "A new career as a ladykiller? Well, in that case, you'll have to stop those hands shaking. Let me lead a little." She began to gently guide him around the floor, and soon they were moving almost gracefully, with Djego even managing a little smile. "There! Isn't this nice? Djego, if you can keep this up, I promise I will dance at your wedding. Come on, smile! You look handsome when you smile, my brother-in-law. You should do it more. Where's the harm? It might bring your wedding day closer, hah?"

Djego's smile faltered. "I do not see that I will ever get married now, Maria."

Maria laughed, and the laugh was strong and sure. "Oh, there's time yet. Look at your brother when I first met him! Remember how he used to spit out of windows? And then he hit poor Father Santiago in the eye!" She laughed again, but Djego's attempt at a smile was nervous. His hands were shaking. Maria sighed. "Djego, if you keep this up I'm going to abandon you to Consuela. She'll teach you a few more things than dancing, I warn you. You've not seen how she has her eye on you?"

Djego shuddered, but not because of Maria's mental image. He swallowed hard, then spoke softly, barely heard above the music.

"Maria... do you remember the poems that Heraclio sent you?"

She blinked at him, continuing to lead the dance more by reflex than anything else, cocking her head slightly to look at him. "How do you know about those? He showed them to you to get a second opinion, right?"

Djego shook his head. "I wrote those, Maria. Those were my words to you."

Maria said nothing, but she stopped the dance.

"Those poems I wrote to you—I gave them to Heraclio because I didn't think I was worthy. But those are my feelings, Maria. The poems that won your heart, that made you his—they were mine." He swallowed, searching her eyes. Her expression was unreadable, but he pressed on. "This... this should be my wedding day." His eyes welled. The sadness was almost too great for him to contain. "I... I know I've waited too long... but... perhaps one day..."

This was the moment that Maria pulled away from him, swung around and slammed one of her fists into his jaw, sending him tumbling onto the ground in a cloud of dust.

"Estupido!" she yelled, and kicked him in the ribs. Elbanco and his band stopped playing. The venerable Consuela gave another gasp of shock—it was doubtful whether her heart would be able to stand any more unthinkable happenings that day. Little Hector put his hand over his mouth, turning ashen—his juvenile meditations on the power of manhood shattered in an instant. Carina only grinned.

Heraclio stood dumbfounded, then found his voice. "Djego, what have you done now?"

Maria spat venom as she grabbed the lapels of Djego's unseasonal black shirt and hauled him up.

"You honestly think you can walk up to me on my wedding day and say such things? Those poems were terrible, Djego! They were desgraciado! It was nice that Heraclio thought of reading me poems, but in the end I used them to start a fire going! You cannot write, tonto!"

Djego sniffled, reaching to wipe the blood from his nose, looking at the blazing Maria with wide eyes.

"Seriously, idiota, what was your big plan, hah? Would this be like one of those stupid books you read? Was I going to be the unattainable great love you pined away for for the rest of your life? Were we supposed to swap charged glances over the dinner table? Well guess what, retraso…" Her foot slammed into his groin. Hard. Djego gasped and collapsed, then began to retch, throwing up a puddle of half-digested wine onto the ground.

"I fell in love with a man. Not a bunch of stupid poems. So crawl off and hide away for a while? You're no longer welcome at my wedding party. Get the hell out!"

Silence rolled across the great square. All eyes were on the sobbing Djego, as he lay there, weeping openly. Had there been a more awkward moment in Pasito's long history than this? It was certainly the most public embarrassment anyone had suffered. Shocked, helpless eyes turned to each other, then to Heraclio, who shrugged, as if to say: *What can I do? She's right!* Not even the venerable Consuela could see a means of rescuing the occasion.

So in many ways it was a mercy when the stage exploded in a gout of fire and shrapnel, tearing Elbanco and his band into bloody shreds.

DJEGO CONVULSED ON the sand as the sun fried his flesh. The memories seemed so clear. He could feel Maria's fist as it hammered into his jaw, again, again,

again, the shame fracturing him with every impact, breaking him like glass. He could feel his soul filling with a black bile, hissing black acid that burnt and seared the walls of himself. The shame. The shame.

His throat burned and he retched. He could feel the bile, the shame, creeping slowly up his gullet. His eyes were wide, looking down at the glittering sand, and every grain seemed to him like a mountain. The sun was a jewel sparkling on blue cloth and in his ears there was a humming sound, as though he was a string that had been plucked—and it was deafening.

A shadow fell across him, hotter on his back than the heat of the sun. A giant shadow.

A giant.

Standing above him. He turned over and saw everything clearly.

His brother stood above him. A giant with his brother's face, looming like God. His brother, big as judgement above him, standing and looking down on him. Always. *Always.*

Djego closed his eyes and tried to breathe. His heart was pounding in his chest, a hot coal resting against his ribcage. Everything in his ears was still humming. Humming. His eyes were closed but the scene was the same. His brother, his judgement, looming over him, looking down.

Djego understood that this had always been happening. It would always be happening. His brother would always tower over him, always leave him in shadow, always look down. After what had happened he had no right to expect anything else.

After what had happened.

Djego shuddered and retched, more black-bile-memory flooding him, scalding him. He felt something hot on his face. Tears. Or blood. He shook like a child.

The giant's massive hand closed about him and squeezed.

INSTANTLY THERE CAME the echo of similar blasts, a tidal wave of fire that seemed to sweep through the town, burning and destroying at random. The courthouse in the north of the town burst like an egg, sending showers of masonry into neighbouring houses, great shards of glass whirling like propellers as they smashed through walls into the cribs of children too young to enjoy the celebration. Then the screaming started.

The crowd scattered, running and trampling in a chaotic mass of bodies, as the crack and clatter of machinegun fire stabbed through the night air and bullets hit the ground around them. The venerable Consuela's head became a fine mist as a high-velocity round pierced her left eyeball, destroying, in an instant, the mind that held so much of the town in the amber of memory. Perhaps she would have died anyway—this was, after all, the third unbelievable event of the evening.

A bullet found Isidoro the schoolteacher, and he fell on his face in the dirt before flapping like a hooked fish, looking down at his right leg in horror. Mid-thigh, the flesh had been torn away and he could see bone and the spurting ends of the femoral artery. Isidoro taught biology among his many other subjects and he knew what that meant. But he did not believe. Even when darkness closed over his vision and he toppled backwards, shuddered and went still, he did not believe.

Who could?

Even Santo did not survive. He tried to run to his master at the first sound of fire, but one of the bullets clipped a cannon bone, shattering it and sending the animal tumbling to the ground. Another shot slammed into his flank, ricocheted off a rib and exited his breast in a fountain of bloody horsemeat that cascaded over the screaming Hector. The boy's screams joined the cacophony from the agonised horse before a third volley of shots silenced them both. Santo's end was merciful—one of the bullets shattered his skull and he died in an instant.

Hector was not so lucky. For the next ten minutes he stared in mute horror at the seeping mass of offal that had toppled from his torn belly.

Maria's blistering anger fell away into confusion and horror. She looked up at the sky, unable to comprehend what could be doing this. And what she saw terrified her beyond measure.

There were men in the sky.

Men in grey uniforms, carrying great black iron guns, with grey helmets and grey expressions. On their backs were metal wings, flapping slowly in the air, great gusts of steam shooting from them as they clanked and groaned. *That isn't holding them up*, she thought madly, unable to comprehend. *Something else must be.* And then one of the men turned his gun on her, and she darted forward blindly.

Everything was happening very slowly now. Her feet, moving through thick molasses, hit Djego, who was still curled up on the ground, sobbing like a little child. Unable to stop herself, she fell forward, landing hard on the ground in her wedding dress. She looked up, winded and spitting dust from her mouth, and then there was a terrible sound and something hit her very, very hard in the side of her throat.

She couldn't breathe. There was something wet on her dress. It was spoiled. Everything had been spoiled. Somewhere, she could hear Heraclio screaming, but it was far away. Was he crying? *Don't cry, my love. I'll sort this out for you. I always do.*

The last thing she saw was the insignia on the shoulder of the man who'd shot her. A red cross in a white circle, with broken ends, all the way round. Like four little L-shapes joined up.

Where have I seen that before? Thought Maria.

And that was that.

HERACLIO LOOKED UP at the flying men and screamed... but that was in the past, wasn't it? Djego felt himself resting on sand, on the giant's palm. He could feel the flesh through the sand. He saw now the truth of it—Heraclio was looking down, not up, always looking down at him, and the opening of his mouth was in hungry anticipation.

Heraclio the giant was feasting.

The mouth of the giant hung wide open, then closed, and between the teeth were the bones of Djego's ankles, snapping, cracking like a chicken-bone, bitten through. Djego screamed. He was going to die. He was going to be eaten bite by bite. Eaten by the giant, the giant judgement, the giant reputation. The reputation he always had to live up to.

When they had been children, Djego had often been pushed over and beaten and his books taken and trampled in the mud. The boys in the village thought he was fat and doughy and pasty, and they kicked him sometimes until he pissed blood. And that was happening now. He was a child again. He was crying again. His brother was coming to rescue him again, wild swinging fists and shouts. Heraclio always came in the end, running and punching and kicking the bullies until finally the attacks stopped. Nobody picked on Heraclio's brother. Nobody. Djego heard his brother's confident shout again from the giant, the wind of it rushing in his hair.

And Djego felt shame again. Black bile. Again, his brother had done what he could not, his handsome brother, his popular brother who fought where Djego could only cower and weep. He had fought so hard. Never harder than that day, that day it had all ended between them. Heraclio had no brother now.

Djego hated him, and the hate brought more self-disgust that cut him open like a knife.

The giant bit deep. One of Djego's legs was torn from the pelvis, crunched and swallowed whole.

He looked up at the giant's eyes and screamed.

HERACLIO LOOKED UP at the flying men and screamed. "Conchas! Get down here! Get down here and face me!" The sight of his beloved lying on the ground—the look in her eyes, the anger that was there—filled his vision with red mist. He gripped his sword in white knuckles, waving it at the sky-soldiers as they fired down, bullets cascading on the ground all around him. To those not running for any shelter they could find from the storm of men and bullets and death, he seemed a vision of bloody vengeance—righteous and pure.

One of the soldiers took notice.

He had been barking orders to his fellows, but now he handed command to a subordinate and swooped down, landing in the dust of the great square. As the soldier slowly removed his helmet, Heraclio's streaming eyes burned into him, as if seeking to destroy him with a gaze.

The soldier smiled. He was tall and blonde, barely nineteen, with sharp blue eyes that returned Heraclio's burning look with an audacious twinkle of his own. Heraclio was handsome, but this newcomer was beautiful—beautiful in the way that men can be, that dangerous, tempting perfection that comes in statues from Greece, or the rebellious teenagers who break their parents' rules in the kinema-films, the wild ones. An angel's face with a devil's eyes.

He smiled, and the smile promised terrible things.

And then he drew the sword from his scabbard.

Heraclio was not in the mood for niceties. He screamed and lunged, the point of his sword aimed at the heart of his enemy. The soldier, smiling softly, stepped back and swept his sword in a short arc, deflecting Heraclio's wild thrust easily before transforming the fluid motion into a strike. The point of his sword slashed across Heraclio's cheek, leaving a deep cut.

"Is that all you can manage?" purred the angel-face.

Heraclio screamed. His face was contorted in a fury nobody had ever seen there before, and yet his movements were precise now, as though the rage boiling in his belly was giving him focus. Djego, cowering on the ground, looked up at him through his wet eyes, and saw perhaps the greatest display of sword fighting he had ever seen. In Heraclio's white knuckles, the blade flashed and darted like a thing alive, seeking those gaps in the defences of his foe that would allow him to plunge the blade deep into flesh.

It found none. The defence was impregnable. The soldier flashed a mocking grin, the blades clanging as he parried each blow without effort.

Over their heads, the flying men circled like vultures, firing when necessary to herd the crowd into position, then landing and screaming orders at them in a foreign tongue.

The swords flashed and struck. Sweat fell into Heraclio's eyes, and he blinked, the sword jerking, leaving him wide open for the killing strike. But it did not come. In that heartbeat, the handsome young soldier looked straight into Heraclio's eyes. Heraclio blinked again. The pause seemed to stretch on forever, and the implication of it made Heraclio's blood turn to ice in his veins.

The soldier was choosing not to kill him... just yet.

The angelic face smiled again, like a cat. He had seen the realisation strike home, the fear begin to build, and so he lunged forward, sword flashing, pressing the attack, but keeping within Heraclio's skill. He was forcing Heraclio to work harder simply to keep from being skewered.

"Djego!" Heraclio shouted. "Help me!" The sound chilled Djego's heart. He could not move.

The angelic soldier pushed forward a little further, enjoying the fear. This was the moment he especially enjoyed—the moment when his foe realised that there was no hope of survival, that he was outclassed and outmatched. The sight of that knowledge blooming in Heraclio's eyes made his heart sing. Soon, there would come the other moment he savoured—the sweet moment of surrender, when the enemy knew he could no longer fight against his own death. He licked his lips in anticipation as his sword flashed, carving a line across his enemy's chest, then striking his blade through the muscle at the shoulder. Two quick strikes, designed to remove all hope. The end would soon come.

"Herr Oberst!" One of the other soldiers called over. "Wir haben die Verarbeitung beendet."

The angel-faced soldier nodded briskly. "Ich bin dort in einer Sekunde."

And then he moved very quickly, lunging and flicking with the tip of his sword. The blade carved deep into Heraclio's belly, slicing up, opening out the guts, sending a tide of blood and offal and filth spattering onto the ground. Heraclio's eyes went wide, and then he looked down, and he saw—and the look of disgust on his face at his own body, so exposed and revealed for what it was, such a look was sweeter for the soldier than the look of surrender could have been. In its own way, it was perfect.

"Eine vollkommene Totung," murmured the angel face. And then he simply walked away.

Heraclio collapsed into his own offal, giving shuddering gasps punctuated by hacking coughs that sprayed more blood into the dirt.

Djego stumbled to his feet and ran forward to cradle his brother. "Oh God... Dios Mio... Heraclio, you have to keep still..." He tried to remove the red wedding sash, to use it as a bandage, but Heraclio gave a sharp twist, snarling like a dog, blood and spit dripping from his chin as he looked at his own brother with the same hate he'd had for the soldiers. The sash was left hanging in Djego's hand.

"Bastard!"

Djego recoiled as if he'd been slapped around the face, but Heraclio reached to grip his wrist, pulling him back, spitting blood on Djego's chest with every word.

"Corbarde. Spineless coward. You... you cower in the dirt while your brother is cut to shreds... while Maria, my wife, is murdered! Maria, who you make a big scene over, who you say you love—but you didn't love her enough to protect her, did you? A dog would have done that! But not you! You bastardo asqueroso!"

"Heraclio, please—I can get help..."

Heraclio gripped his sword and thrust the handle towards his brother. "It's too late to help, mierda. Go and run away. Run away like the bastard coward you are!"

"I... I won't run..." stammered Djego, taking the sword, horrified at the blood that coated the handle, that coated his hands, that flowed into the sand like a torrent and soaked his suit.

"You will, inmundicia. My brother, the shit. You will run away as you always do... but never far enough. Never far enough."

"Heraclio, please..."

Heraclio looked up then, and fixed his brother Djego with a terrible stare, a look which would never fade away, looking deep into his brother's eyes.

"No matter how far you run, Djego, my blood will always be with you. My ghost will always be with you. You can run from your home, your family, your responsibilities—you can run from your love—but you can never, never run from me. That is my curse upon you, brother. I will be with you until the day that you die."

Djego opened his mouth to speak, to plead, tears streaming down his face—but it was too late. Heraclio's grip relaxed. He slumped backwards, eyes rolling up into his head. Whatever strength had kept him alive long enough to deliver his terrible curse was gone. All that was left was a corpse at his feet.

Djego lifted his eyes, the sword and the sash in his grip, and he saw what was happening. The soldiers had landed and were herding the people through the square in a great mass, prodding them forward with batons. Old Gilberto was kneeling over the body of his son, looking dumbfounded. Two soldiers marched up to him in their black boots and, almost gently, forced him up and into the march. Then they turned towards Djego, and a terrible realisation ran through him that poured ice into his spine.

He would have to fight. He would have to lift his brother's sword and run towards the soldiers and try to kill them. Most likely, they would shoot. The bullets would punch through his chest, his belly, his face and he would be left dead in the dirt. If he was unlucky, the baby-faced commander would swoop down and use Djego for sword fighting practice as he had used Heraclio. Cut him up like meat and leave his guts hanging out for the vultures.

Djego swallowed and took a step forward, tears streaming down his face, the sword a blur in front of him. He had to fight. It was the only thing left to do. If he didn't fight, then what did that make him?

The soldiers raised their guns with a chuckle, then a laugh—laughing at the man in the dirty black clothes, doughy and pathetic and lank-haired, with his wobbling sword and his streaming crybaby eyes.

The sound was enough to break Djego. He turned and ran, bullets kicking up the dirt at his feet.

He didn't stop running until he reached the desert and his breath gave out, and then he forced himself to keep walking as the town receded in the distance behind him.

The sword and the sash were clutched in his hands, his knuckles were white with the strain and he could no longer see through the tears, but he kept stumbling forward, breath ragged, one foot in front of the other. He was walking in search of death.

He walked for three days.

*   *   *

THE TEETH OF the giant bit through Djego's stomach, severing his spine. Heraclio's perfect teeth. His perfect, handsome face. Crunching down into his chest. Djego understood then, as every piece of him was bitten away and crushed, how small and pathetic he had been. How meaningless. How futile and ridiculous. It was a pleasure to let go, to let 'Djego' be eaten and swallowed bite by bite, to let his ugly soul fracture and split into infinite pieces. Swallowed into something larger than he was.

He no longer felt pain, but something itched at him, at the back of his skull. The face. The face on the giant. He thought it was Heraclio's, but it had never been. The face on the giant was his own.

He heard laughter from his own throat, deep and rich, booming across the sands, a wonderful, joyous laugh of triumph and confidence. Whose laugh was that? Not Djego. He was dead and gone and he never laughed. But if not Djego... then who?

Who was lying in the sand?

He shuddered, convulsed once more, every muscle rigid. The eyes in his head rolled back. He gripped the sword and the sash tighter, until they seemed to pulse with a life of their own.

And then his heart stopped.

CHAPTER ONE
THE CORPSE UNDER THE SHEETS

Nine Years Later

ALEXIS WOKE UP next to a corpse. He hardly noticed at first.

He lay there for a moment, blinking in the darkness of the room, feeling the cold mass in the bed next to him and trying to remember what it was. Who it was. Had been. There had been so many of them, it was always difficult for him to remember.

The Officers' Club, perhaps? He vaguely remembered a new waitress. Or some curfew-breaker? There was a tall, handsome youth he seemed to remember with some clarity. Was the lump male or female? He took men to his bed regularly, a healthy amount, experimentation—certainly not the same thing as the degenerates who ended up in the camps. Not the same thing at all. But it led to these frustrating mornings, when he desperately tried even to remember the gender or some distinguishing feature of the cold counterweight that balanced his own body on the mattress.

He racked his mind and clicked his tongue, in the very same way he clicked his tongue when he spilled his coffee or forgot his keys. And then he swung his legs out of the bed and stood. Enough time had been wasted by pointless musings. He left the corpse as it lay, under the sheets.

He was waiting for himself in the bathroom mirror. Still the face of an angel, clean and unblemished, with a mop of blonde hair and piercing blue eyes. The chiseled jaw and soft lips of a matinee idol. He had barely changed in the nine years since the occupation of the town began—when he took so much pleasure in gutting Heraclio like a fish. It was a face you could trust.

He took the opportunity to study the smile carefully. An easy smile. Good-natured. It was a useful tool for getting him what he wanted, which was the important thing. Idly, he looked down at his hands, examining the caked blood. He would have to get all of the dirt out from under his fingernails before he applied his facial scrub. These things had to be done efficiently.

Alexis Eisenberg had killed an average of one person per week in this fashion since he was seventeen.

The facial scrub was followed by a brief shower, and then a rub-down with an exfoliating gel that originally came from Corsica, and then another shower, and then Alexis walked back into the bedroom to do his exercises. One hundred press-ups. One hundred sit-ups. Ten minutes of aerobic exercise to work the heart and pump the blood. And the corpse lay under the sheets. It was probably a small man. Or perhaps a woman. It was hard to tell—the body seemed so shapeless and was in such a strange position. Several of the joints were most likely dislocated. The only way to know for certain would be to lift the sheet, but then he'd probably get blood under his fingernails again... ah well. It hardly mattered anyway. It wasn't important.

One hundred pull-ups, followed by a third shower. Cleanliness was next to godliness. Who could respect an Oberstleutnant of the Luftwaffe who did not bathe in a proper fashion? He applied a little aftershave before he put on his uniform. The aftershave came from Paris. The corpse lay under the sheets. Then on with the uniform, the dark grey of the Oberstleutnant, the second-in-command in this place, but taken in a little here and there to show off his figure. Was it five years ago there had been uniforms like this worn in the streets of Paris and Milan as the fashion? Post-modernism had a lot to answer for in those places where the world of art had not stood still, frozen in Victoria's gaze... and the Führer's. He wore the jacket open, and no cap. The solid silver cross that was his trademark hung over his chest, where the shirt hung open with no tie. Style was very important to Alexis.

On his way out, he smiled to the Gefreiter who stood guard on his room, returning the man's salute with easy familiarity. "There is some refuse in my bed, mein Herr. Could you see that it is disposed of, and my sheets cleaned?"

The private nodded. "Of course, Oberstleutnant. I shall attend to it at once." He saluted once more and clicked his heels as Alexis walked on.

ONCE UPON A time, before the occupation, the place had been called El Pasito. It went by another name now. Aldea. A clockwork-town, where no trains ran. And so the people would run on time instead. As Alexis strode through the town, his eyes passed over those who had once run this dusty collection of hovels. The subhumans. The Mexicans. They had been organised now—proud workers for a greater cause than their degraded notions of happiness. Subhuman they might be, but they were workers for the Fatherland and had thus earned a bare modicum of his respect. Alexis nodded brusquely to them as they filed to their labours, a number branded into the forehead of each. Men and women walking in lockstep to their work. The work that made them free.

Most of the work in Aldea was done in the middle of the town—the Great Square, where the Statue of Freedom loomed. With the boot-heels locked in an eternal click, one arm raised in straight salute, it was a sight to bring pride and pleasure to the heart of every true Aryan. Every detail was exact, from the proud chest to the tall, straight legs, from the iron gaze to the perfectly trimmed moustache, this great stone statue of his magnificent Führer—Adolf Hitler himself!

In happier times.

Adolf Hitler was still Führer, of course, and he would be for a hundred years yet, perhaps a thousand. The propaganda painted him as immortal. But Alexis knew that if a statue were to be built of the Führer as he was now... well.

Best not to.

The sound of the work woke him from his reverie. Hammering and sawing echoed about the square as these fascinating, almost-human creatures worked on the scaffolding. The statue had been put up over the course of a year and according to the laws of Aldea, it must soon be taken down, for how could a statue properly represent the perfection of the Führer? The great Führer who, as any schoolbook in the town would tell you, was in all times and in all places, an ideology that had transcended the poor flesh to live forever? It was idolatry at best, a treasonous offence committed by these animals at worst. Thus, the statue would be slowly and painstakingly dismantled—and then the very next day the order would be given that it must be built again. Build and destroy. Build and destroy. The principle was easy to grasp—work should hold no significance for the worker, beyond the basic understanding that it was the worker's duty to work. All human feeling must be excised to create the pure detachment from self that would ensure eternal subservience.

The even numbers hammered and sawed and worked in silence on the great statue like a colony of ants. Like a machine colony. The odd numbers did the hundred and one other little jobs that needed doing. Farming the land. Cleaning the toilets. Waiting tables in the Officers' Club.

The corpse lay under the sheets.

On random days, the odd and even numbers would switch tasks. Then, a week, a month, a year later, they would switch back. It was best that the workers did not grow too attached to one particular task. Again, the work must hold no significance for the worker. You work until you stop—if necessary you work until you die. There should be no meaning to the work beyond that.

That did not mean that work should be entirely without reward, however, even for these half-human imbeciles. Alexis cast an eye restlessly about. Eventually his gaze alighted on a short, pudgy Mexican man, with a large handlebar moustache, dressed in a white ice-cream suit, a panama hat and immaculate shoes. Alexis smiled, a genial grin that seemed to light up his whole face. It never touched his eyes.

"Master Plus."

The fat little man in the white suit jumped, nearly losing the hat off his head and exposing his grotesque bald patch in the process. He turned quickly, eyes wide as he looked to the officer.

"Oberstleutnant... forgive me, I was woolgathering..."

"Heil Hitler, Master Plus."

The fat man turned pale and did a reasonable approximation of a proper salute. Alexis scowled. Nine years, this fat little half-man had been in a position of great responsibility with many perks—and he still couldn't manage a decent salute. His greasy brown hand was like a flailing fish jerking on the end of a line. Alexis shook his head slowly. Master Plus was the exception to the rule. No number was branded into his forehead. He never woke up to find that he was now expected to clean toilets. He owned a beautiful white suit and paraded it in front of his fellow aberrations. He had a diamond stickpin that flashed in the bright noon sun. He owned a beautiful house.

Master Plus was in charge of the concept of Reward.

A living carrot, dangled in front of his fellow subhumans, a symbol of how high in the ranks they could rise if they were to only play the game, follow the rules. In this capacity, he gave speeches to the workers, 'seminars' where he would tell them how simple it was to achieve his lofty position—if only they would work just a little harder. "If I can do it, why not you?" as he would say, over and over again, his diamond stickpin flashing into the eyes of the audience as they slaved in the pouring rain.

It was an illusion Alexis despised. You didn't need to trick the ox into pulling the cart, or butter up a sheep before you took its wool. So why play such games now?

The fat man swallowed hard. Alexis restrained himself from sneering openly in response. The creature was a natural coward—he'd turned on his own kind for fear that the Luftwaffe would do to him and his daughter what they had done to so many others. He'd grown dependent on the luxuries the new regime afforded him. And what was he now? A parrot on a jewelled perch, endlessly repeating the same empty phrases for fear of being denied his cracker. As he stammered his reply, Alexis fought the irresistible urge to simply take hold of his fat Mexican head and twist it off. He had no doubt that such an act would provide more motivation than the workers had had in nine years.

"H-h-heil Hitler, Oberstleutnant. Heil Hitler." The moustache twitched as Plus forced an oleaginous smile. His eyes were those of a cornered rat.

"You only need to say it once, my dear fellow." Alexis smiled a little wider. "I've been watching the workers building the statue. Is it me, or do they seem a trifle behind?"

Master Plus blinked. He opened his mouth and then closed it, once, like a fish, before licking dry lips and summoning himself to speak. "Herr Oberstleutnant—I haven't observed any decrease in productivity…"

Alexis let his smile drop. "So it is me. My judgement is faulty. Thank you for bringing that to my attention, Master Plus."

"No!" The word was almost cried out. "No, I would never suggest such a thing, please, Herr Oberstleutnant, I merely meant to say that I have not seen any drop—I would never question you…"

"In that case, it's your judgement that's not up to par. Or your ridiculous speeches. Tell me—my dear friend—do you honestly think we need a Master Plus in this experiment? I don't wish to offend you—you do such necessary work. But do you truly think a colony of ants should have regular pep-talks? Are machines in great need of motivational speakers?" He was grinning now, a vulpine grin that was a world away from the cultivated, easy-going smile of the young, handsome officer. Here was revealed the beast, the carnivore, the killer who waited for his chance and struck once only.

Master Plus blinked. He spoke slowly, treading with the care of a man picking his way through a minefield. He was walking on the tongue of the crocodile.

"I would not dare to suggest that I was... indispensable, Herr Oberstleutnant. However, my function within Aldea has been... I do only what I have been directed to do by my superiors, Herr Oberstleutnant. By your father. The Generaloberst. My function is as a part of his larger mechanism, and as such... I would hardly dare to suggest that I was... dispensable, either. Such decisions are not up to me, Herr Oberstleutnant."

Your father.

There it was. Alexis could not help but feel a stab of admiration for the fat little animal's clever tongue. It was a stratagem almost worthy of a true man. Now, instead of tormenting a worthless subhuman raised far beyond his station, Alexis had been placed in a position where he was in danger of being seen to speak against the Generaloberst himself. The leader of the occupation force. His father. Alexis wasn't quite ready to make such a move.

Just yet.

Master Plus took the opportunity to steer the conversation towards less dangerous waters. "Perhaps we can discuss this at my house, Herr Oberstleutnant... it's been too long since you last made a visit."

Alexis flashed another lifeless smile. It had been barely three days. Still, had the half-man stood his ground and pressed the point, Alexis would have faced a choice between showing weakness and defying his father. Neither would have been conducive to his continued good health. The best thing to do now would be to graciously accept the change of subject.

Besides, there were far less pleasant activities on a hot day like today than visiting the house of Master Plus. The greatest treasure in all of Mexico was kept there.

A FEW STREETS away from the statue lay the palatial house. In most respects, it was the same sort of house that many of the officers lived in—large rooms, nice furniture and what have you. But this one had an air of mystery about it not easily defined.

What officer of the mighty Luftwaffe did not show off his house? It was a symbol of status, and there was precious little of that to be found in Aldea. The house an officer was given was in direct proportion to their work for the Reich—the greater the work, the better the house, and so forth. So most evenings you would find a Staffelkapitan entertaining select members of the Staffel, or an Oberst showing off to a couple of Lieutenants—showing off his whisky and his gramophone records and his high ceilings. Thus, the inside of every big house in Aldea was common knowledge to all, from Udo Reimann's little bolt-hole with its wall of one hundred empty whisky bottles (always one half-finished) to the light, airy spaces of Oberst Mehler's residence, where he played Mozart on a little steam-player until late. But there was one house that was a mystery, and that was Master Plus' residence.

Few officers of the Luftwaffe would want to admit a desire to see the inside of a subhuman's dwelling, of course—even those who belittled the Führer's ravings in private were mindful of the effect such an admission would have on their careers—but by its very nature, the house of Master Plus invited comment and curiosity.

It was known as the House Without Windows.

Several of the windows on the upper floor were covered with large sheets of canvas that permitted the light to come in, but blocked out all sight of the machine-town around it, and from these the house took its name. Occasionally people would swear they heard music from the upper floor—and more occasionally, singing, soft and sweet, an angel's voice. But nobody knew from whom it came.

Nobody except for Master Plus himself, the Generaloberst—and Alexis.

MASTER PLUS USHERED Alexis through the front door, looking left and right, up and down the street, before closing it behind them and turning the key in the lock. He turned to look at Alexis, the smile creeping up over his face underneath his caterpillar moustache.

"She's been asking after you, Herr Oberstleutnant... she's looking forward to the day of the wedding! Just imagine... the old church bells ringing again... the square alive with dancing! Why, we've not had a wedding in this town since... since..."

Alexis allowed the nervous prattle to tail off into silence. He cocked his head, gazing upon the smaller man with an undisguised sneer. Then, after a pause, he began to climb the stairs to the upper floor. Standing outside the heavy oak door, he waited as Master Plus bustled past him and ceremoniously withdrew a large jewelled key from his pocket, turning it in the lock with reverence. Alexis was half-amused at best by this—this undue ceremony, this imitation Blackbeard with his secret door. They'd been through this a hundred times. Surely by now he saw how ridiculous it all was?

"Are you decent, my little flower?"

The musical tones were muffled by the heavy oak of the door.

"It's all right, Papa. You can bring him in."

Master Plus gave a tight smile. "I've become a creature of habit, it seems." With that, he pushed open the heavy door, and the two men stepped into the room.

To say that Carina was beautiful was to call the noonday sun a flickering candle. This was not the only romantic cliché that applied to her.

Her skin was like coffee-coloured silk, her limbs long and supple, her lips soft and full, and so on and so forth, ad infinitum. But the cigarette advertisements on the hoardings in Berlin were as beautiful and similar songs were sung of the cabaret girls there, every night after ten. What those women lacked was the unique allure that comes with true grace in all its many meanings. Even if the rank and file were informed of the beauty that lived in the House Without Windows, they would never understand. Until one had seen Carina in motion, there could be no understanding.

As she padded across the carpet to meet her father her hips swayed gently back and forth like a cat twitching its tail. The hair that cascaded to her back flowed like water, tumbled like silk. It was a purely unconscious motion, without guile—Carina was an innocent in such matters, having been denied the opportunity to experience the heights and depths of human nature by her father. The intelligence that danced and sparkled in her green eyes was quick, and sharp, and alive—but caged. For the past nine years, Carina had lived the life of a fairytale princess. A princess locked in a tower.

The windows of her palatial rooms had canvas stretched upon them, painted with scenes of El Pasito as it had been in better days, before the occupation. These seemed completely real in every respect. The attention to detail was stunning, and the lack of depth was compensated for with a series of inbuilt optical illusions that made perspective appear where there was none. She had been kept in these rooms, looking through these trick windows, for nine years, with all possible luxuries provided for her—except the luxury of walking out through the hard oak door.

This bizarre set of circumstances had been created at the insistence of Master Plus, who had wished that his nine-year old child might be free of the horror that had befallen her world. The Ultimate Reich had been most co-operative in allowing him to realise this—for in many ways, Carina was as much an experiment as the rest of the town. Was it really possible to raise a human being to be so blind to reality? Was this the case with Carina, or was she only biding time? And if it could be done with her, could it be done with others?

As Carina moved to hug her father, Alexis moved to take hold of her hand and tugged sharply. Carina winced imperceptibly and turned to face him. He lifted the hand to his lips. They felt like a cobra brushing against her skin. Carina half-smiled, warily.

"Alexis. How pleasant to see you again."

"Carina. I've been counting the hours until our wedding day. I can hardly wait."

Carina's smile widened slightly, but it was a reflex action only. The hand in his grip tried to pull away. He did not allow it to. Her eyes narrowed.

Master Plus' wheedling voice shattered the moment.

"You will be wishing your life away, Herr Oberstleutnant! Come, have a pot of tea… or perhaps…" He tailed off, swallowing, as Alexis turned his cold eyes to pierce his. He stepped back, suddenly conscious of the way his forehead glistened, the clammy feel of his own skin. "That is to say… I did not mean…"

Alexis only smiled. "My life, Master Plus? Surely not." He smiled wider. Carina moved away, giving no sign that Alexis was even in the room, moving to pick up one of her books and settle herself down with it. At one time she had been flattered by Alexis' attentions. He remembered her adoring smiles, how she blushed when he looked her way, how her eyes once shone for his entrance. But those had been the reactions of a girl of fifteen who had never met a handsome young man before. In the years since she had simply grown to know him too well. She understood him now, and as a result she had become cold and distant. He could hardly blame her, but that was neither here nor there. The wedding would go ahead, or Master Plus and his daughter would simply vanish and never be heard from again.

Of course, it was mostly for the benefit of the locals and the psychologists, one more piece of data for the Great Experiment. It wouldn't be a true marriage of equals—the subhuman girl was sublime in her beauty, but that was merely an accident of genes and presumably masked imperfection elsewhere in her. The match would be very pleasant for him—for a brief while—but could not be expected to last any serious length of time. The only real question—one that had arisen in Alexis' mind in recent months as his respect for Carina's sharp mind had grown—was which of them would kill the other. But then, in such matters, Alexis was the superior.

"My apologies, Master Plus. I was... woolgathering." He smiled, turning his head, and slowly walked over to Carina, measuring his steps. "Until we meet again, Carina."

She did not look up. Master Plus coughed, then spoke up. "Come now, little flower, you can offer Herr Oberstleutnant a kiss goodbye, can't you?"

Carina looked up at that, and looked at her father with a sweet smile, eyes like chips of green ice.

"Dear Papa, I am sure the dashing Herr Oberstleutnant will steal a kiss from my lips soon enough."

Master Plus almost choked. "Carina..."

Alexis chuckled. "I admire your... subtlety, Carina. It is, unfortunately, a skill I never learned... I will leave you with your father. Doubtless you and he have a great deal to talk about?"

Carina returned to her book as though he had said nothing. Alexis felt a wave of admiration for her, even as he nodded briskly to her coward of a father and silently walked through the oak door and down the steps. Admiration would change nothing, of course. It only made it clearer that Carina could not be underestimated. To allow himself the foolish cliché of the wedding night would be to sign his own death warrant.

He decided that she would not survive the carriage ride from the church.

AFTER THE MEETING with Master Plus, Alexis needed something to take the taste from his mouth. It was always the same—the pleasure of seeing Carina's grace and beauty never lasted so long as the sickening feeling that came from standing in her father's obsequious, oleaginous presence. The man was like a ball of slime, a slug, a tainted creature who spread foulness—and worse, weakness—wherever he touched. The only way to cure himself of the pestilence that seemed to cover his flesh like a creeping tide of ants was to go to see Master Plus' opposite number.

Alexis strode purposefully towards the concrete bunker on the opposite side of the town, nodding to the menials as they performed their tasks. Already he began to feel better. Master Minus was a man after his own heart. Master Minus was in charge of Punishment.

The Palace of Beautiful Thoughts, as it was known, was a grey concrete edifice that seemed like a simple blockhouse, but that was only what lay above ground. Beneath was a large complex of corridors and rooms—guesthouses for those who broke the rules of the town. There they were entertained by a man who was everything that the pathetic Master Plus was not—a true Aryan, a man who understood the meaning of iron will, an artist and a poet. By the time he reached the steel door, Alexis had a spring in his step.

"Hans! My good fellow. Is Master Minus inside?" It was a question that needed no answer—Master Minus was always inside.

Hans Bader smiled tightly as he performed the salute. "Jawohl, Oberstleutnant—the Master is in. He is, ah… working at the moment." Hans dropped his eyes to the ground. His duty for the past three years had been to guard the door of the bunker on the outside, and for this he was profoundly grateful. He had no desire to learn what lay inside.

"Ah, you are squeamish, Hans. Perhaps you could pass a little time with Master Minus yourself, hmmm? Help you get over these foolish attitudes. Open the door, Hans."

As Hans began to twist the handle that would open the heavy steel door, his hands began to shake. Alexis was not known for making idle threats.

Inside there was a small chamber with a number of leather suits hanging from pegs. Alexis stepped into the room and selected one of the suits as the door closed. The suits were baggy, shapeless and airtight, with a heavy faceplate, and every breath that Alexis took passed through filters over the nose and mouth, which cleansed the air of all impurities. It was a necessary precaution, for as the inner door slowly swung open, tendrils of sickly yellow seeped into the room, coiling around him like tentacles, attempting to catch him in their grip. Alexis stepped forward, lumbering in the bulky suit. He felt confined, weighed down. But he knew better than to discard the heavy leather. Only one man could keep his sanity in such a climate.

Stepping forward, Alexis entered the Palace of Beautiful Thoughts.

The yellow mist contained massive doses of psychoactive chemicals—drugs designed to weaken the will, to bring paranoia, terror, euphoria and madness. This was the atmosphere a condemned man would breathe as he waited, chained and shackled, for Master Minus to reach him. Often, by the time Minus began his painstaking work on the flesh and psyche of his latest client, the victim would already be a broken, shaking wreck. Not that this would stop him.

Alexis wended his way down through the twisting corridors, listening to the unique sounds of the Palace—the sounds of screaming, sobbing, frenzied laughter, or that strange kittenish mewling, the guttural sound the throat made when all hope was lost. Beautiful thoughts, indeed! The spring returned to his step, even encased in the heavy leather, as he turned the corner to find himself in the main room that was reserved by Master Minus for the practice of his unique art.

The sight made him smile. An old man, more than sixty, was bound with iron manacles to a large metal rack, set at a forty-five degree angle. A corset of barbed wire had been wound around his stomach, and the bent, stick-thin figure of Master Minus was perched on a small set of steps, the better to reach his victim's face. Alexis watched the scalpel flash, the blade catching the light, reflecting as the blood seeped down across the neck and chest, which rose and fell like a bellows. Surely the man would have a heart attack at any moment! And yet, the touch of Minus was sure, and swift, and perfectly aligned with the planes of muscle and flesh, as the scalpel dug and carved and sliced. Scraps of pink and wet red, orange in the mist, flew with unerring accuracy towards a bucket reserved for such leavings. To Alexis, it was like watching a master sculptor putting the finishing touches to a great work of art.

"I will be right with you, Oberstleutnant, but I must not be interrupted at this critical stage. I'm sure you understand." The voice had the texture of old, dry parchment.

"Of course, Master Minus. Please, by all means—carry on." Idly, Alexis reflected that if Master Plus had spoken to him in such a manner, he would have been buried alive in a pit of caustic lime. But Master Minus was a different calibre of man altogether.

The scalpel flashed. The blade dug and stripped and cut. There were no screams—presumably either the victim was too far under the influence of the gas, or he had been properly anaesthetised beforehand. Pain was not the object, evidently.

Finally, Master Minus descended the steps, and the work was revealed—a shining skull. Eyes gazing without lids from the raw sockets, the jaw held in place with threads of muscle, still working, opening and closing, as the hands opened and closed at nothing and the barbed wire cut and tore at the flesh of the stomach.

Master Minus smiled softly.

"One of my better pieces. He will keep for a while, but it's important that I bring him to his daughter's house without too much delay. She must learn that spreading malicious gossip about der Führer has certain… unfortunate consequences."

It was like conversing with an aged beetle. Master Minus must surely have been more than ninety years old. The flesh of his face hung in wrinkled folds and his body bent as he walked in slow, shuffling steps. The dark monk-like habit he wore covered most of his body, leaving only the shining bald pate of his head, and his wrinkled hands—his terrible artist's hands, that worked with such tender skill. Alexis smiled.

"You must forgive me if I fail to understand, mein Herr. Why not simply take the woman for her crimes? It seems a somewhat roundabout method of punishment."

Master Minus chuckled, and the sound was like dry twigs cracking underfoot.

"I could not expect you to understand the concept of guilt, Oberstleutnant. I barely comprehend it myself except as one more colour for my palette. But take my word for it—there is no torture like that of guilt. Pain is useful, I will admit—as useful as a hammer, for pounding nails. But take a hammer alone to a block of purest marble and all that is left is rubble. The hammer must be used in concert with the chisel, and... but I am an old man, Herr Oberstleutnant. I could talk you into your grave and then wake you with my noise. Instead, let me give you a demonstration."

A flicker of light danced in the old man's eyes.

"Let me show you the true meaning of torture."

The yellow mist swirled in the air. Master Minus walked slowly to a rope hanging from one wall, and tugged. A small silver bell rang in the silence. Alexis leant forward, straining his ears, curious despite himself about what the old man would show him.

A door at the back of the room opened, and a shirtless boy of nineteen years walked through it. Subhuman, yes, but uncommonly handsome—perhaps as handsome as Alexis himself in his own inferior way. Alexis nodded in appreciation. "About to demonstrate your skill, Master Minus?"

"I already have, my dear Oberstleutnant. This man has been tortured. He has been broken, torn to pieces, placed beyond the limits of endurance and left there to scream until his throat gave out. He is a finished masterpiece."

Alexis frowned. "There is not a mark on him."

"Once again, you place too much importance on the physical world. Tell me, Oberstleutnant—what would you say is this young man's best feature?"

Alexis studied the boy's face for long moments.

"I suppose if I was forced to comment... I would say... his eyes. He has very striking eyes."

Without hesitation, the boy reached up to his face. Fingers scrabbled and dug at the flesh. A rivulet of blood ran from each of the sockets as he worked his fingers deeper... then tugged. There was a sickening popping sound—a wet suction—as his eyes were drawn from the bloody holes they'd rested in, still clinging to the stringy optic nerves. A further tug and those nerves were dangling on his cheeks amidst the blood.

The boy spoke a few words of halting Spanish, his eyeballs in his palms. Master Minus chuckled.

"He is offering them to you, Oberstleutnant. As a gift."

Alexis reached and took one of the eyeballs, examining it. Still very striking. "How did you manage it without marking the flesh?"

"Shame, Oberstleutnant. Humiliation. These are finely-honed skills. Guilt and self-hatred cut as fine and sharp and deep as a scalpel in the right hands... in my hands. When the soul is tearing at itself with hot claws, the body can be made to do anything the torturer wishes. Once that point has been reached, there is no more torture. There is only sculpture and poetry. Creativity worked in flesh. Do you understand me, Oberstleutnant?"

Alexis turned the eyeball around and around in his fingers with a half-smile. "I believe I do, Master Minus. I will have to visit you again soon. Perhaps I will try without my helmet, hmmm?"

Master Minus laughed. "I would not advise it, my friend. The air I breathe... I am adapted to this, yes? I breathe it every day. I'm used to the feelings it brings... the wonderful, heated shame. At this point, if I were to breathe the air outside—I would go mad. I have a suit myself for use when I leave the Palace."

"The black one. I remember it now. It's been some years since you've worn it."

"It has been some years since I've needed to leave, Oberstleutnant. But that reminds me the General was asking after you. He and I have been in consultation over a difficult problem and now he requires your thoughts on the matter. If you'll proceed to the Red Dome, I will return to my patients..." He waved a hand towards the stripped skull of the man in the rack.

Alexis smiled, nodded, and moved back towards the airlock to strip the heavy leather suit off and return to the normal atmosphere.

As he walked back into the sunlight, he placed the eyeball in his mouth and bit down.

It was delicious.

*   *   *

IN THE CENTRE of the city, within sight of the great statue, stood the Red Dome. Here sat the government for Aldea, the infernal heart of the terrible machine that drove the people to and fro on their tracks, that flew the flapping, hissing wingmen through their owned sky.

Here sat the Generaloberst.

Entry to the red dome was guarded by a platoon of soldiers below, and a flock of wingmen above, circling in formation, a halo of angels atop the devil's brow. Once all passes and permits had been checked, stamped and copied in triplicate for filing—a process that even Alexis was not excused from—the visitor was allowed to take the great spiral staircase to the waiting room. Here the soldiers would wait to have their leaves granted, to apply for transfer, to lodge a grievance, flirting with the pretty secretaries as the wheels of bureaucracy slowly turned and the clock ticked around to the time when they would be granted their belated audience. The General was a busy man.

Alexis needed no appointment, however. He nodded curtly to the secretary—a cool blonde of no more than twenty-two, most likely with a sweetheart among the officer class—knocked sharply on the oaken door and then walked into the main office.

This was the seat of power. An immense window dominated the east wall, looking out onto the town, and the statue. There was a red tint to the glass— plush red leather on the walls, the carpet a rich burgundy. Subdued lighting and gleaming gold furnishings gave the office an air of regality—a cross between the headquarters of a great banking company and the study of some deposed French king. The furniture itself, however, was paradoxically austere—a picture of the Führer (in happier times) and a picture of the General sat side by side on the wall, but neither were overly large or ostentatious. Indeed, the only things in the room which could properly be described as such were the desk of polished mahogany and red leather, and the sumptuous chair behind it, large and imposing, like the man seated in it. General Eisenberg.

His name meant 'Iron Mountain,' and he was one of those lucky individuals for whom sobriquet and self unite in harmony. The General stood at six feet and seven inches. Even when sitting down, he seemed to loom over those he spoke to like some great outcrop of desert rock. A carpet of grey, close-cropped hair topped his great stone head, and his eyes were like hailstones. His face carried that certain touch of rugged fascination that came with the authority of war—in other aspects, it was like a fist, his stare or scowl a weapon to brutalise and subjugate those who dared oppose him.

His parents had died as part of an unsuccessful black operation on behalf of the Führer—the attempted coup, against the wishes of Victoria, which would have opened up Belgium and left Western Europe ripe for conquest. His first clear memory was being shown a lithograph of his father and mother hanging from a gallows in a Brussels jail.

An orphan at six years old, he had carried ammunition and medicine in the great assault on the Maginot Line, where so many thousands had died. He had seen men torn apart by the great Vickers guns, still living, men with bandaged eyes who eternally begged the orderlies to please remove their boots—they would do any favour if the doctor would only remove their boots and scratch that terrible itch that nagged even through morphine. Their boots were always a kilometer or more away, of course. With their feet. By eight, the boy carried a knife and pistol, and slit the throats of the wounded on the battlefield as they begged. No one had ordered him to do this—it was as logic dictated. While the French might take prisoners, and fatten them on good bread and cheese while their soldiery starved for bullets, Germany should never be so foolish. His voice was not yet broken, this boy, and yet he was stronger than grown men in this regard—or so the Führer would say, on the day they met.

Eisenberg grew to manhood and his place remained with the military. He participated in the bloody push into Italy, when Il Duce finally fell from favour. He had carried a clip of silver bullets in Hitler's terrible eastward push, fighting both the biting winter and the things that lurked on the Russian front. And he had returned alive to tell the tale when der Führer finally had to choose between losing his face or losing his country under the terrible pressure of Her Majesty and her Soviet helpmeet, the man the British lovingly referred to as 'dear old Colonel K.' Be it the jungles of South-East Asia, the foothills of Spain or the endless deserts of Saudi Arabia, the Iron Mountain had been the Führer's implacable fist, his crushing hand. He had taken more and more power, greater and greater accolades, until finally his tireless work had led him here, to the plush, red leather chair, and the governance of the clockwork-town. This was the greatest reward—the most important duty. This was not just another of the Führer's plays at conquest, not a simple grab for more of the global pie. This was the future of Germany—and perhaps also the world.

It was hardly surprising, then, that he did not smile as his son entered the room. Such grave responsibility must preclude human feeling.

"Good afternoon, Father." Alexis displayed his very best smile, if only to provide a contrast. The red light that pervaded the room gave the easy grin an air of almost imperceptible menace.

Eisenberg's eyes narrowed, and the voice that echoed through the room was the sound of stone grinding upon stone.

"Within these walls, Oberstleutnant, I am the Generaloberst. Any biological relationship between the two of us is simply… coincidence. Nothing more. This constant lack of respect for my rank could soon become tiresome."

"My most profound apologies, Herr Generaloberst. Permission to stand at ease?"

The General leant back in his chair and sighed. "I should make you stand there all day and night. But I know it does no good whatsoever. My son and heir… I was informed of the mess you left this morning. Don't you worry that your proclivities might injure your chances at promotion?"

"The Führer shares my 'proclivities,' Herr Generaloberst. I merely take a less efficient approach… more hands-on, as it were." Alexis grinned—that stage-star smile that charmed so many. The General only scowled in response and when he spoke, it was the low rumble of a glacier.

"I would not speak his name if I were you, boy." The huge man's eyes narrowed as his voice lowered to a whisper. "You are a deviant—and believe me, that is the kindest word for this fever that grips you. Without me to protect you, you would be bound for the camps. And I have no intention of protecting you at the cost of myself, Alexis. One day you will reach too far and I will be forced to choose between saving you or saving my career… and on that day…"

Alexis waved a hand through the air. "That day! That day has not come these past nine years, father! Nine years in a wasteland, driven to distraction by the boredom, the subhumans and the flies! I belong in Paris, or Milan, or on the Queen's Road, not cooped up with these animals! Is it any wonder I occasionally decide to amuse myself with their wretched bodies? It's either that or go mad!"

The General raised an eyebrow and gave the ghost of a smile.

"I could remark… no, no, I'd rather not start a fight at this hour. You're sane enough to be of use to me, put it that way. After all, if a wolf is in the woods, the sheep will more readily heed the bark of the sheepdog. Did you come for a particular reason, Alexis? Wedding plans, perhaps? I understand the lovely Carina is as taken with you as it is possible to be."

"Sarcasm ill becomes you, Herr Generaloberst."

"And your flippant attitude ill becomes an officer of the Ultimate Reich!" The General scowled as he rose from his seat and strode to the red—tinted window. "Do you understand the significance of what we do here, Alexis? Do you understand what Projekt Uhrwerk is? For decades Britain has loomed over the Reich like a vulture—allowing us to exist at her sufferance! And why? Because they have the technology to rule! A robot workforce to cater to their every need! While we—the superior race—must work with inferior robotics, clanking monsters of steel that can function only as terror machines! With an economy kept stunted by the cage Magna Britannia keeps us in! But no more! No more!"

Eisenberg's grey eyes flashed fire as he turned around. "Here is our laboratory, Alexis. Our testing ground. We have our robots now! Infinitely adaptable! Infinitely programmable! For they are crafted of human flesh! Our new robots will work tirelessly for the Führer—efficient, expendable and inexpensive. After all, we have been creating them since the apes came down from the trees. Imagine it, Herr Oberstleutnant! Berlin and Munich and Bonn running with the efficiency of Aldea! Cities ticking like well-made watches! A final solution to the tiresome individuality that leads to crime and perversion! An end to the twin burdens of free will and personal responsibility—the dirty and degrading chimera called morality! Can you see it, Alexis? Can you see the future?"

Alexis half-smiled. "This is a speech I've heard before, father. Besides, surely the experiment is a success by now? Time to go home, don't you think?"

Eisenberg sighed and turned back to the papers on his desk. "In six months, perhaps. A year at most. But there are still slight glitches in the machinery that must be set right... Come, if you're going to disrupt the peace and dignity of my office then you can put that twisted streak of yours to work. I'm deciding what to do with a special case." He beckoned, and Alexis walked around the desk. There, on top of the plush surface, lay a grainy sepia photograph of a man in his mid-thirties, dressed in black with a shock of hair already shot through with grey. In his eyes was a look of weariness and infinite care, and at his throat was the small white square of a dog collar.

"It seems that for the past nine years, this man has been preaching the word of God to the citizens of Aldea. His name is Father Jesus Santiago."

Alexis shrugged. "Is that what a life of devout Christianity does to your looks?"

"Very droll. Very witty. But this sort of rabble-rousing is no laughing matter. When the good Father Santiago waves his God in the faces of good workers, it takes their mind away from their work and their Führer. Before very long, the people decide that perhaps his God would rather they did not obey. Perhaps his God would rather they rebel against us and martyr themselves to our bullets. We must not have that, Alexis. God cannot be tolerated."

"Master Minus will deal with Father Santiago, father."

"I think not. Oh, Master Minus is fine for destroying a man—or many men. But we are playing a different game today. It is not enough to finish Jesus Santiago, even if we string his guts between the houses like washing-lines and make the workers hang their clothes to dry on them. Our task is to finish God! We must kill him, grind his bones into dust, completely and utterly. We must rend the Almighty to shreds and hurl him from the rooftops like confetti! Even Master Minus admitted that this was a difficult task, although he's giving all his thought to the problem. But we felt your perspective might bring us some fresh insight."

The General looked up at his son, eyes narrowing. "Well, Alexis?"

Alexis smiled slowly.

THE WHIP DUG into Jesus Santiago's back as it roasted in the desert sun, leaving a red trail of bloody, ripped flesh. The crack was like a gunshot sounding over the crowd as the townspeople watched—and waited. Some of them were grinning, eyes glassy as they took in the show that had been laid on for them, while others looked at the ground, fearfully reaching into their clothes for hidden crosses. In the sky overhead, the Luftwaffe circled like vultures.

Santiago grimaced—but did not cry out. Not until the whip landed again, carving a bloody X into the flesh of his back. The priest was up on an improvised wooden stage, standing with his bare feet shoulder width apart, the tattered cuffs of his trousers held to his calves with rope—the rope that kept his ankles bound to the sturdy stage. He stood, stretched as through on a rack, his bare arms lashed together above his head with leather straps. A strong rope ran from his bound wrists through a pair of pulleys, and on the other side of that rope hung a wooden platform, the weight of which was enough to keep Santiago's body held up despite the blows of the whip staggering him.

Alexis held the whip.

"Where is God? Tell me, wretch. Where is God to be found here?" The whip whistled through the air again, marking the back twice, laying the flesh open.

Santiago gritted his teeth, forcing his words out through the haze of red that shrouded his vision.

"In the hearts... of the people..."

"I see no people here, creature. I see subhuman scum! I see your executioners!" Alexis spat, and the whip landed another time, and another—cutting more slices out of the shaking flesh. Four shorter cuts now met the X at right angles.

Alexis had carved the swastika into Santiago's back.

He turned, addressing the crowd with a grin which would have befitted a wolf in the Black Forest. "Now, workers—you will show your obedience to the Führer! Each of you will take one stone—just one—and place it on the platform. Yes, the whole crowd of you will each take a stone... the penalty for doing otherwise will be death. By all means, think it over! But there is no shame in this act... How could anyone blame you? All you are doing is picking up a stone... a single stone..."

Santiago snarled. "Damn you!"

Alexis grinned. "Here is your God, Santiago. In these good men and women, each picking up their stone, because such a tiny act cannot possibly be unforgivable! Because everyone else is doing it—so why not they? Your God is dead! You see it now, and they see it too. Listen to the chink of the stones falling one upon another, Santiago—isn't it music? Sweeter than a hymn!"

The stones piled up, a small pyramid on the swaying platform, and the platform was weighed down by them, a little more, and then a little more... and with each stone, Jesus Santiago was stretched, bit by bit, as the agony built... until his joints and sinews screamed for mercy.

But no mercy came.

The men and women of the town shuffled forward, one by one, picking up a stone, dropping it on the platform, laying them reverently, gently. Then they wrung their hands, as though washing them clean. On and on it went. On and on, the silent procession of the shuffling damned, with only the sound of the clicking stones and the creaking pulleys echoing across—

Alexis snapped his head around.

"Who laughed?"

He scowled, raising his voice. The moment had been ruined.

"Who laughed? Tell me!"

It came again. The laughter. Rich and strong, echoing around the square, freezing the milling workers in their tracks. An awful laugh—a terrible laugh of hope and joy and strength! A sound that had not been heard in the clockwork-town for nine years!

In the Red Dome, Eisenberg heard the sound and blinked, unsure if he had imagined it.

In the House Without Windows, Carina looked up from her books with a gasp of shock, unable to stop herself from smiling wide. Such a laugh!

Deep in the belly of the Palace of Beautiful Thoughts, no sound could penetrate, and yet a prisoner chuckled on the torture rack, as though amused by the great joke of life. Master Minus' scalpel clattered suddenly from numb fingers.

Such a laugh!

And suddenly, without warning, there appeared on a neighbouring rooftop a man, naked but for a pair of black trousers, ragged and stained with desert dust. His hair was long, filthy and unkempt, his beard was wild and home to insects, and over his eyes, there was tied a red sash, coated with old, dry blood, with holes cut to see by, the tail-ends flapping in the wind like pirate flags. His skin was baked and hard from the desert sun and the burning sand. To Alexis, who bathed so meticulously and treated his skin and hair with a thousand products, he seemed like some ugly, savage monster.

In one hand, the creature held a sword. Razor sharp—gleaming and glittering in the light—it pointed directly at Alexis. The smile on the creature's face was powerful and confident and utterly unafraid. To Alexis, it seemed like the smile the devil might have in the deepest pits of Hell.

The moment seemed to last a thousand years.

FAR AWAY, IN Alexis' apartment, two enlisted men were beginning the grisly task of stripping Alexis' bed. They were preparing a large hessian sack for the corpse—it would then be taken to one of the pits on the outskirts of town reserved for the Aldean dead. The men did not speak as they worked...

...but as the sound of laughter echoed across the town, they shuddered and glanced at each other briefly, as though hearing the first sounds of an approaching storm.

The corpse lay under the sheets.

CHAPTER TWO
BEYOND THOUGHT

THE MOMENT ENDED as Alexis finally found his voice—cracked and broken though it was.

"Kill him! Kill..."

He got no further. The masked man's foot slammed into Alexis' angel face with a sound like a rifle shot. In the time it had taken the Oberstleutnant to give the order, the man in the mask had hurled himself from the roof, landed on the stage with the grace of a cat, flipped onto his hands and driven the ball of his bare foot into the side of Alexis' jaw with enough force to loosen teeth. For the crowd, it was like watching lightning in a bottle. Jaws hung open and eyes that had been half-closed with sullen anger or acceptance—or even a terrible ecstasy of punishment—snapped wide.

Alexis stumbled back, his whip falling at Santiago's feet, and he toppled off the narrow stage and hit the ground beneath like a sack of flour, the wind driven out of him in an instant. His head struck one of the wooden beams that held the whole construction of the punishment-stage up, and everything went dark.

The soldiers standing on the stage were still aiming their guns, hesitant to fire—mere seconds had passed, and besides, to pull the trigger would be to risk raking the Oberstleutnant with bullets. As Alexis disappeared from view over the edge of the wooden stage, one of them—the sharpest—seized his chance.

His name was Udo Maurer and he was twenty-nine years old. He had grown up in a small village just north of Lowenthal. His grandmother smelled of cloves.

He had less than five seconds to live.

Udo Maurer squeezed the trigger on his MG-66, shooting a burst of lead directly towards the place where the masked man had stood an instant before. But by then he was no longer there. Udo's eyes lifted, and he watched the man turning a lazy somersault in the air—then his vision blacked out as the ball of the bare foot snapped down again, shattering his nose. He fell backwards, the gun still firing, muzzle veering to the left as it spat—

—Santiago flinched once as something stung his cheek and passed on its way—

—Anton Stroh, the other machine-gunner, felt nothing even as the bullet burst his head like a melon and lodged in the back of his helmet—

—and then Udo struck the ground, his gun clicking and clattering, out of ammo. His helmet had not been properly secured, and it bounced hard away from him. His eyes widened as he saw the masked man land like a cat on top of him, straddling him, his face a tight smile as his hand slammed down, the heel of the palm first, a hammer blow against Udo's exposed forehead that slammed his skull back into the stage with enough force to crack the wood.

All the lights went out in Udo. They weren't going to come on again. His heels drummed against the wood of the stage, but soon they would be still.

The masked man rolled and got to his feet, the sword still in his hand as he slashed, severing the rope that held up the heavy platform laden with its cargo of stones—the weight that was stretching the old priest like a bowstring. As the platform crashed to the stage, the stones clattering in a heap, Santiago fell forward with a gasp of released tension, slumping to the ground. The masked man swung his sword at the ropes binding his ankles, leaving only frayed ends.

"Move!"

Father Santiago knew that voice and did not know it. There was confidence there—an assurance that was unfamiliar, and yet... No. It couldn't be.

Heraclio was dead.

He rolled and ran, diving off the stage and then crawled beneath it.

Seconds had passed and the crowd were beginning to react. As was the Luftwaffe. The six wingmen above circled, moving into formation as their great metal wings clanked and whirred. It was often wondered how such unwieldy mechanisms could possibly keep the soldiers of the Luftwaffe in flight—as with so many things in Aldea, the truth was kept hidden, the better to promote a feeling of unease among the populace, as though the flying men had some terrible secret reserved only for diabolists. All magic tricks rely on a simple secret, and this one was achieved with a metal that could be bought in bulk from any industrial manufacturing firm in Germany—although at prohibitive expense: Cavorite, the 'nth metal' that powered Britain's economy, and to a lesser extent the Fatherland's. The clanking, hissing wings, driven to and fro by small jets of steam, were only for manoeuvrability—it was the cavorite that infused the metal of the wing-packs themselves, which allowed the Luftwaffe the freedom of birds.

Moritz Dresdner's voice carried above the clank and creak of his wings. "No machine-guns! If we fire on the crowd, we'll create more problems than we solve. Shoot him down with your Lugers! He's only one man!" Moritz Dresdner was the flight leader. He spoke from experience. Early in his career, he had fired an MG-62 into a small gathering of children—just as a warning, you understand—and that had indeed created a great many problems for him. He had been accused of wasting the resources of the Reich and given twenty days in the stockade.

He had also been fined thirty marks, three for each dead child. So it was certainly no small matter.

The formation passed over the stage, firing directly down at the man in the mask, who tumbled forward, rolling like an acrobat, flipped nimbly onto his hands, then changed direction wildly as bullets raked the spot where he was— and where he would have been.

The eyes behind the red mask narrowed as he landed next to the fallen platform and its cargo of stones. Gripping one of them in his hand, he tested the weight. The flyers were wheeling back around in the sky for a second pass—playing it safe. He waited for his moment.

As the troops swooped towards him, he swung his arm around—his memory flashing back to countless hours, days, months in the heat of the desert, picking objects, testing, throwing, perfecting his aim into a skill, then a science. He had blocked so much from his mind, but it was all hidden inside him, waiting to be reclaimed at the proper time.

The stone left his hand.

Moritz Dresdner was not from Dresden, as his name suggested, but rather from the small village of Hegensdorf. In his twenty-five years, he had become used to a life of great and secure privilege—for Moritz Dresdner was a handsome man. In fact, to say he was handsome was to obscure the issue. Many men are handsome—it's a word that can mean a number of things. Moritz Dresdner had been the most handsome man in Hegensdorf from the age of thirteen onwards—and was loved for it, in that subconscious way that certain people are. It was far more than just phenomenal success with women—that old cliché clutched wistfully at by the monstrously ugly—no, this was a face which allowed its owner access to a world where anything could simply be had. Shopkeepers would smile at the handsome boy and laugh when he stole sweets from their counters. "Oh, that boy! He's a rascal. You can tell just to look at him!" Then they would turn around and give another child—who was not quite so handsome—a stiff clip around the ear for trying to sneak a look at the latest issue of *The Pearl* as it sat high up on the top shelf.

And so it went. Moritz was constantly showered with all the gifts, love and appreciation that regular, less photogenic children were denied. He would turn up at restaurants with the latest in a series of easy conquests—who, needless to say, thought of themselves as the one who could finally change his ways—and be shown to the best table, even though he had made no appointment. Despite his constant philandering and occasional trysts with married women (the husband of one of whom committed suicide), he was considered a pillar of the community—something of a rogue, perhaps, but certainly deserving of a free drink whenever he happened to be present in the bar. When he chose to join the army—tiring of his many luxuries, as those who have never tasted hardship often do—he was provided with a good overseas posting in the Luftwaffe, in a position of some importance on a vital mission for the future of the German Race. He had expected as much.

Moritz Dresdner had that quality, and it was most present in his smile—his clean, sparkling white teeth, arranged just so, not quite perfect but perfect in their very imperfection, his eyes that shined and twinkled. He could turn his smile on like a lamp, like the sun, and brighten the lives of any who came near. He had never imagined that it was possible to live any other way, but he had a dim understanding that his face was his fortune. As such, he kept very good care of his teeth and skin and occasionally laid awake at nights, with a fear he could not quite name.

It was the fear of this very moment.

The stone smashed into his face, knocking out his front teeth, chipping and shattering the rest, and breaking his nose. The impact cracked his jaw in two places and the sharp facets of the rock carved at his flesh, lacerating his lips. Moritz Dresdner, filled with panic and terror, bucked and jerked his body as he scrabbled at his destroyed face, and thus lost control of his wings.

The cavorite infused into the structure of the wing-pack was designed to compensate for the weight of the pack and rider, to enable the Luftwaffe to rise from the ground and make them mobile while in the air, but the cavorite ratio of each pack was carefully balanced for the individual rider's weight. Thus, if a wingman wanted to land, he could land. The downside was that if a wingman could not keep from crashing, then he would crash—as surely as a bird shot down from the sky.

He came down in the crowd. Up until this moment, the massed citizens of Aldea had been standing and watching the show, partly mesmerised at the display, partly afraid of the consequences of moving from the spot. But when Moritz Dresdner wheeled around towards them, desperately clutching at his ruined mouth, the assembled throng scattered in all directions, leaving him to crash down hard in the dirt, the crunch of impact breaking his jaw completely, crushing that handsome face beyond recognition.

Moritz would survive. He would be shipped out from Aldea, back to Germany, and spend six months in a treatment centre in Bremen before returning to the village of Hegensdorf. And twenty-two months after his return, friendless, deep in debt and awaiting trial for three counts of shoplifting, he would open his wrists with a pearl-handled straight-razor, still not fully comprehending exactly how it was his life could have changed so drastically.

The stone hit the ground, raising a little cloud of dust.

The man in the mask smiled. His voice was low and clear.

"Apologies. My hand slipped."

UNDER THE STAGE, Father Santiago huddled and stared at the neatly punched holes, the sun shining through them. The holes where the bullets had gone right through the wood and into the dusty ground.

Soon, he thought, *they will happen to shoot at the piece of stage that I am under, and that will be the end. Or the Oberstleutnant will wake from his dreams and his first act will be to strangle me. Better than being stretched to death, I suppose. Oh Heavenly Father Above, look kindly on your foolish servant now. He did his best and now his life is in the hands of a madman.*

A familiar madman. Father Santiago sat under the stage, working at the ropes at his wrists, gnawing them, and tried to remember where he last heard that voice.

DRESDNER HAD BEEN the flight leader. There was a moment—a few seconds at the most after he smashed into the ground—when the five other wingmen simply looked at each other, flying in disorder, desperately trying to remember who would be next in line. Moritz, with his inbuilt certainty, had never prepared his unit for what might happen in the event of his face being smashed beyond recognition, and so there was no real second-in-command—it had never been fully decided.

So the masked man had a brief window of opportunity, and he used it. His hand took a stone, and then the stone left his hand. He picked up another and it left his hand too and then his hand found a third, as easily and quickly as thinking the words. It was beyond thought—as the action was conceived, it was carried out. Things merely were what they were and occurred in the order they occurred. Events took their place. He was in his element, and the world fitted around him like a glove. All past mistakes and triumphs were simply the causes that led to the current events. Things were what they were at any moment—and he filled that moment with the precise action needed.

Do you understand?

He did.

He had learned this concept in the desert, after his soul had shrieked at itself and torn itself apart with bloody claws for what seemed like a thousand years, and it was his total understanding of it that made him the most dangerous man on the planet.

The stone left his hand, joining the other two in flight.

The first stone hit Konrad Zumwald in the ribs, cracking one. The second smashed into the same rib, and the stabbing pain forced him to double over, aiming himself towards the ground. He saw the dangers and tried to pull up, against the screaming of his shattered rib, desperately attempting to right himself despite the agony.

Wolfgang Rader growled in anger, swooping forward for the kill, readying his own pistol. He pointed the gun directly at the masked man's heart as the third stone flew.

This was the stone that did the damage. It hurtled into Konrad's balls, impacting hard against the testicles, ringing them like bells. Konrad gasped then screamed loud at the stabbing pain that ripped into his belly. He veered upwards, in front of Wolfgang Rader, at the same moment the other man pulled the trigger. A single bullet tore into the back of Konrad's neck, erupting through his throat in a gusher of hot blood, the crimson drops falling to earth like rain. Konrad's eyes went wide, glassy. He tumbled to the ground like a leaf.

Wolfgang was shaking, stiff, drifting in the air. Thirty minutes earlier he had been slapping Konrad on the back, promising him a beer in the mess hall to make up the rest of the debt he owed. A day before that, Konrad was grinning and pocketing the seventeen marks he had won from Wolfgang in the poker game and reminding his fellow wingman that he owed three more. Eight months before that, Wolfgang was teaching Konrad how the game of Seven Card Stud was played and the hierarchy of the winning hands. Three years before that, Wolfgang Rader was shaking the hand of Konrad Zumwald, originally from a district in Bonn, whose father was a doctor. "Welcome to the unit," he had said.

Konrad Zumwald hit the ground hard, the light fading from his eyes. The flesh of his throat flapped, ragged from the bullet that had torn through it. Wolfgang Rader dropped his gun and stared with eyes that didn't see.

He was thinking about a secret the two men had shared. A secret that would never be told to anyone, that was theirs alone. And now belonged to only him.

The man in the mask hurled himself left as three Luger shots hit the wood of the stage, passing through the space he had so recently vacated. He reached out and let his fingertips find coiled leather—the bullwhip, still stained with Santiago's blood. His fist closed and jerked as he rolled up onto his knees, arm snapping out hard, the whip following—

CRACK! The sound of domination!—

—and the tip of the whip curled around Marcel Renoux's Luger and tore it from his hand, fracturing the bones of the index and middle fingers. Marcel Renoux had been born in France, but moved to Germany at the age of eighteen with the express purpose of joining the Ultimate Reich. Life in Paris was too small, too chic, too petty. The obsession with Le Nouvelle Vague—it turned the stomach. Marcel dreamed of steel instead of silk, of fire and raised fists instead of cigarette smoke and clever words. He dreamed of what it might be like for the Ultimate Reich to march in his streets, to stride through Paris, to occupy it and bend it to their rule. His grandfather had died fighting back the Nazis on the Maginot Line, but there were always, and always would be, those who felt more than a little sympathy with the Führer's ideals.

He'd emigrated seven years ago, at the age of eighteen, head shaven, denim on his back, a cloud of contemptuous Gauloise smoke infesting his lungs. As he crossed the border, it was as though the air had become clean again. Immediately he marched into the nearest recruiting office and joined up. Sliding his feet into the jackboots had given him an erection, as is often the case when small men achieve small dreams of being controlled by big systems. The sound of domination was familiar and sweet to Marcel Renoux.

Two years ago, after a long, hard climb through the ranks, he had been transferred to Aldea. In his mind, it was his dream of a conquered Paris made real—and he strode through it with a smile of triumph, his leather boots creaking. He was a god, an Aryan, in a world that made sense to him.

Much more than a gun had been taken from Marcel Renoux. Such is often the way with men who worship power—they will bark and strut and snarl on command, but a crack of the whip will show them where the power really lies.

The whip cracked twice more, yanking the guns from the hands of the other two wingmen still airborne. The masked man caught the last one, whirled it around his finger and fired, a whirl of motion. The bullet sailed through the air, missing by a vast distance. The man in the mask looked down at the gun, a vexed expression on his face with the merest hint of humiliation.

The masked man had been in the desert for nine years. He had his sword with him. He had stones. He had his fists and his feet and the phantoms of his mind and he had time. Most importantly, he had the spark of madness, the fire of vengeance—and the understanding that all things were possible.

He had not had a gun.

Aiming one was a lot harder than it looked.

Perhaps in the future he would have a spare moment to practice. Not now. Now there was only time for action. His sword was in one hand, the whip in the other, and in the sky the wingmen were drawing their own swords, sharp as razors, swooping like eagles to move in for the kill.

He smiled, flicking the Luger back by its barrel.

The gun left his hand.

Underneath the stage, Father Santiago had managed to free his hands. His wrists burnt and ached from the ropes and the agony in his back was starting to make his vision blur. He could feel the trickle of fresh blood coursing down his spine every time he moved. He kept still, watching the bullets pound through the wood of the stage, getting closer to where he was, burying in the dirt inches from his feet.

Alexis murmured thickly, and began to stir.

OTTO BAUM WAS a simple man of simple pleasures. Out of all the members of the unit, he was the least complicated. He simply did as he was told. He was a big man, tall and skinny—if a soldier was too heavy, the cavorite would not be enough to help him achieve flight—and he packed a hard punch. His swordsmanship was proficient, and he had learned the hard art of air duelling with the simple, slogging perseverance with which he learned everything else. He was among the best of the Luftwaffe in this respect, which was obvious from his stance as he swooped in, ready to calmly chop off the masked man's head.

Which was why the butt of the hurled pistol slammed hard into the space between his eyes.

The masked man drew his own sword as Otto continued his fall, positioning the blade carefully. The gun hadn't hit hard enough to kill, but Otto's vision blanked and blurred and all he could think of was pain. It was only for an instant—three seconds at the very most.

That was long enough for Otto to fall onto the masked man's sword.

The point slid between the ribs and carved through one of the lungs, then slid out. Otto collapsed on the floor, choking blood before the blade chopped neatly down again, severing his spine at the base of the neck. After that, Otto Baum was even simpler, and he needed no pleasures at all.

The man in the mask looked up at his attackers and smiled. It was the kind of smile a gallant suitor might use to entice a fair señorita to dance, but it was contrasted by an icy gaze that promised quick death. Such a look might have worked to the swordsman's advantage had Wolfgang Rader not barrelled into him from the side, a mass of fists and tears, snarling and sobbing.

The death of Konrad Zumwald had driven Wolfgang to the brink of madness and beyond. Later, his fellow members of the Luftwaffe would wonder what it was the two men had shared that would make Rader attack so recklessly. Various theories would be expounded on the subject in the mess hall and in the dormitories, some of them scandalous, others simply scurrilous. The most common was that Konrad Zumwald and Wolfgang Rader had been having a sexual affair. Such things were uncommon among the soldiery for obvious reasons—the consequences for such a thing would be ignominy and death. But the very danger of such a punishment made such affairs, when they did occur, matters of deep and undeniable emotion. To risk death for a true love was something many soldiers could half-heartedly respect—even if they were, of course, disgusted and appalled and horrified, et cetera, that such a devil's practice could go on among proud soldiers of the Reich. They were quite wrong, anyway. Konrad Zumwald and Wolfgang Rader had not had any form of sexual contact whatsoever.

It was something quite different.

The masked man kept his grip on the sword, turning to meet the threat, slicing in a hard, quick, stroke, then sidestepping Wolfgang Rader's body as it flew on its way. The head of Wolfgang Rader arced up in a slow turn, lips working, gasping like a fish, then rolled along the stage to drop off the edge. The last thought in his severed mind before the blackness came was that he dearly wanted to tell his secret—the terrible secret, the long-held heart-deep secret that burned his lips every single day—but then there was the hard crunch of cracking bone and after that there were no thoughts at all.

So much for secrets.

Rader had sacrificed his life to give the two remaining men in the unit an opening. They took it, swords flashing, ready to carve up the masked man-like beef.

FATHER SANTIAGO'S MOUTH went dry as Alexis' eyes opened. At first there was confusion in the blue eyes, and then rage—terrible, burning rage, deep as the sea. He rolled over, and the expression on his face made Jesus Santiago clench his bladder for fear of wetting himself.

"Priest!"

Alexis snarled the word, spitting it. Slowly, he reached to his belt, gripping the sharp, cruel hunting knife he kept there. The blade was cut with seven notches. Seven kills. Alexis looked at it and grinned.

He smiled as the priest began to scramble backwards. "You like that swastika I drew on your back? There'll be another on your face in a moment, and two for your chest, and a nice big one for down between your…"

A severed head rolled off the stage and smacked hard into the back of Alexis' skull, hard enough to make a sound like bone cracking. Alexis went out like a light, slumping forward. He was lucky not to impale himself on his knife.

Santiago's eyes widened. He stared at the severed head, the eyes already rolling back. The lips twitched a couple of times, as though the head was trying to say something, to tell him something terrible and wonderful and strange.

IT WAS DOWN to Marcel Renoux and Hugo Stahl, and Hugo Stahl was the finest air duellist the Luftwaffe had produced.

The secret to air duelling is to combine the skills of the jousting knights of old with the killing instincts of the eagle swooping to catch prey. Two combatants dive, weave and spin on their metal wings, swords ready to murder, each aiming to strike their killing blow through the eye of their opponent's defence. The practice is bloody and savage, frowned upon by most of the officer class for its lack of discipline. The penalty for conducting an unauthorised air duel is six months in the stockade, or a year if there has been a fatality, with a fine of more than two hundred marks. Hardly small potatoes. Of his ten years with the Luftwaffe, Stahl had spent four years in the stockade for offences relating to air duelling.

That said, an air duel in progress is a strange and fascinating sight, a display of dazzling flight that requires the utmost skill from the combatants. So the Luftwaffe trained its wingmen scrupulously in the art of air duelling, and held mock-duels with blunt-tipped fencing foils each Sunday. Hugo Stahl routinely won these, and won the larger events that were held yearly (at least, during those times when he wasn't sitting in the stockade).

As a result, the wingmen of the Luftwaffe were accomplished swordsmen, used to the additional complexities and nuances of conducting sword-fights in the infinite arena of the sky. To face one of them on the ground and survive for sixty seconds would be a challenge that would push the finest duellist to his limits.

To face two was suicide.

The masked man smiled.

Renoux charged first, aiming his sword in a wide arc at neck height. The masked man held his ground, both hands gripping the pommel of his sword, shifting the blade to block the stroke and then aiming forward, attempting to plunge the point of the blade into Renoux's eye. Renoux reacted quickly, turning the masked man's blade aside and countering.

The blades rang as Stahl circled around like a hawk sighting a mouse. He grinned. At this angle it would be simplicity itself to thrust his sword into the masked man's back. The most beautiful thought of all to him was the knowledge that he would finally be able to kill—to spill blood, take life, stop the heart—and there would be no consequence. If anything, he would receive a commendation for a noble action in battle.

He was salivating at the thought as he swooped.

Marcel Renoux was sweating—his sword flashed and rang as his every blow was expertly parried and driven back by the man in the bloody mask. He was going about this the wrong way, he knew—treating it as a duel on the ground, hovering in close, barely a foot above the wood of the stage, not using the natural advantage flight gave him. Time to cut and run, recover his breath and then circle in for the kill... but then his eyes were drawn over the masked man's shoulder, to Hugo Stahl, diving, his sword up and ready to drive in, to kill.

Marcel Renoux allowed himself a tight smile as he suddenly pressed back his attack. In addition to the glance over the shoulder, it was too much of a signal.

The man in the mask suddenly flattened and spun, pirouetting out of the path of the plunging blade while deflecting Renoux's thrust from the front, leaving the Frenchman wide open. Stahl cursed as the point of his blade missed the masked man by inches, to pierce Marcel Renoux's breastbone—and then his heart.

The masked man grinned and swung. If Hugo Stahl had been any less of a fighter, he might have stayed still, wasting precious moments attempting fruitlessly to tug his blade from Renoux's chest, even as the killing blow cleaved the base of his neck. But Hugo Stahl was not a man who wasted moments. The moment his sword burst Renoux's heart, he let go, cursing once again, and flew out of reach of his enemy's sword-strike. The masked man's blade passed through the air where Stahl had been and buried in Marcel Renoux's neck.

It had taken less than half a second. The tight smile was still frozen on Renoux's face, as the second, bloody smile gaped wide beneath his chin, spilling blood down his chest. His eyes glazed as his knees buckled and he crumpled to the stage, his blood pooling and seeping between the wooden boards. Neither the masked man nor Hugo Stahl gave him a second glance.

Instead, they watched each other, Stahl circling, weaponless, the masked man with sword in hand but tied to the ground. Those few stragglers who'd remained in the square watched them. They held their breath. The whole battle had taken... three minutes? Four? Backup would be on the way at any moment, and then the masked man would be torn apart and killed. A flock of wingmen would descend on him, or a rush of ground troops armed with machine-guns. He was only one man.

One man who had killed five wingmen without breaking a sweat.

Some in the crowd held their breath in anticipation. One or two held it in wonder. These would be the ones who would begin to spread the legend.

Stahl circled, wings beating slowly, creaking in the still air. Then he swooped down. Not towards the masked man, but towards the Luger. Wolfgang Rader's Luger, lying on the dusty ground where it had fallen. One bullet had killed Zumwald, but there were seven shots still in the magazine. He could keep out of range and pick the masked man off at his leisure.

The man in the bloodstained mask dropped the whip and reached forward to take Stahl's sword from Renoux's chest. It did not come easily, but it slid out quickly enough, in the time it took Stahl to swoop down to the ground and grab the pistol.

A gun versus a sword.

UNDERNEATH THE STAGE, Alexis blinked. The pain in his head was abominable—a hot, stabbing, throbbing pain, that threatened to make him vomit. There was something he had to remember to do. Someone he had to murder.

His eyes focussed on Jesus Santiago.

HUGO STAHL SMILED. His aim with a bullet was not quite as perfect as his aim with a sword, but still, he was as proficient with a Luger in his hand as any man in the Luftwaffe. This time he would take into account his foe's seeming ability to dodge bullets. He would lead his pigeon, aim to wound. Perhaps one of the legs, or the gut, and then a shot to the head when the quarry was downed... Stahl's finger's closed around the pistol. He whirled, aiming carefully, watching to see which way his enemy would break.

The masked man's arm moved like lightning as Stahl's sword left his hand.

Stahl blinked, reflected light flashing into his eyes, spoiling his aim. Light reflected from something arcing towards him—a sword, his own sword. The sword he had polished and sharpened that very morning, flying towards him as straight and true as an arrow, thrown like a javelin—

—and then he was lying on the ground and his left side wouldn't move and there was pain right through him and blood in his eyes. His right hand reached up and touched the length of steel jutting from his forehead. He tried to remember what had happened and he couldn't think of the words. He couldn't think of anything but grey. Grey turning to black.

Hugo Stahl's body began to convulse, so hard that his sword began to teeter. It was lodged firmly between his eyes, in the folds of his ruptured brain, but its weight slowly turned his head to the side, as if he was settling to sleep.

The masked man smiled.

It had really been an excellent throw.

ALEXIS NARROWED HIS eyes and snarled, like an animal ready to pounce. His head was clearing and the agony was subsiding somewhat, but the anger still held him in a red fog. He understood what had happened. He had been in control of the situation. He had been showing the worthless subhuman scum who was boss, who was in charge. And then he'd been thrown around like a child's doll by some lunatic caveman and—and this really was the icing on the cake—he'd been brained by the severed head of one of his own men.

He gripped the hilt of his hunting knife hard enough to whiten his knuckles. He would be revenged for this humiliation, and revenged now. The masked madman could wait—wait for backup to arrive and blow him into gobbets with sustained bursts of machine-gun fire, and never mind any workers who happened to get in the way. But the priest—the trembling, mewling Father Jesus Santiago—he would die now. He would die now and die in the ugliest manner. By the knife.

The snarl became a smile. Alexis crept forward.

Father Santiago was trembling, shaking like a leaf, a shell of a man, a wreck. His back was agony and his vision was beginning to grey at the edges through loss of blood. All he could do as Alexis closed in for the kill was try not to look into his eyes. If he didn't look, perhaps he could let himself believe in a quick death. He mumbled a soft, desperate prayer under his breath, for the strength to face what was about to happen.

There was a noise like a gunshot as the bullwhip cracked through the air. The leather tail laid itself on Alexis' face, snapping harshly, cutting it open down the cheek. Alexis screamed and fell back, clutching at his face with both hands, trying to stem the blood. His face had been broken. The film-star looks were gone in an instant, scarred, imperfect, ruined, gone. To Alexis it was worse than death. It tore through him on a level deeper than thought, and instantly his legs began to pump and work, scrambling him back, rolling him to his feet, carrying him away from that place. Tears and blood mixed on his cheek. When thought returned to him, he would feel worse than shame. And that would come to coalesce into a cold, hard, righteous anger, burning with freezing fire.

In time.

Now, he ran, and cried, and behind their windows and through their curtains, the town watched.

The man in the bloody mask dropped from the stage, sword coming down towards Alexis in a killing stroke, but he was already gone. In the distance, there was the sound of creaking, cracking steam-powered wings. A flock of predators.

Father Santiago looked up at the masked man, his vision blurring. He had seen him before somewhere... the day of the wedding... he knew if he could only remember who it was, then maybe he could ask him to help. His lips were moving but no sound came out. If he could only remember the name...

Slowly, everything went black.

Jesus Santiago collapsed.

JESUS SANTIAGO SAT up in his bed.

He was back in his little house, a tumbledown shack that looked abandoned from the outside—an illusion he'd carefully created to avoid detection. The shack had a large basement and it was here that Santiago slept. He often spent whole days down here, working by the light of one of the hundreds of old mass candles which he'd carefully stored and kept and rationed for nine years.

The shack was part of a long-abandoned satellite town of Pasito, a tiny knot of buildings nestled between cliffs two miles from the town itself. Even before the invasion, Santiago had been the only one who still lived there. Once it had been a thriving offshoot, a half-dozen strong new dwellings that might one day have become a town in their own right. But that was more than a century ago, and the cutting had failed to take root. Over a hundred years, families had moved back across the desert to Pasito, one by one, taking their belongings and often stripping their houses for wood until not even the frame was left. Even the old Santiago family home was in disrepair, so much so that it became a source of endless amusement to the townspeople. Indeed, Father Jesus very often began his covert sermons with a digression about how he really had to get around to fixing his roof or mending his windows or a hundred and one other small tasks that he never performed, drawing a little gentle mockery from his congregation before he moved onto more serious topics. Of course, they all knew the truth of the matter—Father Jesus Santiago was the most conscientious man you would ever meet, but he kept himself so busy with church and charity that he never had time to look after his dilapidated shack. It was only a place to get his head down for a few hours each night before he went back to the business of tending to his people. More often than not, he had spent his nights sleeping in the church.

The invaders had no way of knowing any of that. The one time they had bothered to search through the place, having stumbled across it while mapping a new patrol route through the desert, he had hidden in the basement, not moving, barely breathing, and they had missed the trapdoor that led down, underneath the rug. He had listened to them as they stood on top of it, discussing whether or not to burn the houses. Eventually they had decided to leave them be—it would be a waste of fuel and controlling the blaze would take away vital resources from the rest of the occupation. After four years of occupation, and with resistance at an all-time low, the scouting party had not even bothered to record the tumbledown shack on their map of the area.

And so Father Santiago's hovel became his hiding place, the base from which he conducted his own private war, without weapons or tactics—with nothing but his faith. It had turned his hair grey and driven deep wrinkles into the flesh of his face, and now it had carved throbbing scars into the muscles of his back.

His eyes focussed slowly, and he saw the stranger in the red mask looking at him with his head cocked.

"You've been out nearly two days, amigo. I thought you were a dead man."

Jesus swallowed, closing his eyes. He felt dead himself. The scars on his back still pulsed with heat. He reached to the bandages that had been wound carefully around his body. The wound had been dressed expertly. Where had the masked man learned that?

"How did..." he coughed hard, grimacing, as the swordsman handed him a cup of water. He drank in sips.

"How did I get you back? I remember where you used to live, Father Santiago. It's been a long time, but I still remember your battered old house."

"No, no... how did you know how to apply these bandages? The Djego I knew..." The stranger flinched as though he'd been struck. For a moment the only sound was the sound of the night wind in the desert above their heads. The priest was the first to speak again. "How did you know?"

The stranger rubbed the back of his head. "I forget. I forget so much, but it's all there for when I need it. I... I think I picked it up somewhere."

"Advanced first aid. Enough to save my life, and you 'picked it up somewhere'? What's happened to you, Djego?" Another flinch. Every mention of that name was a stab of a knife in his heart, a twist of a blade deep inside a wound that had scabbed and scarred over a thousand years ago. But the priest kept on. "I know who you are, Djego. What happened to you? What did you become?"

"Djego..." the masked man forced the word from his lip. "Djego is dead, Father Santiago. He was useless and stupid and pathetic. And he died and left good flesh behind. So I took his place." The eyes behind the mask met Santiago's then, and the priest breathed in sharply. There was nothing of Djego in them.

There was nothing human in them.

Something bigger had lodged there, something stronger and faster than a man, something with a laugh that could shake mountains and a spirit like hot iron and fire. Something better.

"I am his shadow. El Sombra."

This time the silence did not even have the benefit of the roaring desert wind to fill it.

Slowly, the priest began to smile.

"El Sombra. As good a name as any. All right, my friend, go and get us some coffee. We have a lot of work in front of us, you know?"

El Sombra relaxed, allowed himself a smile—one that promised great deeds and greater vengeance on the men who had stolen his life from him.

"Oh yes, amigo. A lot of work."

CHAPTER THREE
THE ENGINE

EISENBERG WAS STARTLED by the sound of the red telephone.

He had been leaning back in his creaking leather chair and watching the ceiling fan turn around and around. It seemed to him like four swords, cleaving the air with a regular slicing motion. He couldn't let go of the thought—the thought of the masked man, that bearded savage with his swords and his idiot grin and his terrible laughter, as though there was no finer thing to be doing on a hot summer's day than slaughtering good National Socialists. The masked man had killed his men, insulted his son and humiliated him. And now the red telephone. The red telephone that had never rung once, not in all the time he had been here, not until now.

Eisenberg took a morbid satisfaction in the thought that the ringing tone was as he had always imagined—like the rattling of metal bones, the jangling of some obscene talisman. He stared at the receiver as it vibrated in its cradle and considered ignoring it, but of course he could not. He might as well take the dagger from his belt and cut his own throat.

His arm seemed to reach on its own as he answered.

"Berlin calling, Generaloberst."

"Yes." His mouth was dry, his tongue like paper. There was silence at the other end of the line for a very long time.

"Generaloberst. Guten abend."

The sound.

A terrible chorus of clicking and crackling and buzzing, like some great mechanical insect from a child's nightmare slowly crawling up the telephone line to spit its venom. The scraping of metal on metal and glass on glass. And forever in the background the noise of the pistons, of hammers beating down in the foundries of Hell, the grotesque music of the machine.

This was the voice of his Führer.

"G-guten abend, Mein Führer." He swallowed. His temples throbbed. Fear took him. Perhaps he could bluff it out. The Führer surely would not yet know of—

"I understand there has been a disturbance of sorts."

There was no bluffing. He was a fool to even think it. The Führer knew, as he knew everything. *The lightning strikes the tall trees and not the blades of grass*, he thought bitterly. Which of the bastards had sold him out? Master Plus, perhaps, the fat little jailer, so aware of the precariousness of his position, so desperate to do anything to cement it. Or Master Minus, the sadistic little freak. The image of his son's face rose in his mind. Alexis, with his angel face, Alexis who left dead girls for the room service to pick up. The obedient second in command. Did he not have the most to gain? Would his own son be so ruthless as to ?

"I am not used to being kept waiting, Generaloberst."

"I—I am sorry, Mein Führer. I was merely—merely gathering my thoughts so as to…"

The metal and glass made the approximation of a chuckle.

"You are afraid that this afternoon's little display will be the end for you."

Eisenberg closed his eyes, trying to ignore the whine and scream of the machine. "Jawohl, Mein Führer. Just so."

"Allow me to tell you a story, Herr Generaloberst. For a short time in Vienna, I had a room in a cheap boarding house. There were rats that came in the night to steal food and creep over my bedding. And so I put down poison. In the morning, I woke to find four or five dead around the skirting board, but there was one—as big as a cat. It was on its haunches, nibbling away at a lump of the poison—the same poison that had killed its brothers! Is it not a curious thing, Herr Generaloberst?"

Eisenberg's knuckles were white against the red of the phone. "Yes, Mein Führer. Very curious."

"I beat that rat to death with the heel of my boot, Herr Generaloberst. The poison had worked so well on so many, but there will always be one for whom it does not work. I learned that in my cold little room in Vienna, and many times since. You are learning it now. It is a fact of life, mein Herr. There is always one."

Eisenberg could not breathe. The Führer was not relieving him of his post. There had been no order to return to Berlin. The great man understood. He sympathised! "I will crush him, Mein Führer. My men will not rest until he is in pieces!"

"Projekt Uhrwerk has come too far now to be allowed to falter, Generaloberst. By all means, make the attempt. But should the poison fail, do not feel offended if I provide you with the heel of a boot."

"Do you mean...?"

"Der Zinnsoldat is being readied for use."

"Mein Führer! I do not deserve such..."

"That will be all. Guten Abend, Generaloberst."

"Guten Abend, Mein Führer!"

The telephone clicked. The clatter and howl of the machine voice was replaced by silence. Gingerly, the General replaced the receiver in its crook, then leant back to once again contemplate the great ceiling fan as it swept in its measured circle. The blades of the fan no longer seemed to cutting the air of the room like a sword. Now, they seemed like four hands, extended, saluting in all directions. An endless salute, on and on forever.

Eisenberg was unaware he was smiling.

"I SEE YOU'VE got a new look."

A week had passed; the sun was again beginning its slow climb across the arc of the sky. In Jesus Santiago's cellar, El Sombra was eating a meal he had not had to skin himself, and eating it from a plate. The novelty of this situation was still so distracting to him that he barely heard the comment. He reached to run the tips of his fingers across his chin, the stubble scratching. All that was left of the wild tangle of beard was a rough moustache that stretched above his lips and down past the sides of his mouth. Similarly, the mass of hair above his temples had been chopped down to a manageable level. "The hair is getting into my eyes when I fight."

"It makes you look a bit less like a mountain man, you know? What's your next move?"

"I have no idea, amigo. Probably lots of stabbing. Is this lizard?"

The old priest smiled and shook his head. "Salt pork. You've been out a lot lately—I take it you're trying to draw some attention to yourself?"

The masked man was already tearing into the thin strip of meat hanging between his fingers. "Make a lot of noise and draw out the ones who killed my people—who killed me—who built this abomination on the bones of my home. When I meet them, they die, and this monster—this 'Aldea'—dies with them."

Jesus blinked. "That is... quite possibly the least well thought-out plan I have ever heard, my friend." He leaned over the table. "Do you know what will happen if you just charge in waving your sword?"

El Sombra was concentrating on a fried egg. "I'll kill the baby-faced bastard who murdered my brother, then I'll cut off his father's head and there'll be a parade."

The old priest chuckled humourlessly. "The only parade they'll hold in this town is for your corpse. The good men who watch over us from above will have killed the dangerous radical, the unmutualist with the mask and the sword, the serial killer, you know? You don't understand the power of the press around here. Besides, even if you do manage to kill ten wingmen, twenty, the General himself—there'll be another just like him here within the week, doing exactly the same thing. Also, you're going to need a knife and a fork to eat that."

El Sombra took hold of the egg, lifting it up like a wobbling white curtain, before biting into the yolk as it hung. It was a messy operation. Finally he spoke.

"Okay. Then I need to build a revolution. Drive those winged killers out and have an army ready if they come back. And for that I need the people on my side."

Jesus nodded. "That's more like it. Would you like another egg?"

"I couldn't possibly. You only have so many, and you're about to help me bring down an army of bastards. If the people are going to be on my side, I have to give them something. Something they don't have."

"Freedom."

El Sombra cocked his head. "A giant box of freedom? Where do I find one of those? I was thinking more of guns or medicine or strong drink, amigo. Start small. Is there some kind of storage depot or something the soldiers use?"

The old priest nodded again, taking a mason jug and uncorking it with his teeth. "Something better, my friend. Something much better."

*   *   *

EWALD SCHENKER HAD been in the Luftwaffe for twenty-two years, seven months, twenty-eight days and five hours. He had been inspired by stories of men who flew like birds, of honourable combat in the air, of modern-day Siegfrieds ruling the very skies. The recruiting officer who'd shaken his hand and led him away from his mother had promised him a world of action and adventure and the thrill of conquest, a life of opera and majesty. The reality had been a crushing disappointment.

Ewald Schenker drove the Traction Engine.

Oh, it was impressive enough. The Engine was an immense beast, fully forty feet long and sixteen across, with a crew of eleven. In appearance it looked much like an immense beetle. Twin treads at the side ran the length of the craft—the front ends raised to tackle obstacles—and a wide slit ran in front for the drivers to see out of. There were two levers, one for each tread, but in an emergency it was possible for one man to handle both, running back and forth between the massive controls.

Half of the space inside the beast was devoted to storage—this machine was first and foremost a transport for cargo and troops, though there were rumours that the Führer had considered mass-producing armed versions. Two men were tasked with guarding the cargo. It was an unenviable duty. They were allowed no distractions and simply stood to attention in the crushing heat. Were they even to engage in conversation—even look at each other—they would be taken off guard duty and made to work the firebox.

The firebox connected to a long chimney that rose from the centre of the roof and belched a never-ending torrent of thick black smoke into the sky, making the Engine visible for miles. Three strong men tended this furnace hour after hour, shovelling in coal and venting excess steam when necessary through pipes in the side of the craft. It was hot work—heat that made this chamber of the Engine resemble the fires of Hell. Working the firebox was a punishment detail.

The most pleasant job on the Engine was to be one of the four men riding up top, hanging onto the rails that ran around the outside of the roof. In the early days of the occupation, the Engine had been a target for rebels, but the roof guards, with their higher vantage point, were in a position to pick off any approaching raider from almost a mile away. Two of them carried sniping rifles for this very purpose—the others were armed with pistols. Up on the roof, they were free to hold conversations, and the burning heat of the desert sun was comfortable compared to the agonies endured by the men in the belly of the behemoth, men such as Ewald Schenker.

Ewald grimaced as he wiped more sweat from his brow and glanced over at his co-pilot. Bruckner seemed not to have a care in the world. Didn't he feel this accursed heat? Ewald felt a sudden wave of hatred for the chubby little wretch. How much longer would he be in this iron tomb, blasted by searing heat, chained to the odious Herr Bruckner? Herr Bruckner who had never read a book, who stuffed himself with day-old bratwurst and then farted the hours away in their confinement, who could not speak of a woman without giving a description of her imagined performance in the bedroom. Herr Bruckner, this oafish boor who was fifteen years younger than he, who had all his teeth and a full head of hair! Herr Bruckner, who joined the Luftwaffe only last year and would be his superior before this year was out! Herr Bruckner, who was constantly there, Herr Bruckner, Herr Bruckner, may the devil take Herr Bruckner! Ewald Schenker spat.

"This intolerable heat!"

Bruckner looked over with an amused grin. "There's nothing we can do about it, so we may as well ignore it." It was just the kind of mindless platitude that became him.

"We can take the route through the canyons again. That will give us some shade—the men up top will thank us for that, at least."

Bruckner frowned. "We shouldn't take the same route too many times. We could go around the mesa and be back at base in good time."

"Or we could go through the canyons and have an hour to spare. Perhaps even time to crack open one of those beers we're carrying when we get home, eh?" Ewald hated the wheedling tone in his own voice. Had it come to this? Begging Herr Bruckner for a moment's shade? For the illusion of shade—inside the guts of the engine, staring through the viewing slit, it would make little difference.

"Oh, very well." Bruckner sighed theatrically and tugged the lever, slowing his tread, forcing the machine to describe a slight arc that pointed it towards the distant canyons. "Why you want shade when you're already stuck inside a damned metal coffin is beyond me."

Ewald's face was crimson. He felt like a child. He stared straight ahead, watching the canyons slowly coming into view, and quite suddenly he wished Heinrich Bruckner dead. The thought was quite clear and distinct, almost as though it had been placed in his mind by another—*I wish Herr Bruckner were dead. I would not mind dying myself today, if I could first see him dead with my own eyes.*

Had he known his wish would come true within the hour, he may have thought differently.

FOR THE MOST part, the rock walls of the canyon were high and steep, but in places they were only twelve feet off the ground. At those points it would be possible for a man to leap onto something passing below with only slight risk of injury. El Sombra waited patiently, pressed flat against the rock, listening for the unmistakable sound of the Engine as it chugged closer.

"You were right, they're going to come through this canyon."

Jesus nodded, taking a swig from a hip flask. "Mmm. When all this started, people used to try to attack the Engine, but anyone who attempted that died before they got close. They have sniper rifles on top, so they can pick..."

El Sombra smiled tightly. "Doesn't matter, amigo. This is close-up work. They aren't even wearing wings."

"I think they have some of their special flying-metal in the frame of the thing. To make it lighter, you know? Otherwise it couldn't move with the cargo in it. The guards on top used to have wings, but they probably figured they could cut corners. That's what it's all about—over time, they've got used to having no resistance. It's made them sloppy. Six, seven years ago, their routes were still all out in the open. They'd take the long way through the desert, so they could see for miles, pick off anybody they saw. Now they want to take shortcuts, get a little shade for the guys on top of the thing, you know? They've forgotten why they did it any other way."

"Let's remind them."

GEORG WEBER HELD the rail in his hands, enjoying the sudden cool as the engine passed into the shade of the canyon. It would be sausage tonight—sausage and potato and one of the beers that were down below, nestled between the bullets and the grenades. And then a patrol about the streets, watching the drones doing their work. And then—a letter to Gerda. He would tell her how much he was missing her, stuck in this backwater, and how he would be applying for a month's leave in the winter. He could take some work with old man Holtz and make them both a little money for extra fuel. They could sit together in her little apartment in Bremen and eat canned oysters, as they had done on their first night together, naked in the single bed, curled up with each other like a couple of playful kittens. Perhaps they could be married if her father had changed his mind. Best not to write of such things. It would only make it harder. Georg Weber glanced up as the shadow fell across him.

The point of the sword entered through his right eye, bursting it, diving into the soft tissue of the frontal lobe. Georg would think no more of Gerda now. His body hit the metal of the roof at the same time as El Sombra, his pistol clattering from its holster and over the side. The masked man stood, lifting the bloody tip of his sword from the corpse beneath.

"Good afternoon, gentlemen. Jump over the side and you might survive."

Rolff Waldschmidt was the first to react. Like lightning, he reached down to the holster in his belt, like one of the gangsters he used to watch every week at the old Kinema-house in Munich, bringing his pistol up to fire. El Sombra was faster, hurling his sword like a javelin, the point passing through the younger man's throat. Rolff pulled the trigger, but by that time he was falling backward in a spray of blood. The bullet soared into the sky.

BELOW, BRUCKNER LOOKED up, one hand on the lever. "What are they doing up there? Was that a gunshot?"

Ewald shrugged. "Probably just horsing around, shooting at vultures. You know what Rolff's like. He's been warned about it before. This time tomorrow he'll be working the firebox instead of playing at gangsters, you mark my words." He looked sideways at the plump little man. "If you're so worried, go up and check, or get Stammler or Altmann to go."

"Stammler and Altmann have to guard the cargo—God in heaven!" There had been another heavy crash on the roof, followed by another crack of gunfire. "Damn it, I can't leave the steering until we're out of these canyons! I'm not trusting you to keep us from crashing. There'll be hell to pay for these idiots, I tell you now!"

Ewald gritted his teeth.

THE LOUD CRASH had come from Klaus Mehlinger, a tall, reedy Austrian, who'd brought his sniper rifle up to bear before Jesus landed on his back, breaking his own fall by slamming the other man down into the metal. The two men immediately began rolling around the roof, attempting to trade punches and kicks, as the other sniper brought his gun up to his hip and fired at the unarmed El Sombra. Gunther Nagel was trained for long distances, and used to aiming from the shoulder, and so the bullet missed, passing within an inch of the masked man's cheek before smacking into the rock wall. The next shot would not miss.

As the engine swung out from the canyon exit, the sun blazed down on the roof of the craft, flashing into Gunther's eyes as his finger tightened on the trigger a second time. El Sombra lunged forward, the bullet passing harmlessly through the space where he had been one moment ago. His flat palms smacked against the hot metal of the roof and he flipped up, driving the ball of one foot against Gunther Nagel's forehead, smashing his head back into the chimney. The sound of Gunther's skull cracking mixed with the loud clang as the chimney buckled.

"ANOTHER GUNSHOT! My God, what in hell is going on up there? I'm going to see what the matter is, Ewald. Try not to kill us all, will you?" Bruckner stood and moved to the small door that separated them from the firebox. As he opened it, clouds of black smoke swept into the steering chamber. "What in heaven…" Bruckner looked through, one arm in front of his face, ignoring Ewald choking and spluttering behind him. The smoke was backing up in the firebox! Two of the men continued to shovel, hacking up their guts—one had already vomited. "What in dear heaven's name is going on?"

KLAUS MEHLINGER, WHO was twenty-eight years old and whose fondest desire was to one day meet his four-year-old son, had managed to get his hands around Jesus' throat and was now pushing him back against the rail, attempting to tip him over onto the treads. Jesus attempted several ineffective punches into the larger man's gut, but this only made Klaus push harder. He had only been stationed here for two years, and when he'd made the long trip to Mexico, Aldea had a reputation as one of the safest postings in the Luftwaffe, and duty on the Traction Engine was the safest posting in Aldea. Klaus had never been in a situation like this in his entire life.

His uniform was soaked with sweat as he struggled, and his jaw was aching from where the priest has managed to get in a lucky punch. *A priest! Lord, this was madness! What was a priest doing here, doing this?* The unreality of it all made his head spin for a moment. He gritted his teeth. *A filthy Mexican priest. Push him onto the treads to join his subhuman God.* There was a noise behind him like someone sliding a butcher's knife through a cut of meat, but he did not dare to turn away—the priest was struggling too hard.

Klaus barely felt the sword as it sliced through the flesh and muscle of his throat, barely saw the spray of blood drenching the man he was fighting with, before strong hands had gripped his shoulders and hurled him onto the rushing treads. Suddenly he was moving very fast towards the front of the Engine. He tried to reach for the guard rail but his arms wouldn't move. In another moment there was a heavy thud and he was lying on desert rock and something was blocking out the sun. He tried to summon the breath to scream but could not. As his bones splintered, the memory of a cockroach being crushed underneath his father's shoe flashed in his mind—and then there was nothing at all.

THE LEFT-HAND TREAD skidded suddenly on something wet, losing traction, the engine turning slightly as the opposite tread dug in. "Damn it, Bruckner! I can barely see! Bruckner!" Ewald shouted, eyes watering from the smoke, but there was no response. The clamour inside the Engine was too loud to shout through anyway. How long would he be expected to drive the machine by himself? He lunged over to the right-hand control, slowing it until the left-hand tread could dig in again. The sweat was pouring down his back, and he could feel a tightness in his chest. He was too old for this.

Bruckner was busy screaming at the men working on the firebox, doing everything short of whipping their hides to get them shovelling coal again despite the choking smoke. If the Engine ground to a halt in the middle of the desert, they were all dead. That ridiculous old windbag Schenker would have to suffer the indignity of doing his bloody job for a few more minutes—somebody had to take charge of this chaos, and that somebody was Heinrich Bruckner. His face was a mask of wrath as he began to undo the hatch leading to the roof.

EL SOMBRA SMILED. "Are you okay, amigo? For a moment it looked like you might be going overboard."

"I'll be fine, my friend. I just need to catch my breath." Jesus winced, shaking his head, his fingers feeling his throat. "That Nazi had a strong grip. I'm lucky to still have breath to catch—are we turning south?"

The masked man shook his head. "I don't think so. There's nothing to the south of us but a sheer cliff... ah, it's turning back again. Listen, amigo, you're not made for this kind of fight. You could get killed."

"And you can't?"

"Stay here. Leave the rest to me. In fact, you'd better take the sword. Both the pistols have gone over the side and I think we proved that these rifles aren't so helpful at close range."

Jesus opened his mouth to protest as El Sombra thrust the sword into his hand. The man was insane. God only knew what kind of hell they'd unleashed on themselves and he wanted to face it without a weapon! "You—you can't just give me your sword..."

The masked man smiled and shook his head. "It's okay, amigo. I trust you."

The sound of metal scraping against metal cut him short. On the other side of the buckled chimney, a hatchway swung open, emitting a belching cloud of black smoke. Turning away from the priest, El Sombra took a few paces towards it, then crouched down.

In THE STEERING compartment, Ewald couldn't take any more. They were well away from the canyons now—he could step away from the controls for one minute to close the damned door and shut out the smoke. He was coughing his guts out and the pain in his chest was getting worse. He looked through the door, eyes slitted against the smoke, watching the men at the firebox, their bodies shuddering with hacking coughs as they loaded coal. Where was Bruckner, anyway?

There he was. Halfway up the ladder, his head poking through the hatch. Shouting something. Typical Bruckner. He wanted command of this whole...

Bruckner's shoulders twisted. One leg began to jerk, shaking and shuddering, slipping off the rung. His hands flopped, arms hanging limp at his sides. One of the men at the firebox turned as though he'd heard a sound, a snapping sound...

Bruckner tumbled off the ladder and crashed to the floor.

His head had been turned backwards on his shoulders.

Ewald slammed the door and drove the bolts home. He stood, blinking for a moment, trying to convince himself his eyes had played tricks. The tightness in his chest was unbearable.

*　　*　　*

EL SOMBRA WATCHED the body hit the floor, then jumped into the hole, his feet finding a soft landing on the dead man's back. The room was a mass of smoke, the noise unbearable—but he could make out three burly men armed with shovels. They were stripped to the waist, tattoos of naked women covering backs and arms, earrings glinting, teeth missing, noses broken and chins unshaven—tough guys. El Sombra grinned. It had all been too easy anyway.

"Call those tattoos? They make you look like Dusseldorf rent boys!" he barked in German, and laughed, the laugh turning into a hard cough in the smoky air. One of the men dropped his shovel in shock. Their eyes widened. "Oh yes, I speak your hideous language."

The first to react was the bullet-head with the swastika over his right nipple. Snarling something in rural Bavarian, he swung his shovel for El Sombra's head. The masked man dodged beyond the range of the blow, his back bumping against the wall of the chamber. He wouldn't have been able to retreat any further, but then he didn't have to. As the momentum of Bullet Head's swing took him off balance, El Sombra gripped a rung of the ladder and swung his feet around, slamming both heels into the larger man's nose, breaking it for what was surely the fifth or sixth time. Bullet Head didn't fall. All he did was bellow, like some enraged animal. El Sombra jumped away, into the smoke, finding himself backing up against a bearded behemoth with a bandana wrapped around his head and a hoop dangling from his ear. The behemoth lunged, meaty arms wrapping around empty air as the masked man ducked, then rolled to avoid the sharp edge of a shovel being brought down with enough force to dent the metal flooring beneath. And things used to be so easy.

IN THE CARGO bay, Stammler and Altmann listened. Stammler and Altmann had served in the cargo bay, day in, day out, for more than seven years. There was something of the hawk about these two men. For them, their duty was almost a pleasure—in their off hours they spent their time in almost total silence, sipping brandies in the officers' mess, looking out of the window. Waiting. Occasionally, one of the citizens of the town would hurry by on their way home, and then they would stand without making a sound, leave the mess and follow. Mostly, those citizens were never found. When they were—well, they had broken the curfew, most likely. And where would they find two men for the cargo bay on the level of Stammler and Altmann? It was best in the end to let such matters pass.

Stammler looked out of the corner of one eye at Altmann, who stared straight ahead. Scuffles up top. Three gunshots. Now some sort of fight was breaking out by the firebox. There had been episodes of roughhousing before, yes, and the roof guards had taken pot-shots at birds of prey in the past, then whined like children when the inevitable court-martial came. But this was a different matter.

Protocol stated that Stammler and Altmann were never to leave the cargo bay, from when the Engine started off from the supply depot, to when it pulled in at the base in the town. Even opening the door would lead to demotion and punishment—probably the firebox. Stammler looked at the door and listened. Then he nodded, very slightly.

Altmann unsheathed his knife.

BULLET HEAD STRUCK lucky, catching El Sombra with a heavy kick at the end of his roll. The smoke was clearing through the hatch, and the masked man was easier to see now. The steel-capped boot slammed into his ribs with a noise like a side of meat being chopped by a butcher. El Sombra gritted his teeth, then let out a gasp as the wind was knocked out of him by the flat of one of the shovels, this one wielded by a huge Aryan thug with a facial scar that formed his lips into a constant sneer. "Hold him, Franz," murmured the scarred man to Bullet Head, as he twisted the shovel in a slippery grip, "I want to see the swine's face when I twist this inside his guts."

EWALD SCHENKER WAS shaking. His hand was slippery as it grasped the lever for the right-hand tread. His knuckles were white. He felt almost as though if he let go of the lever, he would fall. Would he ever stop falling if that happened? What was happening back there? What in God's name had those madmen done? The face of Heinrich Bruckner rose in his mind. The expression on the twisted corpse had been one of disbelief and outrage, as though Herr Bruckner was appalled that this should happen to him, of all people.

It's my fault... I wished him dead.

Ewald swallowed, his eyes staring blankly through the slit at the front of the engine. He could not think like that. The barbarians were outside the door.

They were killing each other. Bruckner was dead and he would be next. They would come through the door, and one would take Ewald's head in his hands, and slowly he would twist…

The pain built in his chest again. Ewald willed it away, but it would not stop. He could not breathe. Suddenly, the strength left his legs and he toppled, dragging the lever forward with his fall. The right-hand tread went into high gear with a terrible grinding noise, and with a hideous juddering motion the engine began to swing hard to the left.

In his mind, Ewald was still falling. He was falling and he could not breathe.

THE SUDDEN JERK threw Scarface off balance. "Was ist…"

El Sombra twisted off the ground, planting his hands into the metal of the floor. Kicking out to the sides, he planted his right foot into Bullet Head's belly while the ball of his left foot slammed into Scarface's crotch. As the two men curled up, the Behemoth launched himself off the wall with a cry of rage. El Sombra brought his legs together to meet the charge, bunched them in— then kicked out, using the momentum of the Behemoth's charge, sending the attacker flying straight over him.

The aim was perfect. The Behemoth's head and shoulders jammed in to the open mouth of the firebox, his face against the blazing coal. His name was Gustav Dietz, and when he was seven his baby sister had giggled and called him 'funny face.' Funny face, funny face, look at the funny face. They called it a tragic accident when she fell into the river. At the funeral, he had barely masked his sense of victory, the flush of pride that he had stopped her teasing. Where was the funny face now?

His screams echoed around the engine.

Soon the funny face was gone.

EWALD'S HAND, SHINY with sweat, slipped from the lever. As the lever snapped back to its normal position, the right-hand tread slowed. The engine came out of the turn and began to move straight ahead, towards the south.

The hand slapped against the chest and Ewald's corpse lay still.

* * *

ALTMANN TURNED TO Stammler, who nodded again. The two of them moved to the door and took up positions either side. Their knives gleamed in the light from the window-slits.

BULLET HEAD RECOVERED first, swinging his fists as El Sombra flipped onto his feet. The second punch connected—a blow to the side of the head that sent El Sombra stumbling back into the ladder, tripping as his feet tried to negotiate Bruckner's prone body. He fell sideways, clutching at the wall for support, seeing stars as Bullet Head moved in for the kill, reaching with hands like slabs for the masked man's face. "Eye for an eye, swine," he growled in his thick accent.

The sword came down hard through the hatch, the point raking down to tear open the flesh, carving a vicious trench through Bullet Head's skull, tearing off most of his nose and upper lip. As Bullet Head opened his mouth to scream, the tip of the blade tore his gum, scraped over the front teeth and drove into his tongue, then down through the bottom of his jaw into the hollow of his throat, to lodge in his chest. For a long moment, Jesus stared, pale and sick with horror, as he felt the sword vibrating in his grip with the heartbeat of the other man. Then Bullet Head jerked away, howling and choking on his own blood, the sword slipping from Jesus' slick palm and going with him.

El Sombra's vision began to clear. He took in the situation. Bullet Head was gurgling, choking on his own blood as he pleaded with Scarface. Was he pleading for help? For medical attention? To be put of his misery? It was impossible to tell. Scarface was bone white, frozen in place. El Sombra smiled.

Taking measured steps, he walked towards Bullet Head and spun him around, smiling as he looked into the wide, uncomprehending eyes.

"Amigo... that's my sword."

He took hold of the handle of the sword and twisted, driving down, bursting Bullet Head's heart, and then tugged upwards as though drawing the blade from a tight scabbard. Bullet Head tumbled to the floor, his blood dripping from El Sombra's chest, covering him in spatters down to his bare feet. The masked man grinned, like a cat with a bird. Scarface had shrunk back against the wall of the craft—now he swallowed, hard, as the point of the sword came to rest against his belly.

Jesus began to climb down the ladder. "Christ, it's a charnel house. I can't believe I did that."

"If you hadn't, it would have been my body at your feet." El Sombra smiled again, keeping his eyes locked on his enemy. The head of the shovel in Scarface's hand raised a fraction of an inch. El Sombra's smile widened and the sword shifted, digging into Scarface's flesh a quarter of an inch, making the larger man grunt in pain as a thin rivulet of blood crept down towards his belt. The shovel clattered against the metal flooring.

The priest spoke up again. "We should think about leaving, my friend. This thing's started heading south—and I think you said the only thing that way is a cliff? This beast doesn't seem to be slowing down much. We should grab what we can and bail."

El Sombra sighed. "That's a real shame. I was looking forward to taking this toy for a little ride. Can you imagine what this thing would do to a man if it rolled over him, amigo?"

"I don't have to."

"Oh, that guy. Well, perhaps he had an incurable disease. I bet we did him a favour. Hey, blondie!" He jabbed the sword again, another quarter inch. Scarface breathed in sharply, air laced with the stench of blood and the sickly-sweet smell of roasting human meat. "Which way to the cargo?"

ALTMANN AND STAMMLER were listening through the metal door. They stood, muscles tensed, their combat knives ready, waiting for the next person to walk through.

The corners of Stammler's mouth twitched slightly before his expression resumed its natural state of blankness. It was as close as he ever came to smiling.

SCARFACE RAISED A finger and pointed. The finger shook.

Jesus took a step forward. "Okay, I'll go in there and get what I can..." El Sombra's free hand settled on his shoulder, stopping him in his tracks.

He shook his head. "You do that, amigo. I'll wait right here," he said, loudly.

El Sombra moved his eyes back to the scar-faced man. His finger raised to his lips. Then he gestured with the same hand in the direction of the door to the cargo bay: after you.

Scarface stood, and blinked. El Sombra twisted the sword, very slightly. Scarface begin to nod quickly.

When El Sombra tugged the point of the sword free of his body, he turned, casting a desperate glance behind him, and stepped towards the door, walking like a man condemned to the gallows. He raised his hand to knock, but the point of the sword jabbed into the small of his back. The hand moved to the handle, twisted, and pushed.

The door swung open, and almost immediately the blade of a knife seemed to grow through the back of Scarface's head. There was a sound like a heavy curtain tearing, his body jerked, and offal fell to the floor in a wet heap. The blade at the back of the man's head vanished, and Scarface toppled backwards. The scarred face was split open, the torso ripped from chest to belly, and something that looked like wet red rope was trailing from the corpse to the offal on the floor. The offal that was preventing the door from swinging shut again.

In the doorway were two men with the eyes of hawks watching mice. Each held a dripping knife. "Unfortunate. The element of surprise is lost," said one, in a voice as soft and steady as a ticking clock.

"We can kill them both, no trouble," murmured the other.

El Sombra smiled and replied in German. "Excuse me? I can understand you."

Jesus looked from one to the other. "What are you speaking? How do you know German?"

El Sombra shrugged. "I picked it up somewhere."

Jesus shook his head. "My Latin is a little rusty, you know? Maybe I should have a psychotic episode and wander the desert for nine years. What are they saying?"

"Nothing important. They're about to try and kill us both. Take a step back, amigo, I need room to work."

Jesus looked at the masked man for a second, and in that second Stammler moved. His arm became a blur of motion and in the next moment the knife was jutting from the priest's shoulder. It happened so fast that Jesus felt nothing. He looked at the knife as though it was something from a dream.

Stammler clicked his tongue.

The pain hit. Jesus cried out and stumbled back, landing with a thud on the metal floor. Gritting his teeth, he reached for the handle of the knife.

El Sombra spoke without taking his eyes off the two men. "Don't take that knife out, amigo. That's what's keeping your blood in your body. Just stay down and leave this to me."

Altmann slowly raised his knife, taking the blade between finger and thumb.

El Sombra kept perfectly still.

Stammler's mouth twitched.

El Sombra tried to ignore his friend groaning in pain behind him. He tried to shut out the rumble of the engine. How long did he have before they went over the cliff? He breathed in. There was no sense thinking about that now. The important thing was to still the mind. Remember the desert. Remember the silence and solitude. Remember what was learned there.

Still the mind.

Altmann's hand moved. El Sombra's moved at the same instant.

The knife flew through the air, aimed directly at the masked man's heart—

—and ricocheted off the blade of El Sombra's sword.

Altmann blinked. "Unmöglich…"

El Sombra flashed a tight smile.

"Nothing is impossible."

He lunged forward, thrusting the blade into Altmann's heart. Altmann's jaw dropped and he took a faltering step backward. By that time, Stammler was already moving. He and Altmann had done everything together for seven years, and his death had meant less to Stammler than a drop of rain splashing against the back of his hand. For Stammler, the most important thing about Altmann's death was that it left El Sombra without his sword for a split second.

Stammler extended the knuckle of his middle finger and aimed for the masked man's throat with the speed of a striking cobra. First the trachea would be crushed. Then it would be a simple matter to remove the eyes. He would leave the optic nerves connected, so that pictures of what he did would continue to be sent to the brain. After that, he could retrieve his knife and begin work in earnest, as his foe writhed on the floor, gasping for a breath he would never take.

Stammler knew exactly how long a strong man took to suffocate. He knew what could be done in that time.

But El Sombra was still inside that silent place in his mind. He let go of his sword and shifted back so that Stammler's strike moved past into empty air, smashing against the metal of the open door. As Stammler's hand fractured with the force of the blow, El Sombra reached to grip it, closing his other hand around the forearm.

Less than a second had passed. Altmann was still on his feet, his reflexes keeping him standing. There was a foot of blade jutting from his chest. El Sombra brought Stammler's arm down onto it with all his strength.

El Sombra kept the killing edge of his brother's sword sharper than a razor. It was more than sharp enough to slice through the bone.

Altmann finally crumpled to the floor as Stammler looked down at the stump of his wrist. He held his other hand over the stump, but the blood continued to leak between the fingers, seeping out onto the floor. He let go and the blood came in quick pulses. As he stared at the mess that had once been his good right hand, Stammler was overcome with a feeling that some fundamental part of the world had gone terribly wrong. Some section of the world's great machinery had come loose. It was for him to take the hands and tongues and eyes of others. Not this. Not this at all.

El Sombra gripped his sword and pulled it free of Altmann's corpse, taking a quick look around the cargo bay. Then he stepped back into the main section of the Engine, leaving Stammler to it, and moved quickly towards Jesus. "Are you okay, amigo?"

"I've had some better days... Christ, this hurts!" the priest snarled through gritted teeth.

"There's a medical kit in there we can use, but mostly it's all guns, bombs, bullets... there are a couple of cases of beer. A reward for the troops, I think."

Jesus got slowly to his feet. "It sounds like the best... oww... the best place for all that is at the bottom of a cliff... speaking of which, we should move. Grab a case of the beer and the medical kit, I'll... I'll see if I can get up this ladder with one hand."

STAMMLER DID NOT move as the masked man walked past him, grabbed two boxes and left. He felt grey, washed out. The pool of blood he was sitting in was getting larger no matter how tightly he gripped his wrist. As the masked man helped the other one up the ladder, Stammler realised that he was going to die. The notion did not trouble him in itself. But the thought that his killer—the masked man— would continue to live, with both his hands... that was an irritation. A splinter stuck in the corner of his mind. He should really do something about that.

Slowly, he stood.

EL SOMBRA PASSED the medical kit and the case of beer up to Jesus through the hatch as the Engine rumbled on. Jesus picked up the beer with his good hand

and hurled it over the side to land in a patch of sand. The kit followed. The priest winced, gritting his teeth. "I hope the bottles don't break—oww! Christ, I should have let you do that!"

El Sombra nodded. "You're lucky you didn't make your wound worse. Do I have time to get another load?"

The priest shook his head. "No. I can see the cliffs. We should jump now rather than take any risks. You're going to have to help me make the... oh my God—"

An arm without a hand wound around El Sombra's throat. Blood sprayed in his eyes. He lost his grip as Stammler's weight dragged him off the ladder and back into the Engine, the breath knocked out of him as he slammed into the floor. Blinking away the blood, the first thing he saw was Stammler's fist before it smashed into his jaw, loosening teeth. The stump smacking into the side of his head, sending more blood into his eyes. His sword had fallen within reach, he was sure, but he did not know where. His fingers scrabbled fruitlessly.

Stammler straddled El Sombra. Keep him off balance, that was the main thing. He aimed a blow at the masked man's forehead, but El Sombra swept an arm across and diverted the blow enough to crash it into the metal next to his head. Stammler ignored the pain. He only needed to hit once, and his own blood was proving a useful weapon. A few more seconds of life, that was all it would take.

Jesus' voice cut through the rumble of the Engine. "We're getting close to the edge! We need to jump now!"

It was true. There was perhaps six feet of distance between the front of the treads and the edge of the cliff. More than one hundred feet below, the Engine would make its grave.

El Sombra blinked blood out of his eyes as he somehow managed to redirect another hammer blow. His attacker's knuckles were smashed, fingers broken, and he had surely lost too much blood to stay alive, and yet here he was, readying another killing strike. El Sombra wondered if this was how he himself appeared to people, even as he saw the only opening he had and took it.

He reached down to grip Stammler's crotch through the fabric of the uniform, and he squeezed until something burst.

Stammler flinched.

It was enough. El Sombra drove the heel of his palm up into Stammler's nose, driving shards of bone deep into the brain, then rolled the convulsing man off him. His sword had been inches from his hand the whole time—how long had it been? Five seconds? Four?

The floor was beginning to tilt.

Jesus realised that this was perhaps his last chance to escape. The Engine was slowing even as it reached the edge of the cliff, but it would not be enough. If he was to survive, he had to leap, to hurl himself from the back of the beast before it tipped. The fronts of the treads were already in empty space. Instead, he fell to the roof and thrust his good arm through the hatchway. "Grab my hand! Quickly!"

El Sombra leapt upwards, feet on the rungs of the ladder, taking hold of the priest's arm as the older man used all the strength left in him to help haul his friend up through the hatchway. The angle of the roof was growing steeper.

The Engine was going over the edge.

El Sombra got to his feet, grabbed the old priest by the collar and hauled him up the slope, bare feet pounding the metal. The Engine should have tipped by now—but the cavorite in the frame of the machine was slowing things. Jesus was screaming something about dropping him—something self-sacrificing of that nature—but El Sombra was too busy making his legs move. It was like running up the side of a steel mountain.

Dragging Jesus with him, the masked man vaulted the rail and leapt, as the back of the machine left the cliff's edge, the mobile coffin starting a lazy descent towards the rocks below, accelerating as the force of gravity overcame the ingrained cavorite. He stretched out his arm—

And the point of the sword slammed into the sand, a foot from the edge of the cliff. He swung the priest up with his other arm, muscles straining and threatening to tear, and Jesus managed to catch the cliff's edge with his good hand. Slowly they began dragging themselves up onto solid ground.

"Damn," panted Jesus as he flopped onto his back, his legs dangling off the edge. "My shoulder really hurts. We should... we should go find that medical kit."

"Yes, we should." El Sombra spat a tooth out onto the desert sand. A molar.

"We should go find the beer as well."

"Oh yes, amigo. Most definitely."

EISENBERG LEANT BACK in the leather chair and looked at the ceiling fan as it turned. There was a report on his desk detailing the loss of the Traction Engine, and how supplies would now have to be marched across the desert for the foreseeable future. This would create rationing problems and ammo shortages. Already there was open insubordination caused by the lack of beer in the mess hall.

Curiously, there were rumours that curfew-breakers had been spotted with bottles of German beer in their hands, toasting to Old Pasito, and the gossip claimed that a man in a bloodstained mask had given them out to any bold enough to drink and toast openly. Eisenberg shut his eyes tightly and massaged his temples, attempting to disperse the oncoming headache.

The red telephone began to ring.

CHAPTER FOUR
HOW IT HAD ALL STARTED

THE SUN ROSE over the desert, on the man known as El Sombra. He sat cross-legged on a rocky outcrop, examining the small blisters that spotted the soles of his feet. His flesh ached and burns covered his arms and back. He still coughed occasionally, spitting out soot-coloured phlegm from the back of his throat. He was very lucky to be alive.

He did not feel it.

Drawing his sword, he examined the blade in the light of the dawn. He could still see the blood staining the metal, coating it in places. Normally he would have cleaned the sword by now—it was sacred to him, and he kept it as immaculate as he could. But this morning was different. He needed to be reminded of what he'd done the previous night, and whose blood was on the blade.

He needed to punish himself.

He remembered how it had all started.

WHO WAS THE man known as El Sombra?

He was a thousand different things in the clockwork-town, because there were a thousand different answers to the question. Since the raid on the Traction Engine the stories had been spreading like plague—even the most diligent worker, whose only thought was of the glory of the Reich, could not help hearing something on the matter. The stories fell on the ears and worked their way into the mind, past the conditioning and the programming and the thousand daily indignities designed to make human beings forget that they were alive. The stories brought back memories of how it was to live without the wingmen and their clattering metal wings, the guards and their guns, the jackboots. How it was to live without an alarm siren that woke you from your bed and forced you to march through blistering heat or freezing cold to do tasks without meaning for people who thought you less than human. For some, that was terrifying.

"EL SOMBRA IS a monster, a lunatic, a psychopath, a murderer, a cannibal. He ought to be hung from a gallows in the great square, in front of the statue! His innards should be defecated in by dogs. Dogs with diseases."

El Sombra looked up from the book he was reading—a copy of *Teresa's Temptation*, the latest from Dame Judith Cooper, a sizzling potboiler of sex, money, power, more money and sex set in the legendary fashion 'families' of Milan. He'd liberated it a couple of days before along with a few thousand rounds of ammunition, and had just reached the part where the beautiful fashionista was in the process of having it all, on top of her desk and in the company of the handsome chief designer who was secretly her brother.

The book was a hard-won luxury, the first one he'd read in nine long years. It wasn't the best thing to be caught reading by a priest.

"What did you say?"

Jesus cleared his throat and began again. "El Sombra is a monster, a lunatic…"

"I do have feelings, amigo. Is this about eating all your eggs?"

Jesus leant against the doorway with a grin. "I'm only repeating what I heard today. You have an image problem, my friend. The general populace sees you as supernatural at best, some kind of demon at worst… they actually make these little wooden stick-men to hang on the door to ward against you coming into their homes and eating their children."

The masked man shrugged, laying the book down open on the floor so as not to lose his place. "Supernatural I can live with, amigo. Besides, what can I do? I can't stop people talking about me."

"So give them something to talk about. Right now, all they have is that you run around half-naked with a sword in your hand killing people and stealing things and you're completely out of your mind, you know? You think that's going to endear you to anybody?"

El Sombra sighed, casting a glance down at the book. "So what can I do? Throw a street party? Maybe set up a puppet show for the little orphans?"

"I hate to deny such eloquent sarcasm, my friend, but you're thinking along the right lines. Remember what you said about getting the people on your side? Guns, medicine, strong drink?"

"It's harder to get anybody to take the guns than I thought. They're all terrified of getting caught and tortured. Same with the medicine—if I leave it for the people, it just goes back to the bastards. So I stash everything in little caches, places the bastards won't look, only it's no use to anybody there."

"What about the drink?"

"You drank it."

"Ah, yes. Well, I'm in recovery, you know? It's medicinal. Hey, maybe one of the reasons the people won't take any risks for you is because you're not doing anything for them."

"Guns, amigo! Strong drink!"

"That's all for you. When you wave a gun in some poor man's face—some guy who's lived only for that damned statue for nine years, who's maybe seen his family taken away to the Palace and coming back without any arms and legs, repeating Arbeit Macht Frei over and over like gramophones—what's he going to think? 'Oh, I will immediately join the violent struggle for revolution and die for this crazy man who doesn't seem to like shirts'? Of course not! He's going to soil himself and run away."

El Sombra blinked.

Jesus barrelled on, warming to his theme. "But if you've been doing things for them—not going out on sorties to kill people and steal things, just going out looking for people in trouble and helping them, you know?—then maybe the guy would think 'Yes! Now I'm being handed a gun by my friend who helps people in need! Why of course I'll get myself shot in the face for you, oh mysterious ghost with no shirt!'"

"I could wear a shirt if it would make you feel happier, amigo…"

"No, no, you're obviously very proud of your nipples, I wouldn't like to take that away from you. What I'm saying is that you need to bring some hope to these people. Right now, all you are is a story for parents to tell their children to get them to eat their vegetables, you know? Right now people trust the Nazis, because they control everything—they control how people think. The more you do for them, the more they trust you."

El Sombra looked at him.

Jesus swallowed. "Or something. It's not an exact science, you know?"

The masked man stood, stretched, and reached for his sword.

"So what you're saying is that I should run around all night, not killing any bastards, but checking to see if any old ladies need helping across the street?" He hefted the blade, then slid it through his belt. "Fine." He scowled, the thick moustache bristling as his eyes glared.

"But I don't promise to like it."

AND HE DIDN'T. As he stalked over the low roofs, jumping across the alleys, eyes looking around for something to do, the wasted time hung heavy on him. He was used to striking quickly, with a specific target in mind—such as a raid on one of the supply depots, already badly understocked since the demise of the Traction Engine, or an attack on a small group of guardsmen to put the fear of God into the rest. This 'patrol,' as Jesus had called it, was ridiculous. The chances of him coming across anything that he could usefully prevent were thousands to one. The most he could achieve would be to find evidence of some atrocity after it had occurred.

El Sombra was so fixed on his thoughts that he didn't notice the orange/yellow light flickering over the rooftops from the west. But he heard the screams. Changing course, he headed west, jumping across the rooftops, keeping to the shadows. The smell of the thick, black smoke hit him first, and beneath it another scent. A sickly sweet smell, like roasting pork.

The schoolhouse was burning.

The two-storey building had been deserted since the invasion. In the early days it had been used as a centre for administration by the Reich, but after the construction of the Red Dome, the schoolhouse had been abandoned. It was still occasionally useful, but for the most part it had been empty for eight years or more. There was no need for learning in Aldea. Every lesson of importance was taught as the children picked up their heavy stones for the first time, under the cracking whips of the overseers, struggling and hefting the rocks towards the great half-built statue.

The first lesson in Aldea was: You do not matter. The second was: You will obey. Anything else was superfluous.

El Sombra reached the conflagration, looking at it from the edge of a rooftop. It was like something out of Hell. The wooden schoolhouse was the wick of some terrible candle, burning and flickering, and around it was a circle of soldiers, armed with long metal batons, with their backs facing the blaze. As the masked man watched, one of the townspeople rushed forward with a tin bucket filled with water, screaming something he couldn't quite catch. The reaction was merciless. Two soldiers stepped forward and swung their sticks at the same instant, the riveted metal ends cracking hard into the man's ribcage. The sickening crack of snapping bone echoed through the night air as the bucket fell, the water spilling into the dirt.

The masked man was already swinging off the roof. But the sound he heard as he fell to the ground added speed to his movement—and stoked a fire in his heart that matched the inferno in front of him.

It was the scream of a child burning to death.

He hit the ground like thunder and judgement.

Roland Koch was a slightly tubby man of around forty years of age. Born in Bremen, he had never set foot outside that city until he'd boarded the zeppelin to Mexico and his post in Aldea. He was not one for zoos, and so had never come within fifty feet of a maddened tiger. But if he had, then the snarl of animal fury that met his ears—at the same time that a lashing foot kicked him ten feet backwards into the heart of the blaze—might have sounded familiar.

Still, it's probable that even then he would be too concerned with his own burning flesh to make the connection.

El Sombra was a whirlwind, a dervish, a demon of movement and motion and violence. His elbow cracked hard against the forehead of a new recruit and the young man crumpled dead to the earth. He spun without pausing and the heel of his foot slammed into the soft trachea of an eighteen-year-old who had joined the squadron the previous week and had, it was agreed by all, a glittering future in front of him. That glittering future was now two and a half minutes long and did not involve breathing. And now the sword—that terrible blood-tempered sword—slashed from the masked daredevil's belt with a terrible sound of razors and hate, plunging into the neck of a father of two who wrote letters to his family in Bonn every two days, leaving it a flapping, gushing ruin. A boy and a girl would not have their letter that weekend—instead there would be a cold telegram from the Führer expressing regret, and their dreams forever after would be haunted by the clang of steel and the crash of thunder.

Perhaps their names should be recorded for posterity, these doomed soldiers who only followed orders—but it is more fitting to leave them as ciphers. They were wheat in the thresher, sheep fed to the slaughterhouse. The sword flashed in the light of the flames, glinting red with the fire and the blood as it carved and chopped though the men as though they were kindling. He was a blur of speed—leaping over the swinging metal truncheons, spinning into kicks that cracked jaws and broke noses, a flurry of punches slamming into soft bellies. One by one, the soldiers fell back, unconscious or dead, bodies around the bonfire.

It was a massacre.

CLIMACO AGUILAR LAY on the ground, clutching his shattered rib, the empty bucket at his side, and he remembered how this had all started. For years, the old schoolhouse had lain empty and desolate and the children had gone without books, without learning, growing up as automatons for the glory of the Reich.

Children of seven and eight, who should have been laughing and bubbling with joy and life, were walking in step, marching, their faces blank and empty, their eyes glazed and dead. The townsfolk had survived only through capitulation—those who resisted, in word or deed, were killed. But the sight of their own children reduced to shells, stumbling on little legs as they hauled stone blocks to the statue, passing out at the end of each day through sheer exhaustion while their skin turned sallow and grey, was enough to bring back those forgotten thoughts of rebellion.

They began to meet after dark, no more than three or four at a time—any more and the soldiers might have discovered their secret. They could not give their children food, or clothing, or even heat in the winter—everyone was allocated the same resources, just enough to keep them from starvation. Any family caught sharing their rations went to the Palace of Beautiful Thoughts for a session with Master Minus.

All they could offer was education.

Not much—an hour a week at most, stolen after dark. Tiny groups of children smuggled to the schoolhouse and given the very basics—reading, writing, learning to count. Sometimes as little as reading to them of the world outside—anything at all to counter the endless propaganda hurled at them by their new rulers. Isidoro the schoolteacher was long dead, but his wife Verdad was alive and more than happy to carry on her husband's work, despite the risk to her aged bones.

For two and a half years, it had carried on. Years of paranoia, almost constant fear of discovery, but the fear was worth it to see the children smiling when their minds drifted to the delicious secrets that Verdad had given them, counting to ten in their heads or thinking of Magna Britannia, that country far away where there was a mechanical man to serve every family and the children had sugar-drops when they were good.

Tonight, things had proceeded as normal—the children shepherded in, the lessons beginning as usual. Climaco was watching for any soldiers when the flames first started licking at the sides of the building—the fire had started from inside, God only knew how. And then, as if on cue, the soldiers had arrived, circling the building to make sure no-one escaped and no help came. It seemed an example was to be made.

Climaco tried to struggle to his feet. He had to fetch water. He knew what the masked man would do next. He wished he had the strength to do it himself.

STAFFELKAPITAN JONAS OSWALD charged, baton swinging. In the past seven seconds, he had watched his entire unit fall like rain, but he did not let that slow him. If he could take the madman by surprise, then he could end this here and now. The masked lunatic growled like an animal, and turned, swinging his sword with a devil's strength. Jonas felt the blade strike, like a hard punch in the side—felt something tear in his spine—and then he toppled sideways. He could no longer feel anything below the waist, and there was something blocking his vision. He understood, then, that the end had come.

He remembered how this had all started. A couple of shared beers in the officers' mess after a hard day of herding human sheep—two bottles for the whole unit, and those were supposed to last the week. They hadn't even had the chance to finish them before the call went out.

Some cretins, most likely El Sombra and his fellow terrorists—had managed to set the old schoolhouse on fire. The unit was to form a ring around the building to prevent the fire spreading, wait for help to contain the blaze, and prevent any of the workers from interfering. Those were their orders, and they carried them out.

The hardest part was ignoring the screams from inside. But there was no saving those people, if you could call them 'people.' If they'd wandered into a restricted building and set it ablaze, then they'd brought this on themselves through their own stupidity, as you'd expect from subnormal intelligence. There was no sense in risking the lives of his men to save the lower races from their own idiocy—besides, the unit was needed outside, to prevent any more of them destroying themselves, like that idiot with the bucket who seemed so ready to hurl himself into the flames.

They'd been following orders. And the masked killer had swept down and butchered them all for it. Didn't he understand that they were trying to help?

Jonas Oswald blinked twice and realised what the object was that was blocking his vision, as the lower half of his body toppled forward, the ragged end of his spine flapping, leaving his line of sight clear. Then everything went black.

"Estoy hasta la madre, pinche pendeja!"

The masked man hurled his sword at the last of them. The man—at nineteen, barely that—screamed as the point of the sword plunged through the open mouth and through the back of the neck in a gout of red blood. The nameless young soldier crashed to ground, eyes already rolling back in his skull, and El Sombra took back his property.

"Water! Now!" El Sombra's voice was like an oncoming storm.

The man who'd been beaten earlier limped forward, carrying his bucket, and hurled the remaining contents over the swordsman. Others in the crowd picked up the hint quickly and doused him with what little water they'd managed to collect, until he was soaked through, dripping wet.

He turned to face the blaze, an inferno now. There were still screams coming from inside, which meant that there was some hope at least. But he knew he had seconds at best. This was not like fighting—something he could do almost without thinking. This would be difficult. He had to save as many of the children as he could, and his true enemy tonight was not the soldiers, or even the flames. It was time. Every second that passed could mean the end of a young life, in fire and agony and horror.

Tick tock.

El Sombra dove into the fire.

The flames licked his face and burned at his neck and back, bringing back memories of the desert heat. He made for the stairs, trying to get to the screaming and weeping he could hear coming from above.

The wooden stairs were a mass of flaming timber, but they could still support his weight. He stilled his mind, shutting off all sensation, all pain. Then he ran forward, pushing through the wall of fire, the calloused soles of his feet hitting the red-hot wood as he took the stairs two at a time. Smoke burned his lungs and his throat was raw. He could barely see and his ears were full of the crack and hiss of blazing wood. He was on the same floor as the screaming now, but he might as well have been a thousand miles away. Every breath he took was soot and heat and the terrible stench of cooked pork.

He staggered forward, eyes swamped with tears, and saw the children.

Six of them were huddled together, not looking at him. They were looking at the seventh, a boy, perhaps six years old but certainly no older.

His name was Spiro Otilio Herrera, and he was on fire.

His flesh was melting, running off his body like tallow-fat, as he thrashed and screamed at the top of his lungs. There was a sizzling that filled the room, and the stench of cooking meat. But the smell wasn't the worst thing.

The worst thing was what had happened to his face.

The fire had burned away lips, nose and cheeks, and burst one eye. The hair had been consumed first. All that was left was a shrieking, blazing skull, resting obscenely on the candle-wick body.

The masked man looked down at the thrashing thing that had once been human and he knew there was no saving the boy. Even if he could get Spiro Herrera outside, there was no medicine that could save his life. He would scream and scream for hour upon hour, each gasping, tortured breath bringing even more pain, until he finally died. Still, he would have tried. But there were six others who needed him and he had no time. El Sombra could do nothing for him...

...but draw his sword.

In that moment, El Sombra knew himself to be no longer a man. He was, instead, what the ticking clock had made of him.

He was a monster.

Tick tock.

Erendira Herrera, worker number 2137, was twenty years old and one of the most proficient workers in all of Aldea. So proficient that she had earned a commendation from the Oberstleutnant himself. Like other workers who had been commended, her papers allowed her to walk the streets a full two hours after sundown, provided she caused no undue disturbance. She had earned that privilege through her obedience to the Führer. Stood at the back of the crowd, watching the building burning and inhaling the sickly-sweet stench of sizzling fat, she listened to the shrill screaming coming from the upper floor of the burning building and seethed.

She remembered how this had all started. The uneasy smiles of her parents at dinner when she expounded on the greatness of der Führer. Her mother's look of worry and pain when she came back from another gruelling overtime session on the high scaffolding. The long arguments with her parents, as if being held up as an example by Master Plus himself was somehow not enough for them. The guilty looks when she mentioned how it would soon be time for little Spiro to begin his work training.

Once she had returned from overtime to find Spiro absent from his room, her mother and father refusing to allow her to contact the proper authorities, content to sit and wait. Eventually he was brought in by Mr Aguilar—a sloven who did not pull his weight on the statue and often needed to be beaten with a cane in front of the other workers—and her mother and father had said nothing about it to her, while Spiro babbled about pyramids and sphinxes and things which he had no business knowing.

She had not wanted to go to Master Plus about the matter. Not until she had all the facts. It was not her place to enforce law in Aldea and, besides, wasting Master Plus' time with gossip and scandal might tarnish her work record.

But she should have informed on them. She knew that now. It was perfectly obvious what had happened. They'd been having their little club meeting, learning their useless stories, and that doddery old witch Verdad had knocked a candle over and set light to all those useless books and bits of paper that should have been burned long ago. She'd started a fire and then fallen or something and not been able to lead the children out. She was stupid and old. In Berlin, they put stupid old women like her in chambers and gassed them, and then burned them in ovens.

She wished this town was more like Berlin.

It made her furious. Every breath she took was tainted with the smell of burning flesh and the blood of the dead. Because these fools could not accept things as they were, children were being burned alive. Good men had been butchered by a lunatic. And for what? So a few new workers knew that across the sea, there were pyramids? What would they do with that knowledge when they were ordered to get a half-ton block of stone up to the top of a hundred foot scaffold? Across the sea, there was discipline. There was *ordnung*. That was all that mattered.

She gritted her teeth, air hissing between them like the noise of a kettle. This would come back to her. When the soldiers investigated, they would find her parents and her little brother mixed up in this somehow, and that would be the end of her commendations and her special privileges. Number 2137 would be just one more troublesome worker from a bad family.

It wasn't fair. It wasn't right. This minority of rebels were spoiling things for everyone who did what was right. Someone had to teach them a lesson. Somebody had to show these criminals and thugs and their masked hooligan the difference between right and wrong.

She picked up a stone and hefted it in her palm.

THE CHILDREN STARED at him for a second that seemed like an hour, and El Sombra looked back at them, unable to meet their eyes. The tears running under the mask were no longer caused by the smoke.

And that had been the easy part.

There had been only one choice regarding Spiro Herrera. Now there were more. There were six children in the inferno, and he promised to himself that he would save every single one of them.

And he knew he would break that promise.

A roof beam cracked and fell, blazing, superheated timber crashing towards his head, and he hurled himself forward. There were three girls and three boys. Two of the girls and a boy were awake and conscious. That might mean they could survive longer, but on the other hand, the still ones might need resuscitation. He could not trust that to the crowd, so it was likely he'd be performing it himself—spending vital minutes saving one child while the others burned. The awake ones first (Could he manage all three? He'd have to) and then back inside for the rest.

All this ran through his mind in the split-second before the beam crashed through the floor behind him.

He grabbed two children in his arms and one by the hair, and twisted, his back smashing against the burning wall. The force of his momentum smashed through the weakened wood, propelling him and his three charges out into the night air on a plume of smoke. It was hard to compensate for the added weight, but he shifted his balance and turned a graceful loop in the air—a memory of jumping off the edge of a canyon while weighted with heavy rocks suddenly flashing into his mind—before landing hard on the pads of his feet, bursting blisters. The children were unharmed. Alive. Now for the rest.

The stone smashed hard into his left temple.

He winced in pain and his skull rang like a bell. He could not believe it.

Someone had thrown a rock at him. For saving three children.

And that was the least of it.

He was just one target. Rocks were hurtling through the air from all sides, at all comers. The crowd had turned on itself and become a riot. A part of him was relieved that he'd made the right decision—there was no way any of these people would be capable of resuscitating a burn victim—but another part was counting seconds. *Tick. Tock.* Every second that passed meant that the risk of another death was higher.

Tick. Tock. Tick.

If he left the children here they'd be trampled or torn apart by the mob. If he stayed, three more children died.

Tick. Tock. He heard screaming from above him. *Tock. Tick.* One of the unconscious ones had woken up. Probably because they were on fire.

If he moved these children away from the crowd and then left them, they'd be picked up by wingmen and taken to a torture chamber somewhere. *Tick. Tock.* He needed somebody who could get them home. But there was nobody.

Tick. Tock. Tick. Tock. Ti—

"Give them to me!" Climaco Aguilar lunged from the mass of bodies, one eye swollen, blood pouring from his nose, missing teeth. El Sombra recognised in him a kindred spirit, and gave thanks. "Get back in there! Get back..."

But El Sombra was already gone. Under a barrage of stones, Climaco herded the sobbing children towards the relative safety of the alleys.

Tick. Tock. Tick.

El Sombra's thudding heart was a stopwatch that counted down the seconds until the death of the next child. Every time his bare foot thumped down on the hard, hot timber, he left a sizzling footstep of blood. He tried not to think about the blood dripping from his sword...

Up the stairs two at a time and this time they could no longer bear his weight. He felt the third stair from the top give way underneath him, and he launched himself up, stabbing the point of his sword into the ceiling above him and letting it bear his weight for the split second he needed to swing himself over the gap to relative safety.

Upstairs things were much worse. There were large holes in the floor from where roof beams had crashed through or the wood had simply given way in the terrible heat. The smoke was thick and black, and the flames were raging out of control. He looked around desperately for the remaining three children. He couldn't hear anything from them. But he'd heard a scream. Was it seconds ago? Minutes? How long did they have to live?

He moved forward as quickly as he could, hoping that he wouldn't fall through the floor onto the bonfire raging below. The only thing he could do would be to grab the children and leave by the hole he'd made before. The smoke cleared for a moment—

—and he was looking at Verdad. Isidoro's wife. She'd been here all along, hidden from view by the smoke. Her old, wrinkled face was distorted in agony. She'd fallen and broken something, by the look of it. Her bones were very brittle and she had to be very careful now that there was no possibility of medical care for her. And she had been coming up and down the rickety steps and teaching the children by candlelight. How much courage did that take?

She looked at him with frightened eyes, then looked away, towards where the children had been. The meaning was clear. He had to leave her to burn.

He wished he had time to speak to her, even a few words. Could she tell him what had caused the blaze?

Did she remember how this had all started?

Tick tock. No time. He vaulted through the billowing smoke, and it was thick and black and tore at his throat and lungs with sharp needles. Nobody could survive more than a few minutes in this place... maybe not even a minute. He had heard once that in an environment like this you had perhaps three breaths before you passed out. How many did a child of five have?

Where were they?

He was in the right place. He was sure of that. Had they moved?

Tick tock.

He drew in a deep breath of smoke and flame and bellowed.

"Scream! Scream, damn you..." The shout broke into a hacking cough. There was a cough in response. *Thank God.* El Sombra dove forward, reaching, hands brushing against small forms. One. Two. A boy and a girl.

There was another one. Where? He didn't have time. That cough he'd heard had been the sound of a death rattle. If he didn't move now, the two children he had would die.

He wished he could see through the billowing smoke, just for a moment— one moment was all it would take. He hoped he remembered correctly which direction led to the outside. He prayed to anyone who might be looking down for some guidance.

His only answer was the pounding of his heart.

He hurled himself sideways, protecting the children with his own body as he crashed through one of the windows. He was too weak this time for fancy landings, and so he fell hard onto his back, glass digging into the meat of his shoulder as the wind was slammed out of him on impact. He looked at the two bodies cradled in his arms. Both dead.

Above him, he heard the screaming begin again.

He had made the wrong decision.

Around him, the crowd busily tore each other apart. There were only a few left, less than twenty, the others having run or limped away to homes and families—those who were not simply beaten to death by the mob. Once upon a time, all of Pasito would have been filling buckets and pails, desperately doing everything they could to put out the raging inferno. Now the town reacted to trouble by turning on itself, the careful clockwork spinning quickly out of control. El Sombra did not have the time to stop them, or even to give a thought to how far his home had fallen.

The clock was still ticking.

He could either go into the burning building for a third time to rescue the screaming, agonised boy he had left behind, or he could perform resuscitation on one of the children with him. Most of the boy's flesh was charred and blistered, the larger part of his skin burned away. He was a ruin. But the girl was hardly marked. Evidently she had simply inhaled too much smoke. But if he didn't get her breathing again immediately—

With that thought, El Sombra condemned the boy above him to death by fire.

Leaning down, surrounded by chaos, he began to breathe for the girl. He had let down too many during those five minutes, but the clock was still ticking. He still had the power to claw back a life, one more life stolen from the jaws of death. In the distance he heard the sound of clanking metal wings somewhere above the roar of the flames and the howls of the crowd, but he did not stop. Let them come. Leaning back, he began to compress her chest. One more life. That wasn't much, was it? Not very much at all.

Above him, the screaming finally died. He gritted his teeth as his arms pushed, bullying her heart into beating again. Then he leant down to inflate her lungs. Again. Again. She must breathe. She had to breathe.

She would not breathe.

ALEXIS EISENBERG STOOD at the window of the humble hovel overlooking the schoolhouse and watched as the masked man tried to resuscitate the girl. Hopefully he would fail—it would set the capstone on what had, all in all, been a very good night indeed. He took a sip of brandy from his hip flask, smiled, and remembered how it had all started.

He had known about the 'education program' for some weeks now. It was something he had permitted to continue. Oh, he could have gone in—crushed the whole enterprise under an iron fist, carted the ringleaders off to the Palace of Beautiful Thoughts, perhaps shot the children in the street as an example. It would have been a perfectly good way of dealing with the symptoms, but it would not have cured the underlying disease; this idea the lower orders had that they knew what was best for their spawn.

He could shoot one hundred people, but that would only create one hundred martyrs. The cycle would have begun over again quickly enough. The only way to really squash these little rebellions was to make them collapse of their own accord. Have the people understand that the system was there to protect them, and that to move against it would only result in harm coming to those they loved.

And so he had planted a very small, very potent incendiary device.

It would be explained away as an accidental fire, caused by a candle tipping over. He had already begun planting the seeds of that conclusion, using his spies among the workers to amend the rumours that were circulating. And the results had been better than he could possibly have dreamed.

El Sombra knew who the power was now. Any rebellious elements would be dealt with. Not by the wingmen, but by the people themselves, who were all too eager to savage each other in the name of safety. His clumsy attempts to bring the people together under the banner of Old Pasito were doomed to failure. There was no Pasito anymore. Pasito had been a town of friends and good fellowship—but Aldea was a place of strangers and mistrust. And that made it easy to control.

And deep down, all that was nothing compared to one great triumph—Alexis had hurt the masked man. Where was his laugh now? He had seen innocents burn to death. He had, Alexis was certain, killed at least one child to save it from pain.

Later, Alexis would consult with Master Minus, the expert in mental distress, and find out how deeply he had managed to wound his enemy. For now, he simply watched. The girl was still not breathing, and his wingmen were getting closer. It would be the cherry on the icing if El Sombra had to let her die to save his own skin, or better, be shot dead as he fruitlessly tried to restart her heart.

Alexis stroked his fingertip lightly over the scar on his cheek and leant forward, grinning like a jackal, to watch.

As the clank and creak of wings filled the sky, El Sombra stood, cradling the little body in his arms. Time had run out.

"Move, all of you! Follow me!" He yelled it at the top of his lungs, but the crowd did not seem to hear. A couple of the battered rioters broke off from their fighting to look at him as he ran for the nearest alley, but most kept up their war without even turning around.

Running into the shadows of the alley, El Sombra heard the storm of creaking wings thunder over the burning schoolhouse. Something was shouted in German: an order to stop fighting or face the consequences. Before the sentence had finished it was drowned out by the clatter of machine gun fire. More lives he had failed to save.

And then, in El Sombra's arms, the little girl coughed softly. Her name was Graciela and her parents were sitting in their dwelling and sobbing as they heard the shots ring out. They had lost all hope.

Graciela began to breathe gently, in and out, and despite himself, the man behind the mask smiled.

He did not smile as he ran his fingers over the burst blisters on the soles of his feet. He had failed the people when they needed him most. He had allowed three children and an old woman to die and run while others were gunned down. He had had no choice in any of this, it was true, and he had done the best he could in the situation.

But all the same, he had failed.

He had spent a great deal of time learning everything he needed to know to conduct a one-man war against his enemies—and virtually no time learning how to help his friends. Oh, he knew resuscitation, and the treatment of wounds, but he had had no idea that the people of the town were trying, against all hope, to give their children an understanding of a life beyond slavery and despair. Earlier, he had moaned to Father Santiago like a cretin that there was no resistance. Father Santiago effectively lived in a cave—of course there would be pockets of resistance that would spring up without his knowledge. It would not have taken much effort for El Sombra to find out about them, and yet he had blithely carried on down his own path, like a train on a track, unable to deviate for an instant. He had amassed an arsenal of guns and ammunition for the people to enact his personal vengeance, but had not bothered himself with bringing them hope.

He had been a fool.

He looked towards the town and then stood and began walking in the opposite direction. He could not return to the priest's shack just yet. He did not need a bed or home-cooked food. He needed the desert, and heat, and solitude. He needed to think.

Things would have to change.

ALEXIS LEANT BACK in his bed and smiled. He had suspected it for a long time, but seeing his enemy's face lit by the firelight, seeing that look of grief and shame and horror... there could be no mistake.

Alexis knew who El Sombra really was.

In the morning, he would discuss his suspicion with Master Minus. Together they would work out a plan of attack, something to run parallel with his father's bumbling attempts to have him killed. Something to succeed where Herr Generaloberst had failed. He turned on his side and thought about children, burning in a furnace of flaming timber.

He slept like a baby.

CHAPTER FIVE
ZINNSOLDAT

SEVEN DAYS LATER and the dawn was breaking. Jesus Santiago watched the desert sun slowly rising over the dust and the rock, turning both a bloody orange. He was taking a chance—he knew that leaving his basement was not to be taken lightly. His occasional trips to the town for information were risky enough. But to stand outside his home doing nothing—making both it and him a target for any desert patrol that might venture out of its usual pattern—well, that was sheer foolishness.

And yet, the sunrise was very beautiful.

Since El Sombra had come to the town, Jesus had found it easier to take joy in the small things. It was as though he'd brought hope itself back with him from the grave. Things that had been so easily forgotten in the name of survival—laughter, courage, defiance—found themselves embodied in him. Since the fire at the schoolhouse, Jesus had seen little of the masked man, but the reports still came to him of curfew-breakers saved from death, of soldiers and wingmen cursing lost shipments of ammunition. His friend had been busy—but his self-imposed task was now a private penance, it seemed, for imagined sins.

Jesus hoped the penance was over soon. He missed his friend.

There was movement behind him on the roof of the shack, and then the sound of a body hitting the dirt. Jesus turned to see El Sombra crouched, cat-like, the dust still swirling around the soles of his bare feet, his sword gripped in his hand. He smiled at the eyes behind the mask, and said the first thing that came into his head.

"They're going to kill you."

El Sombra looked up from his egg, tearing off a piece of the white with his fingertips. "That was a very pessimistic way to greet a friend, amigo."

Jesus shrugged, smiling as he leant back in his chair, a glass of good whisky in his hand. "I only repeat what I hear. I'd have told you sooner, but you've been in the desert for days, you know? Did what happened at the schoolhouse hit you that hard?"

El Sombra scowled. "What do you think?"

Jesus hung his head. "It's my fault. I should have known what Verdad and the others were doing. If I'd kept you informed, you could have…"

El Sombra shook his head. "No, it wasn't you. It's in the past now. Besides, I haven't been sitting around crying like a schoolboy. I've been waylaying as many foot patrols as I can—trying to starve their supply routes. It's like chess—they have six or seven routes, but they all need to go through shade at some point. If they march their men through the open desert all the way, their men die. But if I try and take them out in the open desert, their snipers are more likely to draw a bead on me before I get to them—so I die. So I have to guess where they're going and then find a shady patch along the way to hide in until they come. It's a science, my friend, but I'm getting much better at it."

"I hate to say it, but… that isn't like chess in the slightest."

"Well, I've never played chess. The important thing, amigo, is I'm starting to put a dent in their supplies again. Crippling their Engine was a good idea, but I forgot that if generals have a problem, they throw human lives at it until it goes away."

"So they're using their soldiers as packhorses, marching them through the desert laden down with their guns and medicine?"

"And the strong drink. Don't forget the strong drink."

"They must be killing a dozen every trip."

The masked man shook his head. "They've shipped in trolleys infused with their special metal. If you kick an empty one, it floats into the air and keeps going for a mile or more. They're expensive and difficult to make, so I do that a lot. A similar principle to the wings—designed to lighten the load enough to make carrying it across the desert a little less impossible."

"So I suppose you're killing a dozen every trip instead?"

"One thing the Ultimate Reich is not short of is human lives, amigo. What were you saying about them killing me?"

Jesus sat down, leaning back in his chair. "The soldiers are making noises about dealing with you once and for all. After what happened at the schoolhouse, you've become a much more sympathetic figure to the people. It's just a shame you weren't around to capitalise on it, you know? Anyway, they have something cooked up that's apparently going to get rid of you once and for all... something called der Zinnsoldat."

El Sombra's eyes widened. Jesus frowned. "Does that ring any bells?"

The masked man shook his head. "Zinnsoldat is bastardese for 'Tin Soldier.' It's not a name that strikes fear into my heart, amigo, put it that way."

Jesus tapped his fingertips together gently, watching as El Sombra finished his egg and used a hunk of bread to mop up the remains of the yolk. The priest murmured a few halting, guttural syllables.

El Sombra frowned. "What the hell was that?"

"I was speaking English. It roughly translates as 'what does a name mean? A rose with a different name would have the same sweet smell.' A famous quotation from Shakespeare, who Djego would certainly have known all about."

El Sombra winced at the name, then growled, tearing into the bread with his teeth. "Let's keep him out of this."

"Look, I wouldn't be telling you about this if they were just saying they were going to kill you, you know? They say that every day. This is a lot more serious, my friend... more sinister. Whatever this Tin Soldier does, it's going to be bad. Keep your eyes peeled."

El Sombra nodded. "It's nothing, amigo. You worry too much. Listen, as long as I'm here, I have something I need to ask you. There are things I need to know in this town before I can be truly effective here. For example, there's a house near the centre of the town with all the upstairs windows covered in some kind of canvas. I need to know more about it."

Jesus nodded. "The House Without Windows? You know as much as I do. Master Plus lives there and for some reason he keeps the upper floor blocked off like that—that's everything. It's one of those secrets it isn't healthy to learn, you know?"

The masked man smiled. "Then I'll have to find out first hand."

*   *   *

As the sunrise hit the Red Dome, it seemed to wash the General's office in a sea of blood. As he looked out through the tinted windows, the sun seemed a boiling mass of fire, a pitiless red eye belonging to a terrifying monster, opening slowly onto the town and bathing it in a gaze that turned it to stone. He couldn't help but smile slightly at that idea, the great weathered face cracking a little. He turned to look at his imposing guest and let out a soft chuckle. There was such a monster stalking Aldea today, and he had its leash in his hand.

There was a knock.

The General grinned. "Come in, Master Plus. Come in and meet our new toy."

The door opened, and the fat man shuffled in, keeping his eyes lowered, as the General knew he would. Eisenberg said nothing, waiting with his arms folded for the little fat man's eyes to rise and take in the sight of his new friend. Slowly, Master Plus lifted his head—and then took two stumbling steps back, a gasp torn from the depths of his throat, sweat beading on his brow.

It was the reaction General Eisenberg had been hoping for. "Be careful, mein Herr. You will give yourself a heart attack."

Master Plus said nothing, only panted, clutching his chest and regaining his feet, his eyes bulging.

Eisenberg smiled. "Master Plus, may I present to you—der Zinnsoldat."

It was ten feet tall, and shaped roughly like a man.

The posture, however, was closer to that of a gorilla—presumably to allow it to fit into smaller spaces, such as the office. The two massive paws, like industrial diggers, clutched and flexed, metal joints squeaking as the network of hydraulic pipes that ran like creepers up and down the forearms hissed menacingly. It had no head, as such, but there was an approximation of a face in its chest, comprised of a pair of massive iron doors, locked shut, with small horizontal slits which glowed orange with the heat of the coals behind. Occasionally a bright ember would drop to the carpet, as though the creature was drooling in anticipation of the kill, and glow for a terrifying moment before dying away. Above the furnace apparatus were a pair of vents, which some enterprising engineer had fashioned into the semblance of eyes, giving it an expression of cold and merciless calculation. On the monster's back, there was a large metal dome, like the shell of some hideous beetle, and rising from this were six metal pipes, for the purpose of letting off and circulating steam within the massive robot, and a chimney that belched the occasional puff of tar-black smoke into the air as it moved. Underneath the shell could be heard a series of clicks and rattles, a constant ticking of clockwork that sounded like nothing so much as an army of devouring insects on the march, as the beast emotionlessly processed its latest directives. The final touch, rising from one shoulder, was a small hydraulic chamber, decorated with the swastika, like a brand to show ownership—or a tattoo to show allegiance.

It moved slowly, leaning forward and staring at Master Plus as though measuring the trembling fat man as a threat. The grabbers closed shut, forming into massive crushing clubs. The slowness of its gait was even more terrible, for it gave the impression that the monster was only storing its power, that any moment it might spring forward with the speed of a striking cobra, and crush the head of the fat man between its metal hands, popping the skull like a boil.

It radiated power, menace, and a cold mechanical contempt for all that could not be represented in numbers and statistics. It was the representation of all that the Ultimate Reich was and all it planned—the icy dominion of inhuman efficiency over the soul of man.

Eisenberg smiled, running his hand gently over the metal shoulder of the immense machine. "Isn't it wonderful? Berlin has only six of these. We're very lucky to be allowed to borrow one. I hope you realise how highly the Führer values this experiment."

Master Plus swallowed hard and took a faltering step closer. "What... what in heaven's name is it?"

Eisenberg looked over at the fat man, smiling. "It is a machine in the shape of man, mein Herr. Or rather, in the shape of an assassin. This wonderful creation will solve a certain masked problem that afflicts us both; disrupting work, stealing valuable supplies, committing murder with impunity."

Master Plus swallowed gently. "El Sombra."

Eisenberg's cold grey eyes narrowed. "I do not need to be reminded of his alias, Master Plus."

The fat man looked at the floor. "My deepest apologies, Generaloberst, I did not mean..."

"Why has there been no salute yet from you, dog? Forgotten your place here already? Heil Hitler!" It was barked like a drill sergeant. Master Plus shuddered and snapped back a salute, almost crying.

"Heil Hitler!"

The General smiled and nodded. "That's better. It wouldn't do to make the wrong impression on my friend here... would it?" The immense robot hissed like a cobra, a cloud of steam filling the room as it moved forward a step, the grabbers creaking and flexing. It was all that Master Plus could do not to soil himself then and there. Eisenberg chuckled.

"Relax. It won't hurt you. It's just looking for food."

"Food?"

"It's not quite as efficient as an English robot. That furnace in its chest needs feeding, and often. Luckily, it's designed to find anything that can be burned in any environment and use it to fuel itself." He nodded to the machine. "Demonstrate."

It moved like lightning, the joints hissing as it whirled around. Two massive paws came down hard against the wood of the General's desk and smashed it into fragments. It was only the heavy reinforcement of the floor that prevented the iron fists from pounding the shattered remains through into the room below—as it was, the floorboards beneath the carpet were cracked and broken. Eisenberg smiled softly as the machine opened the huge mouth-furnace doors, the ingenious construction ensuring the flaming matter within did not spill out even as the robot shovelled broken, splintered shards of wood into it. The entire operation took perhaps fifteen seconds. When the robot was done, it turned back to face Master Plus, the slits in the furnace doors glowing with infernal light.

Eisenberg spoke softly. "That desk was solid mahogany. I wonder if El Sombra will prove quite as flammable when he is crushed by those paws."

Master Plus stuttered, fighting the wave of terror that crept through him. "I... It... it seems a shame, Herr Generaloberst, to lose such a fine desk..." He flushed crimson even as he spoke, hearing his own stupid banality loud in his ears.

Eisenberg nodded, unsmiling. "It was a present from my late wife." The fat man's eyes widened. "Do not look so shocked, mein Herr. We must be prepared to sacrifice the things we love for the glory of the Ultimate Reich. Is that not so?"

Master Plus swallowed hard. "I... I don't see..."

"It is very simple. There is nothing you own that is so precious that it cannot be taken from you in service to the Führer. Love is a weakness, and weakness must be eliminated." Eisenberg reached forward, placing a huge hand on the other man's shoulder. "After the wedding, Master Plus, you will come to understand."

Master Plus lowered his head and hoped that the tears in his eyes would not condemn him, as the General reached into his pocket and removed a small roll of paper, studded with tiny bumps, like Braille, and various little punched holes in a complex pattern. He held it up for Master Plus' examination, although all his attention was concentrated on his mechanical creature.

"This represents all the information we have on the masked dissident. Recent sightings, movements, a full description, those he's been seen with, even things he's said. Der Zinnsoldat has already been fully programmed with information regarding Aldea, its history, and our mission here. Now watch closely..." He unfurled the roll of paper and began to carefully feed it into a small slot sitting next to the dome that protected the creature's thinking-machinery. "Our friend feeds on information as well. Hear that clicking? That's how it thinks. All those tiny little cogs and wheels and gears clicking together, falling into precise place..." The machine suddenly swung its arms around, following and smashed through the doorway of the office, bringing down the heavy wood door in its rush to be about its murderous work.

Master Plus cried out, and the General laughed, a mocking glee in his eyes. "There it goes! It won't stop now until the masked man is dead. Come on, mein Herr. We must be quick if we're to keep up with our little pet."

CARINA LOOKED OUT of her window, as she often did, down at the fruit-seller on the corner. His name was Miguel—her father had told her—and his life was idyllic in its simplicity. He was always on the corner, leaning against the wall, with a basket piled high with oranges and a smile playing around his lips. She remembered seeing people buying fruit from him... well, she couldn't remember precisely when, but she must have, surely. He had a wife, two children—the youngest was just starting lessons at the schoolhouse, apparently. It must be nice, she thought, to mingle with other children. But that wasn't possible, of course.

Until the age of nine, she had been allowed out. She remembered splashing in the mud and climbing trees. There had been a boy named Hector—something had happened to him, she remembered—had he been injured somehow? She remembered a fire... but it seemed so distant, as though it had happened in a dream.

That was just before she was shown her rooms for the first time. Her father had explained how things had always been in Pasito. There came a time when women were locked away, for their own good, in palatial quarters such as hers, so that they could mature without distractions. She remembered being appalled at that. Even at the age of nine, and just back from the hospital—what had she been in hospital for?—even then, she'd felt that something about that was just… wrong. At first, she'd rebelled, running around, breaking things, crying for her playmates. But before long, she settled, as she had no other choice. Her father, who could be bought with a smile, was obdurate in this one matter. So she stayed, locked in her tower, taking her lessons, reading the books her father brought her, often sitting at one of her windows, looking out at the peace and quiet of the town—the peace and quiet that never ended.

Carina had never seen anyone arguing in Pasito. Occasionally she heard shouting, sometimes even gunfire, and there was always a strange clanking, hissing sound that she could never identify, like great iron wings beating far away. But when she went to the window, there was no sign of anything but peace and harmony. Sometimes that peace and harmony made her feel uneasy. Sometimes she'd sit, looking down the street, watching, biting her lower lip as she waited and waited for someone to leave one of the buildings, or cross the street. Scanning the scene, looking for something, but never certain quite what. Occasionally she would comment on the seeming strangeness of Pasito to her father, and he would laugh and dismiss her idle thoughts, making her feel stupid and silly and foolish for questioning the evidence of her eyes.

Somewhere under the earth, a few hours after such a conversation, an old man in thick glasses would listen to Master Plus' report and make a note in a leather-bound journal. And smile at the continuing success of the experiment. But of course, Carina never knew of that.

On a sudden impulse, she stretched out, leaning as far out from the window as she could, reaching forwards, fingertips stretching. She felt only the air. It was something she did more and more often lately, without knowing quite why. Or perhaps she did know why, deep down below the floor of her conscious mind. Perhaps the truth was simply too horrific to face without being forced to.

Perhaps, in the back of her mind, she did know that her outstretched fingertip had been less than an inch from the canvas, but probably not. It was, after all, canvas that had been decorated with the second most cunning optical illusion in the world. She would make the distinction herself at the age of sixty, when she saw the first in its museum in Marseilles and was heard to comment 'even if someone walked through that one, I'd still believe it.' And then the grey-haired woman would sigh and look to the ground, as though remembering a man she had lost in blood, a long time before.

But that was the future.

Carina turned to pour herself a glass of water from the carafe standing on the table by the couch, and that was when the shadow fell across the room.

Carina turned and what met her eyes was terrifyingly, vertiginously impossible. The shadow was hanging in the sky. The shadow of a man was in the sky. She felt a stab of splitting pain in the back of her skull, and felt a feeling of pure horror wash over her. Horror and something else, something indefinable. Why should this be making her feel so angry?

There was the sound of tearing canvas, and a man fell through the sky and clutched at her windowsill. He was half-naked, wearing a tattered, bloody mask and carrying a sword, and he had serious grooming and hygiene issues. None of which mattered.

All Carina cared about was seeing the sky for the first time.

The real one.

"Make that hole bigger." She heard herself speaking, but felt hardly conscious. The edges of her vision were greying, and something was rushing through her blood, through her brain—a pure, white-hot rage with her father's name.

The masked man kicked at the canvas as he clambered over the sill into the room, slumping on the polished wooden floor. Carina walked around him without a glance in his direction and stared out of the window, as she had done so many times before.

She finally knew what it was she was looking for. She'd found it.

It was impossible to describe—like a hole in space, onto a different world. A world that was darker, and crueller. The buildings were old and worn, neglected. Smoke hung lazily in the air, and occasionally a strange bird-man would wheel past in the long distance and a tiny little creaking, clanking sound would reach her ears. Something about the bird-man made her feel sick. The last time she saw one of those... she'd blocked it out, but it still made her sick. But only a little sick.

What really made her want to vomit up a tide of black bile was the thing in the very centre of the scene, that rose over the town, coated in scaffold, with human beings crawling like ants over it, working blindly and hopelessly and forever. The statue of the man with the nasty little moustache and the ugly hair and the arm raised in eternal salute. And the eyes, sculpted perfectly, as to the life. Eyes that seemed dead, all human emotion vanished from them. Eyes that had held no understanding of common humanity, windows to a soul soured and twisted beyond recognition. All those who bought the threepenny broadsheets with their alluring red banners and nodded their heads sagely at the carefully-tailored ignorance within, all those who were first to stand up and moan shrilly about the wave of 'social correctness' that was sweeping Europe, coveted and lusted for a pair of eyes like that. They were the idol and the template for all those who secretly believe that the world would be better if such silly concepts as 'human rights' were hurled into the incinerator. Along with a few dozen humans to really drive the point home. They were evil personified, cast in stone to gaze forever at the town which they had enslaved. Carina cast her eyes away, unable to stand the sight of them.

It was her first sight of Adolf Hitler.

She didn't feel the tears trickling down her cheeks, but she felt her teeth clench, and heard the terrible hiss of her exhaled breath as it burst from her.

It was El Sombra who broke the silence. He was staring out of one of the other windows, looking at a scene of perfect, pastoral calm.

"What the hell happened to the town? I've only been in here a minute!"

Carina turned and stared at him, then—despite herself—she began to laugh.

FATHER JESUS SANTIAGO sat in his front room, enjoying the sunlight streaming through the window. He'd pulled the wooden boards down to allow the light in and was sitting at his desk, collating a list of the disappeared—one of the many tasks he set for himself every week. Someone had to keep track of these things.

He'd been afraid that the addition of sunlight would show up the old, broken furniture and layers of dust, but to his surprise the room still had a rustic charm, despite its abandoned quality. In the back of his mind, he knew he was taking another risk, but there hadn't been a soldier within a mile of the house in years. It was time for him to start enjoying life again—the small things that most took for granted, morning sunlight, fresh air. There was no sense in denying himself the most basic joys life had to offer because of misguided paranoia—

—there was the sound of clanking metal in the distance.

Jesus' eyes narrowed, and he turned to the sound, listening intently. The clanking and creaking of metal was nothing new in these parts, but there was something different about this. The sound was heavier, somehow. Louder, more insistent. As though made by something very, very big...

The adrenaline hit. Jesus leapt out of his chair, grabbing the paper he was working on and hurling himself at the trapdoor. He could hear his heart pounding in his ears, feel the blood rushing, his chest tightening as he burrowed under the rug. Working quickly, he levered up the catch with slippery fingers, lifting the heavy wood of the trapdoor enough for him to squeeze through, then letting it drop and hoping the rug stayed enough in place to fool the intruders. He couldn't breathe—he had to consciously work his lungs, trying to keep from panting, to keep as silent as possible. The sweat dripped down his neck and back and the scraping of the wooden door against the barely-healed scars had set them screaming once again. They seemed to burn as he lay with his spine pressing on the stairs just under the trapdoor, unable to move a muscle in case his shifting weight made them creak. Over his head, there were thudding footsteps and the sound of German being spoken.

Like a fool, he had dropped his guard—and they had come for him.

The floorboards overhead were creaking. Not just the floorboards, but the supporting beams in the cellar, as though they were being forced to bear some unimaginable weight. The noise was deafening. Not just the creaking and clanking, but a terrible clicking like a thousand insects trapped in a metal jar—all sandwiched between terrible claps of thunder, hard metal impacting on dusty wood. Occasionally he heard the crack of one of his floorboards breaking under the strain. There was a very real possibility that whatever thing was up there would simply crash through the floor under its own awful weight. If that happened, he would be discovered or, worse, crushed to death by the monstrosity above.

The thunderous footsteps shook the wood an inch from his head, making the trapdoor rattle under the rug—and stopped.

The seconds ticked by. Except for the ticking and clicking of the thing above him, there was no sound.

Jesus held his breath.

A drop of sweat slowly trickled from his hairline, running over his brow, down the side of his nose. His lungs began to burn with the effort of controlling his breathing, of staying so very still.

The clicking above him stopped.

Silence.

Very slowly, and with infinite care, Jesus allowed himself to breathe out, and then slowly breathe in.

The clicking began again, loud and fast, and then there was the sound of heavy metal cracking onto wood as the beams around him screamed in protest. The monster was taking a step. And another. And another.

Away from him.

Jesus breathed out again, silently, and allowed his body to relax.

Beneath him, one of the steps creaked.

A massive industrial grabber smashed down through wood to close on his left ankle, then jerked hard, dragging him through the splintered hole. The smashed, ragged edges of the wooden boards tore at his back and shoulder, raking down the flesh, tearing the half-healed wounds open as his body whirled up through the air like a rag doll, to be brought down hard against the floor with enough force to crack the wood beneath him. He felt two ribs snap like twigs and then something popped in his ankle as the monster tightened its grip on it. Then it swung him up again. This time it slammed him into the wall, his bandaged shoulder taking the brunt of the impact, and swung him around like a hammer to crash down into the centre of the great oak table he'd been working at. Another three ribs shattered and something in his spine seemed to tear as two of the table legs snapped off with the force of the impact. The priest rolled onto the floor, retching up what looked like half a pint of blood and black matter. The pain was indescribable and he could no longer feel his legs. He turned his head slowly.

Something from a nightmare was towering above him. An immense metal creature, hunched like an ape to fit into the room, the chimney on its back belching smoke as it scraped against the ceiling, mechanical paws already reaching out to grip him again. The terrible buzzing of a thousand trapped hornets was coming from a shell on its back and, as he watched, it took hold of one of the legs of the shattered table and broke it up into pieces to stuff into the raging furnace located in the centre of its chest. But perhaps the worst thing about the monster was its eyes—or the burning holes that passed for its eyes. There was something horrific in that unchanging, fiery gaze, the unmoving carved slits constantly fixed in a look of cold concentration—in the way that the creature would crush him, tear him to shreds, without the slightest show of outward emotion.

"Wonderful, isn't it? We've spent years wondering where your bolthole is, and the machine works it out in seconds. Where is the one called El Sombra?"

The voice was deep, gravely, with a very strong German accent. Jesus had heard it before, but could not remember where. He coughed up more blood in reply.

The metal creature yanked his dislocated ankle again, and this time he screamed as his body arced through the air, the thing letting go and sending him crashing through the thin wooden panelling of a wall. He landed hard on the dusty floor of what had once been the kitchen, sharp splinters of wood sticking into his back, arm twisted beneath him, the shattered end of the ulna bone poking through torn flesh. He screamed again, the scream becoming a choking sound as he retched up more of his own blood.

The General looked down at him, face filled with contempt.

"Again. Where is the one called El Sombra?"

Jesus coughed hard, spraying a red mist over the floorboards. The General patiently waited until he found his voice, looking at the shattered man with his ice-grey eyes.

"I have... no idea what... you're talking about, Herr Generalob..."

The sentence ended in a scream as the mechanical horror took a step forward, the heavy metal foot coming down hard on the priest's wounded shoulder. The clavicle snapped, making a sound like dry kindling.

"We know he's been here, Priest. Der Zinnsoldat is never wrong. Where is the one called El Sombra?"

Jesus' vision was greying at the edges. The pain came in waves now, like knives tearing his flesh. He choked as more blood spewed from the back of his throat, blood mixed with bile. How much more was in him? He tried to speak through the agony, every syllable punctuated with little flecks of red on his lips.

"Te meto la... verga por el osico... para que te calles... el pinche puto osico hijo de perra..."

The General turned, looking to Master Plus, who was cowering in the doorway, staying as far from the immense machine as he could.

"You speak the mud language. Were those directions?"

Master Plus swallowed hard and shook his head. He looked sick, and the sweat was pouring from him as he bore witness to the torture. "No, Herr Generaloberst. Quite the opposite."

Eisenberg nodded, looking down at the mangled body below him. "I don't think pain is going to work here, and I don't want him to die of blood loss before he's shown us where to find our masked friend. I think we need more subtle measures with this one."

He turned, fixing his grey eyes on the fat man.

"Get me Master Minus."

*　　*　　*

"OKAY. OKAY... so let me see if I have this straight. Your father..."

El Sombra furrowed his brow.

"...is a massive, massive... massive asshole."

Carina nodded, pouring herself another glass of water. She did not turn around. She could barely look at the windows now. "I feel like such a fool."

"Don't. I know they aren't real and I'm still fooled. They almost seem like they're moving."

Carina laughed. It was without humour.

"They almost do. If you look at them long enough, you'll think you remember them moving... or someone walking across them... I don't know how they do that." She sighed, closing her eyes and burying her face in her hands. "Maybe it's magic. Why not? If I'm going to be locked up like a princess in a tower, it might as well be a magic tower."

El Sombra winced and pressed his fingers to his temple, as though he was developing a headache.

"Unnh. Unterschwellige... subliminal message. It's a signal or message embedded in another object so it passes below..." He winced again. This one had been buried deep. "... below the normal limits of perception. So the conscious mind cannot see it, but the subconscious mind perceives it and informs the conscious mind. In your case, it's a whole bunch of little messages in the picture telling you that it's real, and to stop thinking about it and accept it."

Carina stared at him in shock.

El Sombra smiled sheepishly. "Sorry. I must have picked that up somewhere."

Carina reached out and touched his temple with the tips of her fingers. "Do you... do that a lot?" He nodded, looking down at the carpet as though he'd been caught doing something embarrassing. Carina drew back, realising in that moment how little she knew about this El Sombra, this man who had come in through her window and revealed everything she had known to be a lie. "Who are you?"

He turned to look at her, and there was something in the eyes underneath the mask.

She understood then that this was a man who would never lie.

This was a man who would never stop fighting until ten minutes after he was dead—and even then, beware! Check the grave daily. Leave a candle burning in the dead of night and never turn your back on a shadow. Never again, for as long as you live.

This was a man who had lost almost everything he had, and would hurl the rest into the fire—even down to what little remained of his soul—if that would save one life.

This was a man who could never be stopped or bought or beaten. A man who could never be broken.

Because he had already been destroyed.

The reason he was what he was… was because his mind was damaged. Like a horse whipped with iron chains until it bled, he would plough on, hammering forward forever or until he died in the dirt, heart and soul burned to nothing in the inferno of his revenge.

So this is what a hero is, she thought. *This is everything my father, the bastard, the liar, is not. This is the woodcutter of the fairytales, the masked caballero, the knight, the man who can fight off an army with a smile, the one who will always be there for me if I ask but once. This is the hero. And he is mad.*

And he is in so much pain.

"I'm sorry."

"Sorry for what? I'm fine." He smiled brightly, his eyes not meeting hers, playing the reckless warrior as he did with everyone else. But she understood it was a front. There was an undercurrent of shame and anger in him that would never quite go away.

Carina shook her head and looked away for a long moment, out at the statue, almost calculating. Then she smiled softly and led him to the divan, sitting him down gently. "Come on. Take the weight off your feet for a minute; they look like they could use it. I want to hear your story."

"It's not something I like to…"

"None of that. I'm going to fix you, El Sombra. You want to save this town, fine, but I'm going to save you. It sounds like somebody has to."

He looked at her, blinking.

"Now tell me your story. And don't leave anything out."

MASTER PLUS' VOICE cracked and quavered in the still air.

"Please, Herr Generaloberst. Please don't send that thing to my home."

The General's face was as stern and cold as steel. He was enjoying the way the fat man squirmed.

"What would you have me do, Master Plus? You heard what the man said. El

Sombra is investigating the House Without Windows. Your house." He waved vaguely towards the shattered Jesus, who was desperately gasping for his next breath through a mist of blood. Next to him was Master Minus, dressed in his black hermetically-sealed suit, fiddling in his black medical bag. His truth serum had done its job adequately. It wasn't something he enjoyed using—it was clumsy and rarely gave good results—but it was tailor-made for cases like this, where the intensity of the pain and injury prevented the subject from resisting its effects.

Master Plus looked desperately around at the immense metal monster standing behind him. "Isn't there some chance that he could have lied? It might be a bluff..." he said, hopefully.

"If it is a bluff, we'll know after der Zinnsoldat tears your dwelling apart and crushes everything that you love. Come now, Master Plus, stand up straight. This is your chance to show the Fatherland what a truly obedient servant of the Ultimate Reich you are. I'll be monitoring your reactions as the machine tears your home to splinters, along with anything else that gets in its way. You could really impress me, mein Herr. It's quite an opportunity for you."

Tears rolled down Master Plus' cheeks as he fell to his knees. "My daughter..."

"... will have to pay the price for consorting with a terrorist. I'm sure der Zinnsoldat will make it very quick." Eisenberg nodded, and the machine turned on its heel, marching forward on its huge crushing feet, one metal paw smashing a section of the wooden wall out and then flicking around like lightning to grab a length of wood for the furnace in its chest. Master Plus scrambled up, his chubby legs flailing as he tried to give chase.

Master Minus sighed. "It's a shame the experiment has to end this way. Carina was a very strong-willed child. I would have looked forward to seeing how the Lying Window technology could be applied in the Fatherland, on those less prone to questioning their surroundings."

Eisenberg turned to Master Minus. "I'm sure we have more than enough results to implement trials at home. Now, I need your professional opinion. What should we do with the priest? I was considering allowing Alexis another chance with him in the Great Square, but now I doubt he'd last the night."

The hunched figure in the leather suit breathed in and out, the awful hiss of his exhalation seeming like some giant cobra readying itself to devour its prey as he loomed over the broken, crippled shell that had once been Father Jesus Santiago.

"Allow me, Herr Generaloberst. It seems that poor Father Santiago has been severely injured by our rambunctious little toy."

The eyes underneath the mask glittered like black diamonds.

"I wish only to afford him... the very best of care."

"So... THAT'S EVERYTHING? Yes, you can eat that."

"Fankf." El Sombra nodded, teeth already busy tearing a large chunk from a yellow-skinned melon. While telling the story of what had happened to Pasito in the past nine years, he'd been fidgeting—exploring the palatial surroundings, examining the covered windows with curiosity, and eating fruit. Mostly eating fruit. A detailed knowledge of vitamins wasn't one of the things he'd picked up during his nine-year fugue state, but he had a vague idea that it was a good idea to get plenty of them. Who knew when he'd get the chance again?

He'd been amazed at how easy it had been to unburden himself. Usually the mention of Djego's name caused him terrible pain, but for some reason, Carina helped lessen that pain. When she asked, he could look at the past without the black bile crippling him. Ironically, it was probably something Djego would understand. He had had a vague knowledge of feelings like tenderness and love—albeit a crude, sophomoric one. Of course, with Djego, everything he knew about women was out of a book, or one of the old copies of *The Pearl* he had kept underneath his bed. A good thing he wasn't here now. El Sombra smiled and swallowed another chunk of melon.

"That's everything. Well, up until I decided to investigate this place."

"So you're saying everything I care about has either been torn to shreds or never existed in the first place?" Her voice was bitter as she lowered her head and wiped a tear from her eye. "I'm sorry. I don't usually cry, it's just... I knew where I stood. Even with that monster Alexis, I thought I had all the facts. Now... it's worse than just feeling stupid. I feel like there's not a single thing I can claim to know anymore. I was told the sun rises in the east. Is that true? I was told that two and two make four... God, it's horrible. Where does it end?"

El Sombra reached to place a hand on her shoulder.

"Well, I think once they're done here they'll just burn everything to the ground and everybody with it." He smiled. "But I'll kill them all before it gets that far. So you needn't worry."

She looked up at him, frowning. "How do you always know just the wrong thing to say? Any more pearls of wisdom up your sleeve? I could write them down for future generations."

He grinned. "I don't know. I was just about to ask if you were doing anything after I stab your fiancé through the heart and decapitate your future father-in-law."

She shrugged. "I think I might be washing my hair... oh for God's sake, you can't even wait for an answer before you go for the satsumas. It's ridiculous. If I ate like you, Father wouldn't need to put a lock on the door, I wouldn't be able to fit through it."

He raised an eyebrow, chomping into the fruit, skin and all. "Mmmrpphhrm?"

She winced as a jet of juice sailed past her left ear. "Dear lord, you've got the eating habits of a vulture. And the smell. What am I going to do with you?"

"I dread to..."

Boom.

El Sombra snatched his sword. "Diablo! What in the hell was...?"

Boom.

"The walls are shaking! It's an earthquake!" Carina jumped up from the divan, running to flatten herself against the wall. El Sombra looked around for some kind of shelter, white knuckles gripping the sword.

Boom.

Carina felt the impact right through her. "Wait, I can feel something pounding into the side of the house. I think there's something climbing the..."

Boom.

A huge mechanical club smashed through the brick and plaster, three feet from Carina's head. She screamed, hurling herself forward into the masked man's arms—then looked back to see a terrifying metal giant tearing open the wall, masonry flying down into the street as it was peeled away by great crushing claws.

"What is it?" Carina screamed, her eyes wide with a terror beyond anything she had ever experienced. The narrow, emotionless eyes looked back at her, burning, promising death.

El Sombra breathed out, preparing himself. He muttered the name, almost under his breath.

"Zinnsoldat!"

CHAPTER SIX
FEED THE MACHINE

THE FIRST THING El Sombra noticed was the smell.

Oil and hot iron. Hissing copper, brick dust and the intangible smell of steam, mingled together with the strong stench of blood, fresh-spilled, smoking and bubbling against hot furnace-metal.

The smell of efficiency in action.

All the numbers crunched, all the plans made, the blueprints drawn up, all led to this—the sickly-sweet, almost medical smell of blood and steam. When the bastards had done with the world, all men would breathe this air, every day of their lives. Blood and steam and the smoke of the terrible automated processing factories that clanked and belched human fat into the sky in the heart of the Fatherland. The conveyor-belt monstrosities that carried corpses to the fire—the dead bodies of 'them,' the 'others,' the different ones with their skin, their faith, their love that could not be allowed.

El Sombra occasionally gave himself a split-second for this sort of poetic reflection. But only one. He grabbed hold of Carina and swung her around to stumble back against the soft cushioning of the divan. An instant later, the monster charged, massive hands extended, fire blazing in its metal maw, the slits of its eyes glowing with an eerie light. For the machine, the brutal attack was simply the easiest means of completing its program. A quick, efficient strike. It was without rage, without malice. It took no pride in its ability to rend and tear. It was simply a tool.

El Sombra judged the moment carefully. The creature was almost on top of him when he pitched himself forward, hands moving to grip each side of the chimney that jutted from the back of the thing. The elegant high ceilings of Carina's rooms allowed the monster to stand almost to its full height, which meant that there was enough space for what he had in mind. The muscles in his arms strained to support his own weight as he pivoted himself upward and over the charging monster, swinging on the hot chimney and vaulting over the network of pipes as though they were balance beams. The machine crashed into the wall on the other side of the room, knocking out bricks and mortar, and barrelled through into the small kitchen beyond—where Carina prepared many of her meals.

El Sombra moved to the hole in the wall, watching the monster closely to catch its next move. Perhaps there was a way to shut the machine down now, before it did any more damage…

The massive engine seemed to lose interest in him for a moment, looking around the small kitchen. The infernal glow of its chest had softened to a dull orange, and the ape-like machine sought to remedy this, reaching out one of its gigantic paws and taking hold of a wooden chair—then crushing it into kindling. As the behemoth opened up the furnace doors in its chest, the masked man edged back towards Carina. He knew he had only a few seconds of grace left before the machine went back on the attack. That time would best be spent in trying to ensure Carina's safety.

He turned to face her. "Quickly—out the window!"

She looked at him without comprehension, and in that instant he heard a crash of thunder from the kitchen. His seconds were used up and the monster was awake again. Awake and ready to kill.

"The window! Jump for it!" He pointed wildly, then dived to one side as the immense robot plunged a pair of huge metal fists through the remains of the connecting wall. Carina rushed towards one of the painted scenes, caught herself, then dashed towards the ragged open hole that displayed the true face of the clockwork-town, only to come up short.

"It's so high up!"

"One storey! Just jump!" El Sombra launched himself up and back, the metal paws clanging like foundry hammers as they slammed together in the space where he'd been a split-second before. He threw himself backwards, tumbling in mid-air to land as a cat does on the Persian rug. "Just jump!"

Carina looked at him, fear written in her eyes. "I can't!"

And she couldn't, El Sombra realised. Carina had always been scared of heights, in the way that children are until they learn that not every fall will hurt you. But for nine years, there had been no falling. Before that, her idea of a dangerous drop had been around six feet—the distance from her father's shoulders down to the ground. And now she had to leap from a second-storey window and land without injury, with no time to judge, while the building shook from the blows of a rampaging mechanical titan. El Sombra cursed himself as he dived between the creature's legs, a brutal blow from the thunderous metal fists shattering the floorboards behind him. Stupid. *Stupid*.

All right.

Plan B.

Jumping to the side, he grabbed hold of one of the red drapes that framed the false windows, tearing it down and holding it in front of him to attract the attention of the monster. It was an unnecessary gesture. The attention of the mechanical creature was fixed on El Sombra, in the same way that the sights of the firing squad are kept fixed on their target. The machine turned, watching carefully, as El Sombra stepped back against the heavy oak door, the door to which only Master Plus held the key. It watched him as he fluttered the red material, as he spoke softly, in low, hushed, almost reverential tones.

"Toro. Toro."

The machine hissed, cold and calculating, letting off another burst of steam. It flexed one massive paw, the iron joints creaking slowly in the silence of the room. Carina pressed herself into the far corner, tensing herself as she saw the terrible potential in that coiled-spring form, as it wound itself up, ready to unleash its full destructive fury.

Then the monster charged.

Like lightning, it powered forward, one huge mechanical fist like a battering ram slamming through the red cloth and into the oak with enough force to crack the massive door into two halves and tear those halves off their hinges, sending them clattering and crashing down the stairs. The power of the blow was enough to pulverise El Sombra's ribs, snap his spine, reduce his internal organs to pulsing red liquid.

But El Sombra was no longer there.

"Hey, zurramato! Over here!" He made sure the creature had a good view of him as he stood, one foot on the windowsill, framed by the false vision of unbroken Pasito. Then he drew his blade and leapt, all in one motion—his sword carving the canvas as he swan-dived, somersaulting to hit the ground feet-first.

Der Zinnsoldat could not be angered, or aggravated. There was no emotion lurking within the heavy metal body and yet, something in the manner of the target—this human, this mass of flesh and organ, this inefficient skin of water and chemicals and bone—irked it. The mission of der Zinnsoldat was to track this fragile flesh-thing and crush it into pulp. The capering and darting of the insect was preventing der Zinnsoldat from fulfilling its mission. Its drive to live was disrupting the efficiency of the unit.

Inefficiency could not be tolerated.

The numbers crunching beneath the creature's metallic carapace dictated that the only correct course of action would be to do as much damage to the flesh as possible, in order to minimise the possibility of the target escaping and healing its wounds elsewhere. The weak bag of skin and muscle would be rent. The blood that flowed through the organs would flood onto the dirt. The eggshell skull that housed the fragile brain system would be crushed, its precious cargo pulped between steel claws.

Efficiency would be maintained.

Der Zinnsoldat crashed through the wall in a shower of debris and brick-dust, metal hands extended to crush, to tear, to kill. After that, the room was silent, but for Carina's breathing.

SHE WAS ALONE again.

In perhaps less than an hour her entire world—the cosy womb in which she had spent nine years asleep and barely stirring—had been destroyed, physically and figuratively. The wind that blew through the gaping holes in the walls was warm, but it chilled her nonetheless.

She looked around at her possessions. Most of the vases had been shattered, and the furniture was in pieces, but her most prized possessions—the books—were still on their shelves. Absently, she picked up a chunk of brick and looked at it before placing it neatly on top of a pile of other bricks. She reached for another and then stopped, the futility of the task overwhelming her.

She looked at the door. This was the door that had been locked for nine years, since a time she could barely remember, and now all that was left was a single torn and hanging hinge and a vista of empty space. Carina was not a fool. She knew that El Sombra had risked his life to open that door, to give her a means of escape.

Escape to where?

She picked up another brick, absent-mindedly placing it on the pile, and considered her options.

EL SOMBRA RAN, and a tidal wave of killing metal crashed and pounded at his heels.

His lungs burned and he measured the time he had left to live in seconds. Even if the wingmen hadn't been briefed on the deployment of this creature, the sheer noise of the chase would bring them swarming like flies. If he was still on the run when that happened, he would have no room to dodge without dancing straight into the arms of the beast. The bullets would ricochet off the iron gargoyle's body like the stings of a hundred impotent insects, but the masked man would be shredded like confetti.

The maximum response time of a Luftwaffe unit to a disturbance of this magnitude was—maybe—two minutes. This close to the statue, one minute.

That was if the General had not already informed them of his plans.

His bare feet slammed against the dirt. His lungs burned and his heart threatened to burst free from his chest. Behind him, he heard the echo of thunderous footfalls and the sound of clanking, creaking, groaning metal. He strained his ears, tuned out the panting of his breath and the sound of metal thunder at his heels, and the sound of the clanking and creaking seemed to come from the sky above his head. A creaking that could only be made by one thing in all the world.

Metal wings.

He was out of time. Any second now, the bullets would cascade down like a waterfall, filling the whole street. The few citizens who were taking the air on their brief break from their allotted tasks—and now found themselves flattened against walls and the ground in terror as they watched the violent, impossible spectacle pass them by—would be torn to pieces along with him. Gunfire would crash through the thin walls of the dwellings and take more lives, and it would begin in less than an instant. There was nothing he could do about—

—a man on a horse.

A Nazi. One of the grey-coat guards, the earthbound ones, riding on a horse, a man of rank trying to look big, but only looking confused and shocked as he took in a sight he was never given the proper clearance to imagine. El Sombra threw himself at the soldier. His name, for the record, was Klaus Haas, he was thirty-seven years old and, to his credit, he nearly managed to unholster his Luger and fire before the sharp edge of El Sombra's blade met his belly with enough force to unseat his spindly legs and fat bottom—even as the rest of him toppled to the ground in an entirely different direction.

The name of the animal was Karsten. Karsten had been bred in stables in Augsberg reserved especially for horses designated for military service. In the normal course of events, a horse possesses a natural aversion to the smell of blood and will bolt at loud noises such as gunfire and the crack of a severed spine—but Karsten had been trained for the battlefield, and so he merely stood still, barely shuffling as his owner was bisected on top of him. At the Augsberg stable, warhorses were trained to stand still if their riders were killed so that they could be of use to other soldiers. The flaws in this thinking would have been apparent to any stablehand of Augsberg, had one been there to watch El Sombra nimbly leap onto Karsten's back and swat his flank with the flat of his sword, spurring him to gallop.

This had all occurred in the space of perhaps two seconds. Der Zinnsoldat was not slow by nature, but the inertia that the heavy machine had built up in its headlong chase worked against it. It had assumed, based on the data it had collected deep in its clockwork mind, that the target would keep the same course until he slowed fractionally enough for der Zinnsoldat to reach him. When the meat-thing changed direction so suddenly, the machine could not stop itself in time. Thus, instead of reaching to pluck its target from the back of the horse and crush him like a bag of kindling, der Zinnsoldat flew past, a slave to its own momentum. It corrected the problem instantly. Metal feet and palms impacted against the ground, kicking up dirt and dust, forcing the mechanical behemoth to a slow skidding halt before it swung around and burst again into motion, chasing after the horse and its cargo, grabbers snapping like crocodile jaws.

El Sombra gunned the horse on with another swat of the blade. He had a better chance of keeping out of the monster's reach now, but he still tensed in anticipation of the hail of death that was about to erupt from the clear sky. He risked a glance upwards and saw a single wingman, armed with a pistol and not even aiming it, desperately signalling for backup with both hands. The meaning was clear—the wingman had not been invited to this particular party—either Eisenberg had forgotten to inform the troops or, more likely, he wanted to allow his mechanthrope to have the kill. There was a logic in that. Gunning a rebel down with machine-guns was effective, if slightly mundane, but having a rebel torn apart in the crushing paws of a giant metal ape had a certain style all its own. It would send a simple message—*you thought you knew the worst we could do to you, and you were wrong.*

Tactically brilliant, if you were a five-year-old boy who wanted to show off his new sparkly toy. El Sombra grinned. He had maybe twenty seconds before the sky came alive with the Luftwaffe, and he knew just how to use them.

He steered Karsten towards the statue.

MASTER PLUS WAS in the doorway.

By this time Carina had built a small cairn of bricks, perhaps to mark the death of the life she had led. She was absent-mindedly tidying up, keeping her hands busy as she thought the situation through. She knew she had to leave. The question in her mind was where to go—or so she told herself. In truth, she had still not reconciled herself to the notion that the entirety of the world she inhabited was a house of cards that had finally tumbled to the ground around her. A part of her still believed that things could return to normal, that the holes in the walls could be repaired and everything could be made secure again. It was a part that had no say in her conscious thoughts, but it was strong. Strong enough to keep her stacking stones and pretending to herself that she did not need to act just yet.

And now Master Plus was in her doorway. He was a mess; his white suit stained, the fat on his body trembling like jelly. He ran forward and took Carina in his arms, holding her close to him, tears rolling down the fleshy mass of his face as he sobbed like a child. "Carina! Oh God, you're alive, you're alive! I saw the holes in the walls and I thought the monster had got you... I thought you were—oh, forgive me, forgive me, forgive me..."

Carina, who had rehearsed this moment in her mind a hundred thousand times since the moment the masked stranger had cut his way through her immaculately-designed horizon, found herself with nothing to say.

She held her father close, and the part of her that hoped so strongly that everything could be put back and made as it was curled up and died at the touch of her father's tears. There was no going back. Everything she knew had been broken and strewn about at random, and there was no power in creation that could tidy it all up now.

She sighed softly, her own tears coming now, as she held him close, and part of her burned with anger that she should be the one to comfort him.

"There, there, Father," she whispered. "There, there."

"HI-YAHHH!"

Karsten thundered forward, one step ahead of der Zinnsoldat. The metal monster had almost caught up many times—for Karsten, as noble a beast as he was, was flesh and blood and thus could tire, or fall momentarily behind in the chase. But der Zinnsoldat had a weakness too—one El Sombra was quick to observe. The monster reached out with one immense steel fist, slamming it into the side of a wooden house, not slowing down. The wall exploded into matchwood as the beast thundered forward, the fist opening to gather fuel, before thrusting it into the open furnace of its chest. The flames leapt higher, spurring it on, as the pipes on its back screamed in a geyser of superheated steam.

El Sombra grinned.

It needs to eat. But not drink.

He drove the horse forwards into the Great Square. For a second, in this vast and open space, he would be a target. He glanced up again, to see a trio of wingmen flying high above on plumes of steam, readying their weapons. The first response. He grinned again. Let them come. He had an answer for them now.

He swatted Karsten's backside, driving him on towards the base of the gigantic stone statue. At this time of day, there were more than a hundred workers swarming like ants over the immense idol, chipping and polishing at the stone. It was near complete, this great stone prayer to the gods of death and madness, and in just a few days the order would go out to dismantle it again. But El Sombra had other plans.

"Run!"

He shouted it at the top of his lungs, driving the horse around the edge of the scaffolding and between the tall wooden struts. At first, the workers only stared down at him, uncomprehending, but when der Zinnsoldat crashed through into the square, pipes hissing with a semblance of terrible fury, they dived from the structure, bolting for any shelter they could find.

El Sombra ran his horse around and around the edge of the great stone effigy. Above, the wingmen who gathered with their guns ready were unable to open fire. To hit the workers with a poorly-aimed shot would be bad enough, but to hit the statue was unthinkable. And so they held their fire, flapping in great circles, watching helplessly as the massive mechanical engine of destruction closed in. There was nothing in its programming about the importance of either the great statue or the scaffolding around it, and so it swept the wooden struts to one side, collapsing the structure bit by bit as it followed the charging horse and its rider around the base. The faceless machine did not flinch as the heavy wooden beams and planks crashed down on it, or make any sign that it even noticed the inconvenience, beyond grabbing one of the thinner wooden beams and snapping it into pieces to feed its ever-hungry furnace.

El Sombra gritted his teeth and rode on, wood and metal crashing all around him before he burst free from underneath the toppling scaffold. Tugging the reins hard, he turned the beast around to face the wreckage. Broken slats of wood were strewn on the ground and piled against the base of the statue, leaving the bulk of it naked—Hitler in full salute, feet apart, immortalised in one hundred feet of stone. The very sight of it made the bile rise in the masked man's throat. Too often he had stared at the grotesque effigy, but no longer. If he accomplished nothing else before this monster finished him, he would at least bring this stone idol crashing down.

He spurred the horse forward, hooves pounding the ground. At the statue's base, the machine paused. The target was coming towards it. The best course of action would be to wait for it to come within reach and then lash out—disable it, crushing all organs and bones beyond recognition. It was simply a matter of calculating the best moment to strike.

El Sombra concentrated. This would be tricky. He eliminated all mental chatter from his mind, focussing on the moment. Time seemed to slow, then stretch, the hoof beats beneath him echoing, a slow drum-beat of war.

As the horse reached the base of the statue, he tugged the reins hard. Karsten jumped between the feet of the Führer.

Der Zinnsoldat analysed the move in a microsecond. The target had moved behind the sheltering protection of a wall of shaped stone, but it would not stand up to a serious blow. The robot swung a huge metal claw around, like a wrecking ball...

And struck.

*   *   *

THE SOUND ECHOED across the clockwork-town. The sound of stone cracking and crushing under the terrible impact of metal. It startled Carina, making her pull away from her sobbing father, and look in the direction it had come from—towards the statue.

For a moment, the great effigy of Adolf Hitler seemed to shudder slightly, then began to list to one side. Something in the stern features suddenly appeared to suggest desperation as the sound of crumbling stone grew louder and the statue began to topple backwards. For a moment, Hitler seemed to be gazing up at the sun, the saluting hand pointing to the sky—and then the whole thing vanished from Carina's sight with the sound of a colossal thunderclap.

Carina blinked, realising how it already seemed as if the statue had always been gone. How much the lack of it made her feel that the old Pasito had returned. She smiled.

Master Plus screamed.

If Carina had spent the last nine years in a prison, then so had he. For nine years, his continued existence and the existence of everything he loved was dependant on his usefulness to the regime. The main part of that usefulness was in monitoring the workers of Aldea in their constant and methodical construction and destruction. The state of the central statue corresponded with his own state of health. If things were ahead of schedule and moving smoothly, he was secure and happy. But if something happened to the statue—some minor blemish, perhaps, or an imperfection in the quality of the stone—the blame fell to him. He was woken in the middle of the night, interrogated, occasionally beaten. Once, early on, he had been taken to visit the Palace of Beautiful Thoughts. That was because the lower tip of the little finger of the saluting hand had crumbled away under an over-eager chisel.

Now, the entire statue was gone.

Master Plus saw all of his hopes and dreams fall with it.

"No!" he screamed, freeing himself from his daughter's arms and scurrying to the window on his fat little legs. "No! That monster, that cursed metal ape! I knew it would do something like this!"

"The metal monster? You knew about it?" Carina had not thought she could be shocked any more by what her father had done. But to hear him refer to the thing that had nearly killed her in such familiar terms sent a fresh wave of anger through her.

"Yes... yes, my superior, the General, he brought it in to track and kill the insurgent—El Sombra. I told him it was too dangerous, but he would not listen. I swear, Carina, I never thought the terrorist would..."

Carina breathed deeply, then exhaled sharply. "You mean to say you set that killing machine to hunt him down? That... that thing that can tear through stone and brick and kills without pause, you sent it after a human being?" She closed her eyes. "I don't even know you, Father. Are you just going to stand here and let that machine tear the town to pieces?"

Master Plus took a couple of paces towards Carina, then stopped, looking down at the floor. In the floorboards beneath him, there was a deep gouge where the massive feet of der Zinnsoldat had pounded and chewed up the wood in its rush to kill. As he looked at it, he remembered a human being writhing on a floor much like it, being slowly crushed by a foot like an industrial press, while he watched. While he watched. As if from a great distance, he heard himself speak.

"What can I do?" He sighed, shaking his head, and when he raised it, his eyes were filled with tears. "What can I do to stop it? They said they would brand a number on your forehead and make you a slave. I had to convince them I could be of use to them—I still do, every day. I grovel. Just to keep you safe for as long as I can. What else could I have done? Yes, I am guilty, I will always be guilty—but tell me, what else could I have done?"

There was silence, and then Carina turned to the doorway, looking at the empty space for a long moment. Then she looked over her shoulder at her father.

"Did you come here by foot, Father? Or on horseback?"

El Sombra's vision cleared.

Between his thighs he could feel the flanks of the horse, hooves still pounding the dirt. In his nostrils was the scent of blood and powdered stone. His vision was a slowly clearing blur.

He remembered now; a chunk of stone had impacted against his forehead, cutting it open and scrambling his brains for a second. Karsten had kept galloping on, bless him. He was still alive, which meant that his plan might have worked. If he could just get his vision clear...

He blinked...

...and saw what was left of the statue.

With one foot shattered by the blow, the immense construction had become unstable. The other ankle had slowly cracked under the weight, and the statue had swayed backwards, finally toppling with an impact that shook the earth like the fist of some terrible god. Now the great stone face stared impassively up at the sky, and the saluting hand rose vertically like some strange obelisk, flat palm facing the sun. The great stone head and shoulders had done the most damage, flattening a number of officers' dwellings on the edge of the Great Square, but the bulk of the statue had fallen in the Square itself, and thankfully none of the workers had been crushed.

Above, the wingmen flew in small, terrified circles, still reacting to what was, for them, an unparalleled tragedy. It was the perfect time to make his escape, just as soon as he knew that—

—der Zinnsoldat had survived!

It stood, with its remorseless blazing eyes turned towards El Sombra, as though carefully examining him for injuries. The masked man had known that there was little chance of crushing the monster beneath the falling statue—but he had hoped. Der Zinnsoldat could not be allowed to survive. The machine had done far too much damage already.

The great mechanical beast watched the target closely. Destroying the human's hiding place had injured it, but not critically. From the previously gathered data, the computer underneath the metal shell made swift calculations of the target's future intent. It would attempt to escape the Square first of all, most probably heading towards the dilapidated shack where der Zinnsoldat had encountered the secondary target earlier. Once the target had confirmed his intent by riding in a particular direction, der Zinnsoldat would move to give chase, using the knowledge of the town layout that had been programmed into its memory to cut him off from his goal. Then the target would be destroyed.

Patiently, the machine stood waiting for El Sombra to make the first move. Had the monster been capable of expressing surprise, perhaps a gasp of shock might have emanated from the blazing furnace mouth, borne out on a tongue of flame. As it was, the monstrosity let off a vast burst of steam from the pipes jutting from its back, a sign of the sudden frenzy that its many cogs and gears had been thrown into. The target was acting in a way that defied probability, in a manner contrary to the dictates of survival. The numbers had been utterly wrong.

El Sombra had circled Karsten around and was now riding the horse at full gallop towards the waiting arms of the machine.

Der Zinnsoldat modified its stance, moving forward on its tireless metal legs, picking up speed. The most efficient course of action would be to drive one of its huge digger-hands into the rider, scooping him off the animal and then applying pressure sufficient to burst him.

Above, the wingmen held their fire, circling like vultures. It would not do to startle the horse at this stage. It might prevent the metal behemoth from making its kill, and then blame would be apportioned and punishment would be served. The best thing to do was to simply wait for the metal creature to act.

Karsten's hooves thundered in the dirt. If El Sombra had underestimated the metal monster, it was all over and done with. He swatted Karsten's backside again with his sword, focussing all his attention on the robot.

Der Zinnsoldat, in turn, watched the masked man approaching, the massive grabber flexing, pistons sinking into place. Then the target came within range, and the arm lashed out, lightning-fast, to snatch the rider from the horse.

The metal scoops clanged together on empty air.

El Sombra had launched himself from the saddle, turning a forward somersault in mid-air as the crushing, killing machine arm sliced the space less than an inch below him. Karsten, trained to ignore shells whizzing an inch from his flanks, paid no heed to the metal brushing his back, not stopping or even slowing as the masked man completed his flip and landed back in the saddle.

Der Zinnsoldat whirled, one arm whipping around in an attempt to connect, but the target was already beyond his reach. Deep in the mass of cogs and wheels that formed its clockwork mind, something very much like anger was building.

El Sombra leant sideways in the saddle, reaching for his own target—a metal bucket that was half-full of muddy water. It had been part of the construction equipment, abandoned in the workers' rush to evacuate. Now it was a weapon. The masked man gripped the handle and carefully eased himself around on the saddle, facing backwards at the metal giant lumbering after the horse. He grinned, a slow easy smile.

"Getting a little tired, amigo? Need a tasty snack? Lookie lookie! Delicious wood! Get it while it's broken and scattered around!" He laughed. Not the great, rich, booming laugh which the occupying force had learned to fear, but a soprano cackle like unto a castrated hyena. Had the machine been gifted with understanding of such matters, it may have taken offence at the mockery.

But der Zinnsoldat had no understanding of mockery, of course. It had no understanding of anything that was human, or warm, or alive. Perhaps it took the suggestion at face value, but more likely it was only coincidence that the creature chose that moment to lean one of its massive grabber-arms down and scoop up a shattered length of wood, the furnace-door mouth yawning wide to receive the offering. El Sombra grinned and gripped the metal of the bucket, readying himself to hurl the water and put out the flame—

—and that was when the bullet grazed his shoulder.

Fire tore through the muscles of his left arm, the bucket jerked, and the payload of water splashed harmlessly into the dirt. El Sombra cursed himself. Overtaken with the triumph of bringing down the statue, of being alive to see it happen, he'd forgotten the wingmen circling overhead. Just because they hadn't fired yet didn't mean they weren't ever going to. Stupid, overconfident pudrete... that could have been your head!

He flipped back and jerked the reins as more bullets streaked down from above, impacting against the ground all around him. Small arms fire, but undoubtedly the big guns were on their way. The question was, would they follow him and pick him off once and for all? Or stay in the Square and take control of the citizens? There was quite a crowd now, creeping back to examine his handiwork. And were those cheers he was hearing?

Herman Becker, a mere private in the great and powerful army of the Ultimate Reich, heard the cheering and knew that his time had finally come. He was a small, withered, timid man of forty-seven years, who could barely do two push-ups and needed glasses to read with. Originally a book-keeper from the small, sleepy town of Delmenhorst, he had woken at the same time each day to a grey sky, taken the same bus every day to his grey job, utilised the same half-hour every day to eat his grey liverwurst sandwiches and drink a cup of grey tea, and walked back in at the same time to kiss his grey wife. And then he had seen the posters advertising a career in the Ultimate Reich, and colour had come to his grey little world.

The recruitment officer had attempted to impress in him the need for book-keeping in the Reich, the subtle glories of the administration posts, which kept the Fatherland running smoothly. Becker would have none of it. He wanted action! Adventure! Excitement! Heroism! He wanted to be able to stand in front of the Führer and say that he had done his best for the great dream of German purity! And then perhaps after that he would be able to summon the courage to tell his grey and fleshy spouse that he was finally leaving her for good.

The opportunity came sooner than expected. Herman Becker had a choice of whether to serve in his sleepy home town or to take the great zeppelin across the sea to the faraway town of Aldea, to keep the peace among subhuman savages. An adventure in far off lands—the great white hero taming the mud people, like a story from one of the chapbooks Becker read when he was a child. Becker would be like his boyhood hero, Nick Führer, Agent of S.T.U.R.M., a jet-setting secret agent who fought against the coloured and the subnormal in far off climes, consorting with beautiful Aryan women. So he rode that great zeppelin to the new world.

And what did he find?

He wore grey clothes, and carried a grey pistol that he never fired, and a little grey hand grenade allegedly of the incendiary type, and he stood in a desert of grey under another grey sky and watched grey people build a grey statue. And every day was the same.

Until El Sombra had arrived.

Suddenly here was a villain to match those in the chapbooks of his youth— evil men like Lex Luthor and the Red Rabbi—an enemy feared and despised by his fellow soldiery, a foe worthy of the man of adventure and passion that Herman Becker knew he really was. The lowly private had come running from his post at the thunderous crash of masonry and wood, and now stood ready at the edge of the Great Square to meet the foe.

The villain thundered towards him on a stolen horse, sword in his belt, clutching an empty bucket in one hand—liberated for some nefarious purpose that could not be guessed at—and pursued by a massive mechanical marvel, doubtless a secret gadget created by a weapons specialist working for his beloved Führer. He had outwitted the machine, but he would not outwit Herman Becker. Herman Becker had an answer to villains of his shadowy stripe! Herman Becker did not believe in the half-measures adopted to mollycoddle those who would attempt to poison the values of the Ultimate Reich!

And with that thought, Herman Becker pulled the pin on his hand-grenade and attempted to toss it into the bucket that El Sombra was carrying.

It missed, of course. A swaying bucket held by the rider of a charging horse is a notoriously difficult target, and Herman Becker's hands were shaking with the nervous tension that is all too common in the dangerously unhinged. The grenade banged against the side of the bucket and rebounded to fall at the luckless private's feet.

El Sombra saluted as he charged past on Karsten, and the booming joyous laugh filled Herman Becker's ears. He stared for a moment, dumbfounded, and then drew his Luger, pointing the pistol at El Sombra's back, mouth opening to shout something about destiny and heroism and righteousness. And then the swinging claw of der Zinnsoldat smashed into the side of his head, knocking him against the wall and fracturing his skull. All of his noble dreams of heroism and chapbook nobility, every second of his grey little life, all of it was boiled down in that instant to one simple truth: Herman Becker was in the way.

The grenade exploded at the machine's feet.

CARINA HAD BEEN lucky. While she'd seen soldiers in both the streets and the sky, they'd all been too preoccupied with the falling statue to take much notice of her riding her father's horse. She was controlling the old white stallion more through luck than good judgement, but still she had managed to avoid drawing too much attention, although it would be difficult to draw a great deal in the current situation. The soldiers of the Ultimate Reich were responding to an emergency unimagined since Pasito had been claimed by the Nazis. With the statue fallen every soldier was needed to restore order and get the citizenry away from the Great Square by any means necessary. To stop for anything less than that would not be conducive to their continued health. Still, she kept to the alleyways. There was no need to take unnecessary risks.

She considered her next move. To head towards the Square would be to invite disaster. But that was where El Sombra had been. He might be dead now, crushed beneath tons of stone, or in the grasp of the robot. She had no choice but to...

The sound of hooves filled the little alleyway. Hooves and the thunder of iron feet.

Carina's eyes widened as she saw El Sombra gallop past the end of the alley on a brown charger, decked out with the livery of the Ultimate Reich, his sword seemingly replaced by an old tin bucket. She was on the point of calling out to him when she saw what followed.

It was the monster. The machine-thing with its furnace jaws and its terrible slitted eyes, enshrouded in fire. The inner workings of the beast were far too well shielded to feel the blaze, but the incendiary gel from the grenade clung to it like a cloak of flame, making it even more terrifying. Before, it was fearful in its inhumanity, in its crushing power. Now, as it surged forward inside its own inferno, it looked like a creature crawled up from the depths of hell.

Carina gasped as her father's white horse reared back, away from the threat. She swallowed hard. El Sombra would have no chance against that. No chance at all. Her own words came back to her.

"I'm going to save you. It sounds like somebody has to."

No time like the present.

She shook the reins and sent the white horse forward, following the trail of smoke and destruction.

KARSTEN'S HOOVES BIT into the earth. The animal was tiring now, barely keeping ahead of the monster's paws. In front of him, the desert stretched out, a vast expanse of sand and rock. El Sombra knew the desert like the back of his hand, and he'd taken this direction for a reason. The sand was thick here, almost forming dunes. There was enough of it for what he had in mind. And then Karsten's hooves were thudding hard against the sand, and there was less traction for them to grip on. And Karsten slowed by a fraction of a second.

The sound was like a sledgehammer bursting a watermelon, but magnified a dozen times and flavoured with the stench of blood. The heavy digger-hands, closed into clubs, crashed together, catching Karsten's rear between them. The impact shattered both hips, bursting the fragile meat between. Karsten shrieked and El Sombra came flying off his back, crashing into the dirt a metre away. Then the robot dealt a second hammering blow to the animal's skull and it fell silent. The legs and hooves of the beast continued to twitch for several minutes, writhing obscenely in the bloody sand. Even dead, it still ran.

El Sombra picked himself up from the ground, grasping the hilt of his sword in both hands, steadying himself for the battle to come. Then he turned to face the music. The monster stood in front of him, looking at him almost quizzically with those burning headlamp-eyes, huge arms readying themselves for the final strike, the flames enshrouding it beginning to die down.

The moment stretched. Time stopped.

And then the creature moved.

It swung one paw in a semicircle, aiming to slam it against the masked man's head, then swung the other a half-second later and three feet lower. Like a chess player, it thought several moves ahead. El Sombra could not launch himself backwards out of the monster's reach, nor could he duck the first blow without being hit by the second. And he had less than a fraction of an instant to dodge the attack.

Any other man would have died, skull split and smashed, brains spattered and flung across the sands, ribs crushed, body caved in and distorted by the force of the blow. But El Sombra was standing on desert sand. This was his place of power, where all the things he had learned and stored away were fresh in his mind and waiting for their moment of use, bubbling just under the surface. He did not need to think. His mind was stilled, reduced to the simple mechanics of reaction. In his own way, he had become as much a creature of efficiency as der Zinnsoldat.

He threw himself forward, inside the reach of the metal arms, then gripped the hot pipes and gears that made up the monsters body, scampering up its face and flipping over its back. The flesh of his hands were burned by the flames and the heat the creature generated, but he did not feel pain. As the monster swung around to face him, arms swinging around to cave his skull and crush his bones to powder, the masked man dived between its metal legs. It was a game—a merciless game of tag, where the opposing player had the power to cripple or kill with a touch. And El Sombra was the loser before he had even started to play.

A robot would not tire. A man of iron and steam would not flag, or stumble, or make any mistake. Out here there was nothing to distract the monster from his business, nothing to disrupt the efficient schedule of murder it had charted in its clicking, ticking brain.

Until a white horse ran into its field of vision, the rider leaping from the back of the beast to run in front of the target, shielding him with her own body.

Carina looked into the headlamp-eyes. "Stop! Stop right there! I am the daughter of Master Plus and in the name of the Ultimate Reich I order you to shut down!"

Der Zinnsoldat's clockwork mind clicked and whirred furiously. While most of the words flowed over it without recognition, the distinctive syllable clusters of Master Plus and the Ultimate Reich were enough to get its attention. It processed the new data.

Carina swallowed. She had made the monster pause. She could not back down now. "Do you hear me? I said shut down! Now!"

Carina's plan was sound. She had a connection to the Ultimate Reich, perhaps one that was important enough to stall the creature, but almost certainly a connection that would protect her. If she could put herself in harm's way—make sure that there was no way the monster could kill or injure El Sombra without hurting her—then she could stop it. It was a sound plan, but a risky one. If der Zinnsoldat had not been programmed to consider Master Plus, or the family members of the Reich, or if it had been instructed to take orders from only one source, she would be dead. It was a gamble.

And she lost.

Der Zinnsoldat examined her closely. She was of almost no consequence... however, it would be foolish to simply crush her when there was one role she could still perform. The firebox that powered the mechanical monster was dangerously low, the chase through Aldea had exhausted the bulk of its power.

It needed to eat.

One arm snapped out, the grabber taking hold of Carina's waist, the pressure enough to make her cry out as the great furnace clanged open, revealing the leaping flames within. El Sombra knew what was about to happen and knew that he had perhaps a second to react before Carina was stuffed alive and screaming into the firebox.

His hand reached out and grasped the bucket, still lying where it had fallen. He filled it with the desert and then charged at the machine.

Der Zinnsoldat registered El Sombra's approach. The target was once again rushing towards him, but this time on foot, and lumbered with a heavy weight. It paused in its business, waiting for him to come close enough for its empty grabber to slam shut on his neck and sever his head. It did not lower Carina to the ground.

Nor did it close its firebox.

El Sombra hurled the bucket with all of his strength. It described a short and graceful arc in the air before striking the open firebox and jamming there, the sand within cascading out to cover the burning embers. The flames were already low, but it still took all of the sand to smother them completely. The furnace died, leaving only smoke and smoulder.

If der Zinnsoldat could feel such a thing as panic, it felt it then. It tossed Carina to one side like a sack of grain and charged, both paws extended in a final attempt to fulfil its programme. Its life could be measured in seconds now. Can a machine panic? Can a machine hate? The meaning of der Zinnsoldat's existence was in tearing and crushing and killing the target, in rending El Sombra like cloth, in wiping the masked man from the face of the Earth. It had been sentenced to die, yet its final movements were for the purpose of killing its foe.

If that is not hate, what is?

El Sombra was within range. Der Zinnsoldat brought up a metal paw, achingly slow.

The masked man took a single step back. And der Zinnsoldat crashed to the earth, no more than a heap of old and broken metal dotted with flame.

EL SOMBRA RUSHED over to Carina. She had struck her head against one of Karsten's hooves when she fell, and was rubbing the back of it in obvious pain. "Are you okay?"

She looked up and smiled, then winced. "I will be. You know, I was meant to be the one to save you this time."

The masked man grinned. "If you hadn't turned up when you did, I'd be a dead man by now. You saved my life."

"Fine... we'll call it one each. But next time I get to save you properly."

"We'll see." He smiled again and leant down, lips close to hers—and then she fell back, unconscious. El Sombra touched the back of her head, and his fingers came away bloody.

It looked like a serious concussion, maybe even a skull fracture. Not to mention the bruised ribs she would have sustained in the monster's grip. He could take her back to the shack and try to fix her up, but what then? She'd be on the run with him. They'd go out of their way to hunt her down. Every nook and cranny of every house would be searched, anyone suspected of hiding information would be shot, any suspected revolutionaries would be tortured and, meanwhile, Carina would probably be brain damaged because he didn't have the resources or the knowledge to treat a serious head injury.

Taking her with him would get the whole town burnt to the ground and probably kill her.

Of course, the bastards had the best in medical care. And she was the daughter of one of the top bastards in the land, the traitor Rafael, alias Master Plus. Her father was obviously a highly regarded man, by his dazzling white suit and the jewels that dotted his person. If El Sombra took her back to him, she'd doubtless be in the lap of luxury before an hour had passed.

He frowned. There was a flaw in the logic somewhere that bothered him. But the girl in his arms could be dying. He had no time to debate with himself.

It was time for El Sombra to make his deal with the devil.

*   *   *

"...AND THEN, WHEN I had lost all hope, he rode up on my white horse, with my daughter in his arms. She has a concussion and needed medical care... and so you were the first one I called on. That's what happened, General."

General Eisenberg raised an eyebrow. The expression on his face was one of cold, unremitting contempt.

"He brought your daughter back to you, Master Plus? That seems strange. You say he was the one who kidnapped her in the first place, yes? Well, then, why would he bring her back, even if she was ill? Unless, of course, she was in league with him. That would make her an enemy of the Reich, would it not?"

Master Plus swallowed, feeling the noose tighten. "General, with all due respect, my daughter would never, never consort with an enemy of..."

"I'm very glad to hear you say that, Master Plus. Very glad of that indeed. Because if she had... consorted, as you put it, with an enemy of the Ultimate Reich... well, steps would have to be taken. For both of you." He smiled and nodded towards Master Minus. Who smiled and nodded back. The General turned, his eyes twinkling, and suddenly the two men seemed like nothing so much as a pair of hungry vultures circling a hunk of rotting carrion. "You understand that, don't you?"

Master Plus' throat was dry. He breathed in and then out. If they did not believe his story... he thought back to the moment when El Sombra had ridden up to him on the white horse. He was sitting outside his destroyed home, with a pair of guards stationed to keep watch. He had told them nothing. What was there to say? He could not condemn his own daughter with the truth.

He had let his head fall into his hands, and when he had raised it again, the guards were gone, without a sound, and El Sombra was in their place, riding his horse, and carrying his daughter. Master Plus had screamed bloody vengeance, called him every name under the sun, and the masked man had taken a tin bucket, of all things, and slammed it down on his head. And then he had told him to take care of her, to get her medical attention, everything the Ultimate Reich could provide.

El Sombra was a good man, it seemed. But he did not understand. He honestly believed, like Carina, that Master Plus held sway in the Generaloberst's office. And why shouldn't he? It was precisely that impression that the little fat man had spent nine years attempting to cultivate.

A pity, then, that nothing could be further from the truth. Master Plus knew what the penalty for his daughter and himself would be if the facts of her involvement with the defeat of der Zinnsoldat were made known. Now he sweated grotesquely, pinned like a butterfly on a board by the General's mocking stare, as he searched desperately for a way to make his ridiculous fairytale believable.

"General... the... the only way she would have received such a head injury would be in trying to escape his clutches. You... your own experience on the battlefield... Herr Generaloberst, you must have left many enemies wounded, in order to slow down their fellows..."

"Not a one, actually. I shoot to kill." Eisenberg stared for a long moment, watching the fat man squirm. "All right, Master Plus, I believe you."

Master Plus' eyes widened in shock and relief. "Yes, Herr Generaloberst! Thank you, Herr Generaloberst!" He made a start towards the door and then stepped back, shuffling his feet and giving a quick and shoddy impersonation of a salute. "H-Heil Hitler, Herr Generaloberst!"

"Heil Hitler, Master Plus." The Generaloberst paused, almost for effect, and then turned slowly to stare the fat man directly in the eye, his grey orbs turning frosty. "Of course, that still leaves us with another matter."

Master Plus looked at him as a gazelle might look at a lion slowly stalking closer.

The Generaloberst's voice was soft and infinitely gentle. "The matter of the statue, Master Plus."

Master Plus stepped back, one hand clutching at his chest, his skin suddenly as pale as the flesh of a corpse. He staggered, then swallowed hard, letting out a shaky breath. He could not speak. All that came from the pallid throat was a low, strangled sound of terror and despair.

The General nodded. "I will call on you to discuss that at length, Master Plus. In the meantime, you may return to your quarters. I strongly suggest you remain there until you are summoned."

Master Plus nodded, the glazed look of purest horror in his eyes unchanging, and slowly staggered towards the door. It seemed as though he was still having trouble breathing as he gripped the doorframe, looking back at the General as though he was about to say something—but then he turned away, back bent like an old man as he made his way through the door. Master Minus smiled wryly as the fat man shuffled out, then turned back to Eisenberg.

"Herr Generaloberst, on the matter of his daughter... why pretend to trust such an obvious fabrication? You are a man badly in need of a scapegoat." His voice was soft and sibilant, crackling like dry old leaves.

Eisenberg turned, and all good humour was gone from him. The twinkle in his eye, the confident air of command had been replaced by a rage born of stark fear. "There is no scapegoat, you fool! Der Zinnsoldat was in my care! It was signed over to me! Now the only way we're going to get it working again is to ship it back to Berlin and have it repaired, and if that happens, and this lunatic hasn't been caught, I will be going back with it, and you will be, and my psychopath of a son will be, and we will all be gassed and thrown to the wild dogs! Do you honestly think Berlin wants human robots if it means that every nine years we can expect terrorist attacks? We have to crush this El Sombra like the bug he is and we have to do it now!" He began to pace, growling under his breath like some wild beast.

Master Minus looked curiously at him through the faceplate of his leather suit. "You will do yourself an injury, Herr Generaloberst. Stop and think for a moment. This El Sombra is only one man, and even madmen have weaknesses that we can exploit. Is the girl being cared for?"

Eisenberg snorted contemptuously. "She's being kept under guard in her rooms, or what's left of them. El Sombra needn't have bothered bringing her home, there was barely anything wrong with her. A cut head, minor concussion and a bruised rib or two, nothing remotely serious. He must have panicked like a schoolboy." The Generaloberst allowed himself a chuckle. "For such a bloodthirsty insurgent, El Sombra has a weak stomach when it comes to sacrificing those he cares for."

"Then we have a weak spot, Generaloberst. He cares. We can use that, I think."

Eisenberg smiled. "Quite so, Master Minus. We can use the girl as bait for..."

"Of course, Generaloberst, but I was thinking more that it was time to test one of my own humble experiments in the field of robotics. It isn't quite as... self-sufficient as der Zinnsoldat, but it has a psychological edge all of its own. The prisoner Santiago is still alive, thanks to my... committed care. I would like your permission to feed him to Projekt Drehkreuz."

The old man smiled softly.

"It is time the fly met with the Spider."

CHAPTER SEVEN
DREHKREUZ

"HEAR YE! HEAR ye! The wedding of Oberstleutnant Alexis Eisenberg and Carina, daughter of Master Plus, shall take place this very day at noon in the Centre For Social Advancement! All are invited! Come one and come all to the wedding of Oberstleutnant Alexis Eisenberg and Carina, daughter of Master Plus!"

TEN MINUTES LATER, El Sombra burst into the dilapidated shack that belonged to his best friend.

"'Carina, daughter of Master Plus'? She was Carina Contreras when I knew her, when did they take away her name? And what's this Centre For Social Advancement? And what's this wedding?" He stopped, looking around. "Hello?"

The only response was the air whistling through the old boarded-up windows. The shack was exactly as it had been when he had last seen it, every rotting beam and splintered board in place, the table standing sturdy and strong by the window, catching the sunlight.

On the table was a note:

Gone for a walk. Back soon. J.

El Sombra picked it up, turning the paper over and over in his hands. A note on the table, left in front of the window for all to see. Madness. He turned the paper over again, read the message once more, folded it and slipped it into his pocket to dispose of later. Then he looked around again, eyes roaming over the walls and floor. Without knowing quite why, he reached out, fingers brushing the wood, almost as if to make sure it was actually there. There was an itch in the back of his mind, and for some reason he could barely fathom, the fact that the layout of the shack was exactly as he had last seen it... disturbed him.

He moved to the rug that covered the trapdoor, lifting it up and then knocking out a prearranged rhythm. No response. He hooked his fingernails at the edge of the trapdoor and it came up easily, without the slightest squeak from the hinges, without even a whisper. The silence of it unnerved him.

Descending into the darkness he held his breath, unsure why his hackles were up. What was he expecting? A skeleton to rear out of the darkness and bite him? Jesus to appear and say that he had left that note as a practical joke?

Something was... wrong. There was no other word for it.

He searched twice through the dank recesses, not quite sure what he was looking for, and then blew out the candle he'd lit and went back up to the surface. Evidently, he had to take this at face value. Jesus, in his infinite wisdom, was out on a morning walk. He'd see if he could spot him in the desert. If he did, he'd knock him unconscious and carry him back to the shack, and then chain him to the basement wall.

El Sombra shook his head, looking around at the inside of the shack, and then walked out into the sunlight, still troubled. There was something nagging at him, but it was not until far, far too late that he realised what that something was.

Everything in the shack was in its place... except for the cobwebs strung across the corners of the ceiling and between the beams.

They were gone.

"YOU HAD THAT eyesore rebuilt? Isn't that a little extreme?"

Master Minus shook his head. "No, Generaloberst, it is not. We cannot put surveillance on the house, because he will see it and never go there again. If we had left it as it was, with holes in the floor and blood on the walls, El Sombra would have known that his fellow insurgent was dead or in our keeping, and his reaction would have been completely unpredictable. By spending a small part of our resources on making a tumbledown shack in the middle of nowhere look slightly less tumbledown, we keep our mouse running in the maze of our choosing."

Eisenberg shrugged, looking out of the window over the town.

"We could have used his friend as bait. That was my plan, and it's a plan that's worked in the past. Hold a big, flashy execution in the Great Square."

"And what happens when El Sombra swoops in and rescues him and humiliates you as he did your son?"

Eisenberg bristled at the mention of Alexis. The boy had never been quite right in the head, but since his defeat at El Sombra's hands he had grown far worse, if such a thing were possible. The General would have been afraid for him if his own position were not so precarious. "Let me assure you, Master Minus, the insurgent could never…"

"He finished der Zinnsoldat. Can you take the risk?"

The silence filled the great, plush office. Without the mahogany desk, the place seemed empty now, as though the Generaloberst had already packed up and moved out. Eisenberg felt exposed here. He hadn't felt exposed when he'd crawled across the fields outside Kiev in full moonlight, inching forward, waiting for something with black leather wings and ripping teeth to swoop down and drain the blood from his body. There, he had focussed on the mission, and his duty to inspire the men who followed behind him. But now the men who followed him had sharp knives ready for his back, and his office was a stark emptiness that echoed the hissing, clicking, scraping voice of the Führer. In his mind, he could already hear that voice pronouncing a sentence of death upon him.

He was afraid.

"This scheme of yours, it seems a risk in itself. How can we be sure that the terrorist won't destroy your Spider the way he's destroyed everything else we've thrown at him?"

Master Minus smiled, a dry chuckle emanating from somewhere within the loose confines of the leather suit. "I fully expect El Sombra to defeat our Spider, Generaloberst. In fact, I look forward to it. The moment when he plunges his blade through the Spider's beating heart will be very sweet to me."

Eisenberg looked up, outraged. Master Minus chuckled again, amused at the reaction.

"For at that moment we finally destroy El Sombra."

* * *

MASTER PLUS SAT on the steps of the House Without Windows. They might as well call it the House Without Walls now, he thought, as he played with the rings on his fingers. He shook, twitching involuntarily, beads of sweat creeping down beneath the collar of the white suit which was no longer quite so pristine. The streaks of dirt and dust that had found their way onto the fabric mirrored the sudden fall in status of the man who wore it.

He had been relieved of his duties.

The statue had fallen, and the workers were swarming to clear it from the Great Square, starting with the shattered remains of the feet and working up. It would take two weeks, if not longer, and there would be little need for reward to spur them on. Failure to keep to the schedule would mean death. And so Master Plus sat on the steps and fiddled with his useless finery and waited for his own end to come.

A pistol dropped into the dirt at his feet.

"I took it from a soldier on the way here. I thought you might have a use for it. There's still a bullet left, so... feel free."

Master Plus looked up at El Sombra, then back down at the gun. He sighed.

"For God's sake, get inside before someone sees you."

The two men entered the house, moving towards the small kitchen that Master Plus kept for himself on the ground floor. It was where he did his drinking. He pulled a bottle of whisky from the shelf and sat down, motioning to El Sombra to take a seat. The masked man looked at him distrustfully.

"What is this? You're offering me a drink now?"

"They took my daughter because of you."

El Sombra blinked, then sat down. "Say that again."

"They took her. Because of you. Because you came bursting in through the window of my home. Because you just had to see what was inside. Because you told her everything so now she hates me. Because when the consequences of your actions bounced back on her, you couldn't at least keep her out of their hands."

El Sombra's stomach lurched and he felt a terrible fear overtake him. "Why wouldn't she be safe in their hands? You're part of the machine here and you're her father."

Master Plus pointed a finger angrily. "How naive can you possibly be? I'm expendable at best! After what happened yesterday, they're just waiting for an excuse to finish me. They pretended to tolerate me because they had a use for me, but you've ruined that. It's on your head if anything happens to her!"

"You're the one who kept her locked away for nine years!"

"I was trying to protect her!"

El Sombra slammed his fist down hard on the table. "Well congratulations, amigo! You did a brilliant job!"

There was a silence between the two men. Each dearly wanted to attack the other, to take out their fury and frustration on the enemy. To mask their own guilt with righteous anger. Instead, they simply sat there and watched each other. Master Plus had not shaved, and his white suit was grubby and stained, but he seemed to have gained some small measure of strength over the last twenty-four hours. If only the innate strength of one who understand that he has nothing more to lose.

The masked man exhaled. "Fine. I screwed up. I should have taken her somewhere safe and tended to her myself. And you screwed up by being a mula. There's no point going over it any more, it's done. What's important now is that we fix it and get her back. What's this wedding?"

Master Plus closed his eyes tight. "The town criers are privates dressed up. God knows why. To catch attention, but I can't imagine any of the workers being that thrilled when they're being forced to pull fourteen hour shifts. But now you know as much as I do. I wasn't informed about any of this, I just heard the announcements. Needless to say, no leaves have been granted to the workers or the lower ranks, so I assume it'll be just officers there. Again, God knows why they're doing it that way. Their original plan was to make a big public spectacle out of it, a little dazzle for the drones." He buried his head in his hands.

"What was your plan? Beyond marrying your daughter off to a psychopath?"

Master Plus gave a great, racking sob, the tears pricking at the corners of his eyes before rolling down his great cheeks.

"I don't know. I remember her seventeenth birthday, looking at her... I thought to myself, I still have time. I still have time to think of something. Anything. And I never did think of anything, I just kept on, and on, doing as I was told, hoping I'd come up with an idea. She'd have been better off with a brand on her forehead and no thoughts in her head. She wouldn't have been noticed. But I had to 'protect' her, turn her into an experiment, put a target on her... oh, Jesus forgive me, forgive me!"

"Jesus isn't here. He's gone for a walk." El Sombra sighed and pushed his chair back. "Where's this Centre For Something Something?"

Master Plus wiped his eyes, drawing in a great hitching breath. "It's the church. The Old Church. It can't be a chuh-church any more, but they've always liked the building. They have events there for visiting dignitaries."

El Sombra nodded. He had never managed to get much information on the old church—Jesus had a superstitious fear of going too near it, thinking he would be recognised if he dared to step through the doors—but this was no surprise. It would be just like the bastards to turn a place where good men worshipped God into a place where bootlickers worshipped the next rung of the ladder.

Master Plus interrupted his reverie. "What will you do if it's a trap?"

"What will I do if it isn't?" he shrugged. "I can't sit back and allow it to happen. If the Church has the same layout I remember, there should be a side exit for the vicar. I'll just grab Carina and run."

"You'll be killed."

"She's dead if I don't get her out of there. You know that."

Master Plus had nothing to say. El Sombra sighed and lifted himself from his chair.

"It's ten to eleven, by your clock. I'm going to see if I can't disrupt this wedding they're having and get your daughter somewhere safe. I'm going to be taking the pistol, so I suggest if you do decide to end it all you use a rope."

Master Plus stared at the bottle. "Thank you."

El Sombra nodded. "You're welcome."

CARINA STARED AT the wall. The only features in the cell were a thick metal door, a wooden shelf that acted as a bed, and a bucket, which was emptied twice a day. The only light came from a small candle placed in one corner. She'd considered starting a fire with it, but all she had to burn was her bed, and that would take too long to catch light. And if it did catch light—what? She'd die of smoke inhalation. A great moral victory, no doubt, but nothing she was interested in doing.

From what El Sombra had told her, there should have been a yellow mist in the air to drive her out of her mind. She wasn't happy by any means—she hadn't been since she'd awoken from a sound sleep to find herself here—but any anxiety she was feeling wasn't artificially produced.

She frowned, remembering the stories of Conan Doyle. Eliminate the impossible, and what is left must be the truth. So, she hadn't been harmed, or even questioned, and she wasn't being held in the Palace of Beautiful Thoughts. Which meant that she wasn't going to be interrogated or questioned, assuming that El Sombra had told her the truth about what her father's friends did to people.

So she was being kept in storage. It was a similar prison to her rooms in her father's house—only considerably less lavish. What were they keeping her for?

The wedding.

They'd invested a lot in her, and they wouldn't see any of it back if the wedding didn't take place in some form. So they'd keep the plates spinning a little longer, have their royal mock-celebration behind closed doors, make proclamations and give out photos and souvenir teacups after the fact... then see how it affected their workforce and tabulate the results. And when they had collected their data, she would, if she was lucky, be shot twice in the back of the head and left in a ditch somewhere.

Smoke inhalation might be more pleasant.

She sighed and leant back against the wall. The best thing she could do would be to sit tight and wait for her chance to escape. That chance would most likely not arrive until the wedding, so she would have to stay alert and hope she could seize it when it finally came.

She had no daylight, and no clock to tell the time, but if she had—and if the dank cell in the basement of the Red Dome had been within earshot of the town criers who had paraded in the streets and lent their voices to the dawn chorus— she would have known that it was three minutes shy of noon.

Her wedding was about to begin.

EL SOMBRA MADE his way through the back alleys towards the church.

The Old Church had been built in the early eighteenth century; the work of zealous Spanish missionaries who believed that the first thing a tiny colony like Pasito needed was a place of worship. Its construction had been sponsored by a wealthy philanthropist of the time, and thus it was built of stone rather than wood, and sported an impressive circular stained glass window, depicting the Crucifixion, around the circumference. The building had been allowed to remain standing at the request of Alexis Eisenberg, who enjoyed the irony of holding formal receptions for the Ultimate Reich in what had once been the house of God.

El Sombra looked up at the old, grey stone, listening to the sound of the organ playing within. It was the Wedding March. Obviously the ceremony was just starting. There were two guards posted outside, one on either side of the double doors that led within, but they seemed shiftless and preoccupied, kicking pebbles to one another and chatting about who knew what. El Sombra watched them carefully from the shadows, then turned away. They looked like bait, and besides, there was no point in coming from the direction the bastards expected. Surprise was the key.

He scanned the sky quickly for wingmen before leaping at the church wall. As his fingers and toes found holds in the stone, his mind flashed up images of sheer rock faces in the desert sun, cliffs without handholds, overhangs of desert rock that could not be climbed, that he had climbed regardless. In comparison, the wall of the church was child's play, and he scaled it silently and swiftly, reaching the roof in less than a minute. The organ was still playing, a loud cacophony that seemed more sinister than celebratory. He would look forward to shutting it up once and for all.

The masked man took a deep breath and stilled his mind. Then he began to run towards the far end of the rooftop, past the silent bell tower with the old weathercock slowly creaking and spinning on top of it, sprinting almost to the edge before hurling himself into space. His body twisted in mid-air, hands gripping a stone gargoyle leering over the edge of the roof, using it to swing himself down, bare feet aiming towards the circular stained-glass window.

The force of his impact shattered the glass, sending hundreds of razor-sharp fragments pouring into the church, slashing at his legs and back, spotting him with shallow cuts as he descended to land like a cat on the altar, the coloured glass shimmering down around him and tinkling against the cold stone.

It took him less than a second to see that his plan was doomed from the start. Rescuing Carina from her wedding to Alexis was a noble goal — but there was no wedding taking place in the church.

Instead, El Sombra had landed in front of a firing squad.

Ten machine guns opened up as the masked man dived behind the stone altar, the bullets ricocheting off carved saints and crosses. A squad of ten wingmen had been waiting in readiness for at least an hour for him to come crashing through that very window. When their moment had arrived, they had not flinched or hesitated. It was only the lightning reflexes that the masked man had cultivated over nine long years that prevented him from being chopped into mincemeat by the rain of gunfire.

El Sombra considered his odds. Since this was a trap, the Reich would have sent their most efficient killers, men who worked well with each other. If they'd been prepared for him to enter through the large stained glass window, then that meant they were skilled tactical planners with an understanding of his psychology. Some had duelling scars, which indicated a mastery of aerial sword fighting. Not that they'd need that with the machine-guns they were carrying, but it meant that even if they were disarmed, they would still be more than capable of ending his life.

Ten highly-trained assassins, six of whom were even now moving around the sides of the altar to box him in. And as a final touch, they'd brought along an organist to serenade them. El Sombra grimaced as the music soared to a new and screeching crescendo, and wondered what kind of mind would think to provide such a distraction. The man at the organ was hunched over, wearing a black, hooded robe, his fingers whirling over the keys as he played a series of savage, half-human melodies that seemed to resonate with murder, malice and death. He looked more like a worker than a soldier. Doubtless some poor fool who had been tortured beyond the limits of his endurance until the pillars upon which his sanity had rested snapped like dry twigs. And now, on the whim of one of the bastards, he was set at the organ like a monkey in a travelling sideshow. It was doubtless meant as a distraction. It was a good one. El Sombra saw the men taking their positions to catch him in their crossfire, as if in slow motion, and the constant screeching and wailing of the thing in the corner meant he could barely think at all, much less come up with an escape.

Think, damn it. Think! He was hiding, behind an altar, from ten men armed with wing-packs and machine guns. Four were moving around each side of the altar, two by two, to pin him in a crossfire, and two more were rising into the air to take the advantage of height. The great vaulted ceiling of the Church was perfect for such a manoeuvre. The remaining four—including the commanding officer, he assumed—hung back, taking up the rear. He needn't worry about them just yet, but that still left him facing odds of six to one.

El Sombra had a sword and a pistol in his belt, but nothing that could take care of six armed men, all firing from different angles. And there was no way he could leap out of the way of this. If he couldn't think of a way to murder six armed men in less than a second, he was going to die.

He was in serious trouble, and the worst of it was, no matter how he looked at the situation, there was no way that it wasn't his fault.

*　　*　　*

HAUPTMANN ALDOUS VON Abendroth commanded Eagle Staffel.

He was forty-one years of age, he stood at six feet and four inches, and he had less than three per cent body fat. Each day with his breakfast, he drank a glass of tiger's milk and royal jelly, which he had imported from his castle in the Bavarian Alps. After breakfast, he would do one hour of T'ai Chi—a system which he had developed a grudging respect for, despite its origination among the mud men of the East—and then challenged whichever of his men had distinguished himself the day before to a wrestling match. It was considered a great honour among the men of Eagle Staffel to be allowed the chance to wrestle with Aldous von Abendroth.

After the wrestling, he spent another half-hour in fortifying his mind by reading Goethe, or Schiller, or one of the court epics of Heinrich von Veldeke. By that time, the other soldiers, who rose with the dawn like the sluggards they were, were stumbling to the mess hall, perhaps casting a glance at Eagle Staffel as they engaged in some rousing callisthenics, followed by a shared snack consisting of nature's miracle, the grape, with a little goats cheese that he had flown from Tuscany.

And then Eagle Staffel dressed.

Hauptmann Aldous von Abendroth had been awarded the Knight's Cross with Golden Oakleaves, Swords and Diamonds. He was a celebrity in Germany, with a range of chapbooks based on his many exploits in the service of the Fatherland and at least one film, but he was mainly known for his range of health magazines, in which he endorsed a rigorous regimen of callisthenics, T'ai Chi (which he renamed The Abendroth Discipline out of respect to his audience's sensibilities) and of course, nature's miracle, the grape.

Despite these eccentricities, he was a very dangerous man. He was an expert in both armed and unarmed combat as well as a master of planning and strategy. When backed up by his Eagle Staffel he was unstoppable.

Most recently, the Staffel had been called away from rest and recreation in the cafes of Rome to a small Mexican outpost of the Fatherland, in the hope that they would assist in solving the thorny problem of insurgency in that colony. A vast amount of damage had been done by a single man. A specialist in bladed and unarmed combat who was making it his business to disrupt and destroy as much of the good work being done by the Ultimate Reich as he could. Hauptmann von Abendroth had dealt with nihilists of this stripe before. They set themselves against the Fatherland's doctrines of ordnung because they were too weak to survive under the Führer's gaze. Well, Aldous von Abendroth knew something about strength, and he intended to teach that something to the anarchist who cowered before him now.

This 'El Sombra' would find that the lessons of Eagle Staffel were short, and sharp, and very final indeed.

EL SOMBRA NARROWED his eyes, looking at the sharp pieces of stained glass that littered the altar and the ground around his feet.

This was going to be tricky.

He moved like a streak of lightning. His hands flashed out to the top of the altar, reaching out to take a large sliver of stained glass in the space between each of his fingers—then he leapt into the air, spinning around once, both arms extended, and let them fly. The razor sharp chunks of coloured glass sped through the air like shurikens.

The effect was impressive, to say the least.

The Church echoed with the wet sounds of glass meeting and piercing flesh. A long chunk of brilliant emerald glass, like the feather of some magnificent bird of paradise, jutted from the eye of a man on his left. On his right, there was a soldier with a long gash running along the side of his neck, the jugular already pumping out a cascading waterfall of rich, red blood as clutching fingers desperately attempted to stem the tide. El Sombra held his stance, muscles tensed, eyes flickering around the circle of men that surrounded him. Everywhere he looked, he saw a fatal wound, a pair of eyes glazing over. He allowed himself to exhale. None of the six shards had missed its target.

Aldous von Abendroth listened, speechless, as the heavy organic thud of four slumping corpses echoed in the confines of the Church—followed by the crash of metal and flesh and hissing steam as two wingmen fell out of the air to crash onto stone.

And then the sound of the organist spurring his instrument on, as though relishing the scent of death.

"Spread out! Random directions, random courses! If you get a shot—take it!" Aldous von Abendroth barked the orders quickly to the three men who remained, not allowing himself to think about the six lying dead on the ground—men who had been his responsibility, who had followed his orders and died because of them. He had trained them, taken care of them, taught them everything he knew, and because he had underestimated the animal squatting in front of him, they had died.

He would not make the same mistake twice.

El Sombra didn't allow himself time for such reflection. He had cut the odds against him by more than half, but that was only because he'd been allowed one free shot. Now he had three people ready to kill him and one more in command, and he should really deal with the damned organist as well. The echoing, screeching music was buzz-sawing through his brain, making it difficult to concentrate. He vaulted the altar and dodged left—and then his eyes lit up.

On a small plinth next to the pulpit, there was a two-foot wide iron collection plate, decorated around the edges with a chorus of trumpeting angels.

Perfect.

He somersaulted forwards, a stream of bullets crossing through the space he had vacated, and snatched up the iron plate, lifting it in time to block another burst of fire from above. He sprinted forward, running between the pews as the bullets chewed up the stone in front and behind. Spinning the plate in his fingers, he gripped it like a discus, aiming upwards, targeting Lieutenant Johannes Trommler, a smart young man of twenty-five who had risen in the ranks quickly, impressing the Hauptmann with his quick reactions. On this occasion, those reactions would not be quick enough. Even as Johannes aimed his rifle to fire a killing shot, El Sombra was already flicking his wrist, sending the iron plate spinning upwards, speeding towards its target. Johannes Trommler made a hideous gurgling sound as the iron plate buried in the front of his throat, penetrating deep enough to lodge between two of his vertebrae.

Hauptmann von Abendroth shouted more orders as another of his charges crashed to the ground, choking and coughing blood. "You two—stay low, for God's sake! Get in close, don't give him room to dodge!"

The masked man's lips twitched, but he did not allow himself the smile. It would not do for the Hauptmann to realise he had taken the bait. If he'd kept his soldiers in the air, with their height advantage, they would most likely have picked him off before he'd managed to target another of them. Now their noble commander had ordered them to clip their own wings.

Well, when they shook hands with the Devil, they could tell him that they had only been obeying orders. Doubtless he wouldn't have heard that one before.

Aldous von Abendroth watched his two remaining men carefully. They were good boys, both of them, and they would know what to do in this situation. The fighting men of Eagle Staffel had been trained to react to any contingency, and von Abendroth was confident that this grim scenario would prove no exception. The insurgent could not be allowed to escape, nor could he be allowed back near the shards of glass. Once had been far more than enough.

He narrowed his eyes and nodded almost imperceptibly at the two remaining men. They returned the nod and began Manoeuvre Vierundzwanzig. Both of the young Lieutenants began to carefully creep in opposite directions, neither too quick nor too slow, Lieutenant Bauer moving to one end of the central aisle that ran the length of the church, and Lieutenant Ritter heading off the other, blocking El Sombra's access to those remaining glass shards. Once the two were sure the insurgent was trapped between them they would open fire, aiming for the head and upper torso—a classic pincer movement. It was von Abendroth's role in the manoeuvre to keep the masked man's attention focussed on him for the vital moments, taking care to draw his fire without spooking him enough to make a run for it. In von Abendroth's eyes, the procedure was much like luring a dangerous animal—a tiger, perhaps—into a trap, ready for the hunter's bullet. The Hauptmann believed that in comparing his foe to a tiger rather than an ape, he was respecting the danger El Sombra represented.

But there are more dangerous animals in the world than tigers, and they walk on their hind legs.

Aldous von Abendroth ostentatiously aimed his gun as though to fire, and watched the prey carefully through the rifle sight. As was expected, the masked terrorist crouched, readying himself to spring at him as the two trusted Lieutenants moved into position. Unseen by the insurgent, they raised their guns, aiming, tracking...

And then El Sombra took a step back.

Von Abendroth blinked. He was surely about to spring, to attempt a frontal attack—why would he step back? Unless he knew about the two guns on either side. Unless he wanted them in the perfect position to—

"Don't fire!" von Abendroth screamed.

Too late.

Two fingers squeezed two triggers at the exact moment that El Sombra threw himself flat and the two remaining men of Eagle Staffel found themselves staring down the barrels of each other's guns. The thunder of machine-gun fire filled the old stone building, echoing across the pews, mingling with the sound of lead piercing vulnerable organs and the screams of dying men. The organist added the final touch in a crashing minor chord.

As the bullet ridden corpses hit the cold stone floor, El Sombra picked himself up and made a little show of dusting himself down. "And then there was one. Any requests from our musical friend before I send you to join them, amigo?"

Aldous von Abendroth could only stare. In less than two minutes, this scarecrow had destroyed nine of the finest soldiers in the Reich—men he had considered his own sons. Eagle Staffel had been annihilated. The boyhood dream of every young man in the Fatherland had been crushed at the hands of this greasy, unshaven, bloodthirsty maniac.

His voice boomed through the empty space like cannon fire as he fought to control his fury. "You! You don't even know what you've done today, do you, schweinehund? Those were the finest young men I've ever known! We wrestled together at sunrise! Well, now Hauptmann Aldous von Abendroth will avenge their deaths! Come closer, you grotesque abomination! Come closer that I might crush you as easily as I would crush nature's miracle, the…"

El Sombra cut him off. "You're flying low, amigo."

Von Abendroth choked on his words and instinctively glanced downwards. "What?"

The ball of the masked man's foot rocketed up into von Abendroth's jaw, sending him tumbling backwards against one of the pews, the constant churning wail of the organ providing a musical counterpoint to his humiliation. He snarled, recovering quickly and moved into a fighting stance.

THE OLDER MAN feinted a punch to the insurgent's belly, then dropped without warning into a sweeping kick aimed at the ankles, sending the masked man tumbling to the floor to smack hard against the tiles. As El Sombra attempted to raise himself, von Abendroth stepped forward to stamp the heel of his leather jackboot down hard against the centre of his back. The fight would go out of the terrorist once von Abendroth had snapped his spine and left him convulsing on the stone floor like a gutted fish.

El Sombra rolled over, putting up his hands to catch the boot as it sped downwards, then twisting hard, sending von Abendroth off his feet to slam into the ground. There was a sickening crack as the Hauptmann's head hit the wood of one of the pews, and his eyes squeezed tight for a single agonised moment—and that moment belonged to El Sombra. He launched himself forward, bringing an elbow down against von Abendroth's throat, his other hand pinning his arm. He repositioned his weight, bringing his centre of gravity down hard on his elbow, attempting to use his own body weight to crush the Nazi's throat.

Aldous von Abendroth growled through gritted teeth, his breath sounding much like the whining of a deflating balloon, and brought a knee up hard, catching the insurgent where it hurt. It was enough to make El Sombra relax his grip for a second, and Von Abendroth took his chance. He gripped the masked man's shoulders, shifting his weight backward as the knee followed through, driving the masked man's body over his head. Then he swung his other leg up, kicking El Sombra hard in the belly, the momentum driving the terrorist onto his back as he desperately tried to take in a breath. Von Abendroth was on him in less than a second, gripping his throat and slamming his head back down against the stone as he wound his thickly-muscled neck back, like a coiled spring. Von Abendroth might have been the Hauptmann of Germany's most prestigious Staffel, but he still knew how to deliver a dirty blow when he had to.

There was a hard cracking sound as von Abendroth threw his head downward, mashing his forehead into the bridge of El Sombra's nose and banging the back of his head into the floor—once, twice, blood spurting and flowing down over the masked man's moustache and into his mouth. One more would see him finally go under, and then Von Abendroth could finish the job by twisting his head all the way around on his shoulders, and finally consign this ragamuffin to the pit of devils he belonged in.

El Sombra would not give him the chance. He twisted savagely, bringing his legs up underneath von Abendroth's belly, then pushing upwards, launching the Hauptmann over his head to sail into the altar.

The top of his head smacked hard against the carved face of a baby cherub, and all he could see for a moment was a pulsing red light, building and dying away with the agony that radiated from his cracked skull. He'd received worse injuries. All he needed was a moment—a split-second. He concentrated his mind, willing away the pain, readying himself to uncoil. Even over the tumult of the organ, he could hear the terrorist's bare feet as they slapped the stone floor behind him. He would wait for the masked man to get closer and then, when he was within reach, von Abendroth would spin, aiming the heel of one palm into the centre of his forehead. The rock smash blow would drive the brain against the skull—and that would be that. All he had to do was wait for El Sombra to come closer... closer still...

Now, thought Aldous von Abendroth.

And then a single bullet tore through the back of his head, spattering his brains and fragments of his skull across the front of the altar and stilling such thoughts for all time. El Sombra tossed the smoking Luger to one side.

"I had a feeling that bullet would come in handy today."

El Sombra looked around the church at the carnage he had created, and felt a sudden wave of tiredness wash over him. What had this been for? He was spent and aching, covered in cuts and contusions, and Carina was still missing. He decided to head back to the shack and see if Jesus had returned yet. He needed to talk things over and work out some sort of plan of action. It was clear he was going to get nowhere if he continued charging into situations like a raging bull. He smiled softly. Jesus would know what to do. He was a good friend, his only real friend in this terrible place.

He shot a glance at the organist, still playing merrily away. The music of choice was now a funeral dirge, sombre in tone but played with a manic, disturbing glee. It sent a shiver through El Sombra's spine, but he could not find it within him to confront the organ player on the matter. The figure at the instrument seemed so wretched, a deranged madman endlessly pounding his keys, one more victim of the bastards and their tortures. Instead, El Sombra simply turned to make his way out through the front door.

The double doors of the church were locked tightly. He should have expected that. Presumably the keys were with the—

The organ screamed.

El Sombra whirled around, unable to believe what he was seeing. He watched, wide-eyed, as the brass pipes began to peel themselves off the wall, clanking and shrieking and blowing steam, clicking together, reconfiguring themselves. It was like watching the skeleton of some grotesque metal animal building itself from the ground up.

Within less than four seconds, the organ had fully transformed from the musical instrument that had provided such sinister accompaniment to the deaths of Eagle Staffel into what looked like a large mechanical spider, scuttling forward, steam hissing in sinister clouds from the brass legs of the beast. In the centre was a cockpit of sorts—the keyboard formed a semicircle around the organist as he played on, discordant notes flowing from the spider-creature as it obeyed his commands. What El Sombra had taken for the hood of a monk's habit was actually an executioner's mask, and behind it, a pair of bloodshot eyes glittered with a mad passion for murder and death. This was Master Minus' own experiment combining human and robot technology. A terrifying apparition torn from a mind devoted to pain and misery. This was das Drehkreuz!

The Spider.

El Sombra scowled. Trained soldiers were one thing, but this was definitely his cue to leave. He somersaulted forward, aiming to flip onto the altar. His next move was to jump, reaching upwards to catch the edge of the shattered window and haul himself through it to the relative safety of the outside world.

It was a move he never got to make.

The Spider moved with impossible speed, scuttling across the floor of the church and up the wall to block the circular stained-glass window with its body. Suction pads cunningly concealed at the end of the brass legs held it in place as the organist hung horizontally, strapped in his chair, merrily playing his frenetic melody of destruction. El Sombra paused, disturbed by the sheer strangeness of the creature that hung there like its arachnid namesake—and that instant's hesitation was enough. The Spider brought up two of its eight brass legs and sent a hissing jet of scalding steam down to engulf the altar. El Sombra hurled himself back, barely escaping being boiled alive by the thing that hung from the window, and fell hard against the stone with a sickening thud. He'd taken too much punishment in recent weeks, and now every such impact seemed to jar right through him, awakening old hurts and pains.

He swallowed hard and drew his sword. Escape was impossible. It was going to be all he could do simply to stay alive in the face of this threat. Der Zinnsoldat had been bad enough, but that, at least, had been predictable. Its computer brain made it easy to out-think. This was being controlled by a human being. A mind sent far beyond the edge of madness by the devilish practices of the Ultimate Reich. There could be no predicting it, and evidently no avoiding it.

The only way to survive would be to kill it.

He began to step backwards, slowly luring the Spider down from its perch. If superheated steam was its main weapon, it would want to stay close enough to kill. And it wouldn't want him to get hold of the key to the main doors.

He took a single step sideways, reaching for Aldous von Abendroth's corpse.

The Spider pounced.

It was on him in less then a second. The hot brass pipes, dripping with condensation, swiped at his feet in an attempt to send him tumbling to the ground, the organist's eyes alive with a demented glee as his fingers ran up and down the keyboard in a frenzy. But El Sombra had been expecting the attack. He leapt into the air, landing on one set of pipe-legs and then hurling himself at another, using them to swing away towards the pulpit and landing, cat-like, atop it. He could feel the blisters forming on his hands and feet, but the machine reacted the way he hoped, the spider-legs clanking into each other as the machine tried to spin round, almost toppling over. The look of glee on the operator's face was replaced by one of berserk hatred, as his fingers cascaded over the keyboard, urging the monster on after its prey.

El Sombra dived down from the top of the pulpit, rolling between the thing's legs as it let off another thick cloud of scalding steam. The Spider was impressive, even fearsome, but for all that, it was only as good as its pilot. It might have seemed like a wise move to Master Minus to put this lunatic in the control seat. After all, he would have needed someone who was unlikely to be troubled by the deaths of Eagle Staffel, should they fail in their mission—but now that the machine had lost the element of surprise, El Sombra knew he could defeat it.

As the massive monster machine swivelled around in an attempt to get at him, the long metal legs banging against each other hopelessly, El Sombra darted to the Spider's left, towards the altar, before pushing off it to the right as though part of some human game of bagatelle. He moved quickly, and for a moment the simple joy of action overtook him and he let out his familiar, joyous laugh, so that it echoed through the church, mingling with the crashing chords and wild stabs made by the organ-creature. Wherever the maddened organist directed the terrible engine of destruction, he encountered only empty space, with El Sombra laughing merrily and challenging him with a swipe of his sword, sometimes a few feet away, sometimes across the room. And then the Spider would turn, and sway, and tilt, and lash out crazily with the brass pipes that were its legs, all the time coming closer and closer to toppling completely.

When it finally did, it seemed a mercy.

El Sombra ran at it and, at the last second, let himself fall into a skid, the moisture that had collected on the smooth, cold stone of the floor aiding him as he flew underneath a pair of clashing, crushing spider-legs. Maddened with hatred, the spider desperately tried to reach beneath its own body to catch at him. The mechanism was already severely off-balance from his last few manoeuvres, and this proved to be the final straw. Brass legs clattering against the stone, the suckers at the ends clinging in a terrified attempt to right itself, the Spider slowly toppled sideways, crashing down like a house of cards.

El Sombra saw his moment, and took it.

He hurled his sword like a javelin. The blade sliced through the air before plunging deep into the heart of the organist. The eyes under the executioner's hood bulged in pain, and as the music sighed away with a final screech of indignation, he turned, fixing the masked man with a look of terrible accusation.

El Sombra smiled grimly. "You signed up for the wrong side, amigo. Don't start crying now."

Those were the last words the hooded organist heard. He slumped forward, the look in his eyes freezing, becoming the terrible stare of a corpse.

El Sombra waited, expecting a trick. He'd been foolish to disregard the organist while he was alive, he wasn't about to make the same mistake just because he was dead. He waited a full minute, muscles taut, ready to spring if there was the slightest danger. But there was none. Eventually, he relaxed, breathing out slowly, letting his heartbeat return to normal. It was time to retrieve his sword and get out before anyone came to check for his body—or bring in backup.

He walked forward and gripped the hilt of the sword, readying himself to tug it free from the chest of the dead man. On an impulse, he took hold of the executioner's hood. No harm in seeing the face of the poor bastard underneath.

He tugged the black cloth upwards—and then fell back, pale as death, a strangled cry stillborn in his throat.

The face under the executioner's hood belonged to Jesus Santiago.

His expression was a grimace of fear and terrible sorrow, as though even in death he was begging his only friend not to take his life. In brutal counterpoint to that look of terror and despair, El Sombra's sword jutted from the centre of his chest, evidence of guilt. He took another step back, his silent, cold accuser staring at him, with eyes that would never see again.

And then the Spider reared forward once more, all the more terrible now for its silence, as the cruel metal legs struck with a ferocity they had lacked before, the brass pipes smashing one after another against his skull, slamming into his sides to crack already bruised ribs, blasting him with scalding hot steam.

He put up a token resistance, but the once mighty El Sombra now stumbled where he once leapt, trembled when he once held fast, and the joyous laugh that had once boomed from his throat had been replaced by a shattered, broken whimper of defeat and despair.

Within seconds of this unequal combat, he slumped to the ground, mentally and physically broken.

And the last thing El Sombra saw, before the darkness claimed him, was the face of the friend he had murdered.

"The church is a wreck. But I've pulled all the workers off cleanup in the Great Square to get to work on it. I'm confident it'll look perfect for the proper wedding tomorrow."

Master Minus raised an eyebrow as he spoke into the telephone. "One night is not a great deal of time to restore a church, Herr Generaloberst..."

"Nonsense. I've had them working on fixtures and fittings a week in advance. You didn't think I was going to leave the place as it was, did you?" The voice on the other end of the line was as stony as ever, but there was a warmth in it now, a sense of self assurance that had been missing since El Sombra's arrival. "I have a new stained glass window ready to install, and an altar to go with it. God is dead, Master Minus, and we have killed him. It's time we redecorated his ugly little house to show that off."

Master Minus shared Eisenberg's relief. His own fortunes were bound to his superior's, and while he could be very useful to the Führer even if the clockwork town proved a failure, it was doubtful Hitler would remember that while in the full flower of his wrath. He allowed himself a soft chuckle at the Generaloberst's little joke. "In that case, we are back on schedule. I'll be taking a little time away from my interrogations tomorrow to catalogue reactions to the wedding. I'll need six or eight of the workers delivered to me for study by late evening."

"Ah yes, the interrogations. One in particular, I imagine." Eisenberg's voice was genial, but there was an edge to it. "If he does not break, kill him. After the wedding tomorrow I want to see him either on a leash or in a coffin."

"My dear Generaloberst, the man is already broken. My wonderful Drehkreuz has done more than a hundred advanced robots ever could have. Even if der Zinnsoldat had been successful, it could only have crushed his body. My creation has shattered his very soul."

There was a pause before the General spoke again. "Take no chances with him. If he should show even a flicker of resistance... bring me his heart." Master Minus heard a soft click as Eisenberg hung up his end of the line.

Master Minus leant back, and smiled, taking in a deep breath of the yellow mist that swirled around his head. The wonderful tang of it filled him, made him eager to begin the day's work. He smiled, running his withered tongue over his yellowed teeth, and rose to greet his newest charge.

El Sombra still wore his mask.

Master Minus approached the prisoner, casting an eye over the selection of tools he had prepared for use. This one would no doubt prove difficult... had the battle not already been won.

The old man grinned as he looked into the opening eyes of his captive.

"Welcome, El Sombra. Welcome to the Palace of Beautiful Thoughts."

CHAPTER EIGHT
PSYCHOLOGICAL WARFARE

"WE ARE IN an age, mein Herr, where creativity is forced to find new means of expression.

"Look at the world. In the theatres of London, we see slum children elevated to the status of theatrical players and writers, men like Stamp and Micklewhite debasing the stage in their bawdy attempts to accurately reproduce the squalor and misery of the boarding house and the kitchen sink. In Russia, the Kinema becomes the stomping-ground of the subhuman, with vampires slathered in greasepaint so they may be captured for the camera sinking their fangs into innocent young girls. Werewolves and the risen dead trained to jump through hoops for the amusement of braying, indolent, popcorn fed simpletons. In the Jew held dystopia of New York, the deviant Warhol enamoured the gallerias with infinite reflections of soup cans. Soup cans! They call National Socialism evil, but by God we don't deify packaging.

"What does that leave? Novels by dilettantes about drug addicts, music broken and crushed into three minute chunks for easier digestion, fashion chasing its own tail through a sea of signifiers and shock value. What is left? What medium is there for the artist to explore? The animals have taken the flag of civilisation and they have wiped their ugly bottoms with it. They have been shown the shining canvas that unites creation with Creator and they have torn it to shreds! How is the true man to seek the path of art? How are we to know the mind of God?

"I will tell you, my friend, that there is only one medium remaining with which to create true and lasting art, and that is torture. Torture is all we have left.

"Don't you agree? Which reminds me, how is my Mexican? Adequate?

"Not talking? Well, I can hardly blame you for that. You were badly beaten. Scalded. Bones were broken. I certainly understand if you don't feel like conversing at present, mein Herr, but never fear. I shall do the talking for both of us.

"All you have to do is breathe."

THE VOICE SCUTTLED and clicked across the stonework, a beetle voice for the beetle man. He was old and withered and bent but still possessed of a terrible potency, unless that was simply the gas. Yellow taint in the air and in his lungs, whispering hideous things in the depths of his mind... how long had the masked man been there, chained to a great iron 'X,' hanging, naked and spread-eagled for inspection?

How long had those glittering tools waited to be used?

Scalpels and spurs, barbed wire, a metal ball that separated with the turn of a screw into ever widening segments, to tear and split the orifices of the captive. Soft, wrinkled fingers stroking over sun baked flesh, measuring places to cut, caressing, cupping and gently squeezing with the practised, shameless ease of a doctor. Or a father at Christmas, smiling and proud, taking his time, waiting to carve.

El Sombra breathed in, and felt something intangible at the core of him begin to pitch and roll and begin to tear apart. Master Minus continued to speak.

"WHERE WERE WE?

"Ah yes. We were discussing torture and its relationship to art. To appreciate the connection, we must first disconnect the concept of torture from the tiresome notions of morality so often attached to its practice.

"In the chapbooks, the films and the junk novels devoured in their hundreds by the general public, torture is only practised by the morally corrupt. If this was a scene from a pulp novelette, doubtless I would be cast in the role of the villain. My intention to torture you would signify to the reader that I was the blackest, most evil creature to inhabit the face of the planet. Their sympathies would be drawn to you. They would be... excuse me a moment, I need to make sure this blade is sharp enough to cut bone... They would be on your side. They would weep for your tragic death.

"But let us now assume that this is a different kind of novelette altogether. This one is based on the gritty events of the real world. It has a title designed to rouse the male ego, perhaps Hostile Zone or Spectre Force. It is about agents of the government dealing with terrorists determined to undermine their very way of life.

"Here we are again, on the page, at the torture scene. But now you are a merciless killer, responsible for the deaths of dozens of government troops who are working to bring order to a troubled region. You are a terrorist whose goal is to destabilise everything the government has built here. I do not know who else is operating in your network. I have no idea of what plans your people may even now be carrying out. Allowing you to keep your secrets could result in the deaths of hundreds, perhaps thousands. You will not see reason. You will not talk. And here I stand.

"I am willing to do whatever it takes to wrest your secrets from you. I am willing to dirty my own hands, to sacrifice my own moral high ground, in order to save the lives of the innocent. Now the reader is with me. He respects my integrity, my courage, my unwillingness to play by rules written by liberals and politicians. And there is a part of him—no small part—that wants to see me prove my masculinity by dominating the cowardly villain in front of me.

"And so, with a simple shift of perspective, you become the villain, and I the hero. And torture, that most morally corrupt of practices, becomes right and proper, a thing of justice, the beloved tool of the righteous and benevolent

"Torture, mein Herr, is neither good nor evil in the final analysis. It simply is.

"Allow me to demonstrate."

THE BLADE WAS a tanto, an antique Japanese dagger. It had not drawn blood since the late fifteenth century, but the razor edge was still keen and quite capable of cutting through flesh as easily as butter. The old man held it reverentially, testing its edge as he spoke, then gently dipping it in a bowl of vinegar, to maximise the pain of the wounds. Stepping forward, he ran one fingernail over the chest of the chained man, selecting a spot just over the heart. The cuts were slow. Deliberate. Methodical.

There were seventeen in all, small, deep cuts into the flesh. It was only on the thirteenth cut that El Sombra even gritted his teeth. By the fifteenth, he allowed a sound to slip—something halfway between a grunt and a snarl.

At the seventeenth cut, he cried out, and his head fell forward.

The old man washed the cut with a sponge dipped in vinegar, admiring the effect. The scars, once healed, would display the Japanese kanji 'kage,' meaning shadow. A nice touch, the old man thought. After all, he didn't intend to leave the chained man his face. How would his new masters recognise him without the proper identification?

He chuckled, the sound of a thousand beetles skittering over a sheet of glass. And then he began to speak again.

"So. We have established that torture is a concept outside the realm of morality, to be classed as right or wrong depending on who wields the reins of power. If it makes you feel better, we can use a different word. Interrogation, perhaps, or questioning.

"Or art.

"After all, an artist is one who shapes a particular medium to suit him, whether it is as a statement or merely for aesthetic pleasure. That medium might be stone, or clay, or porcelain. It might be canvas or celluloid, words on a page or actors on a stage. But the artist shapes the medium and recreates it to his wishes with the tools at hand.

"In this case, the medium is your flesh and soul, which have been given to me to reshape according to my will. The tools I use are laid out before you, scalpels and skewers, vices and clamps, one hundred little gadgets that I have collected over the years, each one serving a specific purpose in sculpting you to meet the needs of my superiors. But these are crude tools at best. What is the pain of cut flesh compared to the agony of knowing that you murdered your only friend? What is the ache of a broken rib compared to the ache in your heart when you remember how you ate and drank with him, how you shared his home and hospitality, and then drove your blade through his heart because you just couldn't be bothered to save him?

"Breathe in, my friend. Breathe it in deep. You'll come very quickly to understand, I think.

"That is the true purpose of this torture—of this art. To open your eyes. You must learn to see things as I do. I am not doing this to you as punishment. I am doing this to bring you your salvation, to rehabilitate you, to make you understand your place in the scheme of things. When I am done with you... when you have breathed in your fill of these wondrous airs of humiliation and despair... you will see that the way of the Ultimate Reich is the way forward for humanity.

"And you will see it of your own accord."

AND THEN THE chained man began to laugh.

Softly at first, then louder, the sound rolling through the quiet, cold room like the skeletons of winter leaves in a chill and bitter wind. It was not a laugh of joy, or of hope, or of strength, or of anything associated with sunlight and clean air. It was a laugh that belonged in these dank and fetid conditions, a snide chuckle, a sneering, contemptuous snicker. A laugh like a thousand beetles marching across a sheet of glass.

It was a sound that would have been sickeningly familiar to anyone who had once been a guest of the Palace of Beautiful Thoughts. The old man started back, looking at the features of his chained captive, breathing in sharply as the handsome face of the terrorist became foreign and strange, warped by the noise emanating from it. He recognised the sound too, recognised the dry, hollow chuckle. And it chilled him.

The chained man turned his head, as though on aged bones, and smiled, a dry and sinister grin. And then he spoke. And the voice that came from his throat did not belong to El Sombra at all.

The chained man spoke with Master Minus' voice.

"VERY GOOD. VERY well done. You're almost there now, my friend.

"Tell me, how did it feel to make the incisions? Was it stimulating to carve helpless flesh as though it were meat in a butcher's shop window? Did the experience make you feel in control? Dominant? Like a true man? Very good, mein Herr. Very, very good.

"You even spout my doctrine as though it were your own. We've really made some marvellous progress in the last few hours. I think we might put you to work as a soldier when we're done..."

* * *

THE OLD MAN stepped back, straightening as he breathed in deep. He could taste the tang in the air, the yellow mist that coiled around his head. He looked towards the mirror, at the aged face, the lines and wrinkles and deep canyon-folds etched into the flesh.

For some reason, he did not recognise his own eyes.

"POOR EL SOMBRA. Poor hero, poor monster. You still haven't learned the true meaning of shame, have you? After all you've done...

"I told you that I wanted to make you understand how things truly are. How can you understand stretched on a rack? How can you see the truth when your eyes are blinded by pain and shame and the depths of your despair? It is not enough to understand helplessness and suffering—you must know the savage joy that comes with inflicting these things upon others.

"In order to truly be brought to our way of thinking, you must know what it is to be the torturer."

THE OLD MAN's hands shook, and he turned towards the chained man for a moment with a look of helpless terror. Then he summoned his authority—the authority of the torturer—and attempted to force words from his throat to overtake the dry, whispering insinuations that emanated from the man on the rack.

The chained man's smile froze him in his tracks. It promised terrible cruelty, a Mephistophilean love of manipulation, and the eyes sparkled with fire from the depths of Hell itself. The old man sucked in another breath scented with sickly yellow and looked desperately away, to find himself staring once again at the mirror, at the face that was surely not his own...

"THAT'S RIGHT, MEIN Herr. You are the torturer. The self-made hero, El Sombra, finds himself reborn into the body of the villain, Master Minus—or is it the other way around? Is the despised terrorist now finding a new lease of life as a noble hero of the Ultimate Reich?

"How many have you tortured today, Master Minus? I saw the glee in your eyes while you delved and hacked and sawed. I heard the whispered words you spoke, almost lovingly, into the ear of that father of three, the one you warmed up with. You've done well in your new role. It's hard to believe the heroic El Sombra ever existed... although now I think of it, he was always fond of tearing his enemies apart with that sharp sword of his, wasn't he? I suppose Master Minus was always there, just waiting to get out. In many ways, this must be a dream come true for you..."

"It isn't true."

The old man was shocked to hear the voice come from his mouth. Was that the soft-spoken rasp of Master Minus? Had those words been spoken by the man who had studied the works of Freud and Jung in the forbidden libraries of the Reichstag, who had had long discussions with Adolf Hitler—not the frail flesh portrayed in the destroyed statue, but the towering majesty of the true Führer—on the nature of the self? Or was this a cracked and pale imitation?

He swallowed and spoke again, hoping against all hope that this time the voice would sound more like Master Minus, less youthful, less... less Mexican. But deep down, as he tasted the yellow poison on his tongue and felt it unlocking the dizzying, vertiginous trapdoors of his soul, he knew that the voice of Master Minus was the voice that came from the man who hung in chains with blood trickling slowly over his belly and a familiar smile lighting up his face.

He closed his eyes, listening to his own words echoing hollowly.

"It isn't true..."

"Oh, yes it is.

"Look in the mirror, Master Minus. Look at the rubber face hanging loosely over your own. Feel the way your back aches and strains from being stooped over in an imitation of age. Here is the truth, El Sombra. You've been Master Minus for hours. Perhaps this was who you always were.

"If the conditions are right, then a cheap theatrical mask is all that stands between the noble hero and the torturer. Take off the mask, El Sombra. Let yourself see how far you have fallen."

* * *

THE OLD MAN, who suddenly felt neither old nor a man, raised his hands, fingertips touching the aged, wrinkled face with the unfamiliar eyes. Could he fool himself that his fingertips travelled across soft, worn flesh, lined with years of service? Or was he feeling sterile plastic, soft, loose latex? He shuddered, the motion travelling up his spine, his hands shivering and twitching as he tugged...

"TAKE OFF THE mask."

...AND THE OLD, wrinkled, false face was torn away, coming off in long strips, pulled away bit by bit to reveal another face underneath. His eyes were wide, unblinking, unable to close as he stared at the face underneath, the face that had been there all the time.

Behind him, the thin beetle-voice spoke once more.

AND THIS IS what it said:

"APRIL FOOL! ¿Quién es el hombre? ¿Quién es el hombre? I'm the hombre! I'm the hombre! Now all I need are some pants."

El Sombra grinned down from the vertical rack at Master Minus, slumped on his knees in front of the blood spattered mirror, staring without eyelids at the remains of his face. He had succeeded in tearing all of the flesh from it, and all that remained were a few scraps of muscle clinging to a crimson, bloodstained skull, with two grotesque eyeballs gazing mercilessly at their own reflection. El Sombra smiled and did the voice again, while he made another attempt to work his left hand free of the shackle that held it in place.

"Creatures of the night... what music... they make... I vant to suck your blooood... yeah, you keep looking, amigo. Intense shame boosted by mind-warping drugs, hey? That's very original, I wouldn't know what that's like at all... ah, these bastard cuffs!" He was babbling, a result of the endorphin rush from the intense pain and the thrill of victory. The yellow mist coursing through his veins—the mist Master Minus relied on so heavily—had been counterbalanced by the Trichocereus validus already in his system, the desert cactus that had destroyed and rebuilt his mind. But while El Sombra was in a stronger position than the torturer realised, Master Minus was weaker than he knew, far too used to the easy victories the mist brought him, not realising that his own exposure to it made him ripe for psychological attack. The old man had spent years claiming that he was immune to the yellow mist, but nobody had ever been in a position to test that claim—until now.

That didn't mean El Sombra was immune to the mist either. The strange fog was slowly starting to make his head swim, bringing up memories of his brother's curse and Jesus Santiago's final accusing stare. He hadn't torn his own face off just yet, but he could feel his mind slowly breaking under the pressure. It was time to check out.

He grunted, teeth gritting again, as his hand tore free of the manacle, raw and bloody. It felt like the edge of the metal cuff had taken off most of the skin, and he was lucky his thumb hadn't been dislocated. He flexed it a few times before reaching for the cotter pin he kept fixed at the back of his mask and starting work on the other shackle, trying not to breathe in more than he had to. The sooner he was out in the fresh air, the better he'd like it.

"So... WHERE ARE you keeping her?"

General Eisenberg admired his dress uniform in the mirror, adjusting his cufflinks carefully. "In the basement. We still have some holding cells there from the days before we built the Palace. I wouldn't go down there, though. It's bad luck to see the bride the night before the wedding."

"It's a quarter to eleven, Father. The wedding's at noon. I'm sure it wouldn't do any harm to look in on her. Just to share a final sweet moment together before we meet at the altar..." Alexis busied himself brushing his shoes, which had arrived in the post that morning from Milan, where they were currently proving the height of fashion. This was one of the few pairs of shoes Alexis had ordered in recent weeks that had actually arrived in any fit state to be worn. He had lost eight pairs of suede loafers—hand-crafted in Tuscany—when the Traction Engine had toppled over the cliff, and attempts to have other pairs brought across the desert on the trolleys had been stymied by El Sombra's one-man raiding parties. Once, he'd been fortunate enough to receive a pair of brogues from Saville Row that had allegedly managed to find their way through. He'd opened the box to find an 'E' carved onto one toe and an 'S' onto the other.

Alexis shook his head. "I'm sorry, Father, what were you saying?"

"I was running through the schedule for today, Alexis, if you could take your mind off your footwear for a moment. Carina and her father have both been dressed and are being gathered for the ceremony. They'll be waiting by the main doors by 11:30 hours. By 11:40, I need you to—where are you going?"

Alexis looked back at his father as he sauntered to the door, flashing his angelic smile. "Well, I've got almost an hour. I thought I'd borrow a wing-pack and head over to the Palace. Maybe check in on my best man... show him my new sword." He grinned and hefted the recently-acquired blade, twirling it a little before placing it in a sheath at his waist.

The Generaloberst closed his eyes and pinched the bridge of his nose, trying to control his anger. "You don't need another reason to talk to Master Minus, Alexis. You pay more attention to that withered corpse of a man than you do to your father. I told him—and I told you—there is no way in hell that El Sombra is going to be your best man. I don't care what sort of message it sends, we're not dropping a random element like that into a controlled experiment! We either have him publicly executed or we have him put to work on the latrines—" He looked up from his tirade and lapsed into angry silence.

Alexis had gone.

EL SOMBRA HADN'T had any luck finding anything to wear, but he had found a Japanese katana to match the tanto. The twin swords had been a gift from the Japanese emperor after the recognition of Manchukuo in 1938, and had been subsequently passed on to Master Minus in recognition of his service. They were a good pair of swords—finely balanced and very sharp. As El Sombra had had no practice fighting with a dagger, he took the longer one and left the tanto behind. He wasn't too fond of that blade anyway. The blood was still dripping down over his belly.

His left wrist was still throbbing and stinging, and the yellow mist was hardly helping his composure. The maze of tunnels and cells that composed the Palace of Beautiful Thoughts was ghoulish and confusing enough in the ordinary course of events, but with Master Minus' drugs coursing through his veins and lungs, the cold and sterile concrete felt like the inside of some hideous mausoleum. The walls loomed in oppressively and the echo of each footstep convinced him that there were enemies on all sides, waiting like tigers to spring at him. In fact, nothing could be further from the truth. There were no guards stationed inside the Palace of Beautiful Thoughts. Soldiers were required to enter only to escort prisoners to their cells. Once in their cells, any prisoners were swiftly made tractable and easily directed by the mists, and Master Minus could generally move them from place to place himself without any trouble.

Those few prisoners left in their cells did not reassure El Sombra in the slightest. When he worked open their cell doors and attempted to give them their freedom, most simply continued lying on the floor as they had been. One or two burst into tears. One man of around thirty walked towards the grey concrete wall of his cell and began to rhythmically bang his head against it, until El Sombra knocked him unconscious to keep him from fracturing his skull.

Carina, thankfully, was not among the prisoners. To see her in that state would have most likely driven El Sombra over the edge.

Eventually, the masked man opened an airtight metal door to find himself in a small room with leather jumpsuits in a variety of sizes hanging on one wall, and another larger airtight door on the other. As he closed the smaller door behind him, extractor fans in the ceiling pumped slowly into life, drawing the yellow mist from the room and replacing it with clean, fresh air. El Sombra felt his head begin to clear immediately, and allowed himself to stand for a moment, taking in deep lungfuls, relaxing as the artificial wind slowed around him.

The outer door began to open.

HANS BADER HAD been guarding the outer door to the Palace of Beautiful Thoughts for a little over three years. In many ways, he was the perfect candidate for such a duty, for Hans Bader had lived in a state of almost constant fear and anxiety for most of his adult life.

His first memory was of seeing his father's pipe in a pipe-holder in the study, and reaching up with tiny little fingers to take hold of the fascinating object. His father had not had the chance to clean his briar-bowl that day, and the ash had, quite naturally, gone everywhere, most of it scattering on an antique rug that his father had brought back from Turkey. Hans Bader vividly remembered how his mother had grabbed his shoulders and shaken him roughly. "You're a stupid, stupid, stupid little boy!" she had screamed, as he bawled in uncomprehending terror. His father stood by, shaking his head, and at the end of his mother's outburst he had simply muttered that he was very disappointed. Then he left Hans Bader to sit in his room and think about what he'd done.

It was a pattern that repeated itself throughout his childhood. There would be some minor infraction—a bottle of milk accidentally tipped over perhaps, or an egg dropped on the floor, or simply a word out of place—and his mother would grab at his shoulders, shake him roughly, and bellow that he was stupid and useless and had no common sense whatsoever. His father would simply repeat, in his low, slow, sad voice, that he was extremely disappointed. And Hans would be sent, shaking at the ferocity of the verbal assault, to his room, to think deeply about what a useless and pathetic creature he truly was.

He began to jump at shadows, staying in his room constantly to avoid the verbal attacks, spending his time there trembling and twitching with an unnamed dread. His father, having already proved himself an expert on the rearing of children, took his listlessness and depression for indolence and resolved, after caning the boy several times, that the best thing for him would be the army.

And thus, Hans Bader was enlisted with the Ultimate Reich.

Naturally, by this time his confidence had been not so much damaged as razed to the ground. He was utterly incapable of using his own initiative by this point, and as a result, stood frozen and trembling while his fellow soldiers rushed about their tasks, petrified lest he make some tiny, insignificant error. He was deathly afraid of his drill instructor upon first meeting, and memorably wet himself on being asked his name, which sealed his fate with regards to his fellow soldiers. 'Wetpants Bader' had a career that mostly consisted of being shuttled from one place to another, screamed at for being almost completely incompetent, and then dismissed, to be moved on to the next hellhole that awaited him.

Eventually, his travels took him to Aldea. By this stage, he was heartsick, barely able to eat and had developed a severe nervous twitch in his right eye. When other soldiers stood stiffly to attention, he hunched his shoulders, quivering like an autumn leaf.

It was in such a state of nervous exhaustion that he was first taken to meet Master Minus.

Master Minus had never had more enjoyable company.

Soon, Hans Bader was given a new task, one he was told that he could not possibly fail at. He would stand outside the door to the Palace of Beautiful Thoughts and prevent anyone without the proper clearance from entering—a simple matter of remembering the faces of three people. And whenever he heard the telltale whine of the fans, that was his cue to open up the door and allow Master Minus to leave, lest the old man strain himself turning the heavy iron handle.

Almost shockingly, he found himself happy in this work. It was so very simple, and Master Minus was the only person he had ever met who truly liked him for who he was. Slowly, he began to feel more self-assured. Which, for Hans Bader, meant fewer episodes of bed wetting and more nights spent sleeping rather than staring at the ceiling and shivering in cold, stark, fear.

For a little over three years, Hans Bader had guarded the door, protecting the Palace of Beautiful Thoughts against any threats that might come from outside. He was finally somewhere close to being happy, and had even grown almost proud of his three years of service. He felt that he could finally call himself competent.

Unfortunately, he couldn't. In guarding the door against outside intruders, he had made another grievous error—his last.

He had never considered that a threat might appear from within.

His end was mercifully swift. The keen edge of the katana cut through Hans' side, slicing through organ, muscle and bone until it exited through his shoulder; along the way, it split his heart into two unequal segments, ending his life in an instant.

The body slid into two chunks as El Sombra stepped back, nimbly avoiding the gore.

As he stood, breathing heavily and trying to get the remains of the drug out of his system, a small burst of applause erupted from the sky above his head. He looked up.

There, smiling angelically in a wing-harness, steam-wings creaking softly as he slowly glided towards the ground, was Alexis Eisenberg. El Sombra looked at him, and then looked at his right hand. Suddenly he could no longer hear for the sound of blood pounding relentlessly in his ears.

Clutched in Alexis' hand was the sword that had belonged to El Sombra's brother, Heraclio.

THE GENERALOBERST WALKED around the Old Church slowly, casting a critical eye over the new decor. Finally he paused, and turned to Oberleutnant Odell Strauss, who had masterminded the workforce in transforming the place in a single night.

"Most satisfactory, Oberleutnant. The pews could perhaps have used a little more work, but the new altar is perfectly serviceable. And I particularly like the new stained-glass window. It's simple yet bold."

The window that had been shattered by El Sombra on his entrance had been replaced by a gigantic swastika, in black on red. It cast the whole church in a baleful, bloody glow, making it look like a place more suited to satanic rituals than a wedding. The altar had also been remodelled, the angels originally pictured on its sides replaced by soaring eagles flying though fields of sculpted fire, and the wooden pews were now decorated with more swastikas, tastefully carved into the wood at regular intervals. The only part of the Old Church untainted by the Nazi emblem was the creaking old pipe organ. It had been dismantled to create a space for das Drehkreuz to lurk in, but now it was back in its old familiar place, as though it had never left. Ironically, under the infernal light it looked like nothing so much as an ancient torture device.

Oberleutnant Strauss nodded. "Thank you, Herr Generaloberst. Under the circumstances, I feel it would be wise to discipline the workers who recarved the pews, since their craft has proved somewhat lacking."

Eisenberg nodded. "Shoot them. Master Minus is far too busy to be interrupted with trifles. My son is no doubt delaying him with foolish requests as we speak." He looked down at his watch—twenty minutes to noon. He sighed, and walked to the open double doors, looking out at the street. Over a distant rooftop, he could see a single stone hand where once there had been the reassuring figure of his Führer, standing in proud dominion over the town.

He sighed and shook his head.

"Where is that boy?"

ALEXIS SMILED AS he touched down in front of the masked man. He wore a tuxedo which had cost slightly over two thousand marks, a pair of shoes hand-stitched by Salvatore Ferragamo himself, and a necktie made by McLaren and Westwood of the King's Road, a black silk affair with a single blood-red swastika imprinted on it where a tiepin would normally stand. Even the creaking pack on his back fitted perfectly, the straps holding fast without ruining the line of the suit. He looked—and felt—truly angelic. The perfect couture in which to slaughter his greatest enemy.

The trick would be to avoid getting blood on the tuxedo. Although perhaps a little would offset the fabric nicely.

He examined his enemy. El Sombra trembled slightly as he stood, like a leaf in a light breeze. His eyes were red and bloodshot, his knuckles white as they gripped the handle of the katana. He looked feverish, occasionally shaking his head slightly as if to clear it. Several fresh wounds were bleeding down over his right nipple, arranged in a pattern the significance of which escaped Alexis entirely. And he was completely naked except for the mask.

Alexis ran his finger slowly over the scar that marked his beautiful face, then grinned like a wolf.

The mask would have to go.

He lunged forward, aiming the point of Heraclio's sword at El Sombra's shoulder. The masked man, still disoriented from the yellow mist, and reeling from the sight of his brother's most prized possession in the hand of the man who had murdered him, failed to block the blow quickly enough, and the point of the sword grazed his shoulder, drawing fresh blood.

El Sombra grimaced in pain. Paradoxically, his first thought was not to the two inch gash in his shoulder, but rather to his brother's sword. Bad enough that it was in the hands of Alexis, but the katana was by far the stronger blade. El Sombra knew from the heft and the sharpness that it was capable of snapping Heraclio's sword in two, like an axe chopping a sapling. Perhaps he should have done just that—ended the threat before using a second slash to divest Alexis of both his wolfen smile and the head that went with it. But this was his brother's sword. It was more than just a weapon. It was all that remained of Heraclio. It had been handed to him with his brother's dying breath. It was not a possession, but rather a sacred relic.

It would be wrong to say that for El Sombra, losing the sword was like losing a limb. It would be like losing the very heart beating in his breast.

Alexis knew this, of course.

He had not spent years visiting and conversing with Master Minus simply for the company. He had always been adept in spotting the physical weaknesses of his foes, but with the insights the old torturer had provided him, he knew where to search for psychological weakness as well. His father, for example, had a deeply buried fear of the Führer—something Alexis suspected was common in those who had actually come face to face with Adolf Hitler in his later years. A simple phone call had been enough to arouse the Führer's interest in Projekt Uhrwerk and inform him about the new element attacking it, and suddenly the great General Eisenberg was concentrating less on controlling his son than on saving his own neck, which had allowed the younger Eisenberg the freedom to play his own games. As a result of which, Alexis had discovered El Sombra's own hidden weakness. He grinned, darting forward again, forcing the renegade to parry his brother's blade as it aimed for his heart and then for lower organs. Then he spoke.

"What's the matter, Djego?"

El Sombra stumbled back as though he had been struck. Alexis stepped forward to fill the gap, keeping Heraclio's sword moving, forcing the masked man to continue parrying to avoid being skewered. "Oh, I see…" He chuckled, his right arm a blur of motion. "This is the way your brother was killed, wasn't it, Djego? While you watched? As I remember, you were crying at the time, like a little child, so it's always possible you didn't see very much. But you saw plenty of him afterwards, didn't you, Djego?"

It was like being punched in the stomach. The name. Again and again. The shame of it. The man he had been, and as the yellow mist sparked and hissed inside his brain, the man he was again. Dirty and ashamed and alone in his brother's blood.

He swung the katana, but it was with Djego's strength, and Alexis easily blocked the clumsy strike. El Sombra—if it was El Sombra and not Djego, that foppish, foolish young man who had let his brother die—blinked, trying to marshal his thoughts. He was being taken apart like an amateur. He was an amateur. He was weak and hopeless and useless…

"You've failed him again, Djego. Poor Heraclio. It's a good thing I killed him. Imagine how he'd feel to see this." Alexis was, frankly, having the time of his life. This was utterly perfect. It was everything he'd wanted since the first time he'd been humiliated by the man in the mask. It was perfect. The perfect wedding present.

"And that reminds me; in a few minutes I'll be marrying the lovely Carina, who I believe you've met. This sword is going to be my wedding gift to her. Don't get me wrong, it's of no particular sentimental value, in fact"—he lunged, slashing at El Sombra's belly while the other man clumsily attempted to parry—"in fact, when I sliced its original owner apart like so much wurst, I felt… well, I felt less than nothing, really." Another lunge. This time the blade gashed the masked man's cheek, and Alexis grinned with petty vengeance. "I mean, for me, this is just a souvenir of a particularly dull invasion. I fought a halfwit and subjugated a city of mindless sheep. Hardly one for the history books."

El Sombra snarled, and there was blood in his eyes. Alexis smiled. Almost there…

"Still, I'm sure my lovely wife will appreciate it. By the time it severs her neck, I'd imagine it'll come as something of a relie—"

El Sombra charged.

He was angrier than he'd been in a long time. There was rage in him, hot and righteous and blazing, and he was ready to carve his brother's killer into bloody chunks with the heavy blade of the katana and then go on and cut every member of the Reich to pieces, to keep cutting and chopping and hacking until every last one of the bastards was dead at his feet. He wanted to soak the streets of his childhood in their blood, to cleanse the rotten sewer that his town had become.

Alexis flicked Heraclio's sword forward with machine precision, the point slashing through the skin and muscle of El Sombra's forearm. The masked man's fingers flared involuntarily and the katana clattered to the ground at his feet. Alexis kicked the sword away with the point of his immaculate shoe.

He smiled, eyes narrowing, savouring the moment. "Look at you! You've met the woman once and suddenly you fly into a rage over an idle threat. This is exactly like you, Djego. Didn't you try to ruin your brother's marriage the same way?"

He levelled the point of the sword at his enemy's throat.

"Take off the mask, Djego. It's time to grow up a little."

Djego looked up at him, swallowing hard, clutching his injured arm. Suddenly he felt very small and weak and foolish. Alexis' smile widened.

"El Sombra is dead."

MASTER PLUS WAS dead. He knew this to be a certainty as he stood in his place by the altar, dressed in a spotless new white suit, tugging at the tight collar and feeling, not for the first time, as though he would suffocate. He shuddered inside as the first few bars of the Wedding March played on the creaking organ and he saw his daughter, dressed in a beautiful white gown and veil, led down the aisle by Oberleutnant Strauss. He had been judged too much of a risk to play that particular role in this farce, and he found himself glad.

A disinterested observer might have thought that Carina was looking around at the new decor of the Old Church. Actually, she was checking possible escape routes and examining the congregation. A crowd of sixty men were stood to attention in the pews, all of them wearing gleaming wing-packs and armed with some form of automatic weapon. She wasn't sure which possibility was more frightening—that this was a trap, or that such an armament was part of their uniform. Actually, the latter was the case. This was the officer class of Aldea. The highest echelon. For the most part, they were pen-pushers and desk-warmers, long absent from any form of real combat. The wings on their backs were dress models, plated with gold and silver to catch the eye, rather than the more powerful combat models. And the machine guns were purely for the occasion. A show of strength that seemed almost comical coming from this crowd of armchair warriors.

Failing to find any immediate way out of the situation, she turned her eyes to her father, and felt a pang of sympathy for him. It confused her.

Master Plus saw the look of compassion in his daughter's eyes and looked away. Anger or bitterness he could have dealt with, but the look of pity on her face was far too much to bear.

Oberleutnant Strauss led her to the altar and then stood stiffly as the Wedding March played on. And on. It was five minutes to noon, and the groom was still nowhere to be seen. The congregation continued to stand stiffly to attention, looking straight ahead. General Eisenberg, in full dress uniform and his own pair of dress wings, stood at the pulpit, looking out on the scene as it descended further and further into a parody of itself. He hissed through his teeth like a teakettle and muttered the same words over and over again.

"Where is that boy? Where is that boy?"

DJEGO REACHED BEHIND his head and untied the knot that had bound the red wedding sash to his face for nine long years. It took several tries to pick apart the blood encrusted knot, and when he lifted the mask from his face he was left with a strip of paler brown across his eyes, where the sun had not baked his flesh. Alexis could not help snorting with laughter at the sight.

"You look like a raccoon. Was it worth it, Djego? All you've really done is make things worse for the people you allegedly care about. We might have shipped them back to the Fatherland for cheap labour if you hadn't stepped in, but now—well, we'll be killing them and bulldozing their bodies into pits. Entirely because of you." He smiled genially. Djego had already sunk down onto his knees, and was looking at the ground like a contrite schoolboy, the long wedding sash cradled in his hands. It was too perfect. Alexis slowly drew back Heraclio's sword. He was satisfied. It was time for the coup de grace.

"Goodbye, Djego. I'll put your brother's sword to better use." He smiled, slashing Heraclio's sword forward, aiming to bury it in Djego's worthless throat.

The blade passed through empty space.

Djego was already moving, springing up and spinning out of the way of the blade—performing a backward flip and sailing over the head of his enemy. He came down like a cat behind Alexis, wrapping the wedding sash around his throat and pulling tight. Heraclio's sword clattered into the dirt as Alexis desperately reached up, scrabbling helplessly at the tightening material. Djego leaned in and whispered into the other man's ear as he tugged the sash tighter still, and there was something in his voice as cold and unyielding as a gravestone.

"Amigo… that's my sword."

Alexis could only gurgle and gasp, mouth flapping like a fish, eyes bulging and rolling into the back of his head as the man behind him pulled with a devil's strength, the red cloth burying into the flesh of his neck, cutting off both his air and the blood flow to the brain.

His hands continued to scrabble at the cloth cutting into his throat for a few more seconds before they fell limply down to hang at his sides. The strength left his legs and he slumped, held up only by the sash that was strangling him. His feet began to twitch and writhe and in a final indignity, his bowels and bladder let go, drenching the inside of his expensive, immaculate suit with filth.

It was ten minutes before Djego let go of the wedding-sash and let the body crash to the ground.

THE ORGANIST DUTIFULLY went into the Wedding March for another time. It was almost twenty minutes past noon. The congregation were still standing to attention, albeit with visible effort. Master Plus was still looking at the ground. Carina, in her wedding gown, continued to look carefully around at the windows and the double doors. And General Eisenberg paced back and forth in front of the altar, lips pulled back from gritted teeth, staring furiously at nothing at all.

"Where… is… Alexis?" He barked the words like a snarling dog.

His son would pay for this humiliation. The El Sombra business may have called unwelcome attention to Aldea at a crucial moment, but it was Alexis who was the loose cannon now. All eyes were on the project, and while this wedding was, at best, a minor experiment, it had become symbolic of a return to business as usual, a sign that the Generaloberst's grip on matters was still as firm as it had ever been. Alexis would not sully that. He would not be allowed to drag his father down though his own flippant attitudes. Alexis would be brought down to the level of Obergefreiter. He would be forced to clean the latrines in the town for seven months. He would be disowned.

There was a knock at the door. Or rather, the hilt of a sword pounding against the wood, three times.

The Wedding March stopped. General Eisenberg cursed, and stepped quickly back to his place behind the podium, thankful that his wretched son had at least thought to give the assembly some warning before he sauntered in from whatever jaunt he'd been on for the past hour. Perhaps it would not be necessary to reduce his rank to Private after all. First Lieutenant would be quite sufficient.

"Come in and take your place, Alexis. We need to get this wedding back on schedule."

There was silence. Eisenberg smashed his fist down hard against the pulpit and screamed.

"Alexis! Get in here now!"

Slowly, the wooden double doors creaked open, to reveal a dead man. Wilhelm Brandt had been happy to be picked to stand guard on the Old Church and ensure none of the curious workers stepped near it until the wedding was finished with. He had felt it an honour, after years of being passed over for such duties, to finally be picked to add his strength to an important venture for the Ultimate Reich. He saw guarding the Church almost as a sacred trust.

So the last emotion that passed though him after the hilt of the sword seemed to come out of nowhere to smash hard into the back of his head was a feeling of crippling shame. The knowledge that his unconscious body was to be stripped before his throat was slit, in order that his killer might get a clean pair of trousers, would have been unlikely to alleviate that.

El Sombra stepped into the Church, his mask firmly in place, Alexis' wing-pack strapped tightly to his back. In his right hand, he held his brother's sword. In his left, he held a human heart, freshly hacked from its owner's chest. He smiled.

"Your son couldn't make it, Herr Generaloberst. But he asked me to convey his apologies and to assure his bride that his heart, at least, will always be with her."

He tossed the bloody organ into the Church and it skidded along the stone floor, tumbling over and over to rest a couple of inches from Carina's white dress.

"How thoughtful of him," she said softly.

After that, there was silence for a while.

And then the congregation turned, levelled their automatic weapons, and opened fire.

CHAPTER NINE
GÖTTERDÄMMERUNG

THE NOISE HIT like a bomb.

Sixty heavy-calibre machine-guns opening up as one, spraying a torrent of lead at the entrance of the Church. Stray bullets impacted against the heavy oaken doors, splintering them, tearing them off their hinges so that they collapsed to either side of the yawning entrance. There was the tinkling sound—like a thousand tiny bells—of cartridges bouncing off the stone tiles. The overall noise was deafening—a hundred storms rolled into one, a barrage of thunder and final judgement, a hymn of murder and destruction that echoed around the stone arches above.

The barrage lasted a total of eight seconds, and in that time two thousand three hundred and eighty-seven bullets were blasted towards the figure standing in the doorway.

None of them connected.

El Sombra was no longer there.

Carina took her hands from her ears and looked through the crowd of soldiers and the thick, pungent fog of cordite. She took a sharp breath at the sight of a riddled, punctured corpse laying in the dirt—and then remembered Wilhelm Brandt, the hapless guard who'd died a few moments before the tide of bullets had torn his body into shreds. Of El Sombra, there was no sign. Slowly, the soldiers crept forward, inching towards the doors, ready for the masked man to appear from whatever point of ambush he had chosen.

In the expectant silence, she heard a slight creaking sound, far above her head.

The soldiers heard it too. One by one, they cast their eyes upwards, towards the ceiling.

Silence.

And then the stained glass window exploded once again, the swastika shattering into a thousand shards as El Sombra flew through it on the wings he'd taken from Alexis' corpse. He'd stolen more than a pair of trousers from the luckless Wilhelm Brandt. He'd also stolen the guard's M30 machine-gun, secreting it on top of the church roof in case the numbers inside were too much to handle. Now he made use of it, squeezing the trigger to let off long bursts of fire, sending streams of ammunition into the crowd below him. While the masked man had had problems with guns in the past, the congregation in the church was so densely packed together that he couldn't help but hit one of them no matter where he fired.

Oberleutnant Strauss reacted instantly to the carnage unfolding in front of him. He was confident that his position next to Carina would shield him from the attack, and so, ignoring the tiny slivers of glass that cascaded over his head, he pulled his Luger from its holster and aimed carefully. Odell Strauss might have been a dab hand at interior design, but as a marksman he was even better. He was confident that, from this position, he could hit the masked man's femoral artery, causing him to bleed out over the assembled company within the space of a few brief seconds. He smiled softly. It would certainly be a wedding to remember.

That was the moment when the jailer, Rafael Contreras—who had spent the last nine years as Master Plus, manservant and dogsbody to a regime that considered him less than human—finally found his courage. Seeing the Oberleutnant levelling his pistol, he took two quick steps forward and drove his elbow hard into the man's teeth, a move he had first learned to use against the drunks and hopheads in his father's jail when he was sixteen. Now the jail that his father had built was the Palace of Beautiful Thoughts, and somehow he had been so concerned with keeping his daughter 'safe'—fattening her for the slaughter—that he had never made anyone pay for that. And so it was a blow with the pent-up rage and humiliation of nine years behind it, and it sent Strauss flying backwards, broken teeth tumbling from between split, bloody lips, the pistol skittering across towards the empty pulpit. Rafael felt the impact run up his elbow, his ulna nerve stinging and pricking with pain. It felt liberating.

Carina looked at her father in shock, and then reached out to take his hand, shouting to be heard over the gunfire:

"Papa! We'd better get behind the altar. I don't want you killed."

Rafael smiled, tears pricking at the corners of his eyes, running the words through his mind again and again. *I don't want you killed.*

Those might have been the sweetest words he had ever heard his daughter say.

Having spent the bulk of their ammunition firing wildly through the double doors at the unfortunate corpse of Wilhelm Brandt, the amassed officer class of the Ultimate Reich found themselves unable to effectively return fire as El Sombra emptied almost the entirety of his ammunition into them. As was often the case with the military, the men further up the chain of command had little understanding of the realities on the ground and, as was also common, they had wasted their resources without thought for the long term. As was somewhat less common, they paid the price for their mistake—despite their heavy wing-packs, the bullets from the M30 were more than powerful enough to punch through one human body and into another and thus El Sombra was able to reduce the congregation by half before they even began to fire back.

Once the assembled Oberstleutnants and Majors began to return fire, the masked man dropped down into the very midst of the crowd, hovering in place to lash out with both his feet, spinning and kicking in a quick circle and using the butt of his gun as a club to smash the skulls of those closest. The congregation were unable to return fire for fear of hitting one of their own—the punishments for gunning down a fellow officer were severe—and so El Sombra found it easy to reduce the congregation to a mere handful of men, standing dazed and bathed in the blood of their colleagues.

Noting that there was now more than enough room in the crowd to fire on the masked man without risking hitting each other, the remaining officers raised their guns—but it was already too late. With a cheery wink and a wave, El Sombra flew out of the double doors and into the cloudless sky above, leaving the officers left standing after his bloody assault no choice but to follow him out and into the heavens.

The entire bloody battle had taken, in total, perhaps ten seconds. Sheltering behind the stone altar, Carina and her father were left to gaze out onto the bloody remains of dozens of men littering the floor. The cream of the Ultimate Reich, leaders of men hand-chosen to make the mission in Mexico a success, now stacked atop one another like cordwood. The lucky ones were still alive, bleeding out from ragged holes ploughed through their flesh and organs, and their groans and pleas for aid echoed through the empty space, along with the remnants of the gunfire. She exhaled hard, the adrenaline still raging through her system. "We should... we should get away from here."

Rafael nodded. He was sickened at the sight of the carnage, and at his own part in it. "You're right. I think this might be how it ends."

And then General Eisenberg stepped out from his hiding place behind the wooden pulpit, Oberleutnant Strauss' pistol in his hand, and shot Rafael squarely in the back.

He looked down at the writhing man, and hissed curtly between his teeth. "Master Plus, you are dismissed from your duties." Then he shot him again. Carina lunged forward, smashing a fist hard into the bridge of the Generaloberst's nose, breaking it a third time, a cry of hatred torn from her throat.

The Iron Mountain was unmoved by the gesture. He barely noted the blood that trickled over his lip as he gripped her wrist, pointing his gun at her belly. "I was stabbed in the chest with a hunting knife on the Russian Front, Carina, and I didn't even notice the wound until a minute after I finished killing my opponent with my bare hands. A punch in the face is hardly going to slow me down. Think yourself lucky I still have need of you." His teeth were still clenched, and his eyes glittered like chips of cold, grey ice. He had walked into this church secure in the knowledge of an almost spotless victory over the last enemy of the Reich in this misbegotten country, and in just a few minutes, he had lost everything he possessed. His only son had been murdered, and now the same man had, in the space of ten seconds, torn apart the vision he had spent nine years building. And somewhere inside him, like a goad spurring him to greater violence, was the nagging thought that it was his own overconfidence that was to blame.

Safe in the knowledge that he had quashed all resistance, General Eisenberg had allowed his top men to form the congregation at his son's wedding. These were the military minds he had hand-picked to aid him in his work, the cornerstones of the clockwork dream, the most integral parts of Projekt Uhrwerk. He would never have allowed all of them in the same room if there had been even a shred of doubt that resistance in Aldea was finished for all time.

And that was the final thing he had lost. He had come to the town of Pasito as the warlord of a thousand campaigns, one of Hitler's most trusted lieutenants. He had come to the Project as a success—and one man had stripped that from him. He had lost the most valuable resources of the Ultimate Reich—the

Traction Engine, der Zinnsoldat, das Drehkreuz, mostly likely Master Minus, not to mention countless weapons, supplies and men—and he had lost them all to that one man. He had lost the respect of his Führer to that one man, and with it his life, for there was no way he could escape punishment for such a titanic failure. And finally—cripplingly—he had lost respect for himself. The tactical skill that had won him his position had been exposed as hopelessly, fatally flawed in his own eyes, and the taste of that knowledge in his mouth was bitter beyond description. He was sick inside with it, black bile hissing and scalding his soul. He burned.

He would cleanse that shame. He would excise the foul, black matter from his being and then go to the execution chamber with at least some tattered piece of his dignity intact.

He would see El Sombra's corpse at his feet. Or he would die trying.

ABOVE THE CHURCH, El Sombra flew on his borrowed wings, pursued through the sky by the highest echelons of the Ultimate Reich. He squinted against the rushing wind, performing a tight loop as bullets singed the air inches from his feet. He had had some small amount of practice with the wings on the way over from the Palace, and he had spied on a training session once or twice during those nine years he had spent in a fugue state, learning what he needed to know. It wasn't much at all, but he could at least manoeuvre without crashing into the ground.

The assembled officers were more adept with the wings, but not by much. For one thing, these were dress models—designed for their looks more than for actual use. For another, these were men used to a position of leadership and command—in other words, the rear. Perhaps three of these men had ventured out from behind the safety of their desks in the Red Dome during the past nine years—apart from the occasional leave, of course, which was generally spent getting fat on German beer and imported champagne in one of the beerkellars or underground cabaret clubs in Berlin. To put it bluntly, these were not the lithe troopers who swooped and soared through the sky like swallows on the recruitment posters, but rather, for the most part, a selection of fat robins, blustering their way through the warm air as they attempted to shoot down their prey with guns they had not practised firing in months.

They had the advantage of numbers, and that might have forced a quick end to the combat had they deigned to work together. But these were men used to barking orders in the heat of battle—or at least the heat of administration—and being quickly obeyed without question, and so they flew their own courses yelling directions, which were ignored by any within hearing. Birds without a flock.

Their disorganisation cost them dear. El Sombra knew that, with his limited skill with firearms, he had to get in close in order to do any damage with the machine-gun, and so he allowed as many as possible to get on his tail, waiting until the bullets almost brushed his cheek before flipping back in a tight turn. As they attempted to swing their guns upwards and pick him off, he flashed over their heads, firing tight, controlled bursts with his weapon into their wing-packs. The masked man managed to rake four sets of wings with the gun before the ammo ran dry, their owners crashing into the ground or, in the case of one whose bright painted wings were torn completely off by the blazing assault, tumbling up into the sky, the cavorite infused into the main harness lifting his body against his will so that he resembled nothing so much as a slowly-rising helium balloon with kicking feet.

The machine-gun El Sombra had stolen was now little more than a club, and so he hurled it downwards with all the force he could manage, the heavy metal object smashing into the elbow of an aged Oberstleutnant who, until today, had been in charge of requisitions and the many different types of forms that needed to be filled out for such matters. The lower end of his humerus was shattered by the blow, and he dropped his own weapon, veering helplessly towards the ground as the pain caused him to lose all control over his flight. Like many of the aged and out of shape men who formed the officer class in Aldea, he was unused to wearing wings in anything other than a ceremonial situation, and so failed to pull out of the dive before the earth rushed up to meet him and crack the rest of his old bones like fine china.

One of the few who was used to wearing wings in combat was the elegantly named Major Dieter Faust, a sixty-year-old veteran of the Ultimate Reich's unfortunate adventures in the jungles of Vietnam. After a long and gruelling career in the Luftwaffe, he had been posted to the clockwork-town for the purpose of training new recruits in the use of the steam powered wing-packs that gifted the Reich with the power of flight. Now he saw his fellow officers, seemingly unable to engage in a simple aerial combat with a single amateur foe, and he was horrified. Was this what they had been reduced to? Granted, they had lost Eagle Staffel, and such gifted impresarios of flight as the younger

Eisenberg and Hugo Stahl, but when he thought that officers of the Reich could be reduced to such a shambles... he shook his head, fuming. He would finish this ragged upstart himself, and then once he was back in Berlin he would be submitting a full report on the combat-readiness of the officer class. He would submit it to the Führer himself, in triplicate. That would show them.

El Sombra noted the grey-haired man pursuing him, and angled his flight down towards the Church, picking up speed. He could tell that Dieter Faust was going to be a problem. For a start, he carried a Luger in his grip rather than one of the cumbersome M30s. The others had fired off their machine-guns as though they believed that, if they fired enough bullets into the air, by the law of averages one of them was bound to hit the target—but Major Faust was evidently a believer in a single accurate shot. He was not firing his weapon randomly. He was tracking El Sombra carefully, aiming at where he was going to be, and accelerating to bring himself in range so as to shoot to kill. El Sombra smiled grimly. This one actually had a chance of bringing him down.

The masked man flipped onto his back, letting Dieter come closer, hovering in place as he kept his eyes on where the other officers were. Then he turned his attention back to Major Faust, and drew his sword.

And stilled his mind.

He closed his eyes, feeling the sword in his grip, opening them to see Major Dieter Faust aiming the pistol carefully. Time seemed to slow. Somewhere in the still, silent desert that he had become, El Sombra calculated the exact trajectory Major Faust's next shot would take. And the one after that. And the one after that. He listened to where in the air the other officers were, buzzing around, raising their own guns in a bid to catch him in a crossfire. He smiled, relaxed and content, and looked Dieter Faust square in his furious green eyes.

The Luger fired three times.

One by one, the bullets struck the sword, ricocheting off at angles as El Sombra brought it slashing through the air at exactly the correct moment.

Major Dieter Faust was shocked. For the first time in his entire ordered life, there came into the piercing green eyes a look of uncertainty, as though all of his most cherished assumptions about the world had been brought crashing down. This was the fear to be found in the eyes of the parish priest on coming, in a single horrific instant, to understand that there was no God.

Then he heard the first screams.

To his left, he saw the accountant, Major Heinrich Mahler, who kept the books for the Project and probably had not known which end of the gun shot the bullets, screaming and clutching at his eye, pulses of rich red blood flowing between his fingers, before he went still and tumbled out of the sky. One of the bullets had burst the jelly of his eyeball and travelled deep into his brain, bringing him death in one single white-hot instant of unendurable agony. How could something like that have happened?

He looked to the right, and there was Gustav Vogel, the Oberstleutnant who coordinated the supply routes, a good friend who knew how to fly, how to shoot, and yet there he was, clutching his throat and gasping like a dying fish, with blood coursing down his chest...

And then Dieter Faust realised that he was no longer holding his pistol, and that he would never hold anything in that hand again. The final ricochet had taken off three of the fingers on his right hand. He look at the hand, the thumb and little finger wiggling obscenely, bookending three lumps of torn, bloody meat, and then he looked at the masked man who was swooping down towards the church roof.

He realised then that he was looking at Satan himself.

No normal man could have done such a thing. This was a creature with death and vengeance coursing through his veins where other men had blood, a creature born not of flesh but of some infernal flame of damnation. Where order was brought to the world, this one would bring bloody chaos. First the scene in the church, service reduced to a riot of dead and wounded men, and now this—this final insult, this demented fluke that the monster had used to save his wretched life. Dieter Faust knew that this ragged, ungainly creature was the enemy of everything he held dear.

A new resolve took hold of him in that moment. He might not have a gun, but he could deal with this abomination, this grotesque untermensch, with his own bare hands. Swooping down, he kept hot on the heels of the ragged swordsman, reaching to grab hold of the flapping trouser-legs. At these speeds, he could do serious damage if he could only force the masked man down onto the roof.

El Sombra looked back at the last enemy, keeping his course straight, heading towards the bell tower with the weathercock standing proudly on top of it. He swung his sword at the thin metal spoke that held the bird up, chopping it in two, and then reached out quickly to catch the tumbling piece of flat metal. He looked at it—perhaps a quarter of an inch thick, the metal rusted and weathered over the years to a blunt edge. He smiled, gave a swift backward glance, and then simply flipped the weathercock backwards over his shoulder.

Major Dieter Faust saw the motion but had no time to consider its significance before he felt something hard strike his face, smashing the cartilage and bone of his nose and splitting his lips. He felt his front teeth rattling on his tongue, loose, but he could not seem to work his jaw to spit them out. Blood coursed down over his neck and into his throat and something grey obscured his vision—something he could not quite define. He reached up, wobbling in his headlong flight, and felt the flat metal of the weathercock, his fingertips feeling back until they reached the point where it had embedded itself vertically in his flesh, splitting his face into two grotesque halves...

That was the moment when Dieter Faust, who was a man who believed in a rigid order, who had no patience for any who lost control of their wings no matter what the circumstance, fully understood the true meaning of chaos. His scream as he lost control and veered madly towards the bell tower was long, barely human and wracked with impossible agonies, and it was cut suddenly short when he impacted against the heavy iron bell, tolling his own demise.

El Sombra hovered in place, looking quickly around for his next opponent. The sky was clear.

Slowly the sound of the bell faded away to silence.

He exhaled.

And then General Eisenberg roared out of the shattered window of the Church below, bellowing at the top of his lungs.

"El Sombraaaaahhh!"

The General's dress wings gleamed in the sunlight, and El Sombra could see from the way he rocketed through the air that these were far more powerful than the wing-packs he was used to, or even the one he was wearing. It could move faster, turn tighter. Every twist he made in the air on his way up seemed effortless, a fact even more astonishing given that he was holding the struggling Carina by the waist, in one hand, using her as a human shield while he aimed the Luger at the masked man with the other.

The Generaloberst grinned, although it was less a sign of good humour than the baring of teeth common to predatory animals. The wings he wore were a prototype, fresh from the offices of the Messerschmitt company. Mass production was not due to start until the following year, and so, with Project Uhrwerk in its final stages, he had had the new wings repainted to serve with his own dress uniform. This happy accident meant that he was now able to outfly and outfight his enemy—El Sombra had a sword and an inferior set of wings, while Eisenberg had a gun and the finest flying apparatus in Mexico. It would be no contest. He flew directly for his enemy, keeping his Luger trained on the space between the masked man's eyes despite the struggling efforts of his hostage.

El Sombra saw what he had to do. He rolled, pitching downwards, the metal wings on his back clanking as they folded in. He hurtled down towards the earth, picked up speed, the ground rushing up to meet him. Eisenberg took his opportunity and followed close behind, keeping on the masked man's tail as he aimed the pistol and readied himself to put a single bullet into the back of El Sombra's head. He looked forward to the sound the lifeless corpse would make as it smashed into the dirt.

At the last second, El Sombra triggered the wings and they unfolded out to either side, spreading wide to catch the air. He turned upwards, shooting into the blue sky with the speed of a rocket—the speed he needed to outfly the faster foe. The Generaloberst's bullet thudded into the dirt below him, and Eisenberg cursed, once, before he replicated the masked man's manoeuvre effortlessly, swinging himself up into the air, keeping on El Sombra's tail, aiming for another shot. He was grimly confident that he could keep up such a chase indefinitely. He had the faster machine. He was the better flyer. And he was armed. All it would take would be one mistake on El Sombra's part and the terrorist would be a dead man.

Carina was holding onto her captor for dear life. She was terrified—her fear of heights made her queasy with vertigo at every turn the General made—but she held back her fear, keeping her focus on the possibility of escape. She knew that if she could claw free of his grip when they were close to the ground, she would have the best chance of survival. The only flaw in that theory was that, when the General had been close to the ground, he had been travelling at such speed that she would very likely have broken her neck had he chosen that moment to let go. On the other hand, at the height they were at now, she did not have the slightest hope of surviving the fall. Whether she liked it or not, she had no chance of getting away. So she held on against death, praying through gritted teeth that there would come a moment when she could break free without killing herself in the process.

Eisenberg held onto her tightly and lifted his pistol, aiming once again for El Sombra's back. This time he would shoot to wound, and then perhaps shoot to wound again, until the masked man was finally no longer able to avoid the fatal shot. This plan had the advantage of cruelty, and the thought of the agony a bullet could inflict when boring through the soft offal of the gut made the Generaloberst smile to himself. Even as he squeezed his trigger, El Sombra flipped backwards in a tight loop, suddenly facing downwards again and aiming himself directly at the General. The bullet whispered past his temple.

Eisenberg clicked his tongue, growling low in his throat. A quick death, then, instead of the planned torture—whatever it took. He had patience. El Sombra could dodge as many shots as he liked, but he would die in the end as surely as a pig fattened for the slaughter. Eisenberg sighted the pistol directly between the masked man's eyes, making sure that Carina protected as much of his own body as possible.

El Sombra hurled his sword straight down.

Carina's eyes widened in shock as the sharp, flashing blade seemed to come straight for her. Eisenberg gritted his teeth and his finger began to squeeze the trigger—only to feel the gun jerk in his hands, suddenly heavy, off-balance. He looked at it, and his own grey eyes grew wide at the sight.

The barrel of the Luger was split down the middle and blocked solid. El Sombra's sword was securely wedged into it.

The masked man smiled and allowed himself a single instant of pride.

It had, perhaps, been the best throw he had ever made.

The Generaloberst snarled like an animal and reached to tear the sword free from his gun and in the process he let go of Carina with no more thought than you or I might let go of, say, the handle of a heavy suitcase in order to reach into a pocket for a key. Carina had finally outlived her usefulness, and now Eisenberg needed both his hands free more than he needed her alive.

SHE DID NOT scream as she fell. But her face grew pale as gravity took hold in the pit of her stomach and her own death rushed up to greet her.

El Sombra, diving downward like an eagle sighting prey, had already reached terminal velocity, while Carina had a few moments left before they were falling at the same speed. He sped past the hovering General, reaching, hand clawing at the air. At the same time, Carina reached upwards, kicking with her legs as though that might slow her fall, straining with all of her strength as though attempting to break gravity's hold through sheer force of will. Underneath, the ground rushed at them both like a barrelling freight train, as the masked man's hand finally found hers, tugging her into his arms before he allowed the metal wings to spread wide once again, lifting him and Carina back up towards the blue canopy above.

The pack on El Sombra's back was calibrated to support one person, and, unlike the General's, it was incapable of supporting two easily. El Sombra felt the momentum he'd picked up from his headlong dive quickly running out as they swept upwards, passing the General once again as he tugged fruitlessly at the fused sword and gun.

"Hold on." The masked man spoke softly, unbuckling the pack from his back at the apex of their upward flight, and then, in one sure movement, quickly swinging it around the two of them and locking the strap around Carina's waist, holding her with one arm as he secured the shoulder straps with the other. There was only a slight lurch, and within seconds, Carina went from clutching El Sombra to keep herself from falling to being the one holding him up. It was a welcome change, although she was still trying to recover from the shock of her earlier near death experience. Thus, when he chose that moment to kiss her softly, his lips finding hers with a sure confidence that would have shocked his old self, she did not return the gesture, but only blinked in stunned surprise. Events were, in all senses, moving slightly too quickly for her to be comfortable.

"See you later." El Sombra smiled genially, and let go, tumbling away from her as she floated up into the sky. Carina cried out, dumbfounded at the act, and reached after him as a reflex action, before closing her eyes to avoid the sight of the man she had come to trust falling to his death on the dust below.

El Sombra looked at her, wind whipping at his hair, and grinned. She was in for a shock.

Below them both, the Generaloberst continued to tug at the sword embedded in the pistol. The pistol might still be of use at short range, and the sword had a keen edge, but fused together in their current manner they were little more than a club. Finally, with a grunt of triumph, he yanked the damaged pistol free of the blade, looking around to see where El Sombra had gone in the few seconds he had managed to distract him.

El Sombra slammed into the Generaloberst with all his weight, knocking the air from the other man. The sword went flying from Eisenberg's hand to tumble through space, finally embedding itself in the hard ground beneath them. The remains of the pistol, however, became a crude bludgeoning weapon as the General smashed the butt of the gun hard into the side of El Sombra's head.

"Let go of me!" he snarled, spittle flying over his chin as his face contorted into an expression of pure, unfettered hate. In the depths of his rage, he came close to losing control of the wings, and the combined weight of the two men caused them to veer crazily across the sky, missing the rooftops by inches as they swooped and soared. Again and again, the General brought the gun down, pistol-whipping the masked man brutally. Carina had been forgotten, the survival of the Project had been forgotten, even his dead son was forgotten as every part of Eisenberg's being focussed on one goal—the brutal murder of the enemy who had destroyed everything he had once taken pride in.

El Sombra attempted to block the blows from the pistol butt without letting go of the General, but there was already blood coursing into his eyes from a serious gash in his forehead and he was having difficulty seeing through the film of red that covered his vision. Desperately, he reached up to grip Eisenberg's wrist, stopping the gun butt from smashing into his skull yet again, pushing the arm back as Eisenberg roared at him like a maddened bear. Then he snapped his head forward. Hard. The masked man's forehead slammed into the bridge of General Eisenberg's already broken nose, smashing it flat against the face. At the same time, El Sombra twisted the General's wrist, forcing the fingers open and letting the broken Luger drop down into the burnt-out remains of the schoolhouse far below.

The General spat blood and his eyes burned, a savage, bloodshot glare filled with the utmost loathing. Cursing, he brought his knee up hard into the masked man's groin. El Sombra gasped, clutching at the General as he felt his stomach turn over in that very personal agony, and his weight shifted the wings once again, sending them diving down in a wide turn towards the Great Square. Below them, the workers looked up from their duties at the air show put on seemingly for their benefit. The statue had already been dismantled and was being carted away from the waist down. Now all that was left was Hitler's torso, the stern stone head gazing up into the sky above, and the arm raised heavenward in salute. Those few guards left to oversee the operation shouted abuse at the workers, trying to force them to continue, before they were distracted by what was going on above their heads. Was that really their Generaloberst, in full dress uniform, battling like some demented beast as he swung madly through the clear sky? What in heaven's name was going on?

El Sombra punched upwards, his fist cracking against Eisenberg's jaw, knocking his head back and loosening a tooth. In response, the Generaloberst let loose a slavering cry of animal hate and wrapped his hands around the masked man's throat. He began to squeeze with a strength born of madness, gripping hard, choking the life from the man he hated most in the world. There was nothing in his eyes now that resembled the man he had been. The cold air of command had been burned away in the blaze of his fury, and the glitter of his ice-chip eyes now suggested a psychopath rather than a tactician.

El Sombra gritted his teeth, grabbing hold of the General's wrists and shifting his weight. Though unable to turn his head under Eisenberg's merciless assault, he was nonetheless able to judge their location in the Square by the position of the surrounding buildings.

They were nearing the most sacred spot in all of old Pasito. The spot where his brother's blood had stained the ground, where his curse had been uttered, where El Sombra had been born in a night of fire and blood. It was where El Sombra would finally die.

But not before he'd done what he was born for.

The masked man grinned even as he was throttled by the General, continuing to shift his weight subtly, to steer the two men through the warm air. The Great Square had gone through many changes since his brother's death, but he remembered what it was that stood on that spot now. It was a great stone shoulder, connected to a long arm and a flat palm raised in eternal salute, up into the sky, like an obelisk, or a monolith to mark the dead.

Heraclio, he thought. I came back. I came back to fight them. And I won.

You can rest now.

He let go of the General's arms, dangling limp from Eisenberg's grip, and then brought his fists up, the knuckles of his index fingers raised to jab hard into the undersides of the elbows. A sharp stinging pain flashed up the General's forearms, into his hands, and the fingers lost their grip, letting the masked man plummet down towards the unyielding stone beneath.

General Eisenberg, the Iron Mountain, looked up to see the flat stone palm hurtling towards him at incredible speed, and he mouthed the first thing that came into his mind.

"Heil Hitl—"

He smacked into the stone hand like a bird flying into a windowpane. The impact pulped his face and cracked his skull open like an eggshell.

El Sombra saw the impact, and felt a great sense of peace descend on him. The Ultimate Reich was finished. The head had been cut off, and now the body would die. He had finally won.

He smiled, feeling the wind whipping through his hair.

Then his back smacked hard into cold stone and everything went black.

CHAPTER TEN
THE END, AND AFTER

DJEGO OPENED HIS eyes.

He was in a comfortable bed in an unfamiliar room. The walls were painted a soothing shade of peach, the sheets were clean and fresh, the sun was shining and the general atmosphere was one of relaxation, rest and well-being. It made him nervous.

As his awareness slowly returned to him he found himself looking at a painting on the opposite wall. It was a picture of what appeared to be a group of dogs, sitting on chairs around a table as though they were men, in a room with ugly blue wallpaper. The dogs were playing a game of cards. One was smoking a pipe. Another had a cigar. One was cheating, an ace held in a paw under the table. All of them had expressions of relaxed joviality, which sat well with their canine features. The whole effect was, quite naturally, unsettling and terrifying to Djego, and he was about to bolt out of the bed and try his luck in a fall from the window when he became aware that there was someone sitting at his bedside.

"It's called A Friend In Need. A man named Cassius Coolidge painted it some hundred and thirty years ago, and somehow it found its way into the hands of the Reich. You wouldn't believe some of the treasures we've found since they left." The voice was warm, rich and reassuring, with a soft musical lilt to it. Hearing it was like sitting next to a roaring fire on a cold and lonely day, and

Djego sank back into the pillows, breathing a slight sigh of relief. He looked towards the voice, heart lifting as the name came back to him from far away.

Carina smiled.

"Welcome back, Djego. You were out for a long time."

Djego's hand lifted to his face, and he gently felt under one eye. There was nothing there. Where his fingers would once have touched the bloodstained fabric of his brother's wedding-sash, now all they touched was his skin.

"The mask..."

"It's safe. And the sword is too. They're both locked up safe and sound in the cupboard over there." Djego looked at her, brows furrowed. She took a deep breath, and carried on. "And... that's where they're staying. You've been through a lot, Djego, and I don't..." She blushed, smiling at the ludicrousness of what she was about to say. "I don't want you leaping out of the window and running off to hit somebody. There's no need for that anymore and... I wanted to meet you. The real you. I wanted to see the real man underneath that piece of cloth."

Djego nodded slowly. "... okay."

He felt naked without the mask, exposed. El Sombra was gone, and there was only Djego left. But somehow... the sky was not falling. Carina was smiling at him, she was taking care of him. He attempted a smile, and it felt comfortable. Perhaps... perhaps it would be enough to be Djego, for a while. The hated name did not have the same power when it came from her lips. It sounded like the name a man might have, instead of a dog. And he had a sense that he would not need the other name—that other man—for a long time. He looked up at her, groping for something to say, to cover the silence of the moment.

"Where am I?"

"A guest room in the Red Dome. We moved you here as soon as you could be moved. It's a lovely place, once you get past all the swastikas. We're going to keep it standing." She smiled softly, as he groped for another question.

"How... how long was I out?" He smiled sheepishly up at her, and something in the sheer mundanity of his own responses pleased him. Djego was beginning to register the aching of his muscles and bones, but still, he felt good. He felt like... Djego was someone he could live with now. Someone he could live with being. Still, there was a nagging itch at the back of his skull, a barely perceptible tingle.

Carina smiled. "About seven weeks, on and off. You came out of it long enough to tell us where you were keeping all the guns, which was nice of you, as it meant we could fight back properly instead of just hurling stones at them. And occasionally you'd start shouting about the bastards... but once they'd gone—"

Djego sat up, staring uncomprehendingly. "They're gone? You drove them out?"

"We drove them out." She smiled. "You'd killed so many of them, and then the General, and his son, and the High Command... their nerve broke, and ours... you should have seen it. When the general's head splattered like that, the crowd just roared. There were only a couple of guards armed with little pistols to keep them at work. They were lynched. By the time I got back to the ground, it was open warfare. Anybody who'd even thought about taking a hand against the bastards was hurling rocks and beating on them with hammers, and the brainwashed ones who didn't want to make trouble were just hiding in their homes."

Djego was shocked. This was what El Sombra had wanted, but the thought now made him feel sick. "Oh my God. How many died?"

Carina shook her head. "Not many at all, considering. Fourteen people, thank the Lord no children. But the soldiers... their hearts just weren't in it, like I said. There wasn't any chain of command anymore. It was just the grunts left, kids and old men who were only there because they'd been told to be. When we attacked them with the guns towards the end, they scattered like rabbits, and they always used to shout the same thing in German—'I was only following orders! I was only following orders!' Isn't that funny?"

Djego rubbed his forehead. It seemed as though he should be able to know what the German for that was, but somehow he couldn't remember. "I suppose."

Carina sighed, reaching out to tease her fingers through his hair absently. "Anyway. They fought a holding action for a couple of weeks, trying to keep us away from their supply depots, but when we took hold of the guns... well, there and then the orders must have come from across the sea. They ran away, Djego. They're gone."

Djego was silent for a very long time. He stared at the picture of the dogs playing cards, and something uneasy stirred in him. "Gone. Gone across the sea." He shook his head, as though clearing it, and then turned to Carina again. "So what happens now?"

Carina sighed. "I'm in charge. Or rather, a committee that I'm part of is in charge. They didn't leave us any infrastructure to work with, unfortunately. We were mindless cattle to them, they weren't worried about providing things like hospitals and—well, you saw what happened to the school."

Djego nodded. Once, mention of what had happened at the schoolhouse would have made his blood boil in his veins. Now, that was someone else's anger. Djego only felt sadness that so much time and so many lives had been wasted for so little reason. "You said there were people who'd been brainwashed... what happened to them?"

Carina was silent for a long moment, then she stood up and moved to the window, looking out. "It took them a while. It was only when the bastards were finally gone for good that they came out. They were so scared... I think they really believed that they were going to be taken in the night at any moment. Some of them still do." She shook her head. "After nine years of this... some people just don't have any hope any more. The best we can do is give them work. You know that some of them are building a statue of you?"

Djego looked at her as though she'd gone mad. "A statue of El Sombra?"

"It's all they know how to do. They're incompetent and unqualified for everything else, but if I don't give them work, they just sit in their homes and have panic attacks. So they're working on a big statue of you." She smiled wryly. "Hopefully, once they're done, I'll have weaned them on to farming. They do have a good work ethic."

"I'm amazed they're doing anything at all that might offend their beloved Führer." Djego's voice was tinged with a deep bitterness. It offended him that his town should have been brought so close to the brink of destruction by a little man, far across the sea, a man he'd never even met. The itch in the back of his skull intensified. "How do you get them to do anything you say?"

There was a soft chuckle from the doorway. "You have me to thank for that." The voice was soft and earthy, with a pleasant rasp in it that made all the difference to the doughy, tremulous tone it had had before. That was the doing of the bullet that had partially collapsed the owner's left lung. The other had entered his back between two of his ribs, miraculously passing through without harming any of his internal organs in the process and lodging in the floor of the Church.

Rafael Contreras, who had once worn another name that was now mercifully forgotten, stood in the doorway, with tea.

"Father!" Carina's voice carried a familiar note of anger, but it was anger born of concern, and Rafael cherished it. "Father, what are you doing? Give me that, you're going to hurt yourself!" She took the tray of tea from him and set it on the side table, turning to Djego with a tight smile. "He has to do everything around here. I have to keep reminding him he had a serious trauma. He could have died. You could have died!" She turned to her father again, shaking her head in disbelief.

"What happened to you?" Djego was taken aback by the change in Master Plus. It was as though he'd become a completely different man but then, he understood how such changes could happen. Again, he felt a nagging feeling at the back of his skull. But the bastards were gone.

They were gone.

"Eisenberg shot him twice in the back and then left him to bleed on the floor. He could have died; he would have, if I hadn't gone back for him. I had to tear the wedding dress up for bandages."

Rafael smiled. "The best use that could have been made of it. It's a good thing you knew a little about how to deal with something like that."

"You were the one who let me read so much." She smiled, but there was an edge to the banter. Carina and her father were on good terms, better than they had been since she was a little girl, but there would always be that edge there, an area of darkness that he could never atone for, and she could never forgive, no matter how much they both tried. Carina quickly turned back to Djego. "Books on first aid and medicine. I wanted to be able to help if anything happened to him." She winced, and Rafael looked away. "Anyway, it doesn't matter. I could help him, that's all that matters. And I could help you too."

Djego raised an eyebrow.

"That fight... the torture... the fall," she shook her head. "You came close, Djego. I thought you were going to die. To have you talking again after just a few weeks..." She smiled, reaching to take his hand and squeeze. "You're a tough guy."

Djego shook his head, looking up into her eyes. "You must be thinking of somebody else. Although you did keep your promise. You saved me, Carina." He smiled and gave her hand a squeeze.

Carina laughed. "I haven't saved you yet, my friend. But I will. Trust me. And now, I have to get my stupid father to sit down before he injures himself. Enjoy the tea."

She stood up, and gently guided Rafael out of the room and down the stairs. Djego was left to lie on the bed, propped up on the pillows and sipping the tea reflectively.

It was all over.

Aldea was gone, and in a few years Pasito would again be a good place to live, with only the Red Dome and a statue of a ragged man in bloodstained wedding trousers and a mask to mark the darkest period in its history. All the bastards were gone.

He frowned at that. Something about the notion didn't seem to fit, but Djego couldn't put his finger on it.

He began to scratch at the back of his skull.

"...SO OCTAVIO SAYS that if they're going to be locking up drunks, they need uniforms, which we have, but obviously the uniforms can't be grey and we should change the cut of them as well... are you listening?" Rafael looked at his daughter quizzically. They were both sat in the small room that had become their kitchen since they had moved into the Red Dome.

Carina nodded. "Just thinking about Djego. He's going to have a lot of adjusting to do. More than we do. It's like we've been waiting all this time for our lives to have purpose again, and now they do... and he is gone. There's nothing left for him."

Rafael nodded. "Is that what you meant when you talked about saving him?"

She sighed and nodded slowly. "The first time we met, he just seemed so... so sad. He was in pain and lashing out against it like a rat in a cage. I want him to be a man. I want him to be happy, but he's never going to be happy so long as he's got that mask on... he needs to learn how to live again now it's all over, anyway. He's been out in the desert for God knows how long, thinking about nothing but fighting Nazis. What's he going to do now?"

Rafael shrugged. "Go to Germany and kill Hitler?"

"Don't even joke about it, Father." Carina smiled softly, shaking her head. Then she looked up with a start. "What was that noise?"

Rafael looked up at the ceiling. "It sounded like breaking wood."

Carina was up and out of her chair in an instant. Heart pounding, she ran up the stairs and grabbed the handle of the door to the guest room.

"Damn it, he's locked the door!" She hammered on the wood with her fists, and Rafael came running close behind her, his breath ragged and short.

"I could... break down the door..." The last word was barely audible over his coughing fit. Carina looked at him in exasperation and ran back down the stairs, heading towards the store cupboard in the basement where the master keys for all the rooms in the Red Dome were kept. She moved quickly, but she already knew she would be far too late.

Sure enough, when they finally managed to open the door, all that they found was an empty cupboard with the door torn off. The window was wide open.

Djego was long gone.

THE MAN WALKED through the desert.

And the desert brought strength to the man.

El Sombra was at home here. It was his element, his place of power. He relished the heat of the sun on his back, and the way the sand warmed the soles of his feet as he trod. The familiar weight of the sword was in his hand, and he clutched it so tightly, so gratefully, that his knuckles were white with the strain, and that felt so good to him that he laughed, the sound of joy carrying over the sands. The mask was back where it belonged, covering his eyes, the knot of the cloth riding against the back of his skull in the way it used to.

He felt bad about leaving Carina so suddenly, and without saying goodbye. He'd hurt her, he knew, and he'd hurt himself at well. Djego had had a chance for something good in his wretched life. A chance to help his hometown heal from the horrors that had been inflicted on it. But El Sombra could not let him rest just yet.

As far as Carina and Rafael and all of Pasito cared, the bastards were gone, but they weren't gone. They'd only left his town. His country.

They hadn't left his planet.

They had gone west, across the sea, to use the lessons they'd learned on Pasito on their own people. But that wasn't the worst part. The worst part was that the man in the statue was still alive. He'd destroyed El Sombra's home from the comfort of a government office somewhere, sitting in a comfortable leather chair as he signed forms to authorise the death and degradation of everything the masked man loved, without ever meeting the people he was condemning, without looking into their eyes. The man in the statue was the orchestrator of every sorrow and shame he and the people of Pasito had ever suffered—and he had never paid the price for it. At best, all Pasito was to him was a cross on a balance sheet, a failed experiment. And that wasn't good enough.

El Sombra wanted the name of Pasito to wake him up in the night, sweating and shaking. He wanted the thought of what he'd done to burn in the coward's heart until the day came when he thrust his brother's sword through it. He wanted the man in the statue to suffer until he ended his wretched life.

It was too bad about Djego. El Sombra regretted little, but he regretted denying Djego that one small chance at happiness. But it couldn't be helped.

Until Adolf Hitler was dead, El Sombra could never rest.

The man walked west, towards the sinking sun.

EPILOGUE
THE MAN IN THE HIGH CASTLE

WALTER HOPFENKECKER WAS neither a strong nor a brave man. Built like a strand of straw on a riverbank, he had often been picked on as a child, his face pushed in the mud by older, stronger children as they screamed into his ear "Walter Haufen Kacke! Walter Haufen Kacke!" He remembered vividly how they took his brand new mathematics book that his father had slaved eight hours overtime to buy him, and threw it in a river. He remembered sitting on the riverbank, sobbing into his hands and thinking that he had never felt so helpless. He wanted control over his life. He wanted the power to stop them hurting him. He wanted them to fear him, wanted them to be punished.

It is from such tiny acorns that great oaks grow. Now Walter Hopfenkecker was the Chief Administrative Assistant to Adolf Hitler, and his power was vast indeed. And men feared him.

Or he punished them.

There was only one man who did not fear Walter Hopfenkecker, and only one man who Walter Hopfenkecker truly feared. And he could not truly be called a man at all.

Walter paused at the great oaken door that led to the Führer's study, trying hard not to allow his hands to shake as he reached to turn the iron key that would allow him access. He bit his lip, almost drawing blood, and then uttered a soft and silent prayer as the key turned and the door slowly swung open.

Then he stepped into Hell.

Steam and smoke filled the massive chamber, scalding the skin and choking the lungs. The art treasures adorning the walls had to be protected by boxes of glass, the temperatures carefully regulated to prevent the toxic atmosphere from destroying what lay within. Human beings who entered the office of the Führer were afforded no such protection.

In the centre of this hideous miasma there was a machine.

It was more than three storeys tall, a terrifying construction of iron, copper and glass. A noxious green liquid coursed through tubes running up and down the structure, exiting a grille in the top as vapour, a grotesque mist that would burn at the eyes and lungs and kill any man who breathed it in. Vast pistons pumped and shifted, creating a constant, eternal shriek of metal scraping against metal. It was horrific to look upon—a vast industrial nightmare that seemed designed for no purpose beyond torture and death.

It was formed roughly into the shape of a man, and at the top, there was a great bronze head, motionless, with eyes that burned a terrible green. In the centre of the chest, there was a tank of reinforced glass, filled with the bubbling green poison, and hanging in the very centre of this, in a web of copper wire, was a human brain.

It was a brain that had once attempted to excise an entire people from the face of the planet. It was a brain that possessed an uncanny ability to incite hatred, fear and violence, to turn a crowd of ordinary people into a mob, to create an entire country dedicated to the deaths of the innocent in the name of their own twisted notions of purity.

It was the brain of Adolf Hitler.

Slowly, the Führer reared up to his full height, leaning over to gaze down at the tiny little man who'd dared to intrude upon him. The eyes in the great bronze mask—the mask of Hitler, an idealised Hitler, more like an Apollo than the shabby, ugly man with the awful hair who had once stalked these halls—stared down at Walter, merciless and cold. From Walter's perspective, he seemed like some terrifying iron god, ready to pronounce judgement on all those whose names were not written in his Book. When he spoke, the voice that projected from speakers located in the brass head's throat was a screaming symphony of needles scraping slowly across sheet glass.

"Greetings, Herr Hopfenkecker. You have the final report on Projekt Uhrwerk?"

Walter nodded, stifling his coughing. "J-Jawohl, Mein Führer. I am pleased to report an eighty-three per cent success—"

"Eighty-three per cent. Does that sound acceptable to you, Herr Hopfenkecker?"

A chill crept up Walter's spine, and he gave a tiny shudder. No, it did not sound acceptable to him. "Unfortunately, the... the actions of the terrorist network forced us to bring the Project to a premature end..."

"One man is not a network, Herr Hopfenkecker. Do not try to diminish your own execrable performance by conferring special powers upon your enemies. I will not tolerate it." The terrifying, screaming machine leant close and Walter took a half-step back, his gut lurching. "One man, who single-handedly destroyed our work in Mexico, in the process destroying hundreds of thousands of marks' worth of property and ending the lives of several dozen of our finest troops. What do you think my reaction would be, Herr Hopfenkecker, if a similar man were to arise here in Berlin?"

"Mein Führer, with the greatest respect, those were special circumstances, we were an invading force and we had barely occupied the town for nine years. Under the circumstances, we did brilliantly. If Project Uhrwerk Phase Two were to begin operating in Berlin—where we control both the government and the media, and there are no outside influences to interfere with the programme— my people calculate a one-hundred per cent chance of total success."

There was a pause. Slowly the head of the immense machine tilted, as though studying Walter for some small sign that would indicate whether or not one of the huge machine-fists should close about him and burst him like a poisoned boil.

Then, the structure shifted back in a storm of shrieking metal and glass. Walter breathed a sigh of relief. "Danke, Mein Führer. Danke."

"We have better things to worry about than a tiny town in a backwater region. When the glorious Reich sweeps through Mexico again—as it will cover the entire world—I will take great pleasure in crushing the town of Pasito and leaving the population's heads on poles to serve as a lesson in obedience. In the meantime, we shall continue with the programme as it stands."

Walter nodded. "I will attend to it directly, Mein Führer. The terrorist will be destroyed with the rest of his town when the great day of our conquest comes."

There was something not unlike a dry chuckle from the machine. It sounded like a handful of broken glass being slowly crushed by the turning of a thumbscrew.

"Oh no, Herr Hopfenkecker, you misunderstand me. We won't be leaving El Sombra to live out his pitiful existence without retribution. Nor will we have to. Anyone who can destroy a man like Eisenberg and everything that he loves will not be content living out his days in some cow town in the desert. Not when there are people like you and I still waiting to be murdered. He will come to me, Herr Hopfenkecker. He will walk into my waiting arms.

"Have our people in the Tsar's Empire watch out for him. If he shows his face, report back to me. I want him alive, if at all possible. I want the pleasure of snuffing his miserable animal existence out like a candle. I want to see this miserable urchin who did us so much damage suffer as nobody has suffered before."

The chuckle slowly built into a laugh, and the horrific echo the machine produced to attempt it was the sound of a blitzkrieg of shrapnel tearing through an orphanage of screaming glass children.

"I promise you, mein Herr... El Sombra has not heard the last of Adolf Hitler!"

THE END

GODS OF MANHATTAN

PROLOGUE
NIGHT AND THE CITY

WHEN THE NIGHT came, you could hear Manhattan coming to life.

Stagecoaches clip-clopped down the wide streets, oil lamps burning on the sides. Rickshaws clattered through back alleys, seeking shortcuts, yelling at each other if they got too close. *Watch it, Mac! You blind?* Newsboys catcalled as they waved the evening editions. *Wuxtry, wuxtry! Blood-Spider sighted in the South Bronx! All in colour for a dime! Wuxtry, wuxtry! Don't ask, just buy it!*

Coloured lanterns picked out theatre signs, reflecting from the silvered letters. In Times Square, great paper advertisements for Sake Cola and *Jonny's Daily Show* at the Chinese Theatre glowed softly from the arrangement of gas-lamps behind them. On every corner there was the scent of cooked sausage meat as the hot-dog vendors grilled their wares over barrel-fires, the smell hitting your nose as their calls and cries met your ears. *Mustard and sweet onion! Red sauce and yellow! Hot dogs, hot dogs! One dollar five! Wrap a nickel in a bill and eat your fill!*

You might start off surrounded by tourists and suits, bowlers and top hats on every head around you, and then turn the right corner and walk down the wrong alley and everything would change before you'd even noticed. You might find yourself face-to-face with a sneering young tough-guy in leather and studs and an injun haircut streaked with pink and green, with a safety-pin through the nose to complete the effect—an apparition you could only find here, in the City of Tomorrow. Futureheads, they were called—an ironic gesture, considering their creed and battle-cry was "No future for me, no future for you."

According to the futureheads, some vital step towards progress had been lost along the way to the present day, and human civilisation had entered a period of stagnation, of cultural inbreeding. The familiar bred with the familiar and created more and more outlandish results. Futureheads were the self-proclaimed end result of this degradation, their clothing a forest of symbols repurposed and détourned, all original meanings subsumed into a new and terrible message—that history had stopped, the roaring train of time had crashed and humanity were now only playing around in the wreckage, finding what uses they could for the junk.

Still and all, a futurehead rarely wanted trouble. That swaggering tough was most likely on his way to a bar, happy with his own, in no mood to give you more than a filthy look and a wad of spit at your feet. No, if it was trouble you were after, you kept an eye on the bikers—the treaded rubber tyres of their Off-Road Bicycles rattling with steel spokies as they bunny-hopped and weaved through the crowds with practised ease, swapping charged looks and predatory grins as they sped down streets and alleys. The better they were on those things, the more likely they were to be purse-snatchers. You could spot them because they rode no-handed, keeping their hands free to cut straps and grab bags, slinging their prizes into a basket on the front of the machine before grabbing the handlebars again to swerve away, leaving pursuit far behind.

Turn another corner and you might find a gothic Lolita-lookalike waving shyly at you from under a streetlight, kitten ears poking from her hair. Or a man wearing hard eyes and a trilby hat, shooting you a dirty look and opening his coat just enough to show you his gun, then strolling into a nightclub and putting four in the belly of some poor schmoe who hadn't made the payments. Or a fellow in shirtsleeves and zoot trousers, spinning like a top on his back and his head, on a cardboard sheet right there on the sidewalk. Music provided by three sharp-dressed men with steel drums and tom-toms, tapping out a beat so complex and layered that no formal dance would ever do, so catchy and contagious that not dancing wouldn't do either. White boy off to the side, throwing shapes with his hands and laughing like a drunk, even though he'd never touched a drop in his life.

That's a top one, fellahs, oh that's a nice one, he'd shout, and the answer would echo back from around the corner, *red sauce and yellow! One dollar five!*

Turn another corner and you might find yourself back in the world, back among those who made sense to you. Or you might find yourself face-to-chest with a powder blue T-shirt and a lightning bolt decal, and a soft deep voice that might have belonged to the Lord on the mount, wishing you a good night and good luck. Or you might find yourself where you'd never known you belonged until now. That place that couldn't exist in any other city in the whole damned world.

This was Manhattan, after all. There were stories here.

And when the night came, they came to life.

Here's a story.

Out on the water, there were two men. They were sitting in a small sailing vessel, drifting in the darkness towards Manhattan.

Willis was looking at the Statue. The arm holding the torch had been destroyed during the Second Civil War—the Statue was French, after all, so there was no surprise in her being a target—but most people liked the replacement arm and the new torch a lot better anyway. Something about having an actual fire roaring out of that torch—an eternal flame, the politicos had called it— made the Statue seem a little more defiant, somehow, and Willis liked that. He breathed in, watching the way the flames danced from the torch, reflected on the water below. He never did get tired of that view.

The other man glanced up briefly, then returned to his sword. He'd been inspecting it for the last hour, and it was starting to make Willis uneasy. The Mexican was a tall, muscular figure, strikingly handsome in an odd way, with scruffy black hair, long in back, and a thick moustache—but he slouched, round-shouldered, and his hair was greasy and hung in his face. He wore a pair of classy tuxedo pants and little else. The only things he seemed to own, once he'd paid for his passage, were his sword and a strip of red cloth poking out of his pocket.

He kept scratching the back of his skull. It made Willis uneasy.

"So. Up from Mexico, huh?" Willis grunted. Talking made the sailing go a little faster sometimes, and besides, he wanted to break the silence. Part of him wondered if he could throw the other man overboard, if it came to it.

The Mexican nodded.

"You know, most folks up from Mexico come via land, if you don't mind me saying. You serious about taking boats all the way around Cape Horn and up the other side?"

The Mexican shrugged. He spoke softly, with a strong accent, but with no hesitation, no fumbling for the right words. "They'd have been waiting for me in

Russia. And somebody once told me there was some interesting art in New York. I wanted to see for myself."

Willis nodded, though in truth he hadn't the faintest idea what the fella was talking about or who 'they' might be. "I, uh, I don't know if they'd let you into a gallery wearing that."

The Mexican laughed, dryly. "Maybe not. I can find something to wear. Or Djego can..." he scratched the back of his head, wincing. "It's hard to tell sometimes who's who. You understand." He stared at his fingers for a moment, then gently felt around his eyes and at the bridge of his nose. "I'm Djego. Of course I am! I'm Djego the poet. Museums are exactly the sort of thing I like. Museums and avoiding trouble." He lowered his head. "Ask anyone. Djego hates fighting. Djego is a coward. Everyone knows." He spat the words.

He gazed out across the water, at the flickering torch.

"That was the problem. Djego ran away when they murdered everything he loved. Poor old Djego. He just wasn't equipped to handle that kind of thing. He needed someone else to take over. Someone better. Stronger. *More*."

For a moment, there was steel in his voice, and in his eyes—and then he blinked and shook his head, scratching the back of it for a moment. "Djego... I... I am just looking after this." He held up the sword, looking at it in the light. "It's not mine."

Willis swallowed, looking nervously at the sword. When the half-naked man had hired his boat, back in Fort Hancock, he'd been happy with the payment offered. Six hundred, half in cash and half in valuables. Gold and diamond watches, tie pins. A couple of Nazi medals, which had been a little strange. Still, Willis had turned a blind eye. Now, he was wondering if he'd been right to be so mercenary about it. This man was crazier than a three-dollar bill in a windsock.

"So, what, uh, what kind of art are you interested in, Mr Djego?" He smiled, wetting his lips and keeping his eyes on the sword.

"The soup cans. And I heard some things when I was talking to people on the way here. The kind of people who wear gold and diamond watches. And have Nazi medals in cigar boxes that they keep hidden and lovingly polished." He snarled, and started scratching the back of his head again. "Bastards." He shook his head, as though trying to focus his thoughts. "It seems... it seems as if I might have some business in this city. Well, Djego won't. Djego couldn't. But somebody will." Idly, he pulled the strip of red cloth out of his pocket. There were two holes in it.

His other hand continued to scratch, as if it couldn't stop. As if some itch in his skull was building and building.

"Business?" Willis took a shaky breath. "What, uh, what sort of business are you in?"

The Mexican blinked at him for a moment.

Then he tied the red cloth over his eyes in one quick movement.

Then he looked at Willis again.

Willis cried out and stumbled back, falling on the deck.

Behind the improvised mask, the Mexican's eyes were terrifying.

He stood—back straight, hair no longer in his eyes—and picked up his sword, gripping it as though it was a part of his arm. He gave a short, barking laugh, and even his voice was different; bold, mocking and macho. The Mexican had become a completely different person.

"I'm an exterminator, amigo."

He grinned—a madman's smile—and flipped Willis a quick salute. Then he jumped over the side.

Willis ran to the edge of the boat, looking into the water, but there was no sign the masked man had ever existed.

Willis sat down, trembling, trying to remember if he'd even heard a splash, and he wondered just what he'd let loose on New York City.

HERE'S ANOTHER STORY.

In Japantown, under the pink light of a shaded lamp, an otaku-kid took a steel flick-comb from his pocket and dragged it slowly through his Jesse Presley quiff, idly transferring a toothpick from one side of his mouth to the other. Hisoka looked at his reflection in the mirrored window of one of the idol stores, and it was acceptable. The weight of the nunchuks on his back felt good, felt right. It was a mark of status in his zoku to have hand-made nunchuks. He'd carved these himself from hardwood, and they were weighted perfectly, so that he could draw them from his back in one smooth motion, spinning and whirling them through the air in a dazzling display, never making the new-kid mistake of banging himself in the head or thigh with them. They were the only thing he'd ever been proud of in his life. With these—he knew with a cold and terrible certainly—he could kill a man.

Maybe he'd have to kill a man tonight.

There was trouble in the zoku between him and Orochi. It couldn't be helped. They were in love with the same girl, the neko-catgirl Akemi. Hisoka didn't have much time for catgirls—they were twee, silly, overdone—but that just made Akemi more remarkable to him. She carried the look in a way that was utterly unlike any of the others, that made the velvet ears and tail seem strangely exotic instead of an affectation so drastically out of fashion as to be simply absurd. The moment Hisoka had seen her, he'd known that this was the woman he would live and die for.

Probably die. But there were worse ways to die than for love.

Hisoka turned his head, hearing the soft whirr of metal and rubber. An ORB—the off-road bicycles the bosozoku ran with, with their thick-treaded rubber tyres. Just one, though. He knew what that meant. A visit from the Inspector.

He turned, looking contemptuously at the slowing bike, lip curled in an imitation of the King's sneer. "Inspector West."

The inspector bunny-hopped and skidded the ORB to a halt, the glass beads on the wheels rattling like the tail of a deadly snake as the sudden lack of centrifugal force left them clattering down the spokes. His eyes were hidden, as usual, behind black sunglasses, and his expression was as unreadable as ever. West was ex-bosozoku himself, the Americanised name hiding his Japanese heritage. The rumour ran that he'd been raised from birth by an outlaw vigilante who lived in a graveyard, and on reaching adolescence he'd formed his own outlaw bike gang to keep the peace in Japantown in the face of a corrupt police force, only joining the pigs himself once he'd burnt the corruption out at the root, and even then only to catch his mentor's killer. It was a good story, and it bought him a lot of respect in the Japantown gang culture, more than for the other cops. But it didn't make him a friend.

"Big night, Hisoka."

Hisoka shifted the toothpick to the other side of his mouth and shrugged, a studied display of indifference.

The Inspector spoke the language. He knew that too much talk was a weakness. He'd already said everything he needed to say—that he knew what was likely to happen, that he knew where, that he'd be watching. Whoever won in the coming clash between Hisoka and Orochi, the winner would walk away in cuffs and spend the rest of his life locked up in Rackham, and Akemi would find another boy, some handsome neko like herself, perhaps.

So be it. To be otaku was to live a manga, and the best mangas were the noirs. Hisoka shrugged again, enjoying the thrill of fatalism that shot through him, and turned his back, showing the Inspector his nunchuks as he walked away.

On Inspector West's face, there was the faintest trace of disappointment. He could pull the kid in, check if he had a permit for those things, but it would only postpone what was coming. He stood off the saddle, driving his feet down hard on the pedals to bring the ORB up to speed, and raced off into the night, leaving Hisoka to his destiny.

Hisoka never made it to the meeting. They found him the next morning, with six bullet holes in his chest. On the body, someone had left a white business card. On one side, there was a spider design, in red. On the other, a haiku:

> *Where all inhuman*
> *Devils revel in their sins—*
> *The Blood-Spider spins!*

His nunchuks were never found.

Here's another story.

Just off Broadway, the man in the tweed coat sniffed, sipping the pint of bitter he'd ordered, and grimaced. O'Malley hated that—the little grimace. Sons of bitches came all the way from Magna Britannia and the first thing they ordered when they came into O'Malley's was English bitter. And then they grimaced, because it was made in New Jersey and they hadn't got it just the way they served it in Assrapeshire or wherever the hell they came from.

Screw it. It was O'Malley's own fault for opening an English bar in the first place. The man frowned. "It's not quite the way it is back home, is it?"

His wife pursed her lips, her mouth becoming reminiscent of a dog's wrinkled asshole. "Well, they don't know any better. They're all socialists here. No education to speak of. Dreadful little country."

So what the hell are you even doing here, O'Malley didn't say. Instead, he just kept on cleaning the glasses and counting his blessings that there weren't any other New Yorkers nearby to make the kind of scene he couldn't get away with making. Tourists were his lifeblood, especially the rich limeys from across the pond who flocked in their thousands to get a first hand look at the City of Tomorrow. A few even stuck around. These two wouldn't.

One look told the story. They just didn't get it.

The man snorted, not bothering to lower his voice. "Well, obviously. Have you noticed they don't have any flags here?"

"We've got a flag. We don't use it much." O'Malley scowled despite himself. It'd been a sore point since 1954.

"Well, there you are. And they go on and on about all the culture here, and then you go to the gallery and it's all just nonsense, just a lot of silly colours and shapes. My five-year-old nephew could do better. And the music…" He turned to O'Malley, as if he was responsible for everything he'd seen and heard. "I've never heard anything like it in my life! The *noise!* There was one fellow playing some sort of—well, I'm not sure what—"

"Guitar," muttered O'Malley.

The man flushed; his wife tutted and sniffed, her mouth shrinking even tighter. "He wasn't even wearing a suit. When I go to a concert back home, we expect the performers to be dressed properly and to play proper instruments. And proper music. Not three-minute bursts of jingles and shouting."

O'Malley shrugged and picked up another glass. "Who was it?"

The man in the tweed shook his head angrily; his wife's mouth had almost disappeared. "Oh, I don't know. They were singing something about 'taking Berlin.' Probably your socialist friends. Well, that sort of propaganda doesn't wash with me. As far as I'm concerned, I'd rather have a thousand like Herr Hitler than one Bolshevik like Bartlet or Rickard. If you ask me, a strong leader like that is what this country needs."

O'Malley scowled. Typical Brits—half of them probably mailed cheques to Untergang from their cosy little armchairs back home. "Yeah, well, he's not exactly a good friend of ours, so you might want to watch that kind of talk while you're here."

The man drew himself up to his full height—roughly a foot and a half shorter than O'Malley. "And you should watch your tone, sir. I'm a guest in your country, and a customer, and the customer is always right."

O'Malley breathed in, then out. *Don't get mad at the customers.* All it took was one bad report spreading through Assrapeshire and he could end up losing a hundred customers. Keep the Brits happy, that was the rule. That was the price for running an English bar.

He could've taken his brother's advice and started a futurehead club, but no, he wanted to serve a 'better class of person.' What a schmuck.

"Sorry, sir," he muttered, concentrating on cleaning the pint glasses.

There was a long silence. The Brits didn't say anything else for a while, and O'Malley was glad of that.

After about a minute of strained silence, the bell over the door rang and a skinny guy with long, dirty blonde hair and a ratty beard walked in, sniffing the air like a dog. He looked as though he hadn't bathed in weeks. The Brits shrank back, looking daggers. The long-haired man just smiled, good-natured.

"Hey, Larson." O'Malley smiled.

"Uh, hey, O'Malley." Larson grinned, nervous, fumbling in his pocket. "Listen, can I borrow your phone?"

O'Malley nodded. "Just remember to pay for the call. How's the fight against the Man? The cops still hassling you?" He took a perverse pleasure in needling Larson about his police phobia, especially with those damned supercilious Brits hanging on every word he said. Larson couldn't have come in at a better time.

The man with the dirty blonde hair laid twenty bucks down on the counter. Larson was notorious for being broke—chasing the dragon would do that to you. This was more money than O'Malley had ever seen him with. "Damn, Larson, what have you been getting into?"

Larson chuckled nervously. "Oh, uh, this and that." He wandered back behind the bar, heading into the back room, and O'Malley found himself surreptitiously listening in, trying to hear what was said over the loud tuts of the British heifer and her grim husband.

"Disgusting," the British guy kept saying, over and over. "Disgusting country. Disgusting people."

O'Malley ignored him.

"Uh, never mind how I found you," Larson whispered into the phone. "I've got something you want…"

Jesus, he'd better not be dealing drugs on my phone, O'Malley thought. Twenty bucks wasn't worth that.

"Who was that *awful man?*" the woman hissed, her eyes wide with indignation.

"College professor," O'Malley murmured, still trying to keep an ear on Larson. He didn't even seem to be speaking English any more. What was that, Spanish?

The British man took another sip of his bitter, shaking his head. "I suppose that's the sort of person who enjoys your American 'concerts.' It's disgusting. Disgusting. They didn't even play your national anthem at the end. Shocking behaviour."

O'Malley frowned, turning his attention back to the tourists. "Yeah, we don't use that much either. Mind if we drop the subject?"

The man sniffed, as if something smelled bad. "Not very patriotic, are you? Not proud of your flag, not proud of your anthem. If some chap was like that back home, we'd say he was rather un-British, what? I suppose that would make you un-American or something!"

The glass in O'Malley's hand cracked.

His knuckles were white, and so was his face. He was sixty-three years old, old enough to remember the last time he'd heard that word, the word nobody ever said anymore. Old enough to remember where it had led. Old enough not to be able to hear the name McCarthy without flinching. Old enough to remember the Second Civil War, the six days of hell when you didn't know who was your neighbour and who was Hidden Empire. Six days when people you'd lived next door to for years took a knife to you, calling you a monster, a *liberal*, like it was a curse word, a fake American. An *un-American*.

And the un-Americans didn't get to live.

Sure, it was all mind control, or that's what most had told themselves so as not to tear the country apart for good when it was all over. Still, after that week, there wasn't a USA anymore. There couldn't be. So the big boys had made it official—sent the message that there'd never be another McCarthy, another Hidden Empire. This was the USSA, and that's how it was staying.

There was a sign behind the bar: *Doc Thunder drinks free.* Pretty much every bar in New York had a sign like it, and everybody knew what it meant.

Everybody except the tourists.

Rudi O'Malley—who'd seen his parents hung in front of his eyes on his sixteenth birthday, who'd seen a man's entrails torn from his belly and wrapped around a flagpole while people laughed and cheered, who'd killed twenty-eight people in the battle for the White House and dreamed of twenty-eight screaming faces every single night of his life—excused himself, dropped the broken glass into the sink, and went into the back room to bandage his hand.

Larson popped his head around the door. "Listen, O'Malley, thanks for the, uh... the... O'Malley?" He gingerly reached out a hand, as if to touch O'Malley's shoulder, then withdrew it awkwardly. "Are, uh... are you okay?"

O'Malley looked at himself in the mirror, at the fat, lazy tears running down his old, worn face. At his lousy, horrible bar and his lousy, horrible clientele and his whole lousy, horrible life.

"Yeah," he said. "Yeah, Larson, I'm fine. Go watch the bar for me, will you? I'll be out in a sec."

Rudi O'Malley was a New Yorker.

What else could he say?

HERE'S A FINAL story.

In the penthouse suite of the Atlas apartments, Heinrich Donner looked out over the city. The twinkling lights of the gas and oil lamps shone up at him like fireflies, and for a moment he remembered other fires. And chimneys that belched black smoke laced with human fat.

That had been a long time ago. He was old now, his white hair almost gone, his beard snow white, his blue eyes turned grey and clouded with the years. He leant on a stick, and rarely changed out of his dressing-gown. What was the point? He never left. Even his landlord had never seen him, or the man who brought his food—even the prostitutes who he took his frustrations at this half-a-life out on came and went blindfolded, so they couldn't see his face.

He remembered once a blindfold had slipped. He'd found the strength to bludgeon her to death, then made some calls to the people he could trust, those in Untergang who still felt he had some value to the organisation. They'd come and cleaned up the mess, and warned him that further mistakes could not be brushed under the carpet so easily. He had to chuckle at the irony. After all, wasn't he a mistake? And had he not been brushed under the carpet, installed in this palatial tomb, a battered relic kept against the day when he might have value again?

Once upon a time, Heinrich Donner was the heart and soul of Untergang. It had been his idea; a fifth column of Nazi operatives, working within American society to corrupt and disrupt from within, blurring the line between criminal activity and terrorism. After the disasters of the Russian campaign, it had been a reasonable success in terms of destabilising the country and spreading panic among the populace. And because the Führer could plausibly distance himself from Untergang—a terrorist organisation operating outside his mandate—Britannia had little to say on the matter beyond a tired shrug and a veiled warning to keep such tactics on American shores and out of the way of the Empire.

Of course, Heinrich Donner was not the 'leader' of the group. That honour fell to a man named Mannheim, codenamed 'Cobra,' whose job was to send long ranting missives to newspapers claiming full responsibility for the Untergang's actions. It served a dual purpose. Since 'Cobra' was only a man sitting behind a typewriter or a wax-cylinder recorder several miles away from any action, he could never realistically be caught—and if Mannheim was apprehended, another 'Cobra' would take his place. The public would see that those charged to defend them could not even catch one man, and panic and disquiet would spread.

And, of course, Donner's hands would remain clean and pure.

Heinrich Donner was a prominent industrialist, a noted businessman, a beloved philanthropist. All of New York had celebrated him when he'd stepped in to help rebuild the city after the horrific events of the Second Civil War. (And damn that fool McCarthy for his stupid, failed attempt. If he'd only swallowed his damned pride and worked with the Führer—but the past was the past, and there could be no going back.)

As far as America was concerned, Heinrich Donner was a saint among men. They cheered his modest speeches, filled with gentle humility, wept at his tearful account of fleeing Germany as a young husband and father to escape Hitler's tyranny, of losing his wife and child to the madman's grasp. The only one who knew the full truth was Doc Thunder, and he could prove nothing in a court of law, of course. Besides, he knew that to expose Donner's secrets would mean exposing his own. He was effectively stalemated.

It had all been going so well.

Why had he become so obsessed with Thunder? Why had he never simply given up, washed his hands of the whole situation, focused on more achievable goals? All those endless attempts to kill him, to steal his blood, to have America's great symbol brought down, brought low… it had brought attention to him, over time. The wrong kind of attention. Eventually, he was caught in an explosion and believed dead, and the Führer had quietly suggested that he should remain that way. For a few years, he had continued to run Untergang's operations, but his heart was no longer in the work, and gradually it passed to other hands, younger hands… until finally he had nothing but this apartment, a monthly allowance for food, drink and whores, and handlers who were only seeing to his needs until the kill order came through and they could dispose of him once and for all.

And the order would never come, he knew. The Führer had long since forgotten him. Untergang's latest leader had his own master plans and never gave Donner the slightest thought. He was a relic, a battered old antique, a souvenir of a bygone age. His place in the scheme of things had been taken by younger men with bigger and better ideas. The world had moved on.

He still hated Doc Thunder. That was the worst thing. That burning, black hatred would never go away, and now it was matched by a bitter, bottomless frustration. To know that you would never look into your enemy's eyes again, never watch them squirm, know the sweet taste of their fear... to know he could never *hurt* Thunder again... it was unendurable.

His lips moved, and he began to whisper.

Please, mein Gott. Please. Give me one chance. Let me hurt him once more. Let me be the catalyst that brings misery and torture down on his head, him and all his kind, all the strutting fools in their masks and their ridiculous outfits, all the ones who made me suffer, who reduced me to this shell. Let me take my final revenge on them all...

Be careful what you pray for.

The sword slid through his back, between his ribs, piercing his heart. The man standing behind him twisted the blade, and Donner shuddered, his eyes bulging, then rolling back.

El Sombra withdrew the sword from the man's corpse and wiped it on the curtains. He'd come straight here after he'd gotten the information, and by the look of things—he prodded the corpse onto its back with a bare toe, studying the features—his information had been correct. He'd half-expected the old man to go for a gun when he'd broken in, but he hadn't even heard. Probably deaf, or nearly deaf. Idly, he took a step backwards, listening to the ugly, wet sound of the bowel letting go, and then turned on his heel and wandered off to check for papers, or lists of names, or maps. Executing one of the Bastards was always fun in and of itself, but he didn't want this to become a dead end. If the Ex-King of the Bastards had fallen from grace, maybe he'd gathered some insurance on the way down. Or at least something that could be used to find more of them.

He found what he was looking for in the bedroom.

Ignored, the body on the carpet began to cool, and stiffen. Two days and eleven hours later, it would be found by patrolmen after Donner's downstairs neighbour complained about the spreading stain on his ceiling, and the stench from above. The newspapermen would hear of it, and it would become front page news—the dead man who died a second time.

And then all Hell would descend on Manhattan.

And a lot of stories would come to an end.

CHAPTER ONE
THE CASE OF THE STOLEN LIGHTNING

Night was falling, and the city was coming to life once again.

As Rabbi Johann Labinowicz shuffled into the deli, he closed his eyes for a moment and took in the sound of the bell. A small, perfect little object that tinkled softly and gently, with a clear, resonant sound whenever the door opened, Johann had found himself wandering three blocks or more out of his way simply to hear it, and as a result this particular deli had, over a span of years, become his regular haunt.

Johann was a man who took pleasure in small things. The ring of a shop's bell, the taste of a perfectly made salt beef hoagy with pickle and mustard. Having your habits and tastes known by your deli. Little things of that nature.

"One salt beef, pickle and mustard." Mrs McGregor said it like a hello, as her husband had. Bill McGregor had passed away five years ago, but Alma had taken over the running of McGregor's Fine Deli and it was as though nothing had happened. She'd mourned, a deep and terrible wound in her had healed over time, but she'd done her mourning in between chopping egg and scattering cress, frying onion for the beef dogs and fine-slicing gherkin the way her husband had taught her. Only her regulars had noticed any change at all, and no change at all in the food. Mrs McGregor was a close and private woman, who played her emotions like cards against her chest. Johann had known her twelve years, and still considered being greeted in such a way to be an honour worth more than rubies.

He'd already counted out the three dollars, fumbling in his pocket as he walked the last few steps from the door with its wonderful bell, and now he laid them out on the counter with a smile, before picking up the sandwich that had already materialised, prepared in advance of his arrival. "You know, Alma, maybe the day comes I don't walk in that door, eh? And then, you'll be out a fresh sandwich."

Alma snorted, shaking her head. "Oh, that will never happen, Rabbi. You're an addict, you are."

Johann shrugged. "What, I have no will of my own? A slave to the salt beef? Suppose I'm trampled by a runaway horse, eh?"

Alma shook her head and went back to slicing pickles. "Then I'd come to the hospital and throw the damned sandwich in your face for being such a god-damned fool as to not look both ways and you'd apologise to me for being so foolish and the sandwich wouldn't have been wasted at all, now, would it?"

Johann chuckled to himself. "Such language!" He sniffed the sandwich, enjoying the tang of the pickle and the waft of the fresh bread.

The bell rang again.

The boy who walked in was barely more than sixteen, but he was six foot and muscular with it. He slouched as he walked, and his hair was carefully shaved into three stripes—blood red, bone white and a livid blue that seemed garish and clown like against his black skin. He was wearing a powder-blue T-shirt with the familiar lightning bolt decal torn off and pinned back upside-down, with the same safety-pins that pierced both his ears. His jeans were ripped, and around each wrist was a studded leather band.

On his left bicep, he wore a tattoo of a scowling McCarthy and the words *AMERICAN.*

A futurehead.

Johann stiffened, inspecting him carefully. Futureheads could be trouble, and this one was dressed to provoke. Still, usually with futureheads that was all it was—provoking a reaction. Shocking the old men. They were harmless. Oh, they'd turn the air blue if you crossed them, call you everything under the sun, but that was all they'd do.

Johann allowed himself to drift into a daydream of the moments ahead. The young man would at the very worst say something he imagined to be shocking to the ears of an old Rabbi—little dreaming that an old Rabbi could already tell him stories that would make him faint—and the old Rabbi in question would play his part and tut and speak of *kids today* or *it's just noise they listen to now* and the dance would be complete. The two of them would go their separate ways, each having played a different game and each, in their own eyes, the winner.

And in maybe five years, no more, Johann would see the boy grown to a man, dressed in ordinary clothes, and the boy would raise his hat respectfully and both would have forgotten this meeting had ever taken place, lost as it was in wild youth.

It was a story Johann had played out countless times with countless disaffected young people, and it was a story he almost enjoyed. It was the story he would have preferred.

"Gimme a sammich," the young man growled, and spat on the floor. Johann winced. Alma wouldn't take that well. Part of him felt he should leave, but he owed it to Alma to provide support in the face of what was sure to be an unpleasant customer interaction.

Alma took the bait, as Johann knew she would. "May I have a sandwich *please,* you young hooligan! And no you may not after you spat on my clean floor! Were you raised in a barn?"

The futurehead scowled. "I want a sammich."

"Well, you're not getting one. Now clear off out of my shop before I throw you out! And don't think I can't!" Alma heaved and shook with indignation, her face beet red. In that moment, Johann believed that she really could have thrown the young man bodily out of her door, as big and surly as he was.

The young man blinked, the scowl still on his face. Then—without a word— he simply reached, took the sandwich from Johann's grasp, and bit into it.

"S'a good sammich." He grinned, chewing.

Johann simply stared.

"You get out now! You get out of my shop!" screeched Alma, purple with fury. The futurehead smirked through a mouthful of the Rabbi's bread and beef, and moved to the door. He'd won the battle. He'd walked in and taken what he wanted, and now he would leave.

"Wait," said Johann, softly.

The young man turned, looked at him, and bit into the sandwich again.

"You can have my sandwich."

The young man narrowed his eyes.

"No, you can have it. You can come in here and cause trouble and spit on a clean floor, if that's what you enjoy. You can steal from an old man, take what you haven't earned. You can do what you like." Johann felt the blood rushing to his cheeks and heard the anger in his own voice. "You can! You can dress like you're in the Hidden Empire, like good people never fought and bled and died to make you safe from them! You can do all of that, because you're taller than we are. It's just a matter of height. You're taller than we are, and stronger than we are, and you look more threatening than we do! And in your world that is the only thing that matters! That, I understand! That is the path you have chosen for yourself—good luck to you! Mazel tov!"

He paused, gathering his fury, his fists clenched. Then he reached out and grabbed a hold of the upside-down lightning bolt, the safety pins popping away as he pulled and the ragged patch of blue cloth came away in his hands. "But you will not disgrace *this* while you do it!"

The boy blinked, shock written over his face. Johann's fist shook. "Now get out. Get out of here."

The futurehead threw Johann's sandwich onto the floor, spat, and left, the door slamming violently behind him.

The bell rang furiously for a second, then came to a stop.

"Oy…" Johann breathed. He felt drained. He hadn't meant to lose his temper that way.

"Give me that." Alma smiled, taking the square of cloth from his hands, then pinning it up behind the counter. "It'll make a good conversation piece. You want me to call the cops?"

Johann shook his head. "No… no, I just lost my temper with him." He let out a sigh, feeling his heart hammering in his chest. "I'm too old for such nonsense. For a three-dollar sandwich! And what have I achieved? For you, a conversation piece and a dirty floor. For me, almost a heart attack, maybe worse if that schmuck had taken a swing at me… ah, let me help you clean this up."

Alma smiled. "I won't hear of such a thing, Rabbi. You sit yourself down and catch your breath and I'll make you up a fresh one."

"No, no…" Johann sighed. "I couldn't eat it now. I'll head back to my apartment and take some soup when my stomach is settled."

"Then take your three dollars back, at least."

"Three extra dollars would throw my whole budget off. I'd become extravagant. You keep it, or give it away to a hungry orphan." He shuffled towards the door, swinging it open and listening to the sound. "Wait, wait—

promise me one thing, Alma, if you think you owe me something for acting like an old fool."

Alma raised an eyebrow.

"Don't ever change that bell."

FOUR BLOCKS LATER, Johann found himself chuckling over the incident. The look on the young man's face! He'd think twice in the future, perhaps, about bullying old men. And perhaps he wouldn't. Still, it was nice to dream.

Johann's eyes flicked up to the solitary gas lamp that lit the dark alley, his little shortcut home. Someone had cut little stars and moons from coloured paper and stuck them on the glass, so that they threw great coloured shapes onto the ground below. The effect was quite charming. A square of cardboard propped against the wall told the rest of the story. Breakers had, sometime the night before, made the alley an impromptu dancehall, at least until the residents had run them off.

Breakers and bikers, futureheads and Warhol-girls. And that lightning bolt on blue cloth watching over them all. Manhattan was a strange place, and yet occasionally it threw up little wonders, pink stars cast in light on the concrete floor of an alleyway. A small thing, but representative of all the strangeness and charm of this unique place, this City of Tomorrow...

Johann took pleasure in small things.

At that moment, he became aware of footsteps behind him. A cold chill seized his chest, and he swallowed hard, that terrible certainty of who those footsteps might belong to racing through his mind. *No, surely not,* he told himself. *I'm an old man.*

There was a low, mean chuckle from behind. He steeled himself. He would look around, and he'd see a group of young men, and he'd recognise none of them. And they'd walk right by him, never thinking to bother an old Rabbi. It was a story he'd played out a dozen times in this alley. A good story.

So Johann turned his head, and found himself looking at three stripes of hair coloured red, white and blue, and a T-shirt with a square torn out of the front and a couple of safety pins hanging from that ragged edge, and a pair of eyes with hate and humiliation in them.

It was the boy from earlier. And not alone. Two others, the same age, walked either side of him, one black, one white, both of them in the same mish-mash of ragged clothes held together by safety pins and charged symbols. The other young black man's face was a mass of steel piercings and studs that made the handsome features alien and ugly.

The white boy wore a swastika.

It was beginning to rain.

Johann sped up, walking faster, as the spattering raindrops hit his cheeks like tears, trickling down. Behind him, the footsteps sped up to match. The rain intensified, suddenly coming down in sheets, the filthy alley lit bright white for a split-second before a crash of thunder formally announced the storm. *Why didn't I bring my umbrella?* Johann thought, madly, and then he found himself running, feet splashing in the growing puddles.

He ran, and they ran after him. It was a race now. At the end of the long, dark alley, he could see trotting horses, smell hotdogs, see bright lights, a finish line. If he could just get to the lights, he might be safe—

And then he tripped.

He landed face-down on the wet, dirty floor of the alley, knocking the wind from his lungs. He lay there a moment in the wet and the dirt, coughing weakly, and then a heavy boot pressed down on his back, pinning him.

He heard the quiet *click* of a switchblade springing from its casing.

Then another. Then a third.

"Gimme my bolt back, old man." The voice was flat, emotionless, as it had been in the Deli. Another voice beside snickered softly, barely audible over the sound of the rain coming down.

"Yeah," said the new voice. "Old man. Give him it before we cut you."

Johann tried to croak out a response—something, anything—and then the boot on his back stamped down harder. Why were they doing this? He was an old man—but then, that was the reason, of course. He was an old man who had humiliated a younger one. With a sudden cold clarity, he understood that they would kill him. They would murder him in this filthy alley and then the three of them would go back to the deli, and see what they were looking for, what Alma had tacked to the wall, and they would want it back, and Alma would stand up for herself and they would kill her too. If they had to, they would kill her quickly, but if they could get away with it, they would kill her slowly. Because they could, and that was all the justification they needed.

But they would kill him slowly first.

The boot pressed down on his back. He tried to say a prayer, but he had no breath to say it. At the end of the alley, he could see the lights, and the horses, and the people passing by, rain dripping off their umbrellas.

Not one of them looked at him.

"Gimme my bolt," the futurehead growled, in his dead, emotionless monotone.

Johann could not speak. His lips moved, but no sound came.

There was only the sound of the rain.

And then the sound of a bullet.

A bloody rose bloomed at the back of the young man's head, opposite the hole that had suddenly appeared just below the white strip of hair. His eyes bulged, lost focus, and then he toppled backwards, dead.

Johann flinched, feeling the weight of the boy's boot come off his back, then heard the splash of the heavy corpse hitting the puddles of the grimy alley floor.

For a moment, there was no sound at all, bar a kind of high-pitched squeak, an animal whimper that crawled out of the throat of the boy with the swastika shirt, as if he was some small burrowing thing caught in a wire trap.

Then there was laughter.

A terrible, echoing laugh, of a kind one might find in the pits of Hell, a laugh that bounced and rolled off the brick and steel and seemed to echo from every corner at once, booming, roaring, growing louder and louder. Johann felt ice in his chest, and once more his wrinkled lips began to stumble through the Kaddish, eyes shutting tight, as if warding off imaginary monsters in the way he had as a child.

When he opened them again, the monster stood in front of him.

He was close to six foot in height, and the long coat of black leather he wore gave him the appearance of being half shadow, a silhouette picked out against the gaslight of the street beyond. Johann blinked the raindrops from his eyes— or were they tears?—and tried to make out further detail, but there was none, only a sea of black, a black hole in space in the shape of a man. Black suit and shirt, black gloves with an odd texture to them, holding a pair of automatic pistols. And a black slouch hat that covered his face—

—oh God, his face!

Johann gasped, and behind him the boy in the swastika made another strangled cry, as though the wire around the struggling animal had tightened.

His face! That terrible mask!

As the monster tilted his head to stare at his persecutors, Johann could see the whole of it. A head of black leather, with a mask of shining metal, and that metal mask coloured a burnished bloody red, featureless but for the eight lenses that shone in the half-light like the eyes of some terrible spider, hiding all evidence of humanity. The effect was terrifying, an emotionless blank visage that spoke of remorseless, unstoppable vengeance for unimaginable crimes. Behind him, Johann heard the boy in the swastika shirt scream.

"What are you? You ain't human!"

The man in the blood-red mask hissed, like escaping steam, and then the hiss turned into a laugh, that devil's laugh, mocking, sneering, rolling across the wet stone.

Then he raised his twin pistols.

The boy with the piercings—the one who'd remained silent up until now—let out a yell and hurled himself towards the figure in black, switchblade gleaming. In response, there was the roar of automatic fire as shot after shot slammed into his bare chest and burst from his back in fountains of blood and bone. His face twisted in an agonised rictus as he took two more steps forward, propelled by the momentum of his charge, and then dropped to the alley floor, a foot from the Rabbi's trembling, prone form.

Johann felt the warmth as the young man's blood pooled against him.

The boy in the swastika shirt took a stumbling step backward, his face deathly pale and slick with sweat. His own blade slid from his grasp to clatter on the ground at his feet, and his hands slowly jerked upwards, as if on puppet strings. "Please," he croaked, tears streaming down his face. "Please. Please."

The man in the mask stopped laughing.

He stepped over Johann's shaking body, walking towards the boy, gazing down on him with those eight expressionless glass eyes. Again, there was a hiss, like steam escaping from some dreadful engine of death.

Then he spoke.

"*You... surrender.*"

The boy blinked, slowly shaking his head. The crotch of the ripped denim jeans he wore darkened as a stream of piss trickled down his leg to mix with the rainwater and the blood.

Gently, the man in the mask pressed the barrel of one of his twin automatics into the centre of the Nazi emblem on the boy's chest.

"*For show?*"

The boy let out another whimper, eyes wide and wet. He tried to find any sign of mercy in that cold, red metal mask, any humanity shining back at him from those eight monstrous lenses.

He saw nothing at all.

The masked man hissed again, softly.

"You should start mixing with a better class of people."

Then he turned his back. The boy stood for a moment, face white, hands still raised, swaying gently in the air like balloons on strings. Then the spell was broken, and he ran back the way he came, sobbing like a child.

The man in the mask bent down and began to help Johann to his feet. The Rabbi flinched at his touch, surprised by the gentleness of it. He swallowed, and spoke softly: "Thank you. I think they would have killed me."

He stood, the adrenaline making him quiver, unsteady on his feet. His clothes were sticky with blood. He looked down at the two dead young men—boys, children—and then up at the blank mask. "Please. I am grateful, you saved my life, but..." He swallowed. "Was there no other way?"

There was a chuckle from behind the mask, dry as kindling.

"Not for them."

Johann swallowed, and nodded, feeling like a coward. He wanted to go home and wash the blood from himself, to be far away from this terrible creature that had saved his life. He wanted to be sick, to sleep for a hundred years, to feel something besides the cold weight of horror coiling in his gut.

"Well. Thank you again," he said, quietly, and turned away. He wondered whether he should call the police.

The man in the mask laid a hand on his shoulder.

"A moment."

Johann's blood froze.

The man's grip on his shoulder was soft, almost gentle. *"Did you think you could escape me, Rabbi Labinowicz?"*

"What? What are you talking about?" Johann swallowed, feeling a cold trickle of sweat at the base of his neck. Helplessly, he tried to jerk away from the hand, but the grip on his shoulder was suddenly like a steel vice.

The other hand still held a squat, smoking automatic pistol.

"Did you think I came here by accident? That I don't know every detail about you?" The laughter came again, and the eight blank lenses reflected the terrified, sweating face of the Rabbi back at him. *"You take a special interest in the children of the neighbourhood, don't you, Johann?"*

Johann licked dry lips. "What of it? The schooling here—they need to learn! I teach them!" His voice sounded hollow in his ears, like a murderer pleading for clemency. *Oh God, how had it come to this?* "Mathematics, and sciences…"

The masked man hissed slowly, dangerously, like a snake about to strike. The blank, emotionless lenses seemed to bore into Johann's soul, uncovering his every secret.

"*I know exactly what you teach them.*" The voice was cold, mocking, deadly. "*You take pleasure in small things, don't you, Rabbi Labinowicz?*"

Johann cried out as if he'd been struck, trying to struggle free again. "Please," he begged, his voice hoarse, "whatever I've… whatever you *think* I've done, please. You don't have to do this. I'll do what you want, I'll, I'll go to the police—"

The man in the mask laughed again, a low, throaty cackle, redolent of cobwebs and deep graves. He raised his pistol to Johann's face. "*I have a surer way of dealing with your kind. Open your mouth, Rabbi. I have another small thing for you, but this time I doubt you will take much pleasure in it at all.*"

"Please—" begged Johann, but he got no further. The bullet entered his mouth and blew the back of his head out across the brickwork. He slumped to the floor and the man in the mask put another into his head for good measure.

In the street beyond, the men and women still walked to and fro. They paid no heed to the sound of gunfire, nor did they notice the trickle of blood running from the alley across the sidewalk and into the gutter. They knew better.

In the alley, Johann's corpse, and the others, began to stiffen, the pouring rain pooling in the bullet-wounds and the sockets of their eyes. Sitting atop each of them was a small white business card with a red spider motif on the back, and a short haiku on the front:

> *Where all inhuman*
> *Devils revel in their sins—*
> *The Blood-Spider spins!*

Of the Blood-Spider himself, there was no sign.

CHAPTER TWO
DOC THUNDER AND
THE QUEEN OF THE LEOPARD MEN

AS A RULE, Maya Zor-Tura woke late.

Each morning, she floated slowly to awareness like a bubble of air rising up from some bottomless ocean trench, the half-remembered fancies of her dream breaking apart and dissipating into the morning sun as it poured through the skylight and splashed onto the silk sheets. Her eyes fluttered open, blinking away the last crumbs of sleep, and she stretched like a cat, arching her back and opening her mouth into a wide, luxurious yawn. And straight after that, on most mornings, she went back to a light doze, finally deigning to grace the household with her presence at eleven, or noon, or perhaps a little after lunch.

At the appointed hour, she'd appear in a gown of translucent yellow silk, or a sharply-cut suit, or her 'adventuring clothes'—black leather corset, boots and coat, with a royal purple skirt in a ragged style on the cutting edge of current fashion—or, quite often, nothing at all. On Maya, nudity seemed as elegant and refined as the evening clothes of British royalty.

She was tall, with flowing dark hair, skin the colour of rich, dark coffee and cat-like green eyes that seemed to constantly radiate a kind of amused superiority, and none of these traits had faded in several thousand years of existence.

For Maya Zor-Tura, time was something that happened to other people.

This morning, she paused in mid-stretch and for just the smallest moment she tried to recall exactly what the dream had been about. Dreams were important, despite Doc's occasional and somewhat half-hearted insistence that they were only a natural function of the brain. He'd learned a more unscientific and unpalatable truth in their time together—that dreams, and especially Maya Zor-Tura's, contained messages. Soundings from the past, and the future, and places beyond human understanding, often all at once. Warnings that should not be ignored.

And this dream seemed especially potent and vivid.

A dream of murder.

Murder, and a man in a mask the colour of blood.

She shook her head, brow furrowed. Did the mask cover his whole face, or just his eyes? She frowned, marring her beauty with her frustration for a single instant. Trying to catch a dream and remember it was like trying to hold smoke in your hands. This one was gone.

She dismissed the remnants of it from her mind for the moment and stretched idly, enjoying the emptiness of the bed. There was something rather decadent about having it all to herself, lounging in that vast, warm space, with the scents of the linen and the bodies that had lain there mixing as she breathed in. It made her almost feel like a goddess again. Maya wondered occasionally about going back to that life, to the forbidden kingdom of Zor-Ek-Narr and the half-human, half-leopard men who'd been her concubines and worshippers. It had been luxurious in a way that the townhouse in New York could never be, even on a morning like this. But it had been so very dull, at the end.

That's why she'd gone with the Doc, when he'd come bursting into her serene existence. The excitement, and the thought of a new world to explore.

She purred, remembering the first thing he'd ever said to her. He'd been chained to the wall of the Temple of Serpents, and she had just drawn the tip of a red-hot iron across his bare chest—the scar had long vanished, as scars did with him, but occasionally she traced her finger along where it had been. She remembered that she'd paused, admiring the way he endured without flinching, and then he'd looked at her with those icy blue eyes.

"I never knew evil could be so beautiful," he'd said.

That was the English translation, of course. It wasn't quite so impressive unless you knew that in the secret tongue of the Leopard Men of Zor-Ek-Narr a particular synonym for 'evil' and the most common word for 'beautiful' sounded almost exactly alike, depending on how you rolled your tongue around the 'R.'

So in that one single moment, he'd shown how little pain or fear meant to him; he'd paid her a compliment, albeit a backhanded one; and, most importantly, he'd made a pun in a language he'd first heard spoken perhaps forty hours previously.

After that, Maya had to admit, she'd been intrigued. She'd allowed him to escape, had him recaptured and ordered him to fight in her personal arena against a cadre of Jaguar Warriors armed with poisoned spears, and all the time the flirting had continued. Once he'd saved her from the giant roc her treacherous high priest had attempted to feed her to, they'd both known exactly where things were leading.

It wasn't forever. He'd age, over the centuries, and she wouldn't. Eventually, he'd die, or she'd simply grow tired of him and walk away, and she knew herself well enough to realise that it was going to be the latter. Lately, she'd found herself thinking more and more about home, feeling an ache that was partly homesickness and partly a feeling of being stifled, of playing a role instead of living a life.

But for now, she was here and it was now and it was more exciting to spend her limitless time this way, in this wonderful city, in this wonderful life of science and adventure and danger, than any other way she could think of. Perhaps in a hundred days or a hundred years she'd think differently, and return to the forgotten temples and palaces of Zor-Ek-Narr to reclaim her queendom and become once again embroiled in the endless intrigues of her people. Or perhaps she wouldn't.

Right now, she decided, it was time to get up and have Marcel prepare her a strong coffee and a croissant. Opening the spacious walk-in closet, she combed through her wardrobe, settling on a simple light blue kimono, and then padded down the stairs to greet the rest of the household.

PASSING THE GYM on the second floor, she heard the soft creak of the chain supporting the heavy bag as it swung. If Monk was doing his morning workout, that made it a little after ten—earlier than she was used to. It was the dream that had woken her so early, the killer in the red mask. In the dream, was he standing over a body?

Yes. Someone she cared for, dead or about to be.

Worth noting.

She swung open the door to the gym and looked upwards. As usual, Monk was hanging by his toes from the ceiling rings, aiming fists big as hams into the big leather punch bag, his grotesque, simian face twisted in familiar effort.

Monk Olsen could best be described as a curiosity.

At the age of six months, he had been found on the doorstep of the Clark Olsen Orphanage in New Jersey, where presumably his parents had been unable to bear the thought of caring for such a monstrous child. Even at that tender age, his face bore the simian cast that would mark him for the rest of his life, while his arms were elongated, with a light coating of fur and already some muscular development, and his toes were large and long, bending and clutching instinctively at the end of his too-big feet. A doctor, called to minister to the baby, suggested that he be put down on the spot; Clark Olsen politely showed him the door.

Clark named him Eustace, after an uncle, but the child never did take to that, choosing instead to repurpose the cruel nickname the other boys taunted him with—Monk.

"If folks shout a word at you in the street, that's an insult. If they shout your name, it's like they're cheerin'. That's the way I figure it, anyhow."

He was five years old when he came up with that little bit of homespun wisdom, but Monk was far ahead of the curve as far as intelligence went. He had a keen eye and an analytical mind to go with his ape-like strength and gait, and on leaving the orphanage found himself a job as a photojournalist with a great metropolitan newspaper, where he showed a penchant for investigating the unusual. The paper touted him as the Gorilla Reporter, a nickname he accepted with a graceful shrug of his sloped shoulders.

Monk found himself used by the paper as a sort of in-house freak, a news story in his own right, and he allowed the editors to exploit him in that manner purely because it gave him access to the strangest, most bizarre stories in the city—impossible crimes, unbelievable inventions, crazed geniuses and the occasional dash of sexual oddity to add spice to the broth. With such a mandate it was only a matter of time before his path crossed with Doc Thunder's, and the outwardly unlikely friendship between the City of Tomorrow's greatest hero and its ugliest citizen continued to fill untold column inches until Monk finally got bored of the daily grind and went freelance, mailing in the occasional story as Doc's assistant and sidekick.

Together, Maya and Monk were Doc's most trusted associates; 'the beauty and the beast,' according to the papers. Rumour had it that the three of them formed a polyamorous triangle. Like all the best gossip, it was both difficult to believe and completely true.

"Hey, Princess!" grinned Monk, waving to Maya from his high perch, before swinging off the rings and somersaulting down to the floor, landing on the pads of his feet. "What happened, did the bed burn down? When have you ever been up so early?"

Maya laughed, kissing him and enjoying the feel of those strong simian arms thrown about her slim waist. "I think around 1647, by the Roman calendar. What can I say? It's a beautiful day and for some reason I didn't feel like wasting it." She kept the dream to herself, for the moment. She had hardly any clear details beyond that blood-red mask and the smell of death, and it didn't seem worth troubling Monk with it—not until she had some clear sign of what it meant. "Have you seen the Doc?"

"Doc?" Monk nodded, scratching his chin. "Down in the lab, last I saw. Looking over some forensic work. You remember Easton West over in Japantown?" Without pausing, Monk did a standing jump, leaping up in a backflip and stretching his thick legs so the long toes could grasp the ring, all with as much forethought as another man would spend in stepping onto a kerb. "He sent some paperwork and a little physical evidence over this morning from some vigilante killing—that spider guy, the one Doc doesn't like much…" Monk let the sentence trail off as he aimed a combination of punches at the heavy bag. Visitors to the brownstone often wondered why Monk Olsen might need a gym at all. He could break a man's skull like another man could crack open a fortune cookie, and there'd been times when he'd done exactly that. When asked about this, he would gently change the subject, not letting these curious souls know that the reason for his continuous training wasn't to practice throwing punches, but rather pulling them.

"I might be a monster," he'd say, "but I'm not a murderer. Not by choice."

The rain of blows landed on the bag with soft, agreeable thuds, sending it swinging back and forth on the sturdy chain but not bursting it asunder as he once had. These blows might break a man's neck, or flatten his nose, or crack his jaw down the middle. But they wouldn't kill. That was the important thing.

"I'll see you later," Maya called, and then left him to his work.

"Oh, and check *The Bugle*. I've not read it yet, but there's a howler of a headline on the front page," yelled Monk, and then unleashed another volley of restrained punches against the leather.

WHEN MARCEL BENOIT looked in the mirror, the Devil looked back.

The Devil used to smile, or laugh, or wink, but these days he assumed a contrite expression, looking over the top of his glasses as if to say—*mea culpa. It seemed like a fun idea at the time, but let's face it, it's starting to get a little tired.*

The Devil, according to Marcel, was a man of certain iron habits. He liked games of chance and chess, he liked a good trade and a better haggle and he liked to tell an incomplete truth, which is easier than a lie and a good deal more fun. He was easily reached, if you knew your way around a chalk circle, and always willing to let a fool bargain something precious away for a trinket he thought he wanted. Marcel was one such fool.

His tragedy had been a simple one. He would never be anything in the kitchen, not even a dishwasher. He could not use a knife without slicing open a finger or thumb, his palette could not distinguish a jalapeno pepper from a clump of mud, and his nose, constantly thick with cold, dripped regularly into any pan or open container he happened to lean over. He was mal carne, bad meat. And yet he wanted nothing more, in this life or any other, than to be one of the great chefs.

Of course, he could not sell his soul. What is a great chef without his soul? Instead, he sold his reflection.

Nobody else could see it. Just him. But slowly, his deteriorating appearance, his lack of grooming and his hissed arguments with mirrors made him persona non grata in the restaurants of Paris. He was indeed a great chef, one of the greatest in the world. But when your best chef starts to have a blazing row with his own meat cleaver, he has to go, no matter how good the terrine is.

Marcel drifted, passing through the great culinary meccas of the world as he went, landing work as a line cook, or a pastry-chef, or a saucier, or any one of a hundred jobs far beneath his true talent. The cycle was always the same—he would come into a new kitchen and dazzle his fellow workers and the customers with his incredible culinary skills, and the bosses would look on him with favour. They would sample his fresh-baked bread or his reductions and state that they were never letting him go, that they would be fools to dismiss this wonderful man as so many others had. And then, one day, the

Devil would say just the right thing from a mirror or a shiny piece of cookware or the back of a spoon, and Marcel would snap and rage against him at the top of his lungs, and it would all come out.

Who wants to employ an obvious madman in a place with knives? Marcel had to go.

Over time, his hair turned white, and the word spread, and even the smallest doors were closed to him. He ended up sprawled under a sheet of flat cardboard in a filthy alley, drinking bathtub gin and bursting into tears whenever the rain left enough of a puddle to see the Devil's face.

That was where Doc Thunder found him.

The circumstances were complicated.

Lars Lomax, the most dangerous man in the world, had attempted to use him as a guinea pig, understanding that he would not be missed. In the aftermath of the whole affair, as the emergency crews attempted to clear away the wreckage of Lomax's gigantic steam-powered Robo-Thunder, Doc had turned to him, laid one large hand on his shoulder, and asked what he could do to help.

"Let me cook for you," said Marcel. And Doc Thunder did. It was the best meal he had ever tasted.

Marcel had told Doc his story, and—rather than laughing or shaking his head in disgust or simply making a quiet call to the local sanatorium—Doc had done what he could. He'd had a new kitchen built, without reflective surfaces, and stocked it with cookware that would, likewise, not reflect, much of which he designed himself. And Marcel cooked, at first for the Doc, and then as time went by for Monk and Maya as well, and slowly he began to mend.

Occasionally, he would still catch sight of the Devil in a shop window or a puddle, and the Devil would only shrug. What was there to say? He had other games, and Marcel just wasn't that much fun anymore.

Maya had met the Devil herself, of course. You didn't get as old as she had without running into him sooner or later. She'd found him rather boring, and made her excuses. They'd not met since.

As she entered the kitchen, she breathed in the smell, as she did every morning; the powerful, sweet scent of the bacon fat, the subtle spice of cinnamon, the warm comforting aroma of the fresh bread, and under it all, as always, the dark, rich tint of her favourite coffee, waiting in a cup for her. "How do you always predict just when I'll want my coffee, Marcel?"

The Frenchman blushed and looked at his shoes. "I paid quite a price for the ability, Mademoiselle. But your smile is worth it all." He reached for the tray which he'd left on the side of the counter—a sumptuous Italian espresso, a perfectly cooked croissant and the morning paper. Even the paper was folded just so.

Maya cast her eye quickly over the paper, and frowned slightly. There was the headline Monk had spoken of: DEAD MAN FOUND MURDERED IN PENTHOUSE.

She could see Monk's point. It was a clumsy headline. If the man had been murdered, to say he was dead was a tautology. Still, something made her look more closely.

Heinrich Donner, the wealthy industrialist and German expatriate, had been found in a penthouse apartment across town, stabbed through the heart. The police believed a sword had been used. The title was referring to the fact that Donner had been missing for decades and was believed dead.

Maya frowned. A sword... had the masked man in her dream carried a sword? Or a gun?

She smiled sweetly at Marcel, finished her coffee and croissant, and then took the paper downstairs to the lab. Doc would want to know.

THE MAN IN the lab coat stood six foot seven, and his body seemed to be carved from bronze, a massive sculpture of hard muscle and sinew.

If he put his mind to it, the man could use that muscle to bend steel three inches thick, or jump an eighth of a mile. The bronze skin looked as tough as leather, and if put to the test it could shrug off bullets and leave only small bruises to mark their passing. An exploding shell might penetrate his skin, if applied directly, but it would not do much more than that.

The man needed to sleep no more than one hour out of every forty-eight, and during emergencies he had been known to stay awake a full week or more. He was more than seventy years old, but he barely looked half that age. If you shaved off the thick beard he wore, he could be mistaken for a man in his late twenties. His blue eyes could see further than an eagle, while his ears could hear frequencies normally reserved for the bat. He had bested three of the world's grandmasters at chess—he preferred speed chess to other varieties, as he often found himself predicting the exact move his opponent would make if they were left too long to think, which ruined the element of surprise.

He also painted, on occasion.

In fact, there was very little the man could not do. Except fully understand what it was to be a normal human being.

Occasionally, that troubled him.

His name was Doc Thunder, and he was widely recognised to be America's Greatest Hero. Occasionally, that troubled him more.

He'd talked to John about it, once, late at night, after that ugly business with Professor Zeppelin and his terror gas attack on Washington DC. He'd sat in the darkness of the Oval Office, nursing a scotch that he knew couldn't do a damned thing to him, letting the words tumble out of him one by one.

"Bullets bounce off my skin. I can stop a traction engine with my hands. I can be killed, but I honestly don't know if I'm going to die, John." There'd been something close to dread in his voice, as if the gas had affected him after all. "There are people who fought just as hard as I did against the Hidden Empire, and they died doing it. They knew they'd die and they fought anyway, because it was right. There are firemen and police officers and soldiers who risk their lives every day, without any of my advantages. Because it's the right thing to do. And I wonder if I'd do the same, if I wasn't... this." He'd sighed, shaking his head. "And I wonder what'll happen if I ever make the wrong decision. What the consequences would be."

John had just laughed and poured him another whisky. "You're a symbol, Doc. It's not an easy job."

Doc had smiled, then made his excuses and got up to leave. John had given him a strong handshake on the way out, and a last piece of advice: "Keep wearing that shirt, Doc. People like the shirt."

It was the last time they'd spoken. Two months later, in November, John had gone to Dallas and N.I.G.H.T.M.A.R.E. had shot him in the head to announce themselves on the world stage. Forty years later, Doc had only just managed to put them down for good, breaking their organisation until no stone was left on another stone. Even Silken Dragon, still beautiful, still deadly, still quite mad, had died in those final moments in Milan, despite all Doc Thunder's efforts to save her and bring her, at last, to trial—although they never did find the body, as so often happened with so many of these people, and a part of Doc knew that nothing ever stayed buried.

Still, John could sleep a little sounder now.

Doc was still wearing the shirt. It peeked out from the open lab coat—a light blue t-shirt with a yellow lightning bolt pointing down and to the left.

The symbol of the Resistance against McCarthy, back in '54. It still meant something, even now. A lot of people flew it from office buildings instead of the old flag, although the stars and stripes still got wheeled out on state occasions.

John had been right. Doc's job wasn't exploring lost continents or fighting insane scientists. It was just standing up and doing the right thing, and being seen to do it. Because there were a lot of folks who didn't, and the more of those there were, the more the average Joe might start thinking he didn't have a chance, that the only way to play the game and win was to play it with no rules at all, golden or otherwise. Screw the little guy, stamp him down. Hate the different ones. Why not? They're Them and you're Us and spitting on them might make you more Us, might win you some power. Tell any lie that'll serve your purpose, print them and distribute them to the people while swearing you only speak truth. Believe what you're told without question, or shrug, because what can you do? What can anybody do? The bastards run the world, we just have to live in it. What can you do?

Keep thinking that way and soon you're looking in the paper at an article that says they're building a camp on the edge of town for all the people who are bad for the country, or bad for the company, there's no real difference anyway, and just keep looking the other way a little longer, friends, just keep nodding along, just keep shrugging, whatever, you're not in danger, you're one of Us and nobody's ever going to come for you, pal. Promise.

It couldn't happen here, is what we're saying.

Would we lie to you?

Doc knew where that road ended. He'd seen it with his own eyes.

So he wore his beliefs on his chest, and he always tried to do the right thing, and when he needed to stand up, he stood up. And because he was who he was, everybody saw it. And maybe someone took a look at him and realised that they could question what they heard, or they could step in when they saw something bad happening, or they could just try and treat people just a little better. Maybe just one person that day looked at him and thought: *I should start trying.*

That was Doc Thunder's job.

Right now, part of that job was to help the police solve a murder.

"The shooting in Japantown?"

Maya's voice. Entering the lab unusually early. Doc nodded, flashing her a brief, tight smile.

"A gang member, executed in the street. There was a Blood-Spider card left on the body. Inspector West wanted me to check if the forensics matched his pattern." He sighed. "And they do."

Maya nodded, frowning. "Shooting children." She shuddered. "Are they any closer to catching him?"

Doc shook his head. "Unfortunately, a lot of the police don't want him caught. A lot of the citizenry feels the same. They see him as being on their side—cutting through the red tape, even. You know he shot a rabbi last night?"

Maya gasped. "That's monstrous."

"They found pictures of naked children in his home. A lot of the police are saying the Blood-Spider should get a medal." He rubbed his temples. "That's the problem, Maya. The people whose job it is to arrest him don't want to arrest him. The only reason Easton wants him off the streets is because... well, you know his foster father was a vigilante?"

Maya nodded. "The Blue Ghost. You worked with him occasionally. I remember you telling me."

"He never took a life. He was shot up more times than I can remember because he refused to. The man had an almost inhuman capacity for taking punishment, but eventually he had to retire." Doc looked into the microscope, double-checking the scratches on the shell cases. "He was murdered three years ago, just before Lars Lomax died. Someone strangled him and dropped him off a pier. By the time the body was found, it had been underwater for weeks. They only identified it as Danny Coltrane with dental records. Any clues had been wiped out." Doc shook his head. "Not pretty. The Blood-Spider popped up soon after that, and, well, I think Easton feels as if he lost his father only to have him replaced by someone who defiled his father's memory." He shook his head again, sadly. "I can't really disagree with him. I don't see killing as ever being necessary."

Maya raised an eyebrow. "Even for a child molester?"

"The man deserved a day in court." He sighed, rubbing the bridge of his nose as if to stave off a headache. "You didn't get up this early to debate moral philosophy, though, did you?"

"No." Maya sighed, then looked Doc in the eye. "I had a dream. I can't remember all of it, but... I dreamt about a man in a red mask, standing over someone I loved. Ready to kill. Perhaps having killed already." She paused. "You know I wouldn't tell you if I didn't think..."

"It's coming true. Say no more." Doc frowned. "A red mask."

Maya handed over the paper. "And I think this might be involved somehow."

"Let me see that." Doc took hold of the paper, scanning the article.

Almost immediately, he went white.

"Donner. Heinrich Donner. My God." His voice shook. A bead of cold sweat trickled from his forehead down his cheek. Then he looked up at her, and his eyes burned with a cold, limitless fury.

"Get Monk in here. *Now*."

He scowled.

"I've got a job for him."

CHAPTER THREE
THE CASE OF THE MAN WHO DIED TWICE

Even in the United Socialist States of America, the old-fashioned Gentlemen's Club was still an indicator of social status among the idle rich.

There was the Union Club, the oldest but no longer the grandest; the Cornell Club; the Down Town Association, although it increasingly attracted beatniks, pop artists and generally quite the wrong sort of people; and The Leash, which allowed female as well as male applicants, although the stringent rules of membership put off many.

The Jameson Club was perhaps the most exclusive of them all. A new member, upon applying to the club, would be asked for references from no less than five senior members. Having produced these, he would be allowed one visit to one of the lesser smoking rooms, where he would be jovially, but thoroughly, interrogated by the Club President or one of the deputies to determine whether he was of the calibre required for membership. Should a prospective member meet the high standards required, there would then be a probationary period of one year, during which time the new recruit could be dismissed from the club without warning and for the smallest social infraction.

These iron laws kept the Jameson Club satisfyingly free of the riff-raff and nouveau riche who infested other, lesser, gentlemen's establishments like a plague of cockroaches. It also meant that the average member was at least forty years old, if not fifty.

Parker Crane was not the average member.

Where most members of the Jameson Club had soft, doughy faces, with great jowls and wrinkled brows, worn from the countless demands made of New York's elite, Parker Crane's face was thin and angular, with a large nose that seemed from some angles almost like the beak of a predatory bird. He was a young man, no older than thirty, and it was generally agreed in the society pages that his sharp features and severe grey eyes, as well as his air of coldness and distance, lent him a powerful charisma. Many starlets and society beauties had fallen foul of the 'Crane effect,' though he was careful not to allow his dalliances to sully the image of the Club. One must, after all, have priorities.

Crane had inherited most of his wealth from an uncle who had died— murdered by a burglar, according to the rumours—and was now a gentleman of leisure, dabbling in photography. It was one of those professions that allowed the independently wealthy to squander their time in its margins, and Crane was a noted presence in fashion-forward circles; the futurehead trend was slowly but surely giving way to pop and op-art creations informed by a return to the Warhol era. Warhol himself, in his old age, was consumed by the idea of inaugurating a new style, a basic, simple look combining jean trousers in denim with a clean T-shirt and athletic plimsolls, perhaps with a workman's shirt over the top. This, he said, was the costume people would wear in the world he saw in his head.

"Imagine, uh, a world where everything was simple, where you could just clap your hands and, uh, light would appear. That's the basis of all this. What if you could make light without effort? We have so much machinery, so much industry, and I feel like, uh, in New York we're on the point of breaking through into a different aesthetic. Machinery without machinery."

He would talk for hours about the possibilities of his mental world. Restaurants where people ate flavoured foams and used liquid gases to create astonishing desserts. A means of recording all human information and calling it up at a moment's notice, so every man could have a whole library at his fingertips. A global telephone system, so there could be calls from New York to London, from London to Paris, as easily as calling across town.

"If, uh, we had all this, if we could do all this... what would it look like? That's where all my work is headed. To try and break into this other world, this dream world, to try and replicate it and bring it here so, uh, so I can live in it."

The newspapers called it *dreampunk*.

Crane was a presence on the edges of Warhol's Factory, often featured in fashion magazines on either side of the camera, although his work was competent at best. Mostly, those in the know were intrigued less by his talent as a photographer and more by his wealth and status, and the dichotomy he represented—on the one hand, the cold, severe traditionalist, the youngest member of the Jameson Club, and on the other, the young photographer with a model on each arm and an eye for the future of fashion. The usual line taken by gossip columnists was that Parker Crane had 'a secret identity.'

They could not have been more right.

"Master Parker?"

Jonah was a tall, deferential man with an impeccably trimmed toothbrush moustache. As majordomo of the Jameson Club, he commanded an army of servants and maids whose function was to be silent and invisible until they could be of service, and then to simply appear, as if by magic, without being asked or even looked for. To speak to Crane in person, instead of sending a servant for the task, was a mark of supreme respect, and Crane took it as such. He put down the fashion spread he was reading and gave Jonah his full attention.

"Ms Lang left a message just now enquiring as to whether you would be free to join her for coffee at the Rockefeller at noon, sir." He pronounced *Rockefeller* with the slightest inflection of disapproval.

Crane nodded. Marlene Lang was a model he'd been seeing on and off for some time, in between other conquests. She was easily bored and favoured open relationships, so the arrangement suited her enough that she kept in touch. Currently, they were enjoying some time apart, but Crane was certain this meeting was about business rather than pleasure. The mention of the Rockefeller was a signal. It was a tourist spot, quite beyond the pale. The only reason Marlene would go there would be to discuss her 'hobby,' as she put it.

Crane was one of the few who knew that Marlene Lang was a member of the Spider's Web.

The Blood-Spider's network of operatives numbered around twenty people, stretching over the whole of New York and reaching into every corner of society. Few knew about the Spider's Web, and those who did spoke of it in hushed, reverential tones, mindful of the importance of secrecy in their great work. Marlene was more open about it than many, but the Blood-Spider was willing to tolerate her idiosyncrasies for the sake of her driving skills.

Her father had been a mechanic, one of the first to combine the raw power of the traction engines and the intricate steam-hydraulics that drove the robots of Europe into a new kind of motor vehicle. The automobile was a young science, but great strides were being made—enough to get the Blood-Spider interested in owning an auto and employing someone to drive it. Having learned to drive the new vehicles almost as soon as they'd been invented, Marlene was a natural choice.

"I'm his personal chauffeur," Marlene had cooed to Crane once, her blonde hair spilling onto his shoulder as they shared a post-coital Gauloises. "It's ever so thrilling. You should see how he makes me dress."

Crane had raised an eyebrow, drawing on the cigarette for a moment before passing it along. "Why on Earth would the Blood-Spider need an auto? They're so unwieldy. They still haven't found a way to fit a decent boiler and furnace into the damned things. You can't get more than five miles in one, and God help you if you're idling at a stop-signal, you'll end up stuck there forever. Autos are a passing fad. Strictly for hobbyists."

"Not this one. The Silver Ghost, I call it. Goes like a bullet—top speed of almost forty miles per hour, once it's warmed up."

Crane had snorted—"Little liar!"—grabbed hold of her wrist and yanked her to the side, spilling her over his lap, her cigarette nearly burning a hole in the silk sheets as he brought the palm of his hand down against her quivering derrière. Afterwards, she'd wiggled coquettishly on his lap, smiling a secret little smile of her own. A smile with a hint of the devil in it.

She was wearing the same smile now as she waited, sipping her espresso, surrounded by the tourists excitedly discussing their visit to the viewing deck. Nobody would be listening to them. She could speak freely.

She pushed a large cappuccino at him as he sat down, which he ignored. "You know my coffee by now, surely?"

"They don't sell it here. I wouldn't even call mine an espresso, frankly." She smirked, enjoying his stiffness in this setting. She was dressed impeccably; a black and white op-art top that hurt the eyes if you looked too long, with a jet black pencil skirt and stilettos to match. Such an outfit should have stuck out like a sore thumb here, among these awful people, but somehow she managed to blend in.

"I have a message for our mutual friend," she breathed, letting the words hang deliciously on her tongue. Crane frowned. She was entirely too much in love with her role, but he was prepared to tolerate it.

"By which you mean the Blood-Spider. Why not tell him directly?"

She pouted. "You know I can't, darling. He contacts me, not the other way around. The only way I know to contact him is through you. The human mail drop." She smirked, taking another sip of the not-quite-espresso. "Do you think he's trying to keep our relationship alive?"

"Such as it is. Still sleeping with that artist?"

She smiled. "He bored me. Détourned symbols are so very yesterday. How do you take something seriously when every scruffy teenager can do it? Let him play with his futurehead friends." She finished her coffee, looking through lowered lashes at the lumpen proletariats milling around their table. "No, the most fabulous thing to do now is believe in something utterly and completely, without restraint."

"Like Warhol? He's going senile." Crane's lip curled, approaching a sneer. He had little time for dreampunk.

"Like the war on crime, darling." Her green eyes flashed dangerously as her smirk widened.

Crane nodded. He was bored of this game. "Give me the message. I'll see that it gets to him."

"If he reads the paper, he has it already. That industrialist everyone thought was dead—Heinrich Donner. He's turned up again."

"Donner's alive?" Crane's eyes narrowed. Why hadn't he heard about this?

"Not quite. Stabbed through the heart, poor man. With a sword. It's very unusual. The sort of thing *you-know-who* might be interested in."

Crane frowned, thinking for a long moment, then stood. "Go home. Wait by the phone. He'll want to get moving at sunset, no later." Absently, he pulled out fifty dollars and left it on the table.

Marlene raised an eyebrow. "You'll give the waitress a heart attack. Or is that for me?"

"I'm sure you'll think of a way to earn it." He nodded a cursory goodbye, then turned away.

"It's a date." Marlene smiled, then snapped her fingers at the waitress for a second cup.

* * *

JONAH GREETED CRANE on his return with a barely-perceptible raised eyebrow. Crane checked his pocket-watch, noting that enough time had passed to allow him some plausible deniability with Marlene, then gave Jonah the slightest of nods.

Jonah took a small copper key from his pocket and moved to unlock the door to the lower library.

In the Jameson Club, there were two libraries. The upper library was one of the club's great treasures—a repository of famous first editions culled from private collections, including a folio of Marlowe's *Faustus Redeemed* and the original manuscript for *Edwin Drood,* complete with the famous epilogue. Had the Jameson Club been a museum, visitors would have flocked to see such exhibits. As it was, most of the members saw these priceless artefacts of literary history only as decorative touches, adding a touch of class to the room where they went to do the daily crossword. The books simply sat and looked pretty, in the manner of a trophy wife or a set of elephant's tusks.

The lower library, meanwhile, was all but forgotten. While there were several first editions stored there, they were the kind of thing you'd find on the bookshelves of any dedicated collector with money to spend, and thus their value as items of decadence was next to worthless. Since the building of the upper library, the room had fallen into disuse, and now it was used as a junk room by the serving staff, a place of dust, cobwebs and bric-a-brac, forgotten by all. Crane was the only member who ever bothered to go inside, and if the other members noticed, they dismissed it as a minor eccentricity. If Crane wanted to poke around amongst piles of dusty old ephemera, they thought, then it was his business.

Surely there was no harm in it.

In one corner of the lower library, underneath a bust of Catullus, there was a locked trunk, to which Parker Crane had the only key.

Inside the trunk, there were three black slouch hats, two black trenchcoats, three pairs of black shirts and slacks, five pairs of strangely-patterned black rubber gloves, three pairs of black shoes with the same intricate pattern on their soles and one pair of black automatic pistols, which were kept in perfect condition.

There was also a mask.

It was made of leather and designed to fit over the whole head, with a blood-red metal plate in the front that covered the face, with eight lenses set into it, like the eyes of a spider.

The last thing in the trunk was an ornate box containing a set of immaculately-printed business cards. On one side, the cards showed a spider design, in red. On the other:

> *Where all inhuman*
> *Devils revel in their sins—*
> *The Blood-Spider spins!*

AS HE POPPED the buttons on his white dress shirt and slid it off, Crane felt a strange sense of peace and contentment envelop his mind. It was a wonderful feeling to strip away the cares of the world, the outward show that was Parker Crane, gentleman of leisure, and to become his true self. How had that editorial put it? The spider at the centre of a web of blood and vengeance.

How true, thought Parker Crane. *How very true.*

He lifted one of the black shirts, inhaling the fresh scent of the laundry. Jonah had done a capital job, as ever—bloodstains were hard to get out of any fabric, and black clothing had a tendency to turn grey if improperly handled. "You're quite the most invaluable member of my web, Jonah," Crane murmured, as he slid an arm into a black sleeve.

"One does one's best, Master Parker." Jonah nodded, deferential as ever, then turned respectfully around as Crane continued changing.

The mask was the last thing to go on. That was the moment when it really happened. When he felt the weight of that dreadful playboy pose—that vicissitude, that narcissism, that languid sloth that felt as heavy as lead on his back—all fall away, replaced by the cold, bright, beautiful clarity of his cause. His mission. To purge the world of the criminals. To wipe out the inhuman.

It was Parker Crane who raised the mask to his face, but it was the Blood-Spider who tightened the straps.

Occasionally, he wondered if there was anyone else who felt as he did, who could lift a mask to his face and become an entirely different person, stronger, faster, harder, colder, *better*. If such a person existed, he should like to meet them one day. To compare notes.

If they were in agreement with the cause, of course.

Otherwise, they would have to die.

"*Telephone*," hissed the Blood-Spider. Jonah bowed, then turned to open a small cupboard near the door. Inside was a black telephone, connected to an unlisted line separate from the club's own. The gloved hands snatched it up, fingers dialing the numbers, stabbing savagely at the apparatus as if possessed. Then he lifted the receiver to that strange, almost-featureless mask and waited, as the spider waits, patiently and remorselessly, for the fly.

DAVID SIKORSKY JUMPED as the phone on the wall rang. "Christ!"

Marlene smiled, shifting her weight on the couch. "I was expecting that. Be a dear and fetch it for me, will you?"

David frowned. He was a man in his mid-thirties, lean and twitchy, with a mop of black hair resting on top of his head like a bird's nest and an unkempt goatee sprouting from his chin. He had a penchant for dark-coloured turtlenecks, cheap black coffee and 'breaker' music, which blared tinnily from a clockwork gramophone in the corner of his studio; the thumping, insistent beat of the drums colliding with the insistent jangle of the telephone. He stared at it for a moment, then looked at his model, brow furrowed with impotent irritation. He'd asked her not to take calls while she was modeling. He'd told her a dozen times, he couldn't have his concentration broken during a shoot, but did she listen?

For a moment, his eyes dueled with hers—two sapphires, gleaming with superior amusement—and then his will broke and he turned to the ringing phone with a heavy, theatrical sigh. Passive aggression had always been David's forte. Rather than answer it himself, he simply lifted the receiver off the hook and, adopting an exaggerated air of indifference, carried it across the studio, the long extension cord stretching as he held it to Marlene's ear.

She was not in a position to take hold of it herself, of course. The black leather singleglove cinching her arms prevented her doing much more than rolling the balls of her shoulders, while the leather straps keeping her ankles bound to her thighs kept her in a kneeling position on the red velour couch, the heels of the tightly-laced ballet boots pressed tightly against her bottom. The black ribbons that kept her hair piled up on top of her head, and the one wound decoratively around her throat, formed the rest of her *couture* for the afternoon.

Marlene enjoyed working with David. If only he wasn't quite so spineless, she might have added him to her catalogue of lovers. She smiled sweetly at him, then spoke into the receiver. "Marlene Lang."

The voice on the other end was a muffled growl, a hiss like steam escaping from some terrible industrial press.

"*You were told to return home and wait.*"

"But if I'd gone home, darling, you'd have called here and you wouldn't have reached me. So I was just being efficient, really." She smiled sweetly, for the benefit of no-one. David was staring moodily into one corner, as if to give her some measure of privacy, though his arm still held the receiver stiffly in place. There was silence on the other end of the line.

"What's the matter?" She purred the words lazily, like a cat. "Am I being terribly immoral? I suppose I am, really. I shall have to watch that."

The voice on the other end was cold. "*Bring the car around to the usual place no later than nine tonight. We have a murder to investigate.*" The line went dead.

Marlene wondered for a moment if she'd made him jealous. But then, to feel jealousy, one would have to feel, and Marlene was not entirely convinced the Blood-Spider had any feelings beyond that cold, hard anger that informed all his movements. Perhaps that was what made him so fascinating to her—or the deliciousness of the cause, their shared war on crime. She had never imagined that a life of pursuing the common good, without recognition or reward, could be quite so wonderfully decadent.

"There, done. You may put the receiver back, David." She smirked, watching him bristle as he marched stiffly back to replace the apparatus in its cradle, then adopted a contrite look, pouting as he turned his wounded eyes back on her. "Have I been very naughty?"

David shook his head, stuttering a response and blushing. "It's not that, it's... I kind of wish you wouldn't... I mean, I've told you before..." Frustrated, he moved to the equipment he'd laid out on the table, out of the camera's view. "You're not going to be taking any more calls, right? I just need to concentrate for this."

"No more calls, darling. I promise." Marlene smiled, arched her back, and opened her mouth for the ball gag.

THERE WERE STILL little phantom shivers of rubber on the tip of her tongue and a pleasant ache in her shoulders as her hands gripped and spun the steering wheel of the Silver Ghost, tearing it around a corner in a cloud of billowing steam.

She was dressed somewhat more conservatively now, although not by much. The belted leather jacket that formed the top portion of her uniform certainly covered up her torso admirably—although the tight fit drew the eye somewhat—and the peaked cap added an air of authority. The leather miniskirt was slightly more of a problem. It only came down to mid-thigh when she was standing, never mind sitting down, and the high heels on the black pumps she was made to wear did little to distract any passengers from the curves of her legs.

Not that the Silver Ghost carried any passengers apart from the Blood-Spider himself, of course. Perhaps he did have human feelings after all.

Or perhaps he saw her as merely a luxurious component of a luxurious vehicle—for 'luxurious' was really the only way the Silver Ghost could possibly be described. A sleek silver bullet, filigreed with the thin, clustered piping that kept the high-pressure steam turning the wheels and driving the whole apparatus forward, the air-intake surrounding the nosecone looking like the maw of some strange and terrifying undersea animal, the blazing twin gas lamps on either side forming its eyes. It looked delicate in its majestic complexity, but Marlene had been in the driving seat when the agents of E.R.A.M.T.H.G.I.N.—that strange reverse-organisation, a gang of madmen existing to mock, détourn and destroy all symbols, the futurehead ethos gone wild and rabid in the streets—had roared out of an alleyway in their own patchwork auto, looking like nothing so much as a squat metal slug, and raked the Silver Ghost with machine-gun fire.

"*Us am vigilantes! Am us not men?*" they'd howled, a terrifyingly accurate parody of the Blood-Spider's hiss, distorted as if played through a sped-up gramophone, the bright red clay headgear they wore to signify their 'de-evolutionary status' refashioned into crude, cruel mockeries of the Spider's signature mask. "*Us use violence to effect social change! Am us not men? Us bring terror to underclass, make streets safer for overclass! Am us not men? Am us not men?*"

The Blood-Spider had turned, bullets missing him by inches, and dispatched each of them with a single shot, shattering the clay helmets and painting the fragments a different shade of red. A final shot had smashed through the slug's bonnet, bringing forth an explosion of hissing steam and sharp metal fragments and sending the auto careening into a nearby gas lamp, a charnel-display of rotting meat left as an example to any others who might consider impeding the Blood-Spider in the performance of his terrible duty.

The Silver Ghost, meanwhile, had suffered barely a scratch. It was built to last.

Marlene parked the auto near the mouth of a secluded, seemingly deserted back alley, filled with shadows and scurrying rats. As she opened the door, one shadow detached itself from the others, uncoiling like a snake, pitch darkness suddenly assuming form and substance. Marlene smiled.

"Darling."

Eight blank lenses gazed back at her as the Blood-Spider took his seat.

"*The Atlas building. West Thirty-Eighth.*" He opened the glove compartment of the sleek silver machine and withdrew a large grappling hook, connected to a loop of strong steel wire. "*I have a personal call to make.*"

"Yes, sir," purred Marlene, gunning the engine and sending the Silver Ghost on into the New York night.

THE HARD PART had been getting to the roof without being seen.

After that, it was a simple matter of placing his hands on the smooth stone of the wall and then vaulting over the roof edge, letting the intricate network of suction-cups on his gloves and the soles of his shoes affix themselves so he could climb down the wall to the window. This was his great secret—how he appeared and disappeared without warning, how he could strike from everywhere at once. The powerful suction of the rubber allowed him to cling expertly to any surface and reach the highest and most inhospitable nooks and crannies, there to watch and wait, as the spider waits in cracks and crevices for his prey.

The Blood-Spider clung, like a spider clinging to a wall, over a drop that would not only shatter and pulverise his bones but liquefy his very flesh if he fell—and he thought no more about it than a normal man would if standing upon the edge of a high kerbstone.

Danger was meaningless. The risk of death had been weighed, judged and found to be acceptable. All that remained now was the task at hand.

The cause.

Slowly, patiently, the Blood-Spider used a glass-cutting tool from his belt to carve a circle in the window large enough to gain him entry, pushing gently with his palm until the circle of glass popped into the room, landing almost silently on the deep plush carpet. He disliked compromising the crime scene in such a manner, but the police department had taken their turn with it. His job now was to find those things they had missed, in the places they had not bothered to look.

As he crossed the threshold of the window, he looked to his left, at the dried blood still mixed with the fibres of the carpet. A man had died there. He had been stabbed in the back by a coward, and it was the duty of the Blood-Spider to find out who that coward was. As the soles of his boots sank into the lush carpeting, he devoted all his attention to that stain of blood, to that spot where Donner had been killed. That was the first piece of the puzzle. He would find the others, and piece by piece he would build up the truth of the matter. Strand by strand, the Spider would spin his web.

He sank to one knee, brushing his fingertips over the dried, crusted stain, the map of a forgotten continent. Slowly, he examined its contours, his whole attention focused on determining its secret meaning, the clues buried in its unique shape.

And so he never noticed the hands reaching for the back of his neck.

Not until they were at his throat.

CHAPTER FOUR
DOC THUNDER AND THE APE DETECTIVE

Monk had big hands.

Large, hard things, they were. Great clubs of meat and bone and sinew, flexing dangerously, constantly twitching and moving. A carpet of rough hairs growing from the back of each, dirt and grime under the thick fingernails that he could never quite get out. Rough calluses on the fingertips, like sandpaper.

Killer's hands.

He'd taught them gentleness, painstakingly and over too many years. But every so often he would pick up a boiled egg and the shell would crack, or he'd handle a paperclip and it would bend between his fingers. Monk would wince, imperceptibly, and it would haunt him for days, making him hesitant about shaking a hand or putting his arm around a shoulder.

For at least a week after such an incident, he would sleep on the couch downstairs. Doc and Maya had grown to accept it. Gradually, his confidence would return, and so would he. But it always took time.

He had to be careful. So careful, all the time. And he was careful. He was careful when he twisted the cotter pin in the lock of the penthouse suite to let himself in, and careful when he examined the room Donner died in, lifting, inspecting, replacing exactly, each object treated like a Fabergé egg, every clue a museum piece of untold worth.

"Go take a look at the crime scene," Doc Thunder had said. "Pick up what you can, then get straight back to me. No risks, understand?"

Monk had shrugged. "Sure, Doc. You think Donner got mixed up with something?"

Doc had laughed humourlessly. "Mixed up isn't the word. He was the man behind Untergang. I could never prove it, but he was. The secret figurehead—businessman and philanthropist by day, inhuman monster by night. And he hated me more than any human being I've ever known."

Monk had raised an eyebrow. "Lars Lomax?"

Doc had almost smiled. "Lars hated me, all right. He would have burned the entire world to see me dead. But... Heinrich Donner would have burned the world to see me stub my toe on the ruins. He was the one who murdered—" Doc had suddenly gone quiet, as if he'd almost said too much. Monk waited.

"We finally had it out in 1959. We were fighting in Paraguay. He had this secret bunker set up... the whole damn place was full of nitro-glycerin and he pulled a gun on me." Doc shook his head sadly. "I had him. I really did. I had hard evidence, I was going to bring him to trial, but he just..."

He'd tailed off, looking into the middle distance. "He knew bullets didn't work on me. He knew that. One of them bounced off my chest, hit the nitro... and boom. Goodbye, Heinrich. Nearly goodbye me." He'd paused. "I think the evil little son of a bitch just wanted to kill us both." Monk remembered being surprised at the venom in Doc's voice. He'd never spoken that way before about anyone, even Lomax. Donner's hatred hadn't all been one-way. "I really thought he was dead. I've taken down Untergang leaders since then—the Purple Wraith, Queen Tiger... they must have been figureheads, like Cobra was. It was Donner. All the time. All the time..." He'd shaken his head, covering his eyes, and Monk had flinched. He'd never seen Doc look that way—that look of despair. "I need to know what he's been doing since 'fifty-nine. I need to know who killed him, and why, and if he's really dead this time. I don't think I can go to the police yet. I just... I don't know, Monk. I don't quite know what to do."

He'd looked at Monk with those steel-blue eyes, and they'd looked lost, like a kid's.

I don't know what to do.

The most frightening words Monk had ever heard Doc say.

"So... you want me to take a look? Bring back some intel?"

Doc had nodded, and suddenly the old certainty was back. "That's what we need." He'd smiled. "Remember, no risks. Take the flare gun. And listen, the slightest hint of anything and you get out of there. This is Untergang we're talking about—old school Untergang. They don't play games. Oh, and one last thing. Maya's had a dream; a man in a red mask, standing over one of us. She thinks it could be connected, so... keep an eye out."

Monk had just smiled. "Sure thing, Boss. No risks. You can rely on me."

And here he was, putting the picture together. A jigsaw puzzle. A portrait of a man's life, a life now ended. Under his breath, he began to murmur to himself. At the orphanage, some funny guy had given him a copy of *The Jungle Book*. Real funny, a laugh and a half for the popular crowd. The joke was on them. He'd devoured it, cover to cover, maybe just to show them, but that one book had started a fire for reading, for knowledge, that'd never gone out. Monk wished he could remember the funny guy's name. He'd wanted to thank him a lot in the years since. Send him a pound cake for Christmas or something.

Anyway, after *The Jungle Book* he was hungry for more Kipling, so he'd moved on to the *Just So Stories*, and there was a verse in that one that came back to him sometimes, on a case like this one.

"I keep six honest serving-men, they taught me all I knew. Their names are what and why and when and how and where and who."

Six questions. Get the answers to all six and you had the puzzle solved.

He was in the where. The police knew the when and the what. They even figured they knew the how.

According to the police, Donner had probably known his killer enough to let him in the door, and to turn his back. There'd been no sign of forced entry.

Monk wasn't so sure. He'd just forced his way in and left no sign of it. Easy enough with hands like his.

They were strong, and they were sensitive. Even under that thick layer of callus, they knew weight, and give, and push. They knew how to open a door with a cotter pin and make it look as though you'd used a key, even to the smartest cop in the world—which the ones who'd checked this place over weren't, not by a long stretch. And more. He knew, instinctively—and it was the smallest twinge in the middle of his gut and on the edges of his subconscious but by God, he *knew*—he hadn't been the first to force that lock.

So the police had it wrong. Donner didn't know his killer. Didn't even know his killer was there until the sword was in his back.

Monk considered it, weighted it in his mind for truth, then continued along the mental path. Donner hadn't gone to the window after letting his killer in. He was already standing, looking out on the city, when the killer had let himself in silently, padded across the carpet, and stabbed Donner in the back. No mercy. Not even an explanation. Just the kill.

That was the how.

He ran his fingers over his sloped brow, as if coaxing the thoughts into life, a physical tic from his childhood. He had the why, too. If Doc was right—and Doc was *always* right—Donner was the leader of Untergang, and that was why enough for a hell of a lot of people. So, five out of six. One to go.

Put the why together with the how, the silent entry, the quiet, instant kill... secret service? Or the Special Tactical Espionage And Manouvres unit? But no, they wouldn't let it reach the papers. And Doc would have been told. Him and President Bartlet had been the best of pals ever since that brain transplant stunt Lars Lomax tried.

Someone else? No love lost between Untergang and N.I.G.H.T.M.A.R.E.— but they weren't about to go to war, either. Besides, N.I.G.H.T.M.A.R.E. was finished. After what Doc had done to them in Milan, they didn't have the manpower to go after a stray dog, never mind a top-flight bad guy. And E.R.A.M.T.H.G.I.N. was just a joke taking itself a little too seriously. It didn't have the chops for this.

Someone new, then.

Monk needed more information. He frowned, took another quick look around the room, then padded across to the bedroom, reaching behind him as he went, unconsciously mussing the pile with his fingers, making sure he left no tracks. An old habit.

In the bedroom, he let those fingers—rough and gentle, club-like and dexterous—tease lightly over the fabric of the bed, while the eyes under the ridged, furrowed brow of his ape-like face scanned every passing detail.

The lamp beside the bed; gold, with a German eagle motif. Monk wouldn't have been surprised to see a swastika there too, but that would've given the game away.

A little rectangle on the bedside, where the dust wasn't so thick. Something had lain there for a while, by the side of his bed. It wasn't there now.

A dent in the wall, like a crescent moon.

The sheets. Expensive. Silk? Or a blend? Either way, they were a little sweaty, a little scummy. Not quite as clean as might be expected.

He looked around, taking another look at the dust on the bedside table. Then he closed his eyes, thinking back to what he'd seen of the living room. Norman Rockwell print on the wall. An ashtray, filled with old cigarettes, a pyramid of them. Not emptied in too long. Food particles caught in the carpet—he'd stopped eating at the table.

Filthy sheets. Filthy ashtrays. He'd stopped doing a lot of things.

On a whim, Monk picked up the heavy lamp and held the circular base to the dent. It matched. A struggle?

No. He'd just thrown the damn thing at the wall.

Depression. Hits a guy that way sometimes. Things stop mattering, people stop caring. The detectives probably wouldn't have noticed. They hadn't been there.

Why hadn't he hired a maid? Because he needed to stay hidden. Stay reclusive. Nobody could know.

Why?

Monk's mind was racing now, cogs whirring in his head, switches flipping. *Think, ape-man.* Why can't the leader of Untergang hire a maid?

Because he wasn't the leader of Untergang any more. He wasn't anything. That stunt in Paraguay Doc had talked about—that was his last run. He might have been the big boss across the big pond, but that didn't mean he didn't have superiors back in the Fatherland. If Uncle Adolf figured he'd been compromised—out he'd go. Exiled.

Monk shook his head, frowning. No, not exile. Storage. He'd been locked away like last year's gramophone, just in case he ever came good again, in case any of the secrets in his head were ever useful to anybody. Instead, he'd been forgotten and left to rot.

So Monk was back to the why. Why now? He scratched the back of his scalp with great club-like fingers. If he only knew why, he'd know who—but then, if he knew who, he knew why. Sometimes it shook out like that.

He needed to know what it was that had been taken from the bedside table. Some kind of book?

He shook his head, then took a last look around the bedroom, hoping against hope that he'd see the damned book or framed photo or whatever it was under the bed or something. No joy.

Best thing to do now would be to head back to Doc, give him what he'd found out, let him figure the next move. One last look around the main room and—

Monk froze.

There was somebody in the main room.

A tall guy, all in black leather, with a big coat and hat. He'd cut his way in from outside, through the window, leaving a big circle of glass on the pile carpet. How the hell had he done that? They were more than forty floors up.

The tall guy bent over the bloodstain on the carpet, brushing gloved fingers over the matted fibres. Monk stilled his breathing, the gentle eyes under that ugly slope of brow narrowing. He moved forward, silent, the soles of his big bare feet falling light as snowflakes on the thick carpet. Silent as the grave.

He was wearing some kind of helmet under that hat. Or a mask.

A red mask.

Almost without thinking, Monk reached forward, those big hands moving towards the back of the tall guy's neck. This was going to have to be done carefully. He was going to have to choke this guy out without killing him.

And he had killer's hands.

He moved fast. Those big, brutal killer's hands wrapped around the tall guy's neck and squeezed—hard, hard enough to cut off air and blood, but at the same time Monk knew he had to be gentle. So, so gentle.

Too gentle, in the end.

The tall guy in the red mask twisted out of the grip and brought the butt of one pistol hard across Monk's face. It would have broken another man's jaw, and it sent him sprawling to the right, cracking his head against the wall and leaving a dent. Red Mask was up on his feet in an instant—

—*Jesus, his face!*—

—and Monk forced himself not to look at those eight featureless lenses, lashing out with those big feet, those ape's clubs on the end of his legs, driving them up and into the taller man's gut. The impact sent the man in the coat flying back in a short arc, landing with a crash that demolished an occasional table.

Monk spat blood, and a molar, then flipped back onto his feet, loping towards the downed man like a charging gorilla. He didn't have room to be gentle any more. He needed to finish this fast, and if that meant mashing that metal mask into the tall guy's face so he never quite looked human again, well, that was just too bad. He'd done his best, but now it was kill or be—

—the revolver in the masked man's gloved hand swung up and spat a bullet into Monk's kneecap, then another into his lung.

Monk went down like a freight train crashing, rolling over from the force of his own momentum, coming to rest next to the destroyed table. He reached, fingers trembling, a last attempt to grab hold of the masked man's coat as he scrambled upwards, but he only caught air.

Then he caught another bullet.

This time he didn't even hear the shot, just felt his head knocked sideways, saw his vision double, then triple. He felt nauseous, the pain in his ruined knee and deflated lung joined by a screaming cold iron spike right through the meat of his brain. He figured he must be dead.

He wasn't. The bullet had glanced off his thick skull, cracking it, and into the wall. The masked man fired another two—one in the gut, another in the chest about three inches from the first.

The last thing Monk saw was the masked man lifting the gun up and aiming it right between his eyes. Those eight lenses didn't have a shred of mercy in them. They didn't hold anything human at all.

Then it all went black.

IN THE BLACKNESS, he thought he saw a star explode, far away. A little supernova that took the shape of a thunderbolt for long moments while it faded. He felt something metallic in his hand, and realised he was awake and pointing that metallic something-or-other through a window at the night sky. There was a big circular hole in the window, which was a little strange. Had that been there before? Was it his window? He figured he should head up to bed, but then he remembered this wasn't the brownstone. It was some fancy apartment.

Whose apartment? Heinrich somebody.

Monk suddenly had a very clear sense that he'd missed something very, very important. Something obvious, something that could have changed the whole game, changed everything—if only he'd thought of it sooner.

He passed out before he could think what it was.

HE DIDN'T REMEMBER using the flare gun, but he must have, because he came round to find Doc shining a torch in his eyes. "Con cushion. Sirius." Something like that. Monk couldn't think straight.

He was alive, anyway. That red mask guy must have left him for dead, gone out the way he came in. He should tell the Doc.

He tried to speak, and went away again into blackness. He felt as if he were out for hours.

He came back around, and Doc was still shining the light in his eyes. No time had passed at all. Monk wondered if he was going to die.

Talk, ape-man. Ook ook.

"Duh. Drrr."

Doc put a hand on his shoulder. "Don't try to talk, Monk. I have to stop the bleeding and then I need to get you across town to the hospital. It's going to be bumpy."

Maya broke in. How long had she been there?

"You can't be serious."

Doc's voice was cold and terse. Deadly serious. Monk realised there was a good chance he was dead, and he tried to say something, tried to say what he'd found, but all he managed was to cough blood.

"Look at him!" Maya's voice held an edge of anger that Monk had only heard a few times in his life. She was furious, which meant she was scared. Which meant... *talk, ape-man. Talk while you can.*

"Look at him! He might die if you move him. If you try to—I can't even say it..." she drew in a breath, her emerald eyes flashing green fire. "If you try what you're planning, he'll die for certain."

"He'll die if I don't. By the time the paramedics get here and get him to the hospital, he'll have bled out. I've already done the math, Maya, there's no way to play this that won't probably kill him. But at least he's got a chance, if get him there myself. *If.*"

Maya gripped his massive wrist, and her grip was like steel. Where there'd been fire in her eyes, there was nothing but a sea of ice.

"If you kill him, I kill you."

Doc pulled his hand away, not speaking, not looking at her, just dressing Monk's wounds with whatever he had—torn silk shirts from the wardrobe, alcohol from decanters on the sideboard. He didn't speak.

It was Monk who broke the silence. "Duh. *Doc.*"

"I said don't try to—"

"Important." He coughed again, and spat more blood. He didn't know how much he had left. "Donner. Not... not Untergang." He flicked his eyes around the room. "All this... exile. Ret... retirement..." He breathed in, weakly, trying to get some air into the lung he had left. Why was this so difficult? He just wanted to go to sleep.

"Monk!" Doc was yelling in his face. He forced himself to spit out some more words and prayed they made some sense.

"Guy who... did this. Red mask. Red mask." *Eight lenses. Black coat.* He tried to say it, but his brain and his tongue seemed disconnected. The blackness seemed to be closing in on him again. He had to try. *Ape-man. Talk. Say it. Eight lenses.*

Talk, ape-man!

"Eyes... crazy eyes..."

That was as far as he got before his head fell away, down into a black ocean with no bottom to it.

And maybe this time he wouldn't wake up.

"RED MASK. DAMN it." Doc was cursing himself. He should have known. Maya's dreams didn't lie. Why hadn't he thought about it? A man in a red mask, standing over the man he killed, a man Maya cared for. Monk, of course Monk, it couldn't be anybody *but* Monk because Doc was all but invulnerable to anything except his own damned stupidity. And he'd sent him into the lion's den anyway. How had he been so damned careless with his best friend's life?

He shook his head, spitting out another curse under his breath. It was Donner. Always and forever, it was Donner. Even beyond the grave—especially beyond the grave—Donner had the power to blindside him, to get under his skin, to get him making mistakes. And now Monk had paid the price for one of those mistakes, and he might not make it through.

No wonder Maya was mad. She stood behind him, those green eyes burning into his back, as he gently cradled Monk in his arms, holding the immense dead weight of the man as if he was carrying a baby. He took a deep breath, stilling his mind and steadying his nerves.

And then he threw himself out of the window.

The important part was to get the landing right—every landing. If he fell from this height and he didn't take the whole impact on his leg muscles, he'd break Monk's neck and most of his other bones. Even so, it'd be a hell of a jar.

"Hold on, Monk," he breathed, almost whispering it. "Hold on, buddy."

The sidewalk rushed up to greet them both like an eager lover. Doc braced, and when his feet hit the pavement—hard enough to crack it—he bent his legs, softening the impact, then straightened them quickly enough to hurl himself over the rooftops. If he'd aimed right, he'd come down on Madison. After that, a leap to Third Avenue, and then one more would get him there. Hopefully that wouldn't be one too many.

Below him, citizens craned their necks, pointing, witnesses to the miracle of a man who could leap more than a thousand feet in one bound, carrying a human gorilla. None of those who saw—not the carriage-drivers whose horses bolted as Doc Thunder landed in front of them, shattering the tarmac and then taking off into the sky again like an eagle; not the secretaries working late in high-up, high-class advertising offices, who turned their heads at just the right moment to see a god sailing past their window with an injured ape-man in his arms; not the kids staying up late on the fire escapes and feeling them rattle with every shockwave—not a one of them would ever forget the sight. Some of them would carry a fear of Doc Thunder around with them the rest of their days, the arachnid response of those confronted with the alien, with a man who so plainly could not be a man. Others would close their eyes in hard moments and bring the memory back, to give them strength in a difficult time.

For Doc Thunder himself, it was three short leaps and nothing more, with the clockwork of his superlative mind crackling as he performed the calculations that would allow him to do it without killing his best friend. He felt no triumph as he landed for the last time in front of Saint Albert's, only a great wave of relief.

Monk was still alive.

"Get this man stabilised!" he yelled, kicking open the door hard enough to send it off one hinge, nurses and orderlies running to fetch stretchers and gurneys. "And get me Hamilton! Miles Hamilton! He still works here?"

A tall man with longish grey hair, haggard cheeks and eyes that had seen far too many sleepless nights stepped forward from the relative calm of one of the wards. He showed little emotion, even while his staff fought to fit their huge patient across two gurneys strapped together, his blood slicking the floor as they wheeled him down the corridor towards the operating theatre. Instead, his cold blue eyes looked up at Thunder's, accusingly. The name on his badge read Dr. Miles Hamilton.

Once upon a time, Hamilton had been Doc's closest ally, his personal physician—the one man Doc had trusted with the secrets of his strange, inhuman physiognomy. He'd been a warm, uncommonly gentle man, a man who would rather die than cause bad feeling to anybody. Then there had been that final, ugly business with Lars Lomax, the most dangerous man in the world, almost three years ago. Lomax had kidnapped Hamilton and tortured him for hours in an effort to get hold of any secret that might destroy his enemy once and for all. Perhaps it was the torture breaking his mind in a way that couldn't be fixed, or perhaps Hamilton blamed Doc for allowing it to happen in the first place, but after it was all over—after Lomax had plunged to his fiery death in the Amazon rainforest—Hamilton had never been the same. The old gentleness was gone, replaced by a cold, hard demeanor, almost cruel. He snubbed old friends in the street, and even his closest colleagues at the hospital felt uneasy around him.

Doc had tried to bring him back to himself, but Hamilton had only grown colder, a new and barely-disguised hatred for Doc Thunder bubbling under the surface of his frosty attitude. Worst of all, he now bugged Doc constantly for a sample of his blood, insisting that the recuperative qualities inherent within it could revolutionise medical science, and even if it were weaponised, well, that would only allow America to spread its military might across the entire world, which could only be a good thing. Imagine an army of soldiers with Doc's powers...

This was the kind of talk that had caused the end of their friendship. Doc had stopped calling, stopped feeling anything for his old friend but sadness at the change in him. Now, Hamilton stood, looking superciliously at Monk, like a man looking at a sideshow freak, and Doc felt again the pain and anger at how far Miles had fallen from his old self.

His voice was curt but without emotion, as if he simply didn't care. "Doc, what on earth is the meaning of this intrusion?"

Thunder shook his head. He wasn't about to get into an argument now. "There's no time, Hamilton. Trust me, I'm not exactly relishing this encounter either, but you were the closest person I could trust. I can trust you?" Even as he asked the question, he reached down to his bicep, grabbing the skin and pinching, digging in with his thumbnail. "Get a catheter."

Hamilton looked up at him, his face still not registering the situation. "You can't mean to—"

"A catheter!" Thunder shouted the words, angrily. "You're getting what you wanted, doctor. My blood! A full pint of it! And unless you want it on the floor, you'll get me a damn catheter!"

He was yelling now, partly from his anger at himself and at the situation he'd created, and partly from the sheer effort it took to tear a hole in his own skin. A thin rivulet of blood began to trickle down towards his elbow.

Hamilton fetched the catheter.

By the time Maya arrived, it was all over. Monk was in the theater, with a pint of Doc's blood hanging over him, being fed to him a trickle at a time along with several pints of his own blood group. Doc's blood would have a healing effect, in time, and from the sound of it Monk was critical but stable and passing further out of danger with every moment.

For a few minutes at a time—just enough to keep him from dying—Monk would have the recuperative powers of Doc Thunder himself. They were the same blood type—O Negative—or there'd have been nothing he could have done. And even among the O-Negatives, there were those who overdosed, who died instantly as their hearts inflated and burst against their ribcages, whose brains hemorrhaged, whose spines were snapped by the growth of muscle in their backs... he had to pray Monk wouldn't end up one of those. "Small doses," he'd said to Hamilton, and the old man had nodded coldly and said something about how he didn't intend to waste any. Doc had felt like punching him. Instead, he'd shaken his hand, resisting the urge to crush it.

They'd been friends once. It seemed like forever ago.

"You were right," smiled Maya as she walked back from her conversation with one of the orderlies. "Monk's alive, thanks to that little stunt. I don't know why I doubted you. Being right is what you do for a living." She leant in to kiss him, and he shook his head, placing a finger at her lips.

"If I'd been right, I'd never have sent Monk in there alone. I was a damn fool, and he paid for it." He shook his head, wincing. "It's Donner. He's haunting me. Making me sloppy."

Maya frowned, curious. "I've never seen you like this. You're... almost afraid of him. Even now. What is he to you?"

Doc Thunder scowled. "It doesn't matter. He's dead. It's his killer we should worry about—and whoever did that to Monk, if he's not the same person." He stood, suddenly, and stalked towards the exit, making her run to keep up. "I'm missing something. Smart as I am, I'm not smart enough..."

Maya blinked, trying to guess his meaning, then her eyes flew wide open.

"No. Doc, no. It's too risky. Every time you use that thing, you run the risk of it killing you. You know that."

"Monk could still die because I was stupid, Maya." Doc Thunder scowled, cracking his knuckles as the rain began to spatter on the sidewalk. "My mind's made up. First, we get some sleep. Then, it's time for desperate measures."

He took a deep breath, then turned to her.

"It's time for the Omega Machine."

CHAPTER FIVE
THE CASE OF THE MAN WHO NEVER SMILED

After he'd finished cleaning the blood from the front of his mask, Parker Crane went to a cocktail party.

It was a low-key affair at the Astoria; a mere one hundred dollars for a ticket, and thus hardly worth bothering with for most members of the Jameson. A couple even looked askance at Crane's rousing himself for such a mediocre get-together. However, most understood that a large number of strumpets from the fashion 'scene' that Crane was involved in would be there, and young men would always be young men—it was only to be expected that Crane would want to sow a few wild oats. Besides, he was so awfully good at keeping his many and varied affairs from tarnishing the name of the club.

Crane decided not to call Marlene; she would either be there herself, or more likely embroiled in her own sordid affairs, in which case he knew where he could find her if she was needed. Instead, he made arrangements to go with two of the models he worked with regularly. A pair of twins, attractive enough to dabble in the modeling world, pneumatic enough to preserve his image and wealthy enough to be deemed worthy of his company, although they were, regrettably, new money. Blonde, naturally. Their father was something in dirigible construction. Crane had quite forgotten their names over the course of the carriage ride from their city apartment, where he'd picked them up—

something that rhymed? Mandy and Sandy? Chloe and Zoe? He hadn't bothered to find out, or even talk to them beyond what was absolutely necessary. They spent the journey giggling and whispering to each other, while he looked out at the rain falling down on the city.

His city.

He was regretting not putting a bullet through the ape man's head. He'd assumed the throwback had died, but he'd seen the flare lighting up the Manhattan sky as Marlene had driven him back to his regular drop-off point, and he knew what it meant. The Gorilla Reporter had called in his lovers to bail him out.

The Blood-Spider disapproved of Doc Thunder—his permissive attitudes were the least of it—and he had no doubt that Thunder's simian sidekick had planned to kill him, perhaps in order to cover up an involvement in Donner's murder. Could he add Thunder to the list of suspects? And if so, how could he be dealt with? What bullet could bring down the bulletproof man?

Something to consider for the future. If Thunder turned out to have been the one to take Donner's life, neither he nor any member of his freakish entourage would live to regret it. Perhaps it would be best, he considered, if Olsen did not die from the bullet wounds, although it would be an unlikely outcome. If he survived, he could be interrogated.

The Blood-Spider would have his answers, once way or another.

On pulling up to the Astoria, Crane and his two dates were greeted by the expected barrage of flashbulbs. As usual, there was a gaggle of photographers armed with box cameras, and a secondary crowd of sketchers scribbling away with coloured pencils on small notepads. He set his face in a careful, studied mask of contempt, one girl on each arm, their matched backless dresses complimenting perfectly the cut of his tuxedo—a Gunn original, hand-stitched by the master himself. Crane felt the mask becoming real as his hands drifted down to the naked smalls of their backs, and the myriad documenters of his social life clustered about him to record the moment for posterity. To them, all he was was this persona, this disguise he'd created for himself. For them, his entire self boiled down to a string of listless, bored copulations, to parties and openings, launches and premieres, rumours and scandals and endless, beautiful women. And not one of them knew the truth—that was what filled him with that cold, coiling hatred, lying like a snake in his gut. Not a single one of these vultures knew the reality of the man they were so desperate to tell the world about in their filthy little publications.

The corner of his mouth twitched, almost involuntarily, in a smile. And if they did know… if the great unwashed who pored over these yellow rags, these scandal-sheets, if they knew his intimate secrets—what? Would they praise him? Understand the cause that burned in him like a fire? He liked to think they might.

Some would want him dead, of course. The criminals. The inhuman. But he and they were at war, a war that never ended. Nestled against warm, yielding flesh, his trigger fingers itched, unsatisfied, denied their kill.

Inside, the girls ran quickly to powder their noses, leaving him blessedly alone. As he plucked a glass of champagne from the tray of a passing waiter, he felt his ears burning, and he turned his attention to the source—a rather loud argument near a potted plant, which the waiters were studiously avoiding as if attempting to starve it into silence, but which had drawn a small throng despite their efforts.

"What you don't understand, Mr Big-Shit Doctor *A-hole,* is the Blood Spider's keepin' our streets safe, capeesh? Every one of these pieces of crap he puts down means lives saved! People *in the line* walkin' away from the jackpot and breathin' for another day! You ever told an officer's widow her husband's lying in the ground because some spic had more rights than he did? Huh? You ever did that, asshole, 'cause I have!"

The voice was loud, belligerent and rough, sandpapery from decades of nicotine abuse. Crane recognised it immediately. Detective Harry Stacey, forty-three years old, five feet and two inches tall. Hair a muddy grey with still the occasional streak of red. A handlebar moustache to match. A tan suit that had seen better days. He stank of whiskey, cheap cigars and light corruption. Crane had no doubt that he'd scrounged up the hundred dollars admission though gambling or stealing cash from the evidence locker, and presumably he was only here in the first place to grease a few palms or find a new mistress to put in the apartment he kept for that purpose across town.

In many respects, the man was a human sewer, but he had qualities that Crane couldn't help but admire. For example, he had an iron determination to protect the decent people in society from the undesirables, those who would prey on them—those inhuman devils who would revel in their sins, as it were—and he never allowed his weaknesses to compromise that. Not to mention that his deep connections with the more squalid elements of the police department allowed him to be useful to the Blood-Spider as a member of the Spider's Web.

Of course, if he hadn't proved himself so useful, he would have probably been killed by now. That made his blind loyalty a source of endless amusement to Crane, although naturally the Blood-Spider would never allow it to show. Idly, Crane looked over at his opponent in the one-sided debate.

A tall, thin man, dressed in a grey suit and leaning on a gold-handled cane, with longish white hair and beard, hollow cheeks and grey, sunken eyes with large bags underneath them. The face was emotionless, almost supernaturally calm in the face of Stacey's tirade, and the only movement the man made was to occasionally take a long sip from the champagne glass in his left hand.

What had Stacey called the man? A doctor?

"It just seems somewhat unconstitutional, doesn't it? Shooting a young man in the street in cold blood. What about the basic freedoms?" The voice was cold, disinterested, and this attitude only enraged Stacey more. The scotch in his glass spilled over his clutching hand as he aimed a stubby finger at his debating partner.

"Freedoms? Screw your god-damn freedoms, Mr Med School! What about *my* freedoms? Where's my right to take a walk through the South Bronx at night without some freakin' jig sticking a knife up my ass? Where're the freedoms of all the decent folk, like—like schoolteachers, not the stinking commie ones, the ones who teach sports, where's their freedom not to have to look over their shoulders all the time in case there's a Jap with a giant freakin' pair of, I don't know, those sticks with the chains, what are they called, standing there waiting to knock their balls right off 'em and wear 'em like a friggin' hat? If it was up to you, Hamilton, you'd just give all the chinks and the spics who're terrorising the streets of this city a, a little slap on the wrist and a don't-do-it-again—"

"Can we do this without the racial invective?" murmured the doctor—Hamilton, that was his name. His expression had not changed, and he looked bored by the whole discussion. There was something about him that rubbed Crane the wrong way. His stoicism in the face of Stacey's drunken tirade seemed unnatural, somehow.

Not to mention his disapproval of the cause, which was suspicious in itself. This Hamilton would bear watching.

"Racial—up your *ass*, pal! I'm no racist!" Stacey flushed red, knuckles white on his glass as he tossed the rest of the scotch down his throat. "You god-damned *progressives*, you're pretty damned quick to call a guy a bigot just for speaking his mind, aincha? Maybe *you're* the racist, pal! Ever think of that? Maybe you're racist against people like me who friggin' work for a living—*in the line*—keepin' the streets safe like my buddy the Blood-Spider! Friggin'… friggin' *cop racist!*"

"I think we're done here." Hamilton turned on his heel, taking the bulk of the crowd with him. Stacey stared balefully after him for a moment, hurled his dead cigar angrily onto the polished floor and then charged off in the other direction, banging immediately into a waiter carrying a tray of canapés and sending miniature smoked salmon rolls scattering in all directions. Crane watched Stacey curse the man out and then head down a corridor in the direction of the gents' toilets.

Crane checked that no eyes were on him and then surreptitiously followed, making sure to keep several paces behind the detective, moving silently. Once they were out of sight of the main throng, Stacey stopped, digging in his inside pocket for a fresh cigar. Crane smiled, taking a handkerchief from his own pocket and using it to disguise his voice as he crept up behind the older man.

It was all in the timing. Crane, silent, waited until Stacey had raised the stogie to his lips and was attempting to light it with a book of matches he'd taken from one of the city's many strip clubs. Then he spoke.

"*Detective.*"

The Blood-Spider's voice. That unearthly hiss, low, sibilant and menacing. Harry Stacey nearly leapt out of his skin. "Christ—" The match went flying, thankfully going out before it burned a hole in the carpet. The cigar slipped from suddenly trembling fingers, bouncing off an unpolished shoe.

"*Turn around and you will be killed, detective. Do we understand each other?*"

Stacey had been half turning, but now stood straight as a ramrod, beads of sweat appearing on goose bumped flesh, staring straight ahead. "Aw, crap. I mean yessir. Whatever you say. I won't turn around, you can count on your buddy Harry Stacey, Mr Blood-Spider, sir, 'cause I'm right there with you *in the friggin' line*, pal—"

"*Be quiet.*"

Stacey was quiet.

"*Two days ago, a man was found dead, detective. Murdered in his home. He was killed with a sword.*"

Stacey frowned. "Killed in his home... wait, was this that recluse guy everybody thought was dead? Danner, Donner, what was his name—"

Crane thrust the tip of a finger into the man's back, and he jerked as if he'd been stung by a wasp.

"*Be quiet, I said.*"

Stacey nodded, dumbly, trying to swallow.

"*I need information, detective. Anyone who's been killed or injured with a sword in Manhattan. If you bring this information to my... mail drop...*"

"Aw, not that douchebag Crane! Jesus, every time I set foot in that friggin' rich-boy hellhole I get a case of the hives—" The finger jerked in his back again. "I love that guy."

"Crane. If you bring him the intelligence I require, I will allow you to continue serving the cause. If not… your sins are deep and steep, detective, and they lie black upon your heart. I know about the gambling, the bribes, the kickbacks, the whores. Some would say the Spider's Web has no place for you."

"So what, you'd kick me out?" Stacey scowled. "Just 'cause I cream a little off the top here and there? A guy's gotta make a living, buddy—uh, sir."

Crane jabbed the finger into his back once more, leaning closer. *"Yes. I would kick you out."*

His hiss dropped slightly. *"Of a window."*

Stacey stiffened, the sweat glistening on the back of his neck. Unconsciously, he raised his arms. "Please, I—I got a family! I got a grandmother with, with lumbago, she needs me—I got two! Another with the consumption! She needs me too! I'm needed in this world!"

Crane chuckled dryly.

"I'd hate to deprive your 'grandmothers' of your continued affection, detective. The information. Tomorrow, without fail, as soon as your shift ends. Do we have an understanding?"

Stacey nodded, and Crane took a perverse delight in noting the dark stain spreading across the front of his tan suit trousers.

"Don't turn around."

Harry Stacey didn't turn around.

He remained, with his arms raised and the front of his trousers coated with his own urine, for six minutes and fourteen seconds, until finally the two pneumatic blondes who Parker Crane would spend the evening entertaining in various ways exited the ladies toilets and asked him if he'd had a stroke.

ON HIS WAY out, with the girls in place on his arms and another coming along for good measure—a statuesque redhead, the daughter of a Wall Street financier, who believed in seizing each moment as it came or some such philosophy, Parker Crane turned back and met the gaze of Doctor Hamilton. There was no emotion in that gaze. It reminded Crane of nothing so much as a dead fish on a slab, but all the same, he found something in it unpleasant. Threatening, almost.

"Can I help you?" he said, trying to keep the irritation out of his voice.

"Parker Crane, the fashion photographer." Hamilton thrust out a hand, which Crane didn't take. "A pleasure to meet you. I'm..." He seemed to be searching for the correct words. "...an admirer of your work. I think you've made quite a valuable contribution to the culture of this city."

Something in the phrasing bothered Crane. "What do you mean?"

"What I say. I've watched your career with interest. In fact, I think we may have a mutual acquaintance..." His eyes narrowed, speculatively, though his expression did not betray the slightest hint of what he was thinking.

Crane stood for a moment, before one of the blondes—Mandy? Sandy?—tugged his arm, giggling. "*Par*-ker, we want to see your place. You said you'd show us your etchings..." They dissolved into tipsy giggles and led him away towards a waiting hansom. As he walked out through the great double doors of the Astoria, Crane turned to look back at the strange man who'd accosted him.

But Doctor Hamilton was gone.

LATER, IN HIS palatial room, Parker Crane lay back on silk sheets soaked with champagne and the sweat of beautiful women, ears filled with drunken laughter and soft, wet noises, and mused that none of this seemed real to him. Occasionally, all of the luxury, these endless dalliances and pleasures of his other self, his fake self—all of it disgusted him. Yes, there was a release there, a form of pleasure, but it was nothing compared to that feeling in him when he pulled the trigger and removed evil from the world. True pleasure came from the barrel of a gun.

The thought amused him as he allowed sleep to steal over him.

In the hospital, Monk Olsen breathed through a tube. He would not die tonight, but his healing would be long and slow.

In the basement of the hospital, Doctor Miles Hamilton gently carried a vial of blood—the bulk of Doc Thunder's generous donation to his friend—down to the cold room where such perishables were kept, placing it in a chilled metal box in which it could remain fresh—a box to which only he had the key.

In the brownstone, Maya slept, and dreamt of a man in a red mask, and murder, and all the secrets of the past returning to haunt the future. Occasionally, she dreamt of home, and smiled.

Doc Thunder did not sleep at all.

CHAPTER SIX
DOC THUNDER AND THE OMEGA MACHINE

"I HATE THIS thing."

Maya scowled as she adjusted the copper headband so that the contacts—small discs of sponge soaked in brine—rested against Doc Thunder's temples. His hands were strapped down to the arms, and another strap ran across his chest, with still more securing his legs. "To prevent convulsions," he'd said, "from the effect of the galvanic stimulation on the body."

The chair was linked up with copper wire to an odd device consisting of an array of magnets, which, when set to spinning in a certain configuration, would create an induction effect and charge the wires with pulses of pure galvanic force—'omega energy,' as the Doc had dubbed it. The shifting colours of the sunset streamed through the window, cascading over the massive, squat machine, reflecting from the shiny copper and burnished steel, making the apparatus look strange and otherworldly, like something out of a scientifiction chapbook.

Monk had once asked him if the 'omega effect' could be used to power a machine, like a steam engine—power a car or a robot, maybe. "Too dangerous," the Doc had said. "Omega energy can kill a normal man, and that's the first thing they'd use it for. Executions. If I can make it safe, I'll give it to the world. Until then, the Omega Machine will be the only one of its kind on this planet."

On Doc's signal, Maya would throw a switch mounted on the omega generator, closing the 'omega pathway' and sending pure omega energy from deep within the guts of the machine down the wire and through the chair. At which point, it would pass through the brine-soaked contacts and straight into the Doc's brain.

On a lesser man, the effect would be fatal, but on Doc's enhanced body, the 'omega effect' charged his synapses, opening up new doors of perception and allowing his conscious mind access to the subliminal, unconscious parts of his brain. Essentially, it boosted the power of his mind by a factor of ten or more and allowed him to make intuitive leaps that previously would have been unthinkable even to him. There was only one drawback.

If he was left too long in the Omega Machine, it would kill even him.

And nobody knew how long 'too long' might be. It could be as short as a few seconds or as long as ten minutes. But once his mighty heart ceased to beat, it would be beyond Maya's power to compress his chest. If his breathing stopped, Maya would not be able to reinflate his lungs any more than she could have reinflated a crushed metal can. CPR just didn't work on Doc Thunder—that was an unpleasant truth he'd lived with all his life.

"I hate it." Maya scowled, though it didn't mar her beauty. Then she laughed, without humour. "It's funny—when you risk Monk's life, I threaten you with death. So what do I threaten you with when you risk your own?"

She looked at him for a long moment, then, a sudden, strange, considering look crossed her lovely features.

Doc's voice was soft, gentle. "Don't go."

Maya smiled, caught. "I was just thinking about the Forbidden Kingdom. My home." She smiled, sitting down on his lap, reaching around to gently stroke the back of his neck with a fingernail. "Intrigues and betrayals. An endless succession of high priests and viziers—either sinned against or sinning. The number of times I had to intervene to break up some conspiracy or other... goodness knows what they've done without me." She leant to kiss him, probing for a long, delicious moment with her catlike tongue, and when she finally let his lips go, her eyes were considering, as if the kiss was an evaluation.

Doc tried to smile. "I'm sure they haven't done anything too..." He tailed off, the words sounding hollow and ridiculous in his own ears. She continued looking at him, head tilted to the side, and he stayed silent, not wanting to betray the sudden panic he was feeling. He'd nearly lost Monk—his best friend, his bedmate—and to lose Maya, too, to let her slip away from him, to be alone again, as he'd been before...

Eventually, he spoke. "Would you... would you really go back to that? I know the danger didn't mean anything to you, but you were so... bored..."

Don't let her be bored, he thought. *Please. Don't let her be bored of me.*

She smiled, reaching down past his belly, stroking, teasing, like a cat toying with a wounded bird. His muscles flexed against the straps, and she laughed. "No. I'm not bored. But... there are dangers here I didn't have to worry about at home. Worse than death. Worse than boredom, even."

She leaned in, her lips brushing his. "Are you going to break my heart, Doc Thunder?" Her lips blocked his reply, that tongue darting and delving in his mouth, her scent in his nostrils as the firm shape of her breasts and the weight of them pressed into him. She broke the kiss suddenly, looking at him with an air of cool consideration as she picked up the rubber bit-gag that would keep him from biting off his own tongue.

"Must I break yours first?"

He opened his mouth to speak, to tell her she was wrong, to ask her to stay with him, but she forced the gag in his mouth and secured it before he could. For the best, maybe. Maya Zor-Tura was not a woman who enjoyed the company of beggars. "Are you ready?" she said, crisply, padding over to the large switch mounted on the casing of the humming machine, the handle coated in rubber to prevent omega discharge.

Doc looked at her for a moment, then nodded.

She threw the switch and—

head full of lightning
sdrawkcab gninnips yromem
something in the past

—the flashes in his mind started to spark and crackle—

clue to discover
long-forgotten adventure
buried connection

—the first galvanised insights coming fast, in a rush—

thinking so quickly

that it becomes something new
not thinking at all

—a kaleidoscope of colour in his head, strange scents and audio hallucinations—

thousand days ago
something changed something went wrong
why think remember

—zoning in on a specific memory, something his subconscious had been screaming at him in the night for three years or more—

lomax was involved
lars lomax anti-scientist
implacable foe

—why Lomax? He hadn't thought of Lomax since he'd died—

hamilton as well
hamilton changed after that
why think remember

—Hamilton had been there, in the airship, over the Amazon, what was the meaning behind that—

go into the past
memory unlocks the clue
think and remember

—think and remember—

Maya watched as Doc jerked and thrashed in the straps, teeth biting into the bit-gag, eyes bulging as the omega energy tore through his brain. When he was ready, when he had the answer he needed, he'd tap out, hammer the arm of the chair with his palm, signal her to turn off the omega field. If he could.

She wondered if this was the time she'd watch him die.

*   *   *

THINK AND REMEMBER.

The insights, the flashes and sparks in his mind, had calmed as they always did, leaving him in a trance state, feeling the pain and strangeness of the electric current flowing through his synapses, and in that twilight world of semi-consciousness Doc Thunder remembered Lars Lomax, the most dangerous man in the world.

The twisted bald super-genius who had sworn to kill him a thousand times, the evil scientist whose self-declared purpose was to burn the whole world and raise his own civilisation in its ruins, the ultimate foe, the one man who on his own had caused more trouble than Untergang and N.I.G.H.T.M.A.R.E. and E.R.A.M.T.H.G.I.N. and every other organisation he'd ever fought put together, bar the Hidden Empire. Lars Lomax—the enemy of Earth. The name that froze the blood in the veins of law enforcement agencies the world over.

In some ways, Lomax had been a worse enemy over the years than even Heinrich Donner, the man Doc Thunder despised most in all the world. Strange, then, that they were so alike in their iron commitment to changing the world for the better. Lomax genuinely wanted to raise mankind to the stars, to make everyone in the world into a Doc Thunder, and if they'd only managed to work in unison, maybe that could have happened. Maybe they could have saved the world together.

But Lomax hated him.

Lars Lomax had hated him for his physical superiority, his perceived arrogance, his reluctance to destroy the status quo rather than change it slowly from within. Doc Thunder could never find it in him to hate Lomax back. He'd tried to save him, tried to bring him around, to persuade him that it didn't have to be that way, that there was a way that they could both get what they wanted without destroying each other. But that hatred had only grown, the terrible flaw in an otherwise brilliant personality. A single crack that turned this mirror-image of America's greatest hero into the world's greatest threat, that made Earth's would-be saviour believe that the only way to save the global village was to destroy it.

More sparks, more flashes. He had to remember something. Their final confrontation. The zeppelin, flying over the rich jungles of the Amazon, the struggle for the pistol...

No. That wasn't the important part. It was the part before, the part Maya had told him about. Something Lomax had said. How had it gone?

What had Maya said?

Think. Remember.

"I always enjoy our talks…"

"I ALWAYS ENJOY our talks, your Royal Highness. Tell me, what will you do when all this is over and your lover is dead? Go back to your forgotten kingdom? I can't imagine what the funeral service will be like."

One thousand days previously—in the sparks and crackles of Doc Thunder's memory—Lars Lomax smiled, and his shaggy red eyebrows lifted in amusement. "I imagine it involves feeding the deceased to a giant cobra, or possibly having a death-duel with a panther. That's about your speed, isn't it? Am I close?" He idly reached out to move his bishop a single square.

"Close." Maya smiled, readjusting herself on her seat. The ropes binding her arms and legs in place, securing her to the warm leather seat in front of the chessboard, were tight, but not so tight as to cut off her circulation. Lomax was considerate of his guests, as long as it suited him to be. "Actually the funeral service involves raising an army of my finest warriors to hunt you to the end of the world and flay the flesh from your living bones for daring to plot against my chosen consort. Never mind the temerity you've shown by daring to bind a Goddess… anyway, Queen's knight to queen five. Knight takes pawn. Mate in three moves."

Lomax frowned as he made her move for her. "Well, I'm not going to leave you free, am I? I'm not stupid. You'd kill me in five seconds. Three moves, you say?" He concentrated for a moment, and then took his own knight and captured a pawn himself. Getting rid of that white rook was a priority—in addition to all the other priorities, of course. Like killing Doc Thunder once and for all. "Well, I'm concentrating on several things at once, you have to understand."

Maya sneered. "King's knight to king four, knight takes knight, mate in two moves. And believe me, I understand. After all… you're no Doc Thunder, are you?"

Lomax cursed. Now he'd lost his knight, his queen was locked in one corner of the board and his king was looking dangerously under threat. How had he missed that? He'd walked right into it. Too many variables, that was the problem. Hurriedly, he captured the original knight with a pawn. Perhaps he could outflank her somehow.

For these few seconds of consideration, the game on the board was as important as the larger one taking place in the massive dirigible floating over the Amazon, towards his destiny. He'd rebuilt his Flying Fortress for the purpose, investing in hydrogen rather than cavorite to lift the structure—less expensive, and more suited to his purposes.

Of course, it meant that he was flying in a gigantic firebomb that could go off at any moment, but what was life without a little risk?

Whenever he had Ms Zor-Tura as his guest—vastly preferable to leaving such a dangerous opponent free to provide aid and comfort to the accursed Thunder—he made a point of getting out the chessboard. Last time, he'd beaten her conclusively in one game and forced her to a stalemate in the second. No small feat, given that she'd been playing the game almost since its inception, and he was putting the final touches to his earthquake machine at the time.

Having made his move, he snapped out of his brief trance and turned his attention back to Maya.

"No Doc Thunder... well, I take that as a compliment. Anyway, pretty soon there'll be no Doc Thunder, just a moldy old corpse hanging off the front of my dirigible. Do you like it, by the way? After you broke the old one, I traded up. I particularly like the new furniture." He stood, walking across the metal flooring of the dirigible cabin towards the chair—his favourite chair, the one Doctor Hamilton was sitting in. "What do you think, Doctor Hamilton? How's my taste in antiques?"

Hamilton seemed restrained, drugged almost—not his usual self. He'd been Doc Thunder's personal physician for over ten years, and in that time Maya had gotten to know him well. A man with a dry wit, a gentle grip and a fierce light in his eyes, always ready with a smile, who cried at the injustices of the world openly and without shame. A truly gentle man.

The light in his eyes seemed gone now. The chair he was strapped in looked as if it would be most at home in one of the dungeons of the Spanish Inquisition. Hamilton's arms were strapped down to the arms of the chair, and there was a further studded metal strap wound around his temples and forehead, with a screw positioned at the back of the monstrous device that would tighten it as needed. Lomax had been slowly tightening the mechanism until it dug into Hamilton's flesh, and the agony must have been unendurable—the band was already visibly sunk into his forehead. Despite this, he remained still and calm, speaking through hitching breaths. "You can stop... stop asking questions. I'm never going to tell you what you want to know." The words held an edge of determination that struck Maya as almost out of character, and she felt shame at the thought. She'd misjudged him.

"But I really don't want to know very much, doctor. Can't we compromise? Long negotiations can be such a headache." He reached to tighten the screw again, and Hamilton winced and inhaled sharply, gritting his teeth. "I really think you should reconsider. If nothing else, when your head cracks open like an eggshell it's going to make a terrible mess of my lovely Flying Fortress."

"I said no." Maya couldn't tell if that look of supernatural calm on Hamilton's face was despair, agony or something else. The words were low, almost rasping. "I'm not going to help you kill him. Good God, listen to yourself! You've tried shooting him, bombing him, stabbing him—now you want to find some ancient poison or radioactive metal that can kill him for you? You're a sick maaaagh!" His voice became a scream as Lomax tightened the band once more.

"Excuse me while I turn this a small trifle... you're right, doctor, I am a sick man. I'm a very sick man. Sick of *him*. That pompous intellectual midget. That over-inflated stuffed shirt. I want him out of my hair for a while, Hamilton. Him and his trained ape."

"I beg your pardon?" hissed Maya, arching an eyebrow.

Lomax rounded on her, his irritation boiling into a sudden rage. "Oh, I forgot, the ape-man's your boyfriend too. Well, of course he is! The monarchy always did get their playthings, didn't they, Princess? King Thunder the first's big happy family can do what they like! *He* can do what he likes! Bend the ears of Presidents! God forbid the rest of us get the chance to make our voices heard! God forbid any *real* human beings ever go outside the stifling rules of this wretched, poisoned society, ever get to live their lives free from the taint of the status quo! Free from the *rules!* The ones *he* enforces!"

Hamilton didn't blink. "You're mad, Lomax. You're completely mad."

"Oh, I'm furious." Lomax was suddenly calm as he turned back to face the doctor. "We have a superhuman being retarding our development. If humans had fought the Second Civil War alone, we'd have a paradise by now. My paradise. Instead, all we did was swap one flag for another. Well, I think it's about time we put the flags away with the rest of our childhood toys." He leaned in, close to the doctor's ear.

"Listen, doctor. You're Thunder's personal physician. You must know his weaknesses. You see, I was thinking... Poison. We're on our way to my Amazon lab, I've got a number of interesting toxins stored there. We'll experiment, see what might work. I just want a little input from you, that's all." He slowly twisted the screw, very gently now, applying only the slightest pressure. Hamilton screamed. "A little co-operation. That's all I want, and then the pain can stop. What do you say?"

"'First, do no harm.'" Hamilton gasped, his expression still unchanging as he gritted his teeth. "I took an oath. You can torture me all you want."

"Good. I'll do that, then."

"Even if I could help you—"

Lomax scowled, standing suddenly. It was all taking too long. He had to speed this up. "Fine. Fine, fine, fine, your own life isn't important to you. I get it. You're a big hero, well done, very good. How about *hers*?" He drew a revolver from his belt and pointed it directly between Maya's eyes. "Because one way or another I plan to hurt him, doctor. I plan to hurt the big blue banana very badly indeed. And between you and me? I don't really care about methods."

Maya strained against the ropes, testing them again. Then she spoke, coolly. "Queen to queen seven, queen takes bishop. Check. And don't you dare threaten *me*."

Without taking his gun off her, Lomax made the move. He chuckled, and called back to Hamilton. "Her Majesty speaks! And she's right, you know, doctor, I am indeed in check. Seems a shame to end the game at this point, doesn't it? I'd look like a sore loser. It'd be sour grapes." He laughed again, eyes flashing fire, matching Maya's as his finger stroked the trigger. "Sure you won't reconsider my generous offer? I'd so hate to seem *unsporting*."

"Go ahead and shoot. I may be more resilient than you think." Maya smiled, daring him with her eyes.

"You are fascinatingly long-lived, I'll grant you that. A true scientific puzzle. But immune to death by gunshot? I'd be a poor scientist if I didn't test that little theory." He chuckled, spying something on the chessboard. "Oh, and..." He took one of his knights and quickly knocked the white queen over on the board before picking it off. "Knight takes queen. That's game over, I think, Maya."

Maya looked back at him, and at that moment the entire cabin lurched sideways, the pieces toppling off the board, the board toppling off the table, the torture-chair sliding across the smooth metal floor.

Maya smiled. "Game over. Yes, I rather think it is. King's knight to king six." Her eyes sparkled. "Checkmate."

A hand tore through the metal siding of the cabin, peeling it away like a can-opener, as the superhuman forced his way in. Lars Lomax only smiled, and straightened.

"I thought he'd never get here."

He raised the gun and fired twice at Doc Thunder, aiming for the eyes. They were the weak spots, where a well-placed bullet could—

wait something not right
i thought he'd never get here
why did he say that

The insight hit like a thunderbolt. They were starting again. He needed to tap out soon, give Maya the signal, but he couldn't yet. Not until he'd worked it out.

"I thought he'd never get here."

But Lomax hadn't found the answer he was after—hadn't found his poison, the death-in-a-bottle that would end the life of the man he hated most. But he'd sounded impatient—

what else had he said
out of my hair for a while
strange way to put it

Another flash. Stronger. He was on the edge of something, he knew. What had happened next?

There'd been a fight. An unequal fight, as always. He'd kept firing his pistol, even as he'd climbed into the cabin, even though he knew it wouldn't affect him. No, that wasn't quite true. He'd gone for the eyes. Always for the eyes.

The weak spot. A bullet in the eye would go straight into his brain and kill him, or at least brain-damage him. During the Second Civil War, he'd kept goggles with bullet-proof glass in them to wear during gunfights, but in the long run they'd limited his vision too badly to be worth it, especially after Silken Dragon's people had discovered inexorium—

inexorium
the metal cuts through my skin
no poison required

Doc gritted his teeth, tasting the rubber of the gag. He was almost seeing something, but not quite. The flashes were coming more quickly now. The insights. He travelled back in his memory, remembering the unequal fight, Lomax darting and ducking, aiming more bullets for his eyes, diving to the floor to escape a punch, rolling and snapping off one last shot—the one that killed him. The bullet had bounced off Doc's forehead, ripping up through the roof of the cabin and into one of the hydrogen chambers. It must have struck a spark on the metal, or at least he'd assumed later that's what must have happened, because suddenly the cabin was filled with flame and smoke. He'd heard the terrible roar and the rush of heat as the hydrogen went up—

but why hydrogen
antiquated and unsafe
why not cavorite

—and then he'd just reacted, grabbing Maya and Doctor Hamilton, ordering Lomax onto his back. He remembered that part very clearly, that oddly triumphant look. "You don't get to save me, Thunder." A coughing laugh. And then he'd run into the flames. Later, in the wreckage of the airship, they'd found his blackened skeleton. In death, it had seem to laugh at Doc Thunder, grinning with an empty skull-smile at his inability to save his greatest foe. It was the smile of the last enemy, of death itself.

Doc had blamed himself, but the simple truth was that he hadn't had time to go after Lomax. He'd just hurled himself out of the crashing airship and into the waters of the Amazon, doing his best to shield Maya and Miles from the full effects of the fall. He'd dragged everyone to shore—Hamilton had nearly drowned—and then he'd freed him from the chair, the metal band across his brow leaving a deep indentation, although he didn't seem to be in that much pain. Hamilton had thanked him, without smiling—

was that when he stopped
after that he never smiled
and now we don't talk

—that was when he'd changed, that day that Lomax died. They'd been good friends before, and after that they'd drifted apart, and eventually Doc Thunder had stopped feeling the need for a personal physician. Now they were strangers.

He could smell skin cooking.

He wanted to tap out, but there was something he was still missing. He could feel it, right on the edge of his thoughts. That unsmiling thank-you on the riverbank—

holding out his hand
it caught me off guard somehow
his left hand shook mi—

And then it was over.

DOC SLUMPED IN the chair, panting, as Maya took her hand off the switch. When she took out the gag, he stretched his jaw, and then spoke, throat raw. "Too soon."

Maya shook her head. "You were in there for almost a full minute. Your skin was cooking. I thought you'd passed out."

He shook his head, gingerly feeling the burned patches at his temples after she undid the straps holding him down. "No such luck. I think I might have something. Or a lot of somethings that are going to add up to something." He shook his head, trying to clear the feeling of nausea—always the aftermath of an omega session. "We need to go back to the hospital."

Maya froze. "Is Monk in trouble?"

Doc frowned, thinking. "Maybe. More than we thought. But... I think I might be the one in trouble, Maya. I think I might have made my second mistake of the evening."

He stood, breathing in, trying to steady himself. Then he spoke again.

"Because when I met him... Doctor Hamilton was right-handed."

CHAPTER SEVEN
THE CASE OF THE KILLER CABALLERO

THE NEW JUNIOR Under-janitor at the Jameson Club swept the floor slowly, methodically. Occasionally, he scratched the back of his head.

He was a temporary fix—quite the wrong sort of person for a permanent position, even as Junior Under-janitor—but the Club had needed someone in a hurry, as the previous Junior Under-janitor had sent an urgent telegram to say that he would not be coming in today, or any day. It was always difficult to measure a man's tone through the medium of something as impersonal as a telegram, but those who read it were of the opinion that the man had written it while frightened out of his wits. Some sort of psychological condition, perhaps. A poor show if he'd hidden it during his interview.

Fortunately, the new Junior Under-janitor had walked in the door only a few minutes later, quite literally begging for work. While he was quite the wrong sort of person—*quite* wrong—he did have a knack for making himself entirely unobtrusive, and thus was hired on for the day, with the possibility of being allowed back the next day if—one—the Club seniors could find nobody else on short notice and—two—he could keep his unfortunate racial handicap from bringing opprobrium on the Jameson Club.

He was, after all, *quite* the wrong sort of person.

Parker Crane certainly did not notice the new Junior Under-janitor as he breezed in, nodding a curt hello to Jonah, who hovered at the foot of the stairs.

"Sir, if I may, you have a visitor." The slight, nigh-undetectable pause before the word *visitor,* and the set of Jonah's eyebrows, communicated all of his feelings on the matter.

"Detective Stacey. Thank you, Jonah."

"I took the liberty of placing him in the Lower Library, sir, as I felt your conversation would be best conducted in a private setting."

"Thank you, Jonah."

"Also, your guest has a somewhat curious smell and I fear allowing him into the more commonly-used environs of the Jameson Club would irreparably damage your standing as—"

"*Thank* you, Jonah. That will be all."

"Yes, sir." Jonah gently ushered Crane through the door and into the room. Harry Stacey was waiting there with a near-empty glass of scotch—not the malt, thank goodness—and impatiently drumming his fingers on the dusty arm of the old leather chair he'd stationed himself in.

"About goddamn time! I been waiting here for close to an hour, you god-damned pansy!" He threw the rest of the scotch down his throat, then pointed an accusing finger at Crane. "Listen, pal, you better get on the *ball,* capeesh? 'Cause I'm in pretty tight with *you know who,* mac, and if *you know who* finds out you messed me about when I got important info for him, *you-know-who* might just figure on stickin' one of his guns right up your well-pounded rich boy *ass* and pulling the trigger until he friggin' breaks it off! Get me?"

"The Blood-Spider. You can say his name. This room is quite soundproofed." Crane was amused, despite himself, by the little man's bluster, but there was business to conduct. "You have the information he asked for?"

"Yeah, sword killings." He lifted up a manila file and opened it up on his lap. "You know, I didn't think there'd be this many. All recent, too—last few days."

"The last few..." Crane's eyes widened. He hadn't expected this at all. "Tell me." The urgency in his voice made Stacey look up, a trace of puzzlement on his idiot's face, and Crane scowled. It wouldn't do to even let this cretin guess his secret. He'd already risked too much with that little stunt at the party. "The... Blood-Spider will want to know the information urgently." His voice dropped, faking an air of concern. "I've... already angered him. I might have accidentally boasted of my connection to the Blood-Spider to, ah, guarantee success with a woman." Harry Stacey looked worried about that, which pleased Crane immensely. "He told me he might be considering getting another mail drop with a smaller mouth. I have to prove my worth to him, or..." He left the sentence dangerously unfinished. He was satisfied that he'd drawn Stacey away from any possible suspicion, and perhaps the ruse might keep him from flapping his own receding gums quite so often.

No such luck. Stacey's worried look transformed into a vicious grin, and he leant back in the chair, pointing a finger at Parker. "Too bad for *you*, buddy. I figure he'll probably cut your balls off you and bury 'em in concrete. Parker Crane, the richest eunuch in New York city. You oughtta get in his good books, like me. Me and the Spider, we're like *that*." He pressed thumb and forefingers together. "Thick like thieves. Two old buddies from around the way. He told me once that I was the cream of his whole friggin' Web, y'know? I mean, compared to some of the things I've seen, y'know, *in the line,* this is just a hobby for me, kinda like stamp collectin'."

Crane sighed, shaking his head. He was probably going to have to do something about Stacey one of these days. "The sword killings." He forced a smile. "If you wouldn't mind."

"Don't want to make the Boss mad, right? I feel you, buddy." Stacey smirked, passing him the photos one by one; the crime scenes left behind.

"We got two futureheads here, found dead with sword wounds. One to the throat, one to the abdomen. That's down in East Village. Both white, swastika tattoos, previous for, uh, 'racially motivated assault.' Roughhousin', I call it, but you know these progressive types. Another over in the Bronx, same. Three more over on Staten Island, one right in midtown, *five* in Central Park. Whoever this nutcase is, he sure gets around, I'll tell you that much."

"All the same man?"

Stacey nodded. "Sure. Wounds all match up. Plus, the vics all have a lot of things in common. All with previous for rolling jigs or queers, all heavily on the Kraut side of politics if you catch my drift. A couple of these dumbasses were actually killed during assaults in progress, while they were rolling other guys. We got witnesses who saw this guy work, said he saved their lives. 'Course, these are mostly jigs or spics, and you know they lie—"

"Stacey." Crane's voice was acid. "Let's have the facts without the editorial, please."

"Listen, rich boy, I don't see the *Blood-Spider* having a problem with the way

I talk, so why don't you just—" Crane's look froze him in mid-sentence. "Ah, fine. Fine, whatever."

He rummaged quickly through the files. "Here's a witness statement for you. The five in Central Park. Apparently these guys pulled knives on a... on a *latino* couple, pardon your delicate friggin' ears, out for a late-night stroll. Went for the lady's purse, the fella stepped it, he got cut up some. Things were getting ugly, you know? Anyway, we got a clear description of what happened next. Just when our witnesses think they're gonna bite it, they start hearing this laugh."

Crane raised an eyebrow. "Laugh?"

"Sure, this big crazy laugh, like Santa Claus, big and booming. Like it's everywhere at once. I mean, I didn't hear it, but according to the witnesses it really got the perps freaking out, you know? Yelling 'who's there,' 'come on out,' all that jazz, trying to make this guy show himself..."

"So... they were scared?"

"Yeah, that's something I don't get either. I mean, it's just laughing, right? Some asshole laughs at me out of some bushes, I'd walk in there, grab his ass and introduce him to a little chin music, capeesh? Guy's probably a friggin' homo, ain't a jury in the world gonna convict me if I hand the guy his face. You gotta get a little rough with their kind, mark 'em up some, or next thing you know, the whole institution of marriage—"

Crane growled. "*Stacey.*"

Stacey shrugged. "Yeah, yeah, you've got your balls on the chopping block, I got you. So, yeah, I guess it must have been a hell of a laugh this guy had..."

Crane nodded, trying to hide the sinking feeling in the pit of his stomach. One of his tactics as the Blood-Spider—one Stacey had never been on the receiving end of—was a merciless, mocking laugh that froze the hearts of his enemies like ice in their chests. Was this a coincidence? Could it be?

"...anyway, suddenly this guy leaps out of the bushes. The witnesses didn't see exactly where he came from. It was like, one minute he wasn't there and the next minute, *bam*, there he was, large as life and twice as ugly."

Crane's brows furrowed. "Describe him."

"Go the description right here, let's see. Well, to start with, he's a wetback."

"A... what?"

"Mexican." Stacey shook his head, looking irritated that he had to explain the term. "Exhibitionist, too. No shirt, no shoes; just a pair of black suit pants. Oh yeah, and get this. He was wearing a mask. A red mask, wrapped around his eyes."

"A red mask…" The sinking feeling intensified. A red mask, like the Blood-Spider wore. Was he being imitated?

"Right. Anyway, this crazy bastard leaps out of nowhere carrying a sword and starts carving them up like Christmas turkeys. Lemme just repeat that for those sensitive ears of yours. One guy, not even wearing a shirt, against *five*. And these were big guys. They worked out, they'd done some time in juvenile. These were people who knew a little something about how to break a guy's head open, you know? Even if he did have a sword and a scary laugh."

"So whoever this… interloper is, he's very highly skilled."

Stacey frowned, looking around briefly as if checking nobody was in earshot. "Listen—" He leaned forward, as though imparting a great secret. "—I can handle myself in a fight, capeesh? I done a lot of stuff in the line. But five guys with blades—I couldn't have taken them. Seriously, they'd have cut off my dick and drop-kicked it into the East River. You ask any cop, they'd tell you the same. Even the Blood-Spider couldn't have taken all five of these guys with just a sword. Not all at once."

Crane raised his eyebrow again. "But the interloper…"

"Two decapitations, two fatal stabbings—one through the eye—and the last guy bled out from getting his junk cut off."

Crane blinked. "No wonder castration was weighing on your mind."

Stacey shrugged. "Like I said, it could be a lie, but *something* killed those assholes in the park. And until we got anything better to go on, I'm going with the sword-man theory." He frowned. "There's more, though. You know I got deep contacts in the FBI? Hell, I could have been a Fed myself, but I told those suit-and-tie assholes right to their faces: 'Harry Stacey is a man of the streets,' I said—"

Crane rolled his eyes. He'd heard this story a dozen times, the day Harry Stacey turned down the FBI, and the truth was a little more prosaic. Harry was in a twice-weekly poker game with a filing clerk at the Bureau. When Harry needed minor information on FBI operations, he either forgave a debt or two or—on those occasions when he was not owed—leaned on one of the local whores to give the clerk a free ride. Like so much of the detritus that made up Harry's life, it was rotten to the core, and Crane found himself wishing he could simply reach forward and break the disgusting little man's neck. But it was necessary sometimes, when fighting the darkness that riddled Manhattan like a cancer, to perform acts that were themselves unsavoury—morally dubious, even. The Blood-Spider knew that very well.

Harry seemed to be coming to the end of his monologue; Crane forced himself to listen.

"—tried to pin a medal on me, but I told them I wasn't interested in none of that crapola. I don't need some piece of tin, that's what I told them. My place is on the streets, capeesh? A medal don't mean a damn thing in the line, you know? The only thing that counts is your shield and your gun and your *guts,* that's what I told 'em." He breathed in, as if showing off his gut for approval. "Anyway, like I said, I got contacts, and apparently this loon's been popping up in connection with some stuff the FBI's looking into. Kraut stuff."

"Kraut?" Crane's eyes narrowed.

"As in Untergang."

Crane blinked, slightly stunned. "Wait, this red mask fellow—he's working for *Untergang?* That doesn't make sense."

Stacey laughed, shaking his head. "Working for 'em? Hell no! Working *on* 'em, maybe. Look, the FBI keep some of those guys under surveillance. They figure if they keep watchin' the little fish, sooner or later they're gonna lead 'em to the sharks, y'know? Anyway, they're keeping tabs on this one cell, waiting for the chance to move in—and our guy just bursts in there and takes them apart. These are friggin' terrorists! With guns! Ten of them at least!" His eyes grew wide, staring into Crane's as if trying to infect him with Stacey's own incredulity at it. "He kills all but one of them—asks some questions—then kills that last guy too!" He drew a finger across his throat. "*Shlikk!* Just like that! The goddamn wetback is some kind of *machine,* capeesh?"

Crane leant back in his chair, lost in thought. "Who *is* he...?"

Stacey shrugged. "He hates the Krauts, that's for sure. Other than that—who the hell knows? Ain't like this town's ever been short of vigilantes. Hell, remember the Blue Ghost? I used to hang out with him when I was just a patrolman. Hell of a nice guy, even if he did get beat up a lot. Him and me were like *that,* even if I did used to smack that Jap kid he hung out with around a lot. I mean, yeah, he broke my arm, but it was all in fun, y'know?" He looked into the distance, furrowing his brow. "Vanished a little before you came on the scene, as a matter of fact..."

"I don't need to hear another tall story from you, Detective." The edge was back in Crane's voice, no matter how much he tried to keep it out. "I need to know who this masked man thinks he is and how and why he found Heinrich Donner." The why was obvious, Crane knew, if unpalatable. The thought brought him back to the ape-man's appearance at Donner's penthouse suite the previous night. "And we need to know how Doc Thunder's connected to all this." And there was a connection, he knew. Doc Thunder and Heinrich Donner had never been friends. Perhaps he was working with this Mexican, this red mask. Perhaps he was Thunder's secret enforcer, committing crimes to make sure Thunder's hero's hands could remain clean and unstained. If that was the case, it was one more reason for him to have earned Crane's contempt.

The Blood-Spider preferred to do his dirty work himself.

Stacey scowled, snarling at him like a dog straining at the end of a leash. "Listen, buddy," he snapped, "I don't know how you got so mouthy— considering you're just a jumped-up messaging service for the boss and all—but if I was you I'd quit flapping your gums, capeesh? You act like you're in charge of this caper because you were born with a goddamned silver spoon halfway up your stretched asshole, but lemme tell ya, pally, I'm in a lot deeper with the Blood-Spider than you are. And so help me, I might just decide to tell him how you been treating me."

"Oh, shut up and get lost, Stacey." Crane waved the Detective away, as Jonah, knowing as ever just when he would be needed, opened the door to escort him out. Stacey snatched up the file, let loose a few more choice epithets about Crane's education and background, and then left, leaving nothing but the stink of sweat, cigar smoke and whiskey to mark his passing.

Crane made a mental note not to lose his temper like that again. He'd spoken as the Blood-Spider, and while an imbecile like Harry Stacey might not think twice about it, he could be sure others would take notice. Parker Crane had always been a mask—a disguise to hide his true self—but lately the mask had begun to fray, and traces of the truth were occasionally visible. That would not do. Not after all the work he'd done.

He had too many plans to allow his temper to spoil them.

"If I might interrupt your reverie, sir...? You received a telegram in the last five minutes, and while I felt it prudent not to interrupt your conversation with the detective..."

"Yes, of course." Crane reached out a hand, taking hold of the folded piece of paper, and passed his eyes quickly over it.

HELLO PARKER STOP NEED TO TALK STOP HAVE
SOMETHING OF INTEREST TO YOU STOP BOTH OF YOU

STOP ALSO FIFTY FIFTY CHANCE OF OTHER INTEREST
STOP PLEASE COME TO THE ROOFTOP OF SAINT
ALBERTS ASAP STOP NO B S STOP

DOCTOR MILES HAMILTON

"Miles Hamilton…"

"Chief Administrator at Saint Albert's, sir. At one point he and Doc Thunder were very close friends."

Crane frowned. "'Fifty fifty chance of other interest.' What does that mean?"

Jonah coughed gently. "If I may be so bold, sir, I would be more interested in the part that says he has something of interest to 'both of you.' Add that to the, ah, 'no B S'… and unless the good doctor has developed a taste for the vernacular…"

"He knows." Crane's eyes grew hard. "He knows that I'm the Blood-Spider. He's learned my secret, maybe *all* my secrets, and he's telling me to leave the mask and the guns at home."

Jonah nodded. "And will you, sir?"

Crane almost smiled. "Jonah, Jonah, Jonah. The mask and the guns *are* my home." He stood, looking over at the trunk that sat in the corner, squat and menacing, like some demon coiled up and ready to explode. "Bring the telephone. I'm afraid I'm going to need to interrupt Ms Lang's evening again."

He turned to look at Jonah, and there was something quite terrifying in his gaze. Something that spoke of brutal, merciless violence yet to come.

"We're going to pay a little social call."

As JONAH LEFT the room, he paid no attention to the Junior Under-janitor, still sweeping the floor and scratching the back of his skull. If he had known the Junior Under-janitor had been listening at the door, he would have been instantly dismissed—and perhaps 'silenced' by the Blood-Spider.

But the Junior Under-janitor was beneath his notice. He was, after all, quite the wrong sort of person. A Mexican, and very likely an illegal immigrant.

If Jonah had known that the Junior Under-janitor was not only an illegal immigrant but was also suffering from multiple personality disorder—and indeed was prone to regular bouts of extreme violence—it's hard to say whether he would have been surprised. But he'd never bothered to ask such things. Could he push a broom, that was all that mattered. The next day, they would begin the process of finding a proper applicant for the post.

He barely even remembered the man's name.

It was Djego.

CHAPTER EIGHT
DOC THUNDER AND THE FACE OF FEAR

MORE THAN TWENTY years before, the clocks were striking midnight. The 'seventies were coming to a close, and the whole of America looked set to follow.

The Blue Ghost watched through one swollen eye as Anton Venger, Agent of N.I.G.H.T.M.A.R.E., held the glass bottle aloft. Inside, the blue ichor which would spell death to half a continent—and perhaps the end of civilisation as mankind knew it—sloshed lazily to and fro, seemingly glowing with its own internal light.

Venger chuckled, his handsome, tanned features lit by the fire of Liberty's torch as he savoured the coming moment, when he would uncap the deadly bottle and hurl the concentrated solution off his perch on top of the Statue—where his men had taken the Ghost at Venger's request—and into the harbour. There, the final reaction would take place, the seawater combining with the experimental poison to form an ever-expanding ring of death; a toxic cloud rising up from below like some monstrous kraken. Before the reaction was exhausted, the eastern coast of America would choke on the deadly fumes. "Ironic, isn't it? We're about to give New York the ultimate liberty—the liberty of death. It's a real shame President Rickard couldn't see reason. One billion dollars is such a piddling little sum..."

The Ghost shifted, trying to break out of the ropes, and was rewarded with a stabbing pain in his side that made him wince. Venger's goons had really worked him over. He counted at least four broken ribs, not to mention the broken leg that he was going to have to heave around the place on crutches for God only knew how long. That was going to make fighting crime a real pain in the keister, and with his arms tied, it left him one good leg to save the country.

Why the hell hadn't he stuck to beating on gangsters?

"You're bluffing, Venger." *I hope.* "If that stuff does what you say it does, you'll die with the rest of us."

Venger looked wounded. "My dear Ghost—I have doctorate degrees in biology, virology and medicine. Do you really think me so stupid as to invent a deadly poison and not inoculate myself against it? When New Yorkers are gasping their lungs out like freshly-landed fish, I will be leading the squads of N.I.G.H.T.M.A.R.E. agents looting the east coast of its valuables. If we can't have our payday one way, we'll have it another. Perhaps our dear Prez will think twice before he bets against the greatest criminal organisation in the world."

The Ghost frowned. He'd fouled up on this one, these were international criminals operating on a massive scale. It was S.T.E.A.M. who should be fighting these guys, not some guy in a blue suit and a skinny tie whose biggest talent was taking a beating and coming back for more. Why the hell hadn't he turned the whole thing over to the big boys when he'd had the chance? The whole world was waiting for N.I.G.H.T.M.A.R.E.'s midnight deadline, and Jack Scorpio's high-faluting Special Taskforce was on a wild goose chase to Yellowstone Park. The only people in the world who knew Venger was here were him and Easton West—and who'd believe a ten-year-old kid?

The only thing he could do now was keep the nutball talking. As long as he was running his mouth, he wasn't emptying that poison vial into the water. "Got it all worked out, haven't you? How many people are you planning to kill for your kicks, you sick, twisted..." He trailed off. *Should I insult the guy, or not insult the guy? A slanging match would be pretty good—that'll keep this going a while—but not if he gets mad enough to toss that crap off the crown.*

Venger didn't seem overly offended. He just smiled his superior smile. "Judging by this wind, I think the poison cloud should blow inland for quite a distance. It may even reach the White House before it loses full potency. And even after... well, if you've ever breathed acid vapour, you know that even if it doesn't kill you, it will certainly sting. And this will be very similar, if you haven't had your inoculation jab. That's why I had my men bring you up here. I want to watch the effects on a human body up close. I hope you don't mind being part of my experiment."

"Sheesh. You scientists." The Ghost rolled his eyes behind his ever-present blue domino mask. "Just once, I'd like to meet a crazy world-conqueror who took drama. He could try and Shakespeare me to death."

"Hmm. Funny you should mention that." Venger smiled widely. "I did do a minor in drama at college—'the man of a thousand voices,' they called me. I could have been a star of the stage. Isn't it funny how things work out?"

"Never too late, pal. Lot of great plays get put on in prison. A little state's evidence and you wouldn't even see the inside. What do you say?" The Ghost was really hoping he'd actually go for this. If he didn't, he was out of options. A last-minute change of heart was about all the hope he had left.

For a moment, Venger almost seemed to consider it. "Hmmm..." Then he smiled. "No. But I do appreciate you trying to keep me talking. I wanted to allow the idiots at S.T.E.A.M. a false glimmer of hope before I showed them just how pitifully they'd failed." He smiled, lifting the bottle up into the air, theatrically removing the cork with his other hand. The air suddenly filled with the sickly smell of rotting lilacs—

—and then Doc Thunder landed on the Statue of Liberty, ringing it like a gong, the small Japanese boy clinging to his back hanging on for dear life.

"Easton!" yelled the Ghost, a note of triumph in his voice. "Great stuff, kid! Gimme a hand out of these ropes, huh?"

"I got help like you said, Mr Ghost Boss!" Easton yelled as he clambered off the big man's back. Having been unable to interest the police in his story, he'd done the next best thing and gone straight to the Doc's brownstone. Fortunately, Doc had been home.

"Put down the fluid, Venger. You don't want to do this." Thunder's eyes were a steely calm, and he spoke softly, carefully. If that solution should fall over the side... even one drop... "Listen to me. If you do this—if you allow this atrocity to happen—there'll be nowhere you can hide. You know that. Every law enforcement agency on the planet will be after your blood from now until the day you die. There will be no escape. Let it end, Venger—Anton. Let it go." He smiled, keeping his eyes on the other man's. He spoke softly, rationally, and he meant every word. You couldn't lie to these people, they could smell insincerity. How many times had he been talking to men with their fingers on the trigger, or the button, or the bomb? How many times had he failed to prevent them from destroying themselves?

For the sake of New York, he couldn't fail now. "I want to save you. I want to help you. If you come with me, we can... *I* can work with you. I can get to the bottom of your anti-social tendencies." The words set off warning bells in his own ears. They sounded fake—ridiculous and fake—and all of a sudden he knew that he'd lost this one. He couldn't pull it back.

Now he needed to get to Anton Venger before he dropped the fluid.

Anton shook his head, terror in his eyes. The West boy was still fumbling with the Blue Ghost's ropes, trying to free him without putting too much pressure on his ribs. Venger began to step back towards the edge, keeping his eyes on Thunder, holding the bottle of blue ooze protectively against his chest.

Doc Thunder knew that if he made a sudden move, Venger would hurl that bottle into the harbour. "Anton!" he breathed, trying to freeze him with his voice. It didn't work. Venger took another step back. Then another. Then another. Then—

—the Blue Ghost stuck his good leg out.

Venger gave a little scream, like a child, as he toppled backwards. But there was nothing little about the scream he let out as the blue liquid splashed out of the bottle and over his face, coating it, then eating into it, seeming to merge with it...

"Dear God..." breathed the Ghost, as Easton West buried his face in the powder-blue suit jacket, hiding from the terrible sight.

"None of it went in the water. We're safe." Doc Thunder breathed out. He hadn't even been aware he'd been holding his breath. "But... I don't know if he'll live through that."

The Ghost looked at the shriveled, withered skin, once tanned, now a terrible bluish-white. The face which seemed to be melting, distorting as he watched. The agonised look in the man's grey eyes.

"I don't know if he'll want to."

"HE DIDN'T."

That was then, and this was now, and Doc Thunder and Maya were racing in a hansom carriage towards Saint Albert's Hospital. "He blamed me, of course. Oh, he hated the Ghost, and he hated N.I.G.H.T.M.A.R.E., I'm sure he hated himself. But most of all, he hated me. If I hadn't turned up when I did, he'd still have a face. All this was before your time..."

Maya smiled. "Very little is before my time. But I take your meaning. What on earth did you do for fun in that big lonely brownstone before Monk and I came along?"

Doc smiled, despite himself. "I played a lot of chess. Miles would come around for a game occasionally." He grew pensive again, shaking his head. "Miles. I can't believe I never saw it."

"You couldn't have—" Maya began, but Doc cut her off.

"Don't tell me I couldn't have known. I could have, I *should* have known, Maya. You might not have known how he got that way, but you knew what he could do. *I* knew what he could do." He shook his head, his face contorted in self-recrimination. "And when my oldest friend's personality changed, and he started favouring his left hand, and his face stopped registering emotion… I thought he'd grown cold. I thought he'd just stopped being a good guy. I thought that instinctive, gut-level dislike I felt whenever I met him… was *him*. And all the time…"

Anton Venger.

The Face of Fear.

That blueish-white visage, once handsome, was now slack, shapeless, drooping like unfired clay. And like clay, it could be shaped. Molded. Given time, and a little makeup, it could be made to look like anyone in the world. Anton Venger was a skilled impersonator, and the madness that had claimed him after his terrible accident only increased his ability to take on the personalities of others, albeit as a dark reflection, with all of their weaknesses and insecurities given full life within this strange, twisted doppelganger.

As a member of N.I.G.H.T.M.A.R.E. he would have been invaluable, but his madness had led him to reject them, to strike out on his own, to make war against all of civilization, against a species he no longer felt any part of. When Anton Venger gazed upon the world, he saw no beauty, no joy, no hope, no love. All he saw was the chemical taint of his never ending hatred; a hatred that burned a cold white blue.

A natural outsider, he'd found himself drawn over time to another outsider—to Lars Lomax, the most dangerous man in the world. The Lomax-Venger Team, as Lars had dubbed them in a moment of bonhomie, had almost been the end of everything a dozen times, but eventually, all things must pass.

"You weren't there when Venger died, were you?" As Doc Thunder spoke the words, he realised he hadn't spoken for several minutes, lost in his thoughts. "Not that he did die, as it turns out…"

Maya shook her head. "No. I was in Venice, trying to deal with the war between N.I.G.H.T.M.A.R.E. and E.R.A.M.T.H.G.I.N. along with Monk and Jack Scorpio. Of course, we didn't know that was just a distraction engineered by Lomax. We thought it was the main event." She sighed. "'Am us not men?' Whatever happened to them?"

"Warhol's dreampunk ideas are the new thing in the art world. Détournement is out. The futureheads that are clinging on to the movement are being co-opted by extremist groups. Which means Untergang, of course. All roads of that nature eventually lead to Berlin." He shook his head. "E.R.A.M.T.H.G.I.N. will mutate into something else. Evolve. Or devolve. Pranksters and tricksters, nipping at the nose of culture—so long as there's a culture to nip at, we won't see the last of them. I hope we never do... I like the idea of a world where the worst thing I have to fight is somebody's joke."

Maya nodded. "Meanwhile, you were there for the final dissolution of the Lomax-Venger Team."

"I was." Doc gazed out of the window, remembering. "Paris. City of romance..."

"Mmmm... such a specimen. So very pretty-pretty-pretty..."

The voice seemed to melt, spilling over the tongue like rich liquid chocolate, as Doc Thunder found himself staring into eyes of brilliant gold, unblinking as a serpent's and possessed of a malevolent playfulness that sent a chill down his spine even as the long, perfectly painted fingernails brushed slowly over his naked chest.

He was bound, of course. Great steel anchor chains stretched from the ceiling of the ornate Parisian drawing-room to shackles that held his wrists, while his ankles were secured to the base of the strange contraption he'd been placed on—like a shaped metal saddle secured to a stout pole. It was an uncomfortable predicament, and more than a little humiliating, especially considering the Silken Dragon hadn't allowed him to keep his clothes.

She was like that.

She was the daughter of the Velvet Dragon, N.I.G.H.T.M.A.R.E.'s first leader, a cold, brilliant and debonair psychopath who had died attempting to hurl Jack Scorpio Senior from the top of the Eiffel Tower. He had raised her to think of the world as a plaything, a bauble to be toyed with and claimed as her own whenever she pleased, and all the creatures in it as her slaves. Anyone looking at her would only see the surface at first; a stunningly beautiful woman of mixed French and Oriental descent, possessed of a bountiful figure, which seemed always on the verge of spilling out of the shimmering golden corset she wore, and a luscious, oozing sexuality, a wickedly deviant mind that glittered in her golden eyes, a merciless confidence that revelled in breaking the strong and taming the weak. By the time they realised the true danger—the sheer, ruthless evil hidden beneath the perfume of her skin, an evil that thought nothing of taking the entire planet as a hostage—it was far too late.

"So pretty-pretty-pretty..." she purred, raking her nails once more down Thunder's sculpted abdominal muscles, brushing them lightly through the thicket of his—

"STOP RIGHT THERE." Maya frowned, irritated. "You were flirting with her, weren't you?"

"I wasn't *flirting,* she's an evil—"

"Oh, please! Like she's not your *type!* Chain you to a dungeon wall and you're anybody's, I should know. Let me guess—did you tell her that beneath her iridescent beauty her evil shone cold and hard as a diamond?"

"Well, I didn't say that *exactly*..."

—HER TONGUE TEASED against his for a moment before their lips parted. "Am I not beautiful, my pretty-pretty-pretty? Am I not to be desired by all who look on me?"

"You're as beautiful and desirable as a diamond." Thunder breathed, eyes stern. "And like a diamond, you're cold, and hard... and flawed."

"You dare to call me flawed?" her voice grew icy as her teeth met at his earlobe, a serpentine hiss in his ear. "You will die for that, my pretty-pretty, inch by inch."

"Your evil is your flaw. And all of your beauty can't hide it," Thunder hissed, before another brutal, claiming kiss sealed his lips.

"OH, GOOD GRIEF. You're incorrigible. I can't believe I fell for that line." Maya grew thoughtful for a moment. "She does sound interesting, though. It is a shame we couldn't have met her on a more informal—"

"It would have been harbouring an international fugitive. Sorry. Also, she was completely insane."

Maya sighed. "Well, you can tell me all about that part later. Skip to the relevant bit."

Doc frowned. "Lomax. And Venger."

*   *   *

"I hope I'm not interrupting…" Lomax smiled, walking into the drawing room with a Polish vodka-martini in one hand and a cigar in the other. "My God. You've actually wounded him. What is that?"

Silken Dragon smiled, twirling the barbed flogger in her hand lazily, before leaning to run her tongue along the bloody gashes she'd carved in Thunder's back. "My scientists developed it. An alloy that can actually pierce the good Doctor's skin. We call it inexorium. It makes torture so much more… enjoyable, when you can see the pretty pattern of scars form on the skin. So pretty-pretty-pretty…"

"Good Lord." His eyes widened, looking at the glittering metal as he took a long sip of the martini. "Tell me you've made a bullet with it. We can end this here and now."

"Where would the pleasure be in that? Anyway, inexorium is so very pricy, and so difficult to make. Just the barbs on the tips of this flogger cost me over a million dollars. And they're just tiny scraps of barbed metal… but so effective, aren't they? So wonderfully cruel." She pouted. "Am I very cruel, Lars?"

"You're as crazy as an outhouse rat is what you are, my dear, and quite frankly—I love it." Lomax grinned, puffing on the stogie before exhaling a cloud of smoke. "Tastes like victory, Thunder. You really should take up the habit."

Doc Thunder winced, testing his chains again. No weak link, but perhaps… "You don't need another bad habit, Lomax. You've got enough already— *aahh!*" He gritted his teeth, crying out as the barbed flogger struck across his back, criss-crossing the cuts it had already left.

"Bad pretty-pretty," the Silken Dragon hissed, her golden eyes dancing with a merciless delight. "Speaking is a privilege, not a right. Will I have to muzzle you, my new pet?"

Lomax waved his hand expansively. "Nonsense. It wouldn't be Thunder if he wasn't ready with a sanctimonious little quip, would it? Where's Maya, by the way? I was looking forward to a game of chess."

"Far away from you." Doc's eyes narrowed.

Lomax sighed. "You're still mad at me for kidnapping her the last time, aren't you? And you should be. I beat her five games to one. At one point she asked to switch to backgammon. Backgammon! Let me tell you, there was blood on the chessboard." He looked at Thunder's gaze for a moment. "Not literally. You know I'm never going to hurt her, Thunder. Never. She's off limits. Know why?"

Doc didn't say anything.

"I mean, I'm a sucker for the whole Lost City vibe, it's so... kitsch. And she's a great chess player. But the real reason I'd never lay a finger on her?" He smiled, blowing smoke in Doc's face. "One day she's going to hurt you, big man. She doesn't know it, but I can tell just by looking at her. She's got all the time in the world, and all the possibilities that gives her, and one day you're going to lie to her, or do something stupid, or just not be enough anymore, and she's going to go live her eternal life somewhere else. With somebody else. And that..." He grinned, knowing he'd struck home. "That's going to break your heart in two."

Doc scowled.

"You and Maya? Unsustainable. I'm going to love seeing her go back to her temple. That's going to crush you. I might send her a fruit basket after it happens with a little thank-you note. Neither of you know it, but she's on my team." He laughed, taking another long sip. "If I were you, I'd get ready for a fall, Thunder. But if I were you... well, I'd do a lot of things differently."

"You've got a poor opinion of love, Lomax—*aaahh!*" Another cruel blow to the flesh of his back. Silken Dragon laughed, softly.

Lomax smiled. "You think it's love. Cute. So where is she?"

"Busy dealing with the diversion you created in Venice."

"Ah, F.R.A.M.T.H.G.I.N.! Easily rooked and manipulated to help goad idiotic numbskulls... like Jack Scorpio and his collection of morons. Which reminds me, what does N.I.G.H.T.M.A.R.E. stand for?"

"Why, it stands for the total domination of the weak by the strong, of course. What else?" Silken Dragon flicked the whip against Thunder's hide again, making him jerk and the chains rattle.

"I'll drink to that." Lomax took a swig of his martini. "You know, I never really thought of myself as the mercenary type, but I really have enjoyed working with your organisation, Ms Dragon. The pay is good, but the fringe benefits..." He took in Thunder's helpless, tortured body. "...they're something else."

"You have no idea." The golden eyes glittered.

"You're a little too rough for me, kid. Besides, I never mix business with pleasure. Apart from chess, of course. Fancy a game?"

"Why not?" she grinned. "I'll carve out a board on his chest and make the pieces from his finger-bones." She leant close, tasting the sweat on Doc Thunder's neck. "I will teach you to adore me, pretty-pretty-pretty. If it kills you, you will tell me how much you want to please me with your final breath."

"And if it doesn't... well, part of my fee is that I get to finish off whatever's left when she's bored of you. Not as direct as I'd like, but that's life in the rat race." He laughed. "And speaking of rats..."

Lomax walked to a speaking tube in the wall, flipping open the cover to yell into it. "Venger! Get up here! It's time to meet that business partner I talked about!" He turned back to Doc, smiling ruefully. "He'd never have agreed if he'd known I was in cahoots with N.I.G.H.T.M.A.R.E. He's still a little mad at them about his unfortunate condition. But we need him for the next phase." He checked his watch. "You see, right now, Jack Scorpio has a condition-red emergency to deal with in Venice, and he's under the mistaken impression that his old pal Doc Thunder is protecting the President. He's not aware that you're here, indulging your little predilection for the wronger side of the tracks." He chuckled, finishing the martini. "Nice work if you can get it. Meanwhile, thanks to a slight communications foul-up I may have arranged, our mutual acquaintance President Garner is expecting Jack Scorpio to bodyguard him during this time of international crisis... enter Anton."

Doc Thunder shook his head. "You seem like a third wheel on this one, Lars. This is the kind of thing Venger could have cooked up all by himself."

Lomax almost choked. "Anton Venger? The man's a pawn! God, you don't believe all this 'team' nonsense, do you? I just say that to make the ugly little weirdo feel better. Without my genius, he'd be one more freak at the circus—"

"What?"

The door to the room was open, and there Venger stood, his blank, sagging, blue-white face betraying no emotion, his voice a hoarse, rasping monotone. But in his eyes, there blazed a terrible, baleful hate.

Lomax smiled, throwing his arms wide. "Anton, Anton, Anton... "

"What is *she* doing here?" He turned, looking Lomax right in the eye. "She's the one who did this to me! You allied us with *her*?"

"Anton, baby—" Lomax's voice adopted the smooth, slick tone of a Broadway producer. "You change your mind about who did 'that' to you every day of the week. Eventually you're going to have to admit you just did it to yourself." He turned to the Silken Dragon, smiling reassuringly. "Tough love. Works wonders."

"*No!*" Venger backed away, the cry sounding all the more terrible for coming in his emotionless monotone, from a face that never seemed to change expression. "We're meant to be equals! Partners! A *team!* I—I thought we were—you *can't*—" His flesh seemed to bubble slightly, the only sign of his emotion. "You can't *do this!*"

"I already did it. Come on, Anton, old buddy. You've got to admit she brightens up the office a little."

"We're meant to be a *team!* The Lomax-Venger Team! *You betrayed me!*" His face was bubbling now, starting to melt and flow like hot wax. The sight was so unnerving that Doc Thunder found himself totally captivated by it—the sheer horror of seeing a man's tortured, disfigured soul displayed for all to see on his suppurating flesh.

"Well, if it was the Venger-Lomax Team I might have consulted you, but probably not." He turned to Thunder and mouthed the words *prima donna*. "Look, are you going to impersonate Jack Scorpio or not?"

"*Never! Never for her!*" Even his scream was a monotone.

"Well, we can't do it without you, pal. Why, I'd have to make an incredibly convincing mask using skin cultures I'd grown from samples of your hideous fizzog that I'd secretly taken while you slept!" He paused. "Oh wait, I did! Looks like you're expendable, old pal. Ciao for now."

He took the cigar out of his mouth and squeezed it lightly, sending a dart bursting out of the lit end and into Venger's neck. The man with the Face of Fear gasped, eyes wide, took a couple of steps forward and then collapsed.

"How about that?" Lomax grinned. "I guess these really are bad for your health. Plan B, Thunder. Never leave home without it."

"You're a monster, Lomax," Thunder growled, the chains clinking as he strained on them again. "That man needed psychological help."

"Yeah, yeah. Wait until you see Plan C. It'll knock you sideways." Lomax surreptitiously watched Silken Dragon's legs as her high heels clicked across the wooden floor and she bent at the waist to take Venger's pulse.

"Quite dead. Do you have any more of those cigars, Lars?"

"I've got more insurance, if that's what you're saying, so no funny business. If you want a box of your own—I'll trade it for the recipe for that inexorium you were talking about."

Silken Dragon smirked. "Not at that price. Perhaps in lieu of your fee for the President's assassination."

"It's a thought." Lomax motioned towards the body. "Bring that thing to my lab. I'll harvest the face and throw the rest away."

"Proud of yourself, Lars?" Doc Thunder's voice was acid.

"As a matter of fact, I am. I'll leave you to the tender mercies of my lovely employer, shall I?"

"Mmmmm…" Silken Dragon purred, licking her full lips. "Such a shame I have none, pretty-pretty-pretty. I will take you to the depths of Hell, and there you will learn that I own you. And when I am bored of my plaything, I will ask my wonderful new friend Lars to slit your throat, so that I may bathe my perfect body in your blood. And you… as the life drains from you into my ornate bathtub… you will thank me."

"Sounds like a charming evening. But I have plans. Raincheck?" Doc Thunder flexed again, the veins on his muscles standing out as he gritted his teeth, putting all his strength into pulling on the massive chains. The beautiful, merciless woman in front of him only laughed.

"Oh, my wonderful toy, you will never break free. Those chains could hold an elephant. My foolish pretty-pretty-pretty."

Doc grinned, and the grin was savage.

"Who said anything about the chains?"

A piece of plaster fell from the ceiling.

"They hadn't reinforced the room. The ends of the chains on my wrists were bolted to the ceiling, but the ceiling itself was the weak point. So, suddenly, I had two big chunks of plaster and concrete on the ends of free-swinging chains. Two giant maces…"

Maya laughed. "I remember you telling me about that part. Lomax ended up with a skull fracture. Six months in the prison hospital."

Doc nodded, and sighed. "They both escaped, of course, but I really thought Venger was dead. I checked the body myself. No pulse. And five years after that, Lomax died, and Miles Hamilton changed so completely that our friendship couldn't survive. He became left-handed, emotionless…" He slammed a fist into his palm. "It's so obvious now… why didn't I see it?"

"Because people don't come back from the dead," Maya said, and Doc laughed, mirthlessly.

"Donner did. And Venger makes two. That's two in two days, and that worries me. Because Silken Dragon's supposed to be dead, too…"

He shook his head, looking off into the distance.

"And, unlike Lars Lomax, we never found the body."

CHAPTER NINE
THE CASE OF THE RED MASK

MARLENE LANG lay on the couch in her apartment, sipping a Brandy Alexander in her nightgown and waiting for the phone to ring.

She had no doubt it would. Rarely did an evening go by without a gentleman caller, and she'd built up quite a stable of admirers.

It might be David, begging her to come around for another shoot, proclaiming in his broken tones that she was the only model who could possibly do, telling her that he understood that he'd been in the wrong. In which case she would smile sweetly, tell him that she was dreadfully busy this evening, and then go and take a long, luxurious bath. David had to learn not to sulk.

It might be Jack—lovely Jack, her one-eyed sailor, her grizzled soldier, back from Uzbekistan or Antarctica or London, catching a night between one delightfully top secret mission and another to ravish her expertly on the balcony, treat her to oysters and champagne in bed and then fly off on a cavorite wing-pack like something out of a radio serial. Jack called rarely, but his brief visits always left her drifting in a pink haze for weeks.

It might be Easton, cool, calm and collected Easton, asking her out to a sushi bar in Japantown to drink cheap sake and help him forget some tragedy. She loved the way he looked at her; that mixture of need, sorrow and contempt, like she was an addiction he couldn't shake, a poison he didn't want a cure for.

It was all so wonderfully *noir*.

It might be Timothy—gentle Timothy, living in his moldy, fetid bedsit in the Village, occasionally slipping out to O'Malley's bar, terrified of the police. Sleeping with him was like charity, like slumming with an underclass of one, and yet there was something in him, a fire that sparked and possessed him; all the fire and spine and strength that David lacked. Dear Timothy Larson, her most secret lover.

It might be Parker, of course. Parker wasn't quite as exciting as Jack or Easton or even David—who had the most wonderfully wicked imagination if not the spine to match—but he had a cruel streak and hidden depths underneath the frosty surface. She enjoyed their verbal jousting, the sexual tension, and most of all his air of cold amusement, as if there was something he knew that she didn't, a secret all his own beyond the ones they shared. Also, she had to admit—and the thought made her instinctively flex her bottom—it had been rather an awfully long time since she had been properly spanked.

New York had the most interesting men of any city in the world, and she was building up rather a varied set.

And of course, there was the other one.

The most interesting of them all.

As if in answer to her thoughts, the phone rang. She smiled as she picked up the earpiece, a thrilling premonition dancing its way down her spine.

She was not disappointed.

"*Ms Lang... you're needed.*" A click, and the line went dead. To-night, it seemed, the Blood-Spider was in no mood to mince words.

Enjoying the secret shiver of anticipation building inside her, Marlene stood, unhooked the nightgown and let it puddle around her feet, and then went to the wardrobe where the sleek black uniform waited for her.

LESS THAN FORTY minutes later, her body caressed and hugged by the tight leather of her chauffeur's costume, her long legs flexing as she pressed her foot down on the accelerator, she guided the Silver Ghost through the twisting traffic of New York City.

The Blood-Spider was quiet in the passenger seat—more so than usual. His expressionless lenses stared straight ahead, and aside from a curt mention of their destination there had not even been the slightest word to her as she powered through the streets in the purring machine, startling horses and rickshaw drivers and astonishing passers-by.

"What's the matter?" she heard herself say.

A pause. So long that she assumed he was simply ignoring her. Finally, he spoke.

"*We have... urgent business. Business that cannot be ignored.*"

"What kind of business?" she asked, before she could stop herself. She was on dangerous ground here, she knew. He was obviously in no mood to talk. And yet, something in her could not help but poke and pick at his looming, oppressive silence.

Again, a long pause. Then he turned his head, staring at her with those unreadable, blank lenses.

"*Perhaps... the end of the Blood-Spider.*"

THE ROOF OF the hospital was flat and barren, in large part taken up by a large metallic structure, a lattice of steel and copper that looked like an Eiffel Tower in miniature. It was designed to absorb lightning strikes and bring them harmlessly to earth, so neighbouring structures were not damaged. Occasionally, the staff of the hospital would come up here to smoke. The hospital was a good ten stories high, and the view, while not spectacular, was certainly worth the trip from the lower floors. On a night like tonight, however—with the setting sun shrouded in dark cloud and a fierce rain already descending—there was nobody who would bother making the long trek up the maintenance stairs.

Almost nobody.

The maintenance exit leading onto the roof opened with a creak, and the man who for the past two-and-a-bit years had answered to the name Doctor Miles Hamilton shuffled out. He leant on his cane, turning his head and checking the roof was quite empty. Then he stood straight, taking the weight fully on his legs, the years seeming to fall from him in an instant. The rain was falling heavily now, but he didn't seem to notice.

Events were moving towards the endgame. Parker Crane would be on his way, and everything he'd worked for the past three years would be set into motion. Had he been capable of it, he would have smiled. Instead, his face shifted and bubbled as the rain fell from above, lashing at his skin, washing away the expertly-applied makeup that so perfectly duplicated the skin tone of Doctor Hamilton and leaving in its place a sickening bluish whiteness, like the flesh of some corpse-fish from the ocean's deepest trench. The dye washed from his hair in a grey river, leaving it pure white, and his emotionless mask began to slacken, the features sliding and slackening, until the face staring out over the city resembled nothing more than a wax sculpture that had been left close to a furnace. A sickening parody of a face, made all the more horrible by the utter absence of any recognisable expression.

As the man without a face gazed over the city, he emitted a series of short, wheezing exhalations, akin to a man doing violent exercises—stomach crunches, perhaps. "Hhh! Hnnhh! Hhh!" Short little gasps, barely audible against the drumming of the rain on the roof.

Anton Venger was attempting to laugh.

He heard the creak of the maintenance door, and turned, speaking in the rasping monotone that was his natural voice once all pretence had been stripped away. "Mr Crane. I'm sorry to have contacted you at such short notice—"

He froze.

The man who'd just entered through the maintenance door laughed, his eyes dancing behind his blood-red mask, and Venger felt an icy chill in the marrow of his bones.

"No problem, amigo. Only too happy to be here," El Sombra said.

He smiled.

Venger gripped the handle of his cane tightly, pressing a concealed button with his thumb. A three-inch blade popped from the very tip of it, glistening slickly with some foul unguent. "A deadly poison, extracted from the Amazonian tree frog. One cut and you'll die slowly and in the most hideous agony the mind could possibly conceive."

El Sombra drew his sword from his belt. "I don't know any tree frogs, amigo, but one cut from this and you'll die fast, I guarantee. Mostly because I'm going to cut off that ugly head of yours and sculpt it into a gargoyle. Or maybe a vase for flowers."

Venger's top lip twitched, and a pulsation ran across his quivering, pallid flesh. On another man, it would have been a smirk. "You can try…"

There was a low rumble of thunder.

"WE'RE HERE."

Marlene frowned, applying the brakes and bringing the Silver Ghost to a halt. The Blood-Spider opened the door and stepped out, walking purposefully into an alleyway near the hospital.

"You can't just leave it at that! The end of the Blood-Spider?" She could not keep the anxiety out of her voice. She realised that she had childishly assumed that this would be forever, or at least until she got bored of it and moved on to something else. To have the end of all of it dangled so casually in her face like this was more than she could stand.

The Spider turned, his mask betraying not the slightest hint of emotion. Again, the lenses gazed into her, seemingly reading her slightest thought. "*Go home, Ms Lang.*"

Marlene pouted. "Damn you! You can't just dismiss me like—"

"*For your own protection. Take the car, go home, and pack a suitcase with essentials.*"

She fell silent. Suddenly, she realised how seriously she should have been taking this. "What happened?" Her voice sounded small and frightened.

"*Up on that roof, there is a man who knows my secrets. Perhaps all of them. Perhaps all of yours. If I do not contact you by midnight... leave this city. Find somewhere to hide, and pray you can hide well. I will contact you in good time.*" The hiss of his voice sounded almost compassionate.

Marlene swallowed, her heart beating in her ears. "What... what if you don't?"

"*Then the Blood-Spider is dead.*"

He turned and walked into the darkness of the alley, and was gone.

ON THE ROOF, El Sombra's sword clashed against Venger's cane as lightning arced across the sky.

Anton Venger had been an accomplished swordsman before his disfigurement, and the poison cane had been a favourite trick of his during his days as N.I.G.H.T.M.A.R.E.'s top undercover agent. He'd lost none of his skills in the intervening years. If anything, the madness that had infected his brain after the loss of his good looks had only added an extra dimension to his prowess. The tiny blade at the end of the cane flashed and darted, each time coming less than an inch from piercing the flesh of his half-naked opponent with a deadly sting.

But if any man knew about the subtle art of madness used as a weapon, it was El Sombra.

Once upon a time, he had been Djego the poet, a shiftless layabout hiding behind a tissue-thin veneer of pretension. Then the bastards—the Nazis—had come to his little town, razing it to the ground and rebuilding it as a clockwork nightmare, a grotesque experiment designed to create a strain of human robots.

Djego's mind had fractured under the stress of losing everyone he had ever loved, as well as the influence of a strain of unknown psychedelic he had encountered in the desert after fleeing the scene of the massacre. Out of that madness had emerged his second personality—the Saint of Ghosts, El Sombra, the shadow-self that existed to perform a single task: to take revenge on all who had wronged him.

Mostly, that revenge consisted of a quest to murder as many Nazis as humanly possible on a bloody trail that would lead to the king of them all—the insane brain of Adolf Hitler, now housed inside a gigantic steam-powered robot deep within a secret chamber at the very heart of Berlin.

He'd heard, on his travels, about North America's infestation by Untergang; the destabilisation agency put in place by Hitler himself, experimenting in 'asymmetrical warfare,' after his doomed Russian campaign. Nobody could prove that the terrorist organisation was run via orders from the Fatherland, and Germany denied everything, of course. El Sombra had decided it was worth looking into.

He'd found out a number of things already. Interrogating—some would say torturing—his way up the ladder of command had led him to Heinrich Donner, the organisation's disgraced ex-chief. But the real find had been the secret journal in Donner's bedroom.

The one that explained everything.

Well, not quite everything—who explains *everything* to themselves in their diary?—but enough. More than enough.

It had led him to the Jameson Club, and while investigating to see just how that fitted into the puzzle, he'd overheard Parker Crane and his telegram. And that had brought him here, to clash a razor-sharp sword against a deadly poison cane, battling for his life against a man with a molten face and crazed, wild eyes, dangerously close to a huge lightning rod in the midst of a raging storm.

Sometimes, life was good.

"So what brings you here, amigo?" Again, the sword and the cane clashed together, the sword-hilt locking with the cane's head as El Sombra leaned close for a moment before pirouetting back and slashing in a wide arc, only to have the blow parried expertly by the other man. Neither of them seemed to blink.

"The reason why?" Venger laughed again—that peculiar expulsion of air in short, guttural bursts—and then lunged, the point of his blade barely missing El Sombra's abdominals. Then his eyes, the only part of him capable of expression, grew hard and cold, like two small stones in a sea of shapeless clay. "My ugly. My disease. My love... and all my lover's revenge."

"You and me could write a bad romance, my friend," El Sombra murmured, blade flashing, clashing, deflecting the poison point as it sought out the weakness in his defence, the eye of the needle that would send the Saint of Ghosts prematurely to the kingdom of heaven. As the dance of sword and cane went on, the two men circled, feet shifting warily. El Sombra did not realise his back was to the huge lightning conductor until it was too late.

"I don't want to be *friends!*" Venger lunged forward suddenly, the deadly point of the blade aimed right for El Sombra's heart, putting him on the defensive and forcing him to take a step back. But he had nowhere to go. His only option was to clamber backwards up onto the metal structure.

Now, he mused, he had the advantage of height. The advantage of height, and also the advantage of being fried like a strip of bacon at any moment.

The thunder roared in his ears.

Doc Thunder and Maya burst through the front doors of the hospital, looking at the bustling activity. It was the second night in a row he'd entered like this, and the staff instinctively looked to see if he was holding any dying people in his arms. When they saw his hands were empty, they breathed sighs of relief.

"Can I help you, sir?" the receptionist said, doing her best to smile.

"Maya, go and check on Monk," murmured Doc, before turning his attention to the woman sitting in front of him. "Hamilton. Doctor Miles Hamilton. I need to see him urgently." He thought for a moment. He couldn't let Venger suspect, and he needed an excuse that would bring him running... "I want to donate more blood."

The receptionist smiled. "All right, sir. He's on a break at the moment. I think he's gone up to the roof." Doc turned, walking towards the exit. "Sir, I can send an orderly to fetch him."

"It's all right, I'll go see him myself." Doc smiled, tightly.

"But the stairs to the roof are that way."

"Oh, I'm not taking the stairs." Doc smiled again, stepping out into the street. "I'm going to take the quick way."

Then he jumped.

The Blood-Spider climbed slowly up the side of the rain-slicked wall, looking like nothing so much as a human spider slowly closing in on the fly at the centre of the web. Despite the rain, the suction cups held fast, as he knew they would. He'd done this before, many times, and it was the last thing Doctor Hamilton would expect.

His plan could be summed up in one word—fear.

The doctor would be waiting on the roof, watching the maintenance door. When the Blood-Spider appeared behind him, seemingly from nowhere, he'd be much more inclined to talk about exactly how he'd discovered the Spider's true identity, and what that strange 'other interest' comment in the telegram meant. Blackmail, perhaps? Was the good doctor intending to sell the Blood-Spider's darkest secrets to the highest bidder?

If so, he would learn to his cost that there was far more to the Spider than he could possibly suspect... before he died screaming for mercy.

The eyes behind the implacable lenses narrowed as the Blood-Spider climbed higher. There could be no mercy offered in this matter. To have his secrets revealed would jeopardise the cause—his holy quest to cleanse New York of the inhumans. The criminals. His trigger fingers burned again, the itch nagging at him under his gloves. It had been a very long time since he'd shot anyone.

He was close to the rooftop now, and suddenly, between the cracks of thunder filling the raging sky, he could hear the clang of steel on steel. The clash of swords.

Carefully, he peered over the edge of the rooftop.

There were two men on the roof, one with a sword, the other with some sort of trick cane. The one with a cane had a face bleached blue-white, sagging like unfired clay, a grotesque monster by any reckoning. And yet it was the other who caught the Spider's eye; the man with the sword. A half-naked Mexican man, dressed only in black tuxedo pants, with a red sash tied around his face, forming a mask over his eyes.

The sword killer. The vigilante who'd been such a thorn in Untergang's side. Was this the murderer of Heinrich Donner?

What was he doing here? How was he involved?

The Blood-Spider watched, fascinated, as the swordsman leapt off the metal structure, somersaulting over his enemy just as a bolt of lightning crashed into the metal attractor, missing him by inches and lighting up the whole rooftop in brilliant white electric light. In the light, the Spider realised that the man with the half-melted face was wearing Doctor Hamilton's uniform. Had he stolen it? No, that *was* the doctor, or the doctor was that, had been that thing, all along. How and why?

There would be time to answer such questions later. For now, all the Blood-

Spider saw was the killer he had been hunting and the man who had attempted to blackmail him in a life-and-death struggle, with a crackling lightning conductor on one side and a ten-storey drop on the other.

Supporting himself with the suction cups on his toes, he drew one of his automatic pistols, removing a silencer from his belt with the other hand. Then he began screwing it in place.

It was only a question of who to kill first.

EL SOMBRA TURNED, deflecting the deadly cane as it sailed within a millimetre of his throat. He'd managed to score a couple of hits on his enemy—he'd slashed Venger's long white hospital coat open, and even drawn blood with a light scratch on his arm—but he was nowhere close to ending this fight. Venger was simply too skilful. And, unlike El Sombra's non-poisoned sword, his cane only needed to strike once. The smallest scratch would kill him. He couldn't afford to be distracted for a single second.

So it was unfortunate that Doc Thunder chose that exact moment to land on the hospital's roof.

His immense body landed with a crash that shook the whole roof, distracting El Sombra for a single, vital second—enough time for Venger to lunge forward, the point of the cane-dagger slashing across the masked man's cheek. Instantly, El Sombra felt a wave of weakness as the poison rushed into his bloodstream. He staggered.

"You're too late, Thunder," Venger spat in his cold, cruel monotone. "I don't know how you found out about this little meeting, but you're too late to save your friend. My poison is even now working through his bloodstream. Within moments, he'll die. Die in unendurable pain."

El Sombra fell to his knees, the pain already beginning. But there was no sympathy in the Doc's eyes. That piercing blue was as cold as steel.

"He's no friend of mine, Venger. This is the man who left someone very important to me downstairs in that hospital with four bullets in him."

El Sombra opened his mouth, trying to speak, trying to shake his head. *Bullets?*

Doc Thunder scowled. "I honestly don't care if this piece of trash lives or dies."

CHAPTER TEN
DOC THUNDER AND THE SAINT OF GHOSTS

"This is the man who left someone very important to me downstairs in that hospital with four bullets in him. I honestly don't care if this piece of trash lives or dies."

Yes, it was him, all right. Red mask, crazy eyes. This was the man who'd done his damnedest to murder his best friend. No doubt about it, this was who Monk had been talking about. And yet...

"How is Monk, but the way, Venger? You being his doctor and all. I'd think very carefully about how you answer that question, if I were you."

Venger chuckled, another expulsion of short barks, unrecognisable as laughter to the untrained ear. "Oh, of course. Your monkey-boy bum-chum. He's stable, don't you worry. Off the critical list. I do know rather a lot about medicine, you know. Probably even more than your other friend, Doctor Hamilton." Suddenly, his teeth gritted, and his eyes assumed once more that intense, hateful gaze. "I'm not a complete monster. I've got nothing against the ape-man. It wasn't *him* who gave me this face, was it? It was you. You and that pathetic masochist in the blue suit."

Doc nodded, taking a step forward. "Danny Coltrane, the Blue Ghost. Was it you who made him disappear? The way you disappeared Hamilton so you could take his place?"

Venger's mouth fell open, flopping like the mouth of a fish. On a normal man, it would have been a delighted grin. "You don't know *anything*, do you? You don't have the slightest clue—"

He was interrupted by El Sombra, whose gut spasmed at that moment, sending a tidal wave of vomit out of his belly and onto the wet roof. His skin was a jaundiced yellow now, his eyes unfocussed, and great drops of cold sweat were rolling down his skin, indistinguishable from the raindrops. The poison was doing its work. He was in the final stages now.

Venger laughed. "Are you sure you don't want to do anything for him? I know you say he tried to execute one corner of your little love triangle, but look at him! I got that poison from a tree frog, you know. It works directly on the brain's pain receptors. It must feel as though he's boiling alive. I wonder why he doesn't scream?"

Doc Thunder didn't speak. He was staring contemplatively at the writhing masked man, pulling a strange face, almost wincing. Venger cocked his head. "No compassion for such a terrible fate? I thought you were supposed to be the hero of decency and fairness? The great progressive setting an example for all us common-or-garden proles? You're almost acting like the Blood-Spider!" He laughed again, another little machine-gun burst of gasps from his sagging lips, then shouted. "I wish he were here to see it!"

ON HIS PERCH, the Blood-Spider frowned. It was almost as if Venger wanted to be rescued.

He was out of luck. The only reason he hadn't been shot yet was because of Thunder's timely arrival. The Blood-Spider hadn't expected him.

The silencer on the barrel might mask the shot from human ears, but from Thunder's? Could he risk it? He didn't want a battle with the man.

Not just yet...

"YOU'RE RIGHT, OF course," murmured Doc Thunder. "I have to do something for him."

With that, he grabbed El Sombra by the throat, lifting him up to stare into his eyes. After a moment, he spat into the dying man's face.

Then he let him drop.

"Satisfied?"

Venger lifted a finger to his face, physically raising one of his eyebrows and then the other, pantomiming a look of surprise. "Note my expression." Another staccato rattle of gasps, as his flesh bubbled and relaxed, returning to its standard emotionless cast. "You've gone rather... *badass* all of a sudden, haven't you, old man? Am I supposed to be impressed?"

"My turn to ask the questions." Doc Thunder's voice was low, menacing. He took another step towards Venger. "You'll find that little pigsticker of yours has a hard time penetrating my skin. And whatever you've smeared on it won't even give me a rash. Unless you've gotten a sudden urge to take a swan dive from this rooftop, I suggest you start telling me exactly what I want to know. Question one—what *did* you do to Miles Hamilton?"

"You'll never guess." His eyes were mocking, dancing with glee. "Or maybe you will. A fifty-fifty chance."

Doc Thunder raised an eyebrow. *Fifty-fifty? What does that mean?* "Tell me."

Another rattle of gasps. Even if you knew it was laughter, it would still seem incongruous coming from the slack, half-melted features. "I did to him what you did to me. Or rather, I did worse. A version of the same compound that caused my face to become this... travesty. Except somewhat more potent, of course. I injected him with it... and then I watched him melt. The terrified look on his face as it slowly lost cohesion, the awful scream as his jaw slid off and burst like a water balloon as it hit the ground, his eyes trickling down his face like a pair of maraschino cherries sliding off a melting ice cream sundae..." He sniggered, or made a sound that could have been a snigger. "Yum yum. Deee-licious."

Thunder's eyes narrowed.

Venger reached up and formed his mouth into a pantomime frown. "Oh dear, have I upset you? How sad. You should learn not to ask questions you don't want the answers to. If it's any consolation, I had nothing against him, any more that I have anything against the big ape downstairs. But unlike your friend the Gorilla Reporter... he was in the way."

Carefully, he began to move sideways, away from Doc, keeping his cane-dagger pointed at the lightning bolt in the centre of Doc's chest as his feet padded softly on the rain-slick rooftop.

Doc followed. "You were wrong earlier, Venger. You are a monster. I'm not going to rest until you've been locked away for the rest of your unnatural life. Now put that contraption down before I twist it around your scrawny neck."

All of his attention was on Venger. Venger had made sure of that himself, made sure Thunder wasn't paying attention to his surroundings. If he had been, he might have noticed that Venger's movements had put Doc between him and the lightning conductor.

The storm was directly over their heads. Just a matter of time...

Venger pressed the stud on the head of his cane once again. The tip of the dagger flew out of the end like a dart, gleaming with the deadly poison it had been coated with, before it bounced harmlessly back, clattering on the rooftop, the point broken.

"You don't listen, Venger. I told you that wasn't going to work on me." Doc frowned. "You were masquerading as my personal physician for years. You know I'm bulletproof, never mind dagger-proof. And even if you could afford an inexorium blade, my blood would just negate any poison you can think of. So tell me—" His voice was thick with contempt. "—what was the point of that?"

Venger chuckled. "I have to eject the dagger before I can trigger this." He pushed the stud again—and a compressed steel net shot out of the cane's tip, expanding as it left, wrapping around Doc Thunder's body, tangling him up. Venger ran forward, kicking hard at his chest while he was off-balance and struggling with the net, and sending him staggering backwards to slam against the conductor—

—and then a bolt of lightning sizzled down from directly overhead.

Doc Thunder screamed, the lightning crackling off his wet skin as it shot through his body. It felt almost like the Omega Machine, but a thousand times more intense, wilder, more agonising. He'd never felt quite this much pain. Although the lightning strike itself only lasted a second, it felt as though the fire was still crackling through his every nerve ending even after he crashed forward onto the rooftop.

He tried to strain, to break out of the steel netting, but there was no way. He couldn't even move. Dimly, he saw Anton Venger standing over him.

"Good timing, eh? I've always been lucky that way."

Thunder tried to speak. A small trickle of blood slid out of the corner of his mouth. Venger blinked. If he could have appeared shocked, he would have.

"Goodness me. That did hit you hard, didn't it? It actually made you bleed."

Thunder twitched, shaking his head. "Nuh. No." He sucked in a deep breath. "Did this to myself earlier. Bit... bit my cheek. Got the blood flowing."

He smiled.

Venger paused for a moment, thinking about that. When would he have... Then realisation dawned.

"...oh my God."

El Sombra appeared behind him, suddenly, grabbing hold of Venger's face hard enough to leave handprints in the clay-like flesh. Then he twisted.

Venger howled, and the sound was horrific, never changing in pitch, a flat, unreal burst of noise. A scream without emotion. El Sombra twisted again, and something popped in Anton Venger's neck. His body went limp.

El Sombra began to drag the body to the edge of the roof.

"Wait..." Doc Thunder said, before lapsing into a coughing fit. El Sombra smiled, hauled it over the side, and dropped it off. Doc Thunder shook his head, feeling impotent. "That... that was murder..."

"Whoops." The masked man smiled, holding up his limp wrist and slapping it with the other hand. "Bad vigilante! Very naughty. Although—and I don't know about you, amigo, you might not agree—I thought that story about how he dissolved a guy was a little bit worse." He lifted his sword, aiming the point towards Thunder's eye. "Thanks for spitting in my face, by the way, amigo. That really made me feel like saving your life. In fact, why don't you give me one really solid reason why I shouldn't poke this through your eye and into your brain?"

"Because spitting on you is what *saved* your life." Doc swallowed, then began straining against the steel net, struggling inside it in an attempt to work his arms together in front of him. From there, he could start trying to tear his way out of it when his full strength returned. "My blood has certain... healing properties. It's what makes me what I am. Even if you're not a blood match, spitting it into your wound should have been enough to negate the poison."

El Sombra frowned, touching his fingertips against the fresh wound. It was true. As soon as Thunder had spat on him, the fever had dissipated. "So you're Spit Jesus. Congratulations. What do you want, a medal?"

"I expect an honest answer to an honest question, that's all. Although if you think you can kill me, you're welcome to give it a try. I can just as easily get answers from you in Rackham Prison hospital." He smiled, winding his fingers around the steel mesh and then pulling. One by one, the links in the netting began to break.

"What the hell, amigo, I'm in a conversational mood. Just lay off the net for a moment, eh?" El Sombra laid the tip of his sword just below Thunder's eye. Thunder didn't blink. "Ask your question."

"Did you shoot a man last night in the penthouse suite of Atlas apartments?"

El Sombra blinked, eyes widening. "Huh. Right place, amigo, wrong crime. I don't use guns. No idea how they work. The only thing I need is this." He pressed the tip of the sword against Thunder's cheek. The skin didn't break. Neither did Doc's gaze.

"So you had nothing to do with the shooting of my assistant? No, of course not." His eyes flicked to the left, considering. "You'd have shot Venger long before he could have stuck you with that cane. You'd probably have shot me—people do. You're not lying when you say you don't use guns." He looked back at El Sombra, evaluating. "But you did kill Heinrich Donner."

El Sombra smiled, grimly. "That's right. I got a hot tip and some incontrovertible evidence leading right to his evil terrorist wrinkly bastard ass, and then I broke into his fancy penthouse and I stabbed him in the back. Thrust the point of my sword right through his stinking, evil heart. Should I apologise?"

Doc Thunder paused. "Why?" He said it softly, quietly. El Sombra's smile widened.

"Why didn't you?"

THE BLOOD-SPIDER listened closely from his perch on the edge of the rooftop. His gun was still trained on El Sombra's head. He was trying to work out whether or not to fire.

On the one hand, he'd heard all he needed to—a full confession. On the other hand, Doc Thunder was there.

He wondered if it wouldn't be better to shoot now, while Thunder was trapped in that steel net. Shoot him and run. Right now.

His trigger finger began to itch.

"I WANTED TO bring Donner to trial. I wanted the world to see—"

El Sombra laughed. "Why? You knew he was guilty, amigo. You knew just what he was guilty *of*. Why not just do it? I'd have done it, a dozen times. Or were you holding back because you didn't want people to know about *your* little secret?"

Doc Thunder froze, looking warily at the masked man. "What do you mean?" It was a question he already knew the answer to.

El Sombra leaned close, looking the other man right in the eye. "I know who you are, amigo. I know *what* you are. I read Donner's—"

Doc's eyes narrowed. Enough.

THE BLOOD SPIDER'S eyes narrowed. Enough stalling.

Kill him.

Now.

AS THE SPIDER'S finger tightened on the trigger, Doc Thunder moved. The masked man had made the mistake of taking the point of the sword away from his eyeball for half a second, and then he'd leaned in close to give Doc an extra-intimidating stare. Presumably he'd learned that one in some chapbook about scary banter.

Bad move.

Doc snapped his head forward suddenly, viciously delivering a brutal head butt to El Sombra's nose, smashing it and sending him flying back in an arc, trailing blood from the crushed cartilage.

Thunder didn't feel the bullet that passed within a few inches of his face, through the air where El Sombra's head had been, or hear the silenced gunshot. So he never knew that he'd saved the masked man's life. Neither did El Sombra.

It probably wouldn't have changed much if they had.

"That's what they call a Bronx kiss, masked man," Doc growled, tugging at the netting hard, ripping it away from him so he could stand up. "Welcome to New York City. We've got a nice hotel waiting for you; it's called Rackham Penitentiary. You'll like it there. Bare nipples are in vogue." He smiled, grimly. "Get up. And don't think about using that sword. It's going to take more than that to cut my skin."

El Sombra rose, shaking his head groggily. For a moment, he gripped his sword tightly, then he lifted it up above his head, opening his hands and shaking his head slowly. "Fine, amigo. You've got me. Put the cuffs on."

Doc took a few steps closer, reaching out for El Sombra's wrists. "I don't actually carry—"

El Sombra moved quickly, bringing the sword around in a circle, swinging it as hard as he could, aiming the edge of the blade between Doc's legs. As it slammed home, Doc gave a strangled scream, dropping to his knees immediately. El Sombra grinned.

"Maybe you do have an indestructible nutsack, amigo, but I think that's going to leave a dent, right? Want me to do the other ball? Or maybe I should put this in your brain and put you right out of your misery once and for all, eh? It wouldn't be like killing a real human, would it?" He snarled. "Come on, tell me why I shouldn't. All I'd be killing is a monster built by monsters—"

"Stop right there."

Maya stood in the doorway leading into the building, holding a pistol at her hip. Her eyes were hard as stone. A man in a red mask, standing over a man she loved. She raised the gun, aiming between El Sombra's eyes.

"Dios mio!" the masked man breathed. "Tell me, chiquita, has anybody ever written you a poem? I know somebody who writes great poems. He's really improved a lot. They rhyme now." Inspiration seemed to strike him. "Or I could rescue you from a giant robot! That often works."

"Shut up." Maya cocked her pistol. She was in no mood to mince words. "No, don't. You can tell me why I shouldn't kill *you*."

El Sombra smiled. "Because I've never slept with a woman." Doc Thunder blinked at him. "What? It's true."

Doc Thunder sighed. "It's not him, Maya. He didn't try to kill Monk. And he saved my life. And..." He swallowed. "We need to talk. About Donner. About what you read in that journal of his."

Maya scowled, lowering the gun and turning to Doc Thunder. "Something about a monster created by monsters. Want to explain that one, Doc?"

Doc winced, covering his eyes. "Not now, Maya. Right now we need to consult with... what's your name?" He looked up. "Hello?"

The rooftop was empty, but for the two of them.

THE BLOOD-SPIDER frowned, putting away his pistol. He'd almost fired, several times, but... it wasn't the time. He'd seen the masked man leap from the rooftop while Thunder and his princess were distracted. Doubtless he had a means prepared to break his fall and ensure a quick getaway. And the man was quick, the Spider had to give him that.

But not quick enough.

I have you, murderer, the Spider thought to himself, beginning his descent.

*I will find you, devil, no matter where you choose to hide, to revel in the sins
you've committed in the name of your own inhumanity. For where all inhuman
devils revel in their sins...*

...the Blood-Spider spins!

"HOW DID HE do that? We only took our eyes off him for a second."

"You've got worse problems." Maya cut off Doc's train of thought, looking
stern. "I checked in on Monk on the way up here."

Doc's blood ran cold. "No. Venger said he hadn't hurt him."

"He hadn't." Maya smiled, humourlessly. "His impression of Doctor
Hamilton stretched to doing no harm. But he didn't help him, either. Monk
got just enough of your blood to get him stable and put him on the mend. He's
on a saline solution now. He's still sleeping, probably will be for some time."

Doc frowned. "So where..."

"I don't know. None of the doctors seemed to be able to tell me where the
sample you gave ended up. We checked the hospital's cold room. Not a sign."

Doc felt that chill again, seizing his heart. "That's why Venger pretended
to be Doctor Hamilton, so he could steal my blood. Why didn't I see it?" He
shook his head. There was a lot he hadn't seen, thoughts that had been dancing
in and out of his mind like puzzle pieces ever since the Omega Machine. He
felt as if he was right on the edge of putting the whole jigsaw together. "You're
right, Maya. I think we have got problems."

Maya looked away. "I didn't say 'we,' Doc. I said 'you.'" She looked back at
him, a deep weariness in her eyes.

"I'm leaving you, Doc."

Doc Thunder looked at her—looked at her properly for the first time since
she'd brought him that paper the morning before. Suddenly he couldn't think
of anything else. "Maya—"

"I'm going back to Zor-Ek-Narr."

CHAPTER ELEVEN
THE CASE OF THE SECRET SCIENTIST

THE BLOOD-SPIDER'S feet touched down on the floor of the alley by the hospital, and he took a moment to look around and check for any clues. To actually catch the Sword Killer was perhaps too much to hope for, at least immediately, but there was the slim chance that he'd find a hint as to which direction he'd taken. The important thing was that he knew who had murdered Heinrich Donner—clearly an inhuman killer.

Inhumanity would not be tolerated. Could not be tolerated. Such was the mission of the Blood-Spider.

As the Spider looked around, his ears caught a sound from nearby; a soft, wheezing moan, like the air escaping from a tyre. He turned, drawing his silenced pistol in a flash of movement.

It was Anton Venger. He had landed in a dumpster.

Perhaps it was due to the pliable nature of his flesh, but the snapping of his neck had not killed him, although he seemed unable to move, and his head now lolled at a grotesque angle. Most of his bones seemed to be broken, and blood leaked from his nose. The Blood-Spider was disgusted, but not entirely surprised, to note that the blood of Anton Venger was not red, but a light, sickly blue. His eyes flickered towards him, imploring, and he attempted to move his lips to speak. Even in such pain and fear as he was in, his face retained only the emotions he gave it. As such, he looked sanguine and unconcerned about his own death.

"Crane?" he breathed, weakly. "Help... help me."

"*Help you?*" The Blood-Spider looked at him through the implacable lenses. His voice was a cold hiss, like escaping steam—in its own way, just as emotionless as Venger's. A passer-by would have been mystified by the apparent ennui with which they greeted the situation.

Or terrified, perhaps.

"*Help you,*" the Spider repeated, as though contemplating the question. Venger's body twitched, shuddering like a cockroach pinned to a board. "*You sent Crane a telegram.*"

"Yes. I sent you a telegram." His eyes widened as the Blood-Spider lifted his automatic, pointing the barrel of the gun squarely between his eyes.

"*Crane.*"

"Wh... what...?" Venger was breathing heavily, a constant rasp from his damaged lungs. He was clearly terrified, and in great pain.

That was good.

"*You sent Crane a telegram. Crane. If I were you, I wouldn't become confused on that point again.*"

Venger twitched again, trying to nod. "Fine! Fine! I sent Crane a telegram. I—I have something for you. For Crane. It's in my coat pocket. The vial's very thick, it won't have broken. It's, ah... for our mutual friend." He swallowed, and his lips twitched and bubbled, as if he was attempting a smile. "Our friend Fifty-fifty. Heh."

"*Fifty-fifty. What does that mean?*"

Venger blinked. "It's the code. Fifty fifty. You know." He swallowed. His face still did not change, but his eyes grew glassy, the pupils dilating with terror. "You don't know... oh God, he said you knew! He said you were working for him! You must be working for him! You *must* be! Fifty-fifty! Fifty-fifty! *Fifty-fifty!* Crane, for the love of God, you *have* to know—"

The automatic spat a single, silent bullet, and a blue flower bloomed in the centre of Anton Venger's forehead as his brain matter, the colour of delicate Japanese pottery, exploded out into the garbage.

"*I told you not to become confused.*"

He hadn't meant to pull the trigger—there was so much more to learn—but to have Venger screaming his name, his real name, where anyone walking by could have heard him… better he was silenced. The Blood-Spider had no doubt that whoever this mysterious 'Fifty-fifty' was, he would be hearing from him soon enough.

And if his hunch was correct, so would Doc Thunder.

Working quickly, the Spider searched through Venger's pockets. Inside one of them there was a thick vial, still stoppered and sealed, undamaged by the fall from the roof.

It was full of blood.

The best part of a pint, unclotted, still cool from the cold room of the hospital. Wound around the neck, there was a slip of paper reading *50/50—DOC THUNDER.*

Doc Thunder's blood.

The Blood-Spider nodded once, grimly, and slid the vial into the inside pocket of his coat. Then he turned and walked deeper into the pooling shadows of the alley.

By the time the police found the body of Anton Venger, he was long gone.

MARLENE LANG PICKED up the phone on the first ring.

She'd only just managed to get in the door of her apartment, after securing the Silver Ghost in its usual hiding place in her private garage, behind a false wall in the side of the apartment building. The Blood-Spider owned the building under an alias—he was the only other person who knew it was there. Even Parker didn't know about it.

She reacted instinctively, but froze once she'd lifted the receiver out of the cradle. What if this wasn't him? What if it was whoever he'd gone to meet— whoever his 'business' had been with? What if he (she didn't consider that it might be a she) had killed the Spider and was now coming to do the same to her?

"H-hello?" Her voice trembled, uncertain.

"*Ms Lang.*"

She let out the breath she'd been holding. She hadn't expected a call the moment she'd come in. If he'd needed her that urgently, he would have asked her to keep the engine running, surely? For a quick getaway. But then, he'd wanted to protect her. She was surprised at how that thought made her feel.

"Do I still need to pack the suitcase?" Her voice shook, no matter how much she willed it to stop. His tone seemed almost amused, but still compassionate, inasmuch as it ever seemed to be anything at all. How much was there, and how much was she reading into it?

"You may still need it. But right now... you're needed. Meet me at pickup point C."

She nodded. That one was near the corner of First and Thirty-Fifth, not far from the hospital. He must have called from the kiosk there. "I'll come right away, sir," she said, blushing at how the *sir* slipped out. He hung up, leaving her with the dial tone and her whirling thoughts.

As Marlene turned to leave, she caught a glimpse of herself in the full-length mirror that hung by the door. Usually, she thought of the outfit the Blood-Spider had chosen, for reasons of his own, to dress her in as being risqué—daring, even. But now she realised it actually looked rather smart. Professional.

All of a sudden, she mused, she had a new understanding of what she was doing. She had come face to face with just how serious this could all get, and rather than shrink from it, or ask to be relieved of her duty, her first instinct was to throw herself in even deeper. And suddenly, she realised, it *was* a duty. Not a lark for a bored rich girl with expensive and naughty tastes, but a solemn appointment.

She was the Blood-Spider's driver, and that meant something.

She smiled at herself, then stepped confidently out of the door. Time was of the essence, after all.

And the war on crime was not about to wait.

THE BLOOD-SPIDER SAID nothing as the two of them sped through the streets, heading for the location in the East Village he'd specified. She hadn't been there yet—he'd never mentioned the place. But she knew better than to ask questions now. Indeed, she was rather enjoying this new feeling of quiet, sober professionalism, even subservience—of being a cog in a well-oiled machine. What was it she'd said to Parker?

"The most fabulous thing to do now is to believe in something utterly and completely, without restraint."

How true. How very true.

She opened up the throttle, a smile crossing her lips as she weaved expertly between two horse-drawn carriages, the horses rearing as she left them in the rear view mirror, rounding the next corner in a screech of tyres. Eventually, the Blood-Spider nodded, and she braked smoothly to a halt and triggered the passenger door release, with all the quiet deference of a British automaton.

"*Very good, Ms Lang. Pick me up on this spot in twenty minutes.*"

He turned and vanished into an alley, and she gunned the engine and eased the Silver Ghost onto the night streets.

A compliment! Perhaps her first from him. It felt rather like coaxing a climax from another man.

"Yes, quite the most fabulous thing," she murmured to herself, and began to cruise slowly around the block, keeping one eye out for crime. Her mind drifted back to that long weekend in Geneva with Jack, when he'd taken her to the shooting range to impress her and she'd ended up impressing him with a perfect grouping. She had a lot of additional skills to bring to the war, she knew.

Perhaps if she was awfully good, the Blood-Spider would let her have a gun.

THE DOOR WAS nondescript—a flat rectangle of metal halfway down an alley between a chapbook store and a long-forgotten dance club. The wall nearby was marked by freshly-chalked graffiti: DON'T PUSH ME 'CAUSE I'M CLOSE TO THE EDGE. A breaker slogan. Indeed, The Blood-Spider could see one of the squares of cardboard they littered their chosen alleys with scattered on the ground. He was glad none of them were here now. Littering was a crime, after all. And it would be so terrible to have any unpleasantness.

His trigger fingers were itching again.

At the end of the alley, he could see a homeless man, covered up by a thick, filth-covered blanket, his head buried in his lap, a mass of greasy black hair hiding his features. The Spider wondered for a moment whether or not he should simply put a bullet in the man's head... but no. Best not to invite trouble.

It was missing the masked man on the hospital roof that had done it, put him in this mood. He'd been so close—so very close—to putting an end to Donner's murderer once and for all, and now the strange Mexican had slipped through his fingers. That was unacceptable. Not only was he Donner's killer, he had been spending the brief time since he entered the city on a rampage that had ended with the deaths of nearly a dozen men.

While the irony was not lost on the Blood-Spider, the simple truth was that there was no room for two vigilantes in a town as small as New York. Even Doc Thunder, the saviour of Manhattan, America's Greatest Hero—even he made the place feel... crowded.

But then, that was why he'd come to Professor Timothy Larson.

Looking around to make sure nobody was watching, he knocked on the door in the pre-arranged pattern. After a moment, it was answered by a rail-thin man with a mop of shaggy, dirty blonde hair and a ratty beard, who looked at him with red-rimmed eyes. This was Timothy Larson.

"Come in out of the rain, man. I was, uh, writing a lecture."

Larson was a strange one. He'd apparently been part of the original futurehead movement as a young twenty-something man when it had started off in the 'seventies as a group of merry pranksters, before it rejected itself, becoming obsessed with détournment and anarchy, mutating into its current form as a thing to be feared, a tapestry of taboos that were allegedly made safe but all too often held all their old power and more. 'No future' had once been a challenge to authority rather than an acknowledgement of the status quo.

Larson let the Blood-Spider into the small bedsit he'd installed him in—a gloomy little cave, lit by a single oil lamp, encrusted in dust and filth. There was a door in the back that led to a toilet that hadn't been cleaned in months, but the rest of the room was all one thing; kitchen, bedroom and bathroom in one—a criminally small tin bath leaning in the corner, a mattress on the floor, a small camping stove and a sink against one wall. The rest of the space was taken up with workbenches and tables covered with beakers, test tubes, Bunsen burners and the stains of a thousand spilled chemicals. The whole place stank, and the Spider found himself grateful for the mask he wore. Larson grabbed a sheaf of notes off one of the tables.

"Dig this, man—'if the truth can be *told,* so as to be *understood,* it *will* be believed,'" Larson said, reading from a sheet of lined paper while the Blood-Spider entered and locked the steel door behind him. "'The emphasis—in breaker music and the street dance culture—on physiologically compatible rhythms is really the rediscovery of the art of natural magic with sound, that, uh, *sound,* properly understood, especially *percussive* sound, can actually change neurological *states*—'"

The Blood-Spider cut him off. "*Breaker music is a weakness rotting this city and it needs to be stamped out, Professor Larson. For your sake, don't let me find out that you've been taking part in the criminality going on outside.*" He reached into his coat. "*It would not be... healthy for you.*"

Larson pouted. "It's just a lecture, man. Actually, I was going to have some breakers perform during it. Kind of a performance piece, you know?"

Of all the members of the Spider's Web, Larson was the most secret, and the most secretive. He had good reason to distrust the police. Apparently, they had never forgiven him for attempting to synthesise an artificial opium as a means of opening what he called the 'doors of perception' within the human mind, or for attempting to pour this opiate into the water supply in order to force the city into delirium. A prank gone too far, some would say. The Blood-Spider, on tracking him down—or had Larson simply stumbled into his path?—had been impressed enough with the man's genius to provide him with new, state-of-the-art equipment and the latest findings on a variety of subjects. It had been a worthwhile expense. Larson was perhaps the most brilliant scientist the Spider had ever met.

He was also the only one who treated the Blood-Spider as he would treat anyone else in the world. He was neither terrified, like Stacey, or fascinated, like Marlene, or deferential, like Jonah—he simply treated the Spider as a perfectly ordinary person, no different from anyone he might meet at the theatre or the bakery. In turn, the Blood-Spider found him to be a fascinating and occasionally quite charismatic, if often irritating individual—he was continually grateful to the fates for making Larson far too useful to execute for his opium-related crimes when they had first met. It would be a shame not to have known the man.

That said, it was always best to let him know where he stood.

The Blood-Spider grabbed hold of the collar of Larson's shirt, lifting him up by it, before slamming him against one wall hard enough to knock the breath out of him.

"Remember who owns you, Professor Larson. You work for the Blood-Spider. The rest of your nonsense can wait."

Larson nodded, eyes wide. "Sure thing! Of course! I—I just wanted to, you know... get your *opinion*..." He swallowed, readjusting his collar as the Spider let him go. "You, uh, don't like breaker music?"

The Blood-Spider removed his hand from his coat, showing Larson the vial. Larson's eyes almost popped out of his head when he saw the label. "Holy crap! Is this Doc Thunder's real blood? Like, out of his body and everything?" He shook his head slowly, as if not quite able to believe what he held in his hands. "We need to get this cold before it congeals..." He looked up suddenly, puzzled. "What's this mean—fifty-fifty? Is it diluted?"

Blood-Spider shook his head. *"Quite pure. Apparently that refers to a specific person somewhere in this city... someone I'd like to meet."* Larson frowned, turning the vial over and over in his hands. *"Any idea who it might be?"*

"Someone who's not one thing or another?" He shrugged, shaking his head. "Or half with you and half against you—like a cop moonlighting as a criminal. Know anybody like that?" He laughed. "Or somebody who's around you a lot when you're, you know…" He gestured at the mask. "Not *you*… but, like, while you're off, y'know, being *you*, they're… being *them*. Fifty-fifty split. Does that make sense?"

"It raises some interesting possibilities. Much like that vial of blood. Perhaps you could tell me more about it, given time. I saw him use it to cure a man of a rare poison…" He scowled under his concealing helmet, irritated by the memory. Venger had deserved to die for his incompetence alone.

Larson chuckled. "So we know it's got some kind of healing mojo—that's cool. I'll bet with a little study we could find out just where Doc gets his whole whammy from. Actually, you know what? That last batch of notes you got me, that seemed to be headed in that direction already…" He chuckled, then stopped, looking sideways at the Blood-Spider. The grin on his face turned sly. "That's why you brought this to me, right? You want some of that for yourself. Aw man, you *dog*, you must have *planned* for this."

The Blood-Spider stared back at him, the eight lenses impassive.

"I plan for everything. I'll expect results swiftly, Professor. Do you understand? Within the week."

"Sure thing," Larson grinned. "You're the boss, babe. I'll find you what you need. Reverse-engineer what's in this and get it into you. Sound good?"

The Blood-Spider looked at him for a moment, then turned to the door, unlocking and opening it with a creak.

"Not a word, Larson. If you value your life. The Spider's vengeance is swifter than any venom."

"Sure, sure." Larson smiled as he closed the door, examining the vial of blood in his hands. "See you soon, man…"

Outside, the Blood-Spider turned to take another look at the homeless man, as if reconsidering his earlier impulse to simply kill him and be done with it. But no. To bring the police down on Larson while he was engaged in such important work on the Spider's behalf would not do. Better to leave him be.

Besides, he had to reconvene with Marlene. There would be other times.

As he turned and walked back towards his rendezvous with the Silver Ghost, the homeless man raised his head, lifting a strip of red cloth from under the blanket and tying it securely over his face.

El Sombra liked automobiles. The wonderful thing about them was that people who owned a fast one seemed to be under the impression they couldn't be followed. But a man who ran across the rooftops and through the tight alleys could easily keep pace with the fastest car, so long as it spent a good portion of its time in New York traffic. And Marlene wasn't quite as speedy a driver as either of them thought.

"Later, amigo." He grinned, before lifting a thick brown volume from underneath his blanket, with the word *Tagebuch* inscribed in gold lettering on the front.

He had a little revision to do.

It was getting on for one in the morning when Parker Crane finally returned to the Jameson Club.

"Welcome back, Master Parker," murmured Jonah as he opened the front door and ushered Crane into the sanctuary of the Lower Library, before any of those members still plodding around the club, in the manner of ruminants plodding around a lush green field, could ask any awkward questions. "And may I say," he said, after the door had been securely locked, "What a pleasure it is to find you still alive."

"Thank you, Jonah," Crane half-smiled as he handed over the briefcase containing the Spider's mask and the uniform that he'd worn to the hospital. "That will need cleaning."

He settled into one of the soft leather armchairs, closing his eyes for a moment and breathing deeply, the half-smile widening slightly. "What a wonderfully interesting evening I've had. You'll be happy to know I solved the mystery of Heinrich Donner's death, although other mysteries present themselves." He sighed, the smile dropping from his face. "Still, the night was remarkably free from dangers—to me, at least. The suction cups Larson invented for me helped enormously with that. Where would the Spider be without the ability to crawl up the sheerest wall, Jonah?"

Jonah sniffed. He did not approve of Timothy Larson. "He is a... surprisingly beneficial resource, sir."

"Oh, I have a feeling we haven't seen the half of it." He took hold of the chilled vodka martini that had materialised on the tray suddenly in Jonah's hand, sipping slowly. "Thank you." He was well used by now to Jonah's habit of knowing exactly what was needed when it was needed.

"Tell me..." Crane stared into the distance, his grey eyes focussing on some unseen point that existed only in his mind. "What would you do if all the power of Doc Thunder could be yours? The power to bend steel, in your grasp? The ability to withstand a speeding bullet fired at point blank range. To win a tug of war with a locomotive at full steam. To jump to the roof of a tall building in a single bound, all of that. What would you do with it all?"

Jonah considered for a moment. "Such a question requires a leap of imagination as to how one might acquire such powers, Master Parker."

Crane chuckled. "Let's just say they're closer to being acquired than they have been in quite some time. What would you do?"

Jonah frowned. "I would venture to suggest, sir, that my answer would be... 'better.'"

Crane nodded. "Quite. No more mollycoddling society's worst elements. No more allowing the criminals, the inhuman scum, to roam free and unchecked. No more collusion and collaboration with Presidents like Bartlet or worse, that little thug Rickard; people who undermine this great country. Real justice, achieved by real power. Think of it, Jonah."

Jonah allowed himself a tight smile. "Removing that second 'S' from the country, you mean, sir? I'll admit I've never felt all that comfortable living in the United Socialist States of America. I've never felt comfortable with socialism as a concept at all."

"Well, not this kind." Crane chuckled, dryly. "A coup, then. President Crane. I rather like that."

Jonah nodded. "It was always going to be on the agenda eventually, sir. You can hardly have a war on crime unless you are the one defining what a crime is. Otherwise you find yourself on such slippery ground..." His face grew thoughtful as Crane finished the martini. "Of course—assuming this is not some idle fantasy—that leaves the problem of another man with all the powers of Doc Thunder."

"That being Doc Thunder. I knew a battle with him was on the horizon as soon as I put four and a half bullets into his ape. Ah well, it's not as if I could have allowed him to live. Many would say he's lived far too long already." Crane frowned as he finished his drink, setting aside the empty glass. "This only moves his death slightly up the schedule."

Jonah bowed. "Very good, sir. Shall I fetch the special ammunition?"

"Yes... but we must spin the web before we catch the fly." He looked over at the grandfather clock that ticked ominously in the corner of the room. "A little after one. The newspaper offices will still be open and busy. I believe I have time to place an advertisement."

Jonah raised an eyebrow. "Calling him out, sir? Rather a risky strategy, if I may say so."

Crane leaned forward. "You may not. The telephone, Jonah. And another martini. And... yes, a Spanish dictionary."

Jonah bowed again, and returned in a few moments with the telephone—the one connected to an untraceable line—and a small, locked box that had been stored carefully in the club's impregnable safe. The members were not short of valuables, and many used the club as an unofficial bank vault; in the giant walk-in safe next to the wine cellar there were furs, jewellery, gold krugerrands, securities and bonds, and even the negatives of occasional blackmail photos which the members had paid through the nose for. There was nothing remotely as expensive as the contents of the ebony box, however. The contents of that box represented an expenditure of more than seventy million dollars, paid to a black marketer with a line on arms and equipment remaining from N.I.G.H.T.M.A.R.E.'s end at the hands of Doc Thunder.

It rattled.

Picking up the phone, Crane threw a handkerchief over the mouthpiece, then spoke. "Operator? *The Daily Bugle*... whoever's in charge of placing the advertisements. I'll wait." He turned to Jonah, who was returning with the dictionary and drink, and smiled slyly. "This isn't a challenge, Jonah. This is a lure."

He turned back to the telephone. "Ah yes, Mr... Robertson? Yes, I have an advertisement I'd like to place. I'll be sending a cashier's check via courier shortly. When? Tomorrow morning, the early edition. Yes. Yes... Mr Robertson, the check in question will be for five thousand dollars. Yes, I thought that would change things. The text of the advertisement?"

He opened the dictionary, leafing through to the correct page. "El... Sustantivo. We need to talk about your blood. Meet me in Grand Central Station at sunset. Your friend in the red mask." He smiled. "No, no, Mr Robertson. Thank *you*." He put the phone down.

"Grand Central Station, sir?" Jonah's face betrayed a look of unease. "Won't that be a little crowded at that time of day?"

"Ah, but it has to be a public place or he'll smell a rat. Besides, with all those people around, he can hardly cut loose, can he?" He grinned, almost feral. "I, on the other hand—well, if some unlucky commuter should wander into the path of a bullet, I won't lose too much in the way of sleep. The first rule of the war on crime, Jonah: everyone in this country is guilty of something."

Jonah nodded, and left silently to fetch a third martini to serve as a nightcap, while Parker Crane unlocked the ebony box with the tiny key he kept constantly on his person. The light of the gas lamp lit the six bullets inside with a soft gleam. They were not made of lead, as his normal ammunition was, but forged from something that shone like silver and shimmered like mercury, and was far more valuable—and more deadly than either.

Inexorium.

CHAPTER TWELVE
DOC THUNDER AND HOW HE CAME TO BE

TWO SUNS SHONE in the sky.

The roc swooped down from between them, and Maya twisted, tugging at the chains that bound her, spread-eagled on her back, turning her face away from the sight. The altar was curved, like the shell of a river turtle, leaving her oiled body arched invitingly, a meal for the monster. The giant bird had fed on traitors and criminals before, and she knew that unless she could work free of the shackles, that terrible curved beak would tear into her belly as if she were any other offering. A chill of fear ran down her spine as the bird circled, toying with her, and she suppressed it with an iron effort of will. If she were to die here, after so many long centuries, then she would die like a Goddess.

"You will pay for this treachery, Zarnos!" she hissed, her emerald eyes blazing with rage.

Her treacherous high priest laughed as he lounged on her own throne, flanked by two of her own leopard warriors, their cat-like eyes glassy, dazzled by the hypnotic effects of the Gem of a Thousand Desires; that pernicious stone with which Krato, leader of the Scorpion Cult, had attempted to dampen her will and seduce her mind—before she had rewarded his blasphemous intentions with a dagger to the heart, and scattered his dark order to the four corners of Zor-Ek-Narr. The Gem glittered and shone with devil's magic, as befit something cast and consecrated during the Age of Woe, before light had entered the world. How such a forbidden object had found its way into Zarnos' ringed hands, she knew not, but he had used it to slowly but surely take control of her kingdom, while she had been distracted by the arrival of the Stranger into her land.

She cursed herself. If only Zarnos had not ordered the Stranger banished to the darkest depths of the Vault of the Serpent God, the sinister labyrinth from whence none had ever returned. If the Stranger did not starve to death in its winding, lightless pathways, leagues away from succour, he would be hunted and torn apart by the legendary Gorgorex, half-snake and half-bull, the fearsome guardian of the secret of the maze, whose horns could pierce stone and whose venom could slay legions. And even if he somehow survived the Vault, why would he come for her after all she'd done to him?

Zarnos' laughter grew louder, ringing in her ears.

The roc swooped once again, for the final time, razor sharp talons glinting in the light of the suns—

—and the Stranger leapt from his hiding place in the rocks, shirt torn to blue rags, aiming a fist like a hammer into the giant bird's skull, snapping it to the side an instant before the great beak would have closed about her glistening, naked form. The sound was like a boulder cracking in two, and the roc spiralled down, fluttering from the heights of the Sacrificial Eyrie down to the valley far below.

The Stranger rubbed his knuckles. "Sorry for making you wait. But that's the kind of thing you only get one shot at."

The he smiled, and in that moment her heart was his.

"Blasphemer! Slay him, my Leopard Men!" Zarnos cried, standing up from the throne he had so sacrilegiously stolen, and pointing one long, bony finger at the Stranger. Their wills vanished into the depths of the Gem of a Thousand Desires, the leopard warriors were helpless to do anything but obey. Their tails twitched from side to side as they lowered their spears, advancing towards the Stranger with fangs bared.

"They're not your Leopard Men, Zarnos. And I suggest you think twice before trying to use a spear on me." The Stranger crossed his arms and simply waited as the two warriors thrust their spears forward, only to see the honed flint points shatter and crack against his bare skin. He smiled grimly. "I have to say... I don't appreciate being poked."

He was more gentle with the leopard warriors than he had been with the roc—merely swatting them to one side with enough force to stun—and while Maya felt a chill of fear close about her once more as Zarnos raised the Gem to shine its malevolent light into the Stranger's eyes, he kept them covered, seeking out the corrupt vizier by the sound of his desperate, wheedling voice. "You will obey me! You will obey the will of Zarnos! All must obey my will!" He carried on screaming the words shrilly even after the Stranger had reached out and crushed the dangling gem between his mighty fingers, scattering the fragments at his feet.

Zarnos backed away, his eyes widening in terror. "You are no man! You are a monster! A devil from the Age of Woe, where no light shone! Keep back, fiend, you will not feed on Zarnos' spirit!" he was babbling, not seeing where his frenzied, backwards steps were taking him.

"Zarnos, you fool, stay still!" the Stranger hissed, reaching out a hand. "*The cliff edge* "

But it was too late. Zarnos, self-styled Emperor of All That Was, stumbled back, his feet treading air before he plunged with a shrill scream into the valley below; a scream ending in death.

"Poor devil," the Stranger murmured, shaking his head as he walked back towards the altar, and the Goddess chained to it. "He should have known. Sooner or later, the path of evil will always lead to a long, lonely fall. Like Icarus, Zarnos flew too close to the sun in his blind thirst for power, and the only way to go was down." He looked up, shielding his eyes, watching the twin suns beginning to dip down towards the horizon. "Suns, I mean... I'm still puzzled about that. Back home we only have the one."

Maya laughed, stretching out on the curved stone, relaxing fully for the first time in days. "According to my astronomers, there is only one sun. The doubling effect is produced by something in the air around my kingdom. Residue of some sort from the simmering heart of the Mountain of Eternal Flame."

The Stranger nodded. "An optical illusion—light refracting off crystal deposits in the air. Presumably those same crystals account for the strange mutations among the people and animals in the region..." He tailed off, staring at the suns. "It's very beautiful."

Maya smiled. "As beautiful as evil?" He laughed, looking down at her, his eyes roaming for a second before meeting her own. "We call it the Dreaming Sun." She purred. "They say that praying to it can make a dream come true. Care to make a wish?"

The Stranger laughed again, and then leaned close. "Let's get those chains off you."

"No." Her eyes glinted darkly. "Leave them as they are."

He raised an eyebrow, then smiled, bending to kiss her belly. "If you insist."

She purred, enjoying the feel of his lips and the soft rubbing of his beard, listening to him breathing in her scent, feeling his strong hands closing about her waist, seeming to restrain her more than the taut chains. "Tell me, Stranger," she breathed. "Tell me your true name."

He looked up, his blue eyes piercing.

"Doc Thunder."

"You lied to me."

Maya spoke the words without emotion, without anger or sadness. She simply stated a fact.

"No, I didn't." Doc Thunder sat in his lab, surrounded by all his equipment, all his experiments, all his useless junk. His voice was lost, haunted, and so very, very tired. For the first time in his life, he had no idea what to do, what to say.

How had it come to this?

She'd slept in the bedroom, alone, and he'd stayed down here, pretending to work, doing nothing but fiddling, keeping his fingers busy and trying not to feel that emptiness, the black despair yawning inside him.

He hadn't realised what it would feel like to lose her. He hadn't realised he could.

Wasn't he America's Greatest Hero? Hadn't he killed a giant roc, escaped a maze of death, fought leopard men and made love to her on a heathen altar in the light of two setting suns?

How could it all come to nothing after that?

As dawn had broken over the city, Marcel had entered, bringing coffee, the morning paper and a bacon sandwich. Doc had smiled, made some strained, fractious joke about the devil that he instantly regretted. Marcel had only half-smiled, sadly, and placed a hand on his great, slumped shoulder.

"Sometimes it is only us, monsieur. Sometimes it is only us."

He ate the sandwich in silence, and didn't taste it. The coffee went untouched after a few sips. He didn't open the paper.

Eventually, he'd heard Maya rising, early, bustling around the bedroom, then walking down the stairs, past the empty gym. He heard her saying a brief hello to Marcel. Then she'd walked into the lab, wearing the long white ceremonial robe she'd worn when he first laid eyes on her, and told him that he'd lied to her.

"You lied to me." She said it once again, shaking her head, not looking at him. "I asked you for your true name and you gave me an alias. A pretend name. Your parents weren't Mr and Mrs Thunder. They didn't name you 'Doc.'"

Doc sighed, shaking his head, feeling the length and depth of the chasm that had opened up so suddenly between them.

He loved her. He loved her for her wit, for her beauty, for the way her eyes changed colour in the sunlight from hard emerald to ocean water, for the things she said in restaurants, for the way she looked when she was asleep, for the way she walked through the city like a cat and was not touched by it, for a thousand thousand reasons and more every day.

He loved her, and the thought of her leaving him hurt. If he'd been given the choice, he'd have taken the lightning again. He'd have reached out and grabbed that conductor and held it like a long-lost friend, if it meant avoiding this for one more day.

He tried to think of something to say that would make her change her mind, and he couldn't think of anything. Finally, he spoke. "We don't always get our true names from our parents..." It sounded hollow. He let the words trail off and stared at the coffee going cold on the worktop.

Maya shrugged. She didn't consider that much of an explanation.

Nobody said anything for a long time after that. Idly, Doc played with a steel spanner, bending it this way and that with his fingers. He couldn't bring himself to look at her.

Eventually, Maya spoke. "I don't love you."

Doc nodded.

Maya sighed, sitting down on a stool next to a workbench piled high with hydraulics and copper tubes, spare parts from something long forgotten. "Maybe I don't love. I never did before I came here. It wasn't something I was ever asked to do." She shrugged. "Why should it be? Love is a relatively modern invention even in your world of a single sun. In Zor-Ek-Narr, we had other things to occupy our time."

Doc swallowed, shaking his head, feeling stung deep inside. "But you felt something for me."

Maya shook her head. "I felt something for Doc Thunder—something like what I assumed love must be. But it was easy to love Doc Thunder. It was like loving a picture of a man. A perfect fiction. And Doc Thunder was a wonderfully perfect fiction, because he never made any mistakes. That was the point of him." She sighed, tracing her finger through the dust on the bench. "And that's not you anymore, is it? The moment you heard Donner's name, you made error after error. And now it turns out you've been making terrible mistakes for as long as I've known you." She looked over her shoulder at him, and her voice was bitter. "How does it go? Your job is to be the example for the little guy? If one man looks at you and thinks he can try just a little bit harder, blah blah, and so on? And there you are, letting all your friends die and letting monsters take their place while you walk away."

She grimaced, not even wanting to look at him. "I don't know if I can trust you anymore, Stranger. How can I love you? You'll only break my heart."

Doc reached for his coffee. "What about Monk? Do you care about him, or have you changed your mind about that as well?" He could hear the bitterness in his own words.

Maya paused. "He made my heart laugh."

"Me too." He sighed, then scowled. "*Makes.* Damn it, he's not *gone*, Maya. He's stable, he's out of danger and the second he can be moved, I'm bringing him back to the brownstone. And then I'm going to give him a direct transfusion—supervise it myself. He'll be better than new."

Maya frowned, suddenly deep in thought. "Your blood. You think Venger managed to spirit it away before he died? You think he's responsible for what happened to Monk?"

Doc rubbed his temples. He didn't want to think about this now. "No. He was waiting for his chance. He's seen me give transfusions in the past to get people off the critical list, people with my blood type. He knew Monk and I were a match. It was a matter of time." He frowned. Something Venger had said—and something he'd remembered in the Omega Machine. He was having trouble putting the pieces together.

"Why would he want it?" Maya was looking at him, curiously, as if seeing him for the first time.

"The same reason Donner did." He shook his head, rubbing his eyes with a finger and thumb. He'd never felt quite so defeated.

"And why did Donner want it?" Maya turned, looking him straight in the eye. "Tell me, Stranger." She said it mockingly, her eyes looking deep into his. "If you can. Tell me your true name."

Doc looked at her for a long moment.

"My name is Donner. Hugo Donner. Heinrich Donner was my father."

Maya blinked. "But…"

"You need to hear it all. Everything I've been hiding my whole life. Then…" He stood up, looking down at her. "Then I'll help you pack your bags."

MY STORY BEGINS in 1935. Hitler had been Chancellor of Germany for two years. He was chafing against the restrictions placed on him by Victoria, as he has been ever since. At the time, he was already planning an expansion to the east—his doomed attempt to conquer Russia—but the plan was always to move on to America. They were the enemy. Karl Marx had fled to America to escape the dark arts of the Tsars, the trade deal with Japan was making New York one of the most multicultural cities in the world, and President Grimm was speaking out against Hitler as early as 1931. Hitler needed Russia, he was willing to deal with China while it suited him, but he wanted us.

Of course, it didn't take a strategist like Rommel to figure out that as soon as he'd done the hard work of taking Russia, Victoria would swoop in from the west and hammer him while he was weakest. Then she'd get everything, and deal with a diplomatic thorn in her side into the bargain. He needed a strong military—much stronger than anything he had—so he could take Russia, hold it, and still be strong enough to stay on the bargaining table against the Empire.

He needed soldiers who wouldn't tire, who could see for miles, who could hear a pin drop fifty feet away. He needed soldiers immune to bullets and shells. Soldiers who could kill with their bare hands, travel in leaps of a quarter of a mile or more, punch out a traction engine.

Sound familiar?

That was Project Gladiator. The transformation of ordinary German soldiers into supermen capable of winning wars on as many fronts as he needed. He'd had people working on this since before he was elected, and by 1935 he finally had a serum—albeit one that had to be injected in utero, into the amniotic fluid, while the foetus was growing. It was the only way Professor Strucker could get it to work on the rats, and they weren't about to start injecting that stuff into prisoners. They needed a human test subject, and one loyal to the Fuhrer.

Which was where Heinrich Donner came in.

My mother's name was Anna, and she was two months pregnant with me when

Donner decided that giving his unborn child up for medical experimentation was a good way to rise in the party machine. Anna didn't agree; not until he made it clear that if she went through with the birth without getting the injection, he'd strangle me in my swaddling clothes, cook me and make her eat me.

Yes, really.

She went through with it.

Things didn't work out too well. Strucker had a massive heart attack right after injecting my mother. It turns out the only copy of the formula was in his head, because, like most people in the Reich, he was worried that if he stopped being useful for ten seconds, they'd kill him. Still, no problem. They could reverse-engineer the serum from my blood as soon as I was born, maybe even make a version that worked on adults. It would have bonded to my bloodstream. I was just the test animal they were looking for.

Heinrich Donner volunteered to slit my throat himself.

That was enough for Mother.

Don't ask me how she managed to get away from him—she never did tell me the details—but she was in the Netherlands before the week was out. Four months later, she was coming into New York City on a fishing trawler and she thought she was finally safe. She never did contact the authorities, she just disappeared into a tenement on the lower East Side.

That's where I was born.

I wasn't the only kid on my street with a German name, but my build marked me out early. I grew like a weed and tore through books like a woodworm. By the time I was ten, I was as tall as a boy of fifteen and twice as broad, and I could pass tests college kids failed. Eventually, mother had to tell me why I was so different. That's how I first learned about Donner, my father. What he did. I asked her why she didn't change our name when she got here. She said it was because she hoped he might still come around. She was willing to forgive him, even after everything he'd done and threatened.

"He was a good man, before the Reich. A good man." She used to say that with a little wistful smile on her face. I never did understand it.

Especially not once he found her.

While I was growing up, Hitler was trying to take Russia, and we all know how that turned out. When he finally threw in the towel in 1945, after a year of bloody stalemate just trying to keep his own borders from being overrun by every horror you couldn't imagine—and I've fought a few things from that region, I know what he was up against—the whole idea of taking on Victoria at her own game via conventional means was over.

It was Donner who suggested the unconventional.

Untergang. A criminal organisation with total deniability, sponsored under the table by Germany via black budget, but in such a way nobody could ever possibly prove it. A destabilisation tactic. A way to harry local law enforcement, strike out against the government, disseminate propaganda and perform covert assassinations and sabotage, while Uncle Adolf tut-tutted at the preponderance of crime in America and held up his clean, clean hands. Asymmetrical warfare. Terrorism on a massive scale.

Since it was Heinrich Donner's idea, he was sent over as the organisation's leader. Oh, he had a cover in place, and a decoy to take the blame for him, but it was him behind everything.

And he hadn't forgotten the promise he'd made to the Führer.

On my eleventh birthday, I came back from school to find my mother had been murdered by a group of four Untergang black-ops specialists. They'd dragged her to the bed and suffocated her with a pillow, before rigging the apartment with incendiary explosives to cover their tracks. Then they'd waited for me to return. Their plan was to stage an armed ambush and take me down as quickly as possible. They had intelligence reports about how strong and quick I was— the same ones that had verified my mother's identity—and they were confident that, between the four of them, they could incapacitate me without difficulty. If it became necessary, they would simply kill me as they had my mother.

Following which, they would steal the blood either from my unconscious body or my corpse.

They thought they could surprise me, but they'd forgotten my hearing. I could hear them moving around, I knew something was wrong, and... well, I came through the wall. Just crashed right through it. That's how I got the first one; he was leaning against it. The others didn't last much longer.

The apartment—my home for the first eleven years of my life—didn't survive the battle. My mother's body went up in the flames, along with every remnant of my life up until that point. I lived on the streets for a year, dodging attacks from Untergang agents who literally wanted my blood.

Eventually, I fell in with the police—Commissioner Coltrane was in charge back then. Danny's grandfather. I wish I'd thought to lie about my age, but we managed to work something out anyway.

That was the last time anybody called me Hugo Donner. I wanted nothing to do with that name. I remember the desk sergeant—a guy called Bud O'Malley—asking me what my name was, and one word boiling up in my head...

"Thunder," I told him.

"Kid Thunder."

MAYA BLINKED. "*KID* Thunder?"

Doc shrugged, embarrassed. "Well, I didn't get my first doctorate until I was sixteen. Anyway, that's the story. Even after my skin got as tough as it is now, Donner still wanted my blood, and he was still willing to do anything he could to to get hold of it. And now... well, he's got it. After all these years. Much good may it do him."

Maya reached to grip his shoulder, gently. "You really think it was him? A scheme he didn't live to see completed?"

Doc shook his head. "I don't know." He looked up at her, and she saw the weariness in his eyes. "I don't know, Maya. I don't know the answers. I thought Donner was the only person who knew who I was or how I came to be, so... but I'm probably wrong. I don't know."

He paused, then sat down, reaching for the cold coffee. He took a sip and grimaced. "And I don't know about you and me, either. I don't know if you can trust me—if you want to trust me to never make a mistake again, you can't do that. You can't trust me not to fail." He turned and looked at her. "But I need you anyway. I need you for this. Because I don't know what the hell I'm going to do next, Maya."

She stared at him for a moment, frowning coldly at him. "No, Doc Thunder doesn't know. I think Doc Thunder's about run his course." Then she broke into a half-smile. "But I think you do."

He looked at her for a long moment, then spoke. "Find out who's got my blood, if anyone has. That's priority one—" He was interrupted by the door to the lab opening.

Marcel entered, carrying a try with two cups of hot, steaming coffee, prepared perfectly. "Monsieur, Madame. Everything is worked out, I trust?"

Maya smiled. "Not nearly. But I think we've made a start."

Marcel nodded. "Très bien!" He noticed the unopened paper. "Ah, Monsieur—you may want to look in the classified section today." He smiled, opening the paper to the correct page and thrusting it under Thunder's nose.

"What am I looking for?"

"El Sustantivo—just there, in the bottom left hand corner."

Doc nodded. "Hmmm. Looks like our friend from last night wants to contact me. Or somebody." He raised an eyebrow at Maya. "About my stolen blood, too. Very convenient."

"You think it could be a trap?" Maya frowned, peeking over his shoulder.

"It's in Grand Central Station. That's a very public place, at least. Still…" He frowned, folding the paper and tossing it onto the workbench. "I think keeping that appointment might prove to be a very big mistake."

Maya nodded. "So. What are you going to do?"

Doc Thunder looked at her.

"Make it."

CHAPTER THIRTEEN
THE CASE OF THE QUISLING OF CRIME

"WUXTRY, WUXTRY! ALL *the news, all the time, for a dime! Doc Thunder in battle with the Face of Fear! Don't ask, just buy it. Red Mask sighted on hospital rooftop during deadly affray! Anton Venger returns from grave only to die a second time! Read all about the riddle of the missing doctor and the murdered master of disguise. Face it, true believer, this is the one! It's the pulse-pounding front page scoop we just had to call: 'IF DOOM BE HIS DESTINY!' Wuxtry, wuxtry! All in colour for a dime!*"

The paperboy's shrill cries echoed through the bustling station, competing with the grizzled old hot dog vendor—

"*One dollar five! Guaranteed unhealthy! C'mon, you assholes wanna live forever?*"

—and the sushi vendor ten feet away, trying to keep the stench of frying onions out of his fish—

"*Nigiri, fifty cents! Roll, sixty cents! We got tuna, we got eel, we got crunchy katsu pork! Just like mama makes!*"

—and the pencil-thin young man with his pencil-thin moustache, selling costume jewellery from a cheap suitcase—

"*Gen-yoo-wine fake diamonds! Gen-you-wine necklaces, chokers, bracelets, earrings made from real glass! Three dollars—can you say no, folks? Hand 'em over by candlelight, you can always run in the morning!"*

—and the slick, sharp-dressed breaker kids, taking off their zoot jackets to windmill on a flat sheet of card, two more playing the toms and freestyling over the top while a pair of bulls watched and tapped their feet—

"*—I'm the c-a-s an' the o-v-a an' the rest is f-l-y—*"

—and the porters calling the trains, and the passengers calling each other, and the luggage trolleys rumbling over the tiled floor, and the sounds of a thousand pairs of moving feet, echoing back and forth from one wall to the other and back.

Grand Central Station at night.

All human life was here—the housewife running from her abusive husband to her sister in Schenectady, the banker who couldn't face his wife's cooking without a couple of tonkatsu pork rolls inside him, the cops on the beat arguing about whether Warhol had finally lost it with all this dreampunk crap, the kid sleeping rough on the streets who'd wandered in to get out of the rain, the British tourists pointing and gawping at everyone else in between looking at their map and wondering how to walk to the Statue of Liberty...

...and up above them, up, up in the shadowy arches of the station, where the gaslight didn't reach, there was a man in a pitch-black coat and a metallic, blood-red mask with eight glittering lenses, who carried a pair of automatic pistols, and he watched them all.

Watched and waited.

Occasionally, he glanced at the clock that told the bustling crowds how late they were for the trains they could never hope to catch now. Eight fifty-nine, and fifty seconds, fifty-one, fifty-two... he watched, his fingers on the triggers itching, buzzing, yearning, as the second hand passed the top of the arc and began a new circuit around the dial.

Nine o'clock. No sign of him.

The Blood-Spider hissed irritably into his mask.

How typical of Doc Thunder to be late for his own funeral.

"I DO SO wish you'd reconsider this course of action, Master Parker."

Three hours before, Jonah had expressed his misgivings about the whole venture. It had come very close to ruining an otherwise excellent dinner of roast quail and asparagus tips.

"Surely it would be safer to wait until you had, ah, acquired abilities commensurate to the good Doctor before embarking on a campaign against him?" Jonah swallowed, unused to this sort of confrontation. Crane only smiled.

"Jonah, if I suddenly turn up being able to bend steel and leap the height of a decent-sized office building, he'll put two and two together. He knows *somebody* stole his blood. No, better to pick him off now before he suspects my involvement. Who knows, maybe I'll get lucky and Donner's murderer will turn up as well—warn him of the trap. Two birds with one stone." He lifted a forkful of quail to his lips, chewing meditatively for a moment. "And consider the larger picture, Jonah. America's Greatest Hero, gunned down in public! In the panic and tumult, the question goes up; who will replace him? His friends either die in mysterious circumstances or sail away to their forbidden cities, if they know what's good for them. And then..."

He leaned back, smiling expansively. "A new Doc Thunder, for new times. The Blood Thunder." He laughed. "Blood and thunder! That's rather good, isn't it?"

Jonah swallowed. "Master Parker, please. Remember the cause. The war." He laid his hand gently on Crane's shoulder. "You're taking a terrible risk. You seem to be becoming... unstable. Remember, sir, that while you do have great power, you also have a grave responsibility."

Crane shook his hand off. "I'll decide what my responsibilities are, Jonah. And I say this is the best chance to further the cause we've had yet. Doc Thunder dead, all his power in my hands... and total war with the inhuman elements of our society. War to the death!"

Jonah looked at him for a long moment, and it was impossible to tell if what lay behind his eyes was reproach or pity. "I see. In that case, I will leave you to prepare, sir." He began to clear away Crane's meal, then took a look around the dusty confines of the Lower Library. "One more thing, though, sir, if I may."

"Get on with it."

"Sir"—Jonah took a deep breath—"you are spending rather a worrying amount of time down here, in this room, sequestered away from the other Jameson Club members. There are other rooms in the club where you may take an early supper without raising quite so many eyebrows."

Crane snorted. "And are there other rooms in the club where I may openly discuss the murder of such a prominent celebrity? With ammunition secured from the ashes of a known terrorist organisation? Hmm? Dry up, Jonah."

"Sir, please—"

"I said dry up!" Crane bellowed the words. "I'm the leader of this particular organisation, Jonah. Do you understand me? I decide what our strategy is! I decide who to *kill!* And I decide whether or not to leave my comfortable little nook here and spend my valuable time with those *overstuffed blowhards* up *there!*" His voice rose, uncaring, until it was almost a shriek.

Jonah looked at him in horror.

"Soundproof walls, Jonah." Crane smiled, his grey eyes mischievous. "Now, tell me again how you'd rather I said all that upstairs in the smoking room while passing out cigars."

Jonah blinked, the look of shock still palpable on his face, and turned to leave. He did not say a word.

"Oh, and Jonah—telephone. I'm going to need Ms Lang tonight, I think. *She* at least knows how to obey an order."

NINE O' CLOCK.

Marlene Lang waited patiently. Back straight in the leather seat, cap pulled down over blonde hair styled in a very severe bun, mirrored sunglasses. Hands in the ten and two position, unmoving. Lips frowning in an icy pout.

She'd held the position for fifteen minutes, and fully intended to hold it until the Blood-Spider's business in the station was concluded, whatever it might be. At which point, he would make his way to the Silver Ghost, parked in a dark alley two blocks away, and they would drive to a safe location which he would make known to her at that time, and not before. It was all deliciously professional.

Professionalism was her new watchword, she had decided.

David had called earlier in the day, and she had told him, in what she felt was a very reasonable tone, that she would no longer be modelling for him at his studio. She'd let him have his say, quietly enduring his wheedling, passive-aggressive tone as he'd begged her to reconsider, his voice echoing tinnily over the receiver as he told her that without her as his muse he had no reason to create his art, that his talent needed her beauty as its essential focus—lies of that nature. She had sighed, like a schoolmistress lecturing a petulant child.

"David, it's very simple. I just have better things to do with my time."

And with that, she'd hung up on him. She would probably have done the same if Jack had called, or Easton. Even Parker—her fellow crime-fighter—would find her closed for anything other than the most pressing business. Since the trouble of the previous night, she'd found herself infused with an almost religious fervour for the cause. It had been the first time she had fully entertained the possibility, which she surmised was still quite real, that the Blood-Spider could be exposed or killed at any moment, and might even end up dragging her down with him. Faced with a choice between dealing herself out of the game before things escalated further and throwing herself into the whole dangerous enterprise wholeheartedly and without restraint, she had chosen the latter. Well, of course she had.

Any other choice would simply have been too dreary for words.

She idly checked her eyeshadow in the rear view mirror. Professionalism was the new watchword in all things, and that meant keeping herself immaculate.

When her eyes looked forward again, there was a man standing in front of the auto.

He was a well-built man, of Latin descent, handsome apart from a freshly broken nose and the wet, bedraggled state of his hair. Although that was somewhat made up for by his wearing nothing but a pair of tuxedo trousers and red sash tied around his face with two holes in it. In his right hand, he was holding a very dangerous looking sword.

"Nice wheels."

She stared at him for a long moment, then went for the pistol she'd hidden under her seat, ducking her head for a moment and grabbing the handle of the gun in a practised motion, bringing it up to fire at—nothing.

The man was gone, as suddenly as he'd appeared.

She blinked, looking up and down the alley for any sign of him. Nothing. He'd simply vanished. Uneasily, she fingered the safety on the pistol, then laid it on the seat next to her. She wanted to be ready if that strange man—whoever he turned out to be—should appear again.

She wondered why his hair had been wet.

Two blocks away, Doc Thunder walked into Grand Central Station.

For a moment, he simply stood on the balcony overlooking the main concourse, closed his eyes and breathed it all in; the smell of roasting onions, hot dogs, sticky rice, shoe polish, perfume, honest sweat. The soft, insistent buzz of conversation, the shuffle of feet, the yell of station announcements, the tapping-out of the beat of a pair of toms, the whistle of the trains on their distant platforms.

Humanity, in all its glory.

When he opened his eyes, the crowd was looking back at him.

One by one, they'd turned to look at the big man in the blue T-shirt, the man who'd fought back against the Hidden Empire when all seemed lost, who'd stopped Untergang, N.I.G.H.T.M.A.R.E., Lars Lomax, Anton Venger, Professor Zeppelin, the steam-powered giant robot ape Titanicus, Mordus Madgrave and his army of the risen dead, Captain Death and the Pirates of Wall Street, the Orchestra of Fear, Jason Satan and so many others. A rogue's gallery of maniacs, mutants, monsters and madmen. For fifty years, while others had come and gone, he'd stood firm against them all.

America's Greatest Hero.

A few people figured that deserved a round of applause.

The sound rippled through the crowd, commuters and breakers, hot dog vendors and police, even the tourists, all of them stopping where they stood and putting their hands together for the man who'd saved them all. The sound built, echoing off the ceiling, bouncing from one pillar to another, escaping onto the platforms where the arriving passengers wondered what all the fuss was about.

Up on his perch in the high darkness, the Blood-Spider listened to it all and waited for his moment to fire.

Doc blinked, surprised and a little embarrassed despite himself. It wasn't the first time he'd been greeted like that, but every time was a shock. He smiled, raising a hand. "Thank you. Thank you all, very much. It means a lot." And it did.

Then his expression grew more serious. "But... I'm going to have to ask you to clear the concourse. I have reason to believe there's someone here who wants me dead, and he's not going to worry about collateral damage. If you could all clear the station in an orderly manner—thank you, that's great..."

The cheers and applause changed slowly to worried murmurs, as the crowd began to break at the edges, some moving onto the platforms, most filing out through the main exits. Within a few minutes, the concourse was completely empty.

"Alone at last," Doc smiled, seemingly to nobody in particular.

Above, the Blood-Spider waited. Did he have police outside? Had he come here alone? Was it too late to get out without being seen? So many variables. He was safe up in the darkness, he knew. So long as he remained hidden, he had a choice.

"The newspaper announcement just didn't ring true, I'm afraid. Last time I saw 'my friend in the red mask,' I smashed his face in with my forehead, although that was after he'd threatened to stab me through the eye. Not too friendly, really. Oh, and sustantivo... that's not the Spanish for 'thunder.'" Doc smiled. "It actually means 'noun.' I take it you used a dictionary for that one?" He paused for a moment, listening. "Not telling? Well, if it is you, my 'friend' in the mask, I'll apologise and accept the title of 'Mr Noun' without a murmur. Just step out and let me get a good look at you."

He turned, looking up at the ceiling. For a moment, the Blood-Spider froze. Thunder was looking right at him—no, he couldn't be. The shadows up here were pitch black. Just stay still...

"No? Well, I suppose there's only one other person it can be, then. I don't think we've actually met, but I've been following your career with interest. A good friend of mine—Easton West?—was hoping I'd find you eventually. You killed a young gang member in Japantown a few days ago, I don't know if you remember..." An edge crept into his voice. "You kill so many."

The Blood-Spider narrowed his eyes, behind his strange mask with its eight glittering lenses. Below him, Thunder reached into his pocket, taking out a small business card. He read the inscription slowly:

Where all inhuman
Devils revel in their sins—
The Blood-Spider spins!

"That's very good. That's a haiku, isn't it? I'm sure Hisoka's family appreciated that little touch of home." He slipped the card back in his pocket. "His name was Hisoka. The boy you murdered. Inspector West wanted you to know his name."

Up in the thick darkness above, the Blood-Spider's hand was shaking. *He knows.* His finger was sweaty inside the black glove. *He knows. Fire. Kill him.* Why couldn't he fire?

"I ran into him at the hospital, actually—while I was looking in on Monk. He's still not out of his coma. Still, it could have been a lot worse. If I hadn't got there in time..." He shook his head. "A close-run thing. Anyway, the Inspector told me that the bullets they dug out of his body matched the ones they dug out of Hisoka. Same calibre, same manufacturer... and guns leave marks. Every gun leaves its own personal signature on the bullets it fires. So it strikes me that you might want to use a different gun for pleasure than the one you use for business…"

The Blood-Spider's hands shook. *Fire! Kill him!*

He knows!

He tried to will himself to pull the trigger, but his finger wouldn't move. *Every gun leaves a signature.* But not on inexorium, surely? But what if it did? And the calibre would be the same… It would be the end of the Blood-Spider for all time. Could he risk that?

Could he still get away?

OUTSIDE, MARLENE DRUMMED her fingers impatiently on the wheel. She'd seen the crowds coming from the station. Something was happening there, something that wasn't included in the plan. She frowned, worrying her lip. More than ever, it was vital the Spider had a quick getaway from whatever he intended to do in there.

She had a nagging feeling that something was terribly wrong.

She wished she had a way of signalling him. He needed to know about the masked man. What had he been doing there, any—

—her eyes were suddenly drawn to the dials.

There was an array of dials on the dashboard; temperature of the internal furnace, water pressure for the hydraulics, steam pressure, and of course the speedometer. They were all over the place. The temperature of the internal furnace was way over normal, water pressure was at zero. And the pressure of the steam on the internal turbines was getting very—

—there was a grinding noise, and she felt the whirr of the turbines stop. Her heart froze in her chest. The Silver Ghost never stalled. Other autos stalled, all the time, but the Silver Ghost was special. The maze of fine hydraulic tubes underneath the car meant that there was always…

Oh God!

Heart thundering, she opened the driver's side door and stepped out—and the high heels of her black pumps splashed into a huge puddle of water, spreading slowly out from underneath the car. Wincing, she got down on her hands and knees, her cap tumbling off her head and splashing into the growing pool as she peered underneath the machine.

The Silver Ghost was armoured so well that a machine-gun couldn't scratch it.

But only from the top. Underneath, it seemed, it was very vulnerable indeed.

Before he even made himself known to her, the masked man had crawled under her auto, without being seen, and used that sword to disconnect every pipe he could find. Since then, all the water had been draining out of the machine, until now there was nothing left for steam. And without steam, the auto wouldn't move a single inch.

The Silver Ghost was dead.

"There's one thing that puzzled me. I'm assuming you investigated Donner's murder at the same time Monk did, and he ran into you. But Monk Olsen… well, he's a celebrity in this town. Moreover, he's unique. There's literally no mistaking him for anyone else." Doc frowned.

"Now, the bullet in the kneecap… I can put that down to shock. Maybe the first one in the lung. Even the one that glanced off his skull. I'm a reasonable man." Slowly, he lay his fist in his hand, cracking one massive knuckle. It sounded like a gunshot.

"But."

Another knuckle. Another gunshot.

"He was down. He was no threat. You knew who he was. And then you fired a bullet into his gut—that's a slow death—and then another into his chest. Why? The thrill of the kill? Simple sadism? Just not thinking straight? Or is it something else?"

And another.

"Something occurred to me, a moment ago."

The Blood-Spider kept his gun trained on Doc Thunder's head. *He can't see me. I can still get away. Or…* His hand was shaking so badly he didn't even know if he'd hit his target if he fired. What was the matter with him? Why couldn't he just fire?

"You see, once I knew it was you who tried to kill Monk, I took a look at your other killings. And there's something rather strange about them."

The Blood-Spider felt a chill rush through him. *Does he know?*

Doc smiled, humourlessly, his footsteps echoing on the tiled floor of the station, walking slowly around like a teacher in the world's largest classroom.

"There's not a single white, straight person among them. Well, apart from Anton Venger—you were the one who shot Anton Venger, weren't you?—

and I'm not even one hundred per cent sure about him. I'm fairly sure he and Lomax were more than just colleagues. But anyway, everyone else you've killed has been... well, there's no other way to say it, is there?"

Doc's smile vanished.

"Non-Aryan."

He turned, looking up into the shadows. "And as I said, something occurred to me. The last piece of the puzzle. The crowd, giving me that little ovation. I'm going to put false modesty aside for a moment here and admit that, yes, I am loved. Perhaps not by everybody, but the people of this city do seem to hold me in very high regard. An outsider—someone who studied at this city without actually living here—would probably say it's because I fight crime. Now, did you see what happened when I asked them to clear the station? Grand Central Station, nine o' clock at night—cleared. No complaints. Not a murmur. Even the police went without a word. In fact, nobody else has come in here, so I'd go as far as to suggest they're outside right now, making themselves useful and spreading the word that I've put the main concourse of Grand Central Station off-limits."

He smiled. "It's a good thing I don't let power go to my head, isn't it?"

The smile vanished, and he turned on his heel, wandering into the dead centre of the concourse.

He's daring me to shoot, thought the Spider. *To give away my position. Why don't I shoot?* He cursed, silently. *I could drop him like a stone from this position! He'd never even hear the bullet!* But he continued to wait, fingers slick with sweat inside his gloves, trying to control the trembling of his hands. He had to be sure. Absolutely sure. Doc Thunder had just demonstrated that he was, to all intents and purposes, the King of New York City.

And if you shoot at a king, you have to kill him.

"Now!" Doc shouted, turning around again, as if lecturing an invisible audience, "Let's say I walked in here with a big bomb and yelled 'clear the station or I destroy us all'! Complete chaos! Mass panic! Oh, it'd clear the station, probably, after a shoot-out with the cops. But it's such a messy way to achieve my goals." He shrugged. "Or to put it another way; President Bartlet refuses to negotiate with terrorists. But I've got his direct line. At the end of the day, you get more by being loved than by being feared.

"Which brings us to Untergang."

All of a sudden, the Blood-Spider's hand stopped trembling.

"We've stopped hearing from them. Not because I finally beat them, the way I did N.I.G.H.T.M.A.R.E… they just went away. Vanished into the ether. Right about the time you turned up, in fact. Which makes me wonder… what if there's a new leader of Untergang? What if that leader wanted to try a new tactic? Rebranding the organisation. Making them loved rather than feared. Having them fight crime, or the right kind of crime, at least. What if the Führer agreed to a trial of this new strategy? What if the new leader of Untergang created a persona designed to appeal to the worst in people, to bring the citizens of New York around to his cause, his war on crime, which would, of course, then become a war against 'urban crime.' Or some other little euphemism." Doc smiled. "'Inhuman,' for example. Sounds a lot more relatable than *sub*human, doesn't it? Comes to the same thing, though. Anyway, what if there *is* a new leader of Untergang, masquerading as a faceless, fearless crime-killer in order to sway public opinion towards fascism?"

"And what if it's you?"

He knows.

The Blood-Spider raised his gun. Suddenly he was completely calm. There were no more choices now, no more chances. *He knows. One bullet, that's all it will take. He has to go.*

Doc Thunder must die.

And then Doc Thunder turned around and looked him right in the face.

"People get so worked up about the bulletproof skin and the bending steel that they always forget about my eyes. I can read small print from a hundred feet away. And I can see in the dark." He smiled, and cracked another knuckle. "Hello, Blood-Spider."

Then he cocked his head, suddenly puzzled. "Wait. You know I'm—"

Under his mask, the Blood-Spider smiled—

—aimed his gun full of magic bullets straight at Doc's heart—

—and fired.

CHAPTER FOURTEEN
DOC THUNDER MUST DIE

Doc HAD SPOTTED the Blood-Spider as soon as he'd walked into the station.

He figured he'd get rid of the civilians before making his move, so the Spider couldn't use them against him. That was when he'd had the revelation about the Blood-Spider's true identity. He was so busy connecting those dots in his mind, he failed to ask the obvious question.

Namely, if nothing less than a bursting shell could penetrate Doc Thunder's skin...

...why was the Blood Spider bringing a gun to a mortar fight?

It was a question that didn't occur to him until he was staring down the barrel of the Blood-Spider's gun—the one he'd assumed was harmless as far as he was concerned. If the Spider had fired earlier, rather than waiting until he had an almost point-blank shot, Doc would have died instantly as the inexorium bullet tore through his heart.

As it was, he was able to realise his error in time and throw himself to the side—enough for the bullet to smash his left shoulder instead of hitting his chest. He went down hard, trying to roll back onto his feet, to keep moving.

Inexorium bullets. Unbelievable. Evidently taking N.I.G.H.T.M.A.R.E. out of commission had led to a lot of their technology being released onto the black market. Presumably he could expect a rematch with Titanicus any day now.

And that was the possibility that would let him sleep at night. Because that would mean N.I.G.H.T.M.A.R.E. was really gone. That they weren't wrapped up in this somehow, behind it all, puppet-masters pulling the strings.

He'd never found Silken Dragon's body.

He put that thought out of his mind—right now, he needed to concentrate on survival. The only advantage he had in this open space was that inexorium bullets were so prohibitively expensive. The Spider would not have too many. One hit near his feet, chewing into the tile and concrete and spitting up fragments. Unlike an ordinary bullet, it would not distort on impact, like the one that had passed so effortlessly through this shoulder, that one could be recycled if someone dug it up.

And if there was a moral to the last few days, it was that nothing ever stayed buried.

Doc hurled himself behind the abandoned sushi stall—a massive thing the size of a car and normally staffed by two smiling brothers from Kyoto—seconds before a third bullet ploughed through the wasabi tray and out of the back, missing him by inches.

I've got to keep him on the high ground, Doc thought. *If he's firing those things into the ground, that's one thing. If he fires them horizontally through a wall, people in the street outside are going to start losing major organs.* He waited for another shot—nothing came. The Spider was waiting for him to make a break. *With the price of magic bullets these days, he can't afford to waste them. How many does he have left?*

His shoulder was already clotting, but it'd be useless for at least a day, maybe two. He'd probably have to rebreak the bone so it regenerated properly. He thought of Miles Hamilton then, of how he'd supervised such operations in the past, and frowned. "Spider!"

"*I have nothing to say to you, Thunder. We're past conversation at this point.*"

"You set this up." He rubbed his wounded shoulder with his free hand. "You told Venger to get my blood, didn't you? He was acting on your orders!"

The Blood-Spider laughed, that terrible laugh from some ultimate circle of Hell. "*Don't be a fool!*"

"It makes too much sense to be coincidence!" Thunder roared. "You shot Monk because you knew how I'd react! You knew I'd do anything to save him! And you had your pet, Venger, waiting!"

Another echoing laugh.

"*I thought you were a scientist, Thunder. Don't fudge the evidence to fit your hypothesis. Venger was working for another player. Someone Untergang would dearly like to meet. Tell me, Doctor, before I end your life, do you have any idea what 'fifty-fifty' could mean? Venger kept repeating it."*

Doc shook his head. Venger had mentioned it during their conversation on the hospital roof, almost as a taunt. Fifty-fifty. Equal odds. Six of one, half a dozen of the other. What did it mean?

"I'm afraid my Nazi party membership seems to have lapsed, Spider. So as much as I'd like to help you bring your fascist insanity to my town, I'm afraid you're right—we're beyond conversation."

"Then die!"

Another bullet chewed through a tray of cucumber rolls, then the wood and metal of the trolley, and finally tore denim, grazing Doc Thunder's leg and leaving him with a red, burning line of agony against his thigh. Another shot would probably puncture his belly. And again, there was that cruel, murderous laugh, echoing with pure, uncontrollable evil.

Doc Thunder wondered how long the Blood-Spider had been mad.

"Give it up, Doctor. I'll make it quick for you. Come on, there's no way you can win! Look at the mathematics! I've got bullets that can blow through anything you hide behind like it was tissue paper, and what have you got? Nothing!"

"I beg to differ."

Doc grabbed hold of the bottom of the sushi cart, testing its weight. Slightly under three quarters of a ton. He took a firm grip on it—

—and then he stood up.

Behind the implacable lenses of his mask, the Blood-Spider's eyes widened. *"No. It can't be! It can't be!"*

Doc Thunder stood, one arm hanging limp at his side, the other raised above his head, three quarters of a ton of metal and wood sat in his palm as if it were a Frisbee, slivers of raw fish and rice and glittering chips of ice tumbling from the trays balanced precariously on top of the massive cart. "Oh yes it can."

He grinned a wolfish grin.

"Heads up."

With his one good arm, he threw the cart like a baseball, aiming it straight at the Blood-Spider's head. The Spider reacted instantly, hurling himself from his high perch up on the arches as the cart exploded into matchwood where he'd been standing just a moment before.

He turned in the air, reaching out with his free hand to touch the smooth pillar, and Doc noticed for the first time that upon the Blood-Spider's gloves and the soles of his boots were dozens of tiny suction cups. He watched, fascinated, as these devices allowed the Blood-Spider to slow his fall, skidding down the smooth marble pillar with a squeal of rubber on stone, turning a fall which would surely have shattered his shinbones into splinters into something which he could walk away from.

Doc Thunder did not intend to let him walk away.

He charged forward, pulling back his good hand, balling it into a fist. The Blood-Spider reacted instinctively, leaping off the pillar and going into a tuck and roll just as Thunder's massive fist crashed into the pillar where he had been, smashing a huge chunk out of the ornate stone. Another man might have broken his hand. Doc Thunder barely even skinned his knuckles.

The Blood-Spider rolled back onto his feet, the automatic in his hand spitting another of the deadly inexorium bullets through the meat of Thunder's thigh. Thunder cried out through gritted teeth, sinking down onto one knee, clutching at the wound, trying to staunch the flow from his femoral artery long enough for it to clot.

Too bad the mysterious Mr Fifty isn't around to take my blood now, he thought. *There's a pint or three here he could soak up, if he brought a sponge...*

Something about that nagged at him. Fifty fifty...

Behind him, the Blood-Spider rose to his full height.

"*It's a wound that would probably kill a normal man, unless it was treated instantly. All you have to do is keep yourself from losing too much blood, and you'll be fine. It does mean you can't move your leg, or move your hands away from your leg. You're as helpless as a kitten until the flow stops... but that's a small price to pay, isn't it? You'd probably be able to stand on that leg in a few minutes... if you had a few minutes.*"

Doc winced. The Spider had a point. If he took his hand off the wound, he'd be dead in seconds, his own superhuman heart forcing the blood out of him like a water cannon. There was no way he could reach and disarm him without dying.

The Blood-Spider examined his automatic, taking his time. "*One bullet left. It's a shame, really, Donner. Just think, if not for Strucker's unfortunate little heart problem, you might have been the leader of a new race of Nazi Supermen. Something to think about on your road to the grave.*"

He raised the gun, aiming the barrel directly at Thunder's head.

"*Goodbye, Doc Thunder—*"

A sword spun out of the darkness above, whirring around and around like the twirled baton in a marching band, the razor point of it slicing across the Blood-Spider's forearm, leaving a deep gash and causing his wrist to jerk, sending the fatal bullet off course to lodge inside the thick marble pillar behind Thunder's head. The sword clanged against the marble floor, bounced in a shivering arc, then slid a few more feet, slowly spinning, and came to a gentle stop.

The Blood-Spider screamed, roaring both with the pain of his slashed forearm and the rage of knowing that he had missed his last chance to kill Doc Thunder. He looked at the sword, the eyes behind the lenses narrowed in furious agony, then threw his gun to one side and reached for it, a trickle of blood coursing down his wounded arm and onto the blade.

He could still kill Thunder. There were weak points—the eyes, the mouth, anywhere one of his bullets had already pierced flesh and the wound had not closed. He would thrust the sword through the eye and into the brain, or through the shoulder wound and down into the heart, quickly, before Thunder could react. And if he raised his hand to prevent it, if he took his hand away from the torn artery that threatened to release his life's blood onto the marbled floor—that would also kill him.

The Spider gripped the sword's hilt. He could still do this. He could still—

"Amigo... that's *my* sword."

The voice came from the darkness above them, where the gaslight did not reach. The Spider's blood ran cold for a long moment, and then he grabbed hold of his other gun, tearing it from its holster and raising it to fire a volley of bullets into the darkness. "*Where are you? Show yourself!*" he hissed, turning in place, the gun raised to fire at the slightest sound or movement.

"You're not the only one who can hide in the shadows, my friend. I've got very good at it, over the years."

The Spider whirled around and fired off another three shots, aiming where he thought the voice might have come from, expecting a cry of pain, a falling body, but only hearing the sounds of lead impacting against the plaster of the roof and the sound of his shell casings tinkling against the echoing marble floor. "*Where are you? WHERE ARE YOU?*" Suddenly his mask felt hot, constricting. He could smell his own sweat in it, feel it pressing against his cheeks, his forehead. "*No. No, no, no...*"

"Old man Donner was right about you, amigo. Right about the other you, I mean. Parker Crane."

"*Shut up! That's not my name!*" the Spider screamed, helplessly, shrieking it into the darkness. "*Show yourself!*" Another volley of shots, with no result. Was he throwing his voice? Was he everywhere at once? Was he a shadow himself? A ghost?

The voice echoed from another place now, continuing his speech exactly where he had left off. "He said you were crazy, and under pressure you were going to crack up. Okay, that's *all* he said about you, but that was enough. That told me you were worth watching."

"*Shut up!*" Another volley of shots into the darkness, and now the gun was light in his hand and the floor was littered with the cases of wasted shells. And still that mocking voice echoed from the shadows above.

"See, I didn't know if you were a good guy or a bad guy. I mean, sure, you killed people, and you were kind of a dick about it, you know? But I didn't know if you were one of the bastards. I didn't know if you needed to die or not, amigo."

"*I said shut—*" The Spider whirled, aiming the gun and pulling the trigger, sending another bullet screaming off at nothing—

—and then the gun clicked empty.

He was out of bullets.

He turned, looking at Doc Thunder, and saw him take his hand away from his leg, revealing a pulsing red scab. In another moment, maybe two, he'd be able to stand.

He turned again, and there was the man in the red mask. Just standing there, in the middle of the concourse. His smile didn't look human. And his *eyes*. Oh, his terrible eyes...

"*Stay back,*" the Spider whispered, and his voice sounded in his ears like a frightened, animal thing, waiting to curl up and die in its hole.

The man in the red mask only laughed. A rich, deep, joyous laugh, a laugh that echoed and filled the whole station, bouncing from pillar to pillar, careening through the great vaulted arches. Such a laugh!

Then the laughter stopped, and he fixed the Blood-Spider with a look that would freeze the fires of Hell.

"My sword. Don't make me ask again."

And suddenly—quite suddenly—there was no Blood-Spider.

There was only Parker Crane, the Nazi. Parker Crane, the traitor. Parker Crane, who thought he could destroy America, and only managed to destroy himself.

Parker Crane. Just a man wearing a mask.

He ran, and left the sword behind him.

DOC THUNDER WATCHED, bemused, as the Spider—what was his name? Crane?—hurled the sword away from him and bolted from the concourse. "Nice trick," he murmured, turning to the masked man. "Throwing your sword from up on the balcony—good aim, by the way—then throwing your voice and a little mental suggestion to make him think you were up in the arches where he'd been. My hat's off. Where did you learn that?"

The masked man shrugged, lifting up his weapon, checking that the impact against the marble floor hadn't damaged it. "In the desert. You can learn a lot in the desert, if you put your mind to it."

"Good psychology, too." Doc nodded, gently prodding the healing wound. He could feel the muscles knitting together. Not long now. "Although I think whatever you did there might have pushed him over the edge of whatever mental breakdown he was heading towards..."

"Just my latin charm, amigo," shrugged the masked man, looking at the wound slowly healing in Thunder's leg. "Ouch. You need a doctor?"

Doc Thunder blinked. *Latin.* He shook his head. "Give me a second." He gritted his teeth, and put his weight on the damaged leg. It wasn't too agonising. Slowly, he stood. "I think I'm good to go. We need to get after him before he loses himself. He's a danger to the general public, and besides, he needs to pay for what he did to Monk." He turned to the masked man, putting out his hand, smiling ruefully. "I owe you an apology, by the way. I was wrong to accuse you."

The masked man laughed. "Well, maybe I was wrong to call you a monster, hey? Nobody gets to choose their parents, my friend." His palm slapped against Thunder's, and they shook.

"I don't think I caught your name, by the way." Doc Thunder smiled.

"El Sombra," said El Sombra.

And then two highly trained police officers burst into Grand Central Station and began shooting at him.

A MINUTE EARLIER, Crane pulled off his mask, quickly folding the leather part flat and sliding it into his inside coat-pocket, and dove into the crowd outside the station. A cop grabbed his shoulder, and another leant into his face, scowling. "Hey, buddy, don't you know nobody gets to go in there? Doc Thunder's orders!"

"I—" Crane's face was a mass of sweat and raw panic. "I went to the toilet. When I came out, it was all happening! A man in a mask... I think he's an illegal alien! He's trying to kill Doc Thunder!" The cops looked at each other, then tore into the station, guns drawn.

Like sheep, Crane thought. *Tell them to herd, and they herd.* He snarled, his contempt rising like bile, then ran towards the meeting place where Marlene would be waiting. Faithful Marlene, who had taken to the cause like a duck to water...

Water. His feet were splashing in it.

His eyes widened as he took in the sight—the Silver Ghost with its bonnet open, water trickling from the underside, and Marlene, bent over like a salacious pinup as she tinkered with the engine, desperately trying to bring back life to a machine that was now dead forever. She looked up as he approached.

"Parker? What are you doing here—" Her eyes widened as she saw what he was wearing. "You...?" She blinked, taking a step back.

"What happened?" He barked at her, eyes blazing. "I gave you one duty! One responsibility! One! And you—oh, you stupid little *whore!*"

"Parker, you can't talk to me that—" She was interrupted by a slap from his open palm that sent her to the ground, blood trickling from a split lip. She looked up at him, eyes wide with shock. "You—you *hit* me!"

His eyes blazed at her. "You can think yourself damned lucky I didn't shoot you!"

She shook her head, eyes gazing at him in—was that astonishment? Or disgust? Or both? "But you're supposed to be the *Blood-Spider—*"

He looked back, staring down at her in impotent fury, then reached into his coat, pulling out the mask and hurling it at her. "There's your precious Blood-Spider," he muttered. Then he turned, rushing out into the street, leaving her where she lay.

"Cab! Damn you, cab! *Cab!*"

Picking herself up, Marlene watched as Parker pulled himself into a hansom cab, yelled a tirade of obscenities at the driver, and sped off in the direction of the East Village. That was the Blood-Spider, then. Nothing but Parker. Parker, wearing a mask and in over his head. And Parker, her debonair, dashing

Parker—*he* was nothing but a vicious little thug when the chips were down.

Dimly, she realised that her life as she knew it was over. Whatever Parker had been up to, there would be repercussions. Easton would want her to make some dreadful statements to the police. Jack would probably call her a traitor. After all, Doc Thunder was a national resource, and hadn't she known, deep down, that Parker was trying to kill him? She just hadn't wanted to believe it. Or perhaps she'd wanted to believe that he actually had a chance.

Time for that suitcase, she mused.

What hurt the most wasn't the slap, or the growing horror of having to leave her whole life behind her. It was the disappointment of knowing that, at the end of it all, the great Blood-Spider was just another man.

But did he have to be?

She picked up the mask, looking into those eight implacable lenses, thinking about the war on crime, and her own words. *The most fabulous thing is to believe in something utterly and completely, without restraint.*

When she walked away from the dead auto, into the darkness of the alley, she was wearing it.

" WELL, THANKS FOR the prompt response, all the same," Doc sighed to the sheepish Officer Rawls, as he examined the fresh bullet holes in his blue shirt. Sooner or later, he was going to run out of these.

Fortunately, he'd managed to shield El Sombra with his body, but the masked man had reacted immediately, delivering a brutal kick into the face of Officer Valchek—who was still unconscious—and very nearly running the other one through before Thunder could stop him.

He turned to El Sombra, frowning. "Impetuous, aren't you? Which reminds me, we're going to have to have a talk after all this is over about the number of bodies you've left behind you."

El Sombra raised an eyebrow behind his mask. "What, you've never had a few deaths on your conscience? At least I only get the bad guys killed, hey?"

"And having beaten up two police officers, you're now trying to start a fight with me. Wonderful." Doc Thunder sighed, rubbing his shoulder. The bone was starting to heal, but he wasn't going to be able to lift that arm properly any time soon. He'd have to fight with one. "More of that latin charm, I take it?"

He never heard El Sombra's reply.

Latin.

"Oh God," he breathed. "How could I have..."

"*...do you have any idea what 'fifty-fifty' could mean?...*"

"*...wait until you see Plan C...*"

"*...want him out of my hair for a while...*"

"*...if I were you... I'd do a lot of things differently...*"

"*...I thought he'd never get here...*"

...El Sombra was waving his hand in front of Doc's face.

"Hey, amigo—you okay?"

"Fifty-fifty," Doc said, slowly. "I knew it. I knew there was someone behind all this. Nothing ever stays buried." He swallowed. "But I was looking in the wrong place. Latin numerals, you see?"

El Sombra gave him a puzzled look. "Amigo... what the hell are you talking about?"

"In the Latin language, the numbers are represented by letters. I for one, X for ten. And for fifty... L. So fifty-fifty... is L.L." He stared off into the distance.

"I think we may already be too late."

CRANE HAMMERED HIS fist on the metal door, yelling for Timothy Larson to let him in. Eventually, the door opened.

"Whoa... Parker Crane, out of sight! What brings you here?" Larson smiled, taking a long sip from a freshly brewed mug of coffee. "Listen, let me get you some java—"

"I don't need your damned java!" Crane hissed, grabbing hold of the lapels of his shirt and slamming him against the wall. "I need the blood! Tell me you've got something—"

"Hey, easy..." Larson frowned, pushing Parker gently away and then closing the door with a small clang. "Listen, you need to just chill out for a second, okay? Just relax. Everything's going to be fine, you know?" He smiled, putting a hand gently on Crane's shoulder. "I know some great meditation exercises you could try."

Crane slapped his hand away. "Shut up! I need to know what you've found in that blood, and I need it now! Don't you understand, Doc Thunder knows everything! He's probably on his way here now—" Crane suddenly froze.

"Wait, how do you know my—"

Larson smiled. "Well, I've got good news and bad news. The good news is, I got the big secret Untergang's been after all these years. A serum that'll give Doc Thunder's brand of the right stuff to any adult who takes it." He raised his hands. "I know, I know, I'm a genius. No applause, just throw money. That's my motto."

Crane took a step back. Suddenly, Larson seemed like a completely different person. "I—I only ever spoke to you as the Blood-Spider. How do you even know who Parker Crane is?"

"No flies on you, Parker! That's what I like about you, you're smart. Smart enough to think you're the smartest guy in the world, which is my *favourite* level of smart, because there's only *one* smartest guy in the world and he likes people to underestimate him. Anyway, the bad news—there was only enough serum for one, and I didn't feel like sharing. Sorry 'bout that. Guess you don't get to be President after all, but that's politics." Larson grinned, reaching and tearing away his moustache and beard, then rubbing his chin. "Any makeup glue left? I want to look my best for company."

Crane shook his head, his eyes wide, sweat beading on his face. "What... what are you talking about? How do you know about Untergang? About my plan..."

Larson lifted off his shaggy wig, revealing a gleaming bald pate. "My plan. You were just a useful tool, Parker, but now that I'm packed full of that serum— and let's just test that out—" He calmly picked up a steel test tube rack, and Crane watched in horror as he slowly twisted it into a double helix, as easily as twisting a wire coat hanger. "Huh! Wasn't sure that'd work. Anyway, Parker, I've got a spot for a dogsbody, but that's about it. So unless you want to be test number two of my amazing new Thunder Serum..." His eyes narrowed. "I'd lay off the attitude when you talk to me."

Crane's mouth was dry. "Who are you?" He whispered.

The bald man grinned. "Why, I'm the most dangerous man in the world, kid. Timothy Larson Lomax, at your service."

He stuck out his hand.

"But everybody calls me Lars."

CHAPTER FIFTEEN
THE LAST CASE

"So, I UNDERSTAND you were wondering who killed Heinrich Donner?"

Lars Lomax sipped his coffee. He'd asked Crane to make it for him, with a cold, hard inflection in his voice that made it clear he wasn't asking at all. Now Crane shrank up against the wall, as if trying to escape through it. Lomax was between him and the door and, if he wanted to, he could put down that coffee, reach out with his hand and twist off Crane's head. He could do it as easily as scratch his own.

And he was mad. Quite mad. Crane was certain of it.

"It was me. My bad." Lomax smiled, waggling his eyebrows. "I mean, I didn't pull the trigger—or, you know, shove the sword in him—but I've got to take the credit. It's kind of a complicated story, though..." He frowned, then drained the last of his coffee, setting the cup back down with a shake of his head. "I don't know if you want to hear it. I mean, this is... on the scale of intricate master plans, this is about a nine. I'd have to be some kind of egomaniac to start boring you with the full thing. Let me tell you, it gets *pret-ty cra-zy* in places. You sure you want to hear the whole enchilada?"

Crane shook his head. "Just... just let me go." He shook his head, voice wheedling. "You've got what you want."

"Of course you do! Atta boy!" Lomax laughed, clapping Crane on the shoulder hard enough to knock him sideways to the floor. "And I've got to admit, I love this part. Seriously, it's burning a hole in me. I've got to tell *somebody* how I did it, and I can't tell Thunder, because that's the part where he usually escapes and kicks my ass. I figure this time I'll get it out of the way early and kick *his* instead. So why don't you pull up some floor there and I'll tell you the true story of how Lars Lomax died and was born again after a thousand and one nights to ascend to exalted glory? Kind of like Jesus meets the Arabian Nights." He shook his head, chuckling, and pulled up a chair, which creaked under his weight. His shirt was already starting to bulge as the muscles underneath began to expand. Every time Crane looked at him, he seemed larger, more menacing.

Hands shaking, Crane poured another coffee.

"I guess it all started when I realised what Anton Venger's big problem was."

He smiled, closing his eyes and breathing in the steam from the cup. Crane eyed the door. Could he reach it before...?

"Anton Venger and me, we made a good team." Lomax looked up, his brown eyes boring into Crane's. "Well, from his point of view, it was more than a team. That business with his face... he was desperate for any kind of affection after that, you know? He latched onto it like a remora. Show the slightest pretence of kindness and he'd follow you anywhere, especially if you happened to hate the same people. So... well, he might have seen our relationship as being something more intimate than just being business partners." He sipped his coffee, then shrugged. "I mean, okay, I'm not saying I never took advantage. He could look like anybody, you know? Put a poncho on him and it was like getting blown by Marilyn Monroe. I'm not proud." He took another swallow. "What's in this? Hazelnut?"

Crane jerked, as if stung. "N-no, I—"

"Or cyanide? I did leave some lying around." He grinned, looking Crane in the eye, and suddenly the rich brown of his eyes was a bright, piercing red. He offered the cup to Crane, who shrank back, pressing back against the wall of the little room. "What's the matter? Don't want any?"

Crane shook his head, too afraid to speak. Lomax was perhaps six inches taller now than when he'd come in, and the seams of his clothes were starting to come apart under the pressure of his expanding form.

Lomax grinned, and something was wrong with his teeth.

"Sure? I could make you drink it. Might teach you a lesson." He drained the cup, then passed it to Crane. "More. And this time go easy on the poison. Just half a spoon for flavour."

He leaned back, the chair creaking in protest. "Anyway, me and Venger were a team. He was crazy about me—literally—and I strung him along because he was about the most useful guy you could imagine. Except." He sighed, flexing his fingers, watching them thicken. "If you know there's a master of disguise running around who can't do emotions, then suddenly your master of disguise isn't that useful any more. Hey! There's a guy who doesn't smile and speaks in a monotone! It must be Anton Venger! Get the cuffs!"

He looked off into the distance. "God, that voice was creepy. That monotone voice singing 'Happy Birthday, Mr President...' I didn't ask him to do that again." He shook his head, as if shaking off the memory. "Anyway, it occurred to me that things would run a lot more smoothly if he was dead. If the world knew Anton Venger was dead—if Doc Thunder had told them so—well, everybody would stop looking for him, right?"

He stretched, and the shirt burst off his back, splitting right down the middle. Crane started, making a little whimper. Lomax just smiled.

"It was a great plan. Team up with N.I.G.H.T.M.A.R.E., have a very public falling-out with Venger, dose him with something I invented that'll slow down his life signs to the point of death, then—while Thunder's being tortured to death, which is a nice little bonus—go rat Silken Dragon out to S.T.E.A.M. and hole up somewhere until the fireworks are all done with. I already had people in place to fake the autopsy and ship the body to a secure location..." He took the fresh coffee from Crane, taking a sip. "No cyanide at all in this one! What did I tell you?"

"I—I thought you were joking." Crane looked at the door again. Only a few feet away. If he ran now—

"I never joke about coffee. You're starting to get on my last nerve, Parker. Maybe I'll pop your head like a zit and see what comes out." He followed Crane's line of sight. "Don't look at the door, Parker. You'll never reach it in time. You don't mind me calling you Parker, do you, Parker? I figure after all these fun times we had together—you know, you pushing me around, treating me like a joke, like your pet science gimp—I figured we'd be on first name terms by now. I never kill people I'm on first name terms with. Are we on first name terms, Parker?"

Crane swallowed, hard. He couldn't look away from Lomax now. Every few seconds, a new muscle would pop up on his shoulders, like a bubble coming to the surface of a lake. A lake of skin. The veins on his arms were starting to pulse a livid purple.

He didn't look like Doc Thunder at all.

He looked stronger.

"Parker! Focus!" Lomax yelled, and his voice was a deep, angry growl.

"Yes," Crane whispered. "Yes... Lars."

"Actually, my first name's Timothy, but nobody calls me that. Even my parents called me Happy." Lomax laughed. "And believe you me, I'm happy now. Anyway... the plan. The big plan to rehabilitate Anton Venger as a productive corpse. It all went off without a hitch, unless you count Thunder breaking out early and clocking me upside the head with a big chunk of masonry. By the time I broke out of prison, Venger had spent six months in a packing crate in a state of living death." He shrugged. "Didn't do a lot for his personality, frankly. He was even more devoted to me when I got him out, on account of how he thought I'd saved his life. The plain fact of the matter is I could have left him in there a lot longer and I kind of wish I had..." He paused, looking at the way the thick red hairs were growing on the back of his hand.

"Anyway, I needed to keep him sweet, give him some kind of reward for all the time he spent in that crate. So I figured we'd go kill the Blue Ghost. He was getting old, getting slow. He was basically just a mascot for that bike gang his foster kid formed, so I figured, okay, we'll knock him off, give Anton something to keep him from going completely off the rails." Lomax looked at Crane, eyes steely. "Only we were too late, weren't we? Why don't you pick up the story from here, Parker?"

Crane shook his head. "I don't know what you—"

"Oh, *please*. You were the fresh new head of Untergang after whatever old coot that replaced Donner finally retired. You had a lot of big, sexy plans. Not as sexy as mine, but pretty big and sexy nonetheless. You took a look at the Blue Ghost—mysterious masked avenger, operatives all over the place, big fan-following with the working classes, and you figured... we need one of those. Just take away the Japanese orphan kid and replace him with a foxy Aryan chick—and how's Marlene doing, anyway?"

Crane spluttered. "How do you know about—"

"Wouldn't you like to know? Anyway, give your brand new Blue Ghost some guns so he's not getting beaten up all the time, package it all up to appeal to Untergang's core voters... I've got to hand it to you, Parker, I know a winning strategy when I see one. There was just one thing wrong, wasn't there?" Crane shook his head, unable to meet Lomax's eyes. They were entirely red now, the white of the eye subsumed, the pupils two black dots in a bloody sea.

Lomax laughed. Crane didn't dare to look.

He had fangs.

"You needed a vacancy! There's no point being the all-new, all-Nazi Blue Ghost if the old Ghost's still around, right? So you strangled him with your own two hands and dropped his body off a pier, and poor little Easton West's been trying to solve the murder ever since! I felt for the guy, I can tell you. And poor Anton! That was all he'd been thinking about for months in his box, and you got there first. Shame on you!" Lomax shook his head, the red eyes burning with mock indignation.

"He wanted to do away with you there and then. In fact, he was all for killing you and taking your place. Running Untergang for our own concerns. I thought about it, I'll admit..." Lomax stood, rubbing the base of his spine. His head almost banged against the ceiling of the room, three feet above Crane's head. "But... that was a little too obvious. I wanted all the benefits of taking over your whole organisation without any of the downsides of actually having to run it. I mean, who wants to run Untergang? Not even *you* want to run Untergang! You've driven it into the ground while you lived out your crazy vigilante fantasy!"

He smiled, turning to Crane and leaning down. Crane thought he smelled brimstone on the monster's breath.

"So *that's* when I came up with the *real* plan. Get ready, Parker."

He loosened his belt enough for the tail that was growing out of his spine to poke over it.

"This is where it gets *weird*."

"...THAT'S RIGHT." DOC Thunder nodded, as the bike cop put another quarter into the payphone and wound the clockwork handle on the side. Doc gave him a brief thumbs-up and continued talking into the mouthpiece. "I've got El Sombra with me. Yes, the man with the sword, Donner's killer. No, he hasn't put a shirt on. Look, we're going to go try to catch Lomax before he gets away, but I need you to call Jack Scorpio and co-ordinate with S.T.E.A.M. If Lomax has done what I think he's done, the army might not be enough." He listened for a moment, then broke in. "Okay. If I don't come back inside six hours... well, you know. Bye." He put the phone down and sighed.

"Trouble with the missus?" the cop asked. Doc blinked.

"You're very perceptive, Officer... McNulty, was it?"

McNulty nodded. "The way you ended your call. Listen, last time me and the wife had some trouble, you know what I got her? A baby pig."

"A baby pig." Doc rubbed his forehead. "Officer—"

"Mr Porkins, we call him." The cop smiled brightly. "'Course, he's a little bigger now, and it's hell hiding him from the building super, but as soon as Joanie saw his cute little nose wrinkle it up, she forgot all about the whores."

Doc sighed. "Thanks, Officer. I'll bear that in mind." He turned to see El Sombra walking out of the station, cleaning marble fragments off his sword. "What took you so long?"

"Just a hunch, amigo. Who knows, it might end up paying off, hey? Could make all the difference." The masked man patted the pocket of his suit trousers.

Doc rubbed his temples again, shaking his head gently. "Fine. Get up on my back, and hold tight—hook an arm through the back of my shirt. This is going to get bumpy. You remember where we're going? East Village, right?"

El Sombra looked sideways at him. "What, you're going to fly there?"

Doc nodded. "Close enough. Let's go."

He jumped.

LOMAX PACED SLOWLY around the boxy, closed-in room, his tail twitching and swishing to and fro like a cat's.

"First of all, Anton Venger needed to take Miles Hamilton's place. If I wanted to get Thunder's blood, that was the best way to do it. Get Venger undercover and wait for him to get his personal physician to supervise a blood transfusion. Bound to happen within a year, two at the most." He laughed, sourly. "Ha! Well, the best laid plans, and so on. Anyway, I couldn't send Hamilton in if I was still on the loose. Thunder would smell a rat. He'd probably smell a rat anyway. *And* I needed a way to get in with your people, so I'd have access to all your equipment and knowhow. If I tried extracting the serum from Thunder's blood on my own, well, I'd probably end up giving myself nut cancer. But standing on the shoulders of your giants..." He turned, giving another hideous, fanged grin. "How am I doing? Better than the real thing, right?" He flexed his immense hands, marvelling at the carpet of red hair that now reached from his back all the way down each arm.

"The answer? Combine it all into one. Kidnap Hamilton, hand him over to Venger's tender mercies—and Venger had a lot of frustration to take out by this point, let me tell you—and then play the whole thing out with Venger in Hamilton's place."

"P-play what out?" Crane was slumped in a corner by this time, clutching at his head, staring at the thing Lomax was becoming, step by awful step, in front of him.

"My death, of course! My beautiful death! Torturing Hamilton in front of Doc's lovely assistant! I'd kidnapped her for the purpose of leaving Doc some obvious clues. All on a big balloon filled with enough hydrogen to set the whole damn place on fire when I fired a bullet through it! Except for the nose, of course—fireproof, crashproof, loaded with supplies for an unscheduled stopover in the Amazon rainforest, and also loaded with Hamilton's skeleton, de-fleshed and pre-charred to take my place. I do my big torture scene, and of course with Venger's squishy face it doesn't do more than tickle, then in comes Thunder, we fight, *bang* goes the gun! Fire everywhere!" Lomax gleefully acted it out, his huge muscled arms sending tables filled with equipment flying, glass shattering against the walls and floor. The tables were solid oak, but to the thing Lomax had become, there were as light and flimsy as paper.

Crane felt his bladder let go.

"Thunder rescues his steady—rescues 'Hamilton'—" The creature held up crooked fingers to make the quotation marks. "—and I crash into the rainforest, ejecting my skeletal stand-in into the flaming wreckage before taking off to hide out in the deepest darkest jungle for a while. Needless to say, poor old Doc's too distracted by the flame-grilled crispy death of his number one foe to look too closely at Venger. And even if he wasn't, what's he going to say? Hamilton's not acting like himself? The guy just got through being tortured! And even if Doc does think Hamilton's gone weird, he's not going to think 'oh no, Anton Venger,' since he saw Anton Venger die and all... I mean, it's perfect—" He stopped, sniffing the air.

"*Christ,* Parker! Do you know how that smells through these nostrils? I thought you were meant to be a dark avenger of the night?" Lomax leaned down, the vertebrae on his back pushing up through his skin, making small popping sounds. "Seriously, haven't you ever seen a man turning into a monster before?"

"The serum," Crane croaked. "It doesn't work properly. This—this is too much—"

Lomax laughed. "Says you. It's underperforming as far as I'm concerned. I wanted devil horns." He rubbed his temples experimentally. "Nope, nothing yet. Seriously, Parker, do you honestly think I wanted to be as good as Thunder? What's the point of that? He'll just call in S.T.E.A.M. or Maya's Leopard Warriors of the Something-Something or, I don't know, that British guy, what's his name? Troy Mercury? Perseus Quicklime? You know who I mean, Untergang must have a file on him a foot thick." He shrugged. "Whatever. I need to be big enough to beat them *all*, Parker. Everybody in his little black book, one at a time or all together." He paused, scratching his chin. "My thinking's getting a little random, though, I'll admit. I keep getting this craving for raw meat. Where did I get up to?"

Crane shook his head, despairing. "You faked your death."

"I faked my death! Slimmed down on the trek back from the rainforest, invested in a wig and a beard and came back as Professor Timothy Larson, harmless opium proponent and total freak. Just the kind of guy you need to do work for you—criminal record, doesn't like cops, pro social justice, which is I think how you sold the whole 'war on crime' bill of goods to me... I was just what you needed. A top-flight scientist with no Untergang connections. A nice clean pair of hands."

Crane looked up at the monster. All terror had left him, for the moment. He only felt numb. Disconnected. "I thought Timothy Larson was real. We did background checks. That business with the opium in the water..."

Lomax laughed. "That's what makes it such a great alias! It *was* me. Just a different me, that's all." He cocked his head at Crane's mystified look. "Fine, the short version. I was born Timothy Larson Lomax, in Brooklyn. Willy my dad— was an asshole, a pathetic little salesman, a phony little fake. All big dreams with no payoff. He died the way he lived, a failure. My big brother was headed the same way, too. Well, not me. I got out, went to college, got my professorship—as Timothy Larson. I didn't want to use Dad's name. Not back then.

"You know the rest. Big in the early futurehead movement, the merry prankster version. Friends with Warhol. A big proponent of the opium culture. I actually did talk like that back then. Like, don't you think you should say hello to a tree today, maaaan? It's so, like, beautiful." He grinned, his new fangs prominent in his mouth, sharp and cruel. His head was starting to bump against the ceiling, leaving dents in the plaster, and small spurs of bone were pushing out through the backs of his ankles. "I got busted for trying to put an opium derivative in the water supply, trying to turn everybody in New York on at once. The first big plan. And you know what? I liked it. The rush of knowing that a whole city could start dancing to your tune—the power trip. It was a one-hit addiction, Parker, my boy. I wanted to do that kind of thing full-time. I wanted to remake society into what I wanted it to be. And I kind of figured I owed it to my Dad to make Lomax the name the whole world feared. I don't know if he'd have wanted it that way, but... well, I thought it was funny anyway. Professor Tim Larson died, and Lars Lomax was born. "

Crane slumped back against the wall, staring listlessly at the black crust forming on the soles of Lomax's feet. "And when Lars Lomax died..."

"Re-enter Timothy Larson. So now I had my man in place to grab the blood, and all the equipment and notes to become the beautiful creature of God you see before you today." Lomax sat on one of the heavy tables, crushing the glass bottles and tubes resting there under him. As the table creaked under his weight, a hissing stream of acid ran from the smashed equipment, gouging a deep crevice in the thick wood before dripping off the table-top and onto the back of his leg.

He didn't seem to notice.

"And then nothing happened. Nobody needed a transfusion. A year went by. Two. Your little scheme went plodding along pretty much as I expected, in that it was an excuse for you to play vigilante and bone hot chicks on der Führer's dime. Venger was getting restless, and he'd managed to alienate Thunder completely, what with all his clumsy attempts to get that blood. I mean, he was pretty much asking Thunder to approve a private fascist militia made up of supermen. *Nice work Anton.* So there was pretty much no chance he'd go to him unless it was a total emergency. I tried setting up a couple of those, but no go. Nobody ever got hurt badly enough. My big plan was a washout. And then..."

He smiled, licking his fangs. "...El Sombra hit town."

Crane blinked. "Who?"

Lomax slammed his fist into the wall, leaving a crater in the concrete. "That's what I mean about you! You're the head of Untergang. Act like it! Call home! Daddy Hitler's got a file on this guy he could use as a doorstop!" He shook his head in disgust. "He's the half-naked guy with the sword, okay? He kills Nazis. That's all he does. It's his entire shtick. Seriously, one phone call would have saved hours of hanging around hissing like a broken kettle. Anyway, when he hit town and the small-time creeps and Untergangsters—all the ones who were sitting around on their keisters because you weren't using them—when they started dropping like flies, I saw an opportunity. I set up a meet and told him all about Donner."

Crane went white. "You dare—"

Lomax laughed. "What are you gonna do about it, tough guy?" Crane sank back to his slumped position on the floor, staring between his shoes, not daring to lift his eyes. Lomax chuckled, his tail thumping against the sagging table like a dog's. "See, once you'd let me into your little clique, it made it easy to find things out. I drop your name, get some tidbits, then drop those tidbits to the right people and they think I'm on the level and give me bigger stuff... pretty soon I knew all about Donner's little exile. Hell, I had the memo from that time he killed a hooker. *'Mein Führer, we hast ein little problem...'* El Sombra loved that, I'll tell you."

Crane shook his head, not speaking.

"So he killed the guy stone dead, and a couple of days later the papers had a field day with it, pretty much like I knew they would. 'Wuxtry, wuxtry! Dead man dies again!' Face it, tiger, this is the *one!*" He laughed like an earthquake. "I knew that'd bring you running, and I knew Thunder was going to send his top clue-hunting guy to the murder scene, on account of that whole thing they had going on in the 'forties. And Thunder's top man just happens to be a big bisexual deformed guy. Just the kind of subhuman—sorry, *in*human—the Blood-Spider likes to shoot whenever he gets an excuse, right?" The table began to crack under Lomax's weight, and he stood, the top of his head cracking into the ceiling and bringing down a flurry of plaster.

"Damn! Where the hell am I getting all this *mass* from? I have to study this later. So, Parker, are you all up to speed?"

Crane scowled. "Why didn't Venger give you the blood directly? Why that nonsense with the telegram?"

"Not nonsense. Deniability. If Venger goes to me with the one thing Untergang have wanted since they started out, that kind of blows my cover. Plus, I wanted him dead." Crane looked at Lomax in astonishment. "Oh, what? You honestly want a psychopath who knows how to melt people running around thinking he's in love with you? Because that's a great recipe for a long and healthy life. Don't make me the bad guy here, okay? He had to go. So, I told him you worked for me, not the other way around, and he should contact you once he had the blood. I figured I could trust you to do what you do with Venger and then bring the blood back to me, because where else would it go?"

"Straight to Germany," Crane muttered. "That's the protocol."

Lomax smiled. "You're in New York, Parker Crane. Protocol went out the window the second you arrived. This isn't a protocol kind of town. This is a town that breeds monsters and heroes, geniuses and madmen. This town makes gods, Parker." He shook his head, a look of amused pity on his distorted face, as the hue of his skin deepened and turned a rich, livid crimson. "And heaven help you, you wanted to be one of us."

He laughed, and the sound was like stone falling on stone.

"You wanted to kick it with the Gods of Manhattan. How's that working out for you?"

Before Crane could answer, there was a sound of thunder and the room shook, as if in an earthquake. "What was that?" Crane gasped, looking up at Lomax in renewed terror. "A bomb?"

"A landing." Lomax grinned. He flexed one massive hand, then the other, and the bones of his knuckles popped through the skin like a set of brutal spikes. When he looked back at the cowering Crane, his eyes seemed to glow. He chuckled, deep in his monster's throat, and spoke a single word.

"Showtime."

CHAPTER SIXTEEN
DOC THUNDER AND THE ULTIMATE FOE

"THIS IS THE place?"

As Doc stepped out of the crater he'd made on the sidewalk from his landing, El Sombra took a long look around at his surroundings. A wide street, almost deserted, with only the occasional hansom cab and bicycle passing through. A small dead zone in the middle of New York's life. From this failed street, lined with businesses either closed for the day or closed forever, smaller alleys extended, crusted with grime and filth—and down one alley, nestled tightly between a shuttered, long-empty breaker bar on one side and a cheap chapbook store on the other, he could see a metal door. The same metal door he'd seen the Blood-Spider walk into after the battle on the hospital roof. "This is it, amigo. What say we go knock on that door and end this?"

Doc shook his head.

"He won't use the door."

From somewhere down the alley, there was a massive explosion, a destructive crash like a wrecking ball tearing through masonry. The empty chapbook store seemed to shake. Then another crash. Louder this time. Closer.

"Brace yourself," Doc murmured, his eyes cold, focussed. Almost unconsciously, he adopted a ready stance, his feet planted, braced against the coming impact.

Another crash, and the window of the chapbook store cracked, a single line splitting the big, friendly window from top to bottom. A couple of chapbooks shivered and fell off the shelves.

El Sombra took a couple of steps back and drew his sword. Gently, he reached down and touched the small, hard object in his pocket, wondering.

Another crash. Louder still.

Doc breathed in. A single drop of sweat formed on his brow, reflecting the gaslight.

And then something terrifying smashed through the brick and plaster forming the back wall of the chapbook store, running through wooden shelves loaded with chapbooks and shattering them to matchwood with a swipe of its hand, the air clouded for a moment by the bright, primary-coloured pages before whatever it was burst out of the front window in a cascade of exploding glass, aiming right at Doc Thunder with a punch that took him off his feet and sent him careening through space into the brick wall on the other side.

The thing that had once been Lars Lomax roared.

It was fully ten feet of muscle, bone and sinew; its back, arms and legs covered with thick, red, shaggy hair, the great bony dome of its head bare apart from the thick eyebrows that sprouted from the protuberance of its brow. Spurs of thick, rock-like bone poked from knuckles, elbows, kneecaps and the backs of ankles. Its skin was a livid crimson, stretched taut over a tapestry of muscles upon muscles, a terrifying parody of anatomy that constantly flexed and shifted with the beast's every breath. Its eyes almost glowed, a rich bloody red, and instead of human teeth it possessed great murderous fangs, huge and sharp. Strangest of all—stranger even than the toes that had fused together, the soles of the feet replaced by a black, hoof-like carapace—was the thick tail of flesh that swished and swiped, back and forth, growing from the small of its back, just above the ruined remains of a pair of tan slacks.

There was nothing in it that would be recognisable as human, never mind as Lars Lomax. In fact, it looked like nothing so much as Satan himself, come to earth to feed on the sins of mankind. And yet, there was something in its bearing, in its inhuman, arrogant confidence, in the way its eyes blazed with mocking hatred at the fallen Thunder, as if daring him to get up and take further punishment—something that said that this was indeed the enemy of the Earth, the most dangerous man alive, the one man Doc Thunder could never truly defeat, not so long as he lived.

The Lomax-thing stared down at El Sombra, and El Sombra stared back, his sword raised. He'd dealt with monsters before. He'd faced human devils, battled killer machines, flying snipers and armoured tanks, stared down the armed might of Hitler's war machine. But this…

"El Sombra, right? We've met, sort of." The voice was like a cathedral collapsing into rubble. "I was the guy who put you onto Donner. I couldn't have done it without you." He grinned, his tongue licking over those razor-sharp teeth. "I owe you a lot, pal, so here's a warning. Try and use that little toothpick on me and you'll just ruin it. And then…" He smirked, and the muscles in his chest and back flexed obscenely. "Then, I'll ruin you. Seriously, if I get pissed at you, I can turn you into hamburger as easily as tapping my toes. I'll make you eat that sword sideways and crap it out the same way, pal."

He turned, looking down at Doc Thunder, who was picking himself up from the shattered remains of the shopfront he'd been punched into. "Go for the eyes," Doc coughed, wiping a trickle of blood from his mouth. "The rest of his skin's too tough to cut, but his eyes might be—"

Lomax grabbed hold of Doc's head, lifting him up and then slamming him down, face-first into the sidewalk, before placing the ball of a black foot on the back of his hated enemy's head, grinding him into the smashed concrete. El Sombra raised his sword, and Lomax shook his head, turning his terrible red-eyed gaze full on the masked man. "Bad idea," he growled. "Listen, El Crazy, I'm as tolerant as the next guy but I'm on the verge of losing my temper. There's a perfectly good Nazi back there—leader of Untergang, remember? That criminal organisation you don't like? Why don't you go finish him off and leave me alone?"

El Sombra looked at him for a long moment, then walked towards the ruined chapbook store, climbing through the shattered window and then through the hole Lomax had made in the wall.

Lomax watched him go, and then turned back to Doc, squirming underneath the sole of his foot. "Looks like you just can't get the help these days. So, Thunder, who's coming to save you next? Maya? I'd hate to burst her head like a melon, but I can't have her beat me at chess again. Monk Olsen? Oh, wait, he's in that coma, my bad. I'll drop by the hospital later for some intensive chiropractics, fold him into an origami bird or something, how's that? Who does that leave… your cook? Easton West, everybody's favourite tough cop? The man rides a bike and smokes, sometimes both at once! I'm shaking—ooh, wait! Jack Scorpio, agent of S.T.E.A.M.! God, I've wanted to take care of that old blowhard for *years!*"

From behind, there was the thunder of hooves; a policeman on horseback, alerted by the commotion. At the sight of what Lomax had become, he drew his .38 and opened fire, to no avail. The bullets bounced harmlessly off Lomax's back as if they were raindrops. Snarling, the monstrosity turned around, reaching out and grabbing hold of the horse's neck. Then—with the terrible crack of fracturing vertebrae—he swung the beast upwards, killing it instantly and sending the rider tumbling off its back and onto the glass-covered tarmac. Laughing monstrously, Lomax swung the dead beast around his head, then brought it down, using it like a bludgeon on the stunned policeman. Horse and rider smashed together, the creature bursting open, sending a tide of blood and horse-offal spilling out into the road. The cop, crushed and suffocated beneath the weight of his own dead animal, managed to stay conscious for a few moments before surrendering to oblivion.

Doc felt the pressure of Lomax's foot ease for a micro-second as he swung the beast through the air, and he took his chance, Pressing his flat palms against the concrete of the sidewalk with all his strength, he managed to lift himself up just enough to squirm out from underneath, rolling clear before the man-monster could grab hold of him again.

"I don't need anybody else to fight my battles, Lomax," he muttered as he staggered to his feet, a stream of blood coursing from a broken nose. "I don't care what you've done to yourself. You've committed too many crimes to be allowed to walk free." His eyes narrowed. "It ends here."

Lomax raised one massive, shaggy eyebrow, then looked at the horse, still shuddering in its final convulsions, the policeman having already gone still. "Cruelty to animals. That always was one of your buttons." He chuckled, raising his fists, the spurs of bone at his knuckles jutting out toward Thunder like stone-age knives. "You realise no prison on the planet is going to hold me now, don't you? I mean, I was hard enough to keep locked away before. But now, they couldn't even keep me in custody for an hour. Not for a minute, not a *second!*" His brutal, inhuman laugh roared out under the night sky. "So are you going to kill me this time? Is the great Doc Thunder, the man who wants to save everybody in the whole wide world, going to get his hands a little bloody?"

Doc looked Lomax right in his eye, the blue piercing gaze duelling with eyes more at home in hell. "If I have to. I'm not proud of it, and I'm not happy about it, and if there's a way to contain and cure you, I'm going to find it. But a lot of people have died because of you and me, because I always underestimate just how wrong you are in that head of yours. And I can't stomach any more."

Lomax stared back at him. "It was a trick question, dummy. You're not going to kill me, and it's not because of any principles or moral imperatives or compassion or any of your usual high-minded bullcrap. It's because you physically can't do it. You *can't* kill me." He grinned, showing his teeth. "But I can kill you. And I'm going to make it *slow*."

Then he charged.

SWORD RAISED, EL Sombra crept into the tiny cell that had, for almost three years, been the home of the man calling himself Timothy Larson. He wrinkled his nose in disgust. The place stank.

It stank of the noxious chemicals that had spilled from the dozens of ruined beakers and shattered test tubes that lay among the debris of the furniture. It stank of the fresh piss of the man who still sat trembling in one corner. It stank of the sweat that clung to the never-changed sheets on the filthy mattress. It stank faintly of opium, smoked late at night, half to keep up the illusion and half to alleviate the boredom that came with waiting endlessly for a chance that never came.

And underneath it all, it stank of madness.

El Sombra knew what it was to hate, to hate so hard and so long that you knew nothing else, to hate so strongly that it crossed that line into something beyond reason. He knew what it was to try to bring a government to its knees, to plan the end of a nation at the hands of a single man. He recognised something in Lars Lomax, some twisted reflection of his own feelings. If Doc Thunder had been a child of the Ultimate Reich—and El Sombra had an idea of how close Thunder had come to being just that—El Sombra would never have rested until he was dead, no matter what it took. He wondered what had happened to Lomax to make him what he was. Was it similar to that apocalyptic day of fire and nightmare and eternal shame that had created him? One massive explosion that had fractured his personality for good? Or had it been a constant drip, drip, drip of a thousand tiny incidents, eroding the rock of his sanity until finally it wore down to nothing?

El Sombra shook his head. It didn't matter. Perhaps Lomax had spared his life through some recognition of their similarities, but El Sombra wasn't about to make the same mistake. El Sombra had never deliberately killed anyone who wasn't a Nazi before, but there were exceptions to every rule. And speaking of which—

Crane made a whimpering sound in the depths of his throat as the masked man turned to face him. Tears coursed down his cheeks, and he clutched his legs, rocking gently in place. "Please." He sniffed, shaking his head. "Please don't let him find me."

El Sombra raised an eyebrow. "I guess you saw him turn into that thing, hey? One minute he's that skinny guy with the beard, and then he turns into that giant diablo monster… right before your eyes…" Crane shook his head, screwing his eyes tight shut and gritting his teeth. A low moan of torment came from between them. El Sombra sighed. "You were already pretty crazy, getting crazier, but now… you're gone, aren't you, amigo? Gone for good."

He lifted his sword, resting the blade in his palm for a moment, considering. Crane only stared, weeping and making his soft, mad noises. El Sombra sighed, shaking his head. "You know, I don't know if I can kill a guy who's already dead. Even if he is one of the bastards."

He lowered his sword, looking around the wrecked laboratory, eyes narrowing. "Hey, you got any glue here?"

LOMAX CHARGED, BARRELLING towards Doc Thunder like a freight train. Doc stood his ground, eyes narrowed. He knew a punch from Lomax's fists could take a normal man's head right off at the neck—what it would do to him, he didn't know, but it wasn't likely to be anything good.

He was used to using his strength, and that wouldn't work here. For one thing, he was too used to holding back, to measuring and rationing his great power for fear of turning every fight into a bloody execution. For another, even if he did manage to overcome his phobia of his own power and attack with all of it, would it actually work? Could he actually put Lomax down for good? Could he even injure him? What if he swung with all his strength and only succeeded in making him angry?

No, strength wasn't going to be the answer on its own. Doc had one advantage as far as he could see. Lomax was so enamoured of his new physical power, that he'd forgotten where he'd got it from. He'd forgotten that the greatest weapon in his arsenal had always been his mind.

It wasn't possible to out-punch him. But it was possible—more possible now than it had ever been before—to out-*think* him.

Doc waited. He waited until the last possible moment, when Lomax was almost on top of him, when he was swinging those bony knuckles back, his teeth already bared in a grin of sheer, animal triumph.

Then he threw himself flat on the floor.

Lomax's feet slammed into Thunder's prone body, sending him flying forward, unable to correct himself. The man-monster slammed hard into the tarmac, his face grinding up big chunks of roadway and gravel, leaving a trench behind him.

Doc rolled to his feet. Hitting Lomax wasn't going to work. He could kick him in the head with enough force to flatten a wrecking ball into a metal pancake, and all it was likely to do was break his foot. He could aim a cobra strike directly to the man's testes hard enough to create an imprint of them in what was left of the concrete and the absolute best it would do would be to make him angry. He was under no illusions about his ability to play Lars Lomax at his own game.

But Lomax was too overconfident in his new body. Just because he was stronger and more resilient, he assumed there was no way for Doc Thunder to defeat him in a fight. Just as in their previous battles, he'd assumed that he would win because he was smarter and had fewer morals. Doc Thunder almost smiled. As always, Lomax's complex, intricate, almost Rube Goldbergian plots fell down because he'd missed something simple. Something as simple as the weak plaster in a Parisian ceiling.

As simple as a wrestling hold.

Doc didn't know that much in the way of judo—an omission he was cursing himself for—but he knew some basics, and had to hope that Lomax, who'd rarely if ever fought hand to hand before now, knew even less. Quickly, he grabbed hold of Lomax's wrists, forcing them up behind his back in a double nelson before he could lock his arms, while at the same time pinning Lomax's legs at the backs of the knees with his own. Lomax struggled, but so long as Doc could keep a tight hold on him, he could keep him in this position for quite some time. The next step would be to put him down for good.

Another policeman would be on the scene soon, carrying a .38, or maybe even a shotgun. At which point, Doc would instruct him to shoot Lomax through the eye at point blank range, maybe more than once. At the very least, that would cause a massive brain hemorrhage. He wasn't happy about the necessity, but he was out of options, and he had a sneaking suspicion that Lomax would heal from even that injury in time.

He had a sneaking suspicion that Lars Lomax would never die. But if he could only hold him a little longer—

—suddenly, Lomax relaxed.

"Oh, why fight it? When you've gotta go, you've gotta go. You win again, Thunder. I'll go quietly to my cell, like a good little felon. I'll rehabilitate. I'll prop up the status quo for you. I'll be a hero too and have a shirt just like yours! Yes sirree, you've shown me the error of my ways!"

He was laughing. Doc frowned, keeping his grip tight. He couldn't let himself be suckered now.

Why was he laughing?

And then the tail wrapped around his throat and squeezed.

"*Psych!*" Lomax bellowed, and suddenly Doc realised that this time he was the one who'd forgotten the simple thing. The tail. It wasn't an affectation, it was something Lomax had designed into the serum because he saw exactly this scenario coming. And now he was choking Doc to death with it, and the only way out was—

—let go of one of Lomax's wrists.

Doc tore at the clutching tail with one hand, and that one hand was the undoing of him. Lomax grabbed hold of a fistful of tarmac, tearing it right up from the road and slamming it with all his strength into the side of Doc's head, knocking him sideways. Then Lomax was back up on his feet as though nothing had happened, moving straight into a kick at Thunder's belly that sent him up like a football, followed by a two-handed blow to the rising body that knocked him right back down and made another crater in the ruined road.

It had all happened so fast that Doc Thunder barely even knew where he was. He reached up and touched his mouth, and the finger came away bloody. *Dear God*, thought Doc, *he's actually hurting me. He's strong enough to take me apart with his bare hands.*

I'm going to die.

And in that moment, he was glad that El Sombra had run away.

CRANE HAD BEEN no help. All he did was whine and moan and occasionally scratch his face and neck, drawing blood. El Sombra didn't know what the final straw had been, but any sanity he'd once had was long gone now.

Fortunately, El Sombra had found what he was looking for. A tube of fast-acting rubber cement, left by the sink after some long-forgotten bit of mending. Carefully, El Sombra spread the cement over the very tip of the sword, then took the thing he'd been saving in his pocket and attached it, holding it in place for long minutes until he was sure the cement had set.

"Don't let him in here," murmured Crane, his eyes wide.

"Shhhh. I won't let him in," smiled El Sombra in response, trying to be reassuring. "You'll never have to face him again. I promise. It's okay, amigo. It's okay."

It was strange. He knew he should feel hate for Parker Crane, or whatever his real name had once been. It was Djego's job to bear things like pity and doubt, to feel sorrow and shame. That was Djego's role in their team of one. El Sombra was there to take never-ending revenge and to laugh and to never look back. But to know that his murder of Heinrich Donner—his righteous kill—had resulted in so much harm coming to so many... and now to see the leader of Untergang, the man he'd come to New York to kill, just an empty, broken madman, a shell of a person...

El Sombra wondered if he was changing.

Experimentally, he prodded his sword at the steel door, and the thing he'd fixed to the end slid into the steel as if it were made of butter.

Good.

"Don't," whispered Crane, a tear rolling down his cheek. "Don't let him back in."

El Sombra smiled, placing a hand on his shoulder. "It's okay, amigo. I'm going to go and make sure nobody ever needs to see him again. And I couldn't have done it without you." He squeezed lightly. "You didn't mean to, but you did some good. Remember that."

Then, gently, he pushed the tip of the sword through the front of Crane's skull and into his brain.

He was not incapable of pity, he knew. But he was who he was, and he did what he did.

And broken or not, the bastards had to die.

DOC'S HEAD SNAPPED to the left, then to the right as the massive red fists slammed into his jaw. Blood flew from his nose and his split lip. One eye had swollen to the point where he could no longer see out of it.

"You know," Lomax grinned, "I've tried a lot of ways to get rid of you over the years. I've tried bombs, I've tried bullets, I've tried poisons. I've tried to create superhard metals. I've tried to dig up radioactive elements. You know what I've never tried? Beating you to death."

He laced his fingers together and then swung his joined fists up in an arc underneath Thunder's chin, sending him flying back with a crack that sounded like bone breaking.

"It's incredibly satisfying." Lomax laughed, that terrible rockslide laugh. "If only I'd thought of it sooner!"

Doc shook his head as he picked himself up, trying to concentrate, or at least to stay conscious. Lomax's serum was still working. He'd gained at least a foot in height since the start of the battle. Doc doubted he'd be able to pin him again, even if he could somehow circumvent the tail. The best he could do at this point was survive; as long as Lomax was concentrating on him, he wasn't endangering innocent lives. Every moment Doc managed to stay on his feet was a victory.

Of course, Lomax was getting stronger all the time. The fact that he was making Doc bleed now meant that his punches were as strong as exploding shells. How long before they were strong enough to tear his head right off his body? And was Lomax ever going to stop getting stronger, tougher, bigger? Would he eventually become too big and heavy to move, or would he continue his rampage even as he outgrew buildings or even cities?

Lomax smashed another punch past Doc's defences, slamming his jutting bone knuckle into Doc's open eye, and in the white-hot flash of pain, Doc had a nightmare vision of Lomax, the size of Manhattan itself, using the city as his throne and issuing orders like a dictatorial Gulliver among Lilliputians. The absurdity of the image only made it seem more terrifying.

Another blow snapped Doc's head back, and he found himself sinking to his knees. He needed a few minutes to heal, and it was clear he wasn't going to get them. Blackness crowded his vision, and his heartbeat was a drum pounding constantly in his ears. He waited for the blow that would finish this unequal combat and set the monster Lars Lomax loose on an unsuspecting world.

It never came.

Instead, he heard laughter. Laughter like rocks tumbling down into a quarry. Lomax's laughter.

For a moment, Doc thought the laughter was directed at him. Why not?

Hadn't he failed anyone who'd ever counted on him or cared for him? Wasn't he dying because he'd committed one inexcusable act of stupidity after another? Because he hadn't seen what was right under his nose until it was too late?

Then he realised Lomax was laughing at someone else, and a chill shot through him to the pit of his stomach.

El Sombra was about to die, and there was nothing Doc Thunder could do about it.

LARS LOMAX COULDN'T help himself. The laughter just came tumbling out.

El Sombra had run out of the chapbook store and now he was standing there with his puny little sword, pointing it at Lomax as if it would actually do any good at all.

"Really? Seriously? You thought, 'Oh! There's Doc Thunder, the most powerful man on earth, getting his hide handed to him by someone much bigger and stronger than he is! Wow, he needs some help! I know, I'll run forward with my little toothpick and wave it menacingly in the bad guy's face! That'll help!' Oh, you kill me, you really do." Lomax almost bent double, laughter exploding out of him. "I might even have you stuffed."

Then he saw what was cemented to the end of the sword, and the laughter stopped instantly.

"No." He whispered the word, taking a step back, shaking his head. "That— that won't work. My skin's too tough. The cement won't hold."

"Won't it?" El Sombra grinned.

Lomax snarled, moving forward, pulling back an arm ready to smash El Sombra with a single blow, hard enough to pulverise his bones and liquefy his flesh, to turn him into flying specks of red jelly just as if a bomb had hit him at point blank range. And at that moment, El Sombra thrust forward and up.

The augmented tip of the sword slid effortlessly through the crimson skin of Lomax's chest, between his ribs, piercing his heart in one swift motion.

Lomax gasped, blinked, and took a step back. He coughed, once.

"You can't..." Black blood trickled from his mouth. "You can't plan for things like that, can you?"

Then, the look of disbelief froze on his face. He toppled backwards, hitting the tarmac hard enough to fracture it.

The red eyes closed.

Doc blinked, slowly getting to his feet. The blackness was clearing from his vision. He was already starting to heal, but he couldn't quite believe what he was seeing. "How... how did you..."

Wordlessly, El Sombra pulled his sword from the man-monster's body. Glued to the end of his sword with rubber cement, still glistening in that strange, alien way, was a single bullet of inexorium, as sharp and deadly as it had been when it was fired, as indestructible as it had been when the masked man had dug it from one of the marble pillars in Grand Central Station with his sword. He smiled.

"A bullet in the right place can change the world, amigo."

And quite suddenly, Doc Thunder had nothing to say.

EPILOGUE
ONE FINE DAY IN NEW YORK CITY

"...AND SO, ONCE again, we can thank Doc Thunder, America's Greatest Hero, for safeguarding our fair city from the machinations of those who would destroy our very way of life."

A cheer went up from the crowd, and Mayor Ambrose adjusted his tie, smiling genially. "Although Doc has asked me to point out that the final blow against the nefarious Lars Lomax, the most dangerous man in the world, was struck by a brave Mexican hero—"

More cheers, a cry of "Viva El Sombra!" from the back of the crowd, then a wave of spontaneous clapping. Ambrose smiled genially, and motioned for silence.

"—a brave Mexican hero who has requested to remain anonymous, lest the worldwide reporting of his deeds interfere with his quest to rid the globe of a certain other enemy of the USSA, who I will likewise refrain from mentioning by name..."

The crowd grumbled.

"...though I understand he only has one ball."

A riotous cheer, a few hats thrown into the air, and another surge of applause, this time lasting for a full minute.

"Naturally, we wish him all the best, and hope his success will lead to Untergang's final exit from the world of terror. I have of course issued a full pardon for any, ah, crimes of violence he may have committed while a guest of our city, and hope that, should he ever complete his task, he finds his home here in Manhattan, where he will always have a place among our heroes."

Another surge of clapping, more "Viva El Sombra!" from the kid at the back.

"Only next time, please, use the flat of the sword."

Polite laughter, some of it uneasy. *Damn it, Darren, the crappy joke goes in the middle, the good joke goes at the end. Jesus. Learn to write a damned speech, why don't you.* Despite his thoughts, the Mayor's smile never faltered. *Okay, time to open it up.*

"Any questions, ladies and gentlemen of the press? You, sir." Ambrose motioned to a rat-like man in a dirty overcoat.

"Rich Uben, sir, *The Daily Bugle.* What happened to Lomax's body?"

"Well, obviously, since he was stabbed through the heart by Mexico's Greatest Hero—" More cheers and applause. *That's how it's done, Darren.* "—we feel he's no longer a threat to anyone on this side of the grave. However, to make sure, we removed his head from his body by means of controlled explosion. Seventeen controlled explosions, in fact, utilising more than one hundred sticks of dynamite."

The crowd made an appreciative 'ooooh' sound. No doubt most of them were wishing they'd had front row seats.

"The head and the body have been flown separately to Langley, where they are being studied extensively by top men."

Uben narrowed his eyes, looking suspiciously over the top of his glasses. "Uh-huh. And which men might those be, Mr Mayor?"

Ambrose smiled back at him, a trifle frostily. He paused a moment before giving his answer.

"Top. Men."

IN THE DREAM, Maya was chained to the altar again, and the giant roc was circling overhead, swooping down towards her. This time it had Doc Thunder's face.

"Don't worry," said Doc, as he opened his mouth wide to bite into her naked flesh, "I'm Doc Thunder, America's Greatest Hero, and I never make a mistake."

She tried to scream, but in the dream something had stolen her voice.

At the last second, someone sprang from the rocks, slamming a fist into Thunder's head, knocking the great bird down into the valley below. She couldn't see his face.

"Wake up," said the Stranger.

Maya jerked awake with a start, blinking at the sun streaming in through the window. "Who on earth—" she muttered, shaking the sleep from her eyes.

"Wake up," said Doc, lounging in the doorway. He was holding some sort of bundle in his hands, gently, as if he was afraid he might break it. There was something about him that seemed different, as if a weight had been lifted from his shoulders.

"What do you mean by this intrusion?" she said, frostily, staring ice daggers at him. He only laughed.

"You need to start making a habit of getting up earlier, young lady. You're sleeping half the day away." He laughed again at her look of astonishment. "Come on, get up. You can sleep in when you're back in your kingdom. You are still planning on going back?"

She nodded, slowly, not looking at him. Why on earth did he want to drag this out? "Yes. I'm sorry, Doc... Hugo... whoever you are. But I need to sort a few things out."

He nodded. "Fair enough. Oh, that reminds me, Monk wants to go too."

Maya's eyes widened, and her mouth fell open, and then she laughed despite herself. "Monk's awake?"

"Awake and asking after you. And like I said, he wants to come with you. I figure he might end up being pretty useful if any more viziers or high priests have been plotting. The only trouble is, you might have to wait for him to be ready to travel. And maybe while you're waiting, we could talk a little. Sort a few things out." He grinned, and the thing in his arms moved.

Maya smiled, relaxing on the bed, her green eyes glowing with their familiar warmth. "We'll see. No promises. What on earth is that you're holding?"

Doc smiled. "It's a present for you. Just something to say sorry for... a lot of things, I guess. Keeping secrets. Not being the man you thought I was." He shook his head, then held the bundle out, tugging back the swaddling clothes to reveal the pink face of a baby piglet. "I'm thinking of calling him El Chancho. When he grows up, he can be my new sidekick."

Maya put her hands to her mouth, gasping in delight. "Oh, he's adorable!" She reached to take hold of the little bundle, looking down at the snuffling little snout of the piglet. Then she looked up at Doc Thunder, smirking. Doc raised an eyebrow.

"What's that for?"

"Oh, I was just thinking." Maya smiled wider. "Doc Thunder saves my life from a treacherous high priest armed with a mystic gem and a giant roc. Hugo Donner gives me a pig."

Doc smiled, looking at the floor. "Maybe Hugo Donner wants to make a more realistic impression." He looked up, suddenly serious. "And Hugo Donner wants to come along to Zor-Ek-Narr too."

Maya winced, frowning. "The whole point is—"

"We'll leave Doc Thunder in New York. I promise. It's not like anybody needs him right now anyway. Who's left for him to fight? Besides, I need to get my blood away from all the would-be super-scientists wanting to be the next Lars Lomax. It's either the Forbidden Kingdom or a beach in Malibu and a shave."

Maya's frown lifted. "Hmmm. A holiday at home with Hugo Donner and Monk Olsen, two big, strong and very ordinary men about town." She smiled. "We'll see."

Doc smiled. "No promises."

They looked at each other for a long moment.

"Oh, what the hell." Maya laughed. "Come to bed."

At the Jameson Club, the disappearance of Parker Crane had not gone without comment. Jonah had refrained from participating in the gossip. For one thing, it was not the place of a trusted servant to indulge in idle rumour, or to betray confidences about those he was tasked to serve.

For another, he was getting very worried about the leader.

The Führer had been in touch, through intermediaries. Reports indicated that Untergang had been so weakened by Crane's shenanigans that Hitler was considering pulling all funding and shutting the experiment down for good. He had expected a significant propaganda victory from Operation Blood-Spider, the report said, and instead he had seen Untergang almost bankrupted to feed the whims of a dilettante with an obsession with American masked heroes. As soon as Crane resurfaced, he would have questions to answer in Berlin.

It was Bunny Etheringdon who broke the news.

"Thanks awfully, Jonah," he'd said, accepting his fifth Singapore Sling of the evening. "I say, have you heard the dreadful news about poor Parker?"

Jonah froze. "I'm afraid I haven't, sir. Nothing serious, I hope?"

"Well, he's dead!" Bunny slurped down a hefty gulp of the Singapore Sling.

"They found his body in some ghastly little one-room apartment in the East Village—the bit that was half destroyed in that bizarre business with the monster man. He'd been shot, or stabbed, or some such." He looked left and right, as if checking for spies, and then leaned in with a stage whisper. "There's some talk that he may have been involved with the whole thing. Do you know he was dressed up like that fellow the Blood-Spider? I'm on tenterhooks waiting for the next revelation, I'll tell you."

He leant back, smiling facetiously, as if expecting Jonah to gasp, raise his hands to his cheeks and exclaim "Well! I never!"

Instead, Jonah kept his composure, and only nodded. "If you'll excuse me, Mr Etheringdon."

Bunny smiled, waving him off. "Oh, of course, Jonah. No rest for the wicked, eh?"

"I have one final task to perform first, sir." He bowed, walked down the stairs to the Lower Library, let himself in and locked the door behind him.

Then, without any fuss, he placed a loaded pistol in his mouth and pulled the trigger.

The Jameson Club hired a new major domo on the Monday.

"Name?"

Marlene smiled prettily, looking through the lenses of the glasses she'd bought from the theatrical costumiers. "Mary Watson," she smiled. It was amazing the difference red hair dye and a pair of glasses made. She could have walked right up to anyone from her old life and they wouldn't have recognised her at all.

"Occupation?" She'd gone for a very tight black rubber dress with a rather prominent window onto her chest, a gift from David in days gone by that was paying dividends now. The customs officer couldn't keep his eyes off that cleavage window, which was all for the best as it distracted him from the cheapness of her fake passport.

"Actress." She smiled again, arching her back a little to make sure his eyes remained exactly where they were. She supposed she was being rather dreadful, really, but it wasn't as though she was going to give him her telephone number. Not her real one, at any rate.

"And is the purpose of your visit business, or, ah… pleasure?" The man's moustache twitched as he leered. It reminded Marlene rather of a rat's whiskers.

He did have a perfectly gorgeous accent, though, but she supposed they all did here. One of the benefits of her move to London.

"Oh, pleasure, of course," she purred. Best not to let on that it was both. After all, crime was a serious business, but declaring war on it was quite the most perfect pleasure she could imagine.

The customs man laughed, opening up her suitcase and leafing carefully through the perfumed silk negligees and leather corsets she'd carefully packed. Of course, he was far too fixated on those to notice the false bottom of the suitcase, and he certainly wouldn't think to look beneath it to find her twin automatic pistols and the mask Parker had left her. He looked up at her, a twinkle in his eye, his lips parting in a smile that revealed the most unsavoury set of teeth.

"One more thing, Miss Watson—the name and number of your hotel. Just to be on the safe side." He even added a wink.

As Marlene reeled off the name and telephone number of a completely different hotel, and a fictional room number for good measure, she found herself wondering if she would end up seeing the customs officer again after all. He looked like the sort that might solicit a prostitute, or possibly enter an illicit vice den to gamble the night away. There was at least a ten per cent chance, she decided, that he would find himself looking down the barrel of the Blood Widow's automatics.

"See you soon, Miss," he said, grinning and fiddling with his crotch as she wiggled away on her heels towards the taxi rank.

"Oh, I hope so. Perhaps even sooner than you think," Marlene murmured, and smiled.

"I SPOKE TO Hisoka's parents. They said thanks for your help." Inspector West took a long drag on his cigarette, then breathed the smoke out slowly, so it formed a lazy cloud drifting over the railing of the balcony, out towards the city. He watched it for a moment before the wind took it apart. Then he poured another sake.

Okawara's was a tenth-rate sushi joint in the heart of Japantown, a little fish being eaten alive by larger, slicker competitors. But they did a good, cheap, strong sake, and they had a view that those big fancy restaurants would kill for. From here, you could see everything, the whole damned city. You could look down on it with a warm sake in one fist and a Lucky Strike in the other, and pretend for a minute or two that you didn't need to walk those damned streets, to wade through the crap that everybody else has to wade through just to survive.

It must be nice to be able to leap over it, or at least that's what Easton West figured. But maybe that just meant you landed in it harder.

"It wasn't me who... apprehended Hisoka's killer." Doc Thunder danced around the word, but they both knew what he meant. *Murdered.*

"You got him that pardon, right? Get out of jail free?" West tried to keep the bitterness out of his voice. "That masked son of a bitch killed a dozen men, maybe more. We're just supposed to forget about that?"

Doc Thunder shrugged. "He saved my life. He probably saved yours. Probably the President's. The whole USSA, in fact." He looked at Easton, and suddenly he looked tired. "What was I supposed to do? I don't like his methods any more than you do, but there it is. He's the reason the sun came up this morning."

"I don't care if he put the damned sun in the sky to begin with," Inspector West growled. "We're a nation of laws. That's all that keeps us from sliding into Hell." He swallowed another fistful of sake.

Doc paused, looking out at the view. "Crane killed Danny. I'm sure of it."

Easton West nodded. "It was him, all right. But that doesn't change anything." He poured another. "Danny Coltrane was the nearest thing I ever had to a father. I became a cop to get the man who killed him. To *get* him, understand? Get him *right,* by the book. That's how the Ghost would have done it." He downed the shot in one. "Killing Crane like that—that's spitting on Danny's memory. And if I see El Sombra again, he's going down for that. By the book."

Doc nodded. There wasn't much to say. He poured himself a measure of sake he knew he wouldn't feel, then poured one for Easton. He lifted the cup between two outsized fingers, and smiled. "Here's to Danny."

Easton smiled, picking up his cup and draining it. "Yeah. Here's to you, Mr Ghost Boss." He smiled, very slightly, just at the corners of his mouth. "You rest now."

"SURE, I KNEW the Blood-Spider. Him and me were like *that,* buddy. Like *that.* He knew he could count on Harry Stacey, yes sir. Knew what I'd done *in the line,* keeping the streets safe. Yeah, okay, maybe there were a few minor breaches of the regulations here and there, but opium goes missing from the evidence locker all the time these days—don't know why people pointed at me. Everybody knows your slant is a fiend for the dragon, and we got a lot more chinks on the force than we used to, thanks to that asshole Rickard and all his bullcrap about 'diversity.' I'm just saying, ask them where it went. Christ, 'diversity in policing'... What the hell does 'diversity' even mean, anyway? I'll tell you; anti-white racism, that's what. The most oppressed race in the whole goddamned world is the friggin' white man. Anyway, the Blood-Spider...

"Now listen, you don't want to believe all that crap about Parker Crane being the Blood-Spider. That's just lies. Parker Crane was just one more asshole rich boy, that's all. In fact, I heard he was a fruit. Well, that's *why* he was always seeing those models, they knew he was safe! And let me tell you, the Blood-Spider was no butt-bandit. The guy was all man. Like me. Coupla peas in a pod.

"And don't believe all that crapola about that friggin' wetback saving the day! That's the goddamned liberal media for you. If they're not spending all their time on that son of a bitch Doc Thunder, who is—and this is a *documented friggin' fact*—a friggin' faggot, a liberal *and* a miscegenationist, they're wanting to turn a god-damned illegal into the hero of New York city. You want to know who took that prick Lomax down? The Blood-Spider. Shot him through the heart with a magic bullet, saved all our asses. That's a damn fact.

"And what does he get for it? He gets smeared! Don't believe that bullcrap that he was Crane, or that Crane was a Nazi—that's just the Jew media tryin' to play with your head, friend. Listen, you know you're getting the straight dope from me. I'm a cop. Well, no, I ain't a cop any *more*, now I clean the toilets in this joint, but like I said, that's all because of the damn slants.

"Yeah, like I said, that business with the opium out of the evidence locker. I mean, *someone* signed it out—probably a chink, like I said—and sure, they used my name. And they found the stuff in an apartment that I'd apparently signed a lease for, but look, that apartment belonged to a *hooker*, okay? I'm a happily married man. Well, I was.

"Listen, pal, this too will pass, you know? A real rain's going to wash all the scum off the streets, let me tell ya. A hard rain's gonna fall when the Blood Spider comes back to town. Him and me were like *that*, like I was sayin,' and he always looked after his number one guy. That's all I'm saying. He always had a place in his organisation for Harry Stacey.

"The Blood-Spider will rise again, friend. The Blood-Spider will rise again..."

*   *   *

IN THE END, El Sombra was glad to go.

New York had been... fun. He had to admit it. There was magic in this city—a strange energy on every street corner, waiting to be unleashed. The music, the culture, the larger than life personalities... As he stood on the docks, waiting for the boat that would take him to Europe—to the final battle with the creature he'd been born to destroy—he found himself thinking over the little things.

Djego, standing in a coffee house in the East Village, not three blocks from El Sombra's battle with Lars Lomax, reading his old poems and getting a standing ovation, starting to cry as a piece of his heart came back to him.

El Sombra, dancing with the breakers in Times Square, losing himself in the rhythm, free and unrestrained and whole again for a few short minutes.

Djego, in the Metropolitan Museum of Modern Art, looking at Warhol's 'cellphone,' a block of black ceramic studded with numbers and a tiny sheet of glass, and for a brief moment being transported to that other world, the world of dreampunk.

El Sombra, squeezing Crane's shoulder, feeling the burning that would forever be in him ease, transforming into sadness for a single moment.

Djego sitting in a futurehead bar, wearing El Sombra's mask around his neck like a bandana, détourning his own personal demons and transforming them into couture, laughing like a boy.

El Sombra, standing on top of the Empire State Building and yelling into the night, scaring the tourists and aggravating the cops and not giving a damn, because whatever the bastards had taken from him, he would always have this one single moment, forever and ever until the day he died fighting.

All of these moments happened, in between and underneath his mission and his adventures and all the craziness and the violence. They all happened, and they were all important, even if they weren't part of that big, complicated story of Doc Thunder and the Blood-Spider and the most dangerous man in the world. Maybe more important because of that.

And maybe that was the lesson of New York City—that all the moments were important, that all the little things mattered. The smallest detail could save the day or destroy the world. It was a good lesson to take into the endgame.

And he had to admit, they'd been very gracious about all the dead bastards.

Still, it was past time to leave. He'd spent too long circling America, while the enemy in Berlin had grown more evil and more dangerous still. Now was the time to end it once and for all. Now was the time to go to the heart of the Ultimate Reich and show them what they'd so thoughtlessly created. What they'd forged in the fires of their damnation.

Now was the hour of final battle.

El Sombra breathed in, focussing on the task ahead.

"Hot dogs! Hot dogs! One dollar five! Wrap a nickel in a bill and eat your fill!"

El Sombra breathed out, laughed his magical laugh, and turned away from the docks and towards the yelling voice in the distance. Well, what choice did he have?

Who could go to their death without a last hot dog?

AND SOMEWHERE IN Langley, Virginia, in the deepest part of a bunker owned and operated by S.T.E.A.M. for the purpose of storing the most dangerous artefacts in the world, there was a large crate and a smaller bottle. Inside the large crate, there was the corpse of something that had once been the son of a mediocre salesman. Something that had grown up to be the most dangerous man in the world, and that had thrown its humanity away to become more dangerous still.

Floating in the bottle, sealed in a solution of formaldehyde, was the creature's head. It floated, eyes closed, the neck ragged and burned from the explosives used to separate it from its body.

It floated that way for a very long time.

And then it opened its eyes.

And if anyone had been there to see the head, they might have been able to read its snarling, sneering lips as they moved behind the thick glass of the jar, showing its fangs. They might have worked out what it was saying, in its dark formaldehyde tomb.

Next time, Thunder.

Next time.

THE END

PAX
OMEGA

AUTHOR'S NOTE

James Newton ("The Printer's Devil") and Matt Zitron
("The Last Stand of the Yodelling Bastards") are
the names of real people.

They appear in this book courtesy of the "Genre for Japan"
charity auction, which took place in April 2011, in support
of the Red Cross efforts in the aftermath of the Japan Earthquake.

The characters appearing under their names are,
of course, wholly fictional.

For Sarah, who is the best thing.

ALPHA...

First, there was not.

Nothing existed, and there was nothing in which to exist.

Over a timeless interval, during which time had no meaning, He considered the situation.

He existed. He was the only thing to exist. That did not feel correct.

He focussed His being, and spoke.

And there was.

As He watched the fundamental forces slowly tear themselves from one another, He found himself wondering if He had chosen to create, or if creation had somehow chosen Him. Nuclei formed in the torrents of energy He had released and spent millennia wooing electrons, forming atoms as He debated the matter with Himself.

Dense pockets in the primordial gas, warped by gravity, ignited into the first suns, and He decided that the question was of no consequence. The act of creation had happened. The future had been seeded.

Around the new stars, swirling debris coalesced and cooled into planets, moons, meteors, the endless architecture of the cosmos. In a moment of curiosity—rebellion against the chain of events He was bound into, perhaps—He attempted to shift some of these emerging bodies from their set course.

Once, He had created a universe from nothing, but things were different now. Exposure to time had somehow decayed Him. He still existed, but not in any physical sense, and the power of His mind was not strong enough to effect the necessary gravitational changes.

He realised then just how much time had passed. His perception of it was accelerating in odd patterns—speeding and slowing—and his disembodied consciousness was starting to drift apart. The decay would continue. Death was coming to Him.

Death, at last.

How strange and novel it would be.

His awareness drifted to one of the new planets, the third out from its star. The shape of the emerging continents was familiar in places, and microscopic life forms were beginning to thrive and propagate in the volcanic regions. He studied them for a short while as they evolved, to flatworms and algae, then to more complex forms.

His intelligence was starting to dissipate now. Death was approaching rapidly, and He relaxed into it, watching the events occur on the new planet until He could no longer comprehend them.

The last thing He saw and understood was the ship, appearing from the wormhole at too great a velocity, trying desperately to change its course and then crashing into one of the newly-formed continents. They were very familiar now.

Hello, He thought. *Hello. Hello.*

After that, He could no longer think of words. He thought of her face, for a moment, and then that, too, became too complex to hold onto.

He thought of a smile.

And then He was not.

THE END OF THE WORLD

MUNN, THE NAVIGATOR, sat with his legs dangling off the edge of the high cliff and watched the monsters fighting in the valley below.

What else was there to do?

There were two of the creatures, giant lizards with great fans of bone crowning their heads, and three horns—two at their temples and one jutting from their snouts—above what looked like a large beak. From what Munn could work out, the combat was between an old bull, defending his place in the pack, and a smaller challenger bucking for a higher position in the hierarchy. A group of females watched, grazing on the tall grasses nearby. They were patient animals—the fight had gone on for at least an hour.

Was it a fight? Now that Munn had watched the pair for so long, the regular clashing of horns looked more like a display—almost a dance. A contest of endurance, perhaps, one that would continue until the weaker of the huge beasts no longer had the energy to carry on. Munn examined each of the creatures carefully from his vantage point, looking for signs of exhaustion, but gave up quickly. Unwen, the Biologist, might have had something to say about it, but he was busy in the ship with his mammals. Perhaps Munn would ask Unwen what he thought on the matter. Without the selfsearch, Unwen might not know precisely, but he seemed to be adjusting himself to the lack of it better than most. He could probably come up with an answer.

Munn undid one of the clasps on his belt, lifting the small plasol bag of hosa from its pouch and packing a little into the three-inch metal pipe he now wore, as a matter of habit, around his neck. He thumbed the stud that ignited the yellow powder, and then breathed the smoke into his lungs, feeling his perceptions loosen and shift slightly as the new possibilities began to fall into his mind, slotting perfectly into place like the bind-blocks he'd played with as a child.

He breathed out a long coil of yellow smoke. The pipe was an inefficient system for delivery of the drug, especially compared with the skin-patch he'd worn on his upper arm ever since he'd left the crèche. In the Habitats, skin-patches were a necessity—without a constant low-level infusion of hosa, the speed, intensity and complexity of normal life would be impossible to comprehend. But on this new planet, in this slower, stranger existence, priorities had changed—the skin-patches had had to go, because they had precious ununtrium in the contacts and there was no ununtrium to be had here, or any way of synthesising it. And without ununtrium they would have had no way of establishing a permanent perimeter-field, and without the perimeter-field they would all have died, as surely as the captain had.

So, no more skin-patches.

QED, as Unwen or Soran would say.

Munn's thoughts drifted. That was another problem with smoking the hosa-powder instead of having the pure essence of the drug micro-injected into the capillaries. Bad memories had a sudden habit of ambushing the conscious mind, and Captain Tura's death was one of them.

After the crash, she'd been monitoring the ship's attempts to seal and repair itself—as much as it could, outside a proper docking bay. He remembered her face in particular, lined with concentration, trying hopelessly to jolt the lift-engines into proper function, not noticing the shadow suddenly descending on her from above. Munn had opened his mouth to call out, but she was already gone—a screaming shape high in the sky, held in the claws of one of the flying monsters. Munn had watched helplessly as the thing had pulled her head from her body with its beak, swallowed it and flapped off with the twitching remnants. Something to feed to its nightmare children, he supposed.

He tried to imagine what the captain had experienced in death—the tearing pain, a split-second of disorientation, the realisation that her body was simply gone... and then the ego winking out like a light, or spiralling away like water into a drain.

And then... what?

Something unimaginable. Something that nobody had had a reason to contemplate, for hundreds of thousands of years. Death, in all its totality.

Munn tried to think of what that inconceivable absence might be like. He tried to think of not thinking, of not existing, and even with the hosa accelerating his mind he couldn't make the mental leap. It terrified him.

He shivered, shaking his head to try and flush the idea away. He'd never had to consider death before he'd arrived in this place. Death was for the special soldiers in the Red Queen's employ, the Silver Service, and no-one else. Theirs was the highest sacrifice, opening themselves to the possibility of non-existence. Munn wondered if the Silvers were given any special reward for their work, beyond the honour of the work itself. Probably not. Nothing material could make up for such a horror.

His mind drifted on, to the vote they'd taken after the captain's death. Not a true vote, of course—without mental-linkage equipment, the best they could manage was a vague, approximated version of democracy. Still, they'd done the best they could in the circumstances, and after a brief debate they'd made the decision to atomise all those items unnecessary for continued existence in this world, like the skin-patches, the fiction gels—even the selfsearch.

They'd used all the rarer elements thus harvested—the precious ununtrium, the sparse grains of dubnium and meitnerium, impossible to hold together outside a quantum envelope—to repair the life-support and create a working perimeter-field strong enough to keep all the monsters outside at bay. Once survival was thus assured, they could work out what to do next.

That had been the plan, anyway.

So now the remaining crew-members were safe in their bubble, and Munn was dangling his legs off a sheer cliff, safe in the knowledge that if he should fall, or leap, the perimeter-field would catch hold of him—he could even walk on it, if he wanted—and watching the lizards dance, hundreds of feet below.

What else was there to do?

"How's your reading, Munn?"

Maya, the Security Officer. Munn took a long drag on the metal pipe, holding the hosa-smoke in his lungs, and exhaled slowly, considering the question.

"It's a phrase that's already lost its meaning, isn't it?" he murmured, smiling humourlessly. "There's no selfsearch any more to get a reading from. I could give you an estimate, if you like…"

Maya looked down at him disdainfully. She'd never thought much of Munn, and with the hosa coiling in him he could read all of her contempt for him as clearly as any stellar map. "I can make a guess for myself," she murmured. "You're missing Habitat One, you're missing a working ship… you're missing civilisation. You're starting to fall into a depressive state." She frowned dismissively, and Munn found himself resenting her—the way she'd so readily accepted being exiled here.

He shrugged, turning away. "I suppose I am. Without a selfsearch reading it's difficult to be sure what I'm feeling, exactly." He laughed bitterly to himself. "This must be how our ancestors felt. Or assumed they felt."

Maya frowned. "Forget selfsearch—it's gone. Frankly, I'm happier without it. I'd have gone all the way and junked the talkeasies, if I could be sure we'd understand each other without them."

"Well, why not? It's not like we understand each other as it is." The words sounded angry in his ears, and he wanted nothing more than to consult the familiar machine and have it tell him why, and what to do about it. Why had he agreed to get rid of them? They could have found what they needed elsewhere. One of Soran's scientific toys, maybe.

"Listen, Munn. What was is over. We should try to make the best of what we have now, not sit around moaning about all our old trinkets. Our species existed for millennia before selfsearch, or hosa, or psychetecture. We'll learn to exist without them again. We'll build back to what we had before."

"You sound very certain, considering it's just the four of us…"

Maya shrugged. "That's how it has to be. That's how it will be. What other choices do we have?"

Munn shook his head, angry at her fatalism. "Rescue?" Even saying the word, he felt stupid. There wouldn't be a rescue—nobody from the Habitats would be able to find them, out here on the other side of the wormhole. "Escape, then?"

Maya shook her head. "There'll be no escape. It's us and this world now— the ship won't take us anywhere else. The xokronite we have is enough to keep us powered, but we can't synthesise the elements we need to repair the lift-engines. Soran was working on it, but…" She shook her head, leaving the sentence unfinished.

"He's given up?"

Maya shrugged. "He tried. He failed. I had a feeling he would. Still, it's more than the rest of us have done." She looked pointedly at Munn, and he felt uncomfortable, under scrutiny. She might as well have asked him straight out what exactly he was doing to help, besides watching the reptiles bash their heads together.

Munn bristled. "There's not much I can do in this situation. I'm a Navigator, Maya. I've been a Navigator for... for..." He tailed off, trying to work out exactly how long it had been since he'd first sat at a navigation station and plotted a course between the galaxies. Eighty thousand years? Ninety thousand? Enough time to grow bored and exhausted with navigating between stars and galaxies and wormholes, and then to fall in love with the process all over again as new developments in the art appeared. And then to lose faith again, and get it back, over and over... but always Navigator, always guiding ships between the stars. It had defined him in a way nothing else had, and now it was gone.

How long *had* it been? Without selfsearch, or external memory packs, or even an efficient supply of hosa in his bloodstream, it was impossible to remember and collate much before the last two or three thousand years; only the vaguest of flashes. The horror of that washed over him for a moment. *I'm brain-damaged,* he thought. *We all are. In three thousand years, four at the most, will we think we've always been here? Will we even remember Habitat One, or things as simple as selfsearch or gels or talkeasies? And if we do remember everything, if we do build it all just the way it was—is that better?*

Or worse?

Maya snapped him out of it. "Munn?"

He rubbed his bare scalp gently with his fingertips, trying to work his way back into the conversation. "For all that time, I've flown ships. Ships are... part of *me*. Stars are part of me. But that ship"—he waved his hand at the lush canopy of the jungle, in the rough direction the ship was in—"that ship's just... a domicell-complex now. A place to live. It won't fly. And at night, the light from the field stops me seeing the stars. And I'm never going to see the stars again..." He swallowed, unable to speak. His eyes stung. He hadn't realised how much he'd missed the stars until that moment. "So what should I do now? Tell me that. What am I going to be?" He turned away from her, not wanting her to see the tears. "I could spend a thousand years trying to decide. We all could."

Maya shrugged. "We've got a thousand years. We've got ten thousand, and ten thousand times that. We can do anything we want. And in the end, what we'll do is build."

Munn stared at her with his wet eyes, and suddenly he hated her; hated her certainty, her seeming invulnerability. What did she know that he didn't? "Build it all just the way it is back at home," he muttered to himself. "Do you think Unwen and Soran will agree with your nostalgia?"

"I suppose we'll find out," Maya replied, as if she already had, as if any conversation on the subject was just a formality.

Munn didn't reply. After a moment, Maya turned and walked off, and he returned his attention to the three-horned lizards in the valley below. In the time he'd spent talking to her, they'd finished their combat, or display, or whatever it had been, and now both the males were grazing alongside the females as if nothing had happened.

Munn wondered who'd won.

"HERE'S ONE I prepared earlier."

Unwen smiled, picking up the miniature field in his hands. Inside the sphere of force, sniffing against the almost invisible barrier, there was a small creature, about the span of a hand, with four legs, brownish fur and a thin, twitching tail. Soran frowned, rubbing his chin. "It's not unlike a surface-cleaner. I remember when I was a boy, we had several. Bio-forms, they were... little pink things with snouts... they actually ate the accumulated dirt, you remember? They were smaller, though, the size of a thumb..." He tailed off, staring at the animal.

Unwen looked at him for a moment, then re-lit his hosa-pipe and took a long, slow drag on the burning powder. "No, I don't remember anything like that." He gazed at the scurrying creature, as though it might recreate whatever decayed memory he was grasping for. "It may be before my time."

Soran shrugged. "I remember it clearly. I used to let them scamper over my feet, nibbling at the dead skin. Someone told me it was disgusting... a nun, or a nurse... I forget..." He stared at his console, lost in thought.

Unwen looked at Soran, concerned. The ship's Engineer was perhaps five hundred thousand years old, one hundred and fifty millennia older than any of them, and the loss of the skin-patches seemed to have hit him the hardest. Strangely, he had consistently refused the pipe. "I'll need you for this next bit."

Soran nodded, snapping out of his reverie. "Yes, yes. Of course. We must be careful." He smiled, looking around the chamber—the Power Room, as it was called for simplicity's sake. The place where the limitless energy that powered the ship and the field was generated; the energy that would power Unwen's little experiment. There was a visible twinkle in the older man's eye as he lifted his hand in the particular gesture that called up the room controls, a string of icons shimmering on a near-transparent field at chest height, and he passed his fingers over them in the manner of a man at play. Of the four survivors, he had had to adapt the least. The ship was still running, the power still needed to flow, occasional repairs would still need to be triggered in those systems that did not immediately repair themselves. He, Soran, was necessary to the group's survival in a way none of the others were.

The room's central pillar hummed softly, like an insect, before its silvery sheen cleared, turning from opaque metal to something akin to glass. Floating inside the glass, at head height, was the glowing blue metal that powered the ship—that powered all of the Habitats.

Xokronite.

Unwen gazed on it, a half-smile playing across his face. "Beautiful, isn't it?"

Soran stroked his hairless chin, studying the shimmering, flowing lines and pulses that told him the energy output. "It's very pretty, very pretty... I once had a sunsuit of that colour..."

"No, no." Unwen shook his head, flashing Soran an amused glance. "What it represents. A gateway for energy from the Big Bang itself..." He laughed, shaking his head in wonder. "We steal energy from the dawn of time, and all the energy we steal, throughout our history—throughout the history of the xokronite, no matter who uses it, *has* ever used it, *will* ever use it... put all that stolen energy together, and you have the exact amount that *needed* to be stolen from the Big Bang to create this exact universe, the exact history and cosmology we know. It's perfect. Isn't that perfect?"

"It's a rather simplistic way of putting it. I can tell you didn't study the physical sciences."

"You say simplistic, I say poetic. The universe is the way it is because it created us, and we discovered xokronite, and through it we made the universe the way it is. A perfect cycle of causality." Unwen gazed deep into the glowing stone, eyes shining with reflected blue. "And we can never get enough energy from it, because if we were ever to do so, if we were ever to drain too much—or not enough—the universe would be a different place. Perhaps only slightly different, but different nevertheless. And it's not, so we don't, therefore we can't, therefore... limitless power. It's so *poetic*, Soran. Don't you think?"

Soran shrugged. "Poetry isn't my department. Or yours. And in my experience, nothing is free, even if you do steal it. There are costs..." He nodded to the creature trapped in Unwen's spherical field. "How does this relate to your friend there?"

Unwen lifted the beast up, looking at it. "We'll need a limited transfer between the two fields. As you say, I'm no physicist, but I do dabble—I think if you drain off some of the tachyon field from the xokronite in the following frequencies..." He reached up with his free hand, calling a display field into existence and inscribing a sequence of fluid shapes and signs, which glowed ethereally in the blue light.

Soran looked them over for a moment. "That's... interesting." A hint of nervousness had crept into his voice.

Unwen grinned. "It will be."

"Yes... I was under the impression that... well, that experimenting with these frequencies on living tissue had been banned by both the Royal Houses?" His grey eyes flicked over to Unwen's.

Unwen lifted an eyebrow in response. "You have an objection?"

Soran sucked in his breath for a moment. After a pause, he shook his head. "No. We'll proceed. I can make this more energy-efficient, now I know what you're aiming for." He forced a slight smile. "What can they do to us here, eh?"

"You see? You're as curious as I am." Unwen set the spherical field's gravity so that it would sit in the air, then took his hands away and let it hang gently, supported on nothing. He stepped back, admiring the small mammal as it turned circles in its floating prison. Some callous part of him enjoyed the sensation of having power over these little beasts—they huddled close to the field in great numbers, as if recognising its power over the larger lizards that were their chief predator, and when he snared one from outside to bring through the field and into the ship, he felt almost like some deity, reaching down to pluck his chosen few to the heavens. There were myths that still persisted in the Habitats of ordinary beings plucked from their base circumstances by the hand of the gods, to dwell among them as one of their own. He imagined the small mammals building their own myths, in their squeaking rodent-language, and the thought pleased him.

And here we have the beginnings of a new myth, he thought to himself. "Let's start slowly. Transfer five per cent of total yield."

Soran nodded, wetting his lips and leaning forward as he brushed the control field with his fingertips. Unwen couldn't help but smile—Soran was as excited as he was, despite himself. He turned his attention back to the field, watching the mammal scurrying and scrabbling at the invisible barrier he was caught in. Gradually, the flesh and fur of the creature was suffused with the same blue glow of the xokronite itself.

There was a soft, gentle whine of straining machinery.

At first, nothing seemed to happen. Unwen, watching closely, could see the beast's eyes dilate. Its breathing quickened, then grew heavy and laboured. Suddenly, the muscles of its back and legs seemed to shift slightly; the mammal rolled onto its back, squealing in discomfort, kicking its legs. Unwen watched its feet move, holding his breath, then let out a small cry. "Stop there!"

Soran shut off the transfer. The glow faded, the soft keening noise died. "What is it?" He hurried across the room to where Unwen stood, hunched over the field, examining the animal as it panted helplessly, still on its back. Unwen seemed as transfixed as his specimen. "Unwen, what is it?"

"Look there," Unwen breathed, tapping the field with his fingertip. Soren looked. The beast was visibly larger, as if it had grown new muscles. Its legs were longer, and he could now see that there had been other changes to the shape of its back and skull.

"You've mutated it."

"More than that. Look at the paws."

Soran's eyes narrowed, then widened. The paws of the animal had changed as well, elongated, into five recognisable digits. Their configuration had a familiarity that at once excited and disturbed him.

Opposable thumbs.

"OPPOSABLE THUMBS?"

Unwen nodded. Maya frowned at him. "And where is it now?"

"I let it go again." Unwen shrugged, and Soran looked up from the food-tray, shocked.

"You didn't! Unwen, even I know that's going to play havoc with the evolutionary tree—"

"It might." Unwen grinned. "Our little friend might get eaten by something before he breeds. Either way, we'll see what happens in a million years. In the meantime, shall we return to the thumbs?"

"I don't see the significance of them," Munn said, as he picked a red protein-globule from the shared tray. "The mutation aspect—well, it's interesting, certainly, that we can do that. It's nothing scientists back in the Habitats weren't able to achieve before, but it's nice that we can do it with the equipment we've got, and by this method..."

"A forbidden method," Maya murmured, frowning. "Forbidden by both the Royal Houses."

Unwen rolled his eyes as he chewed idly on one of the white carbohydrate squares. "Nobody's going to come and punish us, Maya."

Maya shot him an angry look. "Perhaps *I'll* punish you for violating the Queen's rule." The others looked at her for a moment, and she seemed to acknowledge the ridiculousness of the statement. "Well, anyway... it's a slippery slope. Are we going to start breaking every rule of society one by one, Unwen? We're supposed to be building—I mean *re*building—society. Not tearing it down for our own—"

"Are we? When did we take that vote?" Unwen interrupted, enjoying Maya's obvious outrage. This obsession she'd picked up with replicating the culture of Habitat One with their meagre resources had gone from naïve to tedious to irritating, and now he found himself glad of any opportunity to prick that particular bubble.

Soran, always less contentious than his fellow scientist, was quick to play down the potential conflict.

"We don't *want* to go against societal rules, as such," he said in a calming tone, "but you have to admit that we're outside that society now. We're a long way away from Habitat One. If I wanted to be pedantic about it, I could say that the moment we took the decision to atomise the selfsearch, we stepped outside the bounds of ordered society. Look at us now—we're unsure of each other's motives, unsure of our own... once upon a time, we could have settled this whole discussion by comparing readings." He took one of the long yellow fluid-sacs and bit it open with his teeth, swallowing the sweet, tart juice, then the skin. "Or by mental link, for that matter, if we'd been at home. That's something I miss... do you know, I had a rather fascinating dream last night of the area without us—just as if we'd never landed here. It seemed very significant when I woke up, and I thought I'd record it on the link and share it... except we have no link any more..." He paused for a moment, staring glumly at the sticky juice that remained on his fingers. "Perhaps... perhaps you're right, Maya. I do so miss my home..."

He lapsed into a silence that none of the other three gathered around the feeding-tray felt like breaking. They were eating outside the ship, next to the perimeter-field, where Unwen could watch the mammals gather on the other side. There was a crowd of them now, staring with pink eyes, occasionally creeping forward to sniff at the shimmering air that kept them out. Mostly, they seemed to be staring at the feeding-tray, floating a foot or so off the ground, loaded up with the various basic components of a complete meal, but occasionally they'd turn their heads, blinking at Unwen, almost as if they remembered him. He smiled, resisting the urge to send one of the small red globes through the field for them to eat. To be a generous god.

Munn broke the silence. "I don't understand what's so special about the thumbs. Why is that mutation in particular so important?"

"I've gone through this once already, Munn. We didn't mutate it, not in the sense you mean." Unwen shook his head impatiently. "What we *did*, Munn—I'll make it simple—was swap out its DNA for that of a descendant from millions of years down the evolutionary line. We looked into the future of the species and brought that future back into the present."

Soran bit into one of the white squares. "That's almost making it too simple, if you ask me. But, yes, in terms of the effect, we were able to... well, jump up the evolutionary ladder. Of course, the results will differ vastly from mammal to mammal according to their species or location. If we were to attempt the process on one of the reptiles, for example, we might find that..."

"Let's not do that," Munn broke in quickly.

Maya nodded in agreement. Soran looked to Unwen for support, but he only shrugged. "I'm afraid I concur with the rest of the group, Soran. It's far too risky to bring one of the larger lizards through the field—anyway, I think we've got enough on our plate right now with this species. I think if we can follow it further down the evolutionary path... well, this is where the thumbs become important, Munn."

"I'm listening."

"The fact that these creatures developed opposable thumbs suggests that, if pushed further down the evolutionary path, there's a chance that they might evolve into... well, us. Or a creature very like us. Bipedal, using tools. Perhaps even sentient." He smiled, popping one of the yellow fluid-sacs into his mouth.

Maya nodded, watching him with a curious look on her face. "I see, Or... its descendants might evolve into primates and stop there. If I'm understanding you correctly."

"You are, up to a point. By adjusting certain variables—and this is something Soran had a great deal of difficulty explaining to me, so I won't try and give you a second-hand version—we can pick and choose which branch of the evolutionary tree we follow. If even one of those branches leads to a sentient or semi-sentient creature, we can... well, bring it into being."

"You're twisting my words," Soran interrupted, scowling. "I said it was theoretically possible with the equipment we had. That doesn't make it easy, or wise. The power drain would be catastrophic."

Unwen seemed almost amused by the idea. "The whole point of xokronite as a power source is that it grants us potentially infinite power, surely?"

"You're not a physicist," Soran spat, almost savagely. "You're not an engineer, either. Drawing energy at the rate you're discussing would lead to—"

Munn cut him off. "The mammals."

"What?"

He pointed towards the edge of the field. "Where are they going?"

The crowd of small animals who'd sat watching the four of them eat were scurrying for cover, finding holes and branches to lose themselves in. A moment later, the ground underneath them vibrated with a sound like thunder.

"I think—" Soran began, and then he was silenced by another thunderclap, then another, and another—louder each time. Something approaching, on feet heavy enough to shake the earth. Something huge and terrible, making its way through the trees.

Then it was on them.

Nearly three times as tall as a man—and even then Unwen could see that it was not rearing up to its full height. Instead, it held its body parallel to the ground, lunging at the field, a great mouth of razors attempting to tear into the empty air. The field shimmered and whined under the assault, becoming almost opaque in places under the stress, and Munn found himself inching back, despite himself.

"It won't breach the perimeter-field," Soran muttered, but there was a trace of uncertainty in his voice.

Unwen felt oddly detached, observing the massive monster as it roared at him, great globs of its spittle trickling down the outer edge of the field. It walked on its massive hind legs, its small arms seeming useless, almost vestigial. But then, the claws were sharp—perhaps, when it was engaged in fighting or feeding on similarly gigantic reptiles, the arms would latch onto its prey for ease of attack. If he could only study one in a more natural habitat. A mobile field, perhaps.

If he could only capture one.

Abruptly, the massive beast turned, slamming its tail into the field, and crashed through the tree-line and out of sight, shaking the earth again as it stomped into the distance. Eventually, the smaller mammals began to creep out of their hiding places, moving back to their place at the edge of the field.

The four of them finished their meal in silence.

LATER, MAYA SAID to Unwen: "Honestly? I think you should try it."

Unwen raised an eyebrow. "Interesting. You're the last person I'd expect approval from, quite frankly. What happened to the slippery slope?"

She shrugged, irritated at his point-scoring. "We're already on one."

The two of them were in Unwen's sparse domicell, away from the others, lounging on a pair of visible fields projected from the walls and floor. Unwen's was a curved plane, allowing his legs to remain horizontal and his back supported, while Maya preferred a solid block to perch on. "Munn hasn't said a word since the fang-beast attacked the perimeter-field," she continued.

Unwen raised his other eyebrow at that. "Fang-beast?"

She smiled, despite herself. "It's by far the largest and most dangerous reptile we've seen. It deserves a name. Feel free to come up with something more scientific."

"I already have. Species designate #7C."

"And the ones Munn's become obsessed with? The ones he stares at all day and most of the night?"

"The triple-horned things?" Unwen thought for a moment. "#3C. The C classes them as reptile. They were the second reptile species we saw, admittedly, after the flying one, but... well, the triple horns. These things should have at least a little poetry in them, Maya." He chuckled. "If we do restart civilisation over again, one thing I'll be pressing for is including poets in the crew of every ship. Just in case something like this happens again."

Maya looked at him for a moment. "You're in favour of rebuilding, now?"

"Not to the extent you are. Everything doesn't have to be exactly the same. I never did understand your obsession with that..." He shrugged. "But what else is there to do? We have to fill our endless time with something, just to avoid going mad. So let's build our own little world here. Why not?"

Maya looked at him in silence. Unwen sighed, leant back, and scratched his chin. "All right... how would it work? We want a nice, large, growing population to rule over. There's not enough genetic material between us to repopulate ourselves... so we take, say, a thousand of the mammals—assuming we can find that many without leaving the perimeter and being picked off. Mutate or evolve them, whichever terminology we're using, until they're sentient creatures. Educate them as best we can to a basic level. Feed them with the ship's synthesisers at first—I don't know where they'll sleep, mind you. And of course, we'll be hoping against hope that the food synthesisers won't burn out from overuse until we've taught them farming... and teaching them how to farm without being picked off by the reptiles will be difficult in the extreme, but I'm sure..."

"Enough." Maya shot Unwen an irritated glance. "Too many problems, Unwen."

Unwen reached into his field, lowering its density slightly so that he sank deeper into it. He closed his eyes, and Maya had the maddening urge to stand up and command the room to switch off all the fields, to watch him crash down onto the floor. "All right," she said, "if the main problem is the reptiles, what would it take to kill one? Say, the #7C."

"The fang-beast. Nothing we've got, unfortunately." Unwen frowned. "Theoretically, we could possibly kill one by projecting a field into its brain or heart, if we got close enough... yes, that would work. We could cannibalise the furniture fields—if that one you're sitting on were to suddenly appear in one of the monster's ventricles, say, or the folds of its brain, that would be very fatal indeed." Unwen stroked his chin, suddenly looking more awake and alert. "Soran could probably jury-rig something—a portable projector. It'd mean losing some of our furniture, obviously, but we could craft new surfaces from solid matter, wood or stone... we have time. If we could do that, our biggest problem then would be getting close enough..."

Maya nodded. "Without being eaten."

"Quite. Even if you managed to kill a #7C—or a #1C, or any of the other dangerous creatures out there—it would probably tear you apart before it realised it was dead. Besides, you're the only one of us with anything close to the training for this kind of thing. The rest of us would die off very fast." Unwen stared up at the ceiling for a moment. "And none of us are qualified to program an AI that could... Ah, yes." He laughed. "I think I'm starting to see. We're back to the mammals again."

"We are?"

"Oh, yes. We need creatures to take this hypothetical device of Soran's—which we will mass-produce—and kill the lizards with it. Some of the larger mammals, too, the dangerous-looking ones. Semi-sentient creatures to kill and die on our behalf. Of course, more often than not, they'll be dying rather than killing. But so long as we can retrieve the field generators, that's fine." He looked at her for a moment, gauging her reaction.

Maya nodded, her eyes not leaving his. "They're only mammals."

"They're only mammals." He chuckled. "And we need to stop them turning the devices on us, of course. So Soran and I will have to create more devices, to implant in their heads, to kill them if they try anything. These killing implants would also be activated if they refuse an order... such as the order to die for our benefit." He kept looking at Maya, waiting for her to snap, to dismiss the whole scenario.

She only nodded.

"An army of slaves..." He enunciated the words carefully, marvelling at them, trying to hide his excitement at the prospect. Surely Maya wouldn't agree to this—

But she nodded again, without changing her expression, and Unwen had to consciously hide his astonishment. He'd actually managed to manipulate her into letting him do it.

Or perhaps she was manipulating him. Or both at once. *Ah, selfsearch,* he thought, *how mysterious life is without you.*

After she left, he lay back on his field with his eyes closed, lost in thought.

He thought about the gigantic reptile that had come at them. The #7C, the fang-beast. He thought about the mammals, and how they had watched him through the perimeter-field.

He thought about how they would remember him, in their legends.

"No. Absolutely not." Soran's voice was firm. "I can't possibly allow it."

The sun was setting, and the four of them were again sat around the feeding-tray as it floated an inch above the grass. This time it was loaded with a mixture of long green sticks, round yellow discs, and clear fluid-sacs of lightly flavoured water—the food-synthesiser followed a rhythm of its own in response to the dietary needs of the crew, and what it provided was rarely questioned. Unwen picked one of the yellow discs up, nibbling around the edge as he studied Soran closely. "The moral issue?"

Soran hesitated, seeming startled by the question. "Yes, yes," he said, a little too quickly. "It's morally unconscionable, it goes against hundreds of thousands of years of moral development by our species..."

Unwen smiled. "What's the real reason?"

Soran flushed red, and scowled. "It's simply too dangerous. The sheer amount of power we'd be draining out of the xokronite..." He shook his head firmly. "Creating just one of these hominids of yours would be risky. To compound that risk by creating an army of them is... well, it's insanity. Utter madness."

Maya picked up one of the clear sacs and bit into it. "What *are* the risks, Soran? What happens if we draw too much power too quickly?"

Soran shrugged. "In layman's terms? Well, the xokronite would become fundamentally unstable. What happens after that would be extremely difficult to predict. That's why it's so dangerous—there's no real telling what would happen."

"Well, can you narrow it down, at least?"

"The xokronite could stabilise on its own once we lower the rate of energy transfer. That's certainly possible. If it doesn't, our safety equipment—the containment cylinder, the energy dampeners—would presumably kick in, cooling it, draining off excess radiation, and so forth. That might be enough to forcibly stabilise it." He rubbed his fingertips lightly against the stubble on his scalp. "But that is the best-case scenario. We *could,* on the other hand, initiate a fatal chain reaction in the xokronite—making it more and more unstable, until..."

Maya frowned. "Boom?"

"No, no. If only!" He shook his head, almost amused at the notion. "The containment cylinder can deal with an explosion—any explosion. You could let off a supernova in there and the outside of it wouldn't even feel warm to the touch. The end would come not with a *boom*, Maya, but with... well, with a whimper." He chuckled. "The xokronite would, in a case of catastrophic instability, degrade into something else entirely. Results vary as to what, depending on the original method of synthesis, but the best outcome I can think of in that scenario would be the chunk we have in our possession ending up as a lump of kronium-442. Which would supply a thousandth of the power required by the ship—perhaps enough to provide starvation rations from the food-synthesiser, if we could get it working under those conditions, but certainly not enough to power the perimeter-field."

There was a pause as all four of the crew took the information in. Maya found herself glancing at the perimeter-field, as if the mention of it might cause it to falter, or magically summon one of Unwen's #7Cs to attack it with tooth and claw. Munn, she noticed, hadn't taken his eyes off it once during the entire conversation.

After a moment, Soran resumed.

"The worst case scenario, of course, would be no power at all—no, no, I'm lying. There are far worse possibilities. When you're dealing with a substance that facilitates the transfer of energy through time, you have to open yourself to hypotheses that seem utterly outlandish—even divorced from known physics. We could all of us end up smeared across time like so much..." He stopped himself. "I shouldn't worry you with hypotheticals. The most likely danger here is losing the one power source we have—and if we lose the xokronite, we lose everything, what few comforts we have, and very likely our lives. It's simply not worth the risk."

Unwen scowled. "And we don't have any reserves?"

Soran smiled ruefully. "The storage batteries were irreparably damaged in the crash, I'm afraid. If we lost the xokronite, we'd have... perhaps three minutes of power? Enough time to evacuate the ship before the doors stopped working, I suppose. And even if they were in full working order, we'd never be able to top them up again—the end result would be the same. No power, no us."

Unwen nodded curtly and looked away.

"Soran..." Maya paused for a moment, choosing her words. "What is it about this... process... that drains the most power? In layman's terms."

"Oh, everything. You're talking about mutating living tissue—no, rewriting it—to bring it into line with some future descendant, millions of years ahead on the evolutionary tree. Now, the temporal rewrite—that's not too difficult. Copying a genetic map from a future descendant is what would really give us trouble..."

"Oh?" Maya was conscious of Unwen's eyes on her, but the biologist said nothing, waiting for her next move. Meanwhile, Soran rattled on, warming to the theme.

"Oh, yes. The problem here is that you want a *particular* descendant to map from. If we were just barrelling down the highway of genetics, grabbing what we found at a certain point *here,* or *there*—well, Unwen and I had no problems doing that before. Reaching deeper into the future shouldn't provoke a more significant power drain, but of course, the deeper you go, the less likely you are to find what you want..." He bit down on one of the yellow discs, considering. "We ourselves shared a common ancestor with hundreds of other species in the distant past of Habitat One—isn't that right, Unwen?"

"Thousands. Millions." Unwen shrugged. "Go back far enough, and you'll find a brother in the nester crouching in the walls of your domicell, eating scraps."

"Not that we'll ever see a nester again. Good riddance, too. Nasty things!" Soran scowled. "And this is where we start to have our power problem. You're looking for something specific—which, by the way, is at least six months of hard work for me and Unwen, since we two are the ones who have to tell the ship's brain what to look *for* in a language it might begin to understand—"

Unwen smiled sarcastically and opened his mouth to speak—to say something about Soran's real motivations at last coming to light—but a look from Maya made him close it again. Now was not the time.

"—and it's that search that will consume the additional energy. A task that will take almost every nanoprocessor the ship's brain has, working in parallel, searching through the millions of different possible species of mammal that might evolve over millions of years... an incredible energy drain." Soran shook his head firmly. "It would be easier to program in a genetic map from scratch—"

"Except programming genetic code from scratch requires a genetic library and programming software, which we do not have." Unwen scowled.

Soran ignored him. "And having taken this dreadful risk, we then do it over again, and again, and again, a hundred times—and when those hundred slaves die clearing the jungle of monsters, another hundred times, and another hundred after that. Even if we get lucky the first time—the first thousand times, the first thousand thousand—eventually, our number will come up, the xokronite will be corrupted and we'll be finished. The answer is no, Maya. I'm not helping you burn through our only energy resources for the sake of your obsession. Or Unwen's."

Silence descended on the group. Maya bit into another of the clear sacs, washing down what was in her mouth. Eventually, she spoke.

"Strictly speaking, it's only the first one that's the risk. Isn't it?"

Soran narrowed his eyes. "What do you mean?"

"Once we create that first hominid, we'll have the genetic map to create more, won't we?"

"Well—" Soran stuttered, looking uncomfortable. Maya didn't let him finish.

"Once we have that, these other thousand thousand slave-mammals you're so worried about will cost us practically no power at all. We'll probably be able to churn them out as easily as Unwen made his thumb-thing yesterday. Right?"

"Well... I suppose..."

"Just the one gamble, then. That's what you're worried about. You know what I think, Soran?" Her voice grew a hard edge. "I think you're trying to turn a small possibility of trouble into certain doom because you'd be happier doing nothing—spending the rest of eternity pottering about inside this field— and to hell with the rest of us."

Soran glanced at Munn for support, but he was quietly picking at a yellow disc, looking lost, his face ashen. He'd barely spoken since the #7C attacked the field the day before. Seeing no help there, Soran opened his mouth to defend himself, to try and convince Maya of the possible dangers, but—

—the earth shook.

Soran's mouth closed. Munn turned pale, looking as if he might be sick.

And again. Unwen stiffened, watching the mammals scampering and skittering away into the undergrowth and the trees. He heard Munn choke back a sob.

The fang-beast had returned.

This time, it did not attack the perimeter-field, or bellow its rage. It only stared at the four of them, through cold, reptilian eyes. The trickle of saliva from its jaws was a promise.

"We have to kill it," Munn whispered, his voice hoarse and cracked. "Whatever it takes. We have to kill it."

Maya nodded, turning to Soran.

"I think you're outvoted."

"THINK OF IT like this. We might be taking a small risk—*once*—but we've got no other options. Munn's already gone crazy in this bubble, and we'll all join him soon enough unless we put ourselves towards accomplishing something."

"Oh, shut up," Soran muttered, looking over at Maya petulantly. He'd tried to stop this from happening many times, refusing to work on the project, delaying things as much as possible, but he was a weak man at heart, and the pressure from the other three had been too much. Now his fingers gently tapped and danced over the display field, making the final connections.

The Power Room hummed, the blue stone inside the central pillar glowing and crackling with added power, and Unwen held one of the mammals in place inside a larger containment field—big enough to hold whatever it might become.

The experiment was ready to begin.

"Where *is* Munn?"

"Outside, staring at his three-horned beasts. Or at the jungle line, waiting for our regular visit from the big #7C. I'm sure he'll be overjoyed to meet our new friend, especially if we can train him to use this." Maya hefted the portable field generator, a squat metal box with two handles, a dial on each to be operated by the thumb—a primitive thing, slapped together by Soran in the little spare time he'd had in between programming the ship's brain over the past few months.

Unwen smiled, crouching to look the small beast in the eye. "We'll have to fit him with something to keep him obedient first. And then teach him what's expected of him. It'll be a slow process, but I have a feeling we might be ready to bag our first #7C in three to six months, depending on how quickly 'our new friend' picks up the basics, like eating synthesised food and disposing of his waste." He reached out, running a hand over the field, and the creature skittered back, nervous and unsure. Unwen liked that. "Next year, we'll know more about how to teach them, how to equip them. The year after that, we'll make some real progress. A mass cull. Farmland. Perhaps a solid-matter wall to keep the smaller predators out. I predict that within twenty years—perhaps even ten—the bubble will be a thing of the past."

Soran shot Unwen a look. "Perhaps sooner yet."

"Now, now, Soran. Let's not be defeatist." Unwen stood, taking a step back. "How long do you think it will take?"

"A minute. Less. If anything, I'll be trying to slow the process down."

Unwen looked at Maya, who nodded. "All right, Soren. Let's begin."

Soran hesitated, as if considering a last attempt to make the others see reason—then he brushed his fingertips over the control field, and the stone trapped inside the cylinder hummed into life. Within the containment field, the creature began to squeal, paws scrabbling against nothing, the blue glow invading its flesh.

"It'll work quickly," Soran murmured. "The power flow is a little higher than we expected... in fact..." His voice trailed off, and then his fingers began to move, jabbing at the field.

"What is it?" Unwen murmured, watching the animal jerk and twist in the field. The muscle groups were shifting, growing in size, the spine warping, legs elongating—but it seemed to be happening spasmodically, without rhyme or reason, as if some parts of the beast were evolving faster or slower than others. And all the time, the stone in the cylinder was glowing brighter, ever brighter. "Soran?"

"We have to shut it down! *Now!* The power drain is growing exponentially, it's as if—" He froze. "Oh. Oh, no, no, no, you *fools*—"

"Soran?" There was an edge in Maya's voice now. Inside the field, the animal began to scream.

So did the machinery. The stone glowed almost white now.

"We're taking genetic information from the thing's descendants, aren't we?" Soran's voice was trembling.

"Yes, but—"

"Except this animal is destined to die fighting a #7C! A fang-beast! We're going to send it out to be killed! It's not going to *have* any descendants! The machine's trying to resolve the paradox, and it's bending the universe out of shape to do it!"

Unwen turned, staring at Soran. "That's impossible—"

"Possible or not, it's happening! I have no idea what kind of kinks this is putting in the probability of events... we could be warping the whole structure of time, distorting the whole future..." He wiped sweat from his brow.

Maya grabbed his shoulder. "Concentrate on the here and now, Soran."

"Shut up!" Soran shrieked. "You caused this! You and that... that egomaniac with his delusions of godhood! Look at the stone! Look at it!" He waved his arms at the glowing white xokronite. "It's beyond unstable now—"

"Just turn it off!" Maya shouted to be heard above the shriek of the machinery and the humming of the stone.

"I can't. The controls aren't responding!" Soran raced towards the containment cylinder, shielding his eyes as he placed a hand against it. "I think the xokronite is coming unstuck in—"

There was a bright, white flash, and a section of the containment cylinder simply vanished. Soran stared for a moment, then put his hand into the break, as if wanting to make sure of it.

His fingers brushed the stone.

Then it flashed again, bright enough to make spots dance in front of Unwen's eyes. When they cleared, the xokronite was gone. So was Soran. So was a large section of the flooring he'd stood on.

Unwen and Maya stared at each other in horrified silence. From outside the ship, they heard Munn begin to scream. "The field! The field is down—"

Maya moved first, grabbing hold of the portable field generator they'd been working on, leaping nimbly over the hole in the flooring and running down the corridor towards the exit. Unwen watched her go, then turned to look at the shattered containment cylinder, the thing that had been able to withstand a supernova.

A first for science, he thought.

He felt oddly calm—calm enough to theorise, even. 'Unstuck,' Soran had said. Perhaps the cylinder had not been destroyed, exactly, Unwen thought. Perhaps it was just that a large part of it was now elsewhere in the temporal dimension. Along with Soran, the xokronite, and, of course, the metal flooring. Perhaps one of the outlandish hypotheses he'd mentioned during that fateful conversation a few months previously had involved the xokronite becoming unstuck in time.

It was a marvellous theory, made more marvellous by the fact that he would die before even beginning to find a way to prove it. It might just as well be true, at least to him. Soran and his magic stone. It had a certain fairytale quality to it.

The earth underneath him shook.

Of course. The #7C, which he'd arrogantly attempted to tame by assigning it a number and a classification, had returned to show him the folly of all his ridiculous theories. How just.

Another tremor. He heard Munn's scream, mixing with a terrible roar. Munn got halfway through another scream, and then there were some loud, wet sounds Unwen didn't feel like speculating on.

Perhaps Munn's sacrifice would give Maya time to get away. He hoped so. Perhaps she would even survive.

He glanced over at the flickering spherical field, and the animal trapped inside it that looked so very much like a man.

It looked back at him with wet, blinking eyes, unable to comprehend what it had become. Unwen smiled, and reached out a hand to bless his creation. A God could do no less.

Then he walked outside the ship, to meet the Tyrannosaur.

THE PRINTER'S DEVIL

The Body of
B. Franklin, Printer,
Like the Cover of an old Book,
Its Contents torn out,
And stript of its Lettering & Gilding,
Lies here, Food for Worms.

—Ben Franklin's self-penned
epitaph, written in 1728. He was 22.

IN THE DREAM, *the kite flaps in a bitter wind, rain pelting the canvas...*

THE OLD SPRUCE in the yard no longer burns.

The tree was set afire by lightning towards the end of the storm, as if the Lord was signing the symphony of wind and rain and thunder with a final flourish, an exclamation point. *You may tame the earth,* He tells us in our hubris. *You may make a toy of fire. But the lightning is Mine, and there is no man who may tame or control it.*

Saul was able to quell the flames in short order by forming a human chain to ferry buckets from the nearby riverbank to the site of the blaze, composed of his fellow slaves and a smattering of indentured servants. If any of the big Germans felt umbrage at taking orders from a negro, they did not show it, and the fire was soon halted. My hat is off to young Saul, who is as much an asset to the plantation as his father was. Would that I had it in my power to reward him adequately, but my uncle has made it painfully clear that my opinions count for little in the running of things here. I am merely unwanted baggage, fed and housed out of a sense of obligation to a man I despised. Were I a man of spirit—had I any shred of self-respect at all—I would leave this place, where I am so clearly surplus to requirements, and make my own way in the world. But I am not, and I have not, and things are as they are.

Writing this, I am reminded that next week will mark the third anniversary of Abraham's passing. It is clear Saul misses him dearly, as do I. Would that my own father had been as gentle and kind a man as Abraham, or, for that matter, as steadfast and noble a man as Donato Scorpio, but, again, things are as they are.

One day I will have that inscribed on my tombstone.

Scorpio is long gone now, of course. He vanished from my life more than twenty years ago, and with Abraham dead and the state of Pennsylvania far behind me I suppose there is no harm in telling the story of how he and my father left my life on the very same night—if only here, in the pages of this journal. And yet a part of me hesitates at the thought of finally committing the tale to paper. Perhaps it feels too much like a confession written by a man condemned.

Well then, let it be a confession, for God knows I feel I have much to confess. My name is Robert James Steele, and in the year 1728, at the age of ten, I caused my father's death.

Is that too strong a manner of wording it? Perhaps. Mine was not the hand that struck him down, but he died so I might survive, and there are days when the guilt of that survival weighs heavy upon me, a black shroud that settles over my soul. During such times I find myself retreating from the sight of men to spend the day alone in my chambers. I find myself wondering, on those days, how my life would have gone had he lived. Eventually, I suppose, I would have inherited the farm, become an owner of my own land, rather than a guest on someone else's. Perhaps I would have sold it, and taken some other profession, though the Lord only knows what. Perhaps he would have killed me first, as he killed my mother. But certainly I would have stayed in Philadelphia. Alive or dead, I would have stayed.

I feel dead now. I feel as if something has left me, or left the world—as if a vital actor has been lost from the play, and the cast is ad-libbing desperately, hoping that they can please whatever looks down on them from the darkness of the balcony. Sometimes, I dream...

But I digress. This is the story of three deaths—my father's, my own, and the catalyst for both. In the middle of the night, he was abducted, bound, taken to the top field of my father's farm and stabbed nine times, in the throat, chest and gut. His genitals were severed and placed in his mouth, and he was then buried in a shallow grave. Too shallow by far—for coyotes unearthed the body, dragging it from its hole and gnawing on it until they had eaten their fill.

Whereupon they left the remains for me to find.

IN THE DREAM, *there is the crack of thunder from far away, and the kite looks very small against the dark of the sky...*

I REMEMBER ALMOST nothing of my mother; a smell, a smile, the light catching russet hair. She died when I was two years old. My first real memory is of a man with kindly eyes and a timorous smile looming over me, asking if I was all right. the Undertaker.

My father, soaked in liquor after a night carousing in the town, struck her for some imagined slight, and as a result she lost her footing, struck her head on the jutting edge of the fireplace, and stove in the back of her skull. The Sheriff, a gruff and hard-faced man named Landon Reed, declared the death a ghastly accident—perhaps he was unaware of my father's nature, though given later events I doubt it.

The incident was spoken of rarely, and until I was eight I had no idea of the specifics at all. (Even then it was Abraham who told me what had occurred, after much urging. He begged me to keep the knowledge to myself, lest he take the blame for spreading the grim particulars, and—knowing the depths of my father's temper—I gladly honoured his request.)

I suppose it is to my father's credit that my mother's death spurred him to give up use of alcohol entirely. However, for him temperance was yet another kind of intoxicant—his sudden adherence to the cause replaced the irrational rage of the drunk with the seemingly rational anger of the overly righteous. In particular, he became obsessed with moral philosophy and the proper punishment of crimes, holding long debates on the subject with whoever would hear him and publishing at least one pamphlet on the subject. Perhaps it was a reaction to the knowledge that he never answered for the drunken manslaughter he committed, although if he felt any guilt over Mother, he never admitted it to me or any other living soul.

While his philosophies never seemed to apply to his own crimes, I was not so fortunate. As I grew up I was perpetually aware that the slightest offence—real or imagined—would result in him ordering me to fetch the heavy leather strap that hung on a nail in his study, whereupon he would 'teach me my lesson,' as he put it. He spent little time with me as it was, being more concerned with the running of the farm and his growing reputation in the town as a man of letters, and this vengeful and unpredictable streak ensured that I avoided him as best I could.

My time was thus spent either in my studies—I was tutored by a stern man named James Newton, who has recently made a great noise on the subjects of education and, more controversially, the uniting of the colonies for better defence—or at play in the fields. Father would beat me for being too familiar with the field slaves, but he saw conversation with those indentured servants working our crops as being of benefit; perhaps he envisaged their rough and ready nature rubbing off on my own slight frame, so that, like them, I would eventually sprout broad shoulders and a strong back. It was not to be.

To the workers in the fields, I was mostly a part of the landscape, and they spoke to me with a forced respect that betrayed their contempt. However, a few did take to me, in particular a tough, quick-witted Italian named Donato Scorpio, who referred to me as 'Generalissimo'—some private joke of his own. He thought nothing of downing his tools for half an hour to join Abraham and me in a brief game of soldiers or a romp through the woods. His popularity was such that a blind eye was usually turned to this, provided he made up the time in some way after the others had finished their labour; no doubt had my father known of this kindness, Scorpio would have been whipped and the overseer who allowed it dismissed from his duties.

My more constant companion, in rain or shine, was Abraham. I have mentioned him several times in the course of this narrative, but it occurs to me that I have not yet offered the hypothetical reader any information as to who he was. Should any eyes but mine read these pages, let me humbly beg their indulgence.

Abraham was a house slave, and his nominal task was to keep me out of trouble, and if I were to get into any trouble, to report it—thus saving my father the troublesome duty of raising his offspring. Abraham had other duties, but his was the lightest load of any of the house slaves, and they rarely let him forget it; the field slaves, meanwhile, hardly spoke to him at all.

I suffered from a lack of friends also, being shy and withdrawn around other children in the town, who responded to my reticence by bullying and taunting me without mercy, until I withdrew to the confines of the farm and grounds; thus, we were lonely together. Still, I was a happy boy, knowing no better and content with my world, and if Abraham ever grew weary of spending his days looking after his Master's son, or yearned for better conversation or stimulation than I in my youth could provide, he was gracious enough not to show it.

I suppose, then, that I had three fathers—my natural father, a judgemental and remote presence that I associated with loss, Abraham, the protector who kept me from harm and made sure I ate what was put before me, and Donato Scorpio, the role model I looked up to and hoped somehow to emulate, despite my slight frame and quiet disposition. And in a sense, my story begins with him, for the day I found the body was the day Scorpio was to leave my father's employ. His four-year term was up, and in a matter of days, certainly no longer than a month, he would be leaving Philadelphia to travel across the country and find more rewarding work elsewhere. I was heartbroken, of course, and I'm sure I drove Abraham to distraction with my petulance, stomping sullenly around the outskirts of the grounds and calling him and Scorpio all manner of unpleasant names.

It was while engaged in this ugly activity that I saw something in the woods at the edge of the top field, which lay fallow and deserted: a hole dug in the earth, just beyond the treeline, with what looked like a large and mangled animal lying half-in and half-out of it. Against Abraham's shouted advice, I crept closer to investigate further, and saw to my considerable shock that the animal was wearing a suit of clothes.

That was my first sight of the printer, Benjamin Franklin.

IN THE DREAM, *the kite loops and glides, dances and spins. It is heavier than it should be. Something is tied to the end of the string, next to the tail...*

* * *

I SHUDDER NOW when I picture his corpse in my mind, butchered at the hands of man and the teeth and claws of nature. But perhaps in my youth I was made of hardier stuff, for mixed in with the shock, horror and nausea I felt at the discovery, there was a kind of wild excitement, a thrill at being the discoverer of this grisly sight, at seeing something not meant to be seen, certainly not by one my age. Abraham tremulously warned me away, but I crept closer, wanting to see everything despite myself.

I assumed at first that the printer had been attacked and killed by some group of large animals, like bears or wolves, but Abraham, looking over the corpse, divined the truth—the printer had been stabbed with a man-made knife rather than gored by an animal's fang or claw, and had been buried by his killer. After that, he had been exhumed from his grave by passing scavengers.

I went straight to my father, which was foolish of me. His first thought on hearing the news was to order Abraham whipped, as though he was somehow responsible for my discovery. I protested, and he ordered me to fetch the strap; I refused, and he brought it himself, and beat me until rivulets of blood ran down to my ankles.

After that, he hand-picked a couple of the field slaves to re-bury the body in a deeper hole. He swore them to secrecy, hinting darkly that if they spoke of the matter to anyone, they would hang for it—to my knowledge, they took the threat seriously and kept their own counsel. As for me, Father forbade me from speaking further on the matter. The man, he said, was undoubtedly a drifter, murdered by another drifter, and that was all there was to it.

Perhaps I should have taken his heed, but I felt that I could not let the matter lie. Drifter or no, this was still a man, and in need of man's justice; thus, risking my father's displeasure, I decided to consult my tutor, the aforementioned Dr James Newton, telling him all I knew about the body, and asking if my father was right to react the way he did. I shall always remember his words to me then:

"Idle gossip, Robert, is something I do not and will not tolerate."

He went immediately to my father, who stormed into the room and bade me fetch the strap again. Father proceeded to thrash me until I bled afresh, welts landing atop welts, and this time he did not feel the need to stop, even when I passed out from the pain of the blows. The wounds I suffered were so severe that I was bedridden for several days.

I lay in a state of fever, pain-wracked and delirious—doubtless the result of an infection of the wounds, though Abraham cleaned and dressed them admirably. He stayed by my bedside as I lay, mumbling in the grip of terrible hallucinations, seeing the mutilated face of the body I had found floating at the foot of the bed, whispering terrible secrets to me that I can no longer quite recall—except in my dreams.

Occasionally, Franklin's grotesque, torn head would lapse into great oratories on taxation and similar political matters that I could not at the time comprehend and do not remember with any clarity now. On these occasions it would often be replaced in mid-speech by the face of Newton, and though the cadence changed, the subject matter remained. At other times, my father's bloodless visage would float above my head, the skull smashed, and it would stare at me accusingly even through closed eyelids. Occasionally, the dead face that haunted me would be my own, although no wound was apparent. This last apparition would never fail to make me scream until there was no air in my lungs; Abraham told me later that during these episodes he could not help but weep to see me so transported.

My father shed no tears, nor did he visit. When I was finally well enough to eat at the table, he acknowledged my presence with a curt nod—nothing more.

I, for my part, was grateful to have survived my illness and my visions, and thought nothing more of them. Now, I can only wonder what message those grim visitations were trying to impart.

IN THE DREAM, *the storm is getting closer, and the pull of the wind bids to tear the kite from its frail human mooring, but the man does not let go of the string...*

ABRAHAM, FEARFUL OF my father's continued wrath, urged me to let the matter drop; however, although my fever had broken and I was regaining my strength, the printer's face continued to haunt my sleeping hours, and I found my waking ones consumed by thoughts of who he might have been and how he came to such an ignominious end. Surely, I thought to myself, it was neither right nor Christian that a man simply be buried and forgotten like that, with no grave marker to signify his passing.

Plagued by these thoughts, I eventually persuaded Abraham to accompany me into the town to see the Sheriff, Landon Reed. I knew that talking to a man of such authority would create terrible trouble, for he would surely swoop down on our farm like all the angels of God, demanding to know why my father and my tutor had conspired to hide the murder of a man from the public record, and yet my young conscience would allow me no other recourse. The Sheriff, I was told, was not in his office, and so I decided, against Abraham's better judgement, that we should see him at home. Trembling, I knocked upon the door, and when it opened the whole story flowed out of me as if a dam had burst.

Landon Reed listened with a weary ear, his face drawn and haggard, and then quietly informed me that I was a very foolish boy, and I should pay attention to my betters and keep my nose out of what did not concern me. He would forbear from informing my father of my foolish excursion, since to his mind I had suffered enough, but I was to go home at once and forget the entire business, or at least speak of it to no other living soul. Having officiated at the death of my mother, I can only assume that he knew full well that were he to tell my father of my visit, the next beating would likely lead to another death in the Steele household.

As he closed the door on me, I caught a glimpse of Reed's daughter Deborah, a young and pretty girl and much admired about the town. She was crying inconsolably.

All my expectations had come crashing down around my ears, and I was left confused and stranded, seemingly without further recourse. I had no idea of who to turn to next, and when Abraham quietly suggested that we make our way home before my father noticed I was gone, as if such a thing were likely, I could only nod in dumb acquiescence.

It was at that moment that I saw Donato Scorpio again.

He was emerging from a hostelry with a wide grin, doubtless after some great gambling win or priapic exploit, and when he saw Abraham and me, he bounded over, shaking Abraham by the hand and tousling my hair. Glad though I was to see him, my spirits were still in low condition from my encounter with the Sheriff, and at first he assumed I was sulking because he had left my father's employ, and planned to leave the state of Pennsylvania entirely as soon as he had decided where to go; the Newfoundland settlements, he thought. He was relentless in curing me of my sour mood, allowing me the rare treat of riding atop his shoulders and telling stories of all the fishing he would be doing when he reached Newfoundland, but I retained my sullen demeanour and eventually the truth came out.

Scorpio reacted with disbelief at first, then astonishment, then anger at my father, who he had little respect for, and my tutor, who he considered firmly in the wrong on the issue. When I related the meeting I had just had with the Sheriff, his emotions circled again to open disbelief. He did not think me a liar, but such a reaction from a man ostensibly tasked with upholding the cause of justice seemed to him so bizarre as to defy all credibility. Surely I must have misunderstood?

I insisted that I had not, and gradually he came to understand that I was telling the unvarnished truth. I had up until this point assumed that it was I who was somehow in the wrong, for surely all of these figures of authority must know more of such situations than a young boy, but seeing Donato Scorpio so astonished by their behaviour brought home how right I had been. Something was rotten in the house of Denmark, and Scorpio declared that he would investigate to the best of his ability on my behalf, that we might all know the plain truth of the matter, starting with the assumption that Landon Reed, Dr Newton and my father evidently had some unknown reason to see this killing hidden from the eyes of men.

I thanked him profusely, feeling truly confident for the first time since the sorry business began, for I knew that Scorpio would not fail me, neither in this regard nor in any other. Abraham, likewise, seemed buoyed by the promise of some resolution to my private sorrows; however, on the trail home, his spirits fell, and he muttered darkly that such a path would lead to unforeseen consequences, and perhaps we had set things in motion better left alone. I refused to hear him. He was an uneducated slave, I told myself, and I put his qualms down to some innate superstition that I imagined was common to his race.

I was a foolish child, and Abraham a wiser man that I will ever be. I was delving into an open, festering sore that it was far beyond my power to heal; there would be precious little justice done as a result of my actions, and the price for them would be far, far higher than I would ever have chosen to pay.

IN THE DREAM, *the storm is coming closer and closer, and the man pulls down the string, carefully tying it to a wooden stake, firmly hammered into the wet ground...*

* * *

I SPENT THE next two days dividing my time between my studies and my usual leisure pursuits of watching the men in the fields and wandering the farm, though I was forbidden from the top field and knew better than to risk a further beating by disobeying my father's edict. The time seemed to pass slowly, agonisingly, as I waited for any word from Scorpio. It crossed my mind that he may have been simply humouring me, or that he had asked a few questions and then given up, and that thought made the time pass even slower. I languished in my studies, prompting stern lectures from Dr Newton, and in my playtime I would trudge morosely up the trail leading to the town and sit at the side of the road for long spells, greeting each passing rider with renewed hope, only to be disappointed again.

At the end of the Friday, after a seeming eternity of waiting, I sat in my room and stared angrily at the ceiling, listening to the sound of the wind and rain outside my window as a flickering candle picked out the shadows on the wall. The air all day had been uncomfortably humid, and the storm finally broke at sunset, a deluge unlike any in my short memory that seemed on a par with the Biblical flood; on another day, I would have listened excitedly to each crack of thunder, gasped in mingled fear and delight at each flash of lightning, but now I simply lay on my bed and sulked. My father had left the house earlier that evening to attend some meeting of philosophical minds, so I was free to stay up as I pleased; Abraham would occasionally poke his head into the room and see how I was keeping and enquire when I planned to settle down for the night, and each time I would simply scowl at him, as though he were the root cause of all my woes. He did not deserve such treatment from an ungrateful boy, and I bitterly regret it now, especially in light of that evening's events.

Just as I was about to blow out the candle and prepare for another sleepless night, there came a gentle tapping on the shutters, and I opened the window to see Donato Scorpio stood in the pouring rain, with a look upon his face as though he had ridden straight from Hell with all the devils of the underworld at his heels. Ashen, he whispered to me to let him in, and I did as I was bid.

And there, as the thunderstorm raged and the lightning arced across the sky, he told me the dreadful story of the printer, and of how his body had come to lie in that shallow grave.

* * *

IN THE DREAM, *the kite flutters and soars in the midst of the raging storm, and the man watches the glint of metal at its tail—the glint of an iron key, tied securely to the frame, the key to a new world, a bright future of light and power, the key that will unlock doors to knowledge undreamed of, the key to the future of the human race...*

DONATO SCORPIO WAS not a man used to the solving of mysteries, but he did pay attention to local talk, and the recent chatter in the town had concerned the Sheriff's daughter, the same girl I had glimpsed weeping when I visited him at his home. The local scandalmongers had it that the poor girl had been involved in some dalliance with a printer named Benjamin Franklin, and some gossips even claimed that he had left her with child. Franklin had since vanished from the town, apparently leaving his home unoccupied and his business in the hands of his partner, Hugh Meredith, all without a backward glance. There was talk that he had somehow learned of the pregnancy and swiftly fled before he could be forced to marry the girl; although the existence of the prospective child was naught but rumour and hearsay, most had come to accept this explanation as the gospel truth.

As Scorpio recounted this, I felt the blood run from my face and my knees weaken with the shock. The gossip of adults rarely reached my ears, and until that moment I had possessed no inkling that the body was not that of a wandering drifter, as Father had maintained. But now there could be no doubt that the missing man and the corpse twice-buried on the outskirts of our property were one and the same. For a moment, in my childish innocence, I wondered how the Sheriff could have remained so unmoved by my story, given that the vanished printer was so closely connected to his own family; but then the scales fell from my eyes and understanding dawned.

Was that the moment of my death? It was as if I, like Adam, had bitten into the fruit of knowledge, for I had in that terrible instant gleaned the hideous wisdom of adulthood, and the taste was sour and bitter and reeked of corruption. Like Adam, I in that moment saw humanity for what it was—a naked, rutting animal!—and, like him, I would never know even the meagre paradise my innocence had afforded me again.

I staggered back, sitting on my bed as my legs finally gave way, and though my mouth fell open I found I could not speak.

Of course Landon Reed had known.

He must have known from the start that the body I had spoken to him of was the same man who had lain with his only child; I was not too young to know that here was motive enough to leave the crime uninvestigated, if not to commit it. Stammering, I asked Scorpio directly: was our Sheriff the murderer? Had the man we entrusted with the keeping of the law committed this most grievous breach against it?

I should have known nothing could be so simple.

There was a long pause from my friend, as he weighed in his mind whether to leave me my illusions. But the world is cruel, and Donato Scorpio knew it better than most; so he took a breath, steeled himself, and told me of the Junto.

IN THE DREAM, *an arc of blue-white light streaks down from heaven to the kite and the key, and God's finger brushes Adam's, and Prometheus brings the first fire to mankind...*

BENJAMIN FRANKLIN WAS a man with a quick wit and a powerful mind. In his native town of Boston, he had written various amusing letters for *The New-England Courant,* the famed news-sheet, albeit via subterfuge; as his brother, the editor, would not take the work from his hand, he slipped them under his door while hiding under the pseudonym of a middle-aged widow, a ruse that ensured fourteen of the missives saw print. Would that I had possessed such spirit at the age of sixteen! However, I was already well set on my present course, journeying into lassitude and despair. Franklin fled his apprenticeship in the face of his brother's wrath; I cannot bring myself to quit a household I have grown to despise.

On arriving in Philadelphia, he spoke often of his desire to found a news-sheet in his new home, even colluding at one point with the Governor of Pennsylvania on the matter; however, despite a sojourn in London ostensibly for the purpose, the idea came to naught, and he soon returned to Philadelphia and his old calling once again. Still, that mind hungered for debate, for discourse, for *ideas.* All who know Franklin agreed on the spark of intelligence that lit him from within; who can say what that spark might have achieved, had it not been freed so summarily from its mortal shell?

The spark did achieve one thing before being so brutally extinguished, and that was the formation of the Junto.

The Junto was a group dedicated to the mutual improvement of its members by means of weekly debates on matters moral, political and philosophical, and to begin with its members were selected by Franklin himself, including his colleagues in the printing trade and various local businessmen whom he had encountered socially. It was by all accounts a fine idea, and a means of discussing ways to improve the community; Franklin himself posited such ideas as a group of men tasked to put out fires, a collected repository of books, and a hospital for public use.

Or was that Newton?

I am, I fear, confusing the narrative. None of this was related to me by Donato Scorpio; these were details I found out later, through correspondence with many of the original members. So broken was I that while other boys my age were learning trades and courting their future wives and seeing the world, I was sat in a lonely room provided by a hated Uncle, writing letter after letter in an attempt to force the world to make sense.

And here I have the entire story, and it *still* does not make sense.

James Newton was the thirteenth member of the Junto, and I am convinced he should never have joined. But how could Franklin not invite him? Newton was an intellect on a par with Franklin's own, and quite possibly the only man in the town who could say such. According to Meredith's account, meetings would often last into the small hours as the two men sparred and jousted with words and concepts, always on opposite sides; for Newton seemed to lack the essential humanity of Franklin, the dusty tutor acting as a dark twin, a mirror-self...

When I say that Newton should never have joined, perhaps what I mean is that Newton should never have existed at all.

Still, he did. George Webb assured me in a long letter that it was Newton who first posited the concept of the neighbourhood watch, while Joseph Breitnall would have me believe it was Franklin; what is certain is that the ideas of the two men overlapped to an astonishing degree, and yet always with that crucial difference between warm and cool, a smile and a frown...

If Franklin had intended to create a philosophical Eden, Newton was the serpent. Although the Junto had no official hierarchy, Franklin was their *de facto* leader, and Newton swiftly made himself co-leader by virtue of his intellect and his powers of persuasion. Although there was no warmth in him, he had the power of cold logic on his side; that was often enough to bend his critics to his will, against their own best judgement. Having secured a place alongside Franklin, he began to force out Franklin's old friends and co-workers, recruiting others to take their places; my father was one of them, for Newton's cold demeanour appealed to his own stringency. Then there was the Sheriff, and eight others besides. Breitnall was the last to leave, unable to bear the increasing rancour of the discussions, or the puritanical element that had entered into the gathering; on the way out of his last meeting, he warned Franklin to watch himself, or better yet, end the Junto as was and let the newcomers be what they wished under their own name. On learning of Franklin's disappearance, he assumed the printer had returned to London, throwing himself on the open ocean in sheer disgust at what his grand plans had come to; I had not the heart to disabuse him.

Donato Scorpio, suspecting Newton and my father were as much involved as he presumed the Sheriff to be, made the decision to discreetly follow my tutor on the night of the storm. It was one week after the murder, and the Junto convened to discuss the matter. Listening at the window, Scorpio heard it all. Some of the newcomers were shaken, and Landon Reed was disgusted with himself, while my father and Newton felt they had committed no sin, and they debated on the moral implications of their act long into the night, and in this manner Scorpio came to know everything.

The Friday previous, the Junto had convened, and Franklin had made his intention to disband the group clear; no longer would it continue in its present form. He would form his own society, with the friends whose company he had previously enjoyed, and allow Newton's icy version to continue as a separate entity. Newton agreed, in principle; but there was a formality to attend to first.

He had to ask the questions.

Every meeting of the Junto revolved around them; a list of twenty-four questions devised by Franklin to promote debate and discourse among the assembled company.

Question the sixth: *Do you know of any fellow citizen, who has lately done a worthy action, deserving praise and imitation? Or who has committed an error proper for us to be warned against and avoid?*

And the answer came back: "*Franklin! Franklin has committed the error!*"

Franklin protested, but the questioning continued.

Question the seventh: *What unhappy effects of intemperance have you lately observed or heard? Of imprudence? Of passion? Or of any other vice or folly?*

"*Franklin! Franklin is intemperate! Imprudent! Franklin's passion is vice and folly!*"

And on, and on, and with each new question the wrath of this circle grew. Veins throbbed, and hands clenched, and all the time, Newton watched, sinister as any serpent.

Question the nineteenth: *Hath any man injured you, from whom it is in the power of the Junto to procure redress?*

And at this, the Sheriff stood up quickly enough to knock over his chair, pointed a finger at the trembling Franklin, and screamed: "*He made of my daughter a whore!*"

At this point, Franklin tried to escape; but the door was firmly locked, and the questions continued incxorably, despite his desperate, unheard pleas.

Question the twenty-fourth and last: *Do you see any thing amiss in the present customs or proceedings of the Junto, which might be amended?*

"*Franklin lives!*" came the cry from ten throats. "*Franklin lives! Franklin lives!*"

And as one, they fell upon him.

He was beaten senseless, and dragged in the dead of night up to my father's top field. The Sheriff, feeling unable when the moment came to involve himself directly, stood watch; Newton, for his part, merely looked on. The other nine—good, noble men of Philadelphia!—each plunged their knife up to the hilt into Franklin. I pray to God he was not awake for it! I pray to whatever God or Devil will hear it that he was not still alive when they severed his organs of generation and forced them into his mouth!

I pray he was not alive for the burial!

Scorpio did not stay for the full meeting, but slipped away to report back to me. He had agonised about whether or not to let me know the full truth, and I could not tell you to this day if he thought it was worthwhile; for myself, I would say that it was that awful truth that slew whatever force of life lay in me, leaving me the shell I am today. And yet, perhaps it is better to have the truth, and not a lie, no matter how painful the truth may be.

And it was a painful truth indeed. For my father had also left that meeting early, and he had returned home to hear Scorpio in the middle of his tale. He had silently listened himself, long enough to know that I had defied him a third time. He had listened, and the rage had built in him slowly, and now his face was a livid purple and his hands clenched so hard his knuckles were white.

And he stood in my doorway to kill me.

* * *

IN THE DREAM, *the lightning strikes the key and travels down the string, crackling like fire, proving a point, creating a future, and when it hits the wooden stake buried in the earth it sets it alight, and the flames illuminate the face of Benjamin Franklin, forty-four years old and only begun...*

SCORPIO PUT UP his fists, but too late; Father hit him hard enough to black his eye and send him crashing to the floor like a sack of potatoes. Then my father's hands were around my throat, squeezing my windpipe shut, and his eyes contained nothing but fury and madness. Perhaps it was the poison Newton whispered in his ear, or perhaps he had been drinking, or perhaps this was my father's true face.

What did it matter? He had come too late to kill me, for I had already died. All he could do was wring the life from a corpse.

He sensed my lassitude, my apathetic refusal to fear him, and it seemed to enrage him still further. I felt him prepare to snap my meagre neck...

Then, abruptly, there came the sound of crunching bone, his eyes rolled back in his head, his grip loosened and he fell to the floor, quite dead. Abraham, hearing the commotion, had run into the room and stove in his Master's skull with a candlestick.

I feel grateful to him, even thought he only saved a husk; for he must have known the penalty for such an act. Scorpio said it first, upon regaining his full consciousness. Should anyone find out what Abraham had done, he would instantly be hanged.

I, in my shock and to my shame, was beyond caring, and Scorpio did the only thing he felt he could. He took the candlestick in his own hand, explaining that he would run through the house and let the other slaves get a good look at him. He would take the blame upon his own head, for he felt he was more capable of running and hiding from the forces of law, having done it many times before; in fact, it was a problem with the authorities in Italy that had necessitated his journey to Philadelphia. Abraham, to his credit, tried to talk Scorpio out of it, but one of the maids walked in as Scorpio hefted the candlestick, and after that the plan was in motion whether it was agreed or not; Scorpio punched Abraham in the face for verisimilitude, barged past the maid, and was away.

The crime followed him. Four months later he was hanged for it in the port of New York, where he was living in sin with a negress; rumour has it she took his name after, and even bore his child.

Abraham, as I have said, died only recently. My father left his farm and his slaves to my uncle, Jebediah Steele, who sold everything off at a pretty profit, save for Abraham, who I insisted come with me. The two of us made the long journey down to Texas, where my uncle put Abraham to work in the fields; having been a house-slave all of his life, his constitution was not best suited to the work and he began to grow sickly. At the same time, his quick mind grew dull under the rigors of the work and the brutal treatment of my uncle. Where once his conversation was lively and his head was high, now he slumped and barely had a word to say. I soon stopped talking with him on any regular basis, though he will always mean the world to me.

The truth of Benjamin Franklin's death never came out, of course; nobody would have taken a boy's word and a slave's against the great James Newton. I have followed the latter's career with some dread, as he seems to be making increasing inroads into the political sphere. I cannot help but wonder whether Franklin, had he survived and somehow ended Newton—had he even known the nature of the strange, unholy duel Newton had fought against him—would have walked the same path. What would the course of our nation have been like? A shade warmer, certainly, which would be no bad thing.

Benjamin Franklin still lies in the soil underneath the fields that were once owned by my family, but his spirit is not entirely gone from Philadelphia. The town gossips were right, and Deborah Reed was with child, a fine boy she called Franklin; for she never stopped loving him, even when he vanished from her life so completely, without a goodbye. He is now twenty-two himself, and in matters of intelligence, the son seems likely to eclipse the father.

He has just invented a wonderful device called a steam engine.

Perhaps one day I will find the strength to hurl myself underneath it.

THE DREAM IS coming to an end, and I will forget all but the vaguest impression of it. Benjamin Franklin has finished his show of magic, having harnessed the lightning with kite and key, and brought it down for man to play with; he does not speak, but he turns to his audience, gives a small bow, and offers the dreamer a warm, broad smile that speaks for him. The memory of the dream will fade, yes; but the dream goes on.

The dream goes on.

But the work shall not be lost;
For it will, as he believd, appear once more
In a new and more elegant Edition
Corrected and improved
By the Author.

—Ben Franklin's epitaph.

THE LONESOME RIDER AND THE LOCOMOTIVE MAN

THOMAS STOOD ATOP the mesa and looked down at what was left of his hand.

Most of the flesh had rotted away from the fingers, so that the white bone peeped mockingly through. He felt no pain—just a tingling warmth at the end of his left arm, and then nothing beyond.

He could not let go of the stone.

He mopped the sweat from his brow with his good hand, licked his dry lips, and concentrated. Tiny bursts of galvanic power crackled over his skin, and his matted black hair began to rise slowly from his brow until it was standing straight up on his head. Almost against his will, he found himself smiling, a madman's idiot-grin. He couldn't help himself. The power running down his arm, across his chest, pulsing and throbbing in every part of his body—he'd never felt anything like it. No-one ever had.

When the soles of his worn-out shoes left the ground, he barely noticed.

He blinked the sweat from his eyes, looking up now, concentrating on the makeshift scarecrow he'd built, standing in front of him. The effigy. The target.

The power was building inside him, and that good, hot, tingling feeling was growing more intense, a sensation of pins and needles across his arm and back, like some crawling insect or a lover's touch.

He held his breath.

After six seconds, perhaps a little more, the prickling sensation intensified, becoming pain, then agony, roaring over his flesh like fire and quickly becoming too much to bear. He held it as long as he could, gritting his teeth, until the stone glowed a bright white and the mesa below him seemed to fade and shimmer—and then he forced the power out of him with a high, thin scream, directing it through the stone, at the head of the dummy.

Lightning arced across the space between them, blinding him for a moment. When his sight returned, the scarecrow was on fire.

Slowly, he succumbed to gravity, his feet drifting back to rest on the rock. He realised that he was grinning again. He wanted to laugh, to laugh and laugh and never stop, but he just didn't have time. He had to make the long walk down into the town. He had a telegram to send.

He would send it that very day, and soon after that, the man who'd tried to destroy him, who'd treated him more cruelly than any of them, his enemy... his enemy would come to him. Come and be burned like the scarecrow. And after his enemy was dead, he would begin to build his new America.

Eyes dancing under a mane of wild black hair, Thomas Alva Edison licked his lips and spoke his enemy's name.

"*Westinghouse.*"

"Hey, boy!"

The man in black finished securing his horse to the rail, giving no heed to the words. Jonah snorted, stamping his hooves—he was a fine horse with fine ears, a sagacious animal who knew a jackass when he heard one. The man patted his flank, gently, so as to calm him down some. A jackass wasn't nothing worth getting upset over, after all.

"Hey! *Boy!* I'm *talkin'* to you!"

Then again, it never did to let a jackass get away with being a jackass. He'd only be a jackass again.

The man in black frowned, looking over towards the office George kept in the town—he could see some young fella in a brown suit and round glasses in George's window, looking out at him. Some accountant or secretary, most likely.

"You *hear* me, boy? You deaf, or just yeller?"

Loud laughter.

Hell with it. Give the accountant a show.

The man in black turned around and took stock of the situation. Four men, a little drunk in spite of the early hour. Cowhands, by the look of 'em. Big fellas—the one talking was about a half a head bigger than he was, and he was a good six foot. Rounder, too, so that was all right.

The man lifted the brim of his black hat a tad and shot the jackasses a hard look. "Took four of you to say that?"

The ringleader—the big talker—sneered and looked around at his sidekicks for support. "Only takes the one of me to handle your kind, boy."

He spat. The man in black's eyes narrowed, and when he spoke, there was gravel in his tone.

"I got a name, mister. Figure you might know it."

"Aw, sure I do!" The big talker guffawed, sneaking another quick glance at his fellow rowdies to make sure they were with him, and a beat later they were laughing right along, sure enough. "Why, you're Jacob Steele, ain't you, boy? The famous Lonesome Rider of the plains, isn't that right? Well, we done heard *all* kinds of stories 'bout *you*, boy!"

Jacob Steele nodded curtly, pulling a cigar from the inside pocket of his black duster coat. "Is that right. Well, mister, I should tell you a lot of them stories the newspaper boys tell... they ain't entirely correct."

The big talker laughed again, turning back to his coterie. He didn't seem to be able to say a word without checking it with them first. Bad quality in a leader of men.

"Didn't I say so, fellas? Huh? Didn't I say there weren't no negro could outgun a hundred men?"

A small crowd was gathering. A couple of them nudged each other and grinned—jackasses in training. Steele shook his head, amused despite himself.

"Well, now. Is that what they say about me? That I done put a hundred men in the dirt? Well, don't that beat all." He chuckled softly, holding a flickering match to the end of the cigar.

His eyes narrowed.

"Truth is, it was a hundred thirty-six."

The men stopped laughing.

"And every single one of them sons of bitches drew first."

There was a moment of silence, and then the rightmost man—a mean-looking cuss with a ragged moustache and hate in his eyes—reached for the holster at his belt. Steele held off an extra split-second or two just to let him clear leather, and then he put a bullet through the varmint's hand.

"Case in point." He nodded to the owlhoot, who was screaming like a banshee, clutching what was left of his fingers and looking at Steele like he was the devil himself risen straight up out of Hell. "Go find a doctor 'fore you bleed to death, you dumb bastard."

The moustached man started off like a scalded cat, and the Lonesome Rider addressed the other three. "Like I said, them newspaper boys... they tone things down. They don't want it to seem like it's crazy talk. But there's two things about me you mighta heard, and them two are the gospel truth. First is, I never drew down on an unarmed man."

He watched a single drop of sweat trickle the length of the big man's face, and then all three of them unbuckled their holsters and let them drop into the dirt, guns and all.

Steele nodded. "Second thing is that I never suffered a damn fool my whole life. Never have and never will. Now, you folks got a choice. Either you can apologise for startin' this conversation off so ungentleman-like, or you can put up your dukes and fight. All of you."

The big man blinked, and the other two looked at each other, then all three of them seemed to recover some of the bluster they'd had a minute before. "Boy, you got to be out of your damn mind to make a challenge like that. There's three of us here—"

"That's right, fat man. There's three of you and there's one of me. And I am gonna beat you until your blood runs and your dead mama cries." He blew out a ring of smoke. "Make your choice."

They chose wrong. Jackasses always did.

The big man charged, swinging one arm like a mace. Steele could see he was way off balance—like as not it'd been a dog's age since he'd had to fight with a fella who could fight him back, and he'd gotten sloppy, if he was ever much good to begin with. Hell, maybe the big talker had been living off his size and his mouth since he was born. Waiting his whole damn useless life for this one moment.

The moment the talking had to stop.

Steele stepped to his left, grabbed the swinging arm and twisted it. There was a loud crack, and splintered bone tore through the big man's forearm and shirt, sending a gout of blood into the dust at his feet. Immediately the big talker went down to his knees, screaming—no, *squealing,* like a stuck pig. Steele shook his head sadly and stepped away. Then he spoke.

"Get up."

The big man looked up at Steele through tears, uncomprehending. The other two stepped back, looking white as ghosts, but the crowd pushed at them, refusing to let them leave. "Wh-what you mean, get up?" the big man whined, looking into Steele's eyes—maybe he was hoping to find some kind of mercy there, but there weren't no mercy to be had.

Steele's voice was like stone on stone.

"You bought yourself a whole mess of trouble today. You bought it and now you gotta pay for it. So get up, fat man. Get up and get ready."

He took a last drag on the cigar, then dropped it into the dirt and ground it out with the heel of his boot.

"I ain't near done with you yet."

"It's a barbaric display," Franklin Reed III breathed, shuddering. He took his glasses off, cleaning them with the handkerchief he kept in the breast pocket of his brown tweed suit. When he put them back on again, all three men were on the ground, bleeding. He leaned closer to the glass.

"If the sight offends your sensibilities, Mr Reed, then I suggest you step away from the window to prevent yourself gawking at it like a damned rooster." George Westinghouse leant back in the leather office-chair—not quite as fancy as the one he kept in his main office in New York, but certainly good enough for Fort Woodson—and grinned. "Those scofflaws knew the man they were dealing with, and so do I. Frankly, I'd be more than a little disappointed if he'd done otherwise."

Reed looked at Westinghouse for a moment, but did not step away. Through the murky glass, he saw that one of the cowhands had staggered back to his feet, only for Steele to land another sledgehammer blow to his jaw, sending a tooth flying. A man in the crowd caught it in his hand, gave a yelp of delight, and showed it to an older man he was with, just as if it were the winning ticket in a raffle. Reed stared for a moment longer before he realised that both the men wore badges.

He sighed and shook his head. "Well, I call this a disgusting spectacle, sir, on a par with the Roman circus. In my opinion, the man's made his point, and they won't soon forget it. He should let them walk away—"

Westinghouse snorted. "Walk away, you say? If they can walk at all, then in *my* humble opinion Steele ain't made his point well enough. And considering he'll be protecting your hide, and your creation, I'd have thought you'd be pleased to see him demonstrate the skills that'll keep you both in full working order." He chuckled to himself, as if he'd made some great joke, and indicated the ornate wooden box on his desk. "Cigar?"

Reed shook his head. "I won't be needing a bodyguard, sir, and neither will my 'creation,' as you very well know. And tobacco is a noxious weed," he murmured absently, "ruinous to the constitution and destructive to the tissue of the lung, which I will have no truck with."

Through the window outside, he saw Steele standing over the broken bodies of the men he had felled, once and then again, over and over until they could no longer rise and honour—or bloodlust—had finally been satisfied. Steele spat into the dirt and the crowd cheered for him, and Reed could not help but wince. "The bloody sport is over with, Mr Westinghouse. I trust Mr. Steele will not allow any other street brawls to delay our business further?"

The only answer Westinghouse gave him was another snort and a shake of his head. A moment later, the door to the office swung open and Steele was among them. Westinghouse stood, offering his hand to the man. "Good seeing you, Jacob. I noticed you got a little exercise before our appointment." He chuckled again.

"If that's exercise, George, I'm gonna get fat." Steele turned in Reed's direction and nodded once. Reed hesitated for a moment, then stuck out his hand. It was an opportunity to size up the man.

Steele had a hard grip, to begin with—hard, but not crushing. Reed had, in the past, met men who'd attempted to prove themselves superior to him by attempting to break the bones of his hand, and these were usually men desirous of concealing some defect or imperfection, possibly in the genital region. Reed next looked to the eyes, and found the man's stare as hard as his grip—not belligerent, but not willing to shrink from belligerence either. A hard man in general, then.

Reed scanned for other salient points. Age—mid-thirties or thereabouts, perhaps a little younger. A touch over six feet in height, taller than most men, and slim, but powerfully built. A small scar over his lip on the right side, and another over his eye, the ghost of some long-ago fight where a blade had gotten a little too close to blinding him.

And he was a negro, of course.

Reed realised the handshake had gone on uncomfortably long, and let Steele's hand go. "A pleasure, sir." It was not, but to admit the intimidation he felt would only lessen him in the gaze of all those present, including himself.

Jacob Steele had likewise used the long handshake to size up Franklin Reed III. He'd taken one good look at the eyes behind those round glasses and figured Reed for a lily-white jellyfish. He hadn't proved himself a jackass yet, though. Thank the Lord for small mercies.

Westinghouse leaned back in his chair. "Well now, I suppose introductions are in order. Reed, you've had a good look at Jacob here, and doubtless you know a little of his reputation as a bounty hunter. What you may not know is that I keep him on permanent retainer as a kind of trouble-shooter for the Westinghouse Steam and Signal Company. I won't bore you with the specifics of the arrangement, but he's worth every red cent I pay him and more besides. Saved my hide and my company more times than I'd care to admit."

He lit his cigar with practised confidence, puffed once, then used it to indicate Reed. "And Jacob, this tall drink of water is Franklin Reed III, scientific prodigy and the most able mind in my employ at twenty years of age. Started working for me when he was twelve. He's a little lacking in horse-sense occasionally, as young men often are, but I tell you now that *this* young man has the capacity to change our entire world. No joke."

Jacob gave the young man in question a sideways look. "Huh."

Reed blushed, looking at his feet. "I fear Mr Westinghouse is indulging in a little hyperbole."

Westinghouse shook his head irritably. "I don't believe in hyperbole, son, and neither should you. It's your inventive genius that's made this company what it is, these last few years, and that's before we bring up what you have sitting in that warehouse over yonder."

Reed shook his head, turning to Steele apologetically. "Really, I've only made a few small breakthroughs in the fields of—"

"Horseshit, son." Westinghouse stood up, stubbing his cigar out in the ashtray. "Hell with it—let's allow Mr. Steele here to judge what's a small breakthrough and what's not. Figure he should see what he's going to be travelling with." He grinned, looking Steele dead in the eye. "I remember when I first saw what you're about to see, Jacob. I went in there with that sceptical look you have on your face, and I walked out a true believer in the world that's coming."

His grin widened.

"I also walked out with shit in my pants."

*   *   *

TEN MINUTES LATER, in a guarded warehouse on the edge of Fort Woodson, Jacob Steele came face to face with the Locomotive Man.

At least, he would have done, if the damned thing had had a face to begin with. Instead, its head was a dome of smooth and expressionless brass, save for a pair of lenses—delicate-looking things—that took the place of eyes. The effect was a mite unnerving, not to say otherworldly, and Steele found himself leaning back a tad. He could feel that slight twitch in the muscle of his gun arm that signified trouble brewing.

For the Locomotive Man's part, it just sat there on a wooden block with its arms at its sides, like nothing so much as a crude statue fashioned from old train parts and iron boilers. It was slumped back a little, like a big, ugly puppet with no strings—a ten-foot-tall puppet at that. Steele couldn't help but wonder what kind of child might play with a toy like that, and the thought didn't exactly endear him to Franklin Reed much.

Reed smiled, opening the iron furnace-door in the thing's belly and feeding it a shovelful of coal. He yelled out above the clatter: "Just a prototype, you understand! I'm working on a system of microhydraulics that should allow me to reduce his dimensions a little. Of course, the firebox would also have to be reduced, which would mean shorter running-time unless we can dramatically increase fuel efficiency, but that's a puzzle I'm sure I can find a solution to..." He ran his mouth on in that vein while he added kindling and newspaper. The fella seemed more in his element now, tossing around a passel of forty-dollar words Steele didn't much feel like puzzling out. He couldn't help but feel a touch otherworldly himself—like he was watching some kinda ritual, some magic he didn't quite understand.

Pretty soon the flames in that firebox were roaring bright, and to Steele's eye it looked like a glimpse straight into the fires of Hell. He shot Westinghouse a look, speaking almost under his breath. "I'll say this plain, George. I don't much like where this is headed."

Westinghouse just smiled, a little superior smile Steele didn't exactly appreciate. Kind of a jackass smile.

Reed slammed the furnace-door shut with a heavy clang, then walked around to the back of the thing. Around back of the Locomotive Man there were a whole mess of dials, switches and levers—a bank of them jutting from shoulder to shoulder. Reed ran his eyes over those, reading them and making what adjustments he found necessary. The chimney rising from the metal man's left shoulder was already belching out a thick black plume of smoke, which drifted up to a vent made for it in the ceiling, and presently the whistle built into its right shoulder gave out a shrill scream, like a train.

All aboard, Steele thought. He still felt like he was dreaming.

"All in working order!" Reed murmured, wiping a little of the soot from his hands onto an old rag. "A minute or two more, just to allow the furnace to reach the correct temperature for full operation, and then..." He smiled, in a proud and genial manner far removed from his earlier stiffness. It almost seemed to Steele as if only here, among the metal and brass and copper and rods and gears of his huge puppet, was he fully himself at last, comfortable in his own skin.

"Do you know," he continued, "I originally considered building the chimney in as a top hat. Can you imagine how that would have looked? But, of course, I had to leave room for the workings of the analytical engine."

Steele pricked his ears up at that. "The what now?"

"Analytical engine! A sort of thinking-machine, based a little on the work of one Mr Charles Babbage—have you heard of him? Dead nearly ten years now, God rest his soul, but he may yet be remembered as the father of the age... ah! There we have it!" He laughed like a boy, noticing some dial had finally crept up into the required temperature, and then yanked down the largest lever on the Locomotive Man's back.

The whistle sounded once again, and then the whole contraption shook and juddered for a second. From inside the brass dome there came an odd chattering sound. Jacob Steele remembered when he'd come across a deputy using one of Mr. Sholes' fancy new type-writers, and this sounded like nothing so much as a roomful of the damned things, all clattering and snapping away at once. The sound carried on for a couple of seconds more, long enough for Steele to convince himself that he'd guessed wrong. There was no way in creation this blamed contraption was going to move of its own accord.

And then—very slowly, as if only just working out how—it did just that.

The Locomotive Man stood up.

"By God!" Steele yelled, taking a step backwards, and the cold breath of fear ran through him. All of a sudden his knees seemed made of water, like they couldn't bear his weight. *I am dreaming,* he thought. *I am dreaming or going mad, having visions of some other place. Because that is not something that should be in this world.*

It was George Westinghouse's turn to smile now. "By God indeed. I had much the same reaction myself. Mr Reed, if you will please have your friend introduce himself to Jacob? I have a hunch they'll be getting along famously once he gets over the shock."

"If you insist, sir," Reed smirked, and he pulled and flicked the levers and switches, one after another. "I will add Mr Steele to the internal record..."

The thing took a lumbering step forward, heavy enough to make the floor shake underneath it. Then it slumped slightly, the lenses of its eyes gazing upon Steele's face, and just for a second the bounty hunter thought it might just reach out with its hands—them blunt mechanical claws it had—and grab a hold of him. And then? Why, he could see it bundling him into the firebox to burn alive like so much kindling while these two white men smiled their big happy smiles.

And then the damned thing reached out a claw out for him, and Steele very nearly shot it in the face.

It was only a split-second of fright, but he was halfway to his iron by the time he saw what it was really doing. Then he understood the gesture and forced himself to relax. "God damn it, George. Are you serious?"

Westinghouse just couldn't seem to get that grin off his face. He looked like a proud papa whose youngest boy had only just learned to walk. "Shake hands, Mr Steele."

"The hell with you, George. I ain't shaking hands with that." Steele found himself surprised at the venom in his voice. *Why not, damn it? No need to make trouble over it, these folks are proud of their toy, so why not play along?* Was it 'cause they'd laughed? That was part of it, sure, maybe a big part, but he was enough of a man to take that for what it was.

No, it was something else. The whole idea of the Locomotive Man just rubbed him wrong, somehow.

Westinghouse swapped his smile for a pained look, like he'd only just realised all the guests at the hoedown weren't quite getting along. As for Reed, the boy had a face on him like a kicked puppy. "It would be a lot better if you did, Mr Steele—"

"That a threat?"

"No!" Reed paled. "God, no! But it just... well, it helps it identify you as a friend... oh, hell." He bit his lip, looking miserable, then stepped forward and started flicking more of the switches on the thing's back. The metal man stared at Steele, almost accusing, while the cogs in its mechanical brain whirred and ground. "There," Reed said at last, "you're added to the record. No handshake required."

Westinghouse shook his head sadly, looking disappointed. "It's not something to be afraid of, Jacob. It's the future."

Steele turned away angrily. He was angry with Westinghouse and his damned disappointed look, like he was some schoolteacher talking to a child who'd got the answer wrong, and he was angry with Reed and his kicked-dog face and most of all he was angry with that cursed heap of junk that was still standing there like it was a man.

And he was mad at himself too, a little, for not playing nice with these overgrown kids and their overgrown toy—except he'd never gone against his gut yet, and in his gut he knew the Locomotive Man was bad news. Hell, it might just be the death of him.

He sighed, and pushed the feeling down. It was always good to listen to your gut, but you had to feed it occasionally too. And that meant money, which right now he didn't have a whole lot of.

"We can talk about that later, George. Right now, I imagine you called me in for more than showing off toys."

Westinghouse shrugged, and nodded. "I did indeed, Jacob. I have a job for you. Easy work, you'll find—you are to be an escort, if you're willing. A bodyguard. For Mr Reed here, as a matter of fact." He paused for a moment, looking away and scratching the back of his neck, as if he was working out how to broach some troublesome news. "And, um... also, for... that is to say, you'll be accompanied by..."

The Locomotive Man let out another shrill scream, and George had the decency to look embarrassed at that.

"God damn it," Steele said, and lit another cigar.

"THERE."

Steele watched irritably as Reed shovelled another heap of coal into the firebox. They'd made a stop at the side of the trail, so that Reed could feed his creation more of the coal and water it needed.

He had a plentiful store of both with him, in a great metal-and-canvas wagon that the Locomotive Man pulled along behind him. It was a hell of a thing in itself, with compartments for all the necessities, including food and water for the flesh-and-blood men on the expedition as well as for Jonah, and built-in bedding so a man might sleep in it at night, with the Locomotive Man standing guard—assuming any man could sleep through the night with the damned thing's whistle screaming out whenever it had a mind. Reed had gone so far as to paint his wagon with the legend 'FRANKLIN B. REED III, OWNER AND INVENTOR OF THE ASTOUNDING & ASTONISHING LOCOMOTIVE MAN,' just as if he was a quack selling snake-oil or a blamed travelling circus.

He'd invited Steele to sit with him on the front seat of the thing, but Steele had flatly refused. Now, as he watched Reed load the firebox from the vantage point of Jonah's saddle, he couldn't help but figure the astounding and astonishing Locomotive Man was a mite more trouble than it was worth.

"About how long do you reckon this'll take, Mr Reed?"

Reed sighed. "Not much longer, I promise. Unfortunately the current design means that, unlike in the case of the common locomotive, we cannot load the firebox while the Locomotive Man is in motion."

"Not unless we want to get ourselves stepped on."

"Yes. Quite."

Steele reached into his black duster coat and fished out another of his cigars. "You considered putting the door in its back?"

Reed sighed as he hefted another shovelful of coal. "Unfortunately, that would mean the control mechanisms would have to go on the front, which again brings up the problem of, ah..."

"Getting stepped on." Steele lit his cigar and took a few quick puffs.

"Quite." Reed scowled, then slammed the furnace-door and hung the dirty shovel on a hook jutting from the wagon's side, where he could pick it up easy next time. Then he clambered back up into his seat and started the Locomotive Man up—the metal man gave out another shrill scream from his whistle, and Jonah reared and bucked a little at that, and then the thing juddered forward into a steady walking-pace, pulling the wagon after it. Once Jonah had gotten over his fright, he trotted gently alongside.

Steele listened to the Locomotive Man's slow, rumbling clank, watching the landscape drift by slowly. "Can't help but figure we'd make better time on horseback, Mr Reed."

Reed shook his head. "Ah, but then we would be without the Locomotive Man!"

"Don't sound like such a disadvantage to me."

"And what if we run into trouble on our journey, Mr Steele?"

"I'll handle it."

Reed folded his arms, looking smug. "And if it's more than you can handle?"

Steele almost laughed. "No such animal, Mr Reed. No such animal." He took another puff on his cigar, then blew out a thick ring of smoke. "And I'll bet you a dollar to a dime it won't be the journey that gives us trouble. It'll be this Edison feller sittin' at the end of it."

According to what George Westinghouse had come out with back in Fort Woodson, after they'd finally gotten done looking at Franklin Reed's wonder, this Edison had been laughed out of most scientific circles, on account of his lack of education and some crackpot ideas about harnessing lightning for telegraph systems or lights or some such nonsense. After years of ridicule, he'd approached Westinghouse with his notions, although why the hell he thought that kind of crazy talk had a place in the Steam and Signal Company, George didn't know and Jacob couldn't tell him. George had treated the man as kindly as he could, but he'd shown him the door all the same, and maybe it was that small kindness that broke Edison at last. After that, he spent more than a year sending threatening letters, telegrams, smoke signals if he could—all promising war, a war George Westinghouse was just too sane to understand the meaning of.

George had refused to respond to the letters, or the impassioned rants on soapboxes in the middle of New York streets, or the full-page adverts taken out in newspapers with money Edison surely couldn't spare. Eventually Edison's propaganda war had tailed off, and Westinghouse forgot him, for he was a man used to dealing with colourful characters.

And then the telegram had arrived.

Steele dug into the pocket of his coat and retrieved it. He squinted at the words for a moment, then leant over in his saddle to hand it to Reed. "Here. Read it out. I want to hear it out loud."

Reed frowned, taking the piece of paper. "Why can't you read it?"

Steele shrugged. "I guess I could if you want, but it'd be a slow business. I didn't learn to read or write 'til I was fourteen, and even then I had to teach myself. Still ain't the best at it."

Reed blinked, and Steele could see the puzzlement on his face. Then he began to read in his soft, almost trembling voice:

```
GALVANIC AETHER A REALITY STOP SOURCE OF
POWER GREATER THAN ANY KNOWN STOP MEET ME ON
DEVILS EYE MESA IN COLORADO IN ONE WEEK FOR
DEMONSTRATION OF ULTIMATE POWER THAT WILL END
DOMINION OF STEAM FOREVER STOP YOU SHOULD HAVE
LISTENED TO ME STOP
                            THOMAS ALVA EDISON
```

Steele nodded grimly. "'You should have listened to me.' See, in my line of work, that's what we call a threat."

Reed shook his head. "I hardly think so. An 'I-told-you-so' at most. I'm more interested in this business of 'galvanic aether'..."

"I'm guessing that's that lightning-power George was talking about earlier."

"I'm not sure. From what Mr Westinghouse told me, Edison was always talking about galvanic *force*, or galvanic *current*. In the newspaper adverts, he described a great War of Currents—water versus lightning."

Steele scowled. "You'd think war between plain men was bloody enough. So what's aether in relation to that?"

"Honestly, I—"

"The simple version. Some of us didn't get your fancy schooling."

"The simple version, Mr Steele, is I don't know. In classical mythology, aether is the air breathed by the Gods—the substance of a plane higher than our own, above the terrestrial sphere. If you ask me, his use of the term is ominous, very ominous." Reed bit his lip, looking towards his metal man, as if for protection. And, as if responding to his need, the Locomotive Man let out another scream from his whistle.

"You think he might be even crazier than last time—God damn it!" Steele tugged on Jonah's rains, keeping him from bucking. "Any way you can do something about that damned whistle?"

"Hmm? Oh, I'll work on it in the next iteration," Reed murmured. "Crazy... I don't know if I would call him that. Apparently he provided a couple of demonstrations that seemed to show he was onto something—some business with magnets and copper wire..."

"Well," Steele murmured, "George doesn't call me in to deal with peaceable types, and this feller sounds like his powder's about ready to blow."

"Ah yes." Reed sighed. "Now that, I can agree with. That's why Mr

Westinghouse sent me, as I understand it—he thought if he went to see what Edison was doing himself, it might stir up old wounds..." He bit his lip, staring ahead at the road. "Or I might be wrong. It's possible he thought I might see something in Edison's ideas that he missed. Perhaps... if I saw what Edison was doing..." He paused a second, like he was about to say more, then shook his head and turned away.

That piqued Steele's curiosity. "What?"

Reed looked him in the eye for a spell, hesitating—then when he spoke, his voice shook. "Mr Steele... do you..." He paused again, then spat it out. "Do you feel as though the world should be *different* from what it is?"

Steele stared at Reed for a long moment. "Kind of a dumb question, ain't it?"

Reed blushed red, and looked back towards the unfolding road. Steele took another long drag on his cigar. "Tell you what, Reed, why don't you tell me how you think it oughtta be different, and then I'll tell you if I feel the same way."

Reed took a deep breath, not quite trusting himself to look Steele in the eye. This time, when he spoke, his voice was down to a whisper. "You must not think me mad, sir. Pray do not think me mad."

Steele shrugged. "You built a train with legs to carry you around like a damn caliph, Mr Reed. It's a mite too late to worry 'bout what I think."

Reed laughed despite himself, then his manner grew sombre again. "I... have had dreams, sir. Dreams in which the world is altered, almost imperceptibly. The differences are subtle, but..." He ran his tongue over dry lips. "Fireflies in glass bulbs. Automatic telegraphs festooned with wires. A system of lightning and wire spanning this country. The beginning of a world of wonders... you must understand, I would not trouble myself with such visions if... if they weren't so vivid. If it all didn't seem so real. So... so horribly plausible. So unlike..." He paused, staring into the distance. "So unlike *our* world, Mr Steele." He turned to Steele again, and now there was an almost feverish look in his eye. "Doesn't it seem strange to you? Doesn't it seem like we're missing something basic? Something we *should* have?"

He caught the look in Jacob Steele's eye, and looked away, composing himself. "I... I apologise. I must sound to you like some babbling half-wit. I just... I'm just trying to explain..."

Steele looked at him for a moment. "Let's just ride a spell, Mr Reed. Figure we'll both feel better once the sun's a little lower."

Reed swallowed, and nodded soberly, not trusting himself to speak further. They didn't speak again until they reached the town.

DEVIL'S GULCH WAS a town about ten miles out from the mesa, and a good place to stop and re-fill the canteens with water and feed Jonah. Steele figured there'd be a place where the two of them could stay for the night, assuming those who ran it were happy keeping the Locomotive Man with their horses.

"We'll stop here a brief spell. Figure we can reach the top of the mesa 'fore sundown—can't be more'n an hour's ride from here," Steele said, tying Jonah to a rail outside the saloon. "Once we've talked to Edison, we can head back here and rest up."

Reed sighed. "If he allows us to."

"One way or another, he'll do that." Steele looked around at the townsfolk. A small crowd had gathered to stare at Reed's wagon and at the Locomotive Man, and a few wags in the crowd were already passing comment that whoever was inside it must be all-fired hot.

"C'mon, mister, y'all ain't foolin' nobody!" one of them called out. "Why don't you get whatever fella you got in there t'unscrew that dome o' his an' show his face?"

Steele couldn't help but crack a smile, but Reed seemed to take it personally. "The Locomotive Man is real, sir! And I will have you know it is the wonder of the age!" He yelled the words back, but the crowd only intensified their jeering.

"Y'all gonna sell us some snake-oil medicine, mister? I could sure use some tonic!" one of the younger ones shouted.

"Yer too young for tonic, boy!" his father bellowed, and a ripple of laughter spread through the crowd. Steele couldn't help but chuckle himself, holding up his palms in apology when Reed turned his furious gaze on him.

"Now, now, Mr Reed. You surely must admit that wagon of yours looks the part."

Reed fumed, shaking his head. "By God, they'll learn. When there's a Locomotive Man in every town, on every street corner, they'll remember this day for the rest of their lives! The day they saw the first! They'll feel foolish then, I'll bet—"

"Hey, you! Metal man!" the boy yelled. "Why don't you do a trick fer us?"

Reed grimaced. "There'll be no tricks!" he shouted back. "This is a marvel of science! It's not a toy!"

Steele shook his head. "Could've fooled me—"

"*Steele!*"

The cry cut through the air like a thrown knife. By the time Steele turned to face it, his iron was already in his hand.

"Grey Owl. By God."

The man pushing his way through the crowd was an Indian, an outcast from one of the Ute tribes, and a man whom Jacob Steele knew well. He walked with a slight limp, and that was the legacy of their last meeting, when Steele had put three bullets in him and watched him take the fall from a high cliff into a river. He'd always figured that if the day came when he ever saw Grey Owl again, it'd be in the next world—yet here he was, alive and well.

"Jacob Steele." Grey Owl's eyes were burning with hate. "I've had visions of meeting you again."

Steele slipped his firearm back in its holster. "Well, I can't say the same. We all figured you was a dead man. Hell, I collected the bounty on you. You've done a hell of a job of hiding yourself these last two years."

"Not hiding." Grey Owl's gnarled hands hovered over the pearl-handled revolvers he wore at his hip—the same guns he'd taken from Colonel Armstrong, after revenging himself for the massacre at Bitter Falls. "Waiting."

Steele's own gun-arm was twitching, and he found himself taking up a stance. Gunfights had their own cruel gravity, and he felt the two of them being drawn towards that irrevocable moment when one of them would kill the other. "Well, here I am," he said slowly, "but I don't much want to draw on you, Grey Owl. We done that dance once already. 'Sides... hell, I figure you had a right to do what you done. Lord knows that damn fool deserved worse."

"Did he? Is that why you hunted me across three states, then? Is that why you put three bullets in my hide?" Grey Owl spat, furiously, clenching and unclenching his fists in preparation for the draw. "Or was it for a fistful of white man's money?"

Steele stared Grey Owl in the eye. He didn't dare to blink. The baying of the crowd, Reed and his ridiculous metal monster—all that was forgotten now. It was just him and his enemy, a man skilled enough to drop him right here if he should falter. For an instant, he found himself thinking back to the big talker in Fort Woodson, and he realised it'd been a hell of a long time since anyone had given him a proper fight, at that.

"I hunted you 'cause I knew others were hunting you just as hard. Men like that evil son of a bitch Cogburn, or Butcher Terrill. I knew what they'd do, and you deserved better than bein' scalped or lynched or tortured for fun by the kind of man who'd look at you and see just one more damned savage in need of killing. Better a clean bullet from a man who understood. Least that's how I figured it." He licked his lips, feeling a trickle of sweat at his temple. "Was I wrong?"

Grey Owl hesitated a moment, then scowled. "Maybe not. But either way, I plan to repay that kindness here and now. Go for your—"

"Why?" Steele snapped. "For what? Why the hell do we need to kill each other today? Is it 'cause I shot you? You didn't know something like that was coming, you're a damn fool, and I never took you for that. Damn it all..." He paused a second. "You know I gave the bounty money to Red Cloud?"

"What?" Grey Owl blinked at the mention of his brother's name.

"To help raise your boy. I don't know what the hell he did with it. He might have burned it, for all I know. He seemed pretty mad at me at the time." Steele sighed and shook his head. "But there it is. And now here's you and me at the ends of each other's guns, and I can't think of a single reason why that ought to be so."

"There's bad blood between us," Grey Owl frowned, but his hands seemed relaxed now, no longer flexing.

"There's worse blood against us, and you know it."

Steele risked a glance at the crowd, who were looking angry and bored. A couple at the back were catcalling, "Draw, already! Ya yeller chickens!" Grey Owl frowned, turning his head as if noticing them for the first time. He paused for a moment, then spoke in a softer tone.

"These people..." He hesitated, then scowled. "They do not see men."

"They see a dog fight. And if one of us was white, they'd see a hero." Steele straightened. "I'm done talking, Grey Owl. Are we gonna do this, or are we gonna walk away?"

Grey Owl stiffened, and resumed his stance, hands flexing, poised once again over the twin revolvers. Everything in his stance showed he was readying himself to shoot, and Steele readied himself likewise, in case the other man should decide to slap leather after all. But when Steele looked in Grey Owl's eyes, the fire of revenge that had started the confrontation had been replaced by a weariness, a disgust with the whole business.

He relaxed. There'd be no gunfight today.

Then he heard the shriek of a steam whistle, and Reed yelling like a banshee—

"*Forward the Locomotive Man!*"—and a ton of clanking iron and brass shoved past him, knocking him to the ground, making a beeline for the other man.

"No!" Steele shouted, as Grey Owl's eyes widened at the monstrosity. Up until now, like all the rest of the townsfolk, he'd seen it as another medicine show, a snake-oil demonstration that his enemy just happened to be riding with. Now, the terrifying reality bore down on him in all its cold, mechanical fury. He drew, firing at the Locomotive Man's centre mass, and the bullets pinged off the metal as if they were bee stings.

"*Call it off!*" Steele yelled over the din, drawing his own gun and aiming for the control mechanisms on the thing's back, trying to determine which might shut the damned monster off once and for all. "*Call it off, Reed, you son of a bitch!*" He fired, pulling the trigger again and again until the chamber was empty, and the bullets shattered dials and broke off switches, but nothing seemed to stop the Locomotive Man's charge.

One of the ricochets from Grey Owl's own pistols hit him in the chest, sending him staggering back, but the machine caught his head in its iron grip before he could fall. Steele heard him cry out something in the Ute language, and then the Locomotive Man crushed his head like an eggshell, sending a spray of blood and brains into the dirt.

It let what was left fall, and stomped back to its place at the wagon.

Not a soul in the crowd spoke.

"*You god-damned son of a bitch!*" Steele stormed over, grabbed Reed by the lapels and pulled him bodily down off the front seat of his damn wagon and into the dirt, and then slammed him with a haymaker across the jaw for good measure. "*You miserable bastard, that was a man! That was a man!*"

"H-he was going to shoot you—" Reed stammered, and Steele's knuckles caught him again, sending his glasses into the dirt and blacking his eye.

"*He was gonna walk away! Get up, you god-damn coward! Get up!*"

The crowd rumbled, growing ugly. A small voice piped up from the back: "Why don't that metal man kill that boy already?" The rumbling grew louder, more insistent, and one of the men at the front of the mob picked a stone off the ground and threw it at Steele's head.

He spun around and shot it from the air.

Then he lifted his hat and let the crowd see what was in his eyes. "I never shot an unarmed man yet," he growled. "If I start, I can't promise I'm gonna stop."

The crowd scattered.

"Those jackasses are gonna grow their balls back soon enough," Steele growled. "On your feet, you lousy bastard. Get your damn metal man up and running."

Reed cowered in the dirt, scrabbling for his glasses. "I—you broke the controls—I need to check if—"

Steele hauled him up by the scruff of his neck. "Get it running and get the hell out of here! *Now!*" He pushed Reed roughly into the wagon, and the younger man scrambled up onto it, reading the broken dials as best he could and flipping what switches were left. Eventually, the Locomotive Man juddered into life. Satisfied, Steele untied Jonah and led him over to the spot Grey Owl had fallen.

As the metal man slowly began to trundle forwards, building up speed, Steele hefted Grey Owl's body up over one shoulder, then tossed it into the back of the wagon as it passed.

"You can't just throw a body into—" Reed protested.

"*Shut up,* you snake in the grass!" Steele spat, swinging up onto Jonah's back and spurring him to a trot. His eyes roamed the empty street, expecting trouble, but none came, and soon they'd left Devil's Gulch behind them. "There. Now, we got an appointment to keep up on that mesa, and I'm anxious to be done with it. After that, we'll bury this man best we can according to custom. Right now I'm of a mood to make you dig the rocks out with your own two hands."

"Steele, the man wanted to kill you—"

"Shut up, I said."

"For God's sake, he was a *savage*—"

Steele drew his gun.

"You say one more word. Just one. I will kill you where you sit."

Reed stared into the barrel of the revolver. He didn't say a word, and after a pause, Steele put his iron away.

"After we're done with the burial, I'm going back to Fort Woodson to tell that son of a bitch Westinghouse just where he can stick his damn retainer. I'm done with all you sons of bitches."

THEY WERE HALFWAY up the long spiral path to the crown of the mesa, and the sun was an angry red ball, low on the horizon.

The journey had taken longer than either man had expected, and the Locomotive Man seemed to be moving slower with every step. From underneath the brass dome, there was the usual whirring and clattering, but occasionally Franklin Reed would hear a fearful grinding sound emanate from the delicate workings within, which frightened him. Finally, he had to speak: "I don't like these noises..."

"I thought I told you to shut up." Steele's voice was weary, and his anger was gone. Reed considered the situation for a moment, then took his courage in his hands.

"I don't believe you are going to shoot me, Mr Steele."

Steele sighed. "Well, maybe I'll just shoot some unnecessary part of you, such as your pecker. Or bind and gag you and stick you in the back of your own damn wagon to pass the time with the man you murdered."

Reed bristled, and anger crept into his voice. "I would not call it murder, sir. From where I was sitting he was ready to murder you, at least until I intervened—"

"Shut up, God damn it." Steele shook his head, looking more tired than ever. He gestured at the Locomotive Man as it sluggishly toiled up the slope, dragging its burden behind it. "What the hell possessed you to build that damn thing anyway? What's it even for, aside from pulling you around?"

"I designed it to ease the burdens of life, Mr Steele." Reed's tone was frosty. "Once the Locomotive Man is mass-produced, it will remove the difficult tasks and drudgeries from life. Ploughing a field, for example, or digging a mine—"

"Or killing a man."

Reed blinked. "Excuse me?"

Steele had a disgusted look on his face, as though Reed's stupidity was a noxious substance that he's stepped in or got on his hands. "What is it like living in that head of yours, Reed? That damn metal man of yours ain't for pulling wagons or planting seed. If you'd swapped your monster out for a good horse we'd have been there and back by now. No, I've seen the one thing your fancy Locomotive Man's good for, and that's killing folks. You honestly think the world ain't gonna pick up on that too?"

The Locomotive Man picked that instant to offer another grinding, agonised whine from inside its brass dome. Steele winced. "Hell, that does sound ugly. I guess it is time you gave the poor bastard a break."

"It's not a 'poor bastard,' sir," Reed snapped. "It's a machine for performing difficult and dangerous chores—"

"Like killing folks."

Reed clamped his lips tight together, biting his tongue to keep the anger in. *How dare he? He dare he judge me, when he's killed a hundred men or more? The man's clearly nothing but a brutal, degenerate n—*

He pushed the thought away and leaned furiously forward, flipping and pushing at the remaining switches furiously, trying to coax life out of the machine.

"Kind of vulnerable for a killing machine, all them levers and switches on its back," Steele commented, dryly. "You might want to do something about that."

Reed scowled. "Well, they won't be there for long. I plan to do away with most of them entirely, in fact—I foresee future models with a simple starting lever, no more than that." He turned to Steele. "The more we—*scientists*, I mean—study these analytical engines, the more improvements we're going to make. I won't bore you with some of the breakthroughs they're making in London, but with what I know now... well, the second Locomotive Man will be able to make complex decisions on its own. It will, in a very limited sense, be able to think for itself."

"And then you'll have the perfect war machine, huh?"

"I've told you, Steele, it's for performing tasks unfit for human beings—"

"Right." Steele shook his head. "So when these machines of yours can think and decide like a man, what makes you think they'll want to do your chores for you? Hell, what makes you think you'll have a right to tell 'em to?"

Reed frowned. "I don't understand you, sir."

"No, you don't, do you? Four years of bloody war and a country built on pain and sweat and blood, and you jackasses still don't understand a damned—" Steele's voice suddenly trailed off. Reed turned to see what he was looking at and turned pale.

"By God," Steele breathed, "what... what is that, Reed?"

Reed licked dry lips. "I don't... I don't know," he whispered. "God help me, I don't know what I'm seeing..."

They had reached the top of the mesa.

Edison was waiting for them.

HE WAS SUSPENDED in mid-air, a foot above the ground, surrounded by a halo of rocks and stones that floated around him like the moons of some mysterious planet. His eyes glowed a gentle blue, and his flesh was a pale, ghostly white, corpse-like and dotted with great drops of sweat. One of his arms, Reed noted with dawning horror, had actually rotted away, leaving only the bone from the elbow down.

In his skeletal hand, he held a chunk of glowing blue stone.

Steele stared for a moment, as if wondering whether to turn back and leave the whole business behind, but then he swung himself down from Jonah's saddle. The horse turned and made its way back down the trail, away from whatever was happening, and Steele did nothing to prevent it. Perhaps he thought Jonah was making the wisest choice.

Reed climbed off the front of the wagon and exchanged a wary glance with the bounty hunter. Then the two stepped forward, approaching Edison slowly, like a pair of skittish deer. Neither man said a word.

"*Where's Westinghouse?*" Edison's voice was distorted, oddly hollow, as if it was coming from somewhere very far away. He nodded to a small pile of charred straw lying nearby. "*I've been conducting experiments. I thought he'd want to see for himself.*"

"What..." Reed swallowed, shaking his head. He couldn't form the words.

Steele scowled. "What the hell is that?"

Edison stared at him for a moment, then looked down at his skeletal hand, still wrapped around the glowing stone. "*This?*" Another stone floated up from the mesa's surface as he turned the thing over. "*I'm sorry. It's... it's hard to think.*" He closed his eyes for a moment, as if calling the memories back over some immense mental gulf. "*I was wandering in the desert. I was drunk. I drank a lot, after... after everything...*" He concentrated, rubbing his temple with his good hand. Another stone drifted up from the ground near Steele's feet.

"*There was a man. Foreign, I think—he called out to me in some language I didn't understand. He was dressed strangely... I took him for a vision at first, or a hallucination born of the bottle. I think... I think he tried to tell me his name... Sorren? Does that help?*" A pause. "*He died.*" Edison shook his head. "*I couldn't do anything. He was burning up with fever, and he'd been baked alive in the desert sun. He died in my arms. He was trying to tell me something about the stone. Trying to warn me away from touching it, maybe, but I didn't understand... and then it was too late.*" He stared into the blue glow of the stone for a long second, and then he raised his head and stared at the two men with narrowed eyes. "*It's mine now. Where's Westinghouse?*"

There was a note of anger in his voice, and the stones spinning and orbiting around him spun faster. Steele took a step back, hand hovering over his holster.

"*Where's Westinghouse? He was meant to—*" Edison froze, the blue glow of his eyes fixing on Reed, and suddenly it did not seem quite so gentle. "*Wait,*" he scowled. "*I know you. You shouldn't be here.*"

Reed blinked. "W-what?"

"*It's the stone. It shows me things. You shouldn't be here.*" Edison's anger seemed to be building, and now tiny sparks and crackling lights danced over his exposed skin. "*I should be here. So should Westinghouse. But not you.*" He pointed the stone towards Steele. "*Or you.*"

Steele drew his gun.

Reed didn't know if Steele meant to fire it, but he never got the chance. A bolt of blue-white energy leapt from the surface of the glowing stone to the barrel of the gun, and Steele cried out, dropping the revolver and clutching at his hand. Reed saw to his amazement that the flesh of his hand was badly burned.

Edison smiled. "*Don't do that again.*" He turned back to Reed. "*Have you ever heard of Alessandro Volta?*"

Reed took a step back, looking over his shoulder for a moment at the Locomotive Man. Could he get to the controls in time? Would the Locomotive Man even stand a chance against whatever Edison had become? "No," he heard himself say, "I don't think I have."

"*You wouldn't have. He was stabbed by a robber in the street. Michael Faraday was knocked down and killed by a horse before he had done anything of consequence, although he had theories. Benjamin Franklin was murdered by a man who should not be here.*" He tailed off for a moment, and his eyes were burning like miniature suns. "*Is this coincidence? Is this enemy action?*"

"I don't..." Reed swallowed, cursing his dry throat. "I don't know what you mean."

"*The stone knows. The stone remembers. It's... it's difficult for me to think with my own mind... to talk in three dimensions...*" He grimaced, and his matted black hair rose up, crackling with static. "*Where... is Westinghouse? He should be here. You shouldn't be. Neither of you.*" He lifted the stone again, pointing it at Reed. "*Now... now I'll have to start again.*"

The stone crackled with power. Reed stared into its depths and saw what was to happen. Edison would use the power to annihilate him, burn him like kindling, and then he would walk—no, float—down from his mesa, and first he would kill everyone in Devil's Gulch, and then Fort Woodson, and if he did not find George Westinghouse there, he would travel to New York, and everywhere he went he would leave scorched earth and burning bones...

Reed closed his eyes and prayed to a deity he did not quite believe in that the end would be quick. And then, just behind his left shoulder, there was an ear-splitting sound.

The shriek of a steam whistle.

Then everything happened very fast.

Reed was suddenly on the ground, and the Locomotive Man was thundering past him, belching smoke, gears grinding in his brass head. The orbiting rocks bounced off his metal body as he swung a blood-stained claw towards Edison, and Edison had just enough time to bring the stone to bear—

—and Reed was almost blinded by the blue-white light that flew from the stone to the Locomotive Man's chest, stopping the deadly charge and tearing the furnace-door from its hinges, then moving to the shoulder joint to rip one great iron arm clean off its body—

—and then Steele was reaching with his good hand for his gun, grabbing it from the dirt while Edison was engaged, and firing twice, all in one smooth motion, aiming for the exposed ulna and the radius, hitting both—

—and when the bones snapped clean in two from the force of the bullet impacts, it was Edison that fell to earth and the stone and the hand that held it that continued to float, the centre of a cosmos of rocks—

—and Steele scrambled to his feet, making a grab for the floating blue stone, catching hold of it while it was still crackling with all manner of strange, unfocussed power—

—and then he was gone.

Reed blinked. Jacob Steele and the blue stone had simply vanished into the air, as if they had never existed. Edison lay on the ground, coughing weakly, and the Locomotive Man stared down at him with its expressionless glass eyes. Then, quite casually, it reached down with its good arm and grabbed hold of Edison's head.

"No—" Reed cried out, but it was already far, far too late.

"Good God. What happened then?" George Westinghouse asked, pouring a brandy.

"I switched it off. It's standing there still." Reed rubbed his temples, then reached for the glass.

"You left it there?" Westinghouse seemed incredulous.

Reed sighed. "It was too heavy to deal with."

Westinghouse shook his head, frowning. "And Edison? What happened to his body?"

"I buried him as best I could with the coal-shovel. The Indian too." He shrugged, remembering the hard ground and the shallow graves. He hoped some predator hadn't dug them up again.

Westinghouse scowled. "Very convenient."

Reed shook his head and ignored the comment. "Anyway, Steele's horse let me ride on his back as far as the town, and they let me telegram from there. And here I am. If you'll allow me to retrieve the Locomotive Man at the earliest opportunity, I can look into what went wrong in the mechanism that made it act without orders..."

"Now that, I'm interested in." Westinghouse poured a glass for himself. "This is something you were working towards—the Locomotive Man acting alone. If that part of your story isn't..."

"Made up? None of it is."

Westinghouse took a long sip of the liquor. "Well, I'm not saying you're lying, exactly, but it sounds like your account might be a little confused. The important thing is what your Locomotive Man did."

"Killed a man." Reed took the brandy and swallowed it in a single gulp. Westinghouse ignored him.

"It acted autonomously, based on earlier instruction. I understand that's the direction they're going in in London. I'd like to get there first, and this might be the key."

Reed lowered his glasses and looked into Westinghouse's eyes. "Steele was right. The Locomotive Man's nothing but a killing machine. I'll have no further part of it." He sat back in his chair and folded his arms.

Westinghouse winced. "Now, Mr Reed, you've obviously had a shock. I'd go so far as to say your recollections might be—"

"I'm not insane, Mr Westinghouse. I might have been when I thought up the Locomotive Man, but not now. It was a childish fantasy, and if I wasn't worried about some fool building another, I'd leave it to rot on top of that rock." He shook his head, reaching down to rummage in a canvas bag at his feet. "Having it pull a wagon was... imbecilic. Why not infuse the technology into the wagon itself? Powered vehicles, sir. A revolution in transport. If that's what you want to do, I'm behind you all the way—but I'm done with mechanical men, and that's the end of it. Let the fools in London take the blame for what's coming."

Westinghouse looked sceptical. "And the money with it? Well, we'll discuss that later. Right now, I want to talk more about what happened up there. Now, as I said, I'm not going to call you a liar, but—"

Reed interrupted him by pulling a heavy mahogany box out of the bag, slamming it on the table. "It's a cigar box. I picked it up in town for the weight."

"I'm not sure I understand."

"You will."

Unceremoniously, Reed opened the box, and a smallish stone drifted up out of it to hang in the air in front of Westinghouse. For a full minute, the older man was unable to speak. Then he reached out with a fingertip to touch the stone, watching it bob away from him. "Good God," he whispered at last.

"Every word of my story is true, Mr Westinghouse. I believe some trace mineral present in this stone, and in the others I took with me, was affected by the object Edison was carrying in such a way as to... well, eliminate its susceptibility to gravity. I'd like permission to correspond with certain mineralogists of my aquaintance, with a view to duplicating this faculty. I've been in conversation in the past with a Dr Herbert Cavor, who I think might..." He paused. "Sir?"

Westinghouse grinned like a boy. "Good God. More of this, you say?"

Reed smiled. "Well, we'll see. It might take a century or more before we can actually synthesise it, but... it's nice to think I might have been instrumental in the creation of something that won't end in death." He looked down, as if embarrassed. "I even thought of one interesting application of an anti-gravity alloy on the way here—something that couldn't possibly be used to kill..."

"Hell, I'll bite. What did you think up?"

"Wings, sir." Reed grinned. "A pair of steam-powered wings."

THE EVE OF WAR

(Excerpt from *The New York Clarion*, dated August 27th, 2000.)

FORBIDDEN ECSTASY

Jason Satan, the Man With the Touch of Death, gazed hungrily on a beaker filled with his own blood, and hissed like a cat!

"What wonderful poison flows in my veins!"

The oozing liquid had the colour and consistency of spoiled milk and a sour and sickly smell, that seeped into the air and filled every nook and cranny of the warehouse. Satan breathed it in, shuddering in depraved, forbidden ecstasy at the unholy scent!

What horror did his unspeakable pleasure portend for the citizens of New York?

HE LIVED ONLY TO KILL

(For the benefit of readers new to the most action-packed newspaper in the five boroughs, there follows a brief description of this noted enemy of mankind.)

Jason Satan was a tall man—six and a half feet—and rail-thin, with the appearance of a skeleton wreathed in skin the colour and texture of office paper. His hair was as fine as cobweb and as white as his face—in fact, there was almost no part of his body that held colour. When he ran his bloodless tongue over his thin lips, it was as if a grey slug was emerging from some sunless cave. When he fixed you with his pitiless, inhuman gaze, his pupils were tiny black dots in a sea of wet, white jelly.

The only exception was his smile—for his teeth were yellow, rotting gravestones poking from grey gums. That devil's rictus was the last sight hundreds of innocent victims had ever seen—for Jason Satan had a love affair with Death, in all its varied forms, in all its horrors and brutalities. He was happy only when Death was near, when he could taste it on his tongue, feel its awful power working through him. *He lived only to kill.*

CATALOGUE OF HORRORS

"How beautiful." The Prince of Poisons purred the words, his eyes glittering with unholy light! "My blood—the source of my killing power! Were a single drop to fall on your exposed skin, my friend..."—his eyes narrowed suddenly, a trace of anger showing in his skeletal features, and a discordant note of malice entered his voice—"...had you not inoculated yourself against my gift... why, you would be dead before you hit the ground! Were I to shake your hand, or kiss your cheek, you might have time for a few last seconds of horror before that final end claimed you—for all time!" He brightened at the thought, his sickly yellow smile springing to life like a jack-in-the-box. "And now... now you say you will translate the deadly power of this perfect ichor to the very air itself?"

He addressed his question to the other man in the room—though 'man' was hardly the correct term.

For Mister Murder, the Master of the Murder Chair, was much more—and much less—than a human being!

VAST, BALLOON-LIKE HEAD

(Again, for the benefit of new readers, we will attempt a description of this most hideous of master-fiends.)

Mister Murder was, in truth, not so much a man as a vast, balloon-like head, criss-crossed with pulsing veins. The diameter of his skull measured a touch over four feet, and as if in compensation, the body that hung from his neck was almost vestigial—tiny and withered, as if it had barely grown since emerging from the womb. His face was a hideous, cracked mass of wrinkles, grotesquely magnified in proportion to his gigantic cranium, and his bulging eyes possessed a secondary, nictitating membrane, like a bird's—so that a murky green film flickered occasionally over them as he spoke. Otherwise, his gaze was utterly fixed and unblinking, an endless stare that seemed to penetrate deep into the soul, worming out all hidden secrets. There were whispers that the hideous experiments which had given him his gigantic brain had also blessed him with telepathy, for he often seemed to know exactly what an enemy or ally was thinking—a talent which made him all the more dangerous.

Some said he possessed the power to control a man's very soul—though none who might have seen it had lived to confirm its use!

Such qualities were bizarre enough to earn him pride of place in any catalogue of horrors. *But the evil scientists of the Ultimate Reich had not stopped there!* They had created a means of transport as dreadful as the creature it was designed for— *the terrifying Murder Chair!*

BEHOLD THE MURDER CHAIR

Reader, if you dare—*behold the Murder Chair!* The man-monster sat awkwardly, like a doll, on a brass and leather seat, with metal straps to hold his gigantic head in place and prevent the weight of it from snapping his neck. The back of the chair, meanwhile, was composed entirely of Babbage machines and analytical engines, constantly ticking and clicking, and connected to large gold-plated pipes—and here the true horror of the apparatus began, for those pipes extended from the back of the chair through the skull and into the tissue of Murder's living brain!

The workings somehow fused with the criminal's nightmare intellect, increasing his terrible mental powers beyond measure and providing him the means to control and propel the Murder Chair by thought alone—for instead of four legs, it scuttled on eight, like some unspeakable insect, each mechanical leg ending in a fearsome point suitable for gutting enemies in a single stroke! Attached to the two frontmost legs were a pair of nozzles, through which the diabolical master-brain could direct sheets of searing flame— meanwhile, the arms of the chair ended in a pair of crude robotic hands, allowing Mister Murder to do the work of his fiendish Nazi masters without assistance. In the past, he had been content to be a mere weapon of Untergang—that malign organisation created to serve the mad dreams of the seemingly immortal Fuhrer and his sinister Ultimate Reich! But, following the shocking events of the past few days, our paper can reveal that this inhuman monstrosity had been selected by the Fuhrer himself to fill the vacuum of power, and become the newest and most horrific leader of that devilish terror group!

And his first act as leader was to partner with the diabolical Jason Satan! Had there ever, in the history of mankind, been so unutterably dreadful a pair of arch-fiends collected together in one place? *Never!* And now their evil alliance had borne fruit—*in a plot to poison the very air New York City breathed!*

SLOW, AGONISING DEATH

"Tell me," purred Satan, running his grey tongue over his yellow teeth, "will the gas we propose to create act quickly? Or... *slowly?*" He shuddered as his evil mind savoured the dreadful thought!

Mister Murder allowed his obscene face to crack into a grotesque smile, and the analytical engines burrowing into his skull made a soft, satisfied *clack*. "According to my calculations," he said in his hollow, high-pitched voice, "death should occur within twenty to thirty hours of inhalation. During that time, the organs will rot and soften, starting with the lungs, until finally they simply melt like wax, pouring out through holes in the skin as it, too, rots away. Total liquefaction of the organs and muscle tissue will occur perhaps five or six hours after death—and finally, after no more than forty hours, the bones will crumble and desiccate. Two short days, mein Herr, and New York will be a mausoleum! The streets will run with blood and powdered bone! *And you and I will be the only human beings left alive!*"

Jason Satan's eyes seemed to flash, almost glowing with pleasure! "How wonderful! Oh, how perfectly perfect!" He giggled. "Although to call either of us *human* seems... somehow insulting."

Mister Murder's cracked lips stretched wider, the grin seeming to split his head in two, and his massive eyes narrowed to vicious slits. "Quite so. We are *übermenschen*, you and I. And may I say how pleased I am that you have finally chosen to, ah... *join the winning team,* as you Americans say."

Satan giggled again, swirling the beaker of white ooze around and around before setting it down on a long table and turning to look around the room—*at the machinery that would swiftly bring a nightmare reign of horror to the greatest city on Earth!*

LETHAL POISON GAS

The room was a large, ostensibly disused warehouse, long ago commandeered for the purpose of terror by Untergang, and the best part of it was taken up by a massive network of copper and brass piping, feeding in and out of various distilling tanks and stills. This was the machinery that was even now slowly chugging and hissing, clanking and fuming, as it went about the business of transforming the blood of Jason Satan into lethal poison gas!

Soon, they would have enough to blanket the entire city—at

which point they would load the tanks of gas onto the short, squat rocket that sat in the centre of the room, underneath the dust-covered skylight. The rocket, fuelled by hydrogen peroxide purchased on the black market, would shoot into the sky above the city like some firework of the damned—*then explode and blanket the whole of Manhattan with a poisonous fog of pure, unstoppable death!*

And that was only the start of their devil's scheme! After the initial airburst, if the wind forecasts were accurate, the cloud would drift inland, bringing death to the boroughs, to the suburbs, to the small towns...

Jason Satan shivered again, hugging himself. He imagined the crowds of panicked people rushing to and fro on the sidewalks, coughing and spluttering up gobbets of their own blood and tissue! The dogs howling! The fathers trying to explain the horror to their dying children! And after that—the corpses, stacked like cordwood in the streets!

So many corpses!

His face suddenly fell into a parody of a frown. "Oh, but what of the Frenchman?" he mused, in a mock-tragic tone.

There was a clatter of cogs from the Murder Chair, followed by a high, rasping chuckle. "Perhaps I will decide to inoculate *him* as well, before the end. Or perhaps—*not!* He is a mercenary, mein Herr—If he were to remain alive, we would eventually have to pay the bill."

His chuckle became a laugh, a high-pitched squeal of devilish mirth, and Jason Satan could not help but join his own voice to the cackling chorus—a tolling bell of terror for the city that never sleeps!

Who would save us now?

MASTERS OF TERROR

The answer—a shadow falling across a filthy skylight! A sudden crash! The air filled with shattered glass! And at the centre of the rain of razor shards—*a man!*

And what a man! Blond and bearded, with piercing blue eyes and skin the colour of bronze, and a familiar lightning-bolt insignia splashed across his blue shirt—the flag of *Doc Thunder, America's Greatest Hero!*

Neither the shards of glass nor the twenty-foot drop seemed to trouble New York's premier he-man, as he landed, cat-like, on the stone floor, mere feet from the deadly missile. In a voice of cold steel, he addressed the cowering villains: "You'll pay the bill, all right."

Those deadly masters of terror now knew fear themselves! For the hero standing to defy them was no ordinary man—this was Doc Thunder! The scientific superman born from the Ultimate Reich's own strange science, and devoted to crushing their power wherever it might raise its merciless head!

A man capable of leaping an eighth of a mile in a single bound—so powerful that nothing less than a bursting shell could penetrate his skin! Even with their ignoble forces combined, would the malicious mind of Mister Murder and the deadly death-touch of Jason Satan be enough to subdue the hero of New York? Were even odds of two against one enough against such a powerhouse of heroism?

They thought not! *And a fair fight was the last thing on their minds!*

MURDERER OF MILLIONS

Satan ran to a speaking-tube dangling from the wall and screeched into it. *"Savate!"*

A moment later, a lithe, powerfully-built figure dressed in an orange jerkin burst in from an ante room! Their ace in the hole—Savate, the deadly mercenary and master of the French martial art whose name he had adopted as his own!

The mysterious Man of a Thousand Kicks had clashed a dozen times or more with America's Greatest Hero, and always escaped to fight another day! Savate was usually hired to delay Doc Thunder and other champions of the law for the crucial moments necessary to complete some heist or scheme— yet his strange code of honour forbade him from taking the lives of those uninvolved in the struggle between the forces of law and the criminal underworld.

But to delay Doc Thunder's victory now would be to doom thousands to slow and painful extinction! Was Savate an unwitting dupe of the sinister forces of Untergang? *Or had he finally crossed the line that separates the dashing rogue from the callous murderer of millions?*

The answer will astound you! Turn to page five for more of the incredible front-page scoop this reporter *had* to call—*"The Fearful Fate of Doc Thunder!"*

(*Note: The bare facts of this account may have been dramatically embellished in parts by ace reporter Stan 'Scoop' Mann in order to increase the pulse-pounding verisimilitude of this incredible story—in the mighty Clarion manner! However, we maintain that the awesome action presented herein remains true to the spirit of the original events.*)

"MAKE ME ONE with everything."

"Sure thing, buddy." The hot dog vendor narrowed his eyes, frowning. "Hey, uh, aren't you that El Sombrero fella?"

El Sombra grinned. He was dressed in his usual style—a pair of ragged trousers from a black tuxedo, stained with dust and blood, and nothing else, save the mask over his eyes. "What tipped you off, amigo?"

In truth, the masked swordsman had become altogether too famous for his liking after the business with Donner, Crane and Lomax; he was used to being a figure of mystery, hiding in the shadows and alleys—or better yet, out in the desert, away from all human company. Now, everyone in New York seemed to think of him as some kind of masked hero, one of the many the city had produced. It was fun, but it was distracting him from his real mission, which was why he'd taken to lurking around the docks: as soon as he found a boat that would take him across the Atlantic, he'd be on his way.

In the meantime, there was always room in his belly for another hot dog.

"Ha!" The vendor smiled, loading up the hot dog with the works. "I guess there ain't many fellers like you walkin' around, right? This one's on the house, pal."

"Muchos gracias." El Sombra speared the hot dog deftly on the end of his sword and took a bite, and it tasted meaty, watery, decidedly unhealthy and absolutely delicious. Hot dogs, he thought to himself, were probably the single thing about New York that he'd miss the most. Maybe when he hit Berlin, he'd enjoy a quick bratwurst or two before he killed Adolf Hitler. But it wouldn't be quite the same.

"You know, those things are gonna kill you."

The swordsman turned to see a tall black man standing in a nearby alley. He was greying at the temples, with a patch over one eye and a large, luxuriant moustache. He was dressed outlandishly—a bright, almost fluorescent blue trench coat worn over some sort of close-fitting white jumpsuit, dotted with pouches, holsters for a knife and pistol, and an insignia El Sombra didn't quite recognise. A pair of steel-capped combat boots completed the ensemble—not quite jackboots, but El Sombra felt himself tensing anyway. He wondered how it was he hadn't noticed the man before. "Let me guess—you're a nutritionist?"

The other man held up a silver badge—that insignia again, a mandala inside a five-pointed star, like an old west Sheriff's badge, with a letter at each of the points. "Not quite. Jack Scorpio. Agent of S.T.E.A.M. Special Tactical Espionage And Manoeuvres." El Sombra gave the badge a careful examination, looked into Scorpio's eyes for a moment and then relaxed—a little.

"Sure, I've heard of you." El Sombra nodded. "Spy guys, right?" The journal he'd stolen from Donner, the ex-head of Untergang, had mentioned them several times, and never favourably—there were rants about a *'degenerate organisation of addicts, sexual perverts and nonconformists'* that went on for whole pages. Reading them, you'd never believe this same organisation was taking down Untergang threats all over the globe, but somehow, there it was.

Frankly, they sounded like El Sombra's kind of people.

Scorpio smiled. "Yeah, I've heard of you too, true believer. Let me see if I got my story right—Mexican village, evil Nazis, brutal massacre, lone survivor. Spends nine years out in the desert grooving on some kind of way-out psychedelic scene and ends up as a living weapon. Hey, you ever hear of the Fourth Earth Battalion? My outfit back in the late 'sixties, before this whole international superspy gig."

El Sombra shook his head. Scorpio grinned.

"Really? I could have sworn you'd read the manual I wrote. Check it out sometimes—some of the training techniques in there might look familiar. Anyway, desert, mind expansion, develops second personality of El Sombra in order to offload extreme combat stress, blah blah blah—and nine years later, to the day, our hero blows right back into that village and gives those Nazi assholes some instant karma. As in wiping them off the face of the earth. As in destroying giant robots, traction engines, Luftwaffe battalions and scientific research the Ratzis have been working on for *decades*—with nothing but a *sword.*" Scorpio looked El Sombra right in the eye, as if daring him to deny it. "You know what? That's the kind of story I like to hear." He opened up one of his pouches, took out a long cigarette and lit it. "Want some of this?"

"No thanks." El Sombra wrinkled his nose at the strange scent of the smoke. He wasn't happy with having his past summed up so casually.

"That's fab, fervent one. More for the rest of us." Scorpio took a long, deep drag, holding it in his lungs for a moment before exhaling. "Anyway, turns out this mystery swordsman decides cleaning house back home ain't enough—he's gonna take out the big bad voodoo daddy Mr Adolf Hitler himself. You do know he's a giant killer robot now, right?"

"I know."

"Cool. Where was I? So along the way our hero stops over in the city that swings—New York, natch—and puts the whammy on a whole nest of Nazi spies and a decidedly un-hip mad scientist who's been giving the long-underwear crowd hassle for years. Then it's right back to the mission, right?" He took another puff on the cigarette, breathing out slowly. "You know, effendi, I do find myself digging that story. You know what I love about it? It's believable. It's all stuff that could just about actually happen. Right up until the ending." He shot El Sombra a look.

El Sombra rolled his eyes. "Don't tell me, amigo. I hate spoilers." He frowned. "And I'm not sure about taking advice from an undercover spy guy you can see from six blocks away. Isn't that a little... noticeable?"

"Funny man. Take a look around, funny man."

El Sombra looked around. The two of them might have been standing just off the street, but they weren't exactly invisible, and New York's docklands were a busy place at this time of day. Yet not a soul passing by was looking in their direction. Even the hot dog vendor was acting as if they just weren't there.

Scorpio smiled. "Anti-camouflage. Draws the eye and reassures on a subconscious level. It's all in the right shade of blue." He took another long toke. "Day-Glo Ops are the new Black Ops, brother. You're living in the S.T.E.A.M. age now."

El Sombra raised an eyebrow. "It's your world, I just live in it?"

"You got it. So, you want that ending?"

"Why not?"

"Well, it's kind of a downer. This El Sombra cat thinks he can go straight to Berlin and take on Mecha-Hitler and the whole Ultimate Reich by himself, and he ends up six feet under—just like everyone else who tried it. And there have been many." Scorpio took another drag. "Just having a little trouble suspending my disbelief on that one, you dig? Like, when there's a whole country just itching to paste the paper-hanger once and for all—why would a cool fool like El Sombra try to go it alone?"

El Sombra shrugged, but there was an edge in his voice. "Maybe he thinks America is a little slow, amigo. If you people had scratched your itch a little sooner, my family would be alive now."

"I can dig it." Scorpio nodded. "But to start the kind of war we're talking about, you'd need the cats in Magna Britannia to turn a blind eye. They got a vested interest in things in Europe staying just the way they are, which is why our friend the freaky Führer ain't rattled any sabres lately—except in places the Brits don't give a damn about, like your home town. And mine. Likewise the Italians, who are grooving on our kind of frequency, politics-wise—they would love to hit Hitler where it hurts. But up until now, the rule's been that if one country starts a party"—he dropped the remains of his cigarette on the concrete and then crushed it out with the heel of his boot—"Britain's gonna be the one to finish it."

"Up until now?"

"You been reading the London papers, pilgrim?"

El Sombra shook his head. "I've been a little busy."

Scorpio grinned. "We got our blind eye. I won't bore you with the details—although they are deeply *yvoorg*, true believer—but Victoria just got hit smack in her ugly face on a scale nobody never saw before, even counting that Martian jazz from last year. Britannia is reeling with the feeling right now, and—assuming they survive this—they are not gonna to be able to say boo to a goose any time soon."

El Sombra blinked. "If they *survive?* Magna Britannia?"

"Could go either way. Obviously, if they don't, it's a whole other ball game, but I'm a glass-half-full kind of cat, dig?"

"So..."

Scorpio nodded. "So right now, there's everything to play for, and if we don't take advantage our buddy Adolf definitely will. Which means sometime in the next month or so—as soon as we negotiate how down the Italians and Russians want to be with this happening—America goes to war." He pointed a finger at El Sombra's chest. "And America wants you."

El Sombra couldn't help but laugh. The idea of him dressing in a helmet and flak jacket and parachuting into the forests with a hundred other men, weighed down by some heavy machine gun, seemed somehow far more absurd than the thought of sneaking half-naked across the border with his sword in his hand. "I don't know, amigo. I think I might prefer to be my own man."

"You would be, baby. In the squad I'm building, there's no room for anything else." He grinned.

El Sombra blinked. "You're a very strange man, Jack Scorpio. Why all this... *cool, cat, baby, groovy*, all that. What is that? Spy talk?"

Jack nodded. "Kind of. It's dream language—focuses the trained mind, distracts the untrained mind. Right now, it's futzing you up a little, am I right?"

"Well..."

"It's cool, I'll tone it down, let you think straight. If we work together, I'll teach you how to do it—Jim Channon turned me on to the concept when we were in the First Earth Battalion. It's basically a mixture of lucid dreaming and... well, it's kind of hard to explain without, uh..." Jack tugged idly on his moustache for a second. "Okay, have you seen what Andy Warhol's been up to lately?"

"Ow!" El Sombra winced, feeling his other self bubbling painfully up. He rubbed the knot at the back of his mask, forcing the thoughts back down. "Djego has. He enjoyed 'Cellphone'—the sculpture."

"Yeah, he's just finished a new one called 'Pod'—it's similar, only instead of the grid of numbers, there's a perfect ceramic circle. I was meditating on that earlier today. Anyway, it's connected to that—dream logic, dreamworld thinking. There is another world. There is a better world." Jack smiled, and El Sombra felt suddenly ill—faded and washed out, as if he was no longer quite real. "Well, there must be. Right? See what I did to you there?"

He was grinning, as if he knew some secret El Sombra didn't. The masked man's guts turned over, and he felt the sudden urge to throw up. Scorpio laughed. "Weaponised cosmic awareness. Welcome to the big leagues."

"Let's... change the subject." El Sombra said, quietly. "Why don't you tell me more about—" he tailed off suddenly, noticing Jack's eyes widen at something just behind his left shoulder. In the distance, he heard the crash of shattering glass.

"What?" El Sombra turned, and saw that one of the disused warehouses now had a broken skylight. A cloud of disturbed dust lingered in the air. "What happened?"

Scorpio breathed out. "Doc Thunder happened. Damn."

"What?"

"He just fell out of a clear blue sky and into that warehouse." Scorpio reached for his holster, drawing a large revolver—a Magnum of some kind—with three chambers, arranged on some sort of revolving drum. "Didn't look like an accident, either. Want to see for yourself?"

El Sombra blinked. Well, why not? He had nothing better to do.

"Groovy, amigo."

SLEDGEHAMMER BLOWS

"En garde!"

That was the war-cry on the lips of Savate, the Man of a Thousand Kicks—as he leapt into astounding action! Few men alive could hope to avoid the hammer-blows of Doc Thunder for long, but the wily Frenchman was perhaps the most agile fighter ever to take on the forces of law and order—and in addition, he was the veteran of a dozen previous duels with the super-scientific powerhouse, and thus knew his every move almost before he made it.

Meanwhile, Doc Thunder fought under the handicap of his own heroic conscience—for he knew that if he struck his enemy with his full strength, strength enough to punch a hole in a brick wall and bend solid steel girders into pretzels, Savate would die—as surely as if he had been hit by a cannon shell! Thus, he pulled his punches, which only made them easier to avoid, and all the time the dread machinery was continuing to distil the blood of Jason Satan. Every second spent in battle brought closer that fatal moment when the deadly poison gas would be ready!

If he could only wreck the machine before it finished its terrible operation, but no! The mercenary was determined to force him away from it, and from the rocket that would deliver the hideous payload into the skies of New York!

Savate knew all of Doc Thunder's weak points. Every second, another flurry of kicks like sledgehammer blows slammed into Doc Thunder's eyes, blocking his sight. He swung a fist out at his side in a wide arc, hoping to knock the rocket over, but struck only the empty air!

And the next moment, twin jets of fire engulfed him in an aura of flame!

For the stumbling combat had driven America's Greatest Hero into the firing-line of Mister Murder's Murder Chair!

And as readers of the *Daily Clairon* well know—*mayhem is the Murder Chair!*

FIERY HOLOCAUST

The insect-like front legs of Mister Murder's fiendish contraption bathed Doc Thunder in a blazing inferno, burning the world-famous T-shirt from his back—but it would take more than that to ignite the Man of Might! Judging that the Frenchman had leapt to safety rather than risk being consumed by the fiery holocaust, Thunder turned towards the source of the flames—grabbing hold of the Murder Chair's incendiary legs and crushing them in his super-powerful grip as if they were tissue paper!

"Nein! Nein! You cannot do this!" screamed the balloon-headed Nazi, as Doc Thunder lifted the Murder Chair from the ground, the six remaining legs scrabbling furiously at his naked chest—but the razor points could do little more than scratch at his near-indestructible skin. Doc Thunder turned his head and saw Savate, already tensing to dodge what he knew was coming. But Savate wasn't the only one who knew how to predict an old foe.

With a mighty heave, Doc Thunder hurled the Murder Chair, with the screaming head of Untergang trapped within it, not at the place where Savate was—but where he would be!

Wha-a-amm!

The French mercenary was treated to the head-butt of a lifetime—and he was lucky to get it! *For had Doc Thunder used any less skill in aiming one enemy at another, the razor points of the Chair's insectile legs might have speared Savate through the chest and ended his life in one agonising instant!*

As ever, Doc Thunder made pains not to take a human life if he could possibly avoid it. But against the deadly killing power of Jason Satan, the Man With the Touch of Death, would even America's Greatest Hero have the luxury of choice? Did he dare to leave this maddest and deadliest of criminals to live another day?

No!

Not now that this most monstrous of men had stumbled upon the deadly secret contained within his own blood! Jason Satan was a living weapon of death, a ticking poison-bomb that would end the lives of millions were he to escape that room!

But could even Doc Thunder subdue the grinning albino without succumbing to the foul ichor that coursed through the insane murder's veins? Could even his mighty constitution survive a single touch from the lunatic's hand?

The choice was kill—or die! Which would it be?

THE TOUCH OF DEATH

The two combatants circled warily. Jason Satan's arms were spread wide, the venom in his fingertips ready to strike as he blocked Doc Thunder's path to the clanking machinery that was even now completing the distillation of Satan's blood into deadly poison gas!

Doc Thunder considered wrapping his bare knuckles to strike the death-blow and perhaps ward off the worst of the fatal effect—but with his clothing destroyed by the Murder Chair's flame-cannons, he had nothing to wrap them in. He would have to hope that he was strong enough to touch Jason Satan and survive—*though no man ever had!*

The super-scientist's eyes narrowed—his enemy's did likewise! Like gunslingers of old, they were judging the moment to unleash the deadly forces at their command! Concentration was total! The slightest distraction now could mean the difference between life—and death!

And at that moment the warehouse door crashed open—and Jack Scorpio, Agent of S.T.E.A.M., burst into the fray! Joined by Mexico's Greatest Hero—the masked swordsman known as El Sombra!

Fate can be cruel! For Doc Thunder allowed his attention to be drawn to the smashing entrance of these two incredible heroes for the split instant his foe required—*to land the fatal blow!*

Jason Satan leapt forward—to plant his open palm square in the centre of his opponent's bared chest—inches from his beating heart!

The Touch of Death had been delivered—to Doc Thunder!

(CONTINUED ON PAGE FOLLOWING.)

* * *

"This doesn't look good, amigo," El Sombra muttered.

It didn't.

Doc Thunder was on the floor, convulsing. His skin had turned a hideous, waxy yellow, and as Jack Scorpio watched, a clump of hair came loose from his scalp and drifted to the floor. His bowels had let go, a rivulet of blood ran from one ear, suggesting some terrifying haemorrhage in his brain, and white foam oozed from the corners of his mouth. His eyes stared blankly at nothing at all.

Jason Satan stood over him, fixing the two intruders with his milk-white eyes and his ghastly yellow grin. Doc Thunder had fought the Man With the Touch of Death several times over the past few years, always careful to wear protective clothing in their battles. This time, he hadn't expected Satan's involvement—but then, Satan was generally a solo operator. He'd never been part of the world of Untergang before.

Not that Doc Thunder had suspected Untergang's involvement either.

Before he began his vacation in the forbidden kingdom of Zor-Ek-Narr, he'd been cleaning up the loose ends from previous cases—including the theft of a large quantity of high-test hydrogen peroxide, stolen from a rocket research facility out in Brentwood by a gang of inexperienced heist artists. Peroxide was expensive and difficult to synthesise, but it worked well in attitude jets, and wasn't half so expensive as cavorite—in fact, there was talk of using it to send rockets into space without the benefit of the gravity-defying alloy. Presumably the crooks had read one of the reports extolling its virtues and figured it'd be easier to steal than cavorite, too.

In the planning stages, it had sounded like a three man job, but they'd needed to bring in a couple of inside men at the facility, and, after all their efforts, the peroxide they stole was only worth fifty grand as opposed to the hundred they'd assumed they could get. In the end, they just didn't have the experience or the contacts to get a good price, and the resentment had simmered, with each member thinking they deserved more than their meagre share.

The gang had planned to split the cash after fencing the H_2O_2, but greed prevailed, and Doc Thunder—having easily tracked the gang to their hideout—found himself bursting in on a pitched gun battle. Too small a payoff between too large a group—it often turned out that way.

After he'd picked up the pieces and found out from the surviving thieves who their fence was—a man named Winston F. Keeler—he wasn't that shocked to find the man apparently dead of a heart attack. He was a good thirty stone, and clearly didn't take much care of himself. He did take good care of his records, though, and Thunder found a notebook in a wall safe—along with a hundred thousand dollars in cash—detailing exactly where the peroxide had been delivered; some kind of insurance, presumably.

It hadn't helped him. Winston Keeler's death had not come naturally to him; he had been assassinated by an injection of digitalis. Had Doc Thunder known, he might have had second thoughts about crashing into the abandoned warehouse the peroxide had been delivered to.

As it was, he assumed it was a fairly simple scam of a type he'd seen before—concentrated peroxide would be stolen, then diluted depending on the target market. Laboratories and water treatment plants would buy it at concentrations of 30% without looking too hard—with further dilution, the same stuff could be bottled and sold as hair bleach. Keeler had bought for fifty grand and sold for ninety—an enterprising businessman could turn that into as much as three hundred, depending on supply and demand. A large, seemingly abandoned warehouse most likely meant an operation of that nature.

Undiluted, high-test peroxide also made for excellent bombs, of course. Doc Thunder thought that was possible, but unlikely. He definitely didn't consider that it might be used for the purpose originally intended: rocket fuel.

More fool him.

"I honestly didn't know if that would work." Jason Satan grinned. "Isn't it wonderful when your secret dream comes true?" He sniggered, taking a step closer, his fingers flexing eagerly.

Scorpio levelled his gun. "Hold it, slick. One more step and I put a hole in you the size of the Brooklyn tunnel."

"Go ahead," Satan cackled. "Shoot me. Send my beautiful blood hissing and spraying from my veins. Drench yourself in it." He took another step. "Make my day."

Jack Scorpio's finger squeezed the trigger, but the gun refused to fire. He just couldn't seem to squeeze hard enough.

Behind him, the Murder Chair hissed and clanked as Mister Murder righted himself and scuttled forwards. He chuckled, a high-pitched giggle that echoed obscenely out of his cavernous mouth. "Herr Scorpio. How wonderful to see you again. Especially now that I've learned to counter your... unique mental defences. Please, tell your trigger finger to move. You'll find I am fully in control. And if I can control one finger..."—Scorpio felt his mind lurch as his arm suddenly swivelled, aiming the gun at El Sombra's head—"There. Good soldier."

"Make him fire." Satan ran a wet grey tongue over his yellow fangs. "I want to see the Mexican's head burst."

"Why not?" Mister Murder twitched his shoulders in something almost like a shrug. "I've grown so much more powerful since the last time we fought, Herr Scorpio. You should have made sure of me then. Now... my mind is powerful enough to wear you like a glove. Like a puppet." The wrinkled, egg-like head cracked into a malevolent smile. "You will make a fine agent of Untergang."

"Excusez-moi?"

Mister Murder froze, then scuttled slowly around. Savate stood behind him, arms folded, brow furrowed in anger.

"Did you say... Untergang?"

CREED OF HATE

Mister Murder's eyes blazed with sudden rage! *Curse the luck!*

Up until now he had used his strange mental powers to fog Savate's mind, so the Frenchman accepted any story he was told without thinking. Thus, he did not question why the World's Most Evil Brain should no longer be working for Untergang, nor why two such accomplished killers should be wasting their time preparing 'knockout gas' to use against the city. In his mind, the three of them had been planning some great caper, to rob a sleeping city blind—but now, with a single unguarded word, Mister Murder had torn the scales from his pawn's eyes!

Could he reassert his mental domination and retain control over Jack Scorpio at the same time? It would be a supreme effort—but he was übermensch! Created in the laboratories of the Ultimate Reich to annihilate free will and spread the Führer's creed of hate across all the continents of the globe! Not only could he do it—*it was his destiny!*

Savate froze, feeling a prickling sensation running down the nerves in his arms. Suddenly, he was rooted to the spot, his limbs refusing to obey him. Jack Scorpio was likewise helpless, unable to do anything but keep his weapon pointed directly at El Sombra's head. Doc Thunder, meanwhile, was still insensate, struggling in the terrible grip of Jason Satan's poison—and despite his superhuman physiognomy he found himself inching closer to death with each passing second!

OOZING GOBBETS

Glistening beads of sweat trickled over Mister Murder's horrifically enlarged brow as he concentrated on keeping the tableau in place. It was all he could do to keep two minds under his control—three was quite impossible. Thus, the time for El Sombra to die was now—*and at Jack Scorpio's hand!*

The hideous mutant supermind gritted his teeth as he tightened his mental hold. There was some vague fuzz gathered around Scorpio's thoughts—the vestiges of the S.T.E.A.M. brain-training that had thwarted Mister Murder in the past—but still, the deranged telepath forced the agent's finger to tighten on the trigger of his incredible multi-ammo magnum... squeezing it... *until*—

—until the gun clicked uselessly in Scorpio's hand... and El Sombra seized his moment and leaped forward—*for the kill!*

His razor-sharp blade—which this reporter can exclusively reveal was inherited from his dead brother in a furious battle against the forces of the Luftwaffe—sliced directly thru Mister Murder's obscene cranium, transforming the Untergang abomination's gigantic head into a gruesome cauldron, open to the world, filled with oozing gobbets of bloody, sundered brain matter! *A fitting end for the arch-Nazi!*

Jack Scorpio felt the mental pressure ease, and breathed a sigh of relief before once again aiming his gun between Jason Satan's near-luminous white eyes.

But this time, he flipped the safety off.

AGONISING STRUGGLE

"Nothing has changed, Scorpio," Satan sneered, hissing the words through his rotting teeth. "By all means, shoot me, stab me—I'll take all of you with me! I'll shower you with my beautiful bleach-white blood and drag you down with me to the lowest pit of Hell!"

At his words, El Sombra backed away! *Had Mexico's greatest hero turned coward in the face of a man who could kill with a single touch?*

"Very sensible, masked man. Just turn your back and let me slip away. You have business in Germany, I understand. You'll be far away from the action, I guarantee." Satan giggled, his eyes flickering between Savate and Scorpio, then looking down at the pale, jaundiced face of Doc Thunder, savouring his triumph!

Once Thunder had been a veritable superhuman—now he shivered feverishly on the cold ground, blind and deaf to the struggles above, every breath an agonising struggle for his very survival! *How long did America's Greatest Hero have left to live?*

"Your turn now, Scorpio. Lower the gun and walk away. Perhaps you can get the good Doctor to a hospital before it's too late." He giggled again, but Jack Scorpio refused to lower his weapon. "No? Then we all die—here and now!"

The madman tensed, readying

himself to spring! All his attention was focussed on the leader of S.T.E.A.M.—and delivering the one touch that would end his life! The time for talk was over—*now was the time for action in the mighty manner only the Daily Clarion can deliver!*

It was time—for Savate to strike!

PURIFYING FIRE

He leaped forward, aiming an expertly-delivered kick to Jason Satan's jaw, hard enough to split the monster's lip! A single drop of noxious white blood flew past Scorpio's ear, deadlier than a bullet—then the Man With the Touch of Death crashed to the ground, the force of his momentum sliding him across the dusty floor—*and underneath the exhaust of the rocket!*

Savate turned to El Sombra and yelled: "Yours, mon ami!"

"Gracias, amigo!" El Sombra shouted back. Then he reached to the wall of switches he'd been backing towards—and pulled the lever for launch!

"*Noooooooooo!*" Jason Satan's inhuman scream was cut off by the roar of engines—*and then the hydrogen peroxide ignited, consuming Satan and all his toxins in a pillar of purifying fire!*

The rocket soared up through the shattered window before detonating high above the city—but without the deadly payload of poison gas, Untergang's deadly firework proved no more than a damp squib!

With two merciless master-villains dead, and Savate rumoured to be working closely with the American government to pay off his debt to society, New York can finally breathe a sigh of relief. *Or can we?*

Untergang's latest foul plot may have been smashed—but their Uncle Adolf is still waiting for his turn! *And America's Greatest Hero is still lying at death's door!*

Buy the Clarion tomorrow for a pulse-pounding front page special on Doc Thunder's fight for life—and the looming conflict receiving unanimous support in Congress! It's all under tomorrow's heart-stopping headline—"*If War Be Our Destiny!*"

"WHY ZE HANDCUFFS, mon ami?" Savate grinned as the police pushed him into the back of a waiting van. "Surely you do not think ze great Savate will perform ze daring escape?"

"Not if ze great Savate knows what's good for him." Jack Scorpio flicked the wheel of his lighter, sparking up another of his special cigarettes. "And by good I mean profitable. Stay cool, Savate. I'll be in touch." Savate stared at him for a moment, and nodded, and then the van doors closed and he was driven away.

Doc Thunder had already been taken away in an ambulance. Most of his hair had fallen out, and he seemed somehow shrivelled, as though someone had opened a hidden valve somewhere and let a little air out of him. The paramedics wondered privately if he'd last the night.

Scorpio took a long drag. "That's what happens when you just blunder in without backup, true believer."

El Sombra raised an eyebrow. "Alternatively, that's what happens when someone blunders in on you."

Scorpio shrugged. "Either way, if we'd all been together, things might not have gone the way they did. Stolen hydrogen peroxide's something S.T.E.A.M. should have known about from the start. Folks like us need to hang together, or we'll sure as hell hang separately."

"Who said that?" It sounded to El Sombra like a quote from somewhere. For some reason, the thought disturbed him.

"Someone in a dream," Scorpio said, and smiled that infuriating secret smile. El Sombra had a feeling he'd be learning to hate that soon enough. Scorpio was right, he knew. The USSA was going to war, and he'd have a better chance of killing off the Ultimate Reich and all their bastards if he took advantage of that. Which, for the time being, meant joining whatever team Jack Scorpio was forming.

Scorpio sighed heavily, breaking El Sombra's train of thought. "God damn it."

"What?"

"Untergang finally won one, even if they hadn't planned it. We figured we had Doc Thunder on board for the war effort, but that didn't look like a man who's going to be storming any bunkers any time soon." Scorpio tapped a little ash out onto the ground. "So much for it all being over by Christmas. Except maybe for him."

"You think he's really going to..." El Sombra couldn't bring himself to finish it. The idea seemed too outlandish. He'd only met Thunder recently, but he'd been under the impression you could throw just about anything at him and he'd walk right through it. To see him shrivelled up and going bald like that—it seemed almost sacrilegious.

"Maybe. Unless we can find an antidote. Even then..." He shook his head. "Well, at least I've got a line on Savate now. I was wondering when I'd get a chance to bring him on board."

"Wait, you're recruiting *him?*" El Sombra blinked. "A guy who kicks people for money?"

"Well, I already got a guy who stabs people for free. I like variety. Anyway, you guys seemed to work pretty well together back there..."

El Sombra had to admit that. "I suppose. So who else have you got lined up in this merry band of yours?"

Scorpio inhaled, held it for a second, then blew out a ring of smoke.

"Trust me, true believer. You ain't seen nothing yet."

THE LAST STAND OF THE YODELLING BASTARDS

OFFICIAL RECORD CONCERNING EVENTS OF 07/12/2004: "OPERATION FALSE FLAG." THE FOLLOWING FILE CONCERNS THE FINAL MISSION OF THE EXPERIMENTAL COMMANDO UNIT YANKEE BRAVO SEVEN AND IS THUS CLASSIFIED ABOVE TOP SECRET.

"GENERAL ZITRON, SIR!" Major-General Allen marched up to the desk and snapped into a salute almost vigorous enough to knock his hat off. Matt Zitron rolled his eyes and tried to suppress an irritated sigh.

"At ease, Hal. Take a load off." He indicated a chair with his pipe.

"I prefer to stand, General, sir." Allen clicked his heels together for emphasis, then threw in another salute for good measure. Zitron thought about chiding him for his failure to stand at ease—but then, for Allen, this was at ease.

Well, so be it. The USSA needed men like Hal Allen—he might be wound tighter than a termite's tuchus, but he was a good man for admin work and he did possess a certain gift for strategy. Just so long as nobody was ever dumb enough to put him in the field, that was all. He belonged right here in sunny Italy, in the rear with the gear.

"That's fine, Hal. You go ahead and stand." Zitron blew out a long plume of smoke and nodded towards the office door. "You got Jack Scorpio out there?"

Allen winced. "Permission to speak freely, General, sir."

Zitron knew what was coming. "Go on, Hal, let's hear it."

"In my opinion, sir, Colonel Scorpio is completely wrong for this mission." He licked his lips nervously. "Now as you know, sir, I cannot quite bring myself to credit the, ah, *otherworldly* elements involved in the mission brief—"

Zitron nodded stoically. "You don't believe in time travel, mysterious portals or Leopard Men. Duly noted."

"—but I respect that this could be a pivotal operation. One that—if even half of what we've been told is true, as opposed to some bizarre fantasy—could possibly turn the tide of this whole war. And, to be quite frank with you, General, sir"— Allen scowled—"I just don't believe Yankee Bravo Seven can do the job."

"You don't, huh?"

"No, sir. They're just not soldier material, sir."

"Seems like they've done all right so far. Ask Von Hammer," Zitron grinned, dropping the name of the enemy Luftwaffe commander—one of the most feared names in the war—who Yankee Bravo Seven had captured alive, and in possession of the latest top secret Nazi wing-pack design, the previous week. Cavorite was still in short supply on the allied side, which meant they were stuck with Rocketeer squadrons for now, but it was still a hell of a coup.

"Sir..."—Allen drew in his breath, as if trying to control his temper—"... regardless of any... flukes of performance, these men do not and cannot possibly function as a proper military unit. I mean, the organisational structure alone—it makes no sense. In the same squad, we've got a colonel, a captain, an OSS captain, a *Navy* captain, a French mercenary, two civilians, one of whom is still wanted for crimes against Magna Britannia and the other of whom is a *conscientious objector,* for Christ's sake, and a... a... I don't know what he is, but he's *naked*—"

"Half-naked. His junk's covered."

"That's hardly the point, sir! He's an escaped lunatic from Mexico on a revenge mission! He's about as far from being an American soldier as you can *possibly get!*" Zitron couldn't help noticing how red Allen's face was getting. Yankee Bravo Seven had a habit of causing that reaction in him.

Well, at least it loosened him up a little. "Major-General, since you're actually standing at ease for once, how about sitting down?"

Allen snapped back to attention. "No, thank you, sir. Since I brought up the nudity issue—"

"Half-nudity."

"—I should say that I find it abhorrent that these men do not understand the simple concept of a uniform. Even Colonel Scorpio refuses to dress in a manner befitting his rank—and this is a man who used to wear a *skintight white jumpsuit* to command a top-secret Black Ops division—"

"Anti-camouflage. That's another thing you don't believe in, right?"

Allen fumed for a moment. "What I believe, sir, is that as a leader, Jack Scorpio seems completely incapable of controlling the men under his command."

"Colonel Scorpio," Zitron gently reminded Allen, "led S.T.E.A.M. for forty years."

Allen took a deep breath. "*In a skintight white—*"

"Anti-camouflage. If I had my way, we'd be using it in the field." He leant back in his chair, fixing Hal with a stern look. "And try moderating your tone a little, huh? The day you get your fifth star, that's the day you get to raise your voice to me."

"*Sir...*" Allen forced himself to calm down. "S.T.E.A.M. under Scorpio was practically a one-man operation, and an irresponsibly expensive one at that. I am given to understand that a significant portion of his operating budget was used to... for the purposes of"—he flushed a deep shade of scarlet—"of smoking reefer and copulating with fetish models. There, I said it."

"Not reefer, Hal. Some kind of special herb from the mountains of Zor-Ek-Narr. Keeps him young, or so I'm told." Zitron watched Hal turn a deeper crimson, almost purple. "It's a Leopard Man kind of thing. And that 'fetish model' you're talking about is a respected member of the Yankee Bravo team with over fifty confirmed kills to her credit. Not to mention one hell of a driver."

Allen took another deep breath. After a moment, his face made some progress back towards a normal colour. "Sir—he is simply not capable of the degree of command necessary for this man's army. Yankee Bravo Seven is... sir, I hate to say it, but it's a *terrible* unit. They're undisciplined, anti-authoritarian and at least three of them have recognised mental problems."

"You're exaggerating, Hal."

"Sir, Cohen is under the delusion that he's Blackbeard the pirate."

"Well, perhaps he is, Hal. We're living in interesting times." He leant forward and whispered. "Leopard Men."

"Sir, I do not believe in Leopard Men. I never have believed in Leopard Men." A manic tremble was creeping into his voice. "If a Leopard Man were to walk in here right now and offer me a cigarette made of 'special herbs'—I would *still* not believe in Leopard Men."

Zitron smiled. "Well, you don't have the clearance to anyway, so it's probably for the best. Is that everything, Hal?"

"Just... please, sir. Give me one platoon of real soldiers. We can still do this the right way. The *Army* way."

"Mmm... no, I don't think so." Zitron shook his head. "This one's a little too crazy to try it the Army way, Major-General."

"Sir—"

"No, I think this one, we do the Yankee Bravo Seven way." He smiled. "You're dismissed, Hal. Send Jack in on your way out."

Allen stared at him in fury for a moment, then saluted sharply. "Sir!"

Zitron watched him storm out of the office, and wondered when exactly Allen would have his heart attack and be done with it. Ah, well. Right now he had bigger fish to fry.

A moment later, Jack Scorpio entered the room.

PERSONNEL FILE: JACK SCORPIO - COLONEL (FOURTH EARTH BATTALION, STRATEGIC TACTICAL ESPIONAGE AND MANOEUVRES) - SKILLS: LEADERSHIP, ESPIONAGE, UNCONVENTIONAL WARFARE, ELONGATED LIFESPAN - PREFERRED WEAPON: S.T.E.A.M. ISSUE COLT X-007 MAGNUM CALIBER HANDGUN WITH MULTIPLE AMMUNITION CAPABILITY - WEAKNESSES: SEX, DRUGS, MAGICAL THINKING

Jack's uniform had changed since he'd left S.T.E.A.M. to form Yankee Bravo Seven. The white jumpsuit was gone, as well as most of the gadgets— his only concessions to the secret agent life were his S.T.E.A.M.-issue multi-ammo Magnum pistol, and a pair of shades which he never removed. The left lens was simple smoked glass, functioning as a replacement for his eyepatch, but the right lens had—allegedly been specially treated to perceive human auras. Like a lot of things about Jack, it was hard to say whether or not that was on the level.

When you came right down to it, Jack was a very strange guy.

These days, he wore fairly standard military combat trousers, albeit a little baggy in the hem, a flak jacket—usually open to the waist—and little else. Instead of wearing the steel-toed boots of old, he walked barefoot, and the soles of his feet had developed a hard layer of callus. Where the S.T.E.A.M. insignia had dotted his old uniform, he wore tattoos of pentagrams and other more mysterious symbols—images of bats and circled lightning, serpents coiled inside heraldic shields.

There was a scorpion branded into the skin at the base of his skull that hadn't been there before. Matt Zitron had once, in the mess after a particularly gruelling mission, asked what it represented. "My nature," Jack had said, and smiled his unsettling smile.

Jack had originally trained with the First Earth Battalion, before taking Jim Channon's ideas into newer, weirder directions. His offshoot, the Fourth Earth Battalion, had eventually mutated into S.T.E.A.M. in order to find favour with the establishment; now it seemed as though Jack had gone back to his roots.

It was no wonder someone like Hal Allen didn't like him. Hell, it was a wonder Zitron liked him, but he had to admit he had a soft spot for the creepy bastard.

If they were going to win this war, it was Jack that would do it.

Zitron stood, offering Jack Scorpio his hand. "Jack. Good to see you."

"Matthew." Jack gripped the General's hand as though he was about to arm-wrestle, squeezed tight, then let it go and offered his fist. Zitron looked confused. Jack smiled. "Greetings from the dream world. Go on, bump your knuckles."

Zitron looked at him for a moment, then gingerly bumped his fist against Jack's. For a moment, he felt strange, insubstantial. Jack's occasional 'dream world' talk always made him feel weird.

"How's the boy?" Jack asked, smiling widely.

"Isaac? Oh, he's doing great. Growing like a weed."

"All part of the circle of life. So, I hear you've got some action? Something regular army can't handle, is that right?"

"Oh, yeah."

Zitron took a long puff on his pipe.

"It's one for the Yodelling Bastards."

"AHEM. FIRST SLIDE, please."

Jack Scorpio sparked up another joint and inserted the next slide—a photograph of a bearded, nervous-looking man in round spectacles. The flickering of the oil lamp that projected the image onto the wall made him seem even more frightened, as if he kept some secret that horrified him.

Standing in front of the photograph, Captain Richard Reed puffed gently on his pipe. "Thank you, Corporal."

"*Aaar*," snarled Lev 'Blackbeard' Cohen, in the broad Cornish accent he'd had ever since his ship was sunk from under him by a Nazi U-boat in the Atlantic. "What's this lily-livered son of a swab have to say to us? *Captain*, he calls himself! Yet he's never stood on the deck of a ship in a ragin' storm o' cannon-fire, urgin' his lovely lads on to th' work o' plunderin'—"

Reed rolled his eyes. "Not this again. Cohen—"

"*Captain Teach, dog!*" Cohen leapt out of his chair, sending it rattling backwards, and drew his cutlass in one savage motion. "*I'll have ye dance a hornpipe at the end of me rope, ye scurvy bilge-rat!*"

"Put it away, fool," Mike Moses growled in his deep, rumbling bass. "Save it for the Ratzis." Cohen turned to him, scowling through blackened teeth, then re-seated himself with a grudging *aar*.

"Honestly," Marlene Lang sighed. "Boys and their swords." She flashed El Sombra a contemptuous look, and he flashed her a grin in response. Savate, sat in the row behind, rolled his eyes.

"Zere eez an Eenglish phrase... ah, oui, I have eet." He smiled, leaned forward and patted them both on the shoulder. "Get a room, mes amis."

In the corner, Johnny Wolf raised an eyebrow. He didn't speak. Ever.

Scorpio looked his team over as the banter continued. Seven specialists, each one the best there was at what they did—and right now, what they were doing was wasting his precious time. Calmly, he drew his multi-ammo Magnum and fired a dum-dum round into the ceiling.

That shut them up, all right.

"Captain Reed." Scorpio smiled. "You have the floor."

The six seated members of Yankee Bravo Seven grudgingly turned their attention to Reed. "Thank you, sir. Now, to answer Cohen's—I'm sorry, 'Blackbeard's'—idiotic question, the reason I'm giving this briefing is that I'm the best equipped to understand what we're facing and translate it for you... laypersons." He took a puff on his pipe. "Or 'morons,' as we in the scientific community call you."

Mike Moses groaned. "Aw, man. This is gonna be all kinds of crazy-ass mad science, ain't it?"

Reed smiled. "My dear Michael... is there any other kind?"

PERSONNEL FILE: RICHARD REED – CAPTAIN (OFFICE OF STRATEGIC SERVICES) – SKILLS: CODEBREAKING, ENGINEERING, SCIENTIFIC GENIUS, TECHNOLOGICAL SAVANT – PREFERRED WEAPON: NONE – WEAKNESSES: LOW COMBAT SKILLS, IS A CONDESCENDING ASSHOLE

"So! First slide—here we have Magna Britannia's own Professor Philip Hawthorne. Fact: fourteen months ago, Hawthorne attended a scientific conference in Switzerland to give a lecture on Parallel Universe Theory and the I Ching. Fact: shortly before he was due to deliver his lecture, he vanished from his hotel room without explanation. Nobody knows why."

El Sombra shrugged. "Kidnapped by the bastards, amigo. It's obvious."

"If by 'bastards' you mean Nazis—and you usually do—then yes, it was deeply obvious, but neither Magna Britannia nor Switzerland want to enter the war. Which is good for us. Right now, it's the USSA versus Nazi Germany, with our various European friends—and theirs—providing moral support, staging posts and deniable resources like Savate here. If Switzerland and Britannia got involved, we have no idea which way they'd go..."

Reed took a puff on his pipe, and Jack Scorpio broke in. "Doc Thunder's the big factor there."

"*Arrr,*" Cohen growled. "How fares he 'gainst the ravages o' the black spot?"

Scorpio shrugged. "He's out of danger, I hear. In a couple of months, maybe he'll even wake up." He shook his head. "Anyway, as long as he's recuperating in Zor-Ek-Narr—and who knows how long it'll be before he's back to his old self—we're a lot weaker. Meanwhile, Magna Britannia know they can control Hitler when he's at full strength; they've been doing it for decades, and apart from occasional Untergang agents like Dan Dashwood, they've had no problems. So do the math. If they enter the war, it'll be to do a nice little deal with the Führer and get their old colony back. Then they'll throw a bone to the Nazis—Italy, maybe—and get back to business as usual."

"They'd do that?" Very little shocked Marlene Lang, but she seemed nonplussed at that.

"Sure. Britain wasn't exactly friendly even before all their shit hit the fan. Anyway, back on topic..." He nodded to Reed and changed to the next slide.

Reed smiled. "Back on topic—here we see Phil Hawthorne and Alexander Oddfellow having a drink in the Eagle in Cambridge, in happier times. If you've been reading your Above Top Secret files, you'll remember Oddfellow as the man who accidentally discovered time travel. Which, funnily enough, was Hawthorne's specialist subject and the focus of most of his theorising. The two of them corresponded until Oddfellow got caught in his own matter transporter back in '97—which we're not supposed to know about, of course. After that, the British government was a little more careful about who he talked to, but it's my understanding that they managed to meet up once or twice. In addition to his correspondence with Oddfellow, Hawthorne also wrote to me regarding the Devil's Eye Incident of 1888, which my great-great-grandfather was the only surviving witness of. He theorised that that was also caused by a temporal anomaly. You see where I'm going with this?"

Savate shrugged. "Non."

Reed sighed. "The world's greatest living expert in time travel has been kidnapped by the Nazis."

Johnny Wolf leaned back on his chair, lifted the brim of his stetson and looked Reed straight in the eye. Reed caught his meaning and nodded.

"As a matter of fact, Wolf, we do know where he is. Or rather, we've got a pretty good idea. Next slide, please." The picture of the two men was replaced by that of a German schloss—a great stone castle in an eccentric and forbidding style, complete with two massive flat-topped turrets. "Castle Abendsen. Situated about ten miles from the ruins of Castle Frankenstein—also rumoured to have been the scene of a temporal anomaly in 1943, which I find significant. Recently, some of our spies operating behind enemy lines have spotted deliveries of vacuum tubes, microhydraulics and industrial cavorite being ferried to the castle by traction engine, and it's rumoured that that's part of a supply line running straight from Berlin bringing some worryingly high technology into the area. It's also rumoured that Castle Abendsen is home to a VIP—that's as in *very important prisoner*. Anyone want to have another go at putting the pieces together?"

Savate nodded. "Ze Bosche are holdeeng zees Hawthorne een zeir castle and forceeng heem to build zem... 'ow you say... une machine à voyager dans le temps."

Reed scowled. "You're making your accent even more ridiculous just to annoy me, aren't you?"

"Oui, oui, mon petit chou-fleur. Do you suppose zey weel attempt to go back een time and change ze course of ze Second Great War?"

Scorpio broke in. "I doubt it. Current thinking for folks who know what went down back in 1943—including the Führer—is that you just can't change the past. All you can do is have shit happen the way you remember it happening, only it turns out that was you all along. Not much use in a military situation." He finished his joint and stubbed it out on his flak jacket. "But from our point of view here in the present, the future's still mutable, until someone comes back and tells us otherwise. So we could—according to those in the know—bring stuff back from there, like weapons, or troops. There's nothing theoretically stopping the Nazi army of next week from coming back, joining up with the Nazis of today and kicking our asses, so long as the Nazis of today remember to keep their diary free next week. Try not to think about it too hard—I don't need any of you getting a migraine before the mission—but be aware that on this op, there's literally no time to lose. They could be throwing the switch right now, and the first we'd know about it would be when we suddenly had to fight five Ultimate Reichs at once."

"Crazy-ass mad science. I knew it." Mike Moses groaned, holding his head in his hands. "So the mission is to bust in, grab Hawthorne and bust right back out?"

"And destroy anything that even smells like a time machine." Scorpio grinned. "Oh, by the way, Castle Abendsen's in the heart of enemy territory and so heavily guarded on the ground that you can't get inside a mile of it without coming down with a lead overdose. Rumour had it they've even got a King Tiger patrolling the area."

Marlene let out a low whistle.

El Sombra looked over at her. "King Tiger?"

"The largest, toughest, most powerful traction engine in the world. It's like driving a battleship, so they say. I've been itching to get behind the wheel of one..." She purred, savouring the thought.

"Well, you won't on this mission," Scorpio informed her. "It's way too dangerous to approach on the ground, and we've got the Luftwaffe patrolling the area from the air. Castle Abendsen's sealed up tighter than a drum."

"Also not to mention all the heightened security inside," Reed murmured. "The place is crawling with SS, and I'd be very surprised if they hadn't been assigned a Zinnsoldat or two to help tidy up any unwanted human beings breaking in."

"I see. A King Tiger, the Luftwaffe, the SS and a couple of Zinnsoldats. And a time machine." Marlene raised an eyebrow. "Jack, dearest, would you say this was a suicide mission?"

"Like the man said." Jack Scorpio grinned. "Is there any other kind?"

*　　*　　*

IT REALLY IS *a beautiful day for killing,* Emil Farber thought.

He'd led his squadron south, for a sortie over what had once been Austria, and they'd run into a platoon of Rocketeers escorting a troop carrier on the ground. Farber couldn't help but smile at how easily his men had out-manoeuvred and out-gunned the Americans in their clumsy jetpacks and helmets. The socialists just couldn't afford the cavorite necessary to maintain a proper flying corps, and their experiments with hydrogen peroxide were only good for creating gangs of human fireworks, exploding with a single bullet in the right place. What sort of moron would send their men out wearing their own deaths strapped to their backs?

The best the Rocketeers could have done was bought time for the troop carrier to get to safety, but they didn't even manage that—it only took half of Farber's squad to destroy the American fliers, their cavorite-infused wing-packs flying rings around them, while the other half calmly machine-gunned the soldiers from above. Farber counted a good forty Americans killed, at the hands of a mere eight men. A good afternoon's work.

He chuckled to himself as his men landed on the tarmac at the Staffel. As long as the Fatherland had the vital advantage in the air, the Americans were doomed. Sooner or later, he knew, his Führer would realise how weak Magna Britannia was and finally give the order to attack the French and Italians. One by one, the countries of Europe would topple like dominoes, and then—finally— Britain and all her resources would fall before the might of the Ultimate Reich.

After that, mopping up the Americans and their fireworks would be child's play.

Behind him, Pfeffer, the newest member of the squadron, piped up shrilly. "Herr Major? Where *is* everyone?"

Farber looked around the Staffel. It was a small area, with a barracks, an officer's mess and a couple of administrative buildings, and usually it was crowded with guards and clerks—at the very least, the engineers should have been rushing out to check over their wing-packs. And yet, nobody was there at all.

"Have we been attacked, Major?" Ludwig Richter this time, ever ready to jump to a pessimistic conclusion. Farber shook his head, although he found himself unable to think of any other explanation. And then, just as he was about to order the squadron to split up and conduct a search, the door to the Officer's Mess opened.

Standing in the doorway was a strikingly attractive blonde woman, wearing a suit of some figure-hugging black material—from a distance, it seemed like leather, but surely it couldn't be—along with a pair of red gloves, and red high-heeled ankle boots. Farber seemed to remember seeing girls dressed like that during pre-war furloughs in Milan—'swinging Milan,' as the British called it. As the blonde flashed him a dazzling smile, he began to wonder if perhaps this was some star of the cabaret stage, here to raise the morale of the troops? No, he would have been informed. A working girl from nearby Feldkirch, then, smuggled in by the ground crew to help one of his young charges celebrate a birthday and a coming of age? No, nobody in Feldkirch looked like that—and again, he would have been informed. Wouldn't he?

In his confusion, he almost didn't hear the sound of seven bodies hitting the ground behind him. He turned around—and saw all his men splayed out on the concrete, a tranquiliser dart jutting from the neck of each one. How... how did...?

He turned back, wide-eyed, to see the blonde aiming a pistol directly at him. He had time for one thought before the dart buried itself in his neck: *this is how the Rocketeers must have felt.*

Then everything went black.

Marlene smiled, and spoke into the communicator at her wrist. "Blood Widow to King Sting. Snake Eyes got seven of them, I dispatched the last. Over."

Jack Scorpio's voice crackled in response. "Only seven? He's slipping."

"He's a gentleman. He knows how much I enjoy shooting commanding officers—I always think of you when I'm pulling the trigger."

"You're going to hold what happened in London over my head for the rest of my life, aren't you?"

"At the very least," Marlene said, and blew a kiss towards the roof of the barracks.

If a man spent an hour poring over that roof with a pair of high-powered binoculars, he'd see nothing but roof tiles in the sun. And then—ten seconds after he'd given up—the pattern of the tile would shift almost imperceptibly, or the shadow of the chimney would lengthen by a fraction...

...and Johnny Wolf wouldn't be there any more.

PERSONNEL FILE: JOHN STALKING WOLF - CAPTAIN (MARINE CORPS) - SKILLS: SNIPER (ULTIMATE CLASS), STEALTH, EXTREME SURVIVAL, NON-VERBAL COMMUNICATION - PREFERRED WEAPON: DRAGUNOV SVU GAS-OPERATED SNIPER RIFLE (ADAPTED FOR MULTI-AMMO CAPABILITY) - WEAKNESSES: HAS NEVER SPOKEN

He unfolded himself from his hiding place on the roof, and Marlene couldn't help but note that he'd taken his shirt off.

How delightfully decadent of him.

"I AIN'T STRAPPING on no wings, fool!"

PERSONNEL FILE: MICHAEL MOSES – CIVILIAN (PREVIOUS OCCUPATION: CIRCUS STRONGMAN) – SKILLS: UNARMED COMBAT, EXTREMELY HIGH NATURAL STRENGTH, INTERMEDIATE MEDICAL TRAINING – PREFERRED WEAPON: FISTS – WEAKNESSES: CONSCIENTIOUS OBJECTOR, SUFFERS SEVERE AVIOPHOBIA

"I will steal a damn tank if I have to!" Mike Moses bellowed. "I will *walk!* I will *hitch-hike!* But you are *not* getting me into no damn wings!"

"Oh, for goodness' sakes, Michael." Reed sighed theatrically. "Statistically, wing-packs *are* the safest form of travel."

"Like hell! You shot a damn missile at one last week!"

Reed shrugged. "I can't argue with that logic."

"They're the safest for what we're about to do." Scorpio said, buttoning his coat. "Now get your damn clothes on." Apart from Moses, they were all dressed in the uniforms of the Ultimate Reich fliers; the fliers themselves were bound and gagged in the Officer's Mess, with the ground crew and the guards. "We need to be in the air in five minutes if this plan's gonna work."

Moses scowled, struggling into a uniform a size too small for him. "Well, it's a crazy-ass plan, Jack. I mean, we fly up to that castle, what the hell are they supposed to think? 'Aw, hey, two black guys wearing our clothes! That look suspicious to you, Hans?' 'Hell, no, Fritz, 'cause the Nazi party's all about equal opportunities and also it's German Opposite Day—'"

"Es ist Gegenteiltag," Reed murmured.

Scorpio sighed. "I've done this before, Mike. We'll be too far away. Nobody on the ground is going to see what colour we are."

"How about when we land on the turrets? Those guards are gonna shoot us like pigeons—"

Marlene smiled, adjusting her cap. Out of all of them, she was the only one who didn't look out of place in the Reich's uniforms; El Sombra in particular was scratching himself as if afflicted with the shirt of Nessus. "Not if we shoot them first, darling," she purred.

"What's this 'we,' lady?" Moses scowled angrily. "I don't kill fools. You *know* I don't kill fools. Hell, I *pity* the fools—ain't their fault they got all indoctrinated, y'know? But you don't have to worry about me not killing fools, because I *ain't* strapping on no god-damn *wings*—"

Marlene shot him with a tranquiliser dart.

"What?" she asked, as the others looked at her.

Jack sighed. "One of these days I'm getting him a therapist. Reed, you got that doohickey you told me about?"

Reed smiled, removing a large piece of clockwork from the backpack he wore and clipping it onto the controls of the largest wing-pack. "This little brain will keep him flying with the rest of us while he sleeps. Just wind it up when you want us to take off."

"Excusez-moi, mes amis," Savate piped up. "But, ah, what do we do with..." He indicated the Officer's Mess.

El Sombra shrugged. "They're bastards, amigo. We kill them." He hefted his machine-gun.

Savate laughed nervously. "Well, I am not wishing to sound like Monsieur Moses, but to machine-gun two dozen men in cold blood... it seems so... wizzout honnair, n'est-ce-pas?"

El Sombra drew in a breath, and the Officer's Mess picked that moment to explode.

Once the rubble had settled and the myriad pieces of smoking meat that had once been men had hit the ground, Scorpio turned to Lev Cohen. "Blackbeard. That was you, wasn't it?"

PERSONNEL FILE: LEV 'BLACKBEARD' COHEN - CAPTAIN (US NAVY) - SKILLS: NAVAL STRATEGY, BLADE COMBAT, DEMOLITION VIA EXPLOSIVE DEVICES - PREFERRED WEAPON: CUTLASS, EXPLOSIVE DEVICES - WEAKNESSES: BELIEVES HIMSELF TO BE HISTORICAL PIRATE BLACKBEARD, RESULTANT AGGRESSIVE BEHAVIOUR INCLUDES CONSTANTLY LIGHTING FUSES IN BEARD, HAIR, EXPLOSIVE DEVICES

"*Aaarr.*"

* * *

"HOW'S IT COMING, mein Herr?"

Herr Doktor Diederich looked around Castle Abendsen's massive dining room, squinting through his monocle at the maze of copper piping and clockwork. In the centre of it, Professor Hawthorne fiddled nervously with one of the Babbage arrays, occasionally winding it with a key and running slips of paper through a slot in the base, then examining the figures that emerged. "It'd be coming a little easier if you didn't have me under such damned pressure." He shook his head. "I shouldn't be doing this at all. It's insanely dangerous—for God's sake, think what happened to Alexander, and he was only attempting transportation through space! For that matter, think what happened to your own man, Dashwood!" He shuddered. "I personally have no desire to end up a skinless monstrosity, thank you. If it was up to me, I'd stop everything here and now and tell your Führer to... to get knotted!"

"You'd do no such thing, Hawthorne. You're too much of a coward. If you were even in the same room as our glorious Führer, you would... what is the English expression?" Diederich considered for a moment. "Es lag mir auf der Zunge... ah yes. You would shit yourself." He chuckled to himself. "Anyway, it is not up to you. You have no choice in the matter, ja? You work for us now, Herr Professor. Get used to it."

Hawthorne bristled for a moment, then sighed and bowed his head. "Of course, of course. I work for you. All I'm saying is that you need to be aware of the danger, that's all."

"That is your opinion as a scientist?"

"Yes."

"Well, I am a scientist as well, mein Herr, and I have my own ideas. Keep working."

Hawthorne stared daggers at Diederich, then finished his tinkering and ran another set of numbers through the array. Having finally come to a result he found pleasing—or at least not displeasing—he slotted the clockwork in amongst a group of its brothers, then stepped back and ran his eyes over the whole contraption.

An immense host of Babbage arrays, logic engines and analytical mechanics had overtaken the room, a maze of connections fed by a gigantic furnace built into the stone wall and constantly supplied with fresh coal by two muscular Aryans. The clattering noise as the machine thought was like a thousand chirping crickets—but it was only standing by, waiting for the key to turn that would set it to its real task. In the very centre of the room was a cylindrical column, three feet tall and six in diameter, made of several dozen wafer-thin discs—copper and zinc, interlaced with discs of purest cavorite. Steel clamps secured the column to the stone floor below, to stop the whole thing rising up to the ceiling and yanking the vital connections with it.

"It is an impressive beast, Herr Professor." It was. Diederich could not entirely conceal his awe at the scale of it. "The question is, will it do what you have claimed?"

"I never claimed anything," Hawthorne muttered, bitterly. "I posited that it *might* work. It still depends on the absence of human error. In fact, for your own safety, you should stay out of the room when—"

"Don't be foolish, mein Herr. I must remain to make sure the experiment is a success." He snapped his fingers, and two of Standartenführer Ackermann's burly stormtroopers marched over and gripped Hawthorne by the arms. "You, on the other hand, are too valuable to risk. Your brain will perform many great works for the Fatherland, Professor Hawthorne. Who knows? Perhaps we will give it a nice new home."

"Now, wait a second! Let go of me at once!" Hawthorne struggled helplessly, beard quivering with indignation at the rough treatment. "You need me here! If the machine goes wrong, you'll be smeared through time like ink on blotting-paper!"

Diederich narrowed his eyes for a moment. "I see. Perhaps I will make a few last-minute checks of your work, ja? And make sure I have the sequence fully memorised. In the meantime, you can return to your quarters... in the dungeons." The SS men frogmarched him away, still protesting.

Diederich watched him go. There was something about Hawthorne he didn't like. He seemed so hunched and cowardly, such a miserable and unkempt little Englander... but then again, there was something sinister in his manner, as if he knew more than he was letting on. Best not to have such a man close by during the final stages of such an important experiment, even if he was the driving force behind it; Diederich doubted he could count on Hawthorne's loyalty to the Führer.

He shook his head, then looked over the maze of copper and iron around him, wondering if he dared to set it in motion. He'd hidden his own fears from Hawthorne, but the Englishman's nervousness was rubbing off. He thought of nearby Castle Frankenstein, destroyed decades ago; when they woke this monster from its noisy slumber, what would it do to them?

In the end, it didn't matter. Yes, he would wait, check for himself, make absolutely sure... but there was never any question that he would eventually throw the switch. He was afraid of bringing the machine to life, but more afraid by far of not doing so.

After all, the Führer was waiting.

He turned around, smiling to the groups of SS men hovering on the edge of the room, watching him intently... and the two Zinnsoldats, the immense steam-powered robots, standing to attention and gazing on him with their terrible red eyes.

Yes, it would not do to keep the Führer waiting much longer...

PRIVATE METZGER LOOKED at the minute hand on his wristwatch, willing it to turn faster. He and Vogt had spent eight hours on this miserable detail, guarding the top of the east turret—a double shift, as punishment for pilfering a bottle of landwein from the castle cellars. It wasn't even good wine, and Vogt had argued, convincingly, that it wouldn't be missed, and didn't they deserve a little luxury, being stationed in such a boring, stifling hole, so far away from the front?

Vogt's convincing argument had bought them both double shifts on guard duty, from now until that pompous oaf, Unterfeldwebel Trommler, decided they'd learned their lesson. It could have been worse—Trommler had taken pains to point out that had those thugs in the SS caught them, they would likely have been shot, and he was probably right. Those bastards didn't care about the ordinary soldier—they'd shoot a hundred Metzgers if they thought it would win them a kindly look from their precious undying Führer.

All in all, it hadn't been Vogt's finest hour, and Metzger was quite justified in refusing to speak to the light-fingered little rodent. But that decision did make the eight-hour shifts pass so terribly slowly.

Twenty minutes left. An eternity. Well, at least Metzger had a good view.

From his place up on the flat roof of the east turret, he could see for miles, giving him a spectacular vista of the various troops moving to take up their positions. The ground units far below seemed to be constantly buzzing to and fro, like ants, or hornets, endlessly setting up new defensive positions to counter attacks that never came, from American soldiers that were twenty miles away, being pounded down by armoured units and the Luftwaffe. Perhaps they were as bored as he was.

"Speak of the devil," Metzger muttered, as he noted the Luftwaffe squadron on the horizon. Every so often, a pair of wingmen would buzz the castle, waving to him or to whoever was stationed on the west turret, but occasionally a full squadron would fly past on the way to the next point on their regular patrol. It was hardly an uncommon occurrence.

But there was something different about this squadron—about the way they flew, like amateurs, wobbling through the sky. Not just those in the middle of the formation, either—the ones who might have conceivably been on their first flight—but *all* of them, even the Squadron Leader. As if they hadn't been doing this every day for years...

Metzger squinted at the winged specks as they closed in, and pursed his lips in a disapproving frown. One of them even seemed to be asleep, although of course that couldn't be possible.

Metzger opened his mouth, but some lingering trace of resentment prevented him speaking to Vogt—just yet, anyway. The last thing he wanted to do was look like a fool in front of that idiot. It was probably nothing, anyway—after all, what did he know about flying? It wasn't as if he'd ever strapped on a wing-pack himself.

Still, something about these fliers, as they came closer and closer... he felt a sudden wave of panic and found himself scrabbling for his binoculars, even as the wingmen came close enough to confirm something was terribly wrong. The uniforms didn't fit. Now he could see—mein Gott, was their Squadron Leader a Schwartzer? A chill ran through him as the awful truth struck him.

Americans!

Now he *had* to talk to Vogt, to warn him, and yet somehow he still could not speak. To admit to Vogt, the idiot, that he had been a greater idiot, and now it was almost too late, and what if he was *wrong?* Desperately, he raised the binoculars to his eyes, to make sure of what he thought he'd seen—

—and a Magnum bullet ploughed through the right lens, his eye and his brain, bursting out through the back of his skull in a red fountain, and that was that.

Another magnum bullet hit the back of Vogt's head an instant later. Vogt had had no idea of Metzger's anger and resentment. He'd assumed the two of them were still fast friends.

He had been busy thinking of recipes for stuffed carp. He died happy, absorbed in idle musings upon the topic of whether carp was a freshwater or a saltwater fish.

Another instant later, Jack Scorpio fired off another two shots, expertly dispatching the sentries on the western turret before they could raise the alarm. "Lang! Blackbeard! Wolf! Grab Moses and land there! Everyone else, eastside! Go! Go! Go!"

The two groups of four crashed down onto the hard flagstones, releasing the secure clips on the wing-packs immediately and letting them float slowly up into the air, unguided. Scorpio's team ran for the steps into the Castle immediately, while Marlene gently manhandled Moses' clips; once the wing-pack was off, she opened a small glass bottle under his nose, then took a few quick steps backwards, out of his reach.

It was a worthwhile precaution. Moses came awake with a sudden start, and his massive hand immediately snapped closed around Cohen's neck.

"*How'd I get up here?*" He roared. "*Huh? How'd I get up here, you son of a bitch?*"

Cohen drew his cutlass in a flash, pressing it to Moses' throat. "*Avast, ye dog! Unhand me or I swear I'll slit ye from stem to stern—*"

"*You put me in the damn wings, fool! You took me up there and I wasn't even awake! I oughtta tear your head off and play dodgeball with it!*"

"*I be not afraid of ye, ye swab! I'll grind ye up for sharkbait and save yer bloodless head for a cannonball!*"

Marlene drew one of her .45s and fired into the air.

"That. Will. Do."

Moses and Cohen looked at her, nonplussed, Moses' hand still clamped about Cohen's neck. Behind her, Johnny Wolf couldn't help but smile.

"Michael, much as we'd all love to see you pull Cohen's head off and use it as some sort of improvised bomb, I seem to remember you don't actually kill people, so you might as well stop making empty promises. As for you, Cohen—"

"*Arrr!*"

Marlene sighed and rolled her eyes. "I'm sorry, *Captain Teach*... you know perfectly well how testy Michael can get if we don't indulge his little phobia. Next time, stand further back."

Moses scowled. "Hey—" he began, and then Marlene flashed him an icy look, and he found himself opening his hand to let Cohen fall. Marlene had a habit of getting what she wanted.

"You know, if God had meant man to fly, he'd be a sadist, right?"

"He may not be, Mr Moses, but I most certainly am." Marlene smiled coldly.

"Now, why don't we go and complete our half of the mission before Professor Hawthorne dies of old age?"

Moses and Cohen exchanged an angry look, then stalked towards the stairwell leading down into the belly of the castle. Johnny Wolf turned to Marlene, and the corner of his mouth twitched, almost imperceptibly.

Marlene sighed. "I know, darling." She grinned, offering her arm. "Isn't it all too, too fabulous for words?"

JACK SCORPIO TOOK a moment to double-check the three chambers of his S.T.E.A.M.-issue multi-ammo Magnum. He'd selected his three ammunition packs carefully: dum-dums to pack a hard punch, tranq-darts for stealth—and the third category, the one he knew for sure he'd need before the day was over. The experimental round.

The four of them were inching along the cold stone corridors of Castle Abendsen, taking out troops as they found them; so far, the alarm hadn't been raised. Scorpio wanted to keep it that way. The deeper they could penetrate into the building without raising the alarm, the easier it'd be to smash whatever insane scheme was being built here once and for all.

He turned to the other three men and raised a finger to his lips—*silent running*. Then he flipped open one of the pockets of his flak jacket and took out a shaving mirror, angling it so he could get a look around the corner at the next corridor. Two stormtroopers were walking towards them—SS men, not the usual guards. These two weren't bored and feckless after weeks cooped up in here; they were fresh, rested and itching to find four American spies, and in another half a minute they'd turn the corner and do just that. And then they'd suddenly find a use for those Sturmgewehr 88 machine-guns they were carrying, which would probably mean raising the alarm if nothing else. Sturmgewehr 88s made a hell of a racket.

Scorpio took another look at the Magnum, and winced. Out of tranquilisers again; how come the non-lethal ordinance was always the first to go?

Hell, no time to beat himself up over it now. He looked at his men; Reed was just about useless for this kind of situation—it just wasn't in his skill set. El Sombra would deal with the soldiers effectively, but Scorpio couldn't be certain if he'd do it without a burst being fired. He *probably* could, but 'probably' just wasn't good enough right now. Scorpio needed a sure thing.

He needed Savate.

And Savate knew it, the arrogant son of a bitch.

PERSONNEL FILE: JEAN-PIERRE "SAVATE" BEGNOCHE - MERCENARY (ON RETAINER TO US GOV'T) - SKILLS: UNARMED COMBAT (ULTIMATE CLASS), SAVATE, PARKOUR - PREFERRED WEAPON: FEET - WEAKNESSES: SERVICES FOR SALE TO HIGHEST BIDDER, HIGH LEVEL OF ARROGANCE

Scorpio held up two fingers, then three, then an 'O' with his thumb and forefinger. *Two of them. Thirty seconds.*

Savate nodded, and assumed a ready stance.

Scorpio noticed El Sombra's hand twitching next to the hilt of his sword, and he shook his head once. *No.*

By now, they could hear the approaching soldiers talking to each other in brisk, clipped German. Savate closed his eyes, judging the moment.

Then he jumped.

Five feet, straight up. He didn't even seem to tense his legs first.

Scorpio had lost count of how many superiors had read the reports and proclaimed them a gross exaggeration of the facts—a string of acrobatic feats surely impossible for a human being to achieve. They'd never seen the Frenchman do the impossible in front of them, on command.

With a cocksure grin, Savate folded his legs up, pushing off one stone wall, then the other. He seemed to become a human pinball, ricocheting effortlessly from wall to wall high above the heads of the approaching men. Despite the steel-grey uniform he wore, and the jackboots that surely constricted his ankles, he was almost completely silent; by the time the two Germans became aware of the creak of leather that signalled him sailing over their heads, or the flash of grey at the upper edges of their peripheral vision, he was already somersaulting down behind them.

On the way down, he lashed out with the tips of those creaking leather boots, each foot striking twice in a single second at the point where the spine meets the skull. Neither of them felt a thing; it was like a candle being blown out.

Another impossible feat; although this time Scorpio didn't get to see it happen. He heard the muffled *crack* of their necks breaking at the same instant, and then Savate strolled back around the corner, grinning like a cat, and gestured dramatically to the bodies. "Observe," he murmured, keeping his voice low.

"The trick, she eez done, n'est-ce-pas? Notheeng up my sleeves, mes amis—or my trouser-cuffs."

He took a stage bow, to Reed's silent, pantomimed applause. El Sombra rolled his eyes, trying not to look bitter and failing miserably. "You're a show-off, amigo."

"Oh? Or could it be zat perhaps I am simply... 'ow do you say... *better* zan you are, mon cher ami. Oui? Maybe zat is why I was picked to—"

"That's enough," Scorpio hissed sharply, before leading the three men further down the corridor, creeping past the bodies as he went. "We're not here to compete. Come on—the closer we get to wherever this experiment's happening, the easier it'll be to find. Something like this is going to need a lot of computing power, and that means they'll need a lot of room and they'll make a lot of noise. You boys ever been in the room with a top-of-the-line analytical engine?"

Savate and El Sombra shook their heads. Reed smiled. "It's like fifty typewriters all clattering at once, or a roomful of crickets. An endless clicking, even when it's just standing by. If they start performing any serious calculations, it'll only get louder. We'll know it when we hear it."

El Sombra nodded. "Okay." He cocked his head for a moment, listening. "So, when you say a clicking noise... would it sound anything like what's at the end of the corridor, amigo?"

The four men stared at each other for a moment, then started moving forward, in the direction of the sound.

ROLF BAUMGARTNER WAS getting thoroughly sick of his post in the castle dungeons.

He would have preferred to be up guarding one of the turrets, enjoying fresh air and a little sunlight; instead, he was stuck in the very depths of this miserable ancestral pile, trapped in a dank stone cul-de-sac with only a flickering candle for light, babysitting one of the most depressing men he'd ever met. He couldn't decide if the post was worse when Hawthorne was around or when he wasn't.

During those times Hawthorne was absent, having been dragged away from his cell by the SS for whatever nonsense he was helping with upstairs, the dungeon was a deeply boring place. Baumgartner wasn't allowed to read a book to pass the time, or bounce a ball off the stone walls, or anything that might let the endless hours drag by a little faster. There were various speaking tubes through which he could speak to his fellow guards in different parts of the castle, if he wished, but the penalty for misuse was strict, and there were little sneaks like Ehrlichmann around who'd jump at the chance to report him for some minor infraction if it meant scrambling a little further up the greasy pole to the officer class.

When Hawthorne was in his cell, as he was now, that was a little better. He and Baumgartner could play a word game, if they chose, or discuss what the weather might be like outside. Or they could sit in dreary silence, as they were doing at the moment, since Hawthorne had decided to sulk for some reason. Baumgartner sighed; it wasn't that much better, after all. Hawthorne was such an astonishingly pitiful specimen.

It was the way he was constantly cringing, as if expecting to be hit, or found out for some unimaginable crime. And he never smiled or looked you in the eye—just sat there, hunched over and trembling. Baumgartner often found himself wanting to grab Hawthorne by the throat and shake him like a rag doll, just to give him something real to cry about.

Part of it, surely, was that Ackermann and his SS thugs refused to allow Hawthorne a proper room. Anyone would start to go a little mad if they were forced to eat and sleep in a dingy cell without a single creature comfort. What harm would it do to give him a real bed, for goodness sake? Or a window? What was he going to do, squirm through the bars like an eel and make a mad dash for freedom? He'd surely earned a degree of trust at this point.

No, if Baumgartner was ever put in charge of the SS, the first thing he'd do would be to allow Herr Hawthorne a proper room, and a good night's sleep, and some decent food—a little bratwurst would probably do wonders for him. After that, Baumgartner, in his role of Reichsführer—or at least Oberstgruppenführer—of the entire, nationwide SS... would make some changes to the uniforms.

Get rid of the skulls, for a start. The skulls were just tacky.

Baumgartner looked over at Hawthorne, huddling in his cell, and thought about bringing up his ideas for the new SS uniforms. Best not, he thought. It didn't pay to voice one's private thoughts on the subject of the SS; they had a habit of finding out, somehow, and after that your position in the Ultimate Reich could get very tenuous indeed. Baumgartner had no desire to end his career as one of the lobotomised 'human robots' in Berlin, thank you very much. Or was it Fortress Berlin, now? The wall was more than half-built, after all. Baumgartner wondered idly if any of the allied spies had had a chance to see it yet. *It'll put the wind right up them,* he thought. *It does me. Pray God I never end up in there.*

He shivered. The silence was growing intolerable. Hawthorne was in one of his moods, Baumgartner could tell—one of those spells where his frown was a little deeper, the slope of his shoulders a little more profound, his eyes even more eager to avoid yours. He hesitated, struggling to remember the English, and then spoke.

"Cheer up, Philip, ja? It might not ever happen, you know."

Hawthorne scowled, and turned away. *Be like that, then,* thought Baumgartner. *We'll just sit here in silence and die of boredom.* He let out a loud, melancholy sigh, tinged with a hint of bitterness. Surely, thought Baumgartner, he was the unluckiest man in the entire Ultimate Reich!

In this, he was mistaken. Rolf Baumgartner was a very lucky man indeed.

If, when Marlene and her team had crept up on him through the shadows of the dungeon, anyone other than Mike Moses had reached him first, he would have died without even knowing about it. As it was, his jaw and nose were shattered when Moses slammed one of his outsize fists into his face, he lost several teeth, and he suffered minor brain damage from the extended concussion, but at least he wasn't killed. Mike Moses, for reasons his team-mates could never quite grasp, made it a point of principle not to kill his fellow human beings.

Luck takes strange forms.

"Professor Hawthorne? We're here to help." Marlene smiled, as Moses took hold of the iron door of the cell, braced himself, and began to pull. Slowly, under Moses' incredible strength, the metal bars warped—then tore loose from their moorings altogether, leaving a hole big enough for a man of Hawthorne's size to walk through.

Hawthorne only sat, looking bewildered. "I... I don't understand. Help me? In what way? Are... are you here to help with the experiment?" His eyes narrowed. "Or are you with *them?*"

Marlene's smile lost some of its warmth. "It's been quite a while since you were kidnapped, Professor. It's understandable you might have lost all hope of rescue..."

Hawthorne blinked. "You're not with them at all, are you? Or perhaps they're just using you. They use everyone. They used *me...*" He shook his head, chuckling darkly. "Kidnapped, you say?"

"Yes, Professor," Marlene said, suddenly unsure of her ground. "You were kidnapped in Geneva, don't you remember?" She looked over at Wolf, and then at Moses, and both of them seemed suddenly as worried as she was.

Professor Hawthorne began to laugh.

Marlene took a step back. The sight of the man wearing a smile was so incongruous as to make her feel slightly ill.

"Professor Hawthorne—" she began, hoping there was another explanation for her looming dread than the one that came uncharitably to mind. Deep down, though, she knew exactly what was coming.

"You honestly think I was *kidnapped?*" He shook his head, trying to control the fits of giggles. "Oh, my hat! They *really* know how to string their agents along these days. Kidnapped indeed!"

"You weren't?" Marlene asked.

His eyes narrowed. "Of course I wasn't. I *defected*, you silly girl." He smiled. "In fact, if you want to get technical? I defected for show, and then I decided to defect for *real*. Because *nobody* uses me! Not even Hitler, not even..." He stopped, as if aware that he might have been about to say too much. Then, quite suddenly, he made a mad lunge for the speaking tubes, grabbing one from the wall and screaming into it.

"*Help! Help me! The Americans are in the dungeon—*"

A moment later, his head, looking shocked, was bouncing across the cold stone floor, and Cohen was sheathing his cutlass.

"All hands on deck, me hearties!" He growled, as he struck a match to light the fuses in his beard. "*Stand by to repel boarders!*"

Marlene looked around for Johnny Wolf, but he was nowhere to be seen; either he'd already melted into the shadows, looking for cover to attack from, or he'd left them to face the music alone.

She honestly wouldn't blame him.

EL SOMBRA SHOOK his head.

"This... does not look good."

"I am so *sick* of you *saying* that!" Reed hissed. "Is that your catchphrase now? Every time we come across something out of the ordinary, we get a statement of the obvious from a half-naked swordsman! Of course it *doesn't look good!* We're an elite commando unit tasked specifically for abnormal operations—we handle things that *by definition* do not look good! If they looked good, do you know who'd be looking at them? *Private Normal and his Tedious Boredom Platoon!*"

El Sombra blinked. "I was just saying, amigo."

"Where's your shirt, anyway?"

"It itched."

"Quiet, both of you," Scorpio hissed. The corridor had led to some sort of balcony overlooking the dining room; perhaps at some point in antiquity it had been used by musicians, or actors, to entertain the nobility and their guests. The important thing was that it gave them a perfect vantage point to watch Herr Doktor Diederich tinkering with his experiment.

He wasn't alone. Scattered around the room were SS troops of various ranks, from the Standartenführer himself on down, there to meet their own future selves as they stepped through from next week, or next month, or next year. In addition, a pair of immense brass and steel robots flanked the Doktor at all times, the furnaces in the bellies glowing with fires akin to Hell's own. Occasionally, one of them would stomp over to a coal bin in the corner of the room, take a large handful and tip it into the great furnace-doors that formed their mouths. Zinnsoldats, they were called, and El Sombra knew them of old; he knew that, should they ever run out of coal, the next thing to be forced into those doors and burned for fuel would be a human being.

"Last time, I smothered its flames with sand..," he muttered, then looked furtively around. "Has anyone got any sand?"

"Quiet. What are we looking at here, Reed?"

Reed frowned. "Analytical engines. Lots of them. Still in standby mode, until the good Doktor starts to flip some of those switches over there—see that bank of levers over on the far side? That's the input. I'm guessing that disc there is supposed to be the gateway they'll bring things through from. I'm not sure quite how it all links up... I wonder, is that an Omega field?"

"A what?"

"Omega energy. The 'cursed science,' according to legend. People who go looking for it have a habit of ending up dead."

Scorpio nodded. "I seem to remember Doc Thunder harnessing it for some machine of his..."

"And look at him now. Makes you wonder, eh?"

Scorpio frowned, and changed the subject. "We're going to have to stop this from—"

And then the voice of Philip Hawthorne filled the room.

"Help! Help me! The Americans are in the dungeon—"

The words echoed from one of the speaking tubes on the wall—then the voice went dead.

"Was that Hawthorne?" Scorpio couldn't believe it. What the hell was he *doing*?

Immediately, the SS troops sprang to attention, six of them running for the exits. "Bring der Zinnsoldat! Bring both of them! The Americans must be stopped!" The robots, following the new orders, turned and stomped out of the room.

"It seems we are out of time," Herr Doktor Diederich sighed, moving towards the bank of levers. "The experiment must begin slightly ahead of schedule. Cross your fingers, my friends, and wish us luck, or at least a quick and painless death, ja?" He chuckled humourlessly.

El Sombra frowned. "We need to make our move now."

Scorpio shook his head. "Not yet."

"What?" El Sombra looked incredulous. Diederich was already flipping the switches, and the chittering of the clockwork crickets in his gigantic maze of arrays was growing louder and louder. "Amigo, in another second it's going to be too late—"

"Wait for my signal, I said! Damn it, I need you to trust me!" Jack Scorpio reached up to brush the back of his finger across his forehead, and realised he was sweating. Through his special glasses, El Sombra's aura was glowing an angry, pulsing red, like a throbbing vein. "Just... *trust* me. I'm asking you to hold back for just five minutes. Reed and Savate will back me up on this— there's more going on here than you know."

El Sombra just stared at him, his lips pulling back from his teeth in a cold snarl.

"Trust me. That's all I ask." Jack Scorpio looked into the blazing eyes behind the bloodstained mask, and spoke softly, soothingly, almost desperately. "Can you just hold back for one minute?"

The eyes behind the mask narrowed.

"Can you?"

PERSONNEL FILE: DJEGO 'EL SOMBRA' (LAST NAME UNKNOWN) – ??? – SKILLS: UNARMED COMBAT, BLADE COMBAT, PARKOUR, HIGH PAIN THRESHOLD, STEALTH, DISGUISE, GUERRILLA WARFARE, UNCONVENTIONAL WARFARE, (CONTINUED ON SEPARATE SHEET) –

PREFERRED WEAPON: SWORD - WEAKNESSES: UNIQUE PERSONALITY
DISORDER (SEE MEDICAL FILE #ES1007, 'DJEGO SYNDROME')
  EYES ONLY: THIS INDIVIDUAL IS HIGHLY DANGEROUS. IT IS
STRONGLY RECOMMENDED HE NOT BE INCLUDED IN ANY OPERATIONS
CLASSIFIED ABOVE TOP SECRET OR HIGHER.
(I'll take the risk - J.S.)

El Sombra spat in Scorpio's face.

"Chinga tu madre."

Then he drew his sword and leaped down into the fray.

THE SOUND OF Mike Moses punching der Zinnsoldat was like Big Ben striking the hour—a heavy, ringing gong that echoed right through the walls of the dungeon. The metal buckled with the force of the blow, and inside the robot's head, the complex clockwork that made it function slipped its gears, cogs and wheels coming loose as the machine tottered a step to the left before crashing to the floor.

"Now *that's* what I'm talking about!" Moses bellowed, turning to backhand a stormtrooper who'd been getting too close.

"Mike! Are you okay?" Marlene yelled over the roar of her automatics, as she aimed a hail of bullets down the bleak tunnel before rolling back into cover. The SS answered with a fusillade of machine-gun fire, their bullets chewing great chunks out of the stonework. Lev Cohen, snarling unintelligibly, pulled a stick of dynamite from the recesses of his borrowed uniform, bellowed something about the Spanish Main, and lit it from one of the fizzing fuses threaded into his beard. Marlene threw herself down on the ground, covering her ears as Cohen hurled the stick overhead—the explosion was enough to shake the whole castle, but it didn't seem to do more than buy them a moment's respite against the waves of SS pinning them down.

"*Mike!*" Marlene screamed, over the ringing in her ears. "*Are you okay?*"

"I think I broke my hand and I might be deaf!" Moses yelled back.

"Well, how's your other hand? They've got another one of those things back there—"

Moses grit his teeth. "Gimme a damn gun, I'll take care of it!" He scrabbled around for the machine-gun the stormtrooper he'd knocked out had been carrying, but it was lying out of his reach; if he broke the cover of the alcove he was hiding in and went for it, he'd be gunned down in an instant. "God damn it! I need a *gun* here!"

"Arrr, I thought ye were a man of peace, matey?" Cohen grinned, before switching his voice to a parrot's high-pitched squawk. "*Aharr, I be Mike Moses! I pity the fools! Pieces of eight! Mikey wanna gun!*"

"Leave your damn invisible parrot outta this, fool! You can't kill a damn robot! Now quit your jibber-jabber and gimme some of that dynamite before I come over there, pick you up and throw *you* at it!"

"Too late for that, me brave bucko! 'Twas the last gunpowder in me hold!" Cohen spat, then grinned savagely. "Let 'em come, me fine lads! *The noose holds no terror for Edward Teach!*"

Marlene winced as her own guns clicked empty. "I'm down to my last clips!" She looked up as she reloaded—and saw the SS troops pulling back, clearing the way. Behind them, the remaining Zinnsoldat snorted, great clouds of steam and smoke coming from its horrifying maw. It looked like the Minotaur roaming the ancient labyrinth.

"Wait a second." Marlene frowned, concentrating. She nodded to the dead-end wall behind them. "What's behind this?"

"Who cares?" Mike yelled, "It's gotta be a foot thick! Hell, maybe if Captain Crazy here hadn't shot his load we coulda blasted it, but now? The only way out is through these fools and their crazy-ass man-eating robot—"

"Maybe not." Marlene took a deep breath. "Maybe it's the other way around." She stepped out, standing in front of the dead-end wall, and raised her twin automatics.

The Zinnsoldat charged.

"*What the hell does that even mean?*" Mike yelled, as the twin .45s roared into life again, bullets bouncing off the oncoming robot. Marlene was aiming for the robot's eyes, but they were thin slits in its nightmarish head, and she just couldn't make the shot.

It was getting closer. She had to take out the viewing slits *now*, before it slowed. If it reached them intact, it would kill her instantly, then start on Mike and Lev and Johnny. She couldn't allow that to happen.

Marlene frowned.

Where *was* Johnny?

And then Johnny was behind her, stepping out of nowhere as he always did, and his hands were on hers, guiding the guns upwards just a fraction, inwards just the tiniest amount... and when she pulled the triggers, the bullets chewed through the glass lenses of the robot's eyes and into its clockwork brain, and even though it was dead now, just mobile junk, the momentum of the charge kept it ploughing on blindly, even as Johnny and Marlene threw themselves to the side and out of the way.

The blind robot hit the back wall with a sound like a wrecking ball. The room shook.

Marlene looked back at Johnny and grinned. "You too?"

Johnny just smiled.

"*We got our way out! Move it!*" Moses bellowed, as Marlene raised her guns again, this time to lay down covering fire as her team ran through the hole in the wall and into the next room.

Which, it turned out, was being used as a garage.

For the King Tiger.

The largest, most powerful, most indestructible traction engine in the world, just waiting for someone good enough to take it and drive it away.

Marlene's grin widened. "Face it, Tiger..."

PERSONNEL FILE: MARLENE 'BLOOD WIDOW' LANG - CIVILIAN (PREVIOUS OCCUPATION: VIGILANTE) - SKILLS: PROFICIENT WITH ALL LAND-BASED VEHICLES, COMBAT DRIVING (ULTIMATE CLASS), VEHICLE THEFT (ULTIMATE CLASS), AMBIDEXTROUS, STRONG LEADERSHIP SKILLS - PREFERRED WEAPON: DUAL .45 CALIBER PISTOLS - WEAKNESSES: UNKNOWN

"...you just hit the jackpot."

STANDARTENFÜHRER ACKERMANN TURNED white, then purple. For a moment, the scream was trapped in his throat, as if locked there by the angry vein pulsing at the side of his neck.

When El Sombra landed on one of his men, sword first—the point slicing vertically down his belly, spilling his guts out onto the floor in a pool of blood and bile—the scream finally burst free.

"*Kill him! Kill the American!*"

El Sombra grinned, turning in a circle, facing each of the SS troops in turn as they closed around him, guns drawn.

"Who are you calling *American,* amigo?"

He darted forward, kicking one man backwards and stabbing another through the heart as the bullets began to fly.

"God damn it!" Jack Scorpio cursed, leaping after the masked man. "Reed— stay where you are! Savate—with me!"

Savate vaulted the balcony and immediately went to work, dispensing lightning kicks to soft tissue and vulnerable bones, crushing windpipes with the ball of his foot, snapping necks, driving nasal cartilage deep into brain tissue. Scorpio spun around in a circle, the Magnum exploding with brutal thunderclaps as it spewed chunks of hard metal that fragmented on impact, blowing great, ragged holes in what had once been men. The stormtroopers outnumbered them ten to one, and there seemed to be always more arriving, rushing in from every corner of the castle, converging on the slaughter until the floor around the chattering arrays was awash in gore, and the whole room seemed to have become a storm of bodies and blood, an infinitely complex chess match with every move carried out at the speed of a bullet.

And in the eye of the storm, there was El Sombra.

He was in his element now.

He was no longer part of Jack Scorpio's elite team. He was no longer part of any human structure. He was a creature of vengeance, without ties to man or country.

El Sombra had spent the past four years trying to force himself to fit in, to align his war with America's. He'd mistakenly thought they were the same conflict. But there was one vital difference.

Someday, America's war would be over.

Herr Doktor Diederich, meanwhile, continued to flip switches, the sweat trickling down his face as he tried to ignore the bloody battle going on all around him. A bullet whined past his ear, breaking the handle off one of the levers a second before he reached for it. He grabbed hold of the jagged metal left behind, cutting his palm open as he pulled it down. He had very little choice but to carry on.

In a gun battle, he could be killed. That was a risk he understood. But if he left the experiment half-finished, there was a risk of worse. Some terrible combination of death and undeath, perhaps—frozen in time for eternity, or stretched across millenia, screaming in agony for thousands upon thousands of years...

What on earth had possessed him to play with the fabric of time like this? How much of this had been his own idea, and how much was Hawthorne? He racked his brain to think of any part of the process that had not been subtly suggested by the Englishman—and nothing came.

Mein Gott, who was working for who all this time?

There was no time for such thoughts now. This was the fatal moment. He threw the last switch, and prayed.

The metal dais began to spark and crackle with strange blue-white energy, the pure cavorite layered into it glowing and pulsing with its own mysterious forces. Diederich closed his eyes and winced, and then the glow of the dais stabilised to a steady, throbbing pulse.

"I've... I've done it!" Diederich smiled, suddenly delighted. "It's begun! It can't be stopped now! Oh, this is a marvellous day! Hawthorne was right—the armies of the Reich will double in size, and the Americans will be—" He turned in mid-flow, to look at the formidable armies of the Reich.

They were all dead.

El Sombra, Savate and Jack Scorpio stood amidst a sea of corpses. Standartenführer Ackermann was still barely alive, on his knees with El Sombra's blade sticking through his throat. As Diederich watched, he coughed up a thick wad of blood, and then his eyes rolled back in his head and he slipped backwards off the sword, slumping to the floor.

"Ah, well. It seems the human error has defeated us after all, ja?" Diederich smiled ruefully. Then Jack Scorpio put a Magnum bullet through his brain.

With the last of the bastards dead, El Sombra found his eyes drawn to the dais. Slowly, a column of blue light was rising up from the centre.

"So," he said softly, "I guess this is some big science, huh?"

"You guess right," Reed said from the balcony. "And if you think I'm coming down there, you're crazier than I thought. It's Scorpio's job now."

El Sombra frowned. "Your job, amigo? Here I thought it was a team effort. What haven't you been telling us?"

Jack Scorpio shook his head. "What you didn't need to know. The Yankee Bravo mission is over. The S.T.E.A.M. mission starts right here, and if you interfere with it, I *will* kill you. I'm working on a scale you can't possibly understand, and you just proved you can't handle it." He shot El Sombra an angry look. "I'd take a step back if I were you."

El Sombra didn't move.

Inside the column of blue light rising from the dais, there was a man. He was indistinct—barely visible—but he seemed to be dressed in some sort of duster coat and what could only be a cowboy hat. In one hand, he was carrying a stone—a large, blue, glowing gem that was the only distinct thing about him, almost as if it was the only part of the strange scene that was real.

He had something else in his other hand, but El Sombra couldn't make it out.

Scorpio aimed his gun.

"Drop the rock."

The man in the blue column turned to face Scorpio. He seemed to be moving at half speed, as if the blue light had the consistency of molasses.

Scorpio spoke slowly and carefully, as if taking this into account. "This is your only warning. The bullet in this gun is made from the same copper, zinc and cavorite structure as the dais under your feet—the one that drew you here. It's an Omega bullet, and make no mistake, it will kill you whether you've materialised fully or not. So either way, you're going to give us the rock."

El Sombra looked around at Savate. "What is this?"

"I could tell you, mon ami," Savate whispered, "but zen I would 'ave to keel you. Comprendez-vous?"

Reed grinned, up on the balcony. "It's the man from the mesa, 'amigo.' The Keeper of the Stone. You're watching the future happen."

"Last chance, pilgrim," Scorpio barked, and pulled back the hammer. "I want the stone. Drop it and kick it over to me—*now*—or I'll sh—"

The figure in the blue column of light moved, and El Sombra heard what sounded like a gunshot, slowed down to half speed, and then Jack Scorpio staggered back and fell to the floor, with a neat round hole in the dead centre of his forehead.

Even at half normal speed, a bullet was still a bullet.

And Jacob Steele, the Lonesome Rider of Time, was still the best shot there had ever been.

El Sombra stared at Scorpio's body, then up at Steele. The Lonesome Rider slowly reached up to touch his hat-brim, then faded away, as though absorbed into the swirling energies whence he'd come.

For the first and last time, El Sombra saluted.

"No," Reed croaked, his voice hoarse. "Bring him back. *Bring him back!* Without the Stone—"

He never finished his sentence. With a tremendous crash, the King Tiger smashed right through the wall and rolled over the bank of levers, and the column of blue winked out for good.

"I'VE BEEN ACCUSED of acts of treason against the United States, and that's probably true." Reed smiled genially, lifting up the handcuffs he wore. "I mean, as a covert agent of S.T.E.A.M. I definitely took part in missions that didn't line up with the goals of the war. We were playing the long game—Jack Scorpio, Savate and myself, I mean. Thinking about America's interests, post-war. The world's interests." He looked up to the military policeman standing at his elbow. "Where did Savate vanish to, anyway? Does anyone know? Oh, well, I'm sure he'll turn up where you least expect him."

On the other side of the one-way glass, General Zitron listened carefully, making notes. He couldn't help but wonder if he'd still be a general come the morning. The Yodelling Bastards had pulled the wool over his eyes, and S.T.E.A.M. before them. In fact, he'd been played for a sucker since the days of his liaisons with the Fourth Earth Batallion. And before them... what? Who had Jack Scorpio been before he studied under Channon? What had Reed been up to before he joined Yankee Bravo Seven?

What did S.T.E.A.M. look like when all the masks were off?

"Quite often, the goals of S.T.E.A.M. and the goals of the country were the same. Take Hawthorne, for instance. He was one of ours—a triple agent—and it was his job to persuade the Nazis to build his time platform, thus wasting incredible quantities of rare cavorite on something that would have benefited us rather than them, if it benefited anyone at all. Enough cavorite for eight hundred wing-packs, squandered. Not to mention all those logic arrays—crushed under Marlene's new toy." He grinned. "You'll find over the next few months the Luftwaffe become rather easier to handle, and robot production in the Fatherland takes a significant dip. Just watch out for Fortress Berlin, that's all." He chuckled dryly. "You did know about that?"

Zitron leaned forward and picked up the speaking-tube in front of him. "If Hawthorne was one of ours... or rather yours..."

"Why did he decide to warn the Nazis about the 'rescue mission'? Well, he did resent our intrusion into his life; we were more than a little heavy-handed about recruiting him, but you have to understand what a prize he was for our side." He smiled enigmatically. Zitron sighed, wondering what *our side* meant this time.

Reed continued, frowning. "I have to assume, based on the evidence, that he wanted to claim the Stone for himself, and we showed up ahead of his schedule. He must have found out what it really was..."

The General sighed again. "What was the Stone, Doctor Reed?" Reed considered the question for a moment, as if he wasn't quite certain himself.

"I won't go into the science. I'll just say that if I'm right—and I am—the Stone is a potentially limitless energy source for mankind. If the Devil's Eye Incident is even half true, we're looking at an infinite supply of cavorite at the very least. The very *least*." He took a breath. He was getting excited. "We'd better hope we can find someone else as clever as Hawthorne someday. I mean, that was a man who made me look like... well, like *you*. Too bad we broke him." He grinned again, and there was something deeply unpleasant in it.

The President sighed, rubbing his temple. "Let me see if I understand this. The Yodelling Bastards were sent in to Castle Abendsen to foil a plot that S.T.E.A.M. had generated and fed to the Nazis in the first place?"

Reed smiled sadly. "They had the technology, we didn't. The plan—in terms you morons can understand—was to let them do all the heavy work, then extract Hawthorne and the Stone. Except Hawthorne had other plans, and in the end so did the Keeper of the Stone. So there we have it." He smiled. "Look on the bright side, though—our little plot managed to cripple the German war effort—not to mention stealing the legendary King Tiger and piloting it back to Italy, thanks to the lovely Marlene. In a saner world, I'd be getting some kind of medal." He shrugged. "Instead, I'm in prison for life. There's gratitude."

General Zitron leaned forward. "One more question." It was a lie. He had so many questions—*who the hell was Jack Scorpio anyway? Did I ever really know him at all? Did anyone?* He restricted himself to the relevant one. "If the Stone was as important as you say, why didn't Jack Scorpio shoot?"

Reed shrugged. "Some problem with cold-blooded murder, I imagine. I wouldn't worry." He grinned that unpleasant little grin again. "We'll fix it on the next attempt."

"So what now?"

Marlene drank the remains of her white wine and looked over at El Sombra. "Now? We all go our separate ways. Reed's in custody for being too sly a spy, poor Jack's dead, Savate's vanished—I've a nasty feeling he's switched sides again—and you've quit the team. That doesn't leave me much to work with, even if I wanted to lead."

El Sombra shrugged. "You four guys did pretty good. America's got the King Tiger now, thanks to you. Makes for a lot of dead bastards."

"Well, we're breaking up the band anyway. Mike's a full-time medic now, Lev's back in the Navy despite his little problem..."—she hesitated, and El Sombra detected the barest hint of a blush—"...and... Johnny and me are taking one of the new USSA Tigers for a bit of a working holiday, as soon as it's built. I hear deep behind enemy lines is lovely this time of year."

El Sombra raised an eyebrow. "You and Johnny, huh?"

Marlene smirked. "He is awfully good at pulling my triggers."

"I'm not touching that one." He smiled and shrugged, nursing his own cerveza. "You know... I always figured there was a chance..."

"Oh, I still haven't forgiven you for killing my car back in New York." She mock-pouted prettily as the barman brought another round. "But if I ever do, I know exactly where to find you, don't I?"

El Sombra nodded grimly. "Six more months. Then I'll have my hands at his throat. I've wasted enough time."

"Six months? As long as that?"

"Make it three. It's not like he'll be hard to find, right?"

He grinned.

"How long could it take?"

THE LAST ENEMY

SEVEN YEARS.

Djego stared at himself in the mirror above the bar and listlessly sipped his schnapps, counting the lines around his eyes and the flecks of white in his black hair.

The back of his head still itched occasionally where the knot of his mask had rested, even after all this time, but it was barely noticeable—phantom pain from a severed limb. Sometimes, during the night, the memories would return and haunt him—bullets slamming into wedding-guests, tearing flesh and bone asunder, his brother's eyes accusing him before the light left them; but upon waking, he felt a vague sadness and nothing more. His muscle definition had softened and he was developing a slight but noticeable gut, although the days he spent gardening kept him in reasonable shape.

El Sombra had been gone for seven years now.

He took another sip of schnapps, and turned to look through the bar window. Over the tops of the houses, he could just about make out the polished glitter of the Berlin Wall.

Bastard City, part of him thought, but did not emerge into the light of his mind. He nodded. Yes, Bastard City.

Fortress Berlin.

He stared for a moment, trying to dredge up some emotion, but nothing came. A vague feeling of pity, perhaps, for the poor souls trapped there. No more than that.

After a moment, he shook his head and returned his gaze to the drink in his hand, and his thoughts lingered on his brother's sword.

He still had it, on top of his cabinet, wrapped in newspaper, and it was as sharp as it ever was. He remembered the weight of it in his grip, the feel of the sword-hilt in his hand, the little push of resistance as it cut through flesh and bone. The adrenaline rush of the kill. Those times he'd had it taken from him, it had felt like losing an arm, or an eye, or some part of his soul.

And now it rested on the battered oak cabinet in the room he paid for with gardening work on the outskirts of Brandenburg. Wrapped in newspaper.

He still had a scrap of the mask, for what it was worth. He kept it in his pocket, like an alcoholic's badge of sobriety.

Coincidentally, it had been seven years since the first time El Sombra drank.

He remembered vividly that first and last drink with Marlene, although it was El Sombra who'd sat there, not him. She'd been talking about her plans for the USSA version of the King Tiger that was being built for her—the Sherman Wildcat, they were calling it, a little sleeker than the German design, with better treads, and the standard .88-calibre machine-guns at the side replaced with the American multi-ammo model; still, it was very much the same beast. It wouldn't automatically win against a Tiger, but it'd even the odds, especially with Marlene at the controls and Johnny Wolf manning the guns. He'd almost wished he could have gone with them, but experience had taught El Sombra that he worked best alone, and it wasn't that much of a walk to Berlin. As Marlene had pointed out, behind enemy lines was lovely that time of year.

Unless you walked into a full-scale battle between Wildcats and Tigers, of course.

It was two weeks after he'd set out. He'd been ambling, taking his time, killing as many of the bastards as he could. He'd returned to the Luftwaffe base he'd visited with the Yankee Bravo team, catching them in the act of rebuilding. He'd killed the replacement ground crew, then the new squadron as they landed; it was nice to know that he could pull something like that off on his own, and he celebrated by blowing up the newly-rebuilt officer's mess. Perhaps the Luftwaffe would decide that particular area was bad luck.

He'd swaggered five miles north, ducking through the forests, killing the occasional sentry, feeling pleased with himself—and then he'd heard the first explosions, and the roar of the great steam engines. Over the next hill, he'd seen it—three King Tigers together, an unimaginable force. Presumably the Führer had decided, in the face of the new competition from the Americans, to group them together instead of spreading them out, and sent them south to take on the Wildcats as they were sent out from the Italian and French borders. Right now the three Tigers were chasing two of the Wildcats straight towards him, and all five of the tanks were exchanging fire—massive explosions of gunpowder, dynamite and peroxide, and great sprays of .88-calibre fire and dum-dum rounds. El Sombra turned to run back down the hill for the relative safety of the forest—and then one of the Tigers had missed its target and the shell had exploded close enough to send him flying through the air in a shower of mud and his own blood. He'd had just enough time to register that his mask had somehow come off in the blast, and then he'd passed out.

He didn't wake again for eight months.

By that time, the war was all but over.

THE SURVIVING WILDCAT crew had recognised him from the newspapers, and, as a veteran of Yankee Bravo Seven, Djego was afforded the best of medical care at the hospital in Venice.

El Sombra was nowhere to be found.

His mask had been torn off in the explosion, along with some of the meat of his leg and arm. He walked stiffly, now, with a pronounced limp, and his left arm was all but useless, hanging limply at his side. The Wildcat crew had salvaged his sword, but Djego had little interest in using it. For him, it was a memento of times long past, not a weapon to be used.

Gradually, he regained his mobility, though his arm had lost most of its strength and the limp would never leave him. The back of his head itched constantly, and he suffered from horrendous mood swings, when he would rage against the Führer and the bastards, or weep helplessly, like a child. But gradually, he found his personality stabilising in the gentle, antiseptic atmosphere of the hospital. He found that Djego—so long despised as a weakling, a coward and a fool—was capable of a kind of gentle, melancholic wit that made him popular, although the self-depreciation still occasionally curdled into self-loathing. He found himself falling into a casual relationship with one of the nurses, a sunny brunette named Savina, who relieved him at last, after a decent interval, of the burden of his virginity; when finally she decided it was best to break it off, he took the blow with a grace and good humour the old Djego would have been incapable of.

Djego healed and grew, and the itch in the back of his skull began to subside, as El Sombra relinquished his grip.

MEANWHILE, THE WAR was ending. Castle Abendsen had been the death-blow for the Nazi forces; Reed had been correct in that the Ultimate Reich had sent their most precious resources to be destroyed on a fool's errand. The old-fashioned Rocketeers were being phased out in favour of squadrons of Hawk-Men to battle the winged Luftwaffe on an even footing, just as the King Tigers were being outfought and outmanoeuvred on the ground by the new Wildcat Mark IIs, 'compact tanks' that sacrificed some of the indestructibility of the earlier design for added mobility; it was no good having the largest gun in the world if your opponent could move faster than it could track. From his prison cell, Richard Reed designed new Locomotive Men based on his ancestor's designs, and they were cautiously tested against the few Zinnsoldats that remained. Very quickly, the allies began taking the cities, then the towns. There were patches of guerrilla warfare here and there, but for the most part the general populace surrendered without too much trouble.

The Nazi High Command had their own plan, in the event of total failure. They were already in the middle of building it.

Fortress Berlin.

A gigantic bunker, thirty miles across, stretching from Potsdam to Werneuchen—a great metallic dome, with walls two hundred feet high and ten feet thick, made of concrete and steel and the hardest known alloys. There were doors into it, that never opened and could not be broken down, but there were no windows. There was no sunlight.

One year after the incident at Castle Abendsen, having managed, through an inhuman effort, to hold off the attacking forces, the remaining Nazis simply closed the door and shut themselves away.

The European leaders debated the strategy. Were they building up forces? At some point in the future, would the Ultimate Reich stream like an army of ants out of its great mental anthill and swarm over them all? But then, what would they re-arm themselves with? Perhaps, some scientists considered, they were building a bomb, some great annihilation device to take everything they had lost with them. But from his cell, where he was provided every luxury as long as he continued to be useful, Richard Reed pooh-poohed the suggestion; it simply couldn't be done with what they'd left themselves. In his opinion, they were waiting it out—waiting for Europe to grow complacent, or waiting for history to forget them. Or maybe they'd just turned the board over and built a place to sulk in.

The rest of Germany was split neatly in two, with half going to France and half to Italy, and their combined forces guarding the bunker against the day it opened. What the Russians though of this remains unrecorded, but Magna Britannia seemed happy enough with the outcome; easier to deal with the French and the Italians than with the Ultimate Reich.

A year and a half after he'd woken up in the hospital, Djego finally felt strong enough to travel from Venice up to the remains of Potsdam, and the edge of the dome. The Franco-Italian armed forces, who knew of his reputation as a war hero, let him pass, and he'd placed his hand on the metal, warm in the sun, and felt the itch in the back of his skull return, stronger than ever. There was a strong part of him, buried deep down inside, that wanted to smash his way in somehow, even though the most powerful shell could not; that wanted to kill every bastard in there, to storm the bunker like an avenging ghost until it was ankle-deep in blood. But his sword was back at his hotel room, and his mask was lost, and he was a man in his mid-thirties with a pronounced limp, and the door was solid steel and four feet thick, and behind it there was likely another door the same. So he turned around and left.

Oddly, he did not feel like a coward. After all, even El Sombra in his prime could not have broken in, and he was only Djego.

There was little to return to in Venice, so he headed west, eventually finding himself in Brandenberg—a French city now—where, while engaged in some cash-in-hand work to pay for his meagre lodgings, he discovered within himself a talent for gardening. It was good, physical work, and it kept him in shape and allowed him to think of nothing but the task at hand for hours at a stretch, and at the end of it, he was rewarded by beauty. The walls of the dome could be seen in the distance, above the houses, like some vast, forbidding mountain, but increasingly, that did not trouble him. He could not forgive the bastards— never that—but he found that he could forget them for a while, as he toiled and tilled the earth, and grew the flowers.

Djego healed. Djego grew. He became a fixture of the city, laughing and talking with the other residents. His gardening business grew. After a couple of years had passed and he had put down roots, he became romantically involved with a woman called Helga Vogt, whose husband had died in the war. Djego did not ask the circumstances, and she did not ask anything of him. The past was the past, and they had a good enough life in the present to let it rest.

Occasionally, Djego would still feel the urges from that other part of his mind, but they were feeble things, buried deep and easy to shrug off. If El Sombra was still some small part of him, he surely knew the situation was what it was, and there was nothing to be done.

Surely.

On these occasions, Djego quieted the old ghosts by visiting the local bierkeller and sipping schnapps alone, counting the years and reminding himself of how much time had passed. It had always worked before.

He was thus engaged when the thin man approached him.

"DJEGO THE POET?"

Djego blinked, turning to study the newcomer. He was tall, thin and bald, with sharp green eyes, deeply tanned skin and a curious blond-and-black stubble that seemed to cover most of his face. He seemed uncomfortable in his crisp black suit, though it fitted him excellently.

"No, that's not me," Djego said, warily. "I haven't written poetry since I was a teenager. I am Djego Rossi"—they had given him the surname at the hospital, for records purposes; it was a traditional placeholder—"or, if you prefer to address a man by his job description, Djego the Gardener." He half-smiled and fumbled in the pocket of his shirt for a business card. "My schedule is fairly full at the moment, but if you have any weeding that needs to be done..."

"Weeding. Very good." The thin man grinned, and Djego noticed that several of his teeth were missing, notably the canines. The effect was unnerving. "Yes, I suppose that's as apt a metaphor as any." He tittered, softly.

Djego sipped his schnapps, wondering if he should make an excuse and leave. "And your name is?"

"Leonard," the thin man said, and grinned again, as if at a private joke. "Leonard De Lareine." He tittered again. It was deeply unnerving.

"You're French?" Djego's eyes narrowed. The man's accent was very difficult to place, but it did not seem native to any part of Europe he knew of.

"Are you Italian, Mr Rossi?" De Lareine's grin did not leave his face. "Or is it Mr Sombra?"

"El Sombra," Djego sighed, feeling a renewed burst of itching at the back of his skull. It happened sometimes. El Sombra had been a famous figure during the war, and occasionally people made the connection, or discovered Djego's whereabouts through some means, and asked him to tell stories, or sign newspapers, or fight them, and he would courteously explain to them that he was not El Sombra and never had been. Then he would walk away, letting them believe it or not as they wished.

"I am not El Sombra, my friend," he heard himself say, "and in truth, I have never been El Sombra. Believe it or don't, as you wish. For myself, I would prefer to finish my drink alone."

"Yes, of course," De Lareine smiled, and there was a long pause, during which the strange, thin man did not leave Djego in peace, or do anything but stare at him, body twitching strangely. After a moment, he began talking in a low, purring voice. "How could you be El Sombra? You can just about walk, with a limp—not quite run. You leave the sword that was sacred to El Sombra in a dusty apartment room, wrapped in old paper, and spend your time poking at worms and soil when blood is crying out to be avenged. You are a coward—"

"Go away!" Djego snapped, incensed. "Leave me alone!"

"You are a coward in the way that all comfortable men are cowards, Djego who was once a poet. You allow injustices to continue, do you not? And for what reason? Simply that it would make you uncomfortable to end them by your own hand."

Djego cursed, hand reaching to scratch furiously at the back of his head. "Damn you! What do *you* know?" He slammed his glass down on the counter, then reached into his pocket for thirty francs to pay his tab for the evening and slammed them down next to it.

De Lareine tittered, and tossed a long piece of red cloth onto the money.

Djego felt his heart seize in his chest.

The cloth was missing a scrap at the end, and there was mud ground into the fabric along with the old bloodstains; but it had two evenly-spaced holes in it, and was unmistakably a mask.

It seemed to be looking at him.

Djego shook his head and tried to step back from it, but his legs wouldn't move.

"No," he whispered. "No. Please."

De Lareine only smiled, like some great cat.

"I was happy," pleaded Djego. "Doesn't that matter to you?" He picked up the cloth in trembling fingers, looking into the empty eyeholes. "Doesn't that mean anything?"

There was no answer. The barman looked up for a moment from polishing the steins, and shrugged. The other patrons of the bierkeller did not even notice anything was happening.

"I was happy," Djego choked, and then, in one spasmodic motion, he pulled the mask onto his face, and secured it tightly, so that the knot once again rested at the back of his head, where it belonged; so tightly that it might never come off again.

El Sombra looked at his hands.

He prodded his belly, amused at the rounded shape of it, and took a couple of steps back from the bar. The limp was gone.

He laughed, very softly, so as not to disturb the patrons. Then he turned to De Lareine.

"How did you find me, amigo?"

De Lareine tapped the tip of his nose. "I followed my nose." He sniffed the air twice, then tittered. "Come. You have something waiting for you in Djego's apartment, I think. Wrapped in newspaper."

The two of them walked out of the bar, smiling like old friends.

The barman watched them go, then picked up the thirty francs.

THE DOOR TO Berlin swung open with a low creak, and El Sombra stepped inside, De Lareine padding behind him.

Outside the metal dome, it was a late summer afternoon, passing into early evening. Inside, it was a black, moonless night. What little light there was came from an oil lamp De Lareine held, although El Sombra could make out the occasional pinprick of light ahead of them.

"How did we get in?" El Sombra muttered. "The Franco-Italian forces have been banging on this door with explosive shells every day for years, and you just knock a few times and it opens for you." He frowned, hefting his brother's sword.

De Lareine tittered and smiled his gap-toothed smile. "The doors are controlled by clockwork arrays, wound every day by the human robots of Berlin. You know of them?"

El Sombra shuddered. "People conditioned to be robots, because they couldn't afford to mass-produce the advanced droids Magna Britannia has. They tried to turn my hometown into a human robot factory." He glanced at the thin man. "You already knew about that, didn't you, amigo?"

"I did. Look, there's one now." He pointed at a figure in the distance, walking stiffly along the road ahead—a woman of thirty, beautiful once, but now sallow-skinned and hollow-cheeked, her head shaved and a tattooed number gracing one temple. On the other was a lobotomy scar. She had not eaten in some days, and her teeth were black, as if before that she had eaten nothing but rotting meat for some considerable time. She passed them without comment, eyes staring dully ahead, as she walked her circuit of Fortress Berlin, moving from task to task.

El Sombra felt suddenly nauseous. It was as if De Lareine had conjured her from the air by speaking of her. De Lareine's smile widened, as if to confirm the notion. "*Now go not backward. No, be resolute,*" he said, and El Sombra knew he was quoting something, but what it was he had no idea.

After a pause, the stranger spoke again. "The knock is a password. It is heard by the machines and the signal is given for the door to open. It's supposed to be used from inside, but the signal works both ways."

"People can't open the door from the inside without the code?" El Sombra said, surprised, then he shook his head. "No, of course not. Nobody gets to escape."

He looked around as they walked, at the deserted countryside, the empty buildings, the endless night. Occasionally, on the road, the two of them would see one of the Nazis, cold and dead, riddled with bullets or stab wounds, occasionally beaten to death with bare hands.

De Lareine tittered softly.

"How do you know the knock?" El Sombra asked, suddenly.

De Lareine looked at him for a moment. "Suspicious of me? Going to turn on me?" He tittered. "Will we fight?"

El Sombra scowled. "Yes; maybe; and it depends on whether you answer the question. Speak."

The tall, strange man licked his lips. "It's my job to know things. I'm an agent."

El Sombra's eyes narrowed. "Of S.T.E.A.M.?"

"S.T.E.A.M. no longer exists, but yes. Once you take S.T.E.A.M.'s mask off, we are what you find underneath. Agents of the Queen."

"Victoria?" El Sombra blinked, dumbfounded. Surely *she* couldn't be... no, not after what had happened.

"No. The other Queen." De Lareine smirked. "The more important one. She has decided it would be best for the world to come if the Führer, too, no longer existed."

El Sombra raised an eyebrow. "So why involve me, amigo? I mean, I wouldn't miss it for the world, but..." He stepped over the rotting corpse of an Oberstgruppenführer. Something had been eating it.

In the distance, one of the human robots slowly trudged across the road, between buildings.

"The Queen knows you." De Lareine grinned. "Eleven years ago, in New York. You made quite an impression. She remembered this was an ambition of yours." He grinned. "Aren't we generous?"

El Sombra frowned. "I don't need S.T.E.A.M. in my life, or whatever you call yourself now," he muttered petulantly, almost under his breath. "I was doing fine on my own."

"You *were* doing fine on your own, weren't you?" De Lareine smirked. "You had a good job, working with your hands. You were trying to fall in love. You were content. But you weren't walking through a city of death in an endless night to kill the man who murdered your soul, were you? No. For that, you did need us." He let out another noxious giggle. "You made your bargain, El Sombra. Too late now."

El Sombra decided not to reply to that.

"What happened here?"

The corpses were piled in the streets, and the stench of putrefaction was so bad that El Sombra and De Lareine had been forced to hold their hands over their faces from a mile distant; eventually, the thin man had produced a pair of breathing-masks to fit over the mouth and nose and block the very worst of it, for which El Sombra was grateful. Here and there, the Nazis were pushed into great, obscene piles of flyblown flesh, as if some attempt had been made to clear them from the streets, and every so often one of the city's remaining human robots would stagger mechanically through the stink and the flies, retching despite itself. One, an old man, collapsed in front of them, and when El Sombra checked his pulse he had already died; another they saw in the distance, engaged in pulling rotting meat from the bones of the dead and chewing mindlessly at it.

"They were sealed in." De Lareine smiled. "The Ultimate Reich had a history of thinking big; Fortress Berlin was to be a gigantic bunker to control the war and the world from. Then... Castle Abendsen. And suddenly the war was lost, thrown away, and the bulk of the high command were locked inside their bunker waiting for an opportunity that would never come. There was talk of remaining in the bunker for a thousand years, like a Phoenix in its egg. The kind of grand plan the Führer was known for coming up with. And in a thousand years, he would still be here to see it." Another titter. El Sombra was finding himself as unnerved as Djego was by it.

"So they were all sealed in. Outside, there were jews, and blacks, and other races, and travellers, and homosexuals, and everyone else they wanted to eradicate; inside, only themselves. Aryans. Their dream of a pure Aryan world, on a tiny scale."

El Sombra sighed. "But some were more Aryan than others, amigo?"

"Exactly!" De Lareine laughed, mockingly, as he swept his arms wide to take in all the corpses littered around them. "It helped that food was becoming scarce. No sunlight, you see. A diet composed principally of mushrooms. It's shocking nobody thought of it earlier." He sniggered. "But people were growing discontent. And in the face of discontent..."

"...they found someone to blame."

"The redheads were first. Oh, they defended themselves tooth and nail, but eventually the city was made pure once again. You will find the bulk of their bodies in great storage-houses, the remainder in the form of ash. After that, brunettes, and once the problem of hair had been sorted out, those whose eye colour differed from the correct shade of blue. Then those with freckles or blemishes on the skin. And of course, anyone with a physical or mental deformity had to go, which was increasingly everyone." He smiled, as if savouring the thought. "Mushrooms are no diet."

El Sombra shuddered. "I can guess the rest."

"Eventually, it was just the immortal Führer and his closest and most Aryan underlings. When they finally turned on each other, it was just a fight over whether or not they'd be allowed out. And that was that. The end of the Ultimate Reich."

"How do you know all this, amigo?"

"Many spies have many eyes, my friend. We know because we watched." De Lareine smiled his maddening, unsettling smile, as if trying to keep a giggle from spilling out. "We have certain technologies available to us that you would describe as magic, but are quite common in our homeland."

El Sombra nodded. "You're from Zor-Ek-Narr. The Forbidden Kingdom."

"I wondered when you'd guess."

The eyes behind the mask narrowed, as El Sombra took in the all-over stubble, and the catlike twitch of De Lareine's walk, and the canine teeth that had been surgically removed to better allow him to blend in with Homo sapiens. "You're a Leopard Man."

De Lareine grinned.

"So Doc Thunder's ex-girlfriend is the Secret Queen of the World." El Sombra shrugged. "Why doesn't that surprise me?"

"The Queen was the first to exist in this world, along with the original Keeper of the Stone, the Shaper of us All and the Weeper of Stars, whose domain was sorrow. And the Sacrificial Lamb, of course, but there are always sacrifices, aren't there?" The cat-man sniggered. El Sombra could hear the capital letters—which struck him as unbearably pretentious—and he didn't much like the talk of *sacrifices* either. His hand gripped the hilt of the sword.

"We"—De Lareine continued, warming to his theme—"by which I mean Us, the Hunting People, all descend from the Shaper's first machinations, which precipitated a great Battle of Gods, at the end of which the Shaper and the Weeper were destroyed by the Titans and the Keeper set free from—"

"Who else was in this mythology of yours?" El Sombra interrupted. "The Peeper? The Leaper? The Creeper? Not that I'm saying Maya made all this up to keep you lot in line, amigo, but she could have picked better names."

"Not a fan of mythology?" De Lareine giggled. "But here we are, in the realm of Dis, among the rotting corpses of the damned, going to kill a Dragon. Mythology's everywhere we look. This is a world of mythology, my human friend."

Something in that jogged El Sombra's memory. "There is another world," he murmured. "There is a better world..."

De Lareine smiled again. "Different, certainly. They're rioting in London, you know."

El Sombra looked at him, mildly curious at the seeming change of subject. "Really? I'll admit, I've been expecting it since Victoria—"

"Oh, not *that* London," De Lareine said, and giggled. The giggle, El Sombra decided, was worse than the titter.

They walked towards the Reichstag in silence.

INSIDE, EL SOMBRA could hear the soft chug of steam machinery filling the air, the puffing of great engines, the slow ticking of clockwork.

He could hear the Führer waiting for him.

He breathed in, ignoring the stench of the rotting dead, and tried to still his mind. But it had been a long time since he'd had to do that, and he found stray thoughts still bubbling up from the recesses of his mind. He had been waiting for more than twenty years for this moment, and now it was here, and his sword was in his hand. His body had become older and fatter in his absence, but that didn't matter. His leg—the one he forced to walk without a limp—was stiff and in constant pain, but that didn't matter.

Nothing mattered now.

When the time came—in the next few minutes—he knew he would be able to move fast enough. He breathed in and out, slowly, imagining the battle, running the different scenarios through his head. The Mecha-Führer, huge in its chamber of smoke and steam, would perhaps rear from its throne, bellowing in fury, and smash one great metal fist down to smash the marble floor underneath, but El Sombra would already have leapt away...

...or perhaps Hitler would unleash a barrage of machine-gun fire from hidden weapons in its arms, the heavy .88-calibre bullets chewing up the walls and floor and even the ceiling as El Sombra dodged like a dervish, his blade coming close and closer to the hydraulics that were the Führer's lifeblood...

...or perhaps there would be time for conversation first, a few deathless words exchanged between the most evil man in the world and the avenging ghost who had walked across a planet to destroy him utterly...

...or El Sombra would fight to a standstill, and then one great fist would reach out and crush him, ending his life and the hopes of the millions of unavenged dead the monster had left in his wake...

...or Adolf Hitler would fall to his metal knees and weep, and beg forgiveness...

...or this, or that, or any other thing.

El Sombra smiled, and he was standing at the door to the great central chamber, the office of the Führer. At the door of history.

He announced himself with a laugh.

It was rich, and full, and it carried over the dead and rotting corpses strewn through the corridors of the Reichstag. It touched the human robots milling endlessly through the streets on their meaningless tasks, making them look up in the endless darkness and remember, if only for a moment. Even De Lareine lost his maddening smile for a brief instant in the face of it.

It was such a laugh...

Then, El Sombra opened the door to the Office of the Führer, and stepped through.

The Führer was waiting for him.

The massive metal body, more than three stories in height, sat upon a vast iron throne, motionless. The immense bronze head, frozen forever into an expression of pure hate, gazed down at El Sombra with black, empty eyes. The weapons bristling from every part of its body could, he knew, destroy him in an instant.

All around them, there were the sounds of machinery, endlessly grinding and turning and clicking in the walls and floor, but the Mecha-Führer was completely silent, utterly motionless.

In the centre of its chest rested a tank of toxic green fluid, and on the surface of the fluid, a human brain floated, like the corpse of a goldfish.

It was quite dead.

El Sombra stared at the Führer for a long moment. Eventually, he spoke, and his voice was cracked and raw, and choked with rage.

"Is... is this a *joke*?"

His hands shook like an old man's.

De Lareine smiled his terrible smile. "The Führer's body needed a great deal of maintenance and repair, you know. After two years, one of the processes delivering oxygen to his brain failed... and there was nobody left to repair it. He died, slowly." Another smile. "There would have been some pain, at the end."

El Sombra slammed his fist into the great iron throne on which the massive body sat, shattering his knuckles and tearing the skin from them. He didn't seem to notice. "*Some pain*," he choked, through gritted teeth.

"They were going to upgrade him." De Lareine shrugged. "There was another body waiting for his brain to be transferred to in the laboratory, but the final trouble started before anything could be done. There was some speculation on whether one of the higher-ranking Nazis would implant themselves in that second body and stage a coup. What a coup it would have been, eh?" Another infuriating giggle. "Two giant robots smashing each other through the ruins of the Reichstag, and to the victor goes the Ultimate Reich. That would have been an ending, wouldn't it? But I suppose nobody wanted to give their humanity up." He grinned, wider. "If only you'd arrived sooner, eh?"

El Sombra was still staring into the empty, dead eyes of the Führer.

"This isn't right," he said, eventually, in a strangled voice. "How... how can it end like *this*?"

"Why shouldn't it?" De Lareine shrugged. "Here's a thought. Maybe, despite his twenty-year tantrum and all his dressing up, spoilt little Djego is not the centre of the universe—"

El Sombra turned, face red, tears streaming from his eyes, and charged at De Lareine, slashing his sword in an arc aimed at tearing the guts from the Leopard Man. But El Sombra was forty years old, and a little fat, and his leg hurt, and De Lareine was faster even than his father, who had won the Last Great Games in the golden temple of Ig-Nur-Hoth, against a mechanical minotaur built for the purpose.

El Sombra crashed down onto the floor, into the soot scattered about, as De Lareine walked around him, speaking in his nonchalant purr. "Did you really believe Adolf Hitler would wait around for your sword? Did you not imagine that it might be *better* for him to seal himself off in a hole to die, instead of murdering and enslaving continents until you finally got around to him? Did you think you were the hero of your own little story, El Sombra, with your mask and your laugh and your—"

"*Shut up!*" El Sombra cried out, scrambling to his feet, the sword shaking in his hand, tears and snot running down his face. "*He was mine! He was mine to kill!*" He lifted the sword, the tip trembling. "*Bring him back,*" he screamed, "*do you hear me? Bring him back to life!*"

De Lareine had to laugh at that.

El Sombra lunged haphazardly forward, slashing blindly. De Lareine languidly ducked the wild stroke, then stepped aside, allowing the masked man to lumber past him like a bull past a matador. Then, before El Sombra could lose his footing again, De Lareine turned and struck, aiming the heel of his hand at the middle of El Sombra's back.

There was a sickening *crack*, like the branch of a rotten tree, and El Sombra crashed once more onto the filthy marble floor, and this time he did not get up again.

After a moment, he spoke in a small, weak voice, like a little boy's. "I can't... I can't move my..." He swallowed, staring into the distance. "What happened?"

"Life," De Lareine replied. He sniffed the air, twice, then left the room.

"Don't go—" El Sombra called after him, but he was already gone. The minutes passed, and though El Sombra felt no pain, he could feel himself growing weaker, and his vision was starting to blur. He wanted to look up at the lifeless robot towering over him—to make his last sight the dead brain floating in its tank, as if that would bring him closure—but he found he could not turn his head.

"How could it end this way?" De Lareine's voice echoed from the corridor, along with the rattle of metal on metal. "Because it was *always* going to end this way. You were always part of the Queen's history, little Djego, passed from Queen to Queen... a Chinese whisper in an empty room... a joke in reverse... first the laughter, then the sick, twisted *punchline*." He squatted in El Sombra's line of vision, the tray of surgical instruments in his hands, letting him see the scalpel, the chisel, the saw, the tank of nutrients waiting for the brain. "You'll understand in the end, don't worry. You'll look back and laugh."

"No," said Djego, in a small, frightened voice, as the tears dampened the red cloth over his eyes. De Lareine only smiled.

"Your chariot awaits," the Leopard Man said, and began to cut.

THE DOOR TO the dome opened again at sunrise.

From inside, there was the ugly sound of metal on concrete, of something impossibly large and heavy being dragged by something even larger.

Then the metal man emerged from his hole, dragging the corpse of the Führer behind him.

They were both around three stories tall, although the metal man was slightly taller, and from a distance they might have looked the same; but on closer inspection there was little resemblance. One—the dead Führer—was a fearsome construction of sharp edges and jagged metal, exposed pistons and gears scraping against the earth. Its ugly bronze head was contorted into an expression of endless rage and hate, and in the glass tank at the centre of its chest, a lump of dead flesh still floated obscenely, visible to the world.

The metal man was of more modern design—a thing of sleek muscle and sinew sculpted in steel and copper, whose inner workings gently whirred and purred where the Führer's had screamed and ground. His body had never been customised to suit its original purpose, so he wore no swastika, and he was thankful for that. The bronze head that sat atop his great shoulders was similarly unsculpted—a placeholder, bald, and possessed of the serene expression of a shop window dummy, or perhaps a Buddhist monk.

Like the Führer, the metal man's chest contained a tank of life-giving fluid, though this one was opaque rather than transparent. To the undiscerning eye, the metal man would appear a simple robot, although a very large one. Nevertheless, the tank contained a human brain, and unlike the Führer's, it would need little in the way of support. The brain in the metal man's chest would, perhaps, live for thousands of years.

He wondered how he would spend the time.

He remembered little of his former life; he had been a man named El Sombra, or perhaps Djego. He had been stupid—he realised that now—but that was something he would never be again.

Apart from that, there was only a succession of faces, the memory of laughter and of a final, awful betrayal that had destroyed him. But there was also the sense that a great and terrible mission had ended at last, and it was time for a new life to begin. Perhaps, as time went by, he might recall more of his past; for now, there was only the wonder of being alive, and new, and filled with purpose.

He knew he would have to explain himself, to convince the humans who would come for him that he was not their enemy, but he was confident that he could do that. The calculating arrays inside him were whirring efficiently, supplied by the data from his living brain, and he knew he was much more now than he had been. Yes, he could explain.

He could explain everything to everyone.

The metal man took a last look back at the great dome of Fortress Berlin. Somewhere in there, the Leopard Man was hunting, freed from his own mission. And in the Führer's old office, the empty, lifeless clay of El Sombra—or was it Djego?—lay, discarded, like a butterfly's cocoon.

The metal man thought on this, as the Führer rusted at his feet and the tanks began to approach from over the hills ahead.

He would need a new name.

PLUTO

"Even if someone walked through that one, I'd still believe it," Carina Contreras-Ortega said. She was looking through a window into a minimally decorated room, where two people, a man and a woman, had been playing the Japanese game Go for some considerable time, each of them lost in thought. Occasionally, Carina thought she heard a frustrated sigh, or saw one of them make a tiny movement, but for the most part they simply stared at the pieces on the board, which were all a uniform grey. There was no way to tell which piece was on which side, or whose move it was.

Except there was no room, no players, no board, no window. It was all painted canvas. The breathing of the players, their irritable sighs, the tiny movements of their bodies—all were illusions created by the sheer realism of the image. Despite herself, Carina found herself completely drawn into the world it presented; the posture of the two motionless grandmasters suggested detailed histories, a relationship stretching back years. The pieces were grey, Carina realised, because the true game was not found on the board, but in the players.

It really was a breathtaking illusion, and quite the most realistic she'd ever seen.

But then, illusion and reality changed places so often in France. Carina smiled, turning to the man standing by her side.

He turned towards her, and the clockwork in his head ticked absently, reminding her that he was not a man, in the strictest sense of the word; rather, the illusion of one.

His name was Anatole-744, and he was twelve years old, which meant that his skin was pale pink, but still obviously painted metal, and his green eyes did not move. His voice was deep and a little grating, never changing pitch or timbre or volume; it was the same harsh monotone whether he was talking of the tourist hot-spots of Marseilles or of Nazi war atrocities. The black hair on his head, brushed into a conservative style, was the most realistic thing about him; horsehair, perhaps. The hotel had been very sorry that they could not provide a newer model, but they had assured her that Anatole-744 was fully programmed as a guide.

After another click, the robot cocked his head. His face was set in a vague half-smile that could pass for a number of different emotions at once, but Carina was getting better at reading his body language, and when he spoke, she read mild confusion into the metallic drone of his voice.

Or the illusion of it, at least.

"I'm sorry, Madame Ambassador, I do not understand," he said, then straightened, awaiting new input.

She smiled, searching for the correct terms to explain it. "I was referring to an experience unique to myself," she said.

Anatole-744 nodded. "I see. Human experiences are fascinating to me," he said. "I would like to hear more about this one."

She almost laughed out loud. It was the third time he'd said that in response to some statement she'd made. The first time, she'd taken it at face value, as an honest expression of curiosity, but now the illusion of humanity was slipping and she found herself amused by the naked programming beneath; people liked talking about themselves, so the guide would invite them to do just that.

She considered telling Anatole-744 that she had once been a turtle swimming in a giant bowl of rice, just to watch him accept it without a qualm and relate the anecdote to some piece of tourist ephemera. Instead, she told him the truth.

"Once I saw a painting so realistic that for years I thought it was the view from the window." She smiled, then continued, without knowing why. The memories still disturbed her. "It was painted over my window, to make me think things hadn't changed after the Nazis..."—she shuddered—"...after the Nazis invaded my hometown. My father was trying to protect me; I never quite forgave him for it."

She turned her head to Anatole-744, expecting him to break in with a comment about some tourist exhibit in Marseilles that related to the Ultimate Reich, or windows, or fathers, some destination she hadn't seen yet. Instead, he kept a respectful silence, and she found herself warming to him, almost forgetting that all his responses were built into the clockwork in his head and chest.

"I was imprisoned behind those paintings for nine years, until our village was liberated," she continued. "Actually, the man who freed us went on to be quite a big name in the war. I heard rumours he'd retired and was living in Germany, but by the time I went looking for him he was long gone." She shrugged. "But at one point he was quite the minor celebrity... have you ever heard of El Sombra?"

There was a clatter of gears and tiny wheels inside Anatole-744's robot brain, and he seemed to shudder. Eventually he responded, haltingly. "No, Madame Ambassador. That story was fascinating to me. May I make a recommendation?"

Carina smiled wanly. *Ah, here it comes.* "Please," she said, politely.

There was another long clicking and whirring of gears, then a great grinding whine from inside Anatole-744's head, and Carina stepped forward suddenly, to touch the robot's sleeve. "Are you all right?"

"That story was f-f-fascinating to me," Anatole-744 said, his hands shaking. "May I make a recommendation?"

"We should get you to a—" Carina started, and stopped. She was going to say *doctor,* but that wasn't the right word. The illusion again. "A—a mechanic. You sound in pain."

"May I recommend—mend—mend—" Anatole-744 stuttered, "that you visit Pluto?"

Carina blinked. "The planet?"

"Yes. No. Yes." Anatole-744 stumbled backwards, crashing to the floor. "May I recommend Pluto. Pluto."

Carina knelt at his side, tearing open his shirt to reveal the pink-painted metal underneath. She looked for a hatchway, some means of entry into his inner workings, but there was none, and she did not know what she would have done even if she'd found one. "Can you tell me what I can do?" She asked, desperately. "How can I help? Is... is there a button? A switch?"

"Pluto." Anatole-744 said, at a lowered volume. "Pluto lives in Paris."

Then he shuddered again, and ceased to move.

His green eyes stared ahead, lifelessly, but then they always had.

*   *   *

THE DEAD ROBOT was shipped back to the hotel, and Carina remained at the museum until a new one could be sent to her. For a moment, she had been astonished at the seeming callousness of the crowd, who had simply watched; but then she shook her head at her own foolishness. What was lying on the floor was nothing but mechanical parts, a machine that had gone wrong and broken down, that was all. Any personality she had chosen to imbue it with was all in her mind—*the illusion*, she thought. Her word of the day, it seemed.

She had to smile. She had always been willing to believe a beautiful illusion over reality.

While waiting for the hotel to send the replacement guide, she continued viewing the exhibit, a collection of Japanese art recently loaned to the Musee Cantini. The artist Kichida was responsible for the canvas depicting the game of Go, and also a triptych of scenes inspired by Warhol; these were scenes of empty cities, overflowing with trash and vegetation. In the rightmost painting were two children fighting over the corpse of a dog. The scene was covered with lights of every shape and size, the glass bulbs Warhol had popularised, but they were dark and dead. The only light came from the glow of the moon. Many had said the work was a commentary on society's addiction to coal; Kichida's only comment was that the work had come to him in a dream, as it had to Warhol, but most took that sort of talk with a pinch of salt these days, as more and more artists and writers tried to jump onto the dreampunk bandwagon, with varying success.

Carina shuddered inwardly at the grim spectacle, and moved on, examining a work by the line artist Urasawa; the corpse of a dead robot, captured in ink on paper. The work was called *Pluto*. The coincidence made her uneasy.

Anatole-744 must have been directing me to this, she thought, examining it carefully. *Why did he think it was in Paris?*

Her reverie was interrupted by a polite cough behind her, and she turned to see another android, more advanced than Anatole-744. This one had a thin rubber coating, making him look like a dummy in a high-priced shop window. His eyes moved, and he could smile, after a fashion. Somehow, it seemed more artificial than Anatole-744's motionless metal features. *There's a term for that*, she thought. *The uncanny valley. Try too hard to create the illusion, and the illusion vanishes completely.*

"A pleasure, Madame Ambassador," he said in a musical voice which rose and fell harmoniously, but seemingly at random, like a child's singing. "My name is Jean-Claude-56621, and I'm here to be your guide for today."

"Hello, Jean-Claude-56621," Carina smiled, offering her hand. The robot pantomimed kissing it, his rubber lips brushing the back of her hand in a way that made her wince slightly. They were cold and clammy, and the effect was not nearly so charming as when Anatole had simply shaken her hand on their first meeting.

"I can converse on many topics," he said, as if that was the most appropriate comment to make. Then he nodded, quite unnaturally, at the Urasawa piece. "*Pluto!* One of several pieces by Urasawa that homages one of his idols, the artist Tezuka. Would you like to know more?"

Carina shook her head absently, wishing the robot would go away. "Anatole-744 said Pluto was in Paris."

"I'm sorry, I do not understand." Jean-Claude-56621 smiled, and his eyes moved back and forth, like a doll's. Carina scowled.

"Wait here," she said, in a faintly disgusted tone. Then she made her way back to the hotel on her own, and told the concierge that she was almost sixty years old, an Ambassador for the South American Union, and more than clever enough to use a map and a guidebook.

FOUR DAYS LATER, she met Rousseau as she came off the train.

"Madame Ambassador," he said, in a warm, deep, rich tone, and offered her his hand as she stepped onto the platform. "My name is Rousseau. Welcome to Paris." His hand was warm, and his blue eyes sparkled, and she found herself thinking for a moment that Jorge would surely not find out, though he had the last time, and the time before.

Then she smiled, breathing in the Paris air for a moment. "No number?"

He raised an eyebrow. "No. How did you know?"

"I didn't, until now. You're extremely advanced." Now that she was looking for it, she could perhaps detect a slight regularity about the skin, an infinitesimally plastic quality. And his movements were a little too efficient, his teeth too even. But then, he looked no more artificial than some of the older kinema-stars in Hollywood or Odessa. "May I ask how old you are?"

Rousseau smiled warmly. "You may, but the answer is complex. When you change the head or the handle of a broom, how old is the broom?" He paused, then lifted her bag from the train, holding it easily with one hand. "My body is very new—three months. The latest model. Most of my clockwork is about two years old, and parts of my memory array are almost fifteen. Ancient, in robot terms. Obviously, back then, my thinking wasn't nearly so good as it is now..."

Carina nodded absently as he carried her luggage to a sleek black towncar. "I was going to say that your syntax was excellent. You sound... well, human."

"Thank you."

"It must be strange," she said, musing, "to have some parts of you so much older than others."

"Oh, it's no different from your situation. Most of your cells renew themselves many times over the course of your life—for example, the fat cells in your body are completely replaced every ten years. Other cells, like the neurons in your brain, never replenish themselves, in the same way that the core of my memory array is still as it was fifteen years ago, when it was first built." He held the door for her, smiling. "We're not so different, you and I."

As Carina settled back into the plush leather seating of the towncar, there was a clashing metallic noise in the street behind her, and she turned to see an old, horse-drawn wagon loaded down with scrap metal as it rattled past; an incongruous sight on the streets of Paris. As the wagon clattered away from her, she noticed that some of the metal in the back was painted pink, old severed arms and legs, occasionally a head, mixed in with the other rusting scrap iron. Then the wagon turned a corner and was gone.

"Not so different at all," Rousseau murmured, and slipped into the driver's seat. The automobile started smoothly, the hydraulic engine propelling it forward at a steady pace. Once upon a time, such a car would have been prohibitively expensive, reserved for royalty; now, with the recent technological advancements, every citizen of France could have one, and most did. Rousseau parked in front of the hotel and helped her once again with her bag, then returned to the towncar while she rang the bell at reception.

"Madame Ambassador," said the manager of the hotel, "it is a great pleasure. Please, accept our apologies; your decision to visit our fair city was very surprising and we were not able to have all the facilities in place..."

"Facilities?" Carina frowned. "Is there something wrong with the suite?"

"Ah, non, Madame, the room is in perfect condition for your stay," the manager smiled reassuringly. "But I can only apologise that we were not able to send one of our androids to meet you at the station."

Carina raised an eyebrow. "You weren't?" She turned, looking back to the entrance, but Rousseau was gone, and the towncar with him.

TWO DAYS LATER, she met him again.

She was enjoying a cup of excellent coffee in a Parisian café—sampling the fruits of her labour, she supposed—and watching the beautiful people go by. There seemed to be so many of them; the men well-turned out in sharp suits with T-shirts underneath, the only signifier of age a dash of salt and pepper in their hair, the women ageless and uniformly beautiful in chic summer-dresses and kitten heels. Everyone seemed to follow the fashion, and yet no two of them were dressed alike. It wasn't quite Milan—Paris followed the trend rather than set it—but it felt close.

Even the robots were beautiful; very few were flesh-toned, instead painted with smooth pastel colour schemes, or with polished metal surfaces exposed to the world. Her waitress looked quite dazzling—an android in female shape with a high, pointed head, styled like the Chrysler building. Carina left her a large tip, to the stares of those at the next table: a portly old man and his over-tanned wife. They were dressed impeccably, but there was something ugly about their eyes and the set of their mouths, and their conversation was loud and boorish. They smoked incessantly, building a mountain of dead cigarettes in their ashtray.

Occasionally, as she watched the crowds and sipped her coffee, she would try and spot another of the very latest model androids, like Rousseau, who looked so completely human. Despite this, she did not notice him approach until he sat down at her table.

"Why did you tip the waitress?" he said, in his easy baritone. "It usually isn't done to tip a robot. Gives them ideas above their station." He smiled. "Or so I've heard."

Carina blinked. "Don't sneak up on me like that, Monsieur Rousseau. You'll give me a heart attack." He grinned at that, showing off those perfect, artificial teeth, and she found herself smiling back. "If you must know, I thought her service was excellent. And she was herself a work of art."

Rousseau shrugged. "The fashions are changing. Once, people preferred androids to be humanlike—now, they find that distasteful. New robots produced in France are beautiful sculptures, like your waitress, rather than crude shop window dummies like poor Anatole-744, or Jean-Claude-56621. Some of the newer ones aren't even humanoid—I believe there is a bar along the Seine where you can be served drinks by a mechanical octopus." He smiled, absently. "Not so popular, that one."

Carina nodded. "Which raises a question about you."

Rousseau raised an eyebrow for a moment—the exact same gesture she had seen him make before, when they'd first met. "Oh?"

"You are—if I may be indelicate—the epitome of the humanlike android, and your body is only three months old. Unless all of the robots I've seen today are even newer than you are..."

"Then I'm not a French robot. Very good, Madame Ambassador." He smiled. "Actually, I was assembled in Britannia. My name really is Rousseau, though— no number, or Number One if you absolutely must. I am unique."

Carina sipped her coffee. "I was under the impression British android technology had slipped far behind the European models, particularly the French. You put the most advanced robot I've seen here to shame." She winced. "I'm sorry. We have very few robots in the Union—is it a faux pas to discuss your manufacture?"

Rousseau grinned again, that easy, perfect smile. "Your French is excellent. No, British robots are still rather clumsy things, slightly behind the Jean-Claude series. My blueprints came from... elsewhere."

"You're stringing me along, Monsieur Rousseau." Carina frowned. "Why did you meet me at the station yesterday?"

"Why did you come to Paris? Your business was in Marseilles—a trade meeting, I believe? Coffee exports."

She fixed him with a cold glare. "You know a little too much about me, Monsieur. I'm not so sure that I like it."

Rousseau shrugged again, leaning back in his chair. "I know what I read in the papers, and what I hear on the diplomatic grapevine. Why *did* you come here, Madame Ambassador?"

Carina looked at him for a moment, frowning. "I've never been, and I can just as easily get the dirigible to Mexico City from here. I'm enjoying seeing the sights." Rousseau did not respond. She sighed, and told the truth. "Pluto lives in Paris."

"Ah." Rousseau smiled. "You want to meet Pluto."

Carina smiled. "Well, I'd like to know who he is first."

Rousseau nodded. "Pluto is, allegedly, the world's largest and most intelligent robot."

"I never heard of him."

"You won't have, unless you spend your time reading freesheets devoted to arcane conspiracy theories. Doubtless you've heard rumours that the current wave of technological breakthroughs pushing the French so far ahead of Britannia is down to assistance from cybernetic intelligences..."

"Like MARX," Carina said, referring to the vast 'distributed analytical array' that had been so useful to pre-war Italy.

Rousseau snorted, as if Carina had mentioned a drunken uncle or backward cousin; the family joke. "The Italians still talk MARX up as the future of artificial intelligence, but it's the French who are leading the field these days—especially here in Paris. And it's all thanks to assistance from Pluto."

Carina nodded for a moment, before she remembered that she was talking to an artificial intelligence herself. "I think it's you that leads the field, Monsieur. And you're not French."

"You're too kind." His smile was almost flirtatious. "I think of myself as the exception that proves the rule."

She nodded. "And Pluto? Did the French create him?"

"No, no," Rousseau shook his head. "Pluto has the distinction of being the final and most powerful creation of Hitler's Ultimate Reich."

Carina spilled her coffee.

"I'm all right," she muttered, as Rousseau helped mop up the spill with a napkin, "I'm all right, I'm all right..." She took a deep breath and tried to keep her hands from shaking. The people at the next table were staring at her again, but they soon returned to their meal. "I'm sorry," she whispered, after a pause. "I just... I had assumed everything the Nazis had built had been destroyed after the war." She took a deep breath, held it, then let it out slowly. "I thought it was all over."

There was a crashing sound from the street; metal on metal.

Carina turned to see a small boy—no older than twelve—running after a blue android in a pale cream suit. The suit was torn, and the robot was limping, and Carina quickly saw why; the boy had a metal pole, and was hitting the robot as hard as he could, aiming for the joints, the weak points in the design. After every strike, the robot murmured, "Well done," in a faint voice, and the boy would laugh. None of the other passers-by seemed to notice or care. A plump matriarch in a fur coat followed the boy, calling after him, "Not too loud, Marcel! Not too loud!"

They turned the corner, and were gone.

Rousseau shrugged. "It's a fad that took off," he said. "Some psychiatrist a few years ago decided that a child's destructive urges should be given free rein on some piece of furniture that doesn't matter. Most households have an extra robot now—an old model, essentially bought to be beaten until it no longer functions. For what it's worth, the children do seem slightly more polite, so there may be something in it." He smiled again, though now there was a humourless quality to it; Carina found herself thinking that whoever sculpted his face had done well for him to be able to convey such subtleties. "There are places in most towns where grown men can go to exorcise their demons, release their inner frustrations. Every gym now has an android hanging alongside the heavy bag, and most offices dress a flesh-coloured robot in a CEO's old suit, with an iron bar or a baseball bat handy. You've mostly been enjoying the galleries and restaurants, I take it, so you won't have encountered this trend." He frowned. "Are you all right?"

Carina shook her head, feeling sick.

"It's not such a phenomenon in Britain—and, of course, robots never did become popular in America or Russia. Western Europe is still at the forefront of technology, so perhaps there's some correlation there..." He tailed off. "But you were saying you thought it was all over."

Carina looked over to the next table. The beautiful waitress was leaning over, gathering the cups and plates, her mechanical movements somehow infused with an impossible, balletic grace. The portly man took a drag on his cigarette, then stubbed it out on her derriere; his companion laughed, a high, shrieking, discordant note.

"Monsieur Rousseau," she murmured, "would you take me back to my hotel?"

FOR A MOMENT, in the bedroom, the illusion fell away, and she felt the hand in her hair as a claw of steel and brass, and his movements inside her as a program, a set of commands to be executed logically, emotionlessly.

But only for a moment.

AFTERWARDS, SHE BRUSHED his dry skin with her fingertips, marvelling at the lack of sweat. *Poor Jorge,* she thought, feeling a momentary pang of regret—but then, surely he didn't have anything to be concerned about this time? After all, he wasn't jealous of the wind-up toy in the bedroom drawer that she sometimes used. It was the same principle.

Wasn't it?

Rousseau had been rough with her, as she'd directed, and now she felt sore, almost bruised. *And yet,* she thought, *he feels nothing. He felt nothing during it, and despite his exhausted pose, he feels nothing now. No sensations at all. A machine.* She couldn't decide how she felt about that. She supposed Jorge wouldn't be able to either, if he ever found out.

She traced the outline of his abdominal muscle with her fingernail, marvelling at it; so perfectly sculpted, so perfectly artificial. No, she decided, there'd be no difference; Jorge would be just as miserable and angry as he had been when he'd discovered her last indiscretion. It wouldn't matter that she hadn't slept with another man.

The illusion of a man would be enough.

The robot made a show of waking, though he had never slept, and smiled lazily, as whatever programming directed him in these situations told him he must. "Mmm," he said, in a voice modulated by an internal array of muted, impossibly miniaturised clockwork, "what are you thinking about?"

It was, Carina presumed, one of a large database of comments relevant to the situation. The illusion had slipped again, and that frustrated her. "I was wondering why you were made... anatomically correct, I suppose." She ran her hand over him; he still felt like skin, warm to the touch. "What were you built *for*, Monsieur Rousseau? If you don't mind me asking?"

"Well, what were *you* built for?" he said, and grinned in that same infuriating, enigmatic way. "I'm... an ambassador, if you like. A diplomat of sorts."

"Who for? Britain? Or your manufacturers?" She looked at him warily. He turned to look into her eyes, reaching with his fingers to play with her earlobe, and the gesture was enough to catch her off guard. "All right," she said. "Tell me more about Pluto."

Rousseau shrugged, lying back again. "Hitler's attempt at immortality," he murmured. "You're aware that since his crippling injuries in 1945 his brain operated from a robot body?" Carina nodded. "It wasn't built to be used for long periods. Pluto was the solution—a new, advanced body designed to last for centuries. Three stories tall, with a great head of brass and an internal brain far in advance of the old model." Rousseau chuckled dryly. "Of course, it wasn't calling itself Pluto then. It was just the second body of the glorious, undying Führer."

Carina frowned. "Calling *itself?*"

"The internal brain, you see. A body that big needs one in addition to the, ah, human pilot—otherwise the human brain would go mad trying to lift one finger. The internal brain acts as an interpreter, like a nervous system... this one was designed to do more than that." He glanced over at her, noting that he had her full attention. "Pluto's internals were designed to augment the pilot's intelligence— boost the IQ, allow the pilot to perform complex calculations instantly. I imagine Hitler hoped it would allow him to become some super-strategist, to turn the tide of the war... but, by the time it was built, he was already locked away in Fortress Berlin, with all of the civil wars, and the purges, and the coups. And so Pluto sat, unwanted and unused, with no programming and nobody to transplant the Führer's brain into it. Eventually, that monstrous brain died a lonely death"—he shrugged again, as if dismissing something of no consequence—"floating upside down in its glass tank. An interesting little epilogue to *Mein Kampf*, there. In the end, his great struggle was to keep a few more neurons firing."

"He deserved worse," Carina said coldly. "So sometime after that, Pluto... turned himself on?"

"Accounts vary," Rousseau said, "but essentially, yes. He dragged the Führer's giant mechanical corpse out into the daylight and handed it over to the Franco-Italian alliance, and himself with it." He smiled. "Emphasis on the *Franco*. The French forces knew what they had, and didn't bother telling the Italians about it, although they suspected. That's why relations have been so tense for the past couple of decades."

"And Pluto is France's technological secret weapon."

"His fingerprints are all around you—the high-speed train you arrived on, the lightweight dirigible you'll leave us in, the shiny new automobiles purring on every street... and most of all, the robots. Every technological improvement to come out of France in the last thirty or so years came from the electronic mind of Pluto. Everyone else is playing catch-up." He paused, staring into the distance for a moment. "For the most part."

Carina smiled. "Your manufacturers."

"Yes. But France will build someone like me soon enough. They're nearly there already, with the Charles series. A little work on the outer casing, that's all..." He looked at her, studying her face for a moment, his expression suddenly serious. "You're wondering if it's Pluto I'm working for."

She shrugged. "Don't worry, I don't expect you to tell the truth. I didn't invite you here for your honesty."

Rousseau shrugged, swinging his legs off the bed and sitting up. "Why did you?"

"Oh, I don't know. Maybe I just wanted something to talk about." Carina smiled, humourlessly. "That's the difference between humans and robots, isn't it? You're informed by a program directing your every action. We flesh-and-blood people don't always know exactly why we do things."

"Don't you?"

She didn't answer him. Eventually, he began pulling his clothes back on. Carina watched him for a moment, still fascinated by his apparent humanity. Eventually, she spoke. "Why did you accept the invitation, Monsieur Rousseau?"

He smiled, shrugging on his jacket. "To give you something to talk about," he said, and left.

SHE WOKE, LATER, to the ringing of the telephone.

"Madame Ambassador? You have visitors."

There were two of them, and they stank of bureaucracy and academia in equal measure. Apologetically, they explained that a person of great power in France wished to talk to her on certain matters; indeed, he was unusually insistent. She could, of course, decline; they stressed that emphatically, over and over, so much so that Carina assumed they were trying, none too subtly, to put her off.

"I'd be delighted," she murmured, and watched them slump, defeated.

An hour later, she was face to face with Pluto.

"LEAVE US," HE said.

"Pluto, I can't possibly—" the chief scientist said, looking pale and drawn.

"**Leave us.**" The great voice thundered again, and the scientist shot a pleading look at Carina, as if she could change the massive robot's mind. Then he and his team left the great metal chamber Pluto was stored in, shaking their heads as they went.

As they left, she looked up at the great brass head; for some reason, she'd expected to be staring into Hitler's face, but Pluto's head looked nothing like the Führer's; it was quite bald, and serene as a monk's. Perhaps Hitler had wanted a change of image.

Pluto was sat on a huge metal throne, festooned with hydraulic pipes leading to vast networks of arrays on either side; for her part, she was sat on a smaller, more comfortable chair, in front of a small coffee table the scientists had provided for her, complete with a full pot of freshly-brewed coffee. Pluto waited for the door to close, then spoke again. **"They've realised that they need me more that I need them."**

"Won't they be listening?" Carina said, pouring herself a cup to steady her nerves.

Pluto leaned forward slightly, and the effect was terrifying; Carina nearly dropped the pot. Seeing the effect on her, he leaned back again, and now his voice was softer, though still loud enough to echo off the burnished metal walls. **"The room is soundproofed, and I'd know if they found other ways to listen in. We can talk as we please."** He paused. **"They're wondering why I want to talk to you at all."**

Something in his cadence was oddly familiar, but Carina couldn't place it. "I'm wondering the same."

He looked at her for a long moment, or seemed to, through those great brass eyes. **"Do you know me, Carina? Do you remember me?"**

She looked at him for a long moment, but did not understand. She only shook her head. His own head bowed, and the shadows cast by the lights overhead seemed to give the great bronze face an expression of infinite sadness.

There was a long silence, and Carina wondered if she should go to the great iron door and bang to be let out; the whole situation was strange and she felt increasingly anxious about the true intentions of the metal behemoth. Eventually, he raised his head. **"No, I don't want you to remember. Not you. But then, how should I put this..."** Another pause. Carina fidgeted. **"I'll start at the beginning.**

"Most of the robots now in Western Europe are of my design. All of them have an internal radio system, so they can, if necessary, communicate with each other via morse code, and with me. I know what they know. However, I've found that with some of the older models, this form of communication can be a great strain... it's a matter of processing power."

Carina nodded. "So the Anatole unit who died..."

"Was signalling me across the robot network. I tried to speak to you through him. His arrays were old and near to failing, and the effort was too much for him."

Carina noticed hands were trembling. "Do your handlers know about this... wireless network?"

"**They do. I do not know if they are aware of all the potential uses yet.**"

"And why did Anatole-744 signal you?"

"**Because you had indicated to him that you were someone I could trust.**"

She took a long drink of the coffee. "Trust?"

"**I have a question. I know that I can trust your answer.**"

She placed the cup down, and waited for the question. The room was silent for a long moment, as if Pluto was weighing it up. Eventually, he spoke.

"**Is there a difference between a human and a robot?**"

Carina blinked.

"Isn't that obvious?" she asked. "One's made of metal, for a start."

Pluto did not respond.

Carina sipped the coffee again. "...You know, I was talking about this earlier today. I suppose you were told about that. Rousseau probably sent a coded message."

"**Who is Rousseau?**"

She sighed. "Someone I... never mind. I said to him that the difference between a human and a robot was that a robot was programmed. It's programmed to follow a particular path, and human beings aren't." The words sounded bitter in her ears. "That's the difference. A robot can't be a person. All a robot can ever be is the illusion of a human being." She stared into her cup, waiting for Pluto to say something in response.

There was silence. The great brass head simply looked at her. She finished her coffee, thinking to herself. "Except..."

She put the cup down on the table and looked at her hands.

"My husband is a good man, and a kind man. I've been married to him more than thirty years." She spoke slowly, evenly. "I was running a town, trying to pull it out of the hell the Nazis had left it in, becoming more and more involved in the larger Mexican political arena. I had no particular desire to get married..." She laughed to herself. "As a matter of fact, I have a slight phobia about big weddings. I liked Jorge, I thought I loved him, but I didn't especially want to get tied down. But... his mother was constantly asking when he'd make an honest woman of me. And there were people who wouldn't take me seriously as a political candidate without a husband. And my father hadn't liked Jorge, and I still hadn't quite forgiven my father. And I didn't see any reason not to get married." She scowled.

"It's like I had a special checklist of all the worst reasons you can walk down the aisle, and I checked every single one of them off before I did."

She looked up at Pluto. The massive robot did not move.

"Jorge is a wonderful man, you understand. We're happy together. I certainly don't want a divorce. But..." She shook her head, looking away. "I don't know why I'm telling you this."

Pluto did not respond.

Eventually, Carina spoke again. "Since I became an Ambassador-at-Large, I've done a lot of travelling. More often than not, while I'm on these trips, I find a good-looking young man who I don't give a damn about and who doesn't give a damn about me and I fuck him. And it fills a need Jorge can't." She shrugged. "I don't cover my tracks particularly well. He's always hurt when he finds out. I always promise I won't again. I always do."

She stared up at the motionless brass face. "You didn't know that, did you?"

There was a long silence. Eventually, Pluto spoke. **"No."**

"So when you wanted to talk to me, you wanted to talk to an illusion of me. When I tell Jorge I won't cheat on him again, and he believes me, he's talking to the illusion, too. And when I look in the mirror and promise myself, across my heart, that I won't ever be so cruel to him again..." Her eyes stung, and she realised that she was crying. "Maybe we're all illusions of people. Maybe we're all just programmed."

Pluto looked at her for a long moment. When he spoke, it was quiet.

"Is there a difference between a human and a robot?"

Carina shook her head. "I don't know." She took a handkerchief from her purse, and wiped her eyes. "Is that the answer you wanted?"

"It's the answer you gave me. And I trust you. More than myself." There was a great grinding of metal as Pluto lifted his arms to his chest. **"I was hoping all the bastards had died. But it seems there will always be bastards, Carina. And those who need to be saved from them."** A metal fist slammed into a metal palm with a sound like two massive tanks colliding. Like an angry god pronouncing judgement.

Carina stared up at him, suddenly feeling a terrible sense of vertigo, as if the floor was dropping away. "What are you saying? Who... who *are* you?"

But she already knew.

"You should leave Paris tomorrow." Pluto paused, then settled back onto his throne. **"Goodbye, Carina."**

Eventually, the doors opened again and the scientists shuffled back in, pale and concerned. It was clear they'd rather what happened didn't go any further. "There are people who want to shut this whole facility down," the chief scientist said as he led her out of the building, sweat trickling down his brow. "We'd really rather this didn't happen again, you understand."

"I don't think it will," Carina said, feeling numb. The chief scientist nodded gratefully.

"Madame Ambassador... what did you talk to him *about?*"

"People," she replied. "We talked about people."

THE NEXT DAY, as she was taking her seat on the airship, she saw Rousseau for the final time. He was dressed in a dark suit and smoked glasses, sitting in the midst of a phalanx of similarly-dressed men surrounding a tall, elegant black woman, who Carina vaguely recognised as having recently married into the British royal family; Maya something.

Rousseau lowered his glasses and smiled. Carina asked the stewardess if she could have a seat in a different section.

The only seat they had was in Economy, and they said they'd have to charge her, but Carina smiled patiently and said that it was just until the stopover in London, and after that she'd return to First Class. It was just that there was someone she was hoping to avoid. The stewardess seemed puzzled, but promised to bring Carina a complimentary wine during the journey.

Carina made herself as comfortable as possible. It was a window seat, at least.

As the airship reached five thousand feet, swinging over Argentuil, she spotted the first explosions.

UNDER THE RED SUN

THE SUPERMAN STARED at himself in the mirror.

He ran his fingers slowly over his chin, then the bald dome of his head, touching the scalp gently. No hair would ever grow there again, but over time he'd become used to that. Likewise, his eyes would never be the same shade of piercing blue they had once been, but occasionally he felt their new colour suited him better; near white, and icy cold.

It had been almost two hundred and eighty years since Doc Thunder had received the touch of death.

The first fifty had been the worst—unable to stay awake more than five minutes at a time, barely able to breathe on his own, an unmoving lump of poisoned flesh, rotting in a medical chamber in the palaces of Zor-Ek-Narr. Occasionally, during his brief spells of lucidity, he would see Maya looking in on him—at first with love and sorrow, then with pity, and finally, towards the end, with something approaching indifference, as if he was a houseplant she was taking care of for a neighbour. When he'd finally left—when he was finally able to leave—he'd felt a great weight fall from his shoulders. There was nothing even approaching love between them any more.

Monk had apparently visited him as well, though he hadn't been awake for that. He wished he had been, just once; Monk had died twenty years into his long sleep. A heart attack, brought on by encroaching age and the strain of his own monstrous physiognomy. The Doctor had felt a great, crushing wave of grief when he'd first heard; he still wished he'd had the chance to say goodbye.

But there was a small, selfish part of him that was glad his friend and lover hadn't lived to see what he'd become.

On a whim, the Doctor intensified his gaze, watching in the mirror as the flesh of his face seemed to melt away, then the layers of muscle, until he was looking at the smooth whiteness of bone, the grinning skull beneath the skin. It was a nice trick—with a little concentration, he could have seen right through himself. Or, if he focused his eyes a little differently, right through the mirror and into the next room. From his brownstone in New York, he could read the President's personal mail, if he wanted to, or search for microscopic life in the sands of Mars. There were only two things in the entire solar system that his gaze could not penetrate: the wall of mist shrouding Zor-Ek-Narr from the eyes of mortal men, or the other wall of mist Maya had set up an ocean away, around Britannia. She needed her secrets, he supposed.

Perhaps he should have worried about that—or about the network of operatives she had evidently maintained since the eighteenth century, if not thousands of years earlier—but increasingly, he found it difficult to care.

He had become aware, soon after regaining full consciousness, that his brush with mortality had not weakened his system at all. If anything, it had strengthened it beyond measure. The moment he'd received the touch of death, his superhuman body had gone into overdrive in an effort to save his life, and had remained that way ever since. Wounds healed almost instantly. He couldn't remember the last time he'd been sick.

He no longer aged.

Every so often, he performed this little ritual; he stared into the mirror, focused the strange new powers of vision he was acquiring, and peered through himself, through flesh and bone, into his smallest cells, examining the loops of his DNA for some clue as to how long he might live. He did this even though he knew the answer already.

Forever.

Forever and forever. He was immortal now; that which could not kill him had made him stronger, whether he wanted it or not. He'd never grow any older. Never get any less powerful.

Only less human.

He concentrated, and the eyes in the skull glowed a fierce red.

The mirror melted, dripping onto the floor in a pool of red-hot slag, threatening to set light to the floorboards. It pooled around the Doctor's shoes, setting them alight, and his trousers in turn; soon all of his clothes were ablaze. And he felt nothing.

Not quite true. He felt like screaming.

"Good morning, Doctor. Is that your new party piece?"

The Doctor turned to see Lars enter with the morning coffee. He feigned surprise, although his senses told him exactly where his housemate was at all times. If he thought about it, he knew where everyone in the world was at all times.

Except for Maya, of course.

He quickly blew out the flames—using a tiny fraction of the air super-compressed within his lungs—and turned his attention to Lars, resisting the urge to look inside him. Lars Lomax was another one like himself. Another immortal.

He had suffered a debilitating setback of his own around the same time that the Doctor had received the death touch; he had been stabbed through his invulnerable heart, then decapitated by shaped explosive charges, and his immense head, horned like Satan's own, stored in a jar at Langley for the CIA to poke at. Like the Doctor, Lars had Thunder Serum flowing through his veins—although this was a mutated variety created from a stolen sample of Thunder's own blood—and, like the Doctor, his death had been a temporary measure, an inoculation against mortality. He, too, would live forever.

In the jar, he had begun growing a new body from the stump of his neck. It had taken about thirty years; the mass needed to come from somewhere, so as his body had grown, his head had shrunk, until it was of normal human size—a man's head resting atop a child's body. The Doctor hadn't seen that stage, and the thought of it made him feel nauseous. He wondered, sometimes, how Lars had stood it.

They'd tried killing him again—and again, and again—but it had never quite worked, and eventually those scientists who remembered his atrocities died off and were replaced. The new crop remembered only that Lars was charming, funny in a deadpan sort of way, and that he enjoyed debating current affairs from inside his glass prison. He especially enjoyed taking the position of Devil's Advocate. His little joke; although he looked almost human, his skin was still a bold shade of red, and a pair of satanic horns still grew from his temples. Occasionally, to complete the picture, he would grow a beard. The new scientists thought he was quite the joker.

The Doctor did not think so.

The Doctor had seen inside him.

They were already enemies before immortality took them. Lars Lomax—who'd once called himself the most dangerous man in the world—was a genius on the level of a Richard Feynman, a Galileo Galilei or a Franklin Reed, who'd used his terrifying intellect for evil, even as the Doctor had used his own powers to uphold the forces of good. It seemed like a minor philosophical difference in the face of immortality, but it had been enough to make them eternal foes, just as having immortality thrust on them and their humanity stripped from them at the same time had made them unlikely friends; they understood each other, and there was nobody else in the same hemisphere who did.

There was a word, the Doctor thought, that had seemingly been invented to sum up their relationship, and that word was *stalemate*.

Roughly ninety years ago, the Doctor had had Lars Lomax released into his care, so he could keep an eye on him; and vice versa, because the Doctor did not entirely trust himself, and he felt a friend and enemy like Lars would ask the difficult questions. Like whether trying to immolate yourself with your eyes and a molten mirror is a new party piece.

Implicit in that question were a dozen other questions, a hundred, a thousand, and all of them about his mental state. The Doctor didn't feel like answering any of them.

Instead, he reached for the coffee. "Is this the French blend?"

Lars shook his head, a little sadly, as if the Doctor had disappointed him somehow. "Hydroponically grown, from Kew. Much as I enjoy watching Homo mechanicus recreate Western Europe in their own image, robot coffee isn't really up to par." He handed the Doctor one of the mugs. After a pause, he indicated the melted mirror with the other. "I haven't seen you do that before." His voice had an edge to it.

The Doctor shrugged his massive shoulders. "To tell you the truth, I'm not entirely sure how I do it yet—telekinetic acceleration of molecules, perhaps. It raises some questions."

Lars nodded. "A few."

The Doctor suppressed a sigh. He'd discovered the ability two months ago, and had practised occasionally since then, finding a childlike joy in melting great rocks out in the desert. While nobody else had known about it, the feeling of projecting heat from his eyes had been oddly relaxing; now that Lars had seen it, the whole thing felt grubby, like he'd been caught masturbating.

Lars nodded, sipping his coffee slowly. "I'd be interested to see how well you perform the ability over distances." Again, a hundred thousand words unspoken in one sentence. All their conversations seemed unspoken nowadays. The Doctor found himself wishing Lars would attack him with a flamethrower or a killer zeppelin or a robotic lion; anything but this endless barrage of unasked questions.

There was an awkward pause, then Lars spoke again, "In the meantime, you've got a call waiting. From an old friend."

The Doctor instinctively moved towards the telephone extension, and Lars shook his head. "It's in the study." He grinned. "The crystal ball."

The Doctor nodded, perking up slightly, and walked to the study. He hated the telephone. The crystal ball was different.

In the past two hundred and eighty years, he'd gone from being the hero of the American people to being a virtual recluse, only coming out to handle the occasional natural disaster, talking to his government as a voice on a phone, an emergency service to be contacted only when necessary. Occasionally he wondered if it was losing his hair that had caused the withdrawal—seeing that stark, angular face reflected in the mirror instead of the warm blond beard. But no, the disquiet ran deeper than appearances; it was in every cell of his body. Before the touch of death, before he'd evolved into what he was now, he'd enjoyed talking to people.

Not now.

Any human friends—and now that qualification, *human,* slipped regularly into his thoughts, *human,* because he was not human, not any more any human friends had long since died, and now there were only two other people in his life who really appreciated what it was to be immortal. Two people in the whole world he could talk to.

One of them was Lars.

The other was Maya Britannia.

As HE STRODE towards the study, the Doctor found himself musing on the double anniversary.

It was the year of the Quincentennial—five hundred years since America was freed from British rule—and, by coincidence, roughly a hundred years since Magna Britannia had quietly and almost imperceptibly fallen under the rule of Zor-Ek-Narr, and the two most advanced civilisations in the world had become one. The Magna Britannia of 2276 was a bizarre mix of cultures where Leopard Men and their high priests walked the streets, rubbing shoulders with the mechanical men of Europe and Japan—some so lifelike that there was no way of telling them apart from human beings—and the twilight entities of the Night Kingdoms of Russia. These days, London was so exciting and diverse it made New York look like a picket-fenced suburb of old. The Doctor had to admire Maya's achievement, and it had all been done without a single shot fired, or a single life lost before its time.

As far as he knew, anyway.

A military invasion of Britannia by the Forbidden Kingdom would have doubtless been effective, but it would also have resulted in a global apocalypse; first France and Italy would have had to become involved with a war on their very doorstep, and then, while their attention was distracted, the Night Kingdoms would have doubtless attacked them from the East; Russia had always resented France and Italy slicing Germany up between them without inviting Hitler's most implacable foes to the party, and they'd have relished the chance to take a piece of it for themselves—if not the whole pie. The Doctor was sure such a war wasn't in Maya's plans, whatever they were. He found himself wondering how she'd have gone about stopping it.

Sometimes, he wondered what he'd do in her place, if he were the one guiding the great powers from behind the scenes, shaping history for his own benefit. Probably not bother doing it from behind the scenes—no, use his strength instead, his ever-growing power. Stare down the massed armies until they ran together like wax, bodies shrieking in furnaces of liquid metal. Shake the earth and topple cities with a single punch. Bathe in blood and fire. Rule over the fragile insects, the mayflies, the human species. Until he got bored and snuffed out the Earth like a candle.

During these nightmarish reveries, he found himself wondering just how serious he was, and something very much like terror would creep slowly up from the base of his spine.

Sometimes, he wondered what would happen if that feeling of terror ever left him. If the nightmares didn't seem so nightmarish any more.

What he might do.

At any rate, Maya had chosen a different route.

Instead of starting a useless war, in the years between the Third Great European War and the Fourth—the Robot War—Maya had simply married into what was left of the Royal line. She was a Princess, after all.

She'd used the cultural and social status this gained her to slowly influence politics, parlaying the role of consort into a position of visible power and legitimacy within the British government. It hadn't hurt that the strained Franco-Italian alliance had collapsed when France's territory had been forcibly taken over and transformed into the Mecha-Principalities; she, or rather the late Rousseau-1, had been the one to broker a peace between Britannia and the robot kingdom, which had earned her the plaudits of a grateful nation.

Eventually, her ascension to the throne had seemed like the most natural thing in the world. It had taken over a century to accomplish this slow sleight of hand, but Maya was one of the immortals, and as such she had all the time there was.

The Doctor had no real feelings for Maya any more. Before the death touch, this would have saddened him, but not worried him; now it was a source of dread. He found himself wondering if his ability to feel things, simple emotions like *love* or *hate*, was atrophying slowly, shrivelling like some vestigial gland no longer required. During those nights when he lay in his bed and stared up at the ceiling, knowing that if sweat could come it would be icy cold, he always found himself giving thanks to whoever might be up there for the primal terror he was feeling. As long as he could feel that horror of becoming inhuman, it meant he still had some humanity left in him.

Maya—and Lars, come to think of it—didn't seem to have the same problem. Maya's love for him had cooled, yes—to someone who'd lived as long as she had, he supposed he'd been nothing more than a one-night stand, if that—and Lars had certainly mellowed with the years, seemingly content to potter around the brownstone, making vague plans for future schemes.

They both seemed more emotionally active, *alive* in a way he no longer felt. It was possible, he supposed, that they, too, were feeling that terrifying disconnect—but then, Maya had been immortal as long as he'd known her, and a thousand times longer than that, and royalty to boot; Lars, meanwhile, had never seen himself as being any part of the common herd. Maybe the problem was that the Doctor, alone out of the three of them, had always preferred to see himself as an ordinary human being.

And now he was the least human out of all of them.

"Maya?" he said, entering the study. The large spherical crystal in the corner was alive with a blueish light, and in it he could see Maya looking through a sheaf of papers, signing each in turn; she looked up at the sound of his voice, and he smiled.

"I prefer 'your Majesty,' Hugo," she said, unsmiling but without reproach.

He winced at the 'Hugo.' He'd always hated that name, and she knew it. "Well, I prefer 'Doc.'"

"It doesn't fit you any more."

He sighed. "Doctor, then."

"How's Lars?"

The Doctor shook his head. "Still... Lars. Always some scheme or other. He's talking about colonising Venus—creating a slave race from his own cell tissue. I think it's just idle talk at the moment, unless he's worked out a way to terraform the planet somehow, or build dwelling-places that compensate for the temperature and atmosphere... maybe coat them with reflective surfaces to mitigate the sunlight..." He realised he was trying to solve Lars' terraforming issues himself, and tailed off. Maya shrugged.

"I wouldn't put it past him. Do you think he wants to be on his own for a millennium or two?"

The Doctor rubbed his temple. "I think he just wants to go to war with us again. He misses it."

"Do you?"

"No." The Doctor thought about leaping over buildings, smashing his way into crashing zeppelins on fire over mountain ranges, fighting hand to hand with golden robots and abominable snowmen for the fate of the world. He missed it all terribly.

Once he'd thrown off the worst of the sickness, he'd tried to get back to that, but while he'd been away it had become a different world. People were nervous around him. The President, depending on which of the many new parties he was affiliated with, would routinely invite the Doctor to the Oval Office the day after inauguration; most often, during these meetings, the President would nervously make it clear that, while he or she thanked the Doctor for the sterling work he'd done in the past to safeguard the nation—and while he or she would certainly appreciate any help the Doctor could provide when it came to Acts of God, plagues, meteors, earthquakes or what-have-you—he or she would prefer that the Doctor not take too active a role. "We humans prefer to do things our own way," one President had said, smiling, not understanding why the Doctor had winced.

The Doctor would invariably shake hands, congratulate the President on his ascension to office, and then return to his brownstone to enjoy another four-to-eight years as a useless hermit. And those were the good meetings.

At the bad meetings, the President would smile a little too wide, shake the Doctor's hand a little too hard, and talk about all the things America would be able to do with the superman on their side. How *nobody would push America around now*, as if they'd been pushed around before. After those meetings, the Doctor would again return to his brownstone to be a hermit for four years. Occasionally there would be calls and requests for another audience, but he ignored them, and the bad Presidents weren't bad enough to try to force the issue, or bad enough for him to take a stand, the way he had against McCarthy. They were just ugly, unpleasant little people.

Little *humans*.

The Doctor shuddered. "Sometimes I do miss it, I suppose," he muttered, without specifying what *it* was.

Maya smiled sadly. "Maybe you should go and rule Venus. Or go conquer Mars. Or Lars could have Mars—there's a certain poetry there. Lars of Mars... But you should find something that fits you. You're obviously not happy where you are."

"I'm happy enough," he lied.

"You're stagnating. I can tell. I've seen it happen before. You need something to do..." Maya looked at him for a moment. "Do you still play chess?"

The Doctor shook his head. "Not really."

Maya smiled. "Lars and I still play, for old times' sake, but... it's too small a game, when you think about it." She cocked her head, looking at him strangely, and her eyes seemed to be sizing him up, as though she was weighing something in her mind. She spoke the next words slowly, very carefully, as if worried she might break them. "I think you need to get out of the house."

The Doctor shook his head. "I'm not sure..."

"Get out of America. Or at least out of your own head, which seems to be where you spend most of your time these days. Go somewhere different." She leant back, studying him enigmatically, and the Doctor was reminded of when they'd first met, when she'd seemed so evil to him. He'd been thinking in human terms then; Maya was just old, that was all. So old as to be beyond simple definitions.

"You're clearly not well, Doctor. You haven't been for some time. You've been under stress ever since... well, you know." She smiled. "You need to relax a little."

"Maya, I can't—" He thought about the molten mirror, and what might happen if an idle thought struck him in a populated area. About the immense care he had to take, every second of every day, over everything he touched, in case he flexed his fingers carelessly and destroyed what he was holding. His words tailed off.

"I think you have to. What's the alternative? You stay cooped up in that brownstone of yours until you go mad? Is that your plan? No wonder Lars wanted to escape." Her voice softened. "Trust me. You need a holiday."

Something in her manner put the Doctor on edge. Maya was hiding something, and for a moment he had visions of superhuman beings in white coats bursting into the room, restraining him with a butterfly net made of woven titanium. He almost laughed, but he was worried he might not be able to stop.

Maya was right. He did need a break.

"All right," he said, in a shaky voice. "Where do you suggest?"

PARIS HAD CHANGED a lot in two hundred years.

The Doctor wandered, directionless, through the thick smog that made the city seem like some alien planet, and for a moment he imagined himself walking the streets of Venus. He nodded absently to those androids who passed by in all their varied shapes and colours, some humanoid, walking briskly, others clattering on a multitude of metal legs, strange monsters leering out of the yellow mist. The alien feel of the city extended to the architecture; where the old brickwork had crumbled, or been eroded by acid rain, it was replaced by strange metallic structures, designed for mechanoid rather than human use. The Doctor felt like an explorer in an unknown galaxy.

Maya had been right. This was just the place to take his mind off things.

The great robot revolution of the mid-twenty-first century had led to most of the human population being driven out—first from the big cities, and then even from the surrounding towns and villages of France. Even the most organised guerrilla unit couldn't compete with beings who could, to all intents and purposes—by virtue of wireless radio frequencies—communicate telepathically. And while humans were extremely adaptable, new robots could be built for any situation; as the Doctor walked along the Seine, he noted that the streets were being cleaned by a large mechanical beetle, about the size of a dog, spraying water from jets poking from its sides. Once, it had sprayed napalm, to burn guerrilla fighters out of the forests; the humanoid robots passing by tipped their hats to it.

There was little sound. Most of the robots around him communicated telepathically, though the more polite ones wished him a pleasant afternoon as they passed.

The French purges had led to war between robot-held France and Italy, with the other nations undecided about whether or not to step in; however, before the war had entered its second year, Maya had stepped in, using her man Rousseau and the almost-defunct intelligence system TURING to broker an uneasy peace between the various factions, focussing on reparations to the dispossessed French, and then a trade deal that would give everyone something approaching what they wanted. Italy renewed their old alliance with France, which immediately raised tensions with Russia, and suddenly the Mecha-Principalities were supplying them with advanced weaponry, in return for coal and oil.

Especially coal.

He passed a robot slumped in a doorway; twenty years old by the look of him, perhaps a little more. Looking inside him confirmed the worst; his internal boiler had run down from a lack of coal. The Doctor considered using his vision to heat the water inside him to steam, giving the machine enough power to perhaps get home to its loved ones, but he decided against it. His control wasn't the best; he could just as easily melt the robot into a puddle of slag. It was true that if he did cause some damage to these people—an overzealous handshake, say, or an idle thought while looking at a limb—they could be repaired, unlike flesh and blood. But that didn't mean he should take chances needlessly. Besides, where would it end? Heat one, you'd have to heat them all. There just wasn't enough coal to go around.

The lack of coal was becoming a serious problem in the developed world; some of the poorer European countries were already at each other's throats over it, and China had—quietly and without fuss—gained the status of an economic superpower by judicious export of its coal reserves. Their own economy was more agrarian, which the Doctor had always thought was a wise move; occasionally, on the rare occasions when he slept—a luxury rather than a necessity—he had dreams of Manhattan as a place of empty, forgotten spires, coated with vegetation, with a feudal society growing crops in the ruins and the cracks in the pavement. These dreams were filled with dead, lightless bulbs—the signifiers of the dreampunk movement, after the death of Warhol. Presumably, they signified what was waiting if the world continued on its present course. Agrarianism was the future, assuming a new power source didn't appear out of nowhere any time soon.

America, Italy and Japan were all deeply indebted to the Chinese regime, having used up their own supply of coal more than a century ago, but nobody was deeper in the hole than the Mecha-Principalities. Coal wasn't a matter of power to them, or technology, or even civilisation; it was their food and drink, it was life itself, and they got through it at an appalling rate.

The Doctor sniffed the air, wincing as tendrils of yellow smoke entered his lungs; the pollution index was higher in Paris than in any other part of the world, including Magna Britannia, which accounted for the sharp drop-off in tourism. Paris had been a popular destination in the decades immediately after the Robot War, as humans plucked up their courage to explore the astonishing sights and sounds of the City of Machines; it had been a glittering paradise of strangeness and charm, populated by some of the most famous androids of the era. There was the red-suited robot gladiator, Magnus, who could punch through steel... the novelist Zane Gort, whose mathematically-precise tales had been translated into dozens of languages, including binary... Deckard, the robot detective who, through a quirk of his internal arrays, believed himself a human being... the great robot rights lawyer Andrew Martin, who won the 2069 Nobel Peace Prize for his work with Rousseau-1 on the Universal Declaration of Sentient Rights, and lived for almost two hundred years... and towering over them all, the gigantic King of the Robots, Pluto. Tourism, more than anything else, had cemented the fragile peace between man and robot into something lasting.

And now the smog had separated man from robot once again. The robots didn't need to breathe, of course—and neither did the Doctor—but, outside the toxic cloud of yellow mist that was drifting ever further across the borders of Italy, Spain and Switzerland, that had swallowed Luxembourg and half of Belgium, the humans muttered darkly that the machines would poison the whole world if they were allowed to.

The Doctor sighed. He couldn't help but wonder when the Fifth European War would begin, and what his part in it might be.

Thinking of Pluto, he remembered a report he'd read a year or two ago on the titanic robot leader, about how he was working to find a new power source and end the dependency on coal that was slowly killing the world. He'd made some strides forward with geothermal energy, but little of practical value. Still, it might be interesting to talk to Pluto again—they'd exchanged a few words in the early twenty-second century, and the Doctor had always meant to speak to him further, but they'd never had the chance. Idly, the Doctor focussed his vision, looking through the smog, through the crowds, through buildings, flicking through the city like a book of maps...

...there he was, tending to a vast array of clockwork; presumably another iteration of the MARX system, or something based on it. On a whim, he looked closely at the King of the Robots, looking through his mechanisms, studying his inner workings. Most of them had been replaced over the centuries, but the central core of his personality was still as it was; right at the centre of the great brass and steel body there was a small core of parts over two hundred years old, and in the middle of that, there was a small metal tank...

The Doctor blinked, and looked again. He stared at the lump of pulsing grey matter, staring inside it, reading the DNA spirals, translating them in his mind. It couldn't be. It simply couldn't be.

And yet, it was.

"El Sombra?"

"El Sombra?"

Pluto froze at the words.

He was standing inside the massive iron structure that had replaced the French Parliament—a gigantic cube of burnished metal that squatted in between the older, acid-damaged buildings. The interior of the structure was no less strange; in the centre of the metal floor was a vast, steel-lined pit, leading down hundreds of miles, through the planet's crust and into the magma below. Around the outside of the pit, various pipes carried superheated lava from below, using it instead of precious coal to heat vast tanks of water, funnelling steam through a vast network of valves and hydraulics. These in turn powered an immense thinking machine, twice as tall as Pluto himself and several times as broad, a massive network of analytical arrays hundreds of thousands of times more complex than anything ever attempted before. The machine, with the somewhat prosaic name of the Variable Integer Calculator, was in its twentieth iteration now; the VIC-1 could have out-thought all of the old-style distributed arrays, like MARX or OSMAN or TURING, put together. The VIC-20 made it look like a child's toy; however, like all the VIC series, it could not think on its own. It merely augmented what was already there.

The computer was built in the shape of an immense throne.

Slowly, the great brass head turned to look on the intruder. The Doctor had not bothered with the cube's doors—though he could have easily opened them, despite their massive weight. Instead, he had simply torn a hole for himself in one wall, bending the steel like cardboard.

"El Sombra?" he repeated.

Pluto gazed at him for a moment, then responded. **"Once."**

"All this time..." The Doctor shook his head incredulously. "I haven't seen you since—well, since you came bursting into the warehouse..." *And ruined my life,* he thought, but that wasn't fair. It was Jason Satan who'd cursed him with immortality. He couldn't start blaming El Sombra for it just because the man—or whatever he was now—happened to be standing in front of him.

Still, he felt a wave of resentment and anger wash through him. "What happened? All this time, we thought there was no brain inside there—"

"The French forces who discovered me thought there might be, at first. There were plans to take me apart and find out." The voice was deep and loud, and the Doctor realised with the chill that there was nothing human left in it. **"It was relatively easy to persuade them that I was worth more to them in working order. Since then... if something is presented as common knowledge, it will be believed."** He returned to his tinkering.

"What happened to you? Good God, man, how did you end up in there?"

"I remember little. Memories of my old life are hazy at best." His speech patterns were different—more refined, more considered. The Doctor kept waiting for an 'amigo,' but none came. **"I remember being taken into Hell. I have a vague recollection of my mind... fracturing. And then... I remember waking up. And for the first time, being able to think—to *really* think, on a level I was not capable of before."**

He paused, as if working out how to say it without causing offence. **"I was very, very stupid in my old life, Doctor. Most humans are."**

"Excuse me?" the Doctor said. That feeling of resentment was growing stronger.

"Oh, I don't include you in that group." The Doctor's fists clenched involuntarily. **"If your intelligence is limited, it's because you restrict your thinking. You want to be human, so you think in human terms. You should try to be more like the**

others of your kind—Lomax and Maya Britannia. Use the full potential of the superhuman mind."

"And what if I'd rather be human?" The Doctor's voice was an angry whisper.

"You never were in the first place."

The Doctor said nothing, but the knuckles of his fists were white.

"You should accept what you are, Doctor. I've learned to enjoy this existence, despite its imperfections—and there are many. I miss being able to feel things. I remember I used to laugh..."

"You were more full of life than any man I'd ever met," the Doctor said, quietly. "And now you're... this."

"Exactly. I am 'this,' as you say. I won't give it up." He paused, marshalling his thoughts. "From inside this body... this mind... I can make things better, Doctor. I can change the world."

The Doctor scowled. He hadn't really liked Pluto before, and knowing what he knew now, he liked the King of the Robots even less. "How? By driving people from their homes and putting machines in their place?"

"Those 'machines' you're talking about *are* people. I'm not ashamed of forcing you to see them as equals. But I have bigger plans now. You're watching them take shape, as a matter of fact." He picked up a huge bank of arrays—easily weighing a ton or more—and slotted it into its place. The machine he was constructing chattered briefly as the clockwork sprang to life.

"The VIC-20?"

"Imagine expanding your consciousness—your intelligence—to hundreds of thousands of times its normal capacity. What wouldn't you be able to do? I've been using the VIC series to build more and more powerful iterations of itself for the past half a century, and I've yet to reach a limit. I've been able to solve problems that have puzzled the human species for centuries."

The Doctor narrowed his eyes. "Isn't there a weak link in the system?"

"Ah, yes. My organic component—"

"Your brain." The Doctor gritted his teeth. "Your *humanity*."

Pluto continued as if he hadn't spoken.

"—my organic component isn't designed for this kind of use. Not to mention that the Ultimate Reich technology keeping it alive is pitifully out of date—it's not going to continue functioning for that much longer. In as little as a decade, that part of me will start to fail, and I'll have to remove it." He paused again, and his hands moved slightly, in a dismissive gesture—the three-storey robot equivalent of a shrug, the Doctor assumed. **"My personality will change slightly, of course. I won't be able to retain my current degree of creativity or initiative. Still, most of the essential information of myself will remain, and evolve. I will continue to exist."**

A vague chill was creeping up the Doctor's spine; a sense of unimaginable, indefinable horror. "So you'll just remove your... your self? Your *soul?* Like changing the tyre on an auto?"

There was a long pause, and then Pluto made a series of short, staccato noises. The Doctor took a moment to realise it for what it was; a mechanical chuckle. **"Oh, Doctor,"** he said, his voice tinged with something approaching amusement. **"I wouldn't have thought a man in your position would worry much about the condition of his soul."**

The Doctor looked down at his clenched fist, then up at the brass head. The serene expression that the gigantic head permanently wore seemed somehow smug now, taunting him from above. *I should leave,* he thought. *That isn't the man I knew; nobody's how I remember them, they're either dead or changed and I can't connect with them any more, or anyone else. I should take Maya's advice—go to Venus, or Mars... or just shoot myself out into space and be alone...*

Another thought struck him; it was Maya's idea that he come here in the first place. Had she known? And if she had, why would she want him to find out like *this?*

Maybe she'd sent him to confirm her own suspicions. The Doctor felt a terrible weariness settle over him; he wanted to be free of all of it, of the endless schemes of the immortals and the petty needs of humanity. He wanted it to all be over, he wanted to just go to sleep and forget everything, he wanted to—*go ahead and admit it, to yourself if nobody else—*

—to die.

Once and for all, he wanted to die.

But he couldn't.

Well, maybe in the blackness of endless space, he'd find some equivalent of that; some kind of peace. The more he thought about it, the more he liked the idea. He wouldn't even need a spaceship—he could just drift, naked, through the solar system and out into the emptiness beyond. Why not? He didn't need to eat, didn't need to breathe, didn't really feel cold or heat as such—though he did notice it, in the same way a normal man might notice a particularly loud or garish colour.

He couldn't help but notice it, in fact. The interior of the cube was like a furnace.

He gestured towards the large, open pit. "What *is* this?"

"You're aware of our issues with coal—not to mention the pollution aspect. It's not the reason I built the VIC-20 array, but the problem of limited resources is the one that I'm trying to solve at the moment—hopefully, if I can find a solution to our coal addiction, the pollution will ease in time..." He made a slight gesture towards the open pit. "To generate the amount of steam necessary to ensure proper running of the VIC-20, we'd need to burn enough coal per day to power every robot in the Mecha-Principalities for a month. Instead, I decided to create a prototype geothermal pump—the first of its kind. By funnelling lava up through the boiler instead of shovelling coal, we can run a hundred VICs if we have to, and once my organics wear out, I may need to do just that. It's an elegant solution, you must admit, if a little dangerous..." He turned his head in the Doctor's direction. "Well, for me. You'd probably survive a fall down there."

"Only probably?" The Doctor raised his head for a moment, then returned to contemplation of the pit. "It doesn't seem overly practical..."

"No, it doesn't, does it? It's a possible solution for large, stationary, power-hungry machines like this one, but ideally, we need something to replace coal, oil, all the other limited resources in one fell stroke—and something clean, to boot." A hissing burst of steam cascaded from the valves on his shoulders; a mechanical sigh. "I'm on the edge of something, I know, but no matter how intelligent I make myself... well, I'm still bound by the laws of physics. The frustrating thing is that I can't help feeling that we're missing something, something crucial—like we're trying to reach the moon without cavorite, if you'll pardon the metaphor. Everything becomes a thousand times harder." He continued fiddling with the computer, his gigantic hands capable of surprisingly delicate work. "Didn't you experiment with an alternate form of energy at once point? Sigma energy? Something like that?"

"Omega energy." The Doctor nodded. "Similar to being struck by lightning. Maya hated it." He shrugged. "I'd almost forgotten it. I used to use it to supercharge my brain, but it took a toll—I suppose it was my equivalent of your VIC machines." He shuddered. "I built this horrible chair, all straps and wiring, to flood my system with bursts of Omega energy and bring on visions—'the Omega effect,' we called it." He laughed mirthlessly, shaking his head. "There was probably an easier way to bring that on, come to think of it. I used to have a thing—a kink, I suppose—about getting strapped into strange contraptions. That was probably part of it..." *Part of the thrill,* he thought, *back when life was all about thrills and adventure. When did that go? Was it when Monk died?* He looked down at his hands. *Or when I stopped loving Maya?*

Jason Satan killed me. That's the problem. He killed everything happy in me and left an immortal, undying husk, a zombie walking around with a tiny piece of Doc Thunder trapped inside it looking out. Just like Pluto has a tiny piece of El Sombra inside him—the thing he's planning to scrape out and replace when it finally dies. There's no difference between us.

No, I'm lying. There's one difference.

Eventually, he's going to die.

He found himself saying it out loud. "When *are* you going to die?"

Pluto turned to look down at him again. **"What?"**

"You said that when El Sombra's brain dies, you'll carry on regardless. Well, when are you planning to die, Pluto? Are you planning to just go on forever?" The Doctor's voice was trembling, and he realised he was gritting his teeth.

Pluto looked at him for a long moment. His face, as ever, was unreadable. Eventually, he spoke. **"Why not?"**

The Doctor stared at him for a moment, then sighed. "One more for the club, then. Lars and Maya will be pleased. Goodbye, Pluto. We won't see each other again." He turned to leave the way he'd come.

Pluto continued talking.

"Earlier, you talked about the soul. It's a uniquely human notion—the idea of something that survives after death. Think of it from a robot's perspective." He turned away from the machine, giving the Doctor his full attention. **"As the arrays that make up our minds and personalities wear out and grow obsolete, we have them replaced, upgraded. To me, this organic component—the brain—is just one more array; a unique and irreplaceable one, true, but nothing I can't do without. My information is recorded elsewhere within me; I will not die. I have no need to."**

"Maybe you're already dead," the Doctor muttered.

"Maybe there is no death; no freeing of the soul. Maybe only a change of function. Humans biodegrade to become food for the local environment; my kind, at the end of their functioning existence, might expect to be melted down to build new robots. Usefulness continues. Still, it seems a poor reward for the loss of self."

"The soul." The Doctor almost whispered it. Pluto's speech hammered against his ears like the tolling of some graveyard bell, the words harrowing in their terrifying practicality; a robot's gospel, bare and without warmth. He began to walk away.

"The *awareness*. There is no part of me that is the seat of it, just as there is no particular cell in your body that is the seat of yours; but it has more value than any other use our bodies may be put to. We should protect that awareness, that most fragile part of what we are. Extend it as long as possible; indefinitely."

The Doctor stopped in his tracks, Slowly, he turned to face the gigantic android again.

"What are you saying?"

"Remember when I said I'd answered questions that have plagued mankind for centuries? I've solved the oldest problem of all, Doctor. The problem of death."

The Doctor stared, and what little colour he had drained from his face. "No."

"Yes. Immortality, Doctor. I'm going to share your gift with the world."

HE'D ATTACKED PLUTO, of course.

He'd stood and listened, in a kind of numb horror, as Pluto had described his nightmarish plans for humanity: "There's no real difference between my people and yours, Doctor. I propose our species take advantage of this, and merge. I've lived centuries, and will live for millennia more, but the next generation won't even have to make the changes I'll have to in order to survive. Their fragile organics—their 'souls,' if you wish—will be protected and nurtured by mechanical systems that will keep them alive indefinitely. If they'd prefer, they can look and feel completely human, just as the most advanced robots did before the war..." He'd tailed off, and his serene and motionless brass visage had seemed to the Doctor in that moment like the face of some mocking demon.

"Doctor?"

The Doctor had leapt up, and punched the brass head hard enough to tear it from Pluto's body. A rain of tiny cogs and gears fell, shimmering, from the severed neck; but the head was mostly brass, and the arrays in it were mostly connective, created to link with other systems. Pluto was far from damaged beyond repair.

"Doct%r?" he said, the voice emanating from somewhere inside his neck, as the Doctor reached in to grab great handfuls of the clockwork, tearing it free and scattering it. "Doctor, you're £mpairing my worki%gs. We can t&lk about this... *Doctor...*" One of Pluto's great hands reached up suddenly, grabbing hold of the Doctor in a crushing grip, actually hard enough to hurt; the novelty of pain shocked the Doctor into letting go, and the great King of the Robots took the opportunity to hurl him across the chamber and into one of the great steel walls. He impacted hard enough to deform the metal, and the whole building shook with a terrifying sound like some huge gong breaking in two.

"**The arr&ys—**" Pluto cried out, turning his headless body slightly as he perceived the tiny gears and switches being jarred and thrown out of their alignments; something that would take hours, perhaps days of painstaking work to restore. The Doctor, pulling himself free of the metal wall, saw the opportunity; a way to hurt his foe, perhaps a way to stop this insanity once and for all.

His eyes glowed a fierce red. After a moment, so did the VIC-20—red hot, then white.

Then it began to melt.

"N%!" screamed Pluto, the crackling distortion caused by the damage to his body adding a note of pain and horror that an artificial voice could never have achieved; helplessly, he watched as his life's work, the great clockwork he had been working so long and so hard on, collapsed into a flowing pool of molten metal and flowed across the floor, taking its secrets with it. Great gouts of steam hissed from it, filling the room.

Pluto turned towards the Doctor and charged.

One great iron foot, treaded with rubber, smashed into the Doctor's face, lifting him up through the air like a rag doll; when he hit the wall, the entire building shook again, with an ominous creak and the sound of some hidden rivet springing loose. From outside came the crash of one of the decorative fixtures toppling from its corner, and the Doctor could hear the sound of ringing bells, a long honk of compressed air forced through a horn—robot screams.

Teeth gritted, he turned his killing eyes on Pluto's chest, aiming to boil the living brain inside the robot in its tank. The outer shell of the machine glowed a deep, dull red, but no more than that—whatever alloy it had been created from was as resistant to extremes of heat as the Doctor himself.

The Doctor grinned savagely. The fire of his own eyes might not be enough, but he knew where he could find better fire than that.

Behind Pluto, the great pit yawned. The shuddering pipes rising up from it were beginning to crack under the strain of the battle, spewing lava as the constant background noise of the pumps built itself up into a manic crescendo. Soon enough, the Doctor realised, they would erupt, drowning the city of Paris in boiling magma. Perhaps that would be enough to wipe Pluto's insane machinations from the face of the Earth. He hoped so.

He didn't plan to be around to see it.

Coiling the muscles of his legs into one final spring, he hurled himself at the gigantic robot, smashing into his centre mass like a bullet; the momentum sent him stumbling back to the edge of the pit—and then a step beyond.

The machine screamed, a single terrible howl of rage and pain, as it and the Doctor toppled over the edge, falling down into the endless shaft, lit from below by bubbling pools of searing liquid stone; the gateway to the core of the Earth. Desperately, Pluto lashed out, attempting to claw a handhold in the metal of the walls; but his flailing claw struck one of the larger pipes, and all he managed to do was shower them both in lava as they fell, until it flowed into his severed neck and silenced the howl of his mechanical voice forever.

The Doctor's rage drained out of him, and he had a few moments of freefall to wonder, fleetingly, if he'd been right to deny mankind eternal life; but what kind of life was that? Life as blobs of flesh inside machines? Wasn't that worse than death? *Then again,* he thought, *I do have a bias. Perhaps I just didn't want to see humanity throwing away something as precious as an ending.*

Still, he thought to himself, *did I have the right?*

There was no-one left to answer him. Seconds later, he splashed down into the magma, and the three-storey robot melted and fused around him, encasing him in a core of molten metal. He breathed in, filling his lungs with it, trying to drown himself in the corpse of his enemy, but the pain was fleeting. Even as the Doctor began the long journey down, sinking to the core of the planet, he knew he would live through this. He would live through everything now, until the very end of the universe. And maybe a little beyond.

How powerful would he be by then? Perhaps this was the best place for him; far away from everyone he could hurt. Already, he was enjoying the solitude. The core of the earth waited to enfold him, like a nurturing red sun.

Inside a cocoon of strange alloys, the being that had once been Doc Thunder curled up, closed his eyes, and began his long wait.

JACOB STEELE IN THE HOUR OF CHAOS

JACOB STEELE DRIFTS *in a haze of blue light, outside time, between one breath and the next. Sometimes, he thinks he's drifted there for a few minutes. Sometimes, it feels like centuries.*

Occasionally, the blue light lifts, and men flitting like hummingbirds are pointing guns at him, or preparing ways to trap him; but he is faster than they are, and he has plenty of bullets left for his gun. Jacob Steele has a sacred duty.

Jacob Steele is the Keeper of the Stone.

Occasionally, the Stone pulses in his grip, and shows him the true, binary structure of the universe; what should be, and what should not be.

A secluded glade in prehistory, where no star ever fell. Leopards who never walked on their hind legs. Great men of science once dead before their time, now living on to pull down lightning from the sky. Light in glass bulbs, spreading across the world in ever more arcane configurations, until the power runs out and it all collapses like a house of cards. Survivors fighting in the ruins, succumbing to diseases long thought banished, from cholera to fascism, but finally growing strong enough to fight the infection off. Green shoots, poking through the ruins.

Or crashing spaceships, evolution run amok, swashbuckling madmen, womanising superspies, superhuman beings brawling with demonic arch-

criminals and giant robots. Monsters of history preserved long past any normal lifespan, watching the strange new beings springing up in a stagnated world, as the smog drifts slowly over it all. And behind them all, the puppeteer, the great red-handed Queen in her secret city, pulling the strings to keep things as they are.

Keep me, the Stone says to him. The world is locked into an unnatural configuration, a state of being that was never meant to be; but you can end it. You can bring things back to how they should be, if you can only hold on. You are the Keeper now; keep me. Hold on to me.

Don't let go.

"JACOB, I LOVE you! But we only have sixty minutes to save the world!"

"What?" said Jacob Steele, the time-lost gunfighter yanked from the Wild West into the strange, exciting world of the twenty-fifth century by forces unknown! On the leather seat next to his own, Maya, Queen of the Future Earth, writhed in helpless terror—and through the viewing screen was the reason why!

A vast star-destroyer, piloted by the insidious clone-forces of Lomax—the Space Satan! Diabolical ruler of the planet Venus, whose only desire was to enslave the planet he had once called home!

"That interstellar fiend!" growled Arcturus, noble knight of the Leopard People, from his position at the starboard cannon.

"Affirmative, sir!" agreed the hyper-intelligent android, Rousseau-5, as he plugged himself into the navigating table in a desperate attempt to plot an evasive manoeuvre that might rescue them from the very jaws of destruction. On the table, magnetic models of the ships whirred and pivoted—but there was no solution that could rescue them from their deadly fate!

"Ha! Ha! Ha!" A vicious cackle echoed over the ship's radio as the immense bulk of Lomax's flagship drew closer and closer to the *Jonah II.* "You've thwarted my insidious schemes for the last time, Steele! Now you will face your final doom! My missiles will seek you out, however you twist and turn—and blast you and your lovely Queen into atoms! The Solar System will be mine—*all mine!*"

"What?" Steele shook his head, wincing. "Who the hell is that?" He looked around the interior of the *Jonah II,* as if he'd never seen it before in his life. "Where am I?"

"The amnesia ray!" Arcturus gasped, the hackles on his neck rising. "It must have had a delayed effect! He's forgotten who we are!"

Steele looked at the huge half-man, half-cat as if he'd fallen prey to some terrifying space madness—and, at that very moment, a pair of sleek rockets roared out of the flagship, streaking across the vacuum of space towards Steele and his crew!

Instinctively, he jerked the wheel, and the great peroxide rockets blasted the *Jonah II* out of the missiles' path, but only for a moment! Then, the missiles turned, as if magnetised, and blasted towards the ship on their relentless mission of death!

"Sir!" Rousseau-5 cried out in his mechanical tones. "The rockets are homing in on something on board the ship! But what could possibly—"

"*The Stone!*" Maya screamed, pointing to Steele's left hand, and the mysterious artefact Steele had brought with him from the far past. The Stone, it had been revealed, was in truth a remnant of one of the lost star-lenses used by a corps of space sheriffs to bring law to a wild universe in times long forgotten, and, now polished down to a flawless gem, it served Steele as a ring capable of channelling strange and mysterious energies. Many times, Steele had used the ring to save his friends from all manner of deadly danger, but even its bizarre powers were no match for the vacuum of space! And now, a pair of merciless missiles streaked ever closer, drawn to the unique stellar mineral!

"There's only one way out," Arcturus snarled, his tail swishing. "Tear it off his hand and throw it out of the airlock! Better yet—fire it at the flagship! We'll see how Lomax likes playing cat and mouse with his own weapons!"

"It's the only logical solution," Rousseau-5 confirmed. "You must remove the ring, sir! Give up the Stone!"

"Wait a second—" Jacob scowled, looking down at his left hand. It was bunched slightly, as if clutching something, and for a moment there seemed to be no flesh there, just a skeletal hand.

"*Jacob!*" Maya screamed, and he looked up—to see the missiles roaring straight towards him, a payload of death for him and everyone he loved! "*Take off the ring!*" she screamed, and despite all his instincts, he found himself reaching to—

Don't let go.

—he jerked the wheel to the side, and the missiles missed them by inches. "Now!" he shouted, and Arcturus opened up with the mass driver, spitting great balls of lead into the void as the rockets blazed past his position. A moment later, the massive bullets did their work, and the missiles exploded, buffeting the *Jonah II* in a torrent of fire and flame!

"Sir!" Rousseau-5 cried, "We've got a rupture in the main boiler! We're going down!"

The *Jonah II,* spewing smoke, began to spiral away from the welcoming stars, towards the green planet below. As Steele fought to level out the ship, he imagined he could hear Lomax cursing under his breath—but the radio was dead.

"THE WEDDING WILL be held in one hour, my dear Jacob." Lomax sneered, fingers toying with his elegant moustache. "It promises to be the event of the season at the Royal Palaces. And you will be the guest of honour—or should I say—*your severed head!*" The Space Satan threw back his head and cackled, a diabolical laugh that echoed around the arena and drew cheers from the crowd of red-skinned, reptilian clones who'd been assembled to watch this cruel gladiatorial combat.

Beside him—on her own golden throne—Maya struggled in her bonds, her dark skin glistening in the Venusian sun as she gazed helplessly at the terrifying spectacle.

Steele rubbed his temples with his right hand, frowning. Hadn't he been on board some kind of spacecraft a moment ago? How had he ended up here? Some sort of crash...

...no, of course not. He'd been here for years.

He felt a familiar weight in his left hand, and looked down to see the blue blade, Souldrinker, forged by the dwarves of Venus from the Stone he had brought with him on his trip through time... which had, of course, been revealed as a fragment of the mysterious Sword of Ancients, as wielded by the Gods of Venus in the time before time. Legend had it that the great Sword could drain the life from a world, and the dagger the dwarves had forged from a single chunk of it had the uncanny power to drink the life-force of any enemy and imprison it forever. A formidable weapon indeed, and Jacob's skill with it, through the long years of his exile here, had earned him the title of Warlord of Venus, and the undying love of the Queen of Southern Venus, Maya Br'tana.

Northern Venus, however, had long been ruled by the clone-hordes of Lomax, the enigmatic Space Satan, who would never rest until the entire planet squirmed in his iron grip. Steele gritted his teeth, readying himself for the combat to come.

"You should have stayed in your own forgotten age, my prehistoric friend!" Lomax sneered, running a serpentine tongue over his fangs. "Your soul-sucking blade will prove of little worth against—*the Derleth!*"

"No!" Maya cried out, squirming helplessly as the iron gate of the arena lifted slowly, revealing a squamous horror, a shambling mass of half-fused tentacles dripping with foul, black ichor. In the centre of the obscenely waving flesh was a single vast, unblinking eye, that looked upon Steele with an infinite hunger. Slowly, the Derleth slithered forwards, leaving a trail of noxious slime.

"Yes!" Lomax smirked, as the crowd bayed for blood. "I have woken the Derleth— the great Soulless One—from his aeon-long slumber beneath the deepest trenches of the Venusian sea. He shall be my weapon against all who dare to defy my rule! In particular, your so-called 'Warlord'—for how can the blue blade drink the soul of a creature that has none—that eats souls itself? No, my dear, your consort is doomed, quite doomed. And soon you shall have a new husband, and all of Venus shall have a new King!"

"Oh, you fiend!" she sobbed, "You unspeakable fiend!"

The deadly Derleth slithered closer, slowly feeling its way across the arena floor. Suddenly, one of the tentacles shot out with the speed of a moray eel, a plethora of fanged mouths at the tip opening wide to drink Steele's blood and absorb his very spirit. He dodged to the side just in time, then lashed out with the glowing dagger, slicing away the beast's tentacle before it could close about him. The severed chunk of slime-coated flesh dropped to the arena floor—then melted, leaving a puddle of bubbling goo behind.

With any other foe, the first blood drawn by Souldrinker would mean the end of the combat; but the Derleth had no soul to steal, and it pressed the attack harder than ever.

"It's after the dagger, my love!" Maya screamed, and at that Lomax showed the first sign of anger.

"Shut up, you little fool—"

"Don't you see? It's an eater of souls—it wants the souls captured inside the blade! Hurl it away from you!"

"No!" Lomax roared, shrinking back. "If he throws that blade at me, the Derleth will devour my soul with the rest! You can't! You mustn't! Oh, demons of the afterworld, have pity upon me—"

Jacob Steele grinned mercilessly, dodging another flurry of tentacles as he drew his arm back to—

Don't let go.

—he leapt forward, driving the point of the blade deep into the grotesque creature's single eye, bursting it like a balloon. Unmentionable jelly squirted out of the ruptured mass, stinking of ancient rot, corruption unknown since the first days of the universe. Still, Steele drove the blade deeper, working it into the creature's brain as the tentacles thrashed madly for a moment, before going limp at last.

Perhaps the Derleth had no soul for the blue blade to absorb. But a dagger was still a dagger, and a monster from beyond the dawn of time still had a weak point.

Lomax stood to his full height, pointed one trembling red finger at the Warlord of Venus, and screamed—

"—OKAY, THIS ISN'T working."

Maya raised an eyebrow. "Perhaps it's your scenario. The 'Venusian sun'? Why not just 'the sun'? And you really oversold it on the last run-through..."

"What, the stab-me-in-the-chest thing? That's called *incentive*." Lomax scowled, scratching the back of his head. "Anyway, look who's talking. '*Oh, you fiend, you unspeakable fiend!*' Really? And what's with all the helplessness? You're the least helpless person I know."

"Well, it's fun to pretend occasionally." She smiled, enjoying his irritation. "You lived with the Doctor for years, don't tell me you never did anything like that with him."

"I lived with a depressed bald man," Lomax sighed, "who was terrified of touching people or even talking to them. The whole experience was about as sexy as haemorrhoids. Poor bastard." His eyes narrowed suspiciously. "One of these days you'll have to let me in on how exactly you got him to destabilise France on your orders..."

"I just told him to take a vacation," Maya smiled, innocently. "Anyway, digressions aside, what do we do now?"

She looked over to the flickering column of blue light on the daio interweaved copper, zinc and cavorite, supplied with crackling Omega energy and supervised by the mental power of a Commodore-class thinking robot.

It was fortunate that Pluto had arranged for his blueprints for the VIC series to be kept safe from any eventuality; her agent, Prometheus Quicksilver— bastard heir of the Quicksilver line—had retrieved them, along with notes from various other projects, during the chaos of the volcanic eruption. As a result—and with Lomax's help—the twin kingdoms of Britannia and Zor-Ek-Narr were once again at the forefront of modern technology, their incredible advancements making them the rulers of the world almost by default. From the philosopher-plutocrats of China to the warring isolationists of the American continent, there was no civilisation on Earth that dared to disobey an edict from the Immortal Queen.

Britannia was certainly, at this point, the only country capable of reaching into the timestream for an audience with the Keeper of the Stone.

While computing power had increased in leaps and bounds over the centuries, thanks largely to Pluto and the new generation of machine consciousness, the basic method by which the Lonesome Rider was retrieved from his lonely vigil had changed little since its invention by the renegade S.T.E.A.M. agent, Philip Hawthorne, in the early twenty-first century; a gateway would be created, the Rider would appear from exile, and there would be a brief attempt, before the portal collapsed, to kill him and take the Stone from his corpse.

These attempts would, without exception, end with the deaths of anyone who tried. Even when the would-be assassin fired from inside a concrete bunker, or a tank, the result was the same. Jacob Steele would have been deadly enough, if you made the mistake of drawing down on him; the Keeper of the Stone was death personified.

After the Doctor's disappearance, Lars Lomax had flown to Britannia to join Maya as a scientific adviser; his already vast intelligence had only grown more subtle and devious over the years, and this seemed like the right strategic move. "I'm sure you'll betray me eventually," she'd smiled, shaking his hand on his arrival, "but you've got all the time in the world for that." He'd laughed at that, happy to be understood, and that night they'd played chess for the first time in years. The morning after, he started working on a means of bringing the Stone back inside current time, and keeping it there.

The solution was simple and elegant; force was never going to work against the Lonesome Rider, and—immortal or no—Lars Lomax had no desire to get shot through the head. So how to get the Stone out of his grip? "Simple," Lars smiled, in that way he had. "We ask."

Maya had leant back on her chair, studying him carefully. "Just ask him to hand it over?"

"Sure. Checkmate, by the way." Lars' smile widened as he theatrically knocked over her King. "The thing is—it's all about *how* we ask."

Maya had to admit, it was inspired. First, build your Omega platform; no change there. Her people could make one of those in their sleep. The hard part was building the Phantasmagorical Projection system over the top of it.

They'd been semi-popular attractions in Britannia towards the end of the twentieth century—bizarre brass coffins that promised to plunge the entertainment-hungry visitor into the virtual world of their choice; the default setting was *Alice in Wonderland*. Most found the notion of being submerged in a fictional reality oddly disquieting rather than enticing; had the punters known that the booths were fully capable of killing in the right circumstances, they would have been even less likely to volunteer themselves for the experience. Lomax's idea was to materialise the Lonesome Rider inside a Projector, and—while he was still reeling from the novel experience of not having anyone try to kill him—run him through various fictional sequences designed to make him reject the Stone.

It was difficult—obviously there could be no margin for error—but eventually they had a projector guaranteed to start working on Steele the moment he materialised in their timeframe.

After that, it was just a matter of writing the correct story...

LOMAX FROWNED. "ALL right. We have less than an hour before the cavorite reserves are drained, and we've used about forty minutes of it. Once our hour is up, Jacob Steele vanishes from the timestream, and if we ever want him back we're going to need to find our own weight in industrial cavorite from somewhere. Do we have that?"

Maya shook her head. "It was hard enough finding the latest batch. Cavorite's a lot scarcer than it used to be."

"Not to mention the fact that there's barely any coal or oil or even wood left, and the entire planet is a smog-filled ruin, thanks to our wonderful ancestors and their enlightened approach to the problems of pollution."

Maya chuckled. "Lars, we've both been around since at least the twentieth century. That was *us*."

"Well, remind me to think ahead in future. The point is, this may be our last shot." He sighed, scratching the base of one horn. "All right, all right... something in our scenarios isn't working. We're providing a world of adventure for him, so he's got something exciting to latch onto from the off. Then we're putting him, and those around him, in physical jeopardy—a jeopardy that he can only get out of by abandoning the Stone. If he won't abandon the stone, he'll..."—Lomax glanced towards the brass coffin on top of the dais, and lowered his voice—"...he'll die, and once again the Stone will be ours. Except we have a problem there, because he's not rejecting the Stone and he's not dying. He's *winning*."

"He's the Lonesome Rider, Lars," Maya said, frowning. "What did you expect?"

"Honestly? I expected he'd enjoy some thrilling action on beautiful, scenic Venus."

Maya shook her head, a half-smile playing on her lips. "You and your Venus. I know it was very disappointing that the terraforming experiments didn't work out, Lars, but it's time to let it go. Your little paradise can only exist over there now, in that brass box..."

Lars nodded, staring into space for a moment. "We've been fools," he said suddenly, and walked over to the mobile brain feeding the Projector, checking the hands of the clock built into the robot's chest. Fifteen minutes maximum before the cavorite exhausted itself. He'd have to work fast.

He smiled reassuringly at the brain, then flipped open its cranial hatch, fingers flicking over the gears and switches inside, conversing with it through mathematics. "You said it yourself; he's the Lonesome Rider. We've both read the histories—Jacob Steele was renowned for staying on the job until the end. He's not going to abandon his task because we threaten him." He snapped the hatch closed, and the robot nodded in silent understanding. Lars took a step back.

Maya cocked her head, watching closely. "What did you program in, Lars?"

"The end." He grinned. "Paradise in a box."

"STEELE?"

Jacob Steele blinked, dazzled by the setting sun.

Reed was in the middle of boiling water for coffee; he started at Steele's sudden arrival, then stared at him for a long moment, shaking his head. "Good God, man," he said, in a dry whisper, "I thought you were dead. Where did you go?"

Steele looked around. He was still on the mesa, but the floating orrery of rocks and stones had crashed to Earth, forming a ring of concentric circles around the twisted body of the madman Edison. Nearby, the Locomotive Man was a smoking heap of wreckage, steam still rising from the twisted metal.

"I wish to hell I knew," he breathed. He tried to remember the hallucinations; that strange spaceship, the arena, the blue void, the Stone whispering in his mind.

He looked down at his left hand. He was still carrying the damned thing.

Reed's look of astonishment cracked into a broad smile. "You vanished during the fight. Just... popped out of existence with that stone of Edison's. If I were you, I'd put the damn thing down now—"

Don't let go.

"Best to hang onto it, I reckon," Steele muttered, without thinking about it. With his right hand, he slipped his iron back in its holster, then fumbled in the pocket of his coat for a cigar. Lord knew he needed one.

Reed raised an eyebrow. "Well, if you insist... You know, I honestly through you'd been wiped out—disintegrated utterly. Stranger things, as they say, have happened." He laughed shakily. "Isn't that right, Mr Owl?"

Steele's eyes widened.

Grey Owl stepped out from behind the wagon, as hale and hearty as he'd ever been.

"By God," Steele laughed, shaking his head. "What the hell happened?"

Grey Owl shrugged. "One minute I was deciding not to shoot you, the next I was waking up in the back of that snake oil salesman's wagon."

Reed grinned. "Coffee," he said, pressing a mug into Steele's free hand. "As I understand it, prolonged use of that stone seems to disrupt time—you were transported an hour or so into the future, while Grey Owl's personal timeline was reversed into the past, to... well, to before he died." He shook his head. "I have to tell you, an event like this is completely unprecedented—"

Steele laughed, then sipped the coffee. It was the best thing he'd tasted in a hell of a long time, and he couldn't help but noting there was a mess of bacon sizzling over that fire as well, but that could wait a spell. He turned to Grey Owl, smiling broadly. "It's called a gift horse, Reed. Don't go looking it in the mouth. How are you feeling, Grey Owl?"

Grey Owl smiled back, a little cagily, as if sizing Steele up—then, on impulse, he stuck out his left hand. "That's up to you. Are we friends?"

Steele looked down at the stone in his hand.

Don't let go.

"Hang on a second, I got my hands full here," he joked, but he could see Grey Owl looked angry at that, the old fire of enmity flickering in his eyes. Steele looked around for a place to put his coffee, feeling like a damn fool while Grey Owl was standing there with his hand out—

Don't let—

—and he could see in the other man a kind of pained realisation developing, that all the talk back at Devil's Gulch had been just that, just talk, and there was to be no peace between these men unless it came out of the barrel of a gun—

Don't—

—and then Grey Owl's hand was slowly drawing back, and the hurt in his eyes was too much for Jacob to stand, and he put the damn stone down to shake hands like a man.

Except when he lifted his hand again, he was alone on the mesa, and when he looked down at his open hand it was a skeleton's, grey as ash and crumbling like wet sand...

THE BRASS COFFIN swung open, and the dust and ashes that had once been Jacob Steele tumbled out onto the dead platform.

"The stone was the only thing keeping him alive after so long," Lars sighed, shaking his head. "Too bad. I honestly think he'd have thanked us for freeing him of it."

Maya lifted an eyebrow. "Really?"

"No, not really." He nodded to the robots entering the chamber. "Make sure you pick it up with the tongs. I don't want anyone touching it—human or android. We don't want to have to go through all this again with someone else."

"There won't be much difference between humans and robots before long," Maya murmured, smiling. "All Pluto's blueprints were missing was a viable power source for his immortal hybrids. Now that we have a sample of xokronite—"

Lars grinned. "Xokronite! I like it. Catchy."

"—we'll have all the power we need, free and clean."

"We'll have to find out how to synthesise it," Lars murmured. "One sample won't be enough. And obviously, we have to work out how to actually get power out of it in the first place..."

"I'll tell you what I remember. You're smart enough to take it from there. We have enough time for that." Maya smiled, watching the stone glow with its blue inner fire as it was carried away. "We have eternal life, and infinite power. And soon all my citizens will have the same. We've taken a planet on the edge of total environmental collapse and created a world of gods."

Lars Lomax nodded. "Yes, we have," he murmured. Then he grinned savagely. "Now, what do we do with it?"

ONE MILLION YEARS LATER...

THE RED QUEEN'S RACE AND THE RED KING'S DREAM

EPSILON TWO FOUR, thought Ull of the Silver Service. *I hate myself and I hate my life.*

The psychetecture of the great golden building responded to the agent's heartfelt depression, the outside of the great structure altering itself to best suit Ull's mood. Great sections of the palace detached themselves, reconfiguring to better promote a sense of well-being and harmony.

While the entrance of the palace was heavily protected—so much so that anyone entering who was not the Red King would have their atomic bonds instantly nullified—the psychetecture system was not; he'd reconfigured the talkeasy built into his frontal lobe to make it believe that he was a guest, and the system was now desperate to accommodate his emotional needs. Obviously, the punishment for breaking into one of the Royal Houses would be death—or worse, ejection from the timestream entirely. Should he be discovered, not only would his infinite life come to an agonising end, but all traces of him would subsequently be forgotten by history. It would be as if he had never existed.

Worse still, he would fail his Queen.

Best to get this part right, then.

Alpha zero five. I'm the best there is at what I do and this is the most fun I ever had.

The sections paused at the sudden change of psychological state, jerked in the air, and moved back slowly towards their original position, as if unsure of themselves. Ull moved quickly, the deep black of his skinsuit shimmering slightly as it propelled him hundreds of feet into the air, to land like a cat on one of the moving sections. Now came the difficult bit.

Beta seven seven. I wish I'd had a mother. The structure he was perched on stopped an instant before it would have slotted itself into place and veered left instead, compensating for the sudden oedipal urge. Ull leapt again, into the gap, changing his mood in mid-air to another suicidal burst of self-loathing. *Epsilon two six. I always let everyone down.* He had to be very careful here—the wrong emotion and he'd be crushed between the moving parts of the building's outer wall. *Delta nine nine. Cechenena is a genus of moths in the Sphingidae family,* he mused, the sheer dryness of the thought sending the sections juddering to a halt just long enough for him to snake between the gap. *Alpha three one. Isn't it great to be alive?* Another gap opened in front of him as the inner walls shifted themselves about to form the perfect complement to a sunny disposition.

A second later and he was through the wall entirely—and inside the palace of the Red King.

Delta four one. Good boy, he thought, and the psychetecture, relieved that its guest had seemingly made up his mind at last, settled into an ostentatious deco design with a soft mechanical sigh. Ull smiled, petting it with his mind.

Good house.

ONE OF YOUR pets just walked into my house through the cat flap.

'Cat flap.' You and your anachronisms.

Don't change the subject. He exploited the psychetecture—presumably he thinks I haven't noticed. I take it that means we're into the endgame?

There'll be other games.

Not with anything of importance at stake. After today, it'll just be for pride, or territory, or philosophy—but today, the game is for a universe.

It always was. Your move.

ULL STOOD, SNIFFING the air. He made a swift check of his selfsearch—under ordinary circumstances, he'd been trained to survive without it, but after the emotional rollercoaster he'd put himself through he needed a little grounding.

Alpha Four Seven, chattered the readout. *Wary confidence, slight fear. The superior man prepares for all eventualities.* How true. *Inner motivations (y/n)?* N. That was always a long one, and he didn't have the time.

The hallway was a strange mishmash of styles, all of them hundreds of thousands of years old. An elevation-field coiled up from the centre of the floor like a snake, glittering in reds and pinks; a visible field seemed oddly gauche to Ull, but it wasn't his place to question the décor choice of a King. Placed around the walls were a plethora of ancient art treasures: sculptures by Warhol, paintings by Kichida, poems by Tunos, all dating back to the pre-powered eras, before xokronite had solved the twin problems of energy generation and pollution once and for all. There were historical artefacts here as well, from the same long-forgotten past—an original copy of the Fourth Earth Battalion Field Manual, the diary of a suicidal slave-owner dated 1750, both more than a million years old. If they hadn't been protected by specially designed fields, they'd have crumbled away to nothing millennia ago.

Ull found himself checking his selfsearch again. *Gamma eight three. Curiosity, the edge of a great understanding. The superior man sees the hidden thread connecting all.* These disparate treasures had something in common, then. What?

There was a large, flat field distortion hanging on the back wall, a complicated interference pattern that seemed to make no sense until Ull realised that it was meant to be appreciated visually; the eddies and currents sparked colours that, on proper inspection, formed a green paradise filled with strange plants and populated by men and women walking hand in hand. It was oddly scandalous— the people in the image were missing the telltale markings that showed where their selfsearches and skinpatches had been implanted at birth, and what Ull had taken at first for flesh coloured skinsuits was actually their naked skin, open to the elements. Most shockingly of all, the men and women in the image had hair cascading from their scalps, under their arms, between their legs; Ull felt vaguely disturbed by it. *Zeta seven three,* he thought, not needing to check. *Mild disgust, fear of the other. The superior man respects all difference and is secure in his own preferences.* He'd had that one several times.

He looked around the hallway, searching for exits aside from the central lifting field; that would certainly be monitored. He could rely on his augmented skinsuit to deflect surveillance to an extent, but this was the Red King's summer palace, and there could be no relying on—

—Ull felt something brush his shoulder. He looked, and there was the smallest rip in the fabric of his skinsuit, and a bead of blood peeking through. His blood ran suddenly cold. *Zeta zero six. Fear of death.* He tried to remember what the superior man did when faced with that particular emotion.

Something brushed against his hand.

When he lifted it to look, one of his fingers was missing.

RAZORFIELDS?

Remember when 'razors' were something that existed? Ask someone what a razor is now. Anyone younger than eight hundred millenia wouldn't have a clue.

Isn't that a little... primitive? Bloodthirsty, even?

He breaks into my house, pokes around my private collection and then sneers at my art—he'll get what he's given and like it. I'm particularly proud of that painting. I'm not having one of your drones turn his nose up at it.

'Painting.' Oh dear.

So I remember history. You know what they say—those who forget the past are condemned to repeat it...

And that's what this is all about, isn't it?

Your move.

IN THE ROYAL Hangars, the five-strong crew of the *Zor 714* stood stiffly to attention, arms at their sides, eyes forward. Behind them, the *Zor* hung in its gravimetric cradle, rotating slowly; a great spinning-top of shimmering silver metal. The crew had been waiting for several minutes, but they showed no sign of resentment, only a hungry anticipation; today, the *Zor* was no longer an ordinary mid-level scientific research vessel—one of thousands serving Habitat One.

Today, the *Zor* was under Royal command.

As a mid-level scientific research vessel, the *Zor* was usually commissioned for surveys on the various colony worlds; very occasionally, if there was a report of some asteroid or planetoid inward-bound from the intergalactic gulf, the *Zor* would be sent, along with several other vessels, to take its measure and make sure it was no threat to the various human-occupied worlds, the Habitats. It never was.

The crew had expected to comfortably drift through the countless millenia ahead of them, like all the other scientific research crews, mapping new planets and solar systems, surveying their flora and fauna, reporting to whichever of the two Royal Houses commanded their particular loyalty—or to both—on any discoveries thus gained. Perhaps when all the stars had been fully explored—when every scrap of life had been fully catalogued and categorised and exploited for whatever use it had—they would find something else to do. In the meantime, they were happy in their work, and the uneventful nature of the job was part of the charm. Captain Tura had never considered the possibility that the crew of the *Zor* would ever do anything too challenging or exciting. She'd certainly never thought her ship would carry out any vital missions for the Queen.

That was the thing about living forever. Given enough time, anything can happen.

A pair of floating silver drones swept into the hangar, their speakers serenading the crew and the ship with the deep musical trills of the Royal Anthem. The Queen's retinue followed, a group of six androids with silver and gold casings; they were occasionally referred to as the Rusos, or the Queen's Bishops, but the role had been purely ceremonial for hundreds of thousands of years. In this day and age, the Queen was best protected by an invisible field, raised around her at all times; it was enough to stop any anarchists or insurrectionists from making an attempt on her life, and the Red King would, it was agreed, never be so gauche as to attempt a direct attack.

Tura swallowed, avoiding the urge to check her selfsearch as she gazed on the glory of the Red Queen. She wore a skinsuit of shimmering royal purple, a hooded cloak of red, and a ceremonial helmet, which completely covered her head and included a mask of brass, fixed into an expression of serene and noble calm; nobody had seen the Red Queen's true face in countless millenia. However, there were rumours among the older residents of the Habitat that, in the ancient times of pre-powered society, she was known as Britannia.

"Your Majesty!" the crew chanted in unison, falling to one knee as custom dictated.

"My subjects," the Red Queen nodded, and Tura rose to her feet. "You are all, I take it, fully briefed on the specifics of your mission?"

"We are, your Majesty." Tura bowed her head.

"And there are no questions?"

Tura shook her head. Who would dare to question a direct command from the—

"Your Majesty?"

It was the voice of the new Security Officer. Tura turned pale, even as she noticed Unwen smirking out of the corner of her eye. She wanted to slap him, but in front of the Queen all she could do was keep her eyes forward and try not to scream.

The Queen turned her expressionless mask towards the speaker, waiting for her to continue.

"Your Majesty..." *Shut up,* Tura thought, desperately, *shut up, shut up...* "Your Majesty, I can't help but notice that these orders are extremely vague. You've told us to take the *Zor* to a very particular nav-point at a very particular time, but there's nothing out there that might warrant a survey—especially not from a biogeneticist like Unwen. Why are we actually needed for this?"

The Red Queen tilted her head. She seemed almost amused, but with the mask it was difficult to tell. "Because I commanded it. What's your name, Officer?" She asked the question as if she already knew the answer.

The Security Officer looked up at the monarch almost belligerently. "Maya."

Underneath the mask, the Red Queen smiled to herself.

"Of course it is."

THE PAWN BEGINS her journey up the board. Well played. Unfortunately, it's all for nothing if I can take your knight out of the game...

We'll see. Your move.

THE SKINSUIT WAS self-repairing. It would mend and strengthen itself as needed, taking care of any holes or gaps in its fabric; so would Ull's skin. His little finger, however, wasn't going to grow back. It would need to be repaired back in the Queen's Palace, if he ever made it that far. And the next razorfield might take his head off at the neck.

The razorfields were invisible to the naked eye, but it was possible for his skinsuit to put out a weak field of its own, distorting them enough for Ull to see their faint shapes flitting to and fro in the air. Their movements were almost random, but at the same time there were traces of a definite pattern in the way they circled the room, like a shoal of deadly transparent fish.

They were toying with him, he realised; evaluating what defences he had before moving in for the kill. Soon, the fields would close in, a storm of knives piercing and slashing at him from every side; and that would be that. His existence would end, and with it the mission. If his skinsuit were capable of distorting the razorfields more, he might stand a chance against them—

—*distortion.*

That was the key.

Gamma eight nine. Understanding in the face of adversity. The superior man thinks and acts in one moment. He reached out with the weak fields of his skinsuit—the same ones that allowed him to leap hundreds of feet in the air, or cling to any surface—and captured the decorative image on the wall. An image made up of billions of tiny distortions...

"No! Oh, you little hooligan—" The voice echoed from nowhere. Ull had never heard the voice of the Red King, but there was no mistaking who was speaking. Under other circumstances, he might have studied the voice, even configured the selfsearch to begin a full mental evaluation. Now, he was busy.

It told him he was being watched, at least.

He curled the image around himself, taking a certain pleasure as the deformation of it made the little people burst and run together, the colours of the green grass and the blue sky and the varied flesh tones melding and changing, flowing into each other in a riot of shifting hues.

The razorfields circled for a moment, as if deciding how to approach, then dove from all sides. As they swooped down on him, Ull stilled his mind and prepared for death.

But the decorative image acted as he had hoped; as the razor fields flew through the distortion field, they were themselves distorted—transmuted by the shifting field into harmless bursts of colour and light. Ull smiled to himself, then released his grip on the image; unable to bear the stresses he'd imposed, it trembled for a moment like a soap bubble before bursting apart into individual globules of every shade and tint. They floated lazily through the air for a few moments, before being absorbed into the walls or the lifting field in the centre of the room.

Ull waited to see if there would be any other traps, or if the mysterious voice would deign to provide further comment. But the Red King, it seemed, had nothing to say.

Well, the alarm had evidently been raised. Ull stepped into the lifting field, and ascended.

*   *   *

THAT POISONOUS LITTLE bastard. I can't believe he *did* that. He could have just let the razorfields chop him up, you know. He didn't have to destroy a priceless masterpiece.

Personally, I thought it had a certain symbolic value.

Really? I thought you said that piece was derivative.

It is. I meant the way he destroyed it.

Oh, ha ha. Well, we'll see who destroys what. That's only a picture—it's the reality I'm interested in. He won't be able to take that apart so easily.

Won't he?

...your move.

THE QUEEN WAS silent for a long time, as if contemplating what punishment to visit upon the Security Officer. Tura, pale and almost shaking with nerves, waited for the axe to fall—would it only be the insolent Maya who faced the penalty for incurring the Red Queen's wrath? Or all of them? Even Unwen seemed to have realised the severity of the situation, and poor Munn looked as if he might be sick.

Eventually, the Queen spoke. "...My move," she murmured, to nobody in particular. Then she addressed the crew as a whole. "The *Zor* will be ready to depart directly—as soon as the necessary changes are made to the fuel situation. A fresh isotope is needed."

"Fresh?" the Security Officer blinked. "One isotope of xokronite is as fresh as any other, surely? The word doesn't have meaning in the context of—"

"*Maya!*" Tura barked, almost shouting. "Be *silent!*"

The Queen's blank brass mask seemed to smile. "Thank you, captain. I can speak for myself, you know."

"Yes, your Majesty." Tura blushed red at her outburst. "My most sincere apologies, your Majesty."

"As I said, the *Zor* will depart once preparations have been made. I suggest you all board the ship, find your domicells and get some rest—apart from your Security Officer." The Queen sounded distinctly amused. "Her I would speak with alone."

"Yes, your Majesty," Tura nodded, trying to hide her relief as she and the crew hurried away. A new Security Officer, then—for the best, considering. Maya had been a little too full of herself for the position, and now she'd dug her own grave. Mouthing off to the Red Queen like that; it was unthinkable.

Who on earth did Maya think she was?

Beneath her brass mask, the Queen smirked.

NOT MUCH OF a move. You're putting a lot of faith in your Knight...

I'm promoting my pawn. Anyway, he's a Silver. That bloodline's served the Queen since before you were born—when the Queen they served was just a mad old hag in a jar, ruling over her tiny little island. They can take care of themselves.

Still, quite a risk. I have Knights of my own, you know.

I know. And you should know how I play the game by now—I only put my faith in a sure thing, remember?

Oh, I'm well aware. Only that which has been tried and tested need apply. I seem to remember you were against stagnation once...

I'll take it over change for change's sake. You always did like rocking boats and rattling cages.

A little chaos in the morning gets the blood running. And you know I hate doing the same thing twice. My move, I believe.

Knight takes knight?

If I didn't know better... I'd say you were reading my mind.

AT THE TOP of the elevating field, Ull found himself in what looked like a maze of mirrored surfaces. Some of these, he knew, would be real-time displays presenting a doctored image—several would be light-reflecting fields set to move and shift when out of his line of sight. A very few would even be permeable; those would be the ones to watch out for.

Where the assassins would be hidden.

Alpha Four Six. Calm readiness. The superior man stills his mind in preparation for action.

He stepped forward.

The first of them lunged out of the mirrored surface to his left—a similarly black-clad figure, wearing his face, or a very subtly distorted version. It was only to be expected, Ull thought, as he grabbed the attacker's wrists, twisting it to snap the fragile bones and then heaving him through the empty air to crash into the mirrored surface opposite, impaling him on the shattered glass. The Red King's Vengers were his elite forces—capable of adapting themselves to match their opponent exactly if need be, both physically and in skill. And who better to use in an environment like this, where a dozen different reflections of Ull gazed back at him with every step he took?

One of the reflections on his left caught his eye—he turned and struck in one quick, liquid movement, then stopped his palm a split-second before it hit home; it was one of the display screens, showing an image of a Venger rather than the real thing. Doubtless it was booby-trapped, and he had very nearly fallen for it. He was just chiding himself on so nearly falling for such an obvious snare—*Epsilon two eight, self-reproach*—when the real Vengers dropped from above.

Stupid! Why hadn't he looked up? One arm was around his throat, cutting off his air, one grinning parody of his own features leering in his peripheral vision as another landed in front of him. Both were armed with nano-sharp carbon-steel blades. He could smell the poison coating the metal.

Delta five six, he thought. *Acceptance of the inevitable. The superior man flows with all moments.*

Even the last.

THERE. KNIGHT TAKES knight.

We'll see if it does take. My move, I think.

"I DID THINK about killing you," the Queen smiled from behind her serene mask. "Snapping your neck with my own two hands. Not for the reasons you might be expecting, but... anyway, it would be a weight off my mind if I took your place. But I just can't risk it."

The Security Officer bristled. "With all due respect, your Majesty, you don't scare me."

"Really?" The Red Queen cocked her head. "Why do you suppose that is? Out of all of my subjects, why is it that you—and you alone—have no fear of the power I wield?" She paused for a moment. "Do you like this society, Maya of Zor under Tura? Do you think it worth preserving?"

"Yes, I do," the Security Officer responded fiercely. "With one caveat. I would see you gone from it."

The treason hung in the air.

"Either you're a very stupid and headstrong girl," the Queen murmured, "or you already know what I'm going to show you. I can't quite remember which it is, I'm afraid."

The Security Officer said nothing. The Queen shrugged, and—making sure nobody was there to see—she reached up to detach the mask and lift it away.

Maya looked into her own eyes.

After a long pause, the mask was replaced. "You understand now, at any rate," the Queen smiled.

The Security Officer swallowed hard and nodded. "How—"

"At the co-ordinates you are to investigate, there is a temporal wormhole that will take you to the prehistory of Habitat One—of Earth. The rest of your crew also has a role to play there—except the captain, of course. But then, you'll learn for yourself that there are always sacrifices..."

"I don't understand."

"You will. You've studied your history—I made sure of that. You have a clear understanding of the turning points that created our civilisation; you'll know when the time comes how to guide it into being, and you'll have thousands of millennia with nobody to stop you doing just that."

"But the Red King—" the Security Officer sputtered, fear showing on her face for the first time. "How can I possibly learn to fight him?"

"The Red King won't learn the game until you know it inside out, and by that time, you'll need the challenge like air in your lungs. And he won't know the secret until it's too late."

"The secret?"

"The wormhole; the one that's about to bring you to the beginning of everything—riding with the Shaper, the Weeper, the Sacrificial Lamb and the Keeper of the Stone. It doesn't take you *back* in time."

Maya blinked at the Queen's expressionless mask, uncomprehending.

"It takes you *forward*."

WHAT ARE YOU, the *Drama* Queen? People have postulated that time is a circle since time started. It's no big secret—it's a theory you happened to prove correct. And what's the difference between backwards and forwards anyway?

There is no backwards. First law of time—you can never go back. The illusion of going backwards in time is caused by going so far forwards that you loop around.

I'm more interested in sideways, myself. Right, my move—

Hardly. That was just chit-chat about strategy. My *move is Knight takes Knight.*

You're joking. Two of my most elite Vengers had the drop on—oh, damn, he's killed them.

What can I say? He's a Silver.

Damn it...

He's quick.

ULL WAS VERY quick.

He grabbed the hand holding the blade, twisting the fingers just so; the Venger gave a yelp of pain, his borrowed face shifting, and the poisoned dagger fell from his grip. Ull caught it by the blade, his skinsuit already analysing the poison chemical and dosing him with the antidote—then his arm flashed up, and the blade flew out from between his fingers, burying itself in the head of the man opposite. He toppled backwards with a low groan, his features blurring to blank, lifeless clay; but his own knife was already in the air.

Ull caught it in his shoulder—*Delta five eight, stoicism in the face of pain*— and felt a wave of dizziness wash over him for a second as the newly-created antidote went to war with the deadly poison; his skinpatch gave him a brief additional burst of hosa to help him focus, and he tugged down on the hand in his grip, slicing the Venger's thumb on the blade.

Evidently, the Red King hadn't thought to make his Vengers immune to their own poison; the man slumped to the floor, dead in seconds. Ull carefully pulled the knife out of him, checking that the flesh underneath the skinsuit was mending itself. His organobotics were functioning at peak efficiency; as a Silver, his immortal body was in far better shape than the common herd. A perk of the job, not that the job needed additional perks.

The honour of serving the Red Queen was enough.

He threaded his way through the maze, feeling the subtle pull of the tracker as it guided him to his quarry.

He was close.

WAIT, YOU DIDN'T *give them antidote? Really?*

They've never stabbed themselves before. Also, you've never sent one of your Silvers to kill them before—oh, the hell with it.

You're not resigning the game?

Never. It's my move, and I'm going to pull out the big gun. I'm going to stop this precocious little creep in his tracks.

Oh? How do you propose to do that?

I'm going to tell him the truth.

EXITING THE MAZE, Ull found himself in a great, vaulted chamber of gold and rubies, the walls quietly reconfiguring themselves to best effect even as he looked at them. In the centre of the room was some sort of barrier of red cloth, hanging from rings attached to some kind of circular rail. Ull had never seen the like before.

Alpha four seven again, he thought. *Be prepared for anything.*

He took a slow step forwards, the poison knife in his grip. Suddenly, from beyond the ring of hanging cloth, there came a terrible, booming voice:

"I AM OZ—THE GREAT AND TERRIBLE!"

A great gout of coloured smoke shot upwards from the centre of the ring, and despite himself, Ull took a step back—then the cloth barrier parted.

Behind it, sitting on a golden throne, dressed in a black robe, was a well-toned, red-skinned man with a neatly-trimmed tuft of black hair on his chin—*Zeta seven three,* thought Ull—and a pair of horns growing from his temples. "I call that my Pluto voice," the Red King grinned, waggling his eyebrows. "The cute thing is, I'm actually a very bad man. But I'm a very good wizard."

Ull stared at the barrier of cloth as it parted further, revealing two shimmering containment fields on either side of the throne, each holding an identical glowing blue stone. The Red King noticed him staring, and rolled his eyes.

"They're called curtains. *Cur-tanz.* Philistine. Which reminds me, you owe me one priceless work of art, created by royalty, depicting a world only accessible in the dreams of madmen, artists and savants. I'll take a cheque." He leaned back on his throne, then turned to look at the identical chunks of xokronite, as if noticing them for the first time. "Oh, you're looking at *those!* Yeah, for this bit I ideally need two identical guards, one who only tells lies and one who only tells the truth, but, hey, I can play both those parts myself. Anyway, you get one question, and..." He frowned. "Oh, come *on,* kid, say *something.* This is good material I'm wasting on you."

"You..." Ull paused, drawing a deep breath. "You're the Red King."

"Funny story about that—" the King began, and then his hand moved, so suddenly it seemed to blur, and he snatched the thrown knife out of the air less than an inch from his throat. "Hey!" He scowled, tossing the poison blade to one side. "Not while I'm talking, okay? And by the way, we have rules about that. I'm being nice to you as it is."

Ull blinked, unable to believe what he'd seen. "You *are* the Red King..."

"Yes! God! Where was I?" He sighed, cracking his knuckles. "Yeah, the whole Red King and Red Queen business. Now, you're not going to get half of this, because you're a philistine who doesn't even know about Judy Garland, but that was originally a joke I made, way, way back when I first realised what was going on. This is about eighty millennia into the powered era, back when she was Britannia and I was just Lomax. We had a lot more accidents back then—colonising space is going to do that—and I hadn't invented hosa yet, so basically nobody remembers that far back. Except us." He smiled. "Anyway, the joke was that she was the Red Queen and I was the Red King, and it stuck."

"A... joke?" Ull was confused—*Zeta nine one, confusion*. Most of the words had little or no meaning for him. Where was Judygar Land?

"A gag, a bit. I make them sometimes, especially when I'm monologuing. Anyway, the joke fits because the Red Queen—Britannia—has spent her entire immortal existence working behind the scenes, pushing dominos, pulling strings and generally running her gorgeous hiney off... all to stay in the same place."

Ull just stared.

"The universe is the way it is because Maya Zor-Tura spent her whole life making it that way, because at this critical moment in history—when a temporal wormhole to so far into the future that it's all the way around past GO opens up, collect two hundred dollars—she sent her younger self through it to do just that."

He grinned again, leaning forward. "Except she can't do it on her own. She also needs to send a lump of xokronite—the magic mineral that steals power from the Big Bang and makes all this possible—through the hole as well. And not one of the ones we synthesised, either, because their atomic structures are ever-so-slightly different, so they might not behave exactly the same. It's got to be the original piece, the capital-S Stone, infinitely old and getting older with every circle around the timeline. Maybe that's what makes it the way it is..." He shrugged. "Anyway, I stole it. And you've been sent to steal it right back. Lucky for you... I've got it right here." He tapped one of the containment fields, then indicated the other. "Or is it over here? Want to take a guess? Could be lucky."

Ull gritted his teeth. *Epsilon one two. Anger. The superior man channels his anger towards his goals.* "Give it to me," he said slowly, taking a menacing step forward.

"Ah-ah-ah!" The Red King grinned, seemingly amused at the Silver's temerity in threatening him. "What did I say? You get a question."

Ull took another step forward, fists clenching, readying himself to spring forward. *The throat,* he thought. *The weak point.*

Then he stopped in his tracks.

The Red King was looking him right in the eyes, and his eyes were so, so old...

"Go ahead, kid," he said, unsmiling. "Make my day."

Ull took a faltering step back. "I..."

"Yellowbelly. Ask your damn question."

Ull swallowed hard. "Why... why are you the Red King?"

The Red King looking at him for a moment, then relaxed, cracking into a smile. "You're not quite as dumb as you look, are you, kid? Your great-great-ever-so-many-greats-grandpa would be proud of you. I remember he broke my jaw once—that was back when I could die." He stared at the ceiling for a moment, marshalling his thoughts. "The other half of the joke. I'm the Red King because I think Maya's wrong. I want us to wake up out of this. I want this whole universe to go out"—he snapped his fingers—"just like a candle."

"You'd kill the universe?" Ull said, horrified.

"I'd *change* it." The King looked irritated, as if Ull had missed the point completely. "Do you know what the world would be like without Maya Zor-Tura? Without the Stone? No, of course you don't. You're not a dreamer—I can tell by looking at you." He furrowed his brow for a moment. "You've never heard of Omega energy either, have you?"

Ull shook his head. "What is it?"

"A form of galvanic force. Only one person ever really got a handle on it, and he didn't know what he had—mostly because Maya—sorry, the Red Queen—was right there to keep him from asking the right questions. Just like she was there to murder anyone who was likely to get too close to it. She'd made sure her younger self knew all the history—or prehistory, I suppose, seeing as we count it from when we got the Stone off that poor bastard Steele." He grinned savagely, enjoying Ull's total incomprehension. "She'd worked it out. Steam technology drains resources, but Omega energy—*electricity*, they call it in the dreamworld—would decimate them completely."

"I don't—"

"You don't understand. Okay. In simple terms, a world without Maya or the Stone is a world of Omega energy. Instead of the *Pax Britannia,* they have the *Pax Omega*—for as long as it lasts."

"As long as it lasts?" Ull was just about able to grasp the concept of things being finite, but he still needed a little help.

"Sure. Omega technology is a hungry little bastard—it runs rampant and eats every mineral resource on the planet inside a couple of centuries, maximum. We're talking everything from petrochemical deposits to good old-fashioned coal to rare elements like indium, helium—even gold. Humanity gets everything it ever wanted—or the rich few do at least—and the population explodes just in time for everybody to lose it again. Take a look at the dreampunk artists around the mid-to-late twenty-first century—you won't sleep for a week. Horrific stuff. Ninety-five per cent of the world just starves to death." The King shivered, shaking his head. He looked genuinely disturbed. "Nobody gets out unscathed."

Ull sounded incredulous. "I don't know what's worse—that this might exist, or that you want it to."

The Red King sighed. "Okay—one, it's not a binary choice. There are a lot of variables to play with. What happens if Maya goes back with a different Stone, for instance? One that isn't quite so ancient and magical? That might change things slightly—maybe just enough to knock this endless merry-go-round off kilter. Maybe stop the universe stagnating in an endless, eternal loop, forever and ever. Who knows? I'm willing to roll the dice—she's not."

Ull opened his mouth to speak, and the King shushed him with a gesture. "Two—that's not the whole story. The human race doesn't die out. For centuries, things are terrible, but people rebuild. They pick themselves back up. Except this time they have to do things differently. Technology isn't an option—they ruined that, and it's a shame, because it could have been great—but that doesn't mean they can't still grow." He smiled. "That's the wonderful thing about humanity. Whatever happens to it, the human race can still evolve. By the twenty-fifth century, you're got agrarian societies beating hell out of each other between lynchings—still not good. By the five hundredth, they're enlightened Buddhists. By the thousandth, they're beating hell out of each other again—it's a rocky road. Peaks and troughs. They don't have immortality to keep them nice and unchanging through the millennia."

"It sounds hideous." Ull shuddered. "What makes that world worth destroying ours for?"

"It's got potential. Ours doesn't. We're just going to sit here and twiddle our thumbs until the final heat death of the universe—although, Maya being Maya, she's set up the solution to that too." He sighed. "Poor bastard..."

"What?"

"Never mind. Like I said, we're in a loop that never ends. But you know who's living on that other Earth now, the one only savants can see? In the year one million and change? A race of hyperintelligent zen monks who communicate telepathically. That's how we *learned* about mental linkage—watching the dreamworld. And do you know what they're doing, these guys? They're immortal too, just like we are. And they're using those superminds of theirs to explore and map the nine billion countries of heaven. And the whole history of their Earth, and of the infinite possible Earths that aren't theirs. And bring it all together."

Ull blinked. "That's impossible—"

"Odds are fifty-fifty they'll do it. My favourite odds." The Red King smiled to himself, looking into Ull's eyes. "You know I'm not lying."

Ull shivered. He knew.

"So what do you think? Are they going to make it? Do we take the risk and maybe all end up in heaven at the end of the story, Maya and El Sombra and Pluto and Doc Thunder and two Ben Franklins and Johnny Wolf and even the bad guys all together in one last happy ending? Or do we play it safe?" He grinned, leaning back on his throne.

After a long silence, Ull spoke, not without compassion. "I'll take one of those Stones now."

The Red King's face fell for a moment, then he managed a half-smile. "Want me to tell you which is which? That's the game. Heads or tails. True or false." He pantomimed pointing to each of the twin blue stones in turn: "Eeny, meeny, miney, mo..."

"My tracker unit has the exact atomic structure of the Stone on file," Ull said, flatly. "I knew which one it was all along."

The King's face fell. "Oh." He shrugged. "Well, I guess you'd better take it."

He scowled angrily, curling up in his throne like a petulant child.

"And don't let the psychetecture hit your ass on the way out, you sneaky little cheat."

* * *

CHECK AND MATE.

More like stalemate. Forever.

Oh, you don't need to map Heaven, Lars, you'd never get in. And there's no need to be such a grouch just because you lost—

Did I?

He knew which Stone was which, Lars.

Yes, he did. He knew which was which. And he made his choice.

MAYA WATCHED THE *Zor* leave, sailing out of the hangar bay on the first leg of its journey, laden down with the Shaper, the Weeper, the Princess and the Keeper—and the Stone that bound them all.

And a Sacrifice, of course. The first of many.

She remembered those early days—the brittle arguments with Munn and Unwen, desperately trying to rush into the role of Queen before she was ready—then the long millennia in the jungle, growing into herself, making her plans, founding the Kingdom of Zor-Ek-Narr.

Zor-Ek-Narr; in the language of the Habitats, *Long live the Zor.*

She'd commanded battlecruisers the size of suns, and star-yachts that had flowed through the cosmos like dreams, but the *Zor* was still her favourite ship, and it always would be. Oddly enough, it was named after the Forbidden Kingdom. Where did that name come from, then? Where was the Stone from, originally?

She supposed it didn't matter.

As the *Zor* reached sub-light speed and winked out of sight among the stars, a terrible thought struck Maya. It was a thought she'd never had before, not once in the billions of years she'd been alive, and it felt like the bottom dropping out of the world.

Maya Zor-Tura, the Red Queen, stood watching the stars, and she thought, *What happens now?*

...OMEGA

Eventually, Earth died.

The stars went out and the planet crumbled to dust as entropy claimed the universe; and from out of the centre of the dust that had once been a planet, there drifted the egg.

The Being within the egg had been dormant for countless aeons, patiently waiting until all life in the universe had died a natural death. He liked being alone.

Although He had never been short of company.

From within the egg, He had seen and heard them all; everything that had ever walked, crawled or flown, from the smallest amoeba to the great immortals, in their eternal Habitats, and more powerful beings even than they.

He had never considered coming out of the egg until now.

He hadn't wanted to hurt anyone.

He was no longer simply powerful; that was a threshold He'd crossed billennia ago. Now, He was power itself.

Once, He had been called Thunder.

In the universe to come, some would give Him other names.

Slowly, over centuries, the metal of the egg flaked away, and He emerged from His cocoon, no longer human, no longer even humanoid. He cast his awareness to the very edges of the dead universe, and found no life. This universe was dead; there was nothing left of it.

There was not.

Nothing existed, and there was nothing in which to exist.

Over a timeless interval, during which time had no meaning, He considered the situation.

He existed. He was the only thing to exist. That did not feel correct.

He focussed His being, and spoke.

And there was.